To Elizabeth Milward
with my good wishes –

Vincent Worley

13. 11. '12

THE
DOGE'S CAT

BY

VINCENT WORLEY

THE MISADVENTURES OF A YOUNG VENETIAN

1693- 1695

www.fast-print.net/store.php

The Doge's Cat
Copyright © Vincent Worley 2012

ISBN 978-178035-237-4

First published 2012 by
FASTPRINT PUBLISHING
Peterborough, England.

For my grandchildren
James, David, Emma and Anna

Illustrations by the author

Murano

Piero's Hut

Palazzo Capello

San Donato

Angeli Church

Ca'
da Mula

Dragon Tavern

Palazzo Capello

Trevison Palace

Ca' da Mula
Molin House
St. Peter Martyr
Zanetti's shop

Grand Canal

S. Giovanni Canal

San Stin
Zorzi's
Home

Glassblowers' Canal

Lighthouse

Miotti del Jesu

St. Peter Martyr

Ondello

Zorzi's Home

PROLOGUE

<u>22nd May 1694</u>

A fishing float, no bigger than a soap bubble and blown from pale green Murano glass, bobbed in mid canal, around it danced reflections of the lines of Monday washing strung along the towpath. Numerous mooring posts as well snaked their brightly painted images onto the watery darkness and in the murky depths below the canal surface hung a bone hook, baited with a soggy piece of Parmesan cheese rind that had been carved and scored down to its canvas coating to resemble a wriggling tiddler fish. A flurry of ripples sent the glass float skimming off downstream from time to time as though intent on scoring a goal beneath the broad humped arch of Saint Peter Martyr Bridge. Whenever the float strayed too far into the shadow cast by the bridge it was reined back to duty again by a quick twitch of the toe of a very skinny child.

It was that time of afternoon when neighbours' babies stopped their wailing: the hour when empty-bellied glass workers flopped down on their work benches for some hard earned repose. In the quiet, shoals of tiny fry rose to nibble on a feast of mosquito larvae hatching amidst the slime and the algae of a double line of posts shoring up the margins of the canal. From the worn flagstones, the gravel and the mud patches of the towpath, hot vapour sizzled up to a sky that might well have been as blue as the Madonna's mantle were it not for a haze of chemical smoke drifting heaven-ward from eighty or more furnaces.

The fishing boy's head and shoulders were shaded from the intense sunlight by a filthy felt hat, wide brimmed and several sizes too large for him. Malnourished and deep set eyed though he was, his face gave promise of being handsome, unmistakably Venetian though, with just a slight aquiline prominence to the nose. That face was now screwed into an unhappy scowl and dirt caked cheeks showed fresh tear streaks. The left jaw was greatly swollen with a gum abscess where the last of his milk teeth had wobbled its way out and left behind a raging infection. It was not toothache, however, that caused Zorzi Miotti to be in such a dejected state of mind, nor hunger, for to that he was quite accustomed.

Apart from a desperate spoonful of acid sharp pickled cabbage, no food of any kind had passed his lips since the previous morning when he had gobbled down a slice of over baked yellow crusted polenta. What troubled the thoughts of our young angler was, of all strange things, a psalm: to be more exact a canticle set to music by a long dead Chapel Master to the Doge of Venice.

There were larger fish nuzzling for anything edible amidst the rubbish strewn canal bottom. None were in the least deceived by that cunningly carved piece of Parmesan bait. At last, hot and stiff from immobility, the little lad lifted his foot from the water, flicked away the green algae, untied the fishing line from his big toe and shuffled his body a few yards into the shade of his front porch. Giving a loud sigh of resignation he reattached the line with a firm sailor-like knot to his left toe, rubbing the other to restore the circulation He settled his back against the soft comforting damp moss that, with long centuries of growth, had gradually climbed up a column of grey and waterproof Istrian stone. This was his favourite of all the eight trunks of stone that straddled the towpath in front of his house. The columns and their cross beams propped up the walls of three medium sized upper rooms built of red brick. Elegant, though crumbling, stone window frames in the pointed gothic style lit the three rooms, two of which directly overlooked the Canal di San Stin, now known as the Glassmakers' Canal. With their broad overhang, the rooms made a shady portico from which wide slippery steps descended to water level, leaving ample space on either side for landing goods from canal barges.

Hugging his knees and leaning his head forward for an afternoon snooze, the boy pulled down the brim of his greasy hat against the myriad of dazzling diamond pinpoints reflecting from the water surface. As he did so, a tiny money spider dropped down from the mossy column, ran over the top of the hat and dangled from an invisible thread in front of his nose. Scooping it up gently into the hollow of his palm, he fixed it with a comic furious stare half hoping that the spider might transform into a handful of gold sequins. He tried hard to think up a spell to enchant the spider then decided that there was nothing better to gabble at the creature than that Psalm from the Old Testament he had learned with so much effort, but whose meaning was, at least for the present, quite beyond his ability to comprehend. Nevertheless, the power of a wizard's malediction seemed to reside in King David's song. No benefit whatsoever had come

2

by joining the choir of San Donato Church, no food, no recompense and now their very livelihood was at risk, for after Grandpa lashed out and gave that ill judged thump to the Podestàs arm both of Grandpa's glass furnaces had been shut down. Once charmed, the money spider might oblige by undoing some of the harm caused by Grandpa's foolish swipe: "DIXIT DOMINUS DOMINO MEO SEDE A DEXTRIS MEIS......" he sang to the motionless mini-beast. (*The Lord said unto my lord, sit by my right hand until I make your enemies into my footstool.*)

Lowering the spider carefully to the damp paving on his right, Zorzi let it scurry away down a crack in the base of the column. Tears now welled up between his tightly squeezed eyelids: in vain he tried to force them back. Clutching his knees he began to rock back and forth, humming quietly the exquisite tune that Monteverdi had set to the fateful Psalm.

That Psalm had somehow changed to sour vinegar his once carefree life. He would never sing it again, not even if the Podestà himself were to command him. Nobody, not even Grandpa, had given him a satisfactory explanation as to why his singing had sparked off the riot at San Donato. At the Saturday afternoon rehearsal, just before chaos erupted and the Arsenal workers charged and thoroughly battered Zustinian's heavily armed troop of lancers, his solo performance of the Psalm had been greeted with cheers, with clapping, with stamping feet and cries of "Bis! Bis!" (*Again! Again!*)

Aldo Molin, his closest pal, had just hurried past, pretending not to see him. Normally, they would have gone off together and swapped jokes while dangling for tiddlers off some distant jetty, for the stinking Glassmakers' Canal was the last place anyone would choose. Old Piero, Grandpa's lifelong friend, had promised a boat trip to the Fair at St. Mark's - that too was now cancelled. Don Tranquillo, Sub Prior of the Dominican's at St. Peter Martyr, had ordered him to stay at home, to fish only from his doorstep, a spot from where he had never had a successful catch. Furthermore, Tranquillo had forbidden him chatter to friends about the whole affair or to satisfy the curiosity of neighbours. It was all for Grandpa's safety: at least that instruction was understandable. On the previous morning two of the most feared of the Podestà's 'bulli' had, smashed down the front doors and had threatened there and then to beat to death his brave old Grandpa who had enough ills to complain about already: what with the 'lungs,' not to mention the 'old Anno Domini,' another troublesome affliction of which Grandpa frequently grumbled. A bluebottle was now hovering about Zorzi, trying to make one more landing on that tempting open sore just below his elbow. Several other flies were crawling in exploration of the smells, stains and grease caked patches of his only garment, a pair of goatskin breeches. Laced at the waist and below the knees with hemp strings, the outsize breeches might, with good fortune and the polenta to go with it, fit him in a year or two.

From somewhere across the expanse of salt marsh and mud flat islands that make up the Venetian Lagoon, the dull thuds of a ship's cannons disturbed the afternoon peace. A more distant rumble of an answering salutation followed, it might well have come from one of the immense siege guns of Fort St. Andrew. With its massive low stone walls, 'Forte Sant'Andrea' was the nearest of a twenty-mile chain of star shaped castles and batteries guarding the entrances to the glorious Harbour of St. Mark.

Much nearer came the rattle and splash of a ship anchoring. Harsh words in a foreign tongue drifted across the open water, commanding a ship's crew about its tasks. Could it be a Nordic or a Dutch vessel mooring off shore from the Island? If so, there was the promise of good trading ahead for at least some of Murano's glassworkers, but certainly not anymore for Grandpa.

In recent weeks, the very grandest of Staten Yachts and of Indiamen had been breezing into the Lagoon, firing blank greetings and dipping their flags as they passed the forts. These giants of armed ships, built to sail the world with their cargoes, were not alone. With them came hired security against pirates on the last leg of their voyage: swift, long-oared Venetian or Maltese war galleys, both kinds tricked out in red and white for easy identification. Huge 'First Raters' encrusted with gilded 'gingerbread' carvings on their many windowed sterns and bristling with bronze cannons were arriving with equal frequency. A competing swarm of ferry boats, gondolas and lighters hovered around them eager to disembark their cargoes of satin clad nobility, of ambassadors, of silks, porcelain, parrots, Afghan rugs, powdered minerals and drugs; the trading goods of almost every nation with vessels sound and well armed enough to plough the Corsair infested waters of the Mediterranean. A dozen at a time on some tides, they swaggered in: each hull glistening with fresh paint; each

4

spar and masthead bedecked with signal flags and colourful bunting; copper lanterns polished to a sparkle sprouted like hatpin jewels from the sterns of every vessel. All were constantly tacking and manoeuvring about, often bearing down at threatening speed and jostling one another to gain a good anchorage, a vantage point from whence they might witness or else take part in the two grandest civic spectacles in all Europe: the Trade Fair of the 'Sensa' and the'Sposalizio del Mare.' *(The Wedding of the Sea.)*

Our fisher boy, wriggled his bony back once more to a comfortable spot against the damp mossy porch column, his head nodded forward and was jerked back once or twice, then within a few heavy breaths he drifted into deep and untroubled sleep.

The green glass float on the end of his fishing line vanished with a quiet plop. For a few moments the waters stirred slowly, menacingly, about the spot where it had disappeared: then, racing madly along, the float re-emerged, zigzagging on a fast and frantic course down and under St. Peter Martyr Bridge and onwards towards the Ponte di Mezzo, *(the middle bridge.)* Zorzi's sleep-relaxed leg shot forward from under his folded arms. Toe first, he bumped and hurtled down the landing stage steps, entering the canal with a high pitched yell and a spectacular splash! There was barely time to gasp before the filthy waters closed, hissed and roared about his ears. All was confusion, spluttering, darkness and flailing limbs. Mercifully for the little urchin, his goatskin breeches did not part company with him but acted as a drag weight. As he was about to be towed to his death under the Middle Bridge - notoriously a place where household rubbish was tipped after dark - the line snagged on some sharp metallic object and snapped. An immense catfish flushed out from its riverbed by a torrent of glacial meltwater swam majestically onwards, but before heading out from the canal into the meandering and muddy vastness of the brackish Lagoon it turned with a flurry of great fins, homing in on easy prey. Like most fleeting visitors to Murano, it had been hooked into carrying away a souvenir.... in the form of a hard mouthful of cheese rind, from which trailed that small float of green soda glass. Now its bull whip sized whiskers sensed close by a much meatier morsel!

Zorzi resurfaced, spouting brown water like a Triton. Unblocking his ears, he was greeted by hoots of laughter. Ever eager to gloat at Miotti misfortune, several 'furnace monkeys' young apprentices from the Barovier glassworks were now leaning over the parapet of the Ponte di Mezzo. With nothing solid immediately to hand they either spat, hurled abuse, or offered crude unhelpful advice. Neighbours, wakened by the commotion, rushed from their beds to their balconies and joined in the babble of voices and mock applause.

Sensing that a show of bravado was needed to impress the ever growing number of onlookers, Zorzi flung himself high out of the water, gave a whoop of feigned delight and with confident over-arm strokes powered himself cautiously in mid stream under the crumbling brick bridge and out between the moorings on the other side. Waving an arm occasionally, to acknowledge the clapping and laughter, he swam on hoping to find some unoccupied landing steps or dangling mooring ropes that he might grasp and use to clamber out. It was however far from easy to find even a finger hold. Stem hitched to stern, every single mooring seemed occupied with some steep sided barge or fishing vessel.

"Nice try Zorzi!" yelled one of the more friendly boys on the Ponte di Mezzo, "Next time try using some decent bait. You might catch a real sea dragon!"

A double line of slimy rotten stakes lined the canal, pile driven high enough to prevent the towpath from collapsing. He swam back and forth for several minutes, now feeling the terrible drag of exhaustion creeping upwards, numbing on its way legs, lungs and arms. With mounting dread he realized that he was drifting close to the Bridge of Santa Chiara. Beyond that notorious boundary a fierce undertow ran out from the canal into the Lagoon and swirled and eddied past the high windowless walls of several glass warehouses that overhung the canal. What towpaths there were on either side were narrowed to such a degree that only sure footed bargees would ever attempt to edge their way along them. A tumble in the canal at this end of its meander was the dread of all who walked its banks. Generations of Muranese parents had passed on tales of monstrous unseen hands writhing beneath the waters beyond Santa Chiara, eager to seize and hold for ever unwary young bathers. Zorzi felt that any moment now he too would slip back under and not have enough strength to flail his way upwards again. In despair he clung as best he could to one of the slime clad stakes and screamed for help. A chill, leaden lethargy began to overwhelm his limbs, his mind began to wander with confused concerns, then came a last troubling image of Grandpa, alone and calling to him for help. Spinning dizzily on Grandpa's iron pontil was a great flaming gather of pink hot glass, then all was darkness.

CHAPTER ONE

<u>7th December, 1693</u>

A gentle prod from Grandpa's clog woke Zorzi. It was soon after dawn
and an icy crystalline mist drifted in from the broken shutters of his upper
floor room. It could hardly be called a bedchamber, for there was no bed,
nor even a stick of furniture. Zorzi rolled over on the mangy goatskin
floor mat and clutched his blanket tightly around his bare shoulders. His
nose and lips were purple blue and he had lost all sensation in his feet,
which was only a temporary blessing, for once circulation returned to
normal he would again be tormented with itchy chilblains.

"Get yourself up now Zorzi. Don Tranquillo has just called in with a gift
for you."

"A gift? Great! Why?"

"St. Ambrose day or something….not one of ours….a Lombard saint. He
tells me you come of age today, though I can hardly believe ten years
have gone since we held you squealing at the font."

"Coming of age: what does that mean Grandpa?"

"It means you could have got an apprenticeship if the few ducats I had put
away had not long gone up the furnace stack. Evidently Tranquillo has
something in mind for you. There's a slice of polenta and a tray of
honeycomb downstairs - his and Fra Zeri's birthday gift. It's on the bench
by the furnaces - make sure you return the tray with a proper word of
thanks. Go and warm yourself before the honey melts all over my floor,
I'm off to talk to the Don about your prospects and to light a lamp in
thanksgiving for your coming of age, though I don't suppose it will make
much difference. Now if only there was an apprenticeship in playing
calcio!"

Zorzi sat up, gave a teeth rattling shudder, clutched his blanket around his
shoulders and slid his half frozen feet into his clogs. Delight at the news
quickly gave way to a troublesome thought: he was distinctly
not taken with the idea of becoming a novice friar, a prospect that

8

Grandpa had hinted at on more than one occasion. Hastening down the rough hewn step-ladder leading to the courtyard, the icy cobbles and suspended fog were one last ordeal before he raced to warm himself at the iron shutter of the 'fornace piccolo.'

Sitting as close as he dared to the raging hot annealing furnace, the smaller of the two great beehive shaped glass-making kilns, he contentedly wolfed down the singed and crusty polenta pudding, nibbling from time to time at the honeycomb to make the more crusty, not to say carbonized black chunks of Fra Zeri's offering that bit more palatable. The searing heat began to restore a tingling sensation to his calloused toes and, like a lizard basking on a dawn lit wall, his full faculties and normally cheerful mood were eventually restored in full. Perhaps when the pale sun warmed up Aldo's orchard, he and other close friends could celebrate the day with a noisy kick around with their rag covered pig's bladder. He would save the 'smaller half' of Zeri's honeycomb to be shared around after the match.

Grandpa's longstanding friendship with Tranquillo had helped, of course, to secure for Zorzi the privilege of being servant to the friars. Don Tranquillo was one of the three remaining members of the convent hospital of San Pietro Martire. Not many years back, twelve friars had been stationed there - nine of them had succumbed - just average mortality for any religious community caring for the sick. Smallpox, typhoid and pneumonic plague came and went with as much regularity as galleys in the Venetian Lagoon. The extensive brick built complex of monastic buildings was on the opposite canal bank to Zorzi's house. A hump-backed bridge spanning the busy canal led directly to the side door of the ancient church. San Pietro was very much a neglected outpost of the vast Dominican convent of Venice - the city's main hospital.

A dawn chorus from a hundred or more church belfries called the devout to prayer. Deep melodic booming peals and not a few dull clanking ones echoed out and across the countless islands of the Venetian Lagoon and served too as the workers' waking call. Glassmakers, printers, lace makers, fishmongers, magistrates and alley sweepers all hastened to be on their way before the last bell ceased its clamour. At the first stroke of the 'Marangona,' the greatest of five bells in the lofty tower of St. Mark, all other bells tinkled to a respectful silence. The 'Marangona,' commanded four thousand and more carpenters, rope makers and cannon casters to rise and to run, to row, or to sail to their toil and duties in the vast docks of the Arsenal. Arsenal workers were sometime despised as hard living men, yet all envied them their generous pensions and health care. The Arsenalotti's greatest privilege however was the right to guard their godlike Doge on great occasions and to carry him to his burial place: an honour for which they had battled, snatched from the nobility, and guarded to themselves down the centuries.

The mischievous pleasure of ringing the bells in the tall and tottering tower of St. Peter Martyr ensured that our fisher boy rose early from his warm and smelly blanket. Wakening his sleepy neighbours was far and away the most satisfying task that Zorzi had to perform as servant to the friars. Unwashed, he would bound along the canal path, over the bridge and straight in through the ever open doors of Don Tranquillo's church. Just a dozen or so elderly ladies made up the early morning congregation. Kneeling in their widows' weeds, their damp prayers rose like cold mist to the vault of the nave, as they mumbled the names of lovers, sons and husbands lost in the endless battle with the turband enemy.

The carved Bible scenes and grotesque caryatid figures lining the walnut walls of the vestry were, Zorzi knew, great works of the woodcarver's art, but he was still terrified to be alone with them. If there was no one about, he would hare into the vestry, grab a waist cord, dive head first into his musty smelling cassock and shield his eyes from those disturbing wood wormed caryatids while making straight for the steps to the bell tower. Leaping up for the tenor bell rope he joined in the merry ding dong din of the Angelus calls: three lots of three pulls, a short interval, then nine swift and much louder clangs without any interval. Letting the rope slide through the hands without getting rope burns and then giving a vigorous tug at the right moment was something Zorzi quickly mastered. He was astonished therefore one morning, after a particularly enthusiastic tug, to be floored and half buried by a tremendous roar of falling bell rope. By good chance Don Toma` (*Thomas)* the librarian, was passing in the corridor leading to the vestry and wondered why the Angelus had come to a sudden discordant halt. Hearing Zorzi's yells for help he was able to disentangle him from the heap of rotting hemp, dust him down and escort him and his bruises to the high altar via a narrow corridor, an ambulatory built into the curving wall of the apse. After Mass, Zorzi climbed with

Don Tranquillo, Fra Zeri and grumpy old Don Toma`, puffing and dragging behind them back up to the high gallery the great length of bell rope: the rope had just frayed apart with sea mist rot and constant use. Fortunately the tenor bell itself had not dislodged from its cradle, as might well have happened, and dropped with its enormous weight down through the tower. After much tugging and prodding with a boat hook, Don Tranquillo managed to unsnag the section of rope that had wound itself tightly round the pulley wheels. He then proceeded to make a splice with such skill and speed that Zorzi marvelled, even though he knew that the priest had once been commander of a flotilla of war galleys.

From the dizzy height of the bell chamber Zorzi surveyed for the first time his little universe. As he hastened excited from one stone viewing arch to another Fra Zeri kept a firm grip on the the lad's cowled cassock. Seagulls sailed effortlessly below and through lifting patches of morning mist the glistening mud flats revealed a whole pallisade of church towers sprouting from the countless islands of the Lagoon. Viewed from a distance, all too few of them were perpendicular. Not far off were the docks of the Arsenal, buzzing with activity, with ships, galleys and gondolas skimming around like flies on a millpond. Looming over his own house on the other side of the canal was the vast dull brown brick tower of San Stin. *(Saint Stephen's.)* A good quarter higher than that of St. Peter Martyr, it was the belfry of the church where his ancestors had worshipped for centuries and 'rested in peace' in the good company of the bones of no less than two hundred of the Holy Innocents murdered by King Herod. Zorzi could now understand why Grandpa felt no longer able to do the same: particularly the 'resting in peace' bit and, being on bad terms with the parish priest there, had long transferred his devotions to St. Peter. The San Stin tower leaned alarmingly in the direction of Grandpa's house and there were wide cracks in the brickwork that could not be seen easily from ground level. Some of the pantiles on the roof of Grandpa's house were missing, their wooden retaining pins having long since rotted away, something Zorzi was already well aware of. On rainy nights he had to shift his goatskin and blanket from one place on the floor to another, in order to avoid a soaking.

Pointing out the inscription around the rim of each bell, which read EX DONO REX ANG. ET GAL. HENRICUS VII - LONDINIUM -MDVI, Tranquillo explained that the great bells came from a distant island called

11

London; a place on the far edge of the world, where it was always cold and rain swept and where a fierce piratical people dwelled. These Londinese, in dress and appearance, closely resembled the loathsome Uzkoks of Dalmatia, but differed from them in the unusual habit of chopping off the heads of their kings and queens.

"But, Don Tranquillo, I don't understand. Why do our people want to go and live there then? Only, I've heard...."

"I guess you have Zorzi. But believe me none of it is true. Leastwise, one bit is true; you did have a great, great uncle Antonio who settled there taking with him his mirror making secrets; thus making us all the poorer, but then, I must tell you he was never a Venetian traitor. He was employed by a great nobleman called Buckingham and claimed he was born in one of the Seven States, I have forgotten which.... Middelburg I think.

Zorzi kept silence - embarrassed on hearing this not altogether unfamiliar tale. Whenever he 'fell out' with the local lads, usually over the outcome of some hard fisted and foul kicking game of calcio, they would taunt him, saying that his father too was a traitor to Venice who had gone off to London with a 'puttana,' a bad woman, to live with her on that distant rains wept island. It cut him to the core to be reminded that his father might have abandoned him and worse still betrayed Murano's secret recipes to foreigners. Whenever taunts were made and doubts nagged at his mind, Grandpa and old Piero would assure him that his father, MaestroVincenzo, had been an honest man who would never have betrayed his fellow glassworkers. He had drowned in a storm whilst out fishing beyond the Lagoon: Grandpa was ready to swear by Saint Mark on that fact. However, it was old Piero who also gave confused and contradictory answers when probed by Zorzi about the tragic details.

"This Henricus Septimus," Don Tranquillo continued, was prince far famed for his true Christian generosity. Alas for him he had an infamous son you will have heard of, his name was Bluebeard!"

"Never, Don Tranquillo, you are kidding me again! Not him who decapichopped his wives every night!"

12

"The very same, and these bells were cast in that very same palace were those evil deeds were done. Let me see... it is written here in their strange barbaric language on the inner rim... it says... ve etae capell."
(Whitechapel.)

Zorzi was shrewed enough to notice that there was always an ulterior reason why Don Tranquillo's conversation drifted off at a seeming tangent.

"Guess who brought the bells back from London? Antonio di Brayda an ancestor of yours. And what do you think that old fellow was doing in London about the year 1506?"

"Being a traitor?" suggested Zorzi, reddening in the face at the thought.

The Don guffawed, "Never! No Miotti was ever a traitor! But he was trading in something rather strange, otherwise we Dominicans would never have mentioned him in our convent record book. He may have been one of The Ten's spies of course."

"A spy for The Ten?" Zorzi was keen to hear more.

"You must understand Zorzi that all this information is written in Latin, so you would have to learn the language if you wanted to read about your ancestors."

"I see," murmured Zorzi, knowing the Don had cornered him. He was suddenly far less excited to hear the end of the story.

"These people of yours, so it is written, came into sudden weath, colossal wealth, so much that all the Miotti were able to rebuild their houses and furnaces. Antonio's own work force is recorded as numerous, his furnaces many, and his home filled with tapestries, silver, table-clocks and the like. Evidently he also owned slaves and servants for his every need. You see, in exchange for shipping the bells back to Murano he was given some mysterious information by our librarian of that time - a book or recipes, no ordinary book - a book containing secrets beyond price!"

"Well, I wonder what happened to it all, Don Tranquillo, 'cos we haven't got anything like that now. Some builder came last month and wanted to buy our window frames, but Grandpa said the house would fall down if he took them out. Did you know we had to sell our staircases to pay for aunt Orsola's dowry? Then auntie died soon afterwards.... so did her baby."

"Yes, I knew all that. Indeed, our lot is often harsh, but we must make the best of our lives, in hope of something wonderful hereafter. Listen Zorzi, it is written that your ancestor even sold this King of London fellow a great quantity of something called most white platter - all decorated with his portrait and his portcullis emblem."

"I expect it was lattimo, easy to paint pictures on milk glass....done it myself once or twice, though Grandpa helped just a bit with the firing."

"Don Toma` seems to think it wasn't lattimo glass. He reckons those Miotti's of old had a recipe for porcelain. We can rely on Don Toma's translations....Though I must say I could do with relying more on his help about the place. He is forever in that musty library."

"Well I expect he is getting a bit old, Don Tranquillo... in all this cold weather, I reckon he needs a good rest in the warm."

"A rest? Warm? Why, he is nine years younger than me!"

"Well you look a lot younger, Don Tranquillo. I guess you must still be only about eighty."

"I take that to be a compliment, Zorzi."

So what's special about this porcelain stuff, Don Tranquillo?"

"Porcelain can be worth its own weight in gold ducats: princes have it on their tables. It is hard to break, even when you put hot food in it, it never breaks. My ink pot, the one you are always fiddling with, now that's porcelain. Strange though, it's got a Florentine mark. The mystery is, how your ancestor could have got porcelain in such quantity. Even in those days, the Turks had barred all routes to Cathay."

"Reckon it was lattimo all the same, Don Tranquillo. We Miotti invented it you know, hundreds of years back."

"Your friend Matteo would dispute that, no doubt. He's a Barovier isn't he?

"Sort of poor cousin to the Baroviers... like we are to the Del Jesu lot. But granny's family, now they were very, very, clever....invented loads of things."

"Ah! Yes, the Darduins. Your granny Angela.... she was something of a treasure to us all....generous to a fault, as well."

"Grandpa had granny's book, you know, Don Tranquillo. Perhaps the porcelain recipe was in granny's book? But we haven't got it anymore. Grandpa had to give it to somebody called Rabbi, though I don't know why. Who's Rabbi, Don Tranquillo?"

"A sort of Jewish priest… Grandpa left your Darduin book with him to secure a loan. But don't concern yourself about it; the Rabbi is a reliable old fellow… the local sawbones… a proper university medico, I'm told. I expect Grandpa will redeem the loan some day, but I doubt if there is a porcelain recipe in that Darduin book. It was only put together in '44 by Gianni Darduin, another great uncle of yours. Unfortunately for us all, lattimo glass is no damned use in the kitchen, not even for making decent plates."

"Well I use mine all the time," protested Zorzi. "I've got a lattimo plate that I've used for ages…. shows a monkey climbing up a bush with an apple in his hand… a bit cracked though, so I don't wash it too often, in case it breaks through."

"I can guess who made that." Tranquillo observed, but refrained from saying anything more than: "How fast the years slip by!" He recalled a similar monkey emblem being scratched on a choir stall in San Stin and of a little lad howling from one of Grandpa's well aimed clips on the ear. Ten year old Vincenzo Miotti had just been apprenticed as a 'scimmietta della furnace' in the 'Del Jesu' glass works of his uncle. In a thoughtless moment Vincenzo decided to record for posterity his new status as a

15

'furnace monkey.' It was a fine bit of sgraffito vandalism nevertheless and, had it been perpetrated in San Pietro, Tranquillo would have thought twice before having it planed out.

"This porcelain, it's got to be some sort of lead-tin mix. I reckon your old book told this Antonio fellow where he could buy some special tin porcelain pebbles. I bet there's a secret river of them somewhere." Zorzi was weighing up in his mind the prospect of becoming rich like his namesake ancestor, against the difficulties of having to learn to read, but thought it best not to share too many of his thoughts on the matter with Don Tranquillo.

"Pretty certain of it my lad: certain he found those secret river pebbles by reading in our book!" The wily Don was now chuckling at the thought that Zorzi might soon be disturbing the realm of his quarrelsome old sparring partner Don Toma`. The library of St. Peter Martyr was one of the finest in all Europe: it was in need now of a bit of youthful rumpus to awake it from its centuries old gloom. However, the librarian would never consider teaching a child who had no idea how to cut a quill. With that purpose in mind, Tranquillo picked up his splicing knife, snatched the feather from Zorzi's hat and pretended to trim the end of it into a nib. Zorzi lunged back to retrieve it, but was not swift enough. Waggling the precious hat feather and challenging the little lad to catch him, the lankly old warrior allowed himself to be chased down the spiralling steps of the bell tower: a rather foolhardy thing to do, since there was no handrail between them and the void.

Zorzi was more than ever convinced that Tranquillo was brewing up holy plans for his future. The breakfasts, the friendly conversations and the thrilling stories were all very pleasant, but Zorzi had no desire whatsoever to be a novice friar - a career that he feared might direct him along some dark and diabolical alley leading to a martyr's death. Behind Don Tranquillo's desk hung a painting that in a less squeamish age had once adorned one of the church walls. As he swept and dusted the office each week Zorzi studied the grim scene with growing fascination: it was the stuff of nightmares and made the prospect of holy martyrdom distinctly unappealing. Portrayed by some master of brilliant brush strokes and now buried below a layer of brownish varnish, St. Peter Martyr could still be seen to bear such a strong resemblance to Don Tranquillo that Zorzi

16

concluded that his elderly friend must have posed for the artist. The saint was painted with a balding head fringed with grey hairs and wearing black and white friar's robes: robes that were unpatched and in far better condition than those worn by Don Tranquillo. Zorzi quickly concluded that both strong armed Tranquillo and genial fuzzy bearded giant Fra Zeri would not have knelt down so obligingly for the armoured bandits. In a similar situation, both friars would have made mincemeat of their attackers. Now Don Toma`, on the other hand, he was the sort who might well have knelt meekly for his slaughter, like the saint in the picture, with a butcher's axe blade struck deep into his pate. The martyr saint's other friary friends, painted against a forest background, seemed to have put up a pretty poor fight as well. They were running away while one bandit, armed just like one of the Podestà's 'bulli' guards, was polishing off poor St. Peter Martyr with a large and beautifully painted dagger.

Zorzi spent hours day-dreaming, swinging his legs and weighing up his prospects during unintelligible sermons and endless chanted litanies. He knew well enough that all things of importance had to be spoken or written in Latin, a language that sounded so much grander than the clipped and buzzing Murano slang. Venice had the best spy service in Europe: perhaps he might learn some sort of spy's Latin? He imagined himself posted to that cold misty island called London that grown ups talked so much about, sometimes in anger and other times in admiration, and where in his secret hopes he felt that he might one day meet up with his father.

CHAPTER TWO

It was at one of those early morning banquets with Don Tranquillo - invariably a dish of boiled mussels heaped onto a dollop of sweetcorn polenta burnt in butter and often severely singed once more in the reheating - that the alternative prospect of becoming a chorister in Bishop Zustinian's Choir was put to him. Cracking the last mussel shell with his teeth and handing its gooey contents to the lad, the Don remarked casually: "How far can you spit Zorzi? I bet you can't spit as far as Saint Donato!"

Guessing this was some prelude to a joke, Zorzi replied: "That would depend on how close I was standing to it: most likely I would get a good thumping from Don Tosi as well. San Dona`? Impossible… it's a quarter of a mile… then there's the ferry!"

"Clever thinking, but I've fooled you there! The saint himself slew a fierce dragon with one deadly gob – from over a mile off! Powerful as a crossbow bolt he was, when he spat!"

"Get away, you are kidding me again! Anyway, I thought you said my Saint Zorzi was the one who killed dragons."

Don Tranquillo was a firm believer in bones, preferably dragons' bones rather than human, for he had grave doubts about those of King Herod's victims in San Stin, his rival's church on the opposite side of the canal. In his days as a marauding galley commander, sailing amidst the dreamlike Islands of the Aegean Sea, Tranquillo had dropped anchor on numerous occasions both to fill his water barrels and to admire the brightly painted Orthodox churches: sometimes preserved within them were fearsome-toothed bony remains of immense size to inspect - for a small donation of course. One such triple horned skull that he had lifted himself weighed more than a barrel of lead shot. The Turks treated such relics, and the Christian legends attached to them, with contempt, giving Don Tranquillo all the more reason to believe. After all, the ancient Greeks were no fools, gigantic bones of heroes and monsters were part and parcel of their religion too, and were often the centerpieces around which their fabulous temples were built. The Bible itself affirmed that 'there were giants in those days.'

"You know, Zorzi," Don Tranquillo added with a chuckle, "I reckon San Donato must have had a really hungry dog - but then he lived on a poorly provisioned island – a rather dried-up place called Kefalonia, I've been there."

"Don't tell me his dog ate dragons as well?"

"Must have done. Behind the high altar in San Dona`, there are dragons' bones, left-overs from his dog's dinner."

"How big was this dog then, Don Tranquillo?" Zorzi asked with growing suspicion.

"Pretty enormous, I reckon, given the size of the dragon bones. But then, I guess, you won't ever be able to see them....such a pity."

"Why can't I ever see them, Don Tranquillo?" Zorzi guessed that his question would, as ever, lead him into one of Tranquillo's mental traps.

"Ah! Let me explain." Don Tranquillo's craggy and rough shaven face changed expression from one of mild amusement to a more solemn set. "Let us talk man to man Zorzi, you must give thought to your future. Grandpa is not, shall we say, in the best of health. He's not going to be able to provide for you for many years longer. I guess you already know that your furnaces may not be passed on to you?"

The news about Grandfather's health was not altogether a surprise to Zorzi. He was less sure though about what exactly he would inherit and what this strange tack in their conversation had to do with dragons' bones.

"But you must know, Don Tranquillo, old Piero owns our furnaces. He won't turn me out, whatever happens."

"Perhaps I should not be telling you this, but it seems likely that Piero will no longer be allowed to keep the glassworks for you." His voice hesitated, his hands twitched, pointed heavenward and then pressed hard on the desk top for a second or two: "The Marigola, that is the Glass Guild, has complained to the Podestà obliging him to write to the... to

19

the…. Quarantia Civil. Well, you know full well that they have banned your family from holding…Oh! I shall say no more!"

"To the Quarantia" Zorzi queried, having overheard island gossip about an appeal that the Podestà had made to a far more terrifying authority. Zorzi gave a delicious shudder of feigned fear, something Venetian children were in the habit of doing, on hearing any mention of some mysterious Committee lurking within the gloomy halls of the Doge's Palace: "Quarantia? Aldo told me the Podestà had sent his letter to, to… the The Ten! Is this Quarantia thing more important than them?"

"Heavens no! The Ten would never concern themselves with the humble likes of us: they are only involved in treason and affairs of State and ruling us, and things like that. Some say it brings bad luck even to mention their name."

Why is that Don Tranquillo?"

"Because nobody knows who they are and they have their ears everywhere, Zorzi. They might even be under the desk listening to you right now."

Zorzi instantly dived under the desk and emerged both relieved and just a little disappointed" Don Tranquillo chuckled:"Whatever happens at the Quarantia *(The Forty Magistrates for Trade,)* I'll do what I can to help, that's why I want you to do something for me Zorzi. You must join the choir of San.Dona`. You can see the dragon's bones whenever you like then. As I said, they hang behind the high altar. More to the point, you won't need to gnaw on them; Zustinian provides bread and cheese at every rehearsal. There are going to be quite a few rehearsals, I gather. It would mean that you would get some proper food on most days."

Knowing that Zorzi sometimes took the liberty of having a sip of wine whilst filling the communion cruets, he added temptingly: "Zustinian provides a particularly fine Soave for the boys. We get a flagon or two from time to time as well. The bottles are extra good quality, but you already know that. Fat Luanardo might even let you have some of his empties…he's the choirmaster at San Dona`.."

For as long as he could remember Zorzi had been collecting empty wine

20

bottles to add to Grandpa's cullet. Those from the Dominican convent and from other church porches had decorative glass medallions stamped at the neck: a way of denoting each vintage year. Intrigued by their variety and sometimes their beauty, Zorzi had quite a collection of these strange reliefs. Unknown to Grandpa, he would carefully break off any new device he found and grind down the sharp edges on the discarded millstone at the end of Aldo's garden. Zorzi hoarded his collection, suspecting that Grandpa might well insist that he add it to his ever dwindling stock of cullet. Once crushed to cullet and re-melted, the broken bottles became a free supplement from which Grandpa's little masterpieces of drinking goblets were fashioned. Don Tranquillo lifted up a heavy flask from the floor and poured the last few drops for Zorzi to taste. Most flasks were marked with the Zustinian imperial eagle emblem; an extra decorative device was often added where the bottleneck bulged outwards. Sometimes this device took the form of a kneeling Doge, other times a castle battlement with a tall tower; sometimes an open book appeared, or a peacock, or more rarely the outline of a Virgin and Christ child. Don Tranquillo took scant notice of these well made glass images, but Zorzi was a lad who rarely let cheap, or better still, free curiosities of such kind escape his acquisitive little grasp. Inspired by Grandpa's great hatred of the Noble Bastian Zustinian; that same loathing extending to Bastiano's uncle, Bishop Torcello, Zorzi took great pleasure in crushing up the Zustinian eagle emblem; however, unless he had a duplicate in better condition, he always kept the amusing monkey images that nobody but he had noticed, for when they appeared they were always hidden out of sight inside the foot rings of large bottles or heavier demijohns.

"What's the badge on the bottle today?" Zorzi asked.

Don Tranquillo inspected it and laughed: "Why it's a dog and a ladder! It's the standard of Can Grande della Scala (*Grand Dog of the Ladder,*) Lord of Verona, he built several castles around the Soave wine region… ages ago….rode into battle surrounded by his pack of ferocious armour plated mastiffs. We Venetians beat him though! I'll tell you about him some other day. They had amusing nicknames those old war lords like, Honeycat and Worm, as well an a few extremely rude names like 'Colleo.....' Well, er, never mind! Can Grande of Verona did lots of exceedingly gruesome things. Now listen! About the choir...."

"So was this his wine bottle?"

"Can't you see it's brand new like the others we get? There's some ruin of a Scala castle, I gather, near Zustinian's villa. Listen Zorzi! San Dona` Choir often gets invited to sing at one or other of the Zustinian palaces. I'm told the tables groan with nosebag after concerts. Dona`boys are always allowed to get their snouts in the trough before his servants come to clear up." Calculating that such a prospect would appeal to his ever-famished young guest, Tranquillo sat back and dabbed his mouth on the grubby tablecloth.

"But Grandpa would never let me. Grandpa loathes Zustinian for some reason. Do you know why, Don Tranquillo? Grandpa won't tell me, though he swears he will get even with him one day." (*Zorzi, like most Venetians, just could not get his tongue around the 'Giu' and 'Gio' sounds and pronounced them with a buzzing 'z': hence Zustinian for Giustinian and Zorzi for Giorgio.*)

"Vengeance is for the Almighty, my little son. Best not repeat what Grandpa says. I share his anger too sometimes, but Zustinian keeps the roof on my church and never leaves me short of a sequin when I need it for the old folk. It's never wise to cross a nobleman, not to mention a nephew of two Doges."

"Grief!" exclaimed Zorzi, with a quiet fishy belch. "Two Doges! I thought there was only one Doge."

"There is indeed only one, my clever lad. Our late Doge was his great uncle, Zustinian's other uncle, by marriage, is no less than our present Highness. And believe me, Doge Morosini is tough enough to knock even the likes of Can Grande into the shape of a lady's poodle. Grandpa would be wise to watch his words when complaining about one of his nephews."

"Oh crumbs! I had better run home and warn him!"

"He knows, my little friend. He knows!" Tranquillo laughed. "Take the rest of the loaf to Grandpa and no picking holes under the crust on the way!"

CHAPTER THREE

Saturday 12th May, 1694

Standing in his allotted place in the San Donato choir stalls, beneath that glittering half dome of the church apse, Zorzi was trying to suppress an attack of the jitters: quaking and cold-sweating next to him was his friend Matteo Barovier. Aldo Molin was with them, though he seemed less concerned about the importance of the occasion, for he was instructed to keep his lips moving and his voice unheard. Choirmaster Luanardo*(Leonardo)* had at first rejected outright the burly young fighter as 'having a voice like a marsh bittern with a bellyache,' but he was persuaded by Tranquillo that Aldo had other merits, such as acting as Zorzi's bodyguard, and as a wreaker of revenge on any who interfered with other choir members on the way to rehearsals. Aldo proved to be a useful companion to Luanardo as well. Luanardo could be rather cowardly when traversing dark alleyways, or when encountering idle and older youth who often loitered at the ferry with the sole intention of heaping insults on the bald and overweight Choirmaster.

The Noble Bastian Zustinian was expected to arrive at the rehearsal at any moment. He would select, or reject, their choir as worthy to sing before the throne of his uncle on the Feast of the Sensa. Morosini had made it known to his bishops and his nephew that he had no time for the new fangled modern music he sometimes heard in his Ducal Chapel at Saint Mark's. He would have Monteverdi's Vespers, a splendid sensuous work that he too had sung as a chorister in those carefree days of his childhood. Old Monteverdi knew how to blast out a warlike tune or two as well. It would be an appropriate piece, a suitable send-off: first to his 'Wedding of the Sea' and then straight on to join the battle fleet of galleys and galleons ready assembled beyond the Lido barrier of the Lagoon. The aches and pains of old age now wracked him, but would not deter him. He would sally forth in martial might and flag draped glory with the tunes of Monteverdi humming in his mind, determined to tear back the Isles of Greece from the ever provoking, ever advancing hordes of Allah. His days were on an ebbing tide - a premonition, that this might be the last time he would attend Vespers made him determined to hear some children's voices in the choir. The cause of his depressing abdominal gripe was certainly not cowardly panic: engaging hand to hand, galley to galley, in vicious sea fights was still far and away his favourite diversion. The constant, irritable-making gripe was something more worrying than the prospect of another murderous encounter with the Turk. His doctors appeared to have no real clue as to what caused his symptoms and even if they did know, they were too scared of him and too obsequious to tell him frankly. Having given him numerous potions of crushed sea pearls and gold dust mixed with fresh bull's blood, they now recommended, as a last resort, a long cruise with much merry slaughter of Ottoman Turk, to take his mind off his ailment. If he died in battle then nobody could possibly accuse them and dangle their scrawny necks for having poisoned the Doge of Venice.

Other than Zustinian, nobody knew how many choirs were in the running for the privilege of singing at the Doge's Vespers. There were most likely fifty or more, warbling away in high hopes throughout the islands of the Lagoon. For many centuries the Zustinian family had been patrons of San Donato, the Island's grandest and most ancient church. Surely the Noble Bastian would choose at least some of the choir from his own parish?

His temper ever on a short fuse, Luanardo was glowering at his choristers. He had repeated his threat to skin alive the first boy who dared to whisper, click his clogs or clear his throat in the presence of the Podestà and his illustrious guests. Luanardo clung to his silver-tipped staff: his hands too were clammy with anticipation. That staff was the symbol of his office; his conductor's baton with which he beat time on the marble mosaic floor and when swiped furiously in the direction of some inattentive choirboy, proved most effective.

Now at last, for a brief hour or so, the Choirmaster would bask in the attention and focus, perhaps even the envy and admiration of the shuffling chattering congregation, now jammed shoulder to shoulder in the cavernous church. Half the population of Murano seemed to be there. The excited crowd spilled out through the great west door and into the square outside, all hoping for the rare privilege of a glimpse of their local overlord and his guest.

Unlike his hairy namesake, the Renaissance artist from Vinci, Luanardo was completely without beard, hair and eyebrows. This and his wide girth gave him the appearance of a genie just blown out of Aladdin's lamp.

Though far from being a genius, the Choirmaster was cunning enough to know that he was in with a chance; quietly, pretending to be a casual visitor as well as a peddler of canvas sacks, he had done the rounds of most of the other church choirs, punting and puffing with fatigue from island to island in his leaking flat-bottomed boat. He felt confident that his choir had the edge on all the others; moreover, he held the ace card up the frayed sleeve of his greasy cassock - a boy with such a rare talent - a boy with the voice of an archangel fit to sing at heaven's gate.

This afternoon would be his moment of triumph, in front of the whole mocking, hateful population of Murano. Would they snigger behind his back? Would they call out 'eunuch' and 'fartso' when he waddled through the market or struggled to keep his balance when boarding the ferry gondola? Not when he was promoted Chapel Master to the Doge! To any who then dared he would order a severe flogging! With a confident smirk on his face, he turned to the noisy congregation, banged his stave loudly on the altar steps and yelled,"Silence...Silence!" Those nearest who could hear his high-pitched shriek just ignored him and continued with their loud conversations.

Exasperated, he stalked over to the organ bellows boy and gave him a sharp prod. "Start pumping!" he ordered. The startled boy began to pedal furiously with his bare feet up and down on the double bellows. The ancient organ gave some rude grunts and whistles and then roared into life as Luanardo hit the keys and stops. A quick flick of his hand alerted the choir. A few twiddling notes more and they knew exactly what he wanted of them.

Zorzi drew his deepest 'glass blower's' breath and in perfect timing with his pals sang out - SANCTA MARIA, ORA PRO NOBIS, SANCTA DEI GENITRIX ORA PRO NOBIS. *(Holy Mary, mother of God, pray for us.)*

Within a trice the whole unruly mob, from the rood screen of the choir to those perched on the high walls surrounding the outside square shushed one another into total silence. Venetians adore music, especially their own brand. Music, carnivals, feast days and ceremonies involving splendidly dressed officials were, and will always be their supreme joy and entertainment. As Zorzi relaxed, singing his heart out, confident in words of Monteverdi's wonderful anthem, his eyes roamed sideways and upwards to the ceiling of the apse. There above him was 'Sancta Maria' herself. Streaming in from the Romanesque arched windows, the late afternoon sun lit up the vast sea of burnished mosaic pieces that were set into plaster at cunningly reflecting angles and glistened all around the Madonna's dazzling blue form. Twelve feet tall and proudly erect in her glassy blue and star spangled gown the Madonna was gliding over golden waves, balanced confidently on her tiny magical mosaic raft.

His innocent conclusion was that to be so depicted in church the Madonna must have enjoyed the occasional rafting adventure up in the oceans of heaven. Come the next windy day, he would go down to the lighthouse beach with Aldo, Lucia, Matteo and his other close pals: with driftwood logs, empty barrels and rotting floor planks they would swim out to meet the incoming tide. Not a child in the least given to self-pity, he had no real memories of his own mother to cherish. A hazy memory of a tall man with shoulder length brown hair was all he could conjure up when trying to recollect his late father's features. Zorzi prayed that his own mother too was up there with the Madonna, whom he imagined she exactly resembled. And if his mother were not too occupied with her own heavenly rafting, then maybe she might be smiling down on him, pleased that he was trying his best to be a chorister. *(That his young mother, a few days after her eighteenth birthday, had been tumbled without reverence or requiem into an unmarked plague pit, together with several hundred other victims from the Island, he was not to learn until he was much older.)*

They were near to finishing the anthem when there was a great noise of cheering and clapping mingled with the clatter-clatter of horses hooves, it came booming in through the west door. The organ gave out a last irate wail. Luanardo stood up and walked centre stage in a great huff.

Springing from his saddle with the elegance and confidence of an athlete, the Noble Bastian Zustinian, adjusted his enormous curly brown wig and grabbed his hat from one of his squires. Before assisting his mature, not to say elderly, guest to dismount, he gave him a slow graceful sweeping bow, worthy of a dancing master. Next, he flourished his blue and white plumed hat to the crowd, who responded with a huge cheer - they were the Doge's colours. Young ladies in the throng squealed, waved handkerchiefs to attract his attention, or pretended to faint with delirium at his sight. He truly was a handsome specimen of manhood, head and shoulders taller than anyone present.   Somewhere, under the caked face powder, rouged lips and beauty patches, he had the weather-tanned skin of a sailor.

At the church door he was met by Matteo Tosi, the Archpriest. Several dignitaries of the district were hovering nearby, eager to be introduced. For the most part they were rich glass merchants rather than the less prosperous furnace owners. All secretly hoped that a bit of grovelling and obsequiousness to the great lord and his foreign guest might lead to a profitable export order. The nobility, living in the many grand villas on the island, stayed away. This was not an occasion when they were constrained to mingle with the unwashed mob. The Noble Marco Zustinian, Lord Bishop of Torcello, was some months away in Milan so there was no need to pay their respects to him. Malicious rumour had it that his pilgrimage was for the purpose of renewing his acquaintance with a wayward daughter of the Spanish Governor of that great Lombard city, who in the past was known to have 'assisted him in his devotions.' The Bishop's uncle, the saintly Doge Marco Antonio Zustinian, who had spent more time on his knees than on his throne and had never married, had recommended him for the Torcello living, in hope that he might improve his ways. But Bishop Marco was the son of his father, the noble and naughty Count Peter, known as 'Golden Guts' for his many successes at the card tables and with the ladies of the Venetian Court. As for that other ducal nephew, Bastian Zustinian and his totally evil French guest, most noblemen and their ladies preferred not to be introduced to them.

Fifteen minutes of complete and enjoyable chaos accompanied the arrival of the visitors, nothing unusual at the start of any important event in Venice. The mounted bandsmen, perched on their scruffy marsh ponies, were stuck in the crowd half way across St. Donato Bridge. Unable to move forward, the bandsmen struck up a marching tune just where they were. The crowd joined in: the silver trumpets brayed; the ponies neighed and fidgeted and shied whenever the outsized kettledrums were pounded right next to their sensitive ears. Then some fool decided to deafen everyone by ringing a joyful peal of welcome from the vast brick tower of St. Donato.

A company of heavily armed lancers had dismounted and was busy pushing back the pressing crowd, by linking lances together to act as a makeshift railing. This posed no great problem in the square, where people could shuffle back, but when they entered the church, to clear a path to the altar, people were crushed like sprats in a barrel. Some tumbled down on the uneven floor, others fell into the laps of the aged folk, who by right, sat with their backs to the wall. The walls, for no apparent reason, were lined with decorative iron railing which was painful for old spines to connect with. The younger and fitter tried to clamber onto the marble choir screen that took up far too much space in the nave and blocked off any view of the choirboys. Luanardo was having none of that and was flailing his heavy staff around and above their heads in a paroxysm of rage. He was losing control of the choirboys as well. They were falling about with laughter for some offensive reason, which he guessed had to do with him.

Matteo Barovier, the joker amongst the boys, had loudly proposed that if old Luanardo connected his breeches to the organ pipes he might play a welcome anthem to the Noble Zustinian, without the need for an ugly bellows boy. Aldo added to the boys' now helpless laughter by suggesting that if Luanardo saved his flatus until the moment when he bowed to the Podestà, then all the boys could go and sing hymns outside the jail house door.

In the evening sunlight of the church square, a number of ragged and elderly 'deserving poor' were being presented to Zustinian and to his guest. Each, with some help, got down on both knees and extended hands in supplication. Zustinian spoke kindly to each one, pretended to listen to their pleas and senile mutterings and made a slight gesture to show that he was willing to help them stand up on their rickety legs. Of course, his servants hastened forward to help and to move them swiftly onwards to where Don Francesco stood. Don Francesco's pageboy held a large silver tray piled with small purses made from Burano Island lace. Inside each purse was a small sum of 'piccoli' coins of low silver content, enough though to keep an old person provided with dried cod and chickpeas for half a year or more.

Don Francesco's careworn and somewhat wrinkled face was neither caked in cosmetics, nor was it a face rarely seen. Being the owner of the largest palace on the island, with a long established court room and ample accommodation for staff, he had reluctantly agreed to act as Podestà whilst his friend, Podestà Giulio Bembo, was recovering from a mysterious skin ailment requiring mercury treatment. His term of office would normally have lasted sixteen months, however the Four Deputies and the Grand Council of the Island had insisted that he rather than Bembo should undertake a second term and that thankfully was within a few months of completion, for in truth Don Francesco was near exhausted by the endless burden of daily administration. Over the past two years Francesco had developed into that rare being - an immensely liked Podestà. By nature shrewd and cautious when making decisions, he was both generous and approachable. Sympathy too had its part in bolstering his popular appeal. Before taking up the post of Podestà *(trans:The Power i.e.,Chief Magistrate and Mayor of Murano,)* he had been a lonely and dejected widower of some forty years of age, who had lost all sense of purpose in life, his wife and daughter having died in the epidemic of the coughing lungs. With the new challenge and the long hours of public duties, the sharp edged sword of the Podestàs sorrow was slowly being blunted.

Podestà the N.H. *(Nobil Huomo)* Francesco Capello Benzon led the way down the aisle and came first into sight. Seeing who it was descending on them, the choirboys creased themselves in their efforts to suppress their giggles. The Podestà was wearing his chain of office and was further ornamented by a snuff brown knee length coat of brocade, delicately overlaid with gold thread. Long black 'convent curls' were massed about his head and shoulders, in the form of a full periwig. The finest Burano lace sprouted from the ends of Don Francesco's sleeves, it trimmed his matching brown silk breeches, and fluffed out stiff with starch from around his neck. In dressing for the occasion, he was careful not to outdo his guests: not that it would have been possible for anyone, other than the Doge, to out-dress the French courtier. He was just an unbelievable apparition of wealth, silk ribbons and elegance. His dark blue velvet outer coat was studded with a great fortune of pearls and diamonds and had strange large flapped pouches on either side: such pockets were the very latest invention of Parisian fashion. His waistcoat and breeches were of pale cream coloured satin, amazingly finely embroidered with floral patterns in coloured silk thread. As the party swaggered down the church aisle, the priests, clerks and better educated in the congregation noted with awe that the French gentleman was wearing the Cordon Bleu, as well as the eight pointed cross of a 'Religious,' that is a Knight of the renowned Order of St. John of Malta. His wide sash of pale blue silk was fixed to his coat with a dove shaped Order of the Holy Spirit: the Holy Spirit having generously descended upon the Frenchman in the form of an enormous and spectacular pink diamond, quite the largest in Europe.

The choirboys were not in the least impressed by the show of sartorial splendour. They quietly chuckled at the nobles' powdered and lip-sticked faces. However, what got them gawping with excitement were the noblemen's jewel encrusted rapiers, menacingly quilloned with finest cut steel. Contrary to custom and good manners, neither Bastian Zustinian nor his French guest had bothered to hand these offensive weapons to his page on entering the House of God.

Three carved and comfortable walnut armchairs were now placed at the foot of the choir steps, blocking off completely any view of the boys. The two noblemen lounged promptly into theirs without doing the Podestà the courtesy of waiting. Legs sprawled apart they appeared to be deliberately showing off their fine doeskin riding boots that were tricked out with dainty rosettes and knots of blue silk ribbon and fashioned with ridiculously high soles and heels lacquered in bright red cinnabar. Both rake-hells had been over indulging at luncheon in Brunello wine and garlic risotto. A clergyman standing in the choir just within hearing range of Zorzi murmured: "What insolence! Who's the raddled old jewel peddler?"

"Well desribed Brother Timothy," Archpriest Tosi murmured, "Sacre Bleu! would be my description of him. He's Lorraine.....the Batard of Lorraine...Orleans's fancy boy. A right blue blood too, if ever there was one. He came here in '82, the year Bernard Perrotto and his entire workforce disappered."

"I wonder, whose glassworks he'll buy up this time?" whispered another elderly cleric.

"Capello disappoints me." Tosi commented. "Surprised he lets those two mollies flaunt their vile habits about our Island. Lorraine doesn't only carry off glassworkers - little boys vanish as well when he's around."

"He's a Guise, that's why," another elderly cleric commented. "The Ten don't want to upset Orleans, that fop brother of King Louis. Lorraine is a big spender. The Sensa is more about profit than piety these days."

Archpriest Tosi mounted his ornate marble tub of a pulpit, one of two on either side of the choir entrance. The boys groaned, in expectation of the usual long and tedious sermon. Adjusting his tiny purple silk biretta that was perched like a dainty pavillion atop his fuzzy cloud of grey wig, Tozi gave a polite cough for silence and announced: "On behalf of the Bishop of Torcello, I welcome the Noble Zustinian and his illustrious guest, the Prince Chevalier Abbot Guise of Lorraine Cambout Harcourt. Unfortunately, because of the presence of so many at today's function, our distinguished visitors are unable to admire our wonderful and ancient church floor which is the finest in all...."

Exceedingly peeved that he had not been given a formal welcome by the wise, but nevertheless windbag of a priest, Podestà Capello scribbled a hasty note: now his pageboy was tugging at Tosi's sleeve. Looking down, Tosi snatched the note, gave a great "Hurrumph!" and read it to himself, which was just as well, for it said: 'Cut it short. Just a few verses to be sung. Noblemen going to Casino` in half an hour. Choose three boys.'

Now the Casino` was a gambling den recently set up in the old Soranzo Palace near to San Stin Church. It attracted wastrels from far and wide, like the two noble louts sprawled in front of him, as well as other undesirables both male and female. Infuriated by this news, Tosi struggled to regain his composure, fumbled to control his toppling biretta and announced: "Sadly, the noble gentlemen will be unable to remain with us for the rest of the afternoon, as they intended; they have been summoned to an urgent meeting with the Senate. Signor Luanardo will therefore select some verses from the Vespers to show the vocal range and talents of our young singers." With that he stepped down from his pulpit, but not before giving a long stare at Zustinian, a stare of priestly condemnation and of cold contempt.

Thrown into confusion by these orders, Luanardo struck up the Sancta Maria hymn once again. This finished, he went on to the Benedictus. The boys sang well: he was now confident that his choir would be the winner. Now was the moment to reveal his trump card. Climbing down from the organ bench he beckoned to Zorzi. Zorzi hesitated, unsure of who was

31

being called. After all, he had only just joined the choir and no compliment had ever been paid about his voice, least of all by Luanardo. The fat choirmaster strode across to him, gripped the collar of his long red cassock and propelled Zorzi to the pulpit on the Epistle side of the choir. There was a titter of laughter from the crowd as only the top of his head could be seen. Archpriest Tosi came forward with a wooden footstool for him to stand on.

"Sing boy. Don't you dare let me down," Luanardo hissed in Zorzi's ear. "Sing Psalm 109 - the DIXIT DOMINUS!" Back at the organ he twiddled a few notes then opened up full throttle.

Limpid as the sound rung from a Murano wine glass, Zorzi's voice reverberated around the ancient walls of San Donato. *'The Lord said unto my lord: Sit at my right hand until I make your enemies my footstool.'* The crowd was silent, entranced by him, as he sang alternate verses with the choir. The psalm ended with a tremendous shout of "Bravo!" and a thunderous noise of feet being stamped in applause. Quite unused to any sort of praise, Zorzi was dumfounded. "Bis! Bis! Bis!" they yelled at him. Not being sure what this meant, he bowed low and awkwardly to the congregation several times. Laughter now filled the church - the Noble Zustinian and his French guest jointing in.

Archpriest Tosi, by now as purple as his silk biretta with sacred rage, dashed down on the bench that natty but uncontrollable symbol of his rank, stepped back into the pulpit and thundered: "Where do you think you are?" This is not a concert hall. Remember you are in the house of God!" But cunning Luanardo drowned the priest's cries of outrage with a prompt burst of notes from the organ - the rehearsed and familiar cue to Psalm 112. The choirboys launched with great gusto into their favourite anthem: LAUDATE PUERI DOMINUM. *'Young boys praise the Lord.'* Once again the congregation fell silent. Some way into the long Psalm it came to Zorzi's part - the PULCHRA ES. *'You are fair my love, beautiful and comely. O daughter of Jerusalem.'*

Old ladies mopped their tear-filled eyes with handkerchiefs: tough Arsenal workers cuffed theirs with dirt caked ragged sleeves. It was a moment of pure high emotion - Venetian style. The glorious voice soared heavenwards again and again - trilled like a linnet and ornamented the notes, as only a young and hearty lunged alto singer can do. Dipping his voice to more solemn tones, Zorzi slowly savoured the menacing verses of the Psalm: *'Terrible as an army set in array....'*

"Madonna and Mark, what a discovery! Such limpid crystal! And from such a tin ribbed midget of a boy! Uncle is going to love this!" Zustinian shouted in French to his friend above the clamour of the audience. "Just what the wicked beast demanded: a perfect cherubim from the lower orders; someone he can show off to the mob after his damned Vespers. But Monteverdi....so primitive, don't you think? All those drums and squealing trumpets give me a headache. It's what Uncle wants though.... a racket of martial thunder off set by a bit of childish warbling. I'll soon be back in the Chancellor's appointment book."

"Be under no illusions on that score, cher Bastien. With your debts the Senate could never elect you. But Orleans might offer you something a deal more profitable than a Procurator's purse. Come back with me and to hell with them, Senate and all: just bankrupt your creditors."

Leaning closer and lowering his voice to a level barely audible above the noise Zustinian chuckled his answer: "As you well know, cher Philippe, consorting with foreigners without a blessing from The Ten is the shortest path to the gallows. What restricted lives we Venetians lead... our so called republic.... time we ended it."

"Then get yourself an appointment at our Court, I could persuade Louis to dismiss your tiresome spy of an ambassador. Better still," Lorraine suggested with a grim smile, "Convince your good uncle that the Serenissima needs a more reliable man in Paris: that would suit all our needs to perfection!"

When the applause died down, both noblemen lounged back into their armchairs. Bastian Zustinian then beckoned to Don Francesco to come forward and whispered something in his ear. The Podestà promptly mounted the choir steps and took the by now bewildered Zorzi by the hand. As he led him down the steps, a beaming and perspiring Luanardo came waddling behind them. "Bow to the noblemen," Don Francesco instructed.

Zorzi stretched his left leg out as far as he could behind him and bent his right knee forward, as far as his tight red cassock would let him. Then raising his hand as though taking off an imaginary hat, he gave a slow and low sweep of his arm, bowing his head as he did so. This gallant gesture he had seen gentlemen do many times, but none of them wore tight cassocks and slippery choirboy's clogs. In short, he did the splits and with a thud collapsed in a heap on the glassy mosaic floor. A peal of unrestrained laughter came from the crowd. The priests, noblemen and equerries held their sides with mirth. It was some time before they regained their composure. It was the Chevalier Philippe de Guise Lorraine who gave Zorzi a hand up from the floor. Zorzi smelt his strong perfume, his foul garlic breath - stinking like an open sewer - and looked with astonishment into the nobleman's lustful eyes that seemed to burn out at him from a wrinkled, pock marked and white powdered face. As Lorraine's wig flapped back Zorzi noticed that the upper lobe of the Chevalier's ear was missing and guessed immediately that it had been sliced in a duel.The Chevalier gave him an unpleasant leer, rather than a smile and running his hands slowly down the boy's sides he murmured "vaat a preety child."

"Your name, boy?" Zustinian demanded.

"Zorzi, Vossignoria."

Luanardo bustled forward," His name is Giorgio Miotto, Vossignoria Zustinian. By far my best pupil, but of course Vossignoria, I've given him hours of personal tuition." The choirmaster lied through his misshapen teeth; gave a sigh of fish and cabbage breath and an ingratiating smirk.

For daring to speak to him before being asked, Zustinian gave the sweaty choirmaster a look of utter disdain....of unmistakable haughty disgust. In his noble esteem fat Luanardo was little more than equivalent to an unwelcome slug that had just crawled out of a plate of salad. "Go back to your boys, Choirmaster, and select two more to sing at St. Mark's," he snarled.

Mortified by this cold 'put-down' and with the realization that only three of his boys would be chosen to sing before the Doge, the poor fellow went over to his organ, rested his head on the keyboard cover and sobbed.

34

"Miotti del Jesu?" Zustinian inquired, with a mystified look on his face.

"No Vossignoria, they are our rich cousins. We are just Miotti....I think we are called Miotti di Brayda."

"Ah!" Zustinian exclaimed with deep annoyance," Not that Miotti, surely not!" His eyes narrowed with malevolence: "Well young Miotto, the sins of a stubborn father shall not, for the present, be visited upon the son. You have a half decent voice. We shall forgive you for that...for your fine voice." Turning to Podestà Francesco he ordered: "See that the child is washed and clothed and sent to Ca` Granda for this evening. I have a mind to give a concert in a day or so."

"You shall not! Never! You shall not take my child away!" An infuriated cry came from amidst the crowd. Battering his way like a bull through a thicket, Grandfather parted the packed congregation and took the equerries, servants and guards surrounding the noblemen by total surprise. Shaking with rage, he faced up close to Zustinian and with a hate-filled voice bellowed: "You have taken my son. Now you would have my grandson! I tell you, I am a Citizen of the Golden Book! My family has lived here more years than yours Zustinian, and we are citizens of this island. I have my rights, Zustinian! I have my rights! You shall not....never!"

Hastening forward to intervene, Don Francesco Capello received a heavy chopping blow on his wrist from Grandfather's forearm, as both tried to grab hold of Zorzi. A gasp of horror, of astonishment, went up from all who witnessed this outrage to the Podestàs person. Before anyone else could intervene, Grandfather whisked the boy back into the crowd, burrowing his way down the right aisle so as to avoid the guard of Lancers. For one awkward moment they were trapped behind the base of a stone column supporting the aisle roof. Looking up, Zorzi caught a fleeting glimpse of Saint Donato trampling on his spitted dragon. He had never before noticed the faded and flaking wall painting, having always entered by the Sacristy door. "San Dona` help us!" he pleaded. The Saint obliged, by giving extra thumping power to Grandpa's elbows. Zustinian's guards were fast approaching, forcing their way with their lances through the milling throng.

At the Great West Door, Grandpa and Zorzi's way was barred once again by a number of tough looking Arsenal men, who assumed that they were either escaping cutpurses, or had committed some other crime in the church. They seized Grandpa and pinned his arms, then recognizing him they unhanded him. It was only old Miotti, what harm could he have done? Grandfather chose a moment of shocked silence to shout back with all his fury into the church: "And I would remind you, Bastian Zustinian, of the promise of Our Saviour Jesus.... Take care he does not hang a millstone around your neck and dump you in the Adriatic Sea!"

Shouts of outrage then gave way to murmurs of uncertainty. Had Grandpa dropped an explosive grenade shell in their midst, his words could hardly have had more effect on the congregation. The Arsenal workers may have been illiterate, and in some cases were no more than thick skulled thugs, but most of them knew some of the more frequently used verses from the Bible. Certain sayings of Jesus had been learned from their mothers' lips. Within seconds most of them understood very well the significance of old Miotti's rantings. Their macho suspicions about the painted Frenchman were confirmed. Those crude jokes about Zustinian's lack of girlfriends: the sniggering innuendos passed around whenever the effete Zustinian had occasion to visit the sweaty sheds of the Arsenal; so, after all, they were not unfounded! Old Daniele Miotti was regarded by many as a bit of a grump, his son a traitor to the Island, but he was no raving lunatic, nor in his dotage. Zustinian must have done something unmentionable to his scruffy little scrap of a grandson, to cause the old man to explode in this way.

The Arsenal men formed a double line and blocked the exit, whilst Zorzi, minus his clogs and a few buttons from his borrowed choirboy's cassock, and now being dragged along by Grandpa, escaped over the bridge and into the rubbish strewn back alleyways of Murano. Swords were drawn at the church door and lances pointed in vain, for when the Arsenal men said they would not budge, they did not budge. Just one blood-drawing prod at an Arsenal man would be an invitation to catastrophe on a city wide scale. Zustinian's lancers knew that full well and though under orders to charge, resorted instead to blows and shoves.

CHAPTER FOUR

The witnesses to the 'San Donato Outrage' returned to their dank hovels or to their handsome country villas well contented with the afternoon's entertainment. There would be enough to chatter about for weeks and in the telling, the facts would become as embroidered as a Frenchman's waistcoat. Old Miotti had gone stark raving mad and mortally wounded the Podestà Don Francesco Capello: the choirmaster was about to be hanged for molesting Miotti's grandson; the Arsenal workers had caused a riot and had hurled rotten vegetables and abuse at some twenty or more fleeing foreign noblemen and their escorts; the unruly crowd had enjoyed chucking some of the lancers and bandsmen into the canal; a pony, with a large kettle drum in tow, was last seen swimming for his life out into the Lagoon. There was some truth in the last two of these inflated tales.

However, quite the hottest gossip in the villas and palace salons was about a certain boy soprano just arrived on the island, most probably hired by Bastian Zustinian, the bishop's nephew, from a Milanese opera house. The child had given a magisterial performance backed "Oh so inadequately" by the San Donato Choir. Ladies of fashion were eager to know in which venue he would be singing next. Would it be opera arias in the garden of one of the grander villas, or a far less appealing church recital where they would be obliged to mingle once again with the malodorous and ill mannered? Or would Zustinian just dress the lad in Grecian drapes for one of his notorious bacchanals, reserved for his close associates - those 'butch' looking ladies and effete bachelors? Comments that the little skylark was no more than the son of a glassmaker; a traitor; even a Guildmaster; who had now escaped overseas, were mostly dismissed with ridicule. How could anyone mistake a ragged half starved Miotti brat for the Noble Bastian's latest and most enchanting new talent?

Don Francesco departed soon after the rioting had simmered down. The greater part of the mob had dispersed to their homes and taverns. Evening was drawing-on as he left by the Sacristy door. A lonely, thoughtful figure, he strolled through the little cemetery and opened a wicket gate to the acres and acres of orchards that lay beyond. His indignation, not to say instant rage at old Miotti's impertinence, had now given way to more customary cool reason. By nature he was affable and not swift to take revenge. A more ruthless Podestà might well by now have had Miotti's scraggy old neck in a noose! Though his arm still smarted from the swift and heavy blow, it was his own realization that he had made a complete ass of himself in the church that rankled most. It was not that he was too cowardly to return home mingling with the excited crowds: though he had been humiliated in their presence; and that he felt was a heavier blow to his status than any swipe from Old Miotti. He justified the long detour he would be making with the thought that he would otherwise have been badgered by much public questioning; the answers to which not even he could fathom for the moment.

The Capello Palace was no more than a minute or two of walking distance from San Donato church. As Podestà his person was sacred: that is to all but the terrifying Ten, who doubtless very soon would be calling him to account. What had possessed him to lay hands on that innocent scrap of a chorister? No half decent grandparent would have done otherwise than to leap to the defence of his offspring. Don Francesco well knew that he had merited that thump from Miotti: yet for old Miotti, if The Ten got involved, it might well mean a ghastly death by 'breaking at the wheel' or, if the sentence were commuted, the mercy of the hangman's noose. Fortunately none of his four Deputy Governors had been present in the church, but exaggerated accounts of what had happened would soon reach their ears. In order to restore their esteem as well as the high regard in which the common folk held him, Don Francesco knew that he would have to move swiftly somehow to trivialize the assault, yet at the same time he needed to show that some punishment had been meted out to old Miotti.

The almond and plum trees, in full May bloom, gave off a sweet refreshing scent. The Podestà blew his nose on a large lace handkerchief and took several deep breaths to clear his lungs of the stench of unwashed clothes and dirty bodies which, despite the incense burners, had filled the church. The setting sun was now throwing the fruit tree branches into dark relief, transforming the plum blossom to a tint of deep red wine. Some fifty miles away, across the rich lands of the Venetian Republic, the Alps soared up to make the horizon with their eternal snows. The air between was so clear that the Alps seemed like a row of pink tents camped at the end of the orchard. It was a lovely evening to be out walking and to tumble over in his clever brain the choice of drastic actions he might now need to take.

He would be in no haste to bring together his Court of Four Deputies and would recommend a public, but not too severe whipping of the aged glassmaker. Better still he would make Miotti sweat with anxiety for several days before sending two of his more intimidating bulli to 'visit' the old man's home and glassworks. Meanwhile, he would give orders for a large wagon wheel to be set up somewhere along the path that most people took to the market. It would be bracketed with iron on top of a post driven deep into the ground. Noisy sledgehammers would be used to attract attention and the largest threshing flail that could be found would be left propped-up against it. It would serve as a grizzly reminder to rioters as to the fate that might well await them. Of course not even the Podestà of Murano, had the authority to condemn a person to such a frightful execution. But news would speedily reach the Most Excellent Council: the affront; the insulting blow to his sacred office as Podestà; the humiliating riot involving a visiting foreign nobleman; all would have to be explained in a long and truthful account. Fortune indeed would smile on him if he received just a note in reply from Grand Chancellor Ballarin thanking him for setting up the wheel as a timely warning to the mob. A chill was now drifting in from the Lagoon and with it came to mind another vision. It was of the Ducal Palace Gastaldo, complete with his jailer, a set of leg irons and a warrant. With an escort of marines the Gastaldo would descend at midday when the well trod footpath in front of the Capello Palace was at its busiest. Don Francesco saw himself being dragged forth half naked in those clanking leg irons and to the pitying murmurs of the crowd, rowed away. Damp and hungry days would then pass in the cells before he stood in the presence of....of The Most Excellent Ten! Terrified, he would babble confused answers to their quietly spoken demands.

There were other matters that needed self reproach as well. Why on earth had he permitted young Bastian Zustinian to flaunt his rank and precedence in public and furthermore to humiliate him at every opportunity? He had held silence for these last few days while being treated most contemptuously by Bastian and his French guest as little more than a servant - an errand boy! That too he concluded was down to his own weak kneed tendency to deference. Though he could write no more than N.H. before his name he was, after all, a Capello of the ancient Capulet; a clan that could claim deeper roots than that of Lorraine.

Moreover, as a Podestà of Venice he need bow to no one but to God, The Ten and the Serenissimo Doge himself. The Senate however were well aware that Lorraine acted as the eyes and ears of King Louis XIV wherever he travelled and Don Francesco could excuse himself to some degree by having to accept the Senate's requirement for him to play host to the decadent and outrageously camp Prince and what's more to entertain Lorraine at his own expense.

He had just been dazzled at first, he had to admit that to himself: dazzled by Lorraine's witty conversation; his exquisite elegance and manners and who could fail but to be held stunned and spellbound by those silks and jewels and the gasps of admiration from the crowd as he, the Podestà, entered and left his modest Murano home in the company of such a Prince?

More pressing concerns then entered his evening thoughts as he wandered amidst the brambles and vines, cabbages and carrot tops poking up from the marshy smallholdings. How was it that young Bastian - descended as he was from the Caesars of ancient Rome - how was it that he seemed to know so much about the humble Miotti family? True, he may have heard of the Miotti del Jesu, for they were listed in the Island's 'Golden Book' of distinguished families who had lived on the Island for centuries. Then there was the matter of grandfather Miotti's wild and uncharacteristic behaviour in the church. Don Tosi and some of the other clergy had hastened to assure him afterwards that Miotti was by nature placid, neighbourly and as honourable a citizen as one could wish. They were astonished that an aged man, said to be terminally ill with his lungs, could show such energy in escaping after delivering that swift and violent blow. But then, both they and the Podestà could well understand why the old glassblower had become so enraged at the attempt to take his grandson from him: Bastian was a clever, nasty natured and unbridled pederast who well deserved his foul repute throughout the islands. Old Miotti had shouted: "You have taken my son, now you would have my grandson!" What did he mean by those words? Again the clergymen had reminded him that Miotti's son, Vincenzo, had disappeared many long years ago. A half forgotten report that the Podestà had read on first taking office then came instantly to mind: it stated that that a lady of ill repute had lured Vincenzo Miotti to London, shortly after his wife had died of the pneumonic plague. The report concluded that Maestro and ex

Guildmaster Vincenzo Miotti had been lured and bribed by a certain Ravenscroft, an English glass merchant in order to reveal glassmaking secrets of the Miotti and Darduin families. Vincenzo had been one of the most acclaimed glassblowers on the Island: that made his desertion all the more hurtful to his neighbours and to the Podestà of that time, in the person of his friend Giulio Bembo.

To reveal such secrets, thus ruining overseas trade, was one of the greatest crimes against the Serenissima. Vincenzo was outlawed on pain of death, by Podestà Bembo. Venetian spies in London were instructed to fillet him with their daggers on first sight. All Miotti furnaces were closed down and they were banned from trading in glass. Guards had to be posted to stop their houses and workshops from being torn down by the angry mob. Then the Miotti del Jesu family protested their innocence, as did their cousins the famous and now near noble Darduins, whose secrets and recipes for rare glass Vincenzo took with him to London. Why should they suffer for the misdeeds of their treacherous cousin? Both Darduin and del Jesu factories were promptly allowed to re-open after agreeing to be over charged on their tax bills. They were left seething with anger against their cousin Daniele and his son Vincenzo: but then to appease the two innocent families, the clever Podestà Bembo publicly announced that the thumping tax bill was in fact a noble and patriotic gift by the del Jesu and Darduin families to the war coffers of the Doge and the Serene Republic. Since his own appointment as Podestà, Don Francesco had turned a blind eye when old Daniele Miotti fired-up again his two very small furnaces and quietly began trading in the distant Rialto market rather than from his premises: all bills being paid and issued in the name of an elderly friend. The Marigola, the Glassmakers' Guild of Murano had protested because that friend was not an elected guild member: not even a glassblower - in fact no more than a penniless fisherman! However he, as Podestà had chosen to ignore their complaints, judging that Murano could only hope to escape from its dire poverty by having as many busy glassworks as possible. The collapse of trade could not be blamed entirely on the wars with the Ottoman Turks. Endless religious quarrels between the princes of Europe, as well as the gradual leaking of secrets to foreign glass manufacturers had also taken its toll. And there were other evident facts that the Podestà had to face: there were far too many qualified glassblowers in Murano and too little business. When The Ten had decreed in 1690 that out of work glassblowers had to be supported by operating kiln owners, life had got far worse for everyone. At least those who were lured overseas sometimes sent back part of their wages to support their starving families. Then there was the fact that if Maestro Vincenzo had wanted a job overseas he could so easily have got one with his distant cousins in Middelburg.

Don Francesco tumbled over in his mind all these concerns and as he wandered now under the plum trees and early blooming roses, jumped a sludge filled ditch or two before following the path southwards across a neatly kept vegetable patch. Duty now demanded that he would have to re-investigate Vincenzo Miotti's disappearance. There was clearly a threat to the morals of the Miotti child from his own tenant, the dissolute Bastian Zustinian: the clergy were in agreement with him on that - but how to prove it? Would it be wise to report his concerns directly to the Most Excellent Council of Ten? Should his suspicions prove to be unfounded, then there would be more serious consequences to worry about than the unpaid rent from the rooms he let to young Bastian. The Ten were pitiless about unproven accusation, especially when made against high ranking noblemen. Any such error made by a Podestà invited disgrace from office and several years in a dark dank cell at the very minimum.

A large heap of rags in the middle of a cabbage patch suddenly moved and a long knife flashed in the gloom. He drew and cocked his pistol with equal speed and backed hard against a tree. As the apple blossom floated down onto his wig, he realized, with a laugh, that it was a very old and very bent peasant woman who had just cut a cabbage. Half stooping and racked with arthritis, she turned and recognized him: embarrassed, he hid the pistol under his coat.

"God's blessing be with you signor Podestà," she croaked.

"What are you doing working at this hour?" he inquired.

"Times are hard, signor Podestà," she answered, "and I have got to cut the last of my winter cabbages for tomorrow's market. This is the best of them, take it as my gift. Please accept it noble padrino, and you will do me great honour."

"You have greater need of a fine cabbage than me," the Podestà answered with a chuckle,"but I will buy it from you."

"Then you refuse my gift?" There was a note of reproof and disappointment in her voice.

"Better still, let us exchange gifts, as gentleman to lady."
Out of her sight, he uncocked and returned the heavy weapon to its holster, fished into his newfangled coat pockets and pulled-out two lace bags full of piccoli coins. They were left over from the alms ceremony held outside San Donato church. Giving both bags and a gallant bow to the old lady, he tucked the cabbage under his arm and wandered off home.

CHAPTER FIVE

There is no twilight in Northern Italy. The sun drops over the mountain tops and most nights, moon and stars take over within very few minutes. Don Francesco stumbled in pitch darkness up to the courtyard gates of the Capello Palace. The chill wind had now given way to a drizzling mist. His pistol powder was almost exhausted, having used it so many times in his tinder box to light the way over rickety wooden bridges. He was sorely tempted to dump the bulky cabbage, but something in his heart prevented him from doing so. It would be perhaps a timely reminder to him, a fairly wealthy man, of the grinding suffering of the working folk. They relied on him to bring back the once prosperous times in the glassmaking industry of the island and that, at the moment, seemed a hopeless task. Lorraine would almost certainly leave now with his silk purse still heavy with Louis d'or.

He decided that he would keep the cabbage on his desk for a few days while he mentally drew up an action plan. Any serious misjudgement he knew could lead to a short life and a miserable existence in the New Prisons. But what the devil was going on in comfortable old Palazzo Capello? The whole place was in total darkness. Normally, at that hour, its lozenge glazed window frames flickered with light from log fires and from his enormous and cheerfully florid glass chandeliers cascading down from the high ceilings of the 'piano nobile,' the state rooms. No more than a glow-worm glimmer of a rush light came from the washhouse halfway across the courtyard and near to the great stone wellhead. At that hour too, he would normally have entered his palace stepping from his gondola, his way up the slippery steps from the canal lit by servants carrying tar soaked torches. His evening wanderings had brought him to the rear of the palace and now he was hammering on the finely wrought iron gates with his pistol butt...but to no avail.

Propping his pistol against a piece of gilded ornament on the gates, he cocked it, took aim and let-fly in the direction of the glimmering rush light. There was a thunderous roar, a flash and a cloud of stinking sulphur smoke, followed by the crashing of glass and a terrified scream. A shadowy figure holding a rush light went stumbling towards the kitchen doorway. Though choking with the acrid smoke, Don Francesco managed to bellow out: "It's the Podestà! Unlock these damned gates!"

44

The scurrying servant halted, turned and approached him, hobbling badly and holding high a bundle of lights that gave off a stink of burning sheep fat almost as foul as that of pistol smoke.

"God and Mark forgive me!" exclaimed Don Francesco," Have I injured you, child?"

"No, Excellency," the re-assuring sound of the young girl's voice came out of the gloom,"I was born like this, Excellency, I'm crippled." The child shuffled away to unhook the key from its nail inside the washroom.

"Where is everyone?" asked the Don.

"Noble Zustinian left half an hour ago with the French prince. They went to Ca` Granda, I think. Everyone else is out looking for you, Excellency. We were all so worried."

"For me….why?"

"Some Arsenal men were rough handling anyone in good clothes. We feared for your safety. There's just Gustav and me. He was supposed to guard the place. I tried keeping him awake, but he fell into some kind of trance. I fear he may have been hurt by the mob."

The scullery maid raised her bunch of foul smelling rush lights illuminating one of the two grandiose wellheads: the Capulet and Lipomano family arms were carved into its time worn Verona marble, 1374 Anno Domini still faintly outlined. Slumped on the well step was a grim, muscular and hairy faced colossus of a man: sick dribbled from the corner of his mouth, down over his beard and onto his mud soaked doublet and splattered steel breastplate. Someway out of hand's reach was his hefty pike staff, now trailing green canal slime: a mud caked wheel-lock pistol of great size rested on the courtyard cobblestones together with a pair of filthy slime covered riding boots.

His other pistol, somehow preserved in a better state of readiness, overhung precariously the deep drop of the well.

"Get up, Gustav, you disgust me!" hissed the Don. He recognized one of

45

his 'sbirri' or policemen, better known to us as 'bulli.' At the same time he identified the cause of the bullo's stupefied state. A small bottle of dark green glass was clutched tightly to the chest of the ugly giant. It was the fierce aniseed liqueur once made by the Dominican friars of San Pietro, disarmingly called 'golden dewdrops.' The last friar who knew how to distil it had long since entered the spirit world via the plague. One thimble full of it would be enough to drop an elephant to its knees in cross eyed stupor. This swine of a bullo had obviously stolen the liqueur from the pantry while Big Marta, was out dutifully searching with the others in the darkness and drizzle.

He gave Gustav a sharp nudge in the side with his boot and shouted again "Get up, and get to your bed. I will deal with you when you are sober!"

The beastly Hercules groaned, mumbled some swear words in German and tried to stagger to his feet. In the confuddled process the pistol tipped over the rim of the wellhead straight into the empty water bucket. Another tremendous flash and bang ripped through the rainy night air. Two neat holes were drilled through the fine bronze bucket as the bullet ricocheted around inside. The weighty weapon instantly sent the bucket flying down to a magnificent splash some twenty feet below. Dogs barked: lights came to the windows of Palazzo Trevisan on the opposite side of Murano's Grand Canal. There were distant shouts and the sound of running feet along the canal towpath. Could it be that the mob was now attacking Palazzo Capello?

"Oaf!" screamed the infuriated Podestà. The bullo took two unsteady paces towards who knows where and fell flat on his face into a rainsoaked patch of kitchen herbs.

"Get me a lantern, girl," the Podestà demanded, his voice still harsh with anger, "and light me up to my study!"

Whimpering with fear, the little lass led him through the courtyard, under its cloister like portico and then up three flights of a stone staircase to his suite of rooms on the first floor. Don Francesco noted, as he followed her, that her left foot was turned club-like inwards and was slightly shrivelled; the outer edge thickly calloused. He had never noticed this limping child before amongst his twenty or more domestics, but then the

46

upper floors of the palace would be forbidden space to a scullion.

"Light me a fire!" he ordered and then checked his voice: it was too unjust
to vent his anger on a child - a helpful minion. The girl knelt awkwardly
then leaned forward extending her rush light into the Dutch tiled cavern
of a fireplace. Before she could ignite the kindling sticks and dried moss
at the bottom of the polished steel fire grate she had to shove to one side
the two heavy logs placed on top. She blew hard: the flames leapt high
into life and with more effort she slid back into the flames one of the two
logs. While still on her knees, she then turned to light one of Don
Francesco's fireside candelabra and in so doing realized that in the gloom
she must have snagged the hem of her dress on one of the sharp
projections of the fire grate. Carefully setting down her rush light onto
tiled floor, she tugged with both hands, but to no effect. The weighty log
had trapped the whole front part of her garment onto the sharp metalwork.
The garment, being nothing more than a cut up turnip sack of rough
woven hemp, resisted her desperate attempt to tear it away. But it was not
her Cinderella like gown that went up in instant flame but her head scarf.
Though damp with night drizzle, the scarf was made of fluffy gun cotton
of that kind used for plate drying or firming down cannon balls against a
powder charge. Her head and shoulders now lit up like a pine torch and
her scream of terror brought the Podestà. Ripping away the blazing scarf,
he hurled it into the fireplace almost igniting in the process his own wrist
lace. Then with an almighty tug he brought the maid, the log and the fire
grate tumbling forward onto the hearthstones. Two or three more heavy
bootings freed-up the fire grate and sent it, its fiery contents, and the
smouldering log rolling back into their blue and white tiled cavern.

Dragged violently backwards to a safe distance, the half dazed and
sobbing scullery maid first propped herself up then tried to scramble to
her feet. Extending both hands to help her up, Don Francesco could not
help but notice, despite the feeble lantern light, that the turnip sack
was the girl's only garment and that her hands were scaly and red raw
from long immersion in plate scrubbing soda. Taken aback himself by the
sudden and somewhat pathetic revelation of immodesty, for to add to her
woes the girl was also shaven headed, Don Francesco sought words to
cover both her embarrassment and his own. Evidently it was one of those
days when awkward situations rose up at every hand's turn and in ever
quickening succession. Clearly the child was a complete innocent,

unaware of the perils of exposing her nethers in the presence of men: a convent orphan perhaps? It now irked him greatly that even one of his lowly servants had been made to walk about the palace in a turnip tabard so short as to deny all decency. Big Marta *(Martha)* the cook was the obvious culprit. Very likely she had sold the child's gown for some personal profit.

In a kindly and amused tone he quipped: "Young lass, if you wish to progress in my service it would be wiser for you to keep a cool head and a warm and well covered rump... and not the reverse!" Chuckling quietly at his own wit, Don Francesco strode around the walnut panelled room lighting numerous candles sconced in magnificent reflecting silver girandole brackets.

Shaking and patting the remaining sparks from her scorched garment the girl looked about her and took in the splendours of Don Francesco's study. "Oh! It is like church…. it's like heaven!" she gasped. Books by the hundred were stacked in carved and curious cabinets, their gold embossed leathers glistening in the candle light: a lapis blue and serene 'Madonna in a Meadow;' set in a costly frame delicately decorated with gilded cherry clusters; an enormous bronze of the drunken Farnese Hercules leaning on his club and on his malachite green pedestal. She blushed at the beefy-muscled and very naked demi-god, it reminded her somewhat of the drunken Gustav now sprawled in the courtyard. Portraits of past Capello Admirals and Senators stared down with haughty looks from their golden frames. A painting of a gorgeously bejewelled lady hung on the wall next to the Podestàs desk. The artist had caught a sad and soulful look in her countenance. The Grand Duchess rested a delicate hand on the fabulous Medici Crown. Before Angelo Bronzino had time to add the finishing touches to this last of several portraits displaying her celestial beauty, both she and the Grand Duke were entombed for ever and at great distance from one another. One delicate eyebrow in the portrait was slightly raised: perhaps Bronzino's painterly hint that someone had murdered her. Nearly a century and a half had passed since news of the despicable crime had spread throughout Europe and then onwards to the courts of far off India; yet still her graven image could be found amidst the tobacco and time stained pin-ups decorating Murano taverns. To the Florentines she would ever remain a cursed foreign gold digger, because she was not noble enough to marry a Medici.

Chief suspect, as the arsenic sprinkler, will always be the Grand Duke's brother, thankfully not a Christian priest but a Cardinal all the same. What was her portrait doing here in the Podestà's study? Well, she was his great aunt Bianca of generations past, who had spent her innocent childhood years in that room. Tradition had it that she had also been seduced in Palazzo Capello and ruined by a penniless bank clerk who later abandoned her in Florence. And what 'Romeo' then came 'in soft light' to woo her beneath her balcony? Why, none other than Francesco Medici, Grand Duke of Tuscany!

The Podestà was an obsessive collector of curiosities. There were numerous ostrich eggs, carved and rare coconuts and large mother of pearl nautilus shells, all set upon gem stone encrusted stands, or held aloft by silver gilt mermaids. The long twisted ivory horn of a unicorn hung over the fireplace. Filling half the space of one wall was the Podestàs writing bureau. With its doors inlaid with precious marble mosaics and rare woods; with its gilded figurines and knobs and secret drawers and hiding places for valuables: it rose up against the wall like some altar to the god of hard work and good administration.

"You may go now," he said in a kindly voice, waking her from her trance of wonder at his beautiful knick-knacks. "Tell Big Marta to send me up some cold chicken, fried aubergines and a carafe of Bardolino when she gets back."

The instant that the poor overawed girl heard him, she bent very low at the waist, clasping her hands behind her back, just as she had been taught to do by the nuns at the orphanage. Her eyes looked down on the Persian silk carpet that now had traces of her muddy bare footprints on it: the hearthstones and fireplace were a mess of smouldering charcoal. She wondered anxiously if he would have her beaten: the 'discipline nun' would have handed out a thrashing for far less. Still bent double, she was stepping carefully backwards towards the door, bobbing her head even lower three times, as was the custom, when the Podestà called her back. His curiosity was aroused, or maybe it was no more than that natural bond which draws together survivor and rescuer. Had he not been present in the room, the girl would have gone up in flames together with his library, or at the very least she would have been horribly mutilated - that was for certain. But he had not given her an opportunity to thank him.

"Just a moment...From where do you come?"

"From the Incurabili, Excellency. Pardon my clumsiness, I'll get it cleaned up."
The Podestà was puzzled by this answer, knowing that the Incurabili nuns educated almost every one but the very dullest of their orphans and found husbands for them, or else launched them in careers as musicians. Clearly the girl was much older than twelve, the age of consent: "Tell me girl, were you never offered to a husband?"

"No offer was made, Excellency, the Superior insisted I stay on as a conversa, but the Governors released me on condition that I left the city and found work in Murano or some outer island."

"As a scullion?" he questioned, still doubting her word.

"My handicap, I suppose, Excellency… my fault for having a crippled foot."

"Not your fault. The Almighty made you that way for some purpose. Be content with your lot. Many great people of the past had terrible handicaps to overcome. Those who are born to beauty and wealth rarely do anything with their lives. I too have my burdens, my sorrows, my cross to carry. No doubt you learned to read?"

"Both Latin and Venetian," she replied, directing her words to the Persian carpet. This news came as no great surprise to the Don.

"Write as well?" he queried. Going over to his desk he drew out a sheet of fine paper, dipped a silver pen into his prized and somewhat obscene inkstand, cast in bronze by that priapic Padovan sculptor, Andrea Briosco. A look of amusement came over his hawkish face. He spoke quietly: "Straighten up. Come here and write your name for me."

With a flourish of elegant script she wrote Bianca... and paused.

"Bianca! How fortunate! You will shine whiter still when you wash away

50

the cinders! Did the nuns change your name before directing you to Ca`
Capello?" Don Francesco knew well the stratagems used by orphanages
to place their young charges in employment.

"No, Excellency, it was given me when Mother Superior brought me in. I
came in a white Christening gown. I once had another name though."
"Christening gown?" Now mildly curious, the Podestà continued in his
questioning as he lit the candles on his desk: "You say the Superior
herself brought you... not left in the barrel like their other infants?"

"No, not in the barrel."

"You had another name....how so?"

"If you will permit me to explain Excellecy: the Christening gown has a
tape-lace hem; it's still used for baptisms. I was ironing it one day when
the laundry conversa told me it had once been my own gown."

"And the hem, the tape lace?"

"Spelled VALSILVEST, Vossignoria Podestà."

"So your roots didn't grow from Murano mud, like us mere
 mortals? Val Silvest savours of nymphs and woody glades."

"Excellency, it was an abbreviation. Superior made me swear on a relic of
San Rocco that I would never reveal it. She said it would only get me
into more serious trouble. You see, I got caught looking in the admission
register when cleaning Superior's office. The discipline conversa then
gave me a whipping."

Curiosity now well aroused, Don Francesco insisted: "Come girl, you are
at liberty here, your Mother Superior was sinful herself in demanding a
sacred oath for such a trivial matter. No harm can come to you while in
my household, that is, so long as you are a bit more wary when lighting
fires! Now tell me, what was this lace trimmed name?"

"Well," she replied reluctantly, "It's Silvestra..."

"Silvestra who?" the Podestà now insisted.

"Valier," came the reply.

"Never!" the Don exploded and then began to chuckle, trying in vain to restrain his mirth. The hilarious news however swiftly gave way to a pause, a solemn and silent moment of anxiety: "Oh, dear! Oh dear! With such a name you really are a burden... a heap of troubles, my dear child!"

"Forgive me Excellency... that was the name in the register. Someone had inked it over and scraped at the vellum, but I could read it in reverse by turning the page and holding it to the light. I don't know how I came by such a name, but I guess it once mattered to someone."

Once again she lowered her head in shame, brimming with tears, supposing that he had been mocking her with his laughter. The Don's agile brain was now fired-up by this extraordinary revelation, grasping instantly the advantages to be gained by promoting, at least in his own household, the prospects of this scullion. Any public advance in her status though, might be altogether too fraught with the prospect of violence - not to say a possible minor bloodbath in Venetian high society. It all now made sense to him – of course it would – that clubbed foot! This awkward minion in her singed turnip sack, could well have been the 'inconvenience' of a certain rampant Valier. Rivalry between Valier and Morosini went back centuries. Just a few months back, the Doge had ticked-off Silvestro in front of the thousand-strong Grand Council of Venetian rulers. The handsome rogue was not only foppishly dressed and not wearing his Senator's robe, contrary to State dress regulations, but was blatantly playing cards with a fellow Senator during important proceedings. Humiliating such a 'grandioso' was something that would not pass without consequences, even for a Doge of Morosini's might.

Any possible resemblance to Silvestro needed to be studied carefully. Intermarriage of like-minded Venetian clans had given rise, over long generations, to distinctive faces. Most of those faces needed no introduction. Those with power and influence recognized one another at a glance, hence the need for masks when out walking in public places. At first acquaintance, this scullery maid seemed so unappealing as to be treated with no more reverence than one gave to a stray mongrel. As a minor member of the ancient Capello family he was not strictly entitled to that Nobil Huomo. The N.H. might well drop from his calling cards once he ceased to be Podestà. Given outright proof of parentage to the keeper of the Golden Book, even illegitimate heirs of grand families might claim the right to add N.H., to their letter headings. As the offspring of a Senator, she might still far outrank him, particularly if her mother was of noble blood. In 'bachelor Venice' where only the alpha male in each noble generation was permitted to marry and to pass on the inheritance, it was not uncommon to find N.D. or N.H. embroidered on the wrong side of the blanket. Her muddy prints trailed across his pale silk Tabriz rug: he would later give instructions for them to remain there, unsponged. It pleased him to keep such reminders of extraordinary moments.

Was the Mother Superior of the Incurabili perhaps playing a more subtle game? Had she deliberately sent this Bianca to Murano knowing full well that her Valier parentage would slip out one day? The sparking vendetta between the quarrelsome, effete and politically ambitious young Zustinian, who saw himself as some future Doge and that roving stallion, Silvestro was common enough knowledge. A Valier bastard placed as a servant in a household rented by the Zustinian Bishop of Torcello might well be mischief making on the part of the Mother Superior: a little nunish black humour, perhaps? Valier were not noted for their generosity to the Incurabili, nor any other worthy cause for that matter. It could of course be that the child's mother had been no more than some low born woman who having consorted with a Valier, gave her crippled daughter a better chance of being taken in by the snobbish nuns. The Incurabili could not look after every abandoned little bundle that landed in their baby barrel: sometimes the gypsies took pity on the leftovers and sometimes, alas, the feral dogs did quite the opposite. The child's mother could hardly have stolen such a baptismal gown: then there was that attempt to expunge the girl's name.

Recollecting the damning words shouted by old Miotti at the church door, yet another stony parable of Jesus Christ came to Don Francesco's mind: 'The stone that the builder has rejected shall become the keystone of the mansion.' This rejected scullion could well become his own support should he, through some misfortune, fall from office during the changes in government that were sure to come very soon. All who mattered knew well that Silvestro Valier had been forced into an unhappy marriage at the age of nineteen with Betta Querini. Betta *(Elizabeth)* was an imperious and quick-tempered lady, jokingly known as the Dogaressa *(Doge's Queen.)* Querini gold was now melded with Valier muscle. The Zustinian, similarly allied in marriage to Doge Morosini's family, were at the pinnacle of power at the moment, but the Doge was old, ill and sailing into battle. When a great family lost its grip, old scores were sometimes settled in blood. This child was destined to him for some reason that he could not quite fathom. Perish the thought that he, an old widower, might marry a scullery maid! It was perhaps no more than fatherly concern that was aroused at this stage. Had she lived, his own daughter would have been nearing this child's age. He had wanted to call his daughter Bianca Capello and then changed his mind for fear of inviting tragedy; yet all the same the Fates cut short the thread of his only child's happy little life.

"Well young woman… stand up straight!"

He held up a six light candelabra. Lifting her chin with a gentle touch of his fingers he felt a shiver of anxiety as to his real intentions. The silver sconced lights revealed in full her shaven head with its tufts of ginger gold brown sprouting where the blade had been carelessly applied. A smutty but unmistakable face stared fearfully at him: the face of a lady who in his gallant youth he had admired from far off, admired without any hope of better acquaintance. An involuntary gasp came from his lips. It was he now who trembled somewhat, splattering candle wax onto the desk top…so confused, no words could form themselves in his brain, but when they did, they were: "Madonna and Mark! The ermine will fly if ever the Countess gets to know of this, let alone Silvestro's wife!" An even more disconcerting image then came to mind: "Silvestro's guts would most certainly decorate the duelling ground should Ettore ever discover this offspring of his ladylove!"

Cavaliere the N.H. Ettore *(Hector)* Martinengo was not only a Knight Commander of the Grand Order of St. John of Malta but a battle stained and terrifying monster. It was no secret too that he was chief widow maker to The Ten: their most obliging eliminator of disgracefully behaving or inconveniently nosey foreign nobility.

He did not blame the nuns for the disfiguration of that shorn hair on such an adorable face. They had to raise funds by all means possible in order to take care of the ever-increasing hordes of abandoned children. Since the habit of wearing wigs had descended to the lower ranks of the artisan class, most beggars in town went about shaven headed and were all the healthier for it. He had noticed too that they were more alert and importuning as a consequence. Long locks harboured head lice. Their constant biting made one feel both lousy and drowsy - a good dusting of white lead powder was the only remedy! Though crippled and in that sense no great match in the marriage market, Bianca was uncommonly tall, fair and refined of features for a juvenile waif. A few good meals would soon flesh out her bony frame. The great Titian himself would have rowed ten leagues in his gondola to seek her out for a canvas Madonna. It was fortunate indeed that Governors of the Incurabili had not auctioned her off as a concubine to one of those geriatric merchants of Rialto who were often to be seen sniffing like randy curs at convent gateposts.

Recovering composure as best he could, he said, "We'll keep your name a secret, between you and me. And Bianca, those nuns were wise in their advice: never again reveal your family name… that is until I may ask you to, at some future date." He gave her a beaming and re-assuring smile; "Now take my order to the cook."

As she left, she almost collided on the stairs with two handsomely dressed gentlemen who came bounding up, swords drawn, lanterns in hand.

"Down at once, skivvy! How dare you sneak up here!" one bellowed. The other bravo gave her a violent shove that sent her tumbling halfway down onto the darkened first floor landing.

"God be praised, you are safe Excellency!" they both exclaimed, as they rushed into his study. "Who shot at you? Whoever it was won't live to regret it....damned scum of the Arsenal!"

"Nobody shot at me… just an accidental discharge of that drunkard Gustav's pistol. Ensure that he is brought before me in the courtroom tomorrow. You will have passed a servant girl on the stairway?"

"We saw her Illustrissimo," snarled the elder bravo, "Impudence! You'll want her to get a drubbing as well? Do you really want her in the courtroom though? Best leave her to Big Marta. I'll see that Marta does it," he added with an unpleasant grin of pleasure anticipated. "Total impudence! Nothing stolen, I trust?"

"No punishment required in her case - the child came up on my orders to light the fire. Now gentlemen, I want to take both of you into my confidence. I have made a dreadful mistake and I want you, if you would be so kind, to help me cover my tracks. You see, after questioning the girl, I now realize who she is and can't forgive myself for my own stupidity. A couple of months back, I asked the Superior of the Incurabili to send me a copy secretary, someone with a neat script to keep a record of my correspondence. I then completely forgot to mention it to the housekeeper and to Big Marta. When the girl arrived at the back gate with her orphanage papers, and I suppose her shaven head, they both took her for the new laundry girl Marta asked me to employ."

It was a quickly thought-up and convincing enough lie and had the Podestà left it at that, the two gentlemen bravi would have been taken-in by his explanation, but he continued, elaborating the tale: "You see gentlemen; it also transpires on questioning her that she is the love child of a distant relative. I am duty bound therefore to maintain her in some style. She will remain for the time being in the housekeeper's house."

"By what name shall we address her, Podestà?"

"Ah yes! A good point! She shall be called signorina Bianca Capello - why not indeed! And in future she will be treated with full courtesy as my relative: is that understood?"

"Understood Illustrissimo," both answered with a knowing grin. "We are men of the world ourselves, Podestà....we quite understand."

"You do not understand at all! My intentions for the child are not of that nature, if you don't mind!"

Knowing better than to anger their master, both bravi commenced to bow themselves out.

"Oh, and tell Big Marta to come straight up here with supper, as soon as she has it ready.... And fetch the housekeeper, I want a word with her too!"

The Podestà s feigned annoyance with the two young men was all part of his deception as well. Both of them were well-connected gentlemen, sent to him for training as potential Podestà and as such, were frequently invited to the gossip salons of elderly noblewomen. Neither of them had yet learned the art of discretion. When they bandied aboutthe news of the Podestàs new mistress nobody at all would believe it: on the other hand, a child of a distant relative, taken under his kindly care, sounded much more likely. Bianca's origin would remain a mystery for the foreseeable future, for if it ever became public knowledge there would be blood in plenty on the blades of all three power crazed families involved. The ancient practice of honour killings (it must be said of Venetian custom, never of the ladies involved,) had not entirely died out, despite the harsh justice handed down to lawless young nobles from the Council of Ten.

Descending the stairs, out of hearing range of the Podestà, the younger bravo quipped: "Evidently, the Don has fallen in love with that little scarecrow. It will be silk slippers next and brocade for the raw-armed scrubber.....you mark my words! What the devil has got into him, and at his age?"

Both bravi knew that it was common enough practice amongst the nobility to give their mistresses the title 'signorina,' followed by the family name.

"I should take good care who you poke fun at, if I were you," commented the older man. "Once she's dressed as a lady, she won't forget who shoved her down the stairs!"

"And did you see that wet cabbage on his desk? What in Lucifer's name does that mean? Could it be a love token from his hobbling skivvy?"

"More likely he is going to plant it on German Gustav's neck tomorrow morning, I should reckon: not that anyone would notice the difference if that 'dummkopf' barbarian went around with a cabbage for a head!"

"Which of us is going to try and chain him up? We had best both do it now, while he is having his beauty sleep, before Big Marta gets back. She has a soft spot for Gustav, I've noticed."

(There was little love lost between 'bravi' or high-spirited gentlemen, and the professional security guards, of Gustav's 'bulli' kind, who were sometimes used by the authorities as the equivalent of police constables.)

CHAPTER SIX

In the frought days following the San Donato riot Zorzi and Grandpa kept close company. Signor Molin, Aldo's father, helped them to barricade the downstairs windows and doors and after dusk old Piero would call to share his catch with them, usually eels or sea-bass fried in butter with salty samphire. Two brick and iron hooped furnaces set against the end wall of the glassworks gave security to the rear of the house. As for the rest, high and ancient walls, much in need of re-pointing, protected them at front and sides. Inevitably a warrant would issue from Ca` Capello, Grandpa knew that full well. Following his arrest, a demolition squad would take pick axe and gunpowder to his home and glassworks. By ancient tradition too his boxes of powdered minerals, his metal oxides, his sacks of quartz pebbles, his lime and potash, and his precious array of iron shears, pincers and pontil blowing tubes would be dragged out onto the landing stage and sold at knock down price to any passing vulture of a neighbour.

An iron door gave access from the yard to the garden plot. The heavy plank now barring it was something of an inconvenience when a call of nature required a trip to the 'cesso.' Zorzi's 'cesso' with its two holed seat and its bunch of dock leaves strung up for convenience was a picturesque shambles. A sturdy cage of dog rose and brambles was the only means by which it had survived over long generations from collapse into a heap of matchwood. Supported by six slimy piled stilts, the 'cesso' overhung a malodorous ditch at the end of their weed strewn cabbage plot. Though made of iron studded oak, the double doors giving out on to the portico and canal landing steps were much more of a security risk. Over several hundred years of use, the flood tides of as many springs, and the occasional kick from Zorzi, both doors had well rotted. Grandpa had to wedge them shut and pile pebble filled sacks against them, something they used only to do on windy nights.

With Zorzi's help, Daniele busied himself in those last days making cheap, undecorated beakers for nearby taverns. Drinking vessels were in fair demand after the wild celebrations that followed the Arsenalotti's triumph over Zustinian's lancers. Old Piero took to staying over night to keep them company, leaving at dawn so as not to be seen with the glassware that he sold on Grandpa's behalf. The Glassmakers' Guild, also known as 'The Arte' or 'Marigola', had not specified that Miotti furnaces should be destroyed when, some five years previously, that traitor of a Guildmaster, Vincenzo, fled overseas. The Guild had however banned Grandpa from trading. Nevertheless, months after the disappearance of Vincenzo the Miotti furnaces had been fired up again. Grandpa employed out of work glassmakers a couple of times a year to help him with the complicated task of swapping over the two enormously hot and heavy ceramic crucibles containing the cullet glass: this necessitated demolishing and re-sealing a segment of each kiln. The new mix of 'cristallo' was prepared at low temperature in the smaller annealing furnace and the empty working crucible from the larger kiln was either chipped out or discarded for a new one. Grandpa was expert in making his own crucibles from a half and half mix of fresh Bassano clay and the pulverized remains of old crucibles. A disreputable lawyer, who took more than his fair share of glassware, arranged the deed of sale to old Piero Tacca, Grandpa's closest friend. No real money changed hands and most neighbours shut a blind eye, knowing that the obliging old seaweed burner did not even have two coins for his own funeral, let alone the price of a large house and two furnaces. Official eyes were turned away as well, so long as Piero did not make a public show of the fact that he was trading without a licence. An agreed signal to open up the front door was for Piero to tap his oar three times on the side of his boat. He brought them powdered samphire and the ashes of other marsh plants that produced pure potassium and sacks of white quartz pebble stones harvested from the banks of the River Tagliamento. These pebbles, with lime and a dash of litharge and manganese, were the basic raw materials of the 'cristallo' glassware for which Murano was renowned, but essential too was the human fuel that he traded in: the fish; mussels; edible samphire and the bundles driftwood with which to cook them.

Don Francesco Capello Benzon, Podestà of Murano, was in no hurry to punish Daniele Miotti. He would let a week or so go by, both to heighten the old man's anxiety, for tension to build up in the neighbourhood and for tongues to wag: 'When would the Podestàstrike out at that doddering fool? Would he hang him upside down by one leg, like a thief, from the public gallows? Would he have him tied to the whipping-post on market day? Then there was that foreboding sight, the Breaking Wheel!' It brooded low beside the market footpath: even the most audacious of Murano's youth dared not lift the flail propped against it. Surely the

Podestà would not be so cruel as to have a sick and aged Citizen of the Golden Book slowly mashed to pulp by the public 'Boia?' The Podestà might risk provoking another riot: Miotti was an honest man who had spent the best years of his youth fighting with bravery and with honour for the Serenissima.

Only Don Tranquillo, knew when and how old Daniele would be punished, and he was telling no one. Over a glass of sparkling Soave he and the Podestà had considered what to do for the best. Daniele had provoked a riot: Noble Zustinian was hopping mad. He had been embarrassed in front of his foreign guest. Plans to accompany Lorraine on a tour around the Island's glass furnaces were put on hold, for fear of another riot. People had been injured....well, let us say, there were a few cuts and bruises: then the sheer indignity of two bandsmen, several lancers and one particularly hated bullo being flung into San Donato canal! Steel helmets, side drums and lances had been tossed into the air, then broken and bunged into the canal after their owners. Some of the helmets were now being used as chamber pots under the beds of little boys who had eagerly dived into the canal after them. Others were squirrelled away in back garden sheds, to be used in play fights and future gang battles. In the confusion, a bandsman's pony had gone missing - last seen swimming out to sea. Someone had to pay for that!

Alas for the poor marsh pony! It was the only real victim of the riot. It made its dash for freedom when the fighting was at its hottest by the bridge. Swimming out boldly with its drums in tow, its desire to join its free-range brothers on some distant, uninhabited, island was soon dashed. Two enterprising young fishermen caught it with their net, dragged it into the shallows and promptly sold it to a miller who asked no questions. The rest of its life was spent in semi darkness walking round and round with a creaking millstone beam attached to its harness.

CHAPTER SEVEN

On the morning before the bulli came to punish grandfather, Zorzi was high up on a rickety ladder in a large dusty room leading off the cloister of St. Peter Martyr Convent. The room had once been a dispensary where the poor, the elderly and sick of the parish came for free medicines and advice from the friar chemists. Sometimes, but by no means invariably, both the advice and the prescription put a swift end to their suffering - it so ill advised or so toxic that it killed them! Zorzi was playing a merry game with Don Tranquillo. He was throwing down from the high shelves pottery jars full of damp and congealed ointments, chemical concoctions, dead spiders, dead flies and cobwebs. Don Tranquillo was catching them - most of the time that is - and stacking them on to a dilapidated wooden handcart. Two pots labelled 'Ant. Pulv.' and 'Arsen Pulv.' he fetched down himself, commenting with a laugh: "Grandpa will be glad: the arsenic looks clean enough to use in his lattimo mix, if not, it should go down a treat with your privy rats. I'm not sure this black antimony will be of any use to him though, but there's enough here, I reckon, to send every monk in the Veneto to his heavenly reward!"

Though surprisingly light to handle and nicely decorated in an old fashioned way with painted scenes in blue cobalt and manganese red, the pots were deemed valueless. Several even bore the ancient date of A.D.1485 - all the more reason to dispose of them in Don Tranquillo's opinion. He had plans to clear the place and open it up as a schoolroom, with free teaching for any who wanted to learn. The Podestà had promised support and a decent sum of money to get started, possibly even a schoolmistress to help the young scholars. Toma` had caused a rumpus when asked to adapt his precious library as a school room for "thieving ragamuffins." He wrote to Raimondo, the grand Prior at St. Mark's and so was left alone once more in his library with his sole companions – a wax caked candlestick and toothless skull. From time to time the skull got livened up by Fra Zeri with a spaghetti wig, or dandelions in the eye sockets. Fra Toma` had no desire either to become a 'schoolmaster to scallywags,' his all important concern was to finish writing his 'Meditations on the Brevity of Life.' He had been scribbling away for nearly seven years now - was on his one thousand eight-hundred and twentieth page - and writing paper never came cheap! Don Tranquillo had taken a peep at a few chapters and pronounced them a perfect remedy for insomnia and as sparkling in their obscure theology as a damp pipe spill. In exchange for the Podeta`s generous offer of funding for his ragged school, Don Tranquillo had allowed himself to be quizzed about the strange goings-on in the Miotti family. It was obvious to Tranquillo from the start that neither the Podestà nor Zustinian wanted Miotti to go on trial. Too much dirty linen, too many compromising facts, particularly about Zustinian's lifestyle, would have been aired in public. The Podestà knew that he himself was more at fault than old Miotti. He, after all, was almost complicit in Zustinian's attempt to kidnap the child. Tranquillo politely and cleverly hinted at that fact and suggested some kind of compromise. The Podestà was a man of otherwise spotless honour, and yet the honour of his office had been demeaned by that blow of Grandpa's. Some kind of punishment had to be seen to have been handed down, for the sake of good order. In each of their friendly encounters Podestà Francesco hinted that he would commute the sentence entirely, if old Miotti would hand over to him a book of recipes. Information had been passed to him by the Marigola Guild that Daniele's son, or someone in his family, may have filched the book from San Pietro Library. A recipe book, in exchange for a possible death sentence - for heaven's sake! Daniele was no thief nor was his son, the late Vincenzo. It quickly dawned on Tranquillo that the Podestà was referring to the ancient text given to Antonio di Brayda in exchange for the bells. He promised the Podestà that he would quiz once more Don Toma` and Grandpa Miotti as to its possible whereabouts. Clearly Miotti no longer had it: nor did Zustinian, so it would seem. It was Zustinian who suggested the face saving deal, in a written note from his Ca` Lolin Palace on the Grand Canal: thus confirming the Podestà's suspicions that young Zorzi would have been held to ransom by Zustinian in order to lay hands upon the missing book. What Tranquillo badly needed to find out was how bad a thrashing his old parishioner would get and whereabouts on the Island it would be given. It was then that Tranquillo came up with his bright idea.

When the handcart was loaded, Don Tranquillo covered it with a stained old altar cloth, tying everything down tightly, broken jars and all. He then told Zorzi to wait on the bridge that led to the church side entrance and to give him a hand wave when 'the coast was clear.' In haste, friar and boy bumped the heavy cart over the bridge, along the towpath and in through the Miotti front door. Nobody saw them, to Zorzi's great excitement....but why all the secrecy?

Grandfather came coughing and wheezing into the courtyard from the glass works shed. Understandably he was quite startled, then relieved to see who it was who had barged in. He took off his paper hat, which protected his few grey hairs from the powdered glass and the deadly toxic metal oxides of his trade and bowed low to the priest. Before Grandpa could open his mouth, Don Tranquillo spoke: "Now listen to me old friend, your life may depend on it! Stop everything that you are doing and check all of these jars for me."

Handing the two jars of poison to Grandpa he added: "I have no idea what these are doing in our pharmacy. Maybe we had Lucrezia Borgia as a customer? You are an alchemist. Anything that may be of use for your glasswork you may keep, but scrape it into your own containers. Just tip the rest into your cesso. Zorzi! You will help your Grandpa, but cover your nose with a wet rag. The empty jars must be placed here in the middle of the yard. Be sure to space them so that a man can walk easily between. Most are labelled with their contents so it should be easy enough to check."

"May I ask why I need to do all this? I've got an order from the 'Cock and Snake' for Piero to deliver today."

"Do as I say old friend, it's for your own good!" snapped back the priest. "And there are other things you must do immediately; bring your work bench out here in the courtyard. Put stools behind it so that all three of us can sit and have a clear view of the front door with our backs to the wall. I want a couple of cheap wine-glasses and a gallon sized old jug, if you've got one. I will bring the wine, when I return. Oh! And I may as well leave these, while I'm here."

Don Tranquillo rummaged in his leather satchel - he regarded pockets as effeminate French creations. Two bottle shaped objects emerged, wrapped in crumpled blue paper. Zorzi recognized them instantly. They were thunder flashes - he had seen their like the previous year on St. Peter Martyr's Feast Day.

"Fireworks Grandpa!" he shouted with delight, "Fireworks!"

"What do you want me to do with them?" inquired the old man sarcastically, "Chuck them in the cesso on top of the alchemicals? That will cause a fine colourful stink, no doubt....mostly brown!"
"No, you old mutton head," replied the friar with a chuckle, "Leave them somewhere dry and safe. I'll need them tomorrow when the Podestàs men come for you. God bless and preserve you both!" His hand waved the 'sign of the cross' in the air.

As the friar strode along the short passageway to the front door he took a fleeting look at the contents of the two doorless rooms on either side. One was piled with sacks and boxes of glassmaking materials, the other a rather shambolic shop with glass bowls, cups, jugs, plates and ornaments stacked on an old table top and on the disorderly shelves of large wooden dressers. He called back to old Miotti: "If you have anything valuable in there, stow it upstairs! Best hide away those Satan's crimping irons of yours while you are at it… tongs, pontils, shears, or whatever you call them. You never know who might get hold of them!" With that, he pushed the handcart out onto the towpath and was gone.

Thus forewarned of his close approaching fate, Grandpa hastened to do precisely as he was told.

CHAPTER EIGHT

The bulli departed at nine in the morning. They left Palazzo Capello with much shouting, clattering of weapons and commotion, so as to attract an excited crowd of onlookers. In a large open-topped black gondola they were rowed swiftly and steadily down the middle of Murano's Grand Canal, then, turned left into the Glassmaker's Canal, in sight of the bridges and the bell towers of San Stin and San. Pietro Martire. Other users of the busy canals - barges, fishing boats and gondolas for hire, made haste to steer out of their path. The fit and able, the young, the unemployed and mischief makers, ran fast along the towpaths and over bridges to keep up with the shiny black coffin-like gondola. There could be little doubt about who the two bulli were, but there were differing opinions about the identity of the masked gondolier with the distinctive golden locks flowing shoulder length from beneath his tricorn hat.

Gustav's great bulk made the gondola dip low into the water. Adolfo, a muscular beanpole of a man, even though seated, was almost as tall as the gondolier, who was standing on his little scrap of carpet at the raised stern of the gondola and rowing with ease and skill. Gustav looked astonishingly neat and clean. No surprise, since he had spent four days mostly up to his thick neck in well water. His penance, once he had retrieved that pistol, was to scrub the well from top to bottom and then to empty it. There was also the Podestàs fine of three 'grossi:' (*silver coins, sometimes called groats.)* one grosso for each hole in the bronze well bucket; one to compensate Big Marta the cook for her bottle of Golden Drops that he had guzzled down. Gustav smarted with anger at the Podestà's punishment. He felt it was grossly unfair, because he alone had protected the Noble Zustinian and his mincing French guest from the mob, all the way back to the palace - but, like any other veteran tight lipped trooper before his commanding officer, he took his punishment and failed to offer the Podestà any excuse or plea in explanation.

At the palace steps the Arsenal workers had caught up with Gustav while he steadied the getaway gondola of the two fleeing noblemen. A gang of twenty or more had overpowered him and thrown him three or four times into a particularly foul and shallow part of the side canal, where the palace chamber pots were emptied. He had no choice but to imbibe that quarter pint of 90 proof alcoholic 'Golden Drops' to clear his throat and to bump-off the canal bugs in his belly. Now the Podestà had docked three months wages! Unfair? Yes, but he chose to say nothing - he still had his enjoyable bullying job and the comfortable certainty of free food and lodgings.

Always greatly enjoying public attention, Adolfo flicked a heavy bullwhip over the wavelets from time to time, just to impress the onlookers. He had the smug smile of a contented man, a bright new silver grosso tucked away in his gunpowder pouch and the praise from Don Francesco the Podestàstill glowing in his heart. He knew that he looked slightly out of fashion with that rusting old Spanish morrion helmet perched like a sliced boiled egg on top of his smallish head. His long scrawny, turkey like neck and the plume of blue and white feathers fluttering from the top of his morrion gave him the appearance of some strange jungle bird from Africa: in short he looked ridiculous. What mattered to him however was the prospect of a morning's sport with a defenceless old man. His exact orders from the Podestà would permit him to boss over Gustav and keep him in check. "Lieutenant Gustav, my foot!" Gustav was never a lieutenant in Count Koenigsmark's army, as in a saner moment the German giant had once claimed. Adolfo had seen the scars on Gustav's back - Gustav was no more than a runaway galley slave.

Orders, if carried out to the letter, would bring Adolfo another two promised silver grossi.Then there was another profitable prospect: the brand new halberd and helmet, which he had filched during the riot and had stowed away beneath some rotting wicker baskets in the 'laundry orchard' hut. They might bring him a tidy sum of money. A Greek arms dealer he knew who traded near the Rialto Fish Market might give him a fair price for them. He was a trader with Ottoman 'middle-men' who asked no questions about the source and ownership of weapons and armour.

The gondolier brought up his long sleek gondola with a deliberate bump against the mooring posts sticking out from the canal mud at the bottom of Grandpa's steps. A gaggle of bent old crones, all on their knees, were blocking the way to the front door. They were being jostled by the throng of newly arrived onlookers who came running up, seeking ghoulish entertainment. The ancient ladies nevertheless persisted in sending up a loud mournful chant of prayer, clicking their rosary beads with pale gnarled fingers. They were the 'morning mourning' widows of St. Peter Martyr Church and had followed Don Tranquillo to the Miotti house, at his request. After twenty minutes or more of their high-pitched praying, Zorzi and Grandpa had become extremely unnerved. It was that kind of rhythmic chant which normally came from old ladies waiting for the arrival of a 'late lamented' parishioner's coffin, or for a funeral Requiem to begin.

All three sat close together on a trestle bench behind the work table. Don Tranquillo, in his best black and white Dominican habit, sat in the middle with his arms resting on Zorzi's and Grandpa's shoulders, as though enfolding them in priestly protection. On the table in front of them Don Tranquillo had emptied a pile of thin silver piccoli of Murano minting and an assortment of mostly foreign bronze coins, popularly called baghettini. It amounted to all that had been donated to him in the church collection boxes over the past two weeks. A large jug of ruby red wine and two tall glasses were placed beside the pile of coins. Grandfather had pleaded to let Zorzi go up stairs to safety, but Don Tranquillo insisted that he stay with them.

The gondolier swung his long oar like a flail to clear a way to the door, sending some of the elderly widows toppling sideways. Adolfo rose majestically from the gondola and leapt up the slippery steps. The lumbering muscle-bound bulk of Gustav made the gondola swing out on its mooring rope, but he too managed an impressive entry. He was holding his head high and snorting. Separated wide apart by a deep bullet scar, his piggy eyes seemed almost to have glazed over. Like a cornered boar he snarled at the crowd, who feared and loathed him.

"Come out Miotto Daniele and submit to the justice of the Most Illustrious Don Francesco Capello Benzon, by the grace of our Sovereign Lord Doge and the Serene Republic, Podestà of Murano!" This important sounding command Adolfo knew by heart from long practice as a bullo. It impressed unruly crowds and kept that kind of civic good order that he demanded of anyone other than himself.

Just one cry of: "Murderers! Cowards! Arrest Zustinian!" came from the back of the crowd. An elderly man slunk away along a side alley. Piero the seaweed burner was well enough liked: any attempt to detain him would have been thwarted by those many in the crowd who shared his sentiments.

There was silence and no movement from within. Adolfo nodded towards his colleague, who, with one well aimed kick of his armour plated boot, flattened both of Grandpa's doors in a cloud of dust and splinters. The two bulli raised their spiked maces and stormed in. A murmur of disquiet arose from the crowd which, pressing forward in an attempt to follow, was shoved firmly back by the gondolier barring the doorway with his oar. Some then recognized the tall and handsomely muscled gondolier, even though a black leather mask covered most of his face and he was wearing half armour instead of his customary skin tight and brightly striped rowing strip. A shout went up, "It's Vogalonga!" More youngsters came running to join the throng, now in high hopes of getting a peep at their sporting hero.

True enough, it was Vogalonga - the lanky blond haired champion gondolier - the fastest oarsman in the whole of the Venetian Empire. Don Francesco had hired him, knowing that he was not only an easily corrupted informer to the authorities but that his star status, especially amongst the children and the young ladies, would create a distraction for the mob at a crucial time for the success of his plan of deception.

Don Tranquillo stood, holding his hands high in a peaceful gesture as though bringing down a prompt blessing from heaven onto the charging thugs: "The doors!" he bellowed with firm voice of a galley captain, "The doors!"

Adolfo stopped in his tracks and through some miraculous surge of strength just managed to rein back Gustav, who was by now breathing fire and brimstone.

"The doors?" asked Adolfo, mystified.

"The doors man! Use your addled brains!" Don Tranquillo commanded once again.

"Oh! Yes! the doors!" exclaimed Adolfo as though a moment of great inspiration had come over him. Hooking Gustav by the arm, he gave

69

another jerk of his birdlike head, directing the giant towards the hallway. Both bulli then faced about and walked back along the corridor. Gustav put down his long steel studded club with its star shaped mace head. Without even the slightest effort Gustav propped both heavy oak doors back into position.

Ever the laconic Teuton: "Guard zem!" Gustav growled through to the gondolier now standing on the outside of the splintered doors. Despite much flattery and other cheeky provocations, mostly from the girls, Vogalonga stood firm at his post, defying any approach by using his oar as both flail and barricade.

The two bulli stalked back into the courtyard. Don Tranquillo gave them a smile and an appreciative nod, as though to thank them for a job well done. Adolfo's eyes lit up when he saw the pile of coins. Gustav's saw red, in the form of an invitingly large jug of wine - bread and water for a month had been part of his penance from Don Francesco after that incident with his pistol and the well bucket.

"Not yet gentlemen, not yet!" came the friar's calming voice, "You have your duty to perform."

A high pitched bellow of rage, worthy almost of a prize bull that had snagged its privates on a thorny thicket, made its way up with increasing crescendo along Adolfo's windpipe: it was a roar of authority that he had refined for such occasions with years of practice. The gigantic Gustav then joined in with his deeper, more dangerous sounding rumble of fury. Both men raised their long steel topped maces, swung them around their heads and then directed their violent blows downward...against the ancient pots!

Fragments flew high in the air, bounced off the carved stone ring of the wellhead, scuttled along the corridor and pinged off the walls, as the two bulli warmed to their punishing task. Grandfather and Zorzi ducked under the workbench to avoid the flying shards, but the friar looked on impassively. His centuries old ceramic flasks; the gorgeously decorated tree trunk shaped 'alborelli' jars of the pharmacy now lay in mosaic fragments. In their swatting spree, the two bulli had laid to everlasting waste and ruin Don Tranquillo's pile of old pots. Most likely though, they

70

had destroyed a king's ransom, a mighty fortune in the rarest of all known porcelain - that which some Venetians still claim was first made in 15th Century Murano. Whatever...the pharmacy containers were considered worthless by Don Tranquillo: having once contained toxic chemicals; they could hardly be given away to his needy parishioners for use as storage jars.

Gustav batted one more fat round pot high into the air and as a consequence got a good dusting all over with its ash grey contents. Satisfied with his efforts he swaggered towards the workbench. As Grandfather and Zorzi emerged from underneath it, the brute gave one more lightening and deadly accurate swing of his steel studded mace. Grandfather felt the whoosh of air as it whistled past inches from the top of his thin grey hairs.

"Thirsty work," Tranquillo murmured pointing to the jug of sparkling red wine. Grunting with pleasure Gustav put down his mace and made a grab for the jug. As he lifted the gallon-sized glass jug, three brand new silver grossi appeared glistening on the bench top beneath it. He stared at the coins stupefied.

"A present to you from the Podestà," Don Tranquillo announced, as he flicked the three coins towards the giant.

"Ah! Oo! Ah!" was all that Gustav managed to stammer out by way of thanks. Adolfo chose this moment to snatch the wine jug from Gustav and to pour some of its deep red contents over his own and the giant's mace where, mixing with the thick depost of chemical dust on the weapons, it gave a fair impression of human blood.

"That's something that I hadn't thought about - a nice operatic touch! This Adolfo can't be quite so stupid as he looks." Don Tranquillo mused to himself.

Adolfo, seeing the look of pleased approval on the friar's face, said, "That's it. We'll be off! These are for me."

As he reached out to scoop up the pile of small coins, Tranquillo clamped the bullo's wrist in a firm and painful grip. The friar too was a powerfully built man. "Not quite, my good bravo," he said with a flattering promotion of Adolfo's rank, "You still have the furnaces to blow-up!"

"Oh yes, Your Reverence, I almost forgot." Adolfo rubbed his painful wrist and fished in one of his many pouches for a tinderbox. Nobody had inflicted such sudden pain on him for many years. He looked at the friar with new respect, but dared not retaliate.

"Here, use mine and take care you don't blow that fine helmet and feathers of yours over the rooftops!" Don Tranquillo slid his large brass and steel tinderbox across the top of the workbench, "You'll find them through there." The friar pointed towards the glassworks shed and then to the cobbled section of pavement at its entrance. Just a trace of blue smoke drifted-up to the sky through gaps in the shed roof where some pantiles were missing.

"Please no. Don't let them do that, I'd rather die!" Grandpa stood up and pleaded with the friar. Zorzi felt tears of anger welling up. He attempted to run at and to clasp the legs of the lanky bullo, but Don Tranquillo grabbed and restrained him.

"Calm down little friend. All is for the best. God will protect us!"

Gustav downed in one gulp the remaining quarter gallon of red wine and wiped and preened his whiskers like a panther sated by its kill. Adolfo stalked off towards the two furnaces with the Don's tinderbox: a few seconds later he came running back with his fingers in his ears. There was a bright flash and an explosion worthy of siege cannon on the battlements of Forte Sant'Andrea. This was followed almost instantly by another tremendous flash and thunderous crash. Black smoke poured into the air at the back of the Miotti home. Roof tiles slid down as the house was shaken to its wooden piled muddy foundations. Some in the crowd outside cheered and clapped; others walked away in disgust at the sight of the dusty black cloud. Many protested angrily, dismayed at the terrifying roars from the bulli and the sounds of smashing. "Miotti, after all, was not such a bad sort. He didn't deserve to be beaten to death in his own home for such a minor assault on the Podestà and, what's more, to have his valuable furnaces blown to pieces."

Destruction completed to the friar's satisfaction, Adolfo bowed low to him, turned and, like a puppy that has just been trodden on, let out a high pitched squeal of pain. His fancy Spanish leather high boots were made to impress the ladies, not to resist jagged-edged hard paste porcelain from the year 1485! Adolfo emerged on the towpath limping badly. Gustav cleared the way with a crazed looking, lowering glance of defiance at the crowd. Women screamed abuse, yelling: "Disgraziato Vogalonga!" at their former hero, the champion oarsman. As the bulli stepped into the waiting gondola they chuckled grimly, waving their bloodstained maces. With one powerful sweep of Vogalonga's oar, the gondola took off like a bolt from a crossbow. Skimming along the Glassmaker's Canal, all three ducked low and disappeared beneath the arch of St. Peter Martyr's Bridge. Their duty done, their silence bought, and with permission given to enjoy the rest of the day at leisure, they made for 'The Cock and Snake Tavern.' There they well lubricated their dust clogged throats and glare intimidation at any foolish or inquisitive customer who dared to venture near them.

As the crowd dispersed nobody turned to notice those thin whisps of normal furnace smoke still seeping through the rooftiles and rising in the midst of the sulphurous column of thunder flash cloud.

Zorzi and grandfather wept and danced with joy. They hugged Don Tranquillo and kissed his hands. Their furnaces were intact and other than a hellish smell of saltpetre, two small blackened craters in the cobbles of the outer courtyard and a few smashed roof tiles, there was next to no damage. But there was bad news to follow: "Listen old friend," said the friar, "You must close down your furnaces until I can persuade the Podestà to let you fire up again. There's no hope of that until well after the Sensa. Zustinian will have left then with his French guest. They are crossing the Alps to the Duchy of Lorraine. From Nancy they go to Paris where Zustinian's uncle may even make him Ambassador. It will be reported that you have died after a bulli beating, that your furnaces have been demolished and that no trace could be found of that damned book. Zustinian's prickly honour will be satisfied with the news. Gossip has it that he has big debts. It's unlikely he will ever return."

"It's not so easy to shut down a furnace." Grandpa grumbled.

"Your neighbours will know that. Just stop the smoke rising and keep out of sight for a week or so. Surely you can sell someone your cullet and whatever you have got annealing?" *(Glasswork in progress and finished pieces were left in the annealing furnace to cool.)*

"I'll not let you down," promised Grandpa, "But how we will manage I just don't care to guess. We are down to our last barrel of pickled cabbage."

"I'll send you some polenta flour with old Tacca. There's that splendid glassware in your store. Get Tacca to sell it in some side street near Rialto: there's no shortage of foreign visitors. Cancel any orders from local taverns. Is that clear?"

"Those pieces are all I have left to remember...."

"Look, Vincenzo is in heaven now. You can't live off of memories: poor Vincenzo wouldn't want you to starve. And you Zorzi, keep well away from friends. Stay indoors until I tell you. No bell ringing, no serving at Mass. Fish from your landing stage, if you must!"

Zorzi was already busy sweeping the smashed crockery in a heap to be dumped into the backyard ditch after nightfall. Though downhearted by the thought that he would not be able to go out to play for some while, he did not dare to question the friar's decision. As he swept and kicked the shards towards the glass shed, the thought came to him that he might while away the lonely hours trying to copy some of the decorated bits that had survived Gustav's mace mashing. He might glue together some of the best painted scenes: knights and ladies of olden times; views of landscapes; castles and cascades; ships and mermaids; dragons and arrangements of wild flowers. With Don Tranquillo's permission, he would decorate his bedroom and its empty mantle shelf with the best of the jagged edged bits. It was a bleak place his bedroom - every stick of furniture had been sold to make ends meet when he was still only a toddler. Something gleamed amidst the broken pots. He picked-up a coin, examined it and saw that the usual image of a kneeling Doge, with the flag of St. Mark was not stamped on the silver, nor was it one of the more common silver oselle coins issued by the Deputies to the Podestà, for Murano had minted its own silver and gold currency for many centuries.

74

"This must be yours Don Tranquillo."

The friar too looked carefully at the coin, "It's an ecu, a coin of King Louis," he observed. "Adolfo must have dropped it. I get all sorts of foreign coins in my collection box. You may keep it for being a brave hearted boy."

"Thanks," said Zorzi excitedly. "Was this Louis the king who chopped off the heads of his queens?"

"No, but he ought to!" Don Tranquillo commented, chuckling at his own joke. "King Louis has a brother called the Duke of Orleans. Orleans, well, he's an odd cove indeed, and his closest friend is someone you have already met."

"Never! You are joking again Don Tranquillo!"

"I'm not Zorzi. That friend is the Chevalier who picked you up in San Dona`."

"Oh God! No! Not him!"

"Don't dare blaspheme, young man!" the friar retorted in an angry tone. "Do not use God's name in vain! The Chevalier is a cousin of the Grand Duke Guise of Lorraine whose ducy has been gobble up by King Louis. The Grand Duke has escaped to Austria, but all the other Guises still regard themselves as princes of France. So I suppose you had the doubtful honour of being helped by a prince. I suspect your nibbled eared prince is behind much of the trouble that Grandpa has now got into."

"How's that, Don Tranquillo?"

"Not for you to know. You are too young," snapped back the friar. "I must leave now. I have matters to attend to. And remember Zorzi, no friends calling, fish from your landing steps, if you must!"

Propping back carefully half of the smashed front door, Tranquillo was surprised to find the bevy of black clad widows still on their knees. "God has answered your prayers, dear ladies. Go home now and pray that

Miotto may recover from his ordeal. I am going to the pharmacy to fetch something for him."

Don Tranquillo never lied: well, not exactly. Earlier that morning he had found yet another pot of powder at the back of a cupboard in the future schoolroom - this one marked 'Pulvis Cinnabaris'- and had put it aside, together with the wicked temptation to add it to the others in Grandpa's courtyard, thus causing Adolfo and Gustav to get a good dusting with red and deadly mercuric sulphide.

Whilst plotting the farce of Grandpa's punishment with the Podestà, Tranquillo had learned more than he could ever have guessed about Zustinian's evil commerce in little singing boys. Don Francesco also revealed quite shocking information about the lifestyle of the Chevalier Lorraine - enough to make a friar blush in the darkness of his confessional. And the Podestà did not mince his words either about the example given by the Papal Court: "This problem of child abduction and of squeaking eunuch voices, would be solved if the Pope condemned the disgusting practice out right. There is no shortage of trained young females in our orphanages, why are they confined to sing only in private chapels?"

Don Tranquillo was of one mind with the Podestà on that matter, pointing out that his own Order and that of the Franciscans would have nothing to do with castrati singers and had roundly condemned the practice as a disgrace to the papacy. However, their plan to solve the problem of old Miotti's punishment had gone exceedingly well, thanks to the willing co-operation of Adolfo and Gustav and the promised of a rise in salary in exchange for their eternal silence. Now friar and Podestà had a far more perilous game to play: a game of both revelation and of cautious deception with the Most Excellent Council of Ten.

CHAPTER NINE

Refresh your memory by returning to the 'Prologue' and to Zorzi's fishing misadventure. Floundering and clinging in fainting desperation to a slimy mooring post close to the swift currents flowing under Santa Chiara Bridge, he was about to be attacked by a giant siluro, known now as the Wels Catfish.

Noticing a sudden turbulence in the canal as the ferocious mouthed beast swirled back towards its prey, a youthful looking sailor with extra sturdy arms hauled Zorzi out of its line of attack, first by grabbing at his hair then hauling him clean out of the water by his breeches. Zorzi lay for some moments panting like a beached codfish. Staggering to his feet, he untied the knee laces of his breeches. A gush of dirty water coursed down his legs: had he really been dragged that far along the canal, and mostly under water? His despairing thoughts of a few moments before evaporated with the steam on his breeches. He now felt rather pleased with himself. How long, he wondered, had he held his breath while being dragged under by the monster? After scolding him for falling into the canal, Grandpa would be quietly pleased. Grandpa often boasted that the Miotti clan had the stoutest glassblowers' lungs in all Murano.

The sailor had spoken briefly in a strange language after fishing him out, and had then walked briskly away. Zorzi felt now that he ought to catch him up and thank him, but there were now quite a few youthful and foreign looking sailors busying themselves with unloading along the towpath. In his state of spluttering confusion Zorzi had taken little notice of the appearance of his rescuer. It could well have been any one of them.

Lucia, a girl of about nine years, quite impervious to the filthy murk in the canal, had already plunged in from the Ponte di Mezzo to rescue Zorzi's hat: it was something she had obliged by doing on more than one occasion when the hat had floated off during some scuffle or wild game. It was her curious way of proving her devotion and the thought never crossed her carefree mind that her courageous playmate might be close to being swallowed up like Jonah further along the canal. Undersized and skinny though she was, Lucia could out-kick any of the lads in game of calcio. Whenever discovered scrumping in an orchard she would leap the highest of fences and run with the legs of a gazelle. When neck to neck with Zorzi in a swimming race she invariably eased off towards the end, allowing him to get the better of her. Having rinsed the filth into someone's convenient rainwater butt, she placed the hat on her own head and went to look at a new attraction to be observed through the glittering windowpanes of signora Zanetti's sugar shop. When Zorzi eventually met up with her she delivered up the hat to him with a whoop of delight. But, to his dismay, the hat was now minus its precious plume. The two dripping mud larks exchanged bows and curtseys with flourishes of their hands, as though surrendering the keys of some conquered fortress city. Onlookers enjoyed this comic charade, clapping and chortling with amusement. Some were growing to admire the plucky Miotti boy, though not one had troubled himself to help him out of the canal. Others, had he drowned, would more likely have expressed their "Good riddance to a traitor's son!"

Now elated by his escapade, head held high and flicking dry the wet felt, Zorzi, accompanied by Lucia, trotted back towards home along the towpath. As they went they splashed through warm puddles, hopped over the baking hot flagstones and leapt the sharp gravel - Zorzi pretending to be quite unshaken by his mishap. Calls of, "Well done little 'un!" and "Better luck next time!" greeted him from some balconies and windows, but more than one grim faced glassworker called out: "Miotti's brat! Curse on you and all your family!" At such hateful comments Zorzi felt, not for the first time, a surge of guilt.

Passing again by Zanetti's sugar shop, Lucia alerted him to the lucky chance that Eldeniz was not on guard. Eldeniz was occupied helping some foreign sailors unload heavy canvas covered cones from a large black barge. Eldeniz, with his horse-tailed fly swat and his green Turkish uniform of a bashi-bazuka, defended the entrance of Zanetti's shop from little boys, wasps, flies and anyone shabbily dressed, and as such, indicating that he could only be a window shopper - for Zanetti's was an establishment with high standards and even higher prices. Any child who got within a whip's length of the fascinating multi-paned shop window was whisked away; sometimes receiving a kick in the bottom from the Eldeniz 'Ali Baba' turned-up slippers: a kick which tended to discourage the offender from ever returning. Eldeniz sometimes let better dressed little girls gawp at Zanetti's creations, knowing that they would not be tempted to soil the gleaming glass with grubby fingers. Such courtesy on his part did not apply to the likes of little Lucia, whose sole garments were a knee length 'sailor's shirt' that she had found discarded at the back of a tavern and a rag of printed calico by way of a head shawl, discovered at the end of market day when foraging for food scraps. Both items of raiment were so ripped and frayed and scuffed through and dirt stained that, from a distance, they gave the impression of being fashioned from delicate Burano crochet lace. Lucia's shirt at least had the merit that she would never out-grow its sleeves. Eldeniz was employed by signora Zanetta Zanetti *(Janet or Giovanna)* both as a startling and memorable attraction and as a porter to help gentlemen and ladies with their purchases. Lady customers always admired his handsome whiskers and military stance as he stood sentinel, arms folded at the shop portal.

"What," some wondered, "was an Islamic janissary, an enemy storm trooper, doing outside a smart shop in the middle of Venice, of all places?" But once the Greek cross hanging from a silver chain about his neck was noticed, all then understood well his status. Like hundreds of thousands of strong and healthy young boys, he had been snatched away from his Greek Orthodox parents, in payment of tax to the Ottoman Turk. Eldeniz was trained and beaten in a madrassa to recite verses of the Koran and to treat all Christians as mortal enemies and to fight like a fury in battle, in high expectation of martyrdom and all the sensual pleasures of a Sultan in the 'hereafter.' Eldeniz, however, was kidnapped late enough in his childhood to store up his seething hatred of the Sultan's tax collectors who had so casually and callously slaughtered his elderly parents. When Doge Morosini and his fleet appeared on the horizon, he was more than eager to go over to the Christian side. Now retired from years of active service with Morosini's fleet and never knowing his own family name, he kept his Turkish one.

Both children now had their mud caked paws pressed against the freshly washed shop window panes, entranced by a model of the Doge's State Vessel spun in threads of coloured sugar by some truly talented former glassmaker. The legendary Bucintoro, the Barge of Gold, had just undergone its annual re-fit in its enormous kennel shaped stone shed in the Arsenal. Rigged with silken cord and decked with plush carpets, its anchors plated with pure silver and its gigantic bulk burnished all over with tens of thousands of sheets of fine gold leaf, the Bucintoro would be rowed out in a few days hence to be the floating stage for Venice's greatest spectacle – the annual ceremony of the Wedding of the Sea. The spectacle would be followed promptly by the Doge's departure from Venice with his battle fleet and his swarm of troop transporters. The sugary image in Zanetti's window display was more than satisfying: neither Lucia nor Zorzi could ever hope to come near to the original.

Signora Zanetti's shop was filled with expensively dressed ladies and gentlemen seeking table decorations and other novelties for their Sensa celebrations. She was cautiously contented with the long overdue delivery from Jamaica - it seemed to be clean coned sugar of high refinement. With the ship's lighter, laden with canvas covered sugar cones, blocking the landing stage, her equally refined customers had to moor their gondolas further along and walk the short distance. She would, she determined, make a serious protest to the Podestà about the bad state of the towpath, when he came in to collect the model Bucintoro. The model would be Murano's gift to the Doge, a centrepiece for his state banquet on the eve of the Sensa.

No sugared sweets of any kind were manufactured specifically for children. In that time of frighteningly high mortality, a child's needs were not even considered until he had survived to an age when he could earn his keep. Sugar was used mostly to make elaborate decorations that were rarely eaten by young folk. Servants, perhaps, might be granted a nibble once the decoration got so battered and dust covered that it would no longer be fit to serve as a table ornament.

Shortly after the death of her husband, signora Zanetti made the sensible decision to close the family furnaces. There was little profit in glass manufacture now that the French, the English and the Bohemians were making their own, often using Venetian workmen. She therefore put her glassblowers' skills to better use spinning and shaping sugar. At Christmas they made gossamer thin winged angels and other Nativity Crib inhabitants. At Easter, Pascal Lambs were fashioned carrying the red cross of St. George. For the Feast of the Sensa, miniature images of Jesus ascending into heaven on a cloud of marzipan were pressed out from tin moulds - in bad taste and even worse modelling- they were sold by weight rather than by quality. Her more expensive products included Lions of St. Mark: the yellow marzipan lion with its raised paw resting on an open book; galleons with spider-web thin rigging, set with coloured flags and in full sugary sail; gondolas and 'Doge's Pistols.' This last, a sugar and liquorish paste confection, was an extremely popular joke item. It was common knowledge that Doge Morosini had cut the pages of his prayer book in such a way that he could hide a loaded pistol inside. The Doge was the leading Christian warrior, but he was not a particularly holy man - that is unless you took into account the hole in his prayer book.

Wonders of confectionary, in all sizes and differing colours, filled the shelves and hung from the ceilings of signora Zanetti's sugar shop showroom. For the poor urchins of Murano, the shop was a little piece of heaven come to earth, even though its sugary gates were guarded by a Turk, rather than by St. Peter. The shop was a form of paradise too for Eldeniz. What need had he for seventy-two maidens, when many more than that passed by and flattered him every week, admiring his rippling muscles? With a tall red felt hat, a big tassel and a 'fatwa' on his head as an ex Muslim, Murano was his earthy paradise.

Eldeniz was approaching now, whisking his horsetail fly-swatter in outrage at the scruffy sight of Lucia and Zorzi! It was time for them to beat a hasty retreat. As they ran off, a loud and gruff foreign voice called: "Hey! Miotti bambino! Come here!"

Annoyed at being called 'baby boy,' Zorzi stopped and turned with an angry frown. Sitting on a barrel of brown sugar next to the barge was a heavily built snowy haired old man. With the aid of a thick graphite pencil he was checking-off into his notebook a delivery of sugar cones. A great fuzzy beard covered most of the sailor's face and merged with thinning short locks which sprouted around a tanned and balding head. Heavily armed with cutlass, pistols, dangling powder cartridges and black sea boots thick enough almost to stop a musket shot, he was every child's fear-filled image of an English buccaneer! Thoughts of kidnap and a lifetime of hardship at sea came at once to mind. "How in Saint Mark's name does this pirate know my name?" thought Zorzi. Then he noticed a tall young sailor standing next to the rather stumpy shaped pirate. The sailor was beckoning now for Zorzi to come over to them. To his great relief, he realized that it was the young mariner who had pulled him out of the canal.

"Come on, he will give us some sugar!" encouraged little Lucia, tugging at his hand, "He gave some to Matteo."

Hand in hand, for mutual safety and keeping a wary eye as well on Eldeniz, they walked over to the men.
"You bambino Miotti?" asked the pirate poking him gently in the chest, "You glass Miotti, old man?"

Zorzi took this to mean his Grandpa and nodded his head.

"No death?"

"Not dead," answered Zorzi.

"You, good," and here the pirate made an over-arm swimming gesture: "Bravo! You catch big siluro! You very lucky bambino! Big siluro never catch you!"

"Show me where you live," said the young sailor with a re-assuring smile. His command of Venetian was, Zorzi thought, quite good for someone who seemed an ordinary foreign sailor. The old pirate pointed to one of the heavy cones that had been dropped: the sack covering had split open. The young man drew his dagger and prized off a large glistening chunk from the cone. He offered it to Lucia. She gave a shriek of excitement and after several graceful curtseys, skipped off with her prize.

The old pirate's deep-set brown eyes twinkled with pleasure on seeing the little girl's delight. Turning to his companion he spoke fast and low in a strange language: *"Well done son! Careful note of where he lives, mind! Stroke of luck! Anchored not an hour and looks like we're in sight of the old fellow we've come for."*

The young sailor hoisted the heavy sugar cone on to his shoulder and said to Zorzi, "Home young Miotto, home!"

CHAPTER TEN

Signor Molin with the aid of Bruno, his 'prize wrestler' of an eldest son was busy lowering to the ground the two front doors broken by Gustav just as Zorzi and the sailor arrived. A knot of young boys and girls had gathered, curious to see quite how they would be mended. Catching sight of Zorzi, signor Molin stood up, clapped his hands fiercely and ordered them all to "Clear off home!" They moved away reluctantly with sidelong glances at Zorzi, who thought he heard signor Molin say something like: "Don Tranquillo has already told you to keep away from Zorzi." Amongst the boys was Aldo, signor Molin's youngest, who gave a wave as though to say goodbye for good. Though deeply hurt by this unfriendly reception, Zorzi ran to old Piero who had just clambered out of his boat with a large double-handled saw, and a long iron auger. Avoiding the sharp tools, Zorzi hugged him round the waist and looked up lovingly to that familiar old snuff stained beard.

The young sailor let down the heavy sugar cone with a thud and came across to Piero. He bowed and said, in quite good Venetian: "Good evening signor Miotto. I'm crew of the Raven. I've a gift from Captain Ravenscroft. He is anxious to meet you."

Piero stood for a moment, completely perplexed. Then memory of two long forgotten names came flooding back: "Corvo Nero! Rafen! Capitano Rafenscro!" he gasped in astonishment.

"Yes. Capitano Ravenscroft is here. He wants to meet you," said the sailor, pointing to the sugar cone.

Dropping his buzzing Venetian dialect and trying his best to speak in posh Tuscan Italian, Piero exclaimed: "But how can he be here? Capitano Rafenscro is dead... dead of old age....a good ten years ago."

"His nephew, Captain Andrew - that is signor Andrea Ravenscroft," explained the sailor, adding proudly, "And the Raven, new vessel, Cuban mahogany…. unsinkable! Anchored this afternoon just off the Lighthouse.....unloading at Zanetti's."

"I must go with this man. Can you carry on until I come back?" Almost

beside himself with hopping delight, Piero added: "Tell Daniele!"
"Tell him what?" asked signor Molin.

"Tell him the 'Rafen,' the 'Corvo Nero' is back from London. Tell him there'll be news of his son!"

Old Piero was clearly overjoyed. Then seeing the look of total tearful puzzlement on Zorzi's face, he realized that in his excitement he had foolishly let slip his belief that Zorzi's father was alive: not only alive but in London, an opinion shared by almost everyone else on the Island.

Attempting to cover-up for Piero's thoughtless gaffe, Molin ordered Zorzi to bring a pointed iron spike and some rivets from the boat and to go at once to heat the spike tip in the furnace. He would need it to bore holes in the oak doors in order to re-hang them on their hinges. He gave the dumbstruck boy a shove in the direction of the boat. Without explaining to the foreign sailor that he was not signor Daniele Miotti, Piero took him by the arm and hurried off in the direction of the black barge, outside the sweet shop.

Don Tranquillo had taken signor Molin into his confidence, knowing him to be a devout and level headed family man, as well as being an obliging neighbour to old Daniele. Molin had long experience of how a bright young boy's mind works. "Listen Zorzi," he said, "Take no notice of old Piero. Say nothing at all to Grandpa. Wait till Piero gets back. You wouldn't want to upset your old Grandpa, would you?"

Zorzi shook his head, but was uncertain. He liked signor Molin...but.

"This business with our Aldo and your other friends: they still like you. It's just that Don Tranquillo does not want the news to get out about what really happened to Grandpa and to your furnaces."

"Oh! I see," said Zorzi, the sequin dropping in his mind, "So that's it. Don Tranquillo could have trusted me with the reason."

"Yes, Zorzi, but you know what friends are like. You tell them secrets and do they always keep them?"

Zorzi shook his head.

"Now Zorzi, I promise you a long ride on one of my ponies and signora Molin will make a special fish pie for you and Aldo when you come to our house, some day very soon. Meanwhile, you will have to wait till Don Tranquillo tells us it's safe for you and Grandpa to go out and about."

"Thanks," said Zorzi, much cheered both by this news and by the promise of fish pie and pony.

"Go and heat the tip of the iron. Use Grandpa's annealing furnace, we don't want blisters on our hands. I must bore new holes if I am ever to fix these hinges again. Your oak is harder than iron, Piero's auger will never do the job on its own. Fetch his pillow and blanket from the boat. He will be staying the night with you."

Zorzi hopped in through the gaping doorway, a happy soul again, but not before urging signor Molin to cut off a big lump of sugar for Aldo and his sisters.

"You're a lucky young man. How did you land such a big cone? It must be worth a fortune."

"It's my prize. A pirate gave it for nearly catching the sea dragon," explained Zorzi.

Lifting the heavy wooden lid of the rainwater butt, Zorzi immersed the blunt end of the spike, so that it would not heat-up too quickly and be too hot to hold. He decided against giving his hair and body a quick splash down in the butt. It was too much effort to skim-off the floating insects and a smidgen of mud never did a boy any harm, so he peeled off his breeches and padded across the cobbled courtyard to the fresh water well. A fine copper green lid covered the wellhead into which was punched the outline of a heart surmounted by a cross and the letters IHS. He knew that his rich cousins used the same sign to mark their glassware products. Banging his felt hat back into some semblance of its previous glory, he arranged it lovingly on top of the copper lid to dry in a shaft of sunlight and walked through to the furnaces. With a deft flick of his bare foot he lifted the blisteringly hot latch to the stoke hole of the furnace and shoved the spike part way into the pink glowing charcoal. He then spread his goatskin breeches over a bend in the brick pipe that took the smoke and toxic chemical fumes high above the rooftops.

Though quite unperturbed by the chipping and hammering made by signor Molin and his elder son as they struggled with the broken doors beneath his portico, the distinctive scraping noise of someone touching his precious furnaces instantly woke Grandpa from his afternoon snooze. In no time it had him hastening down the rickety wooden ladder that now sufficed for a stairway. When Grandpa rose, either at dawn or from his afternoon beauty sleep, he was always breathless. Until he had taken a generous pinch of snuff and coughed-his-lungs-up, as he delicately put it, he was never in the best of moods.

"I'm heating an iron for Aldo's dad," Zorzi hastily explained.

"All very well young Adam, but you have left the shutter wide open. We don't want an updraught and any more smoke from the stack. What are you doing in that blackamoor state anyway? Wrap a sack around you for heaven's sake!"

"I fell in. A sea dragon caught me off-guard. " Zorzi found a ragged pebble sack and used a bit of Piero's net cordage to wrap it about his nethers.

"Sea dragon eh! Quite sure it wasn't Jonah's whale on its way to the Sensa Fair? Pity it wasn't, because it would have swallowed you muddy feet and all! That would serve you right for not catching anything worth frying for supper! Thank providence for old Piero and his eels."

"I've lost my feather Grandpa. It must have floated away."

"Well at least I see you've not lost your father's old hat. It's a bit of an omen though. Peacock feathers found or lost always bring bad fortune. They certainly did to your father. Your feather has set me thinking though."

His curiosity thoroughly aroused by Piero's indiscreet remark and never too keen on washing himself, Zorzi tried to keep Grandpa engaged now that he was in a talkative mood. While the iron rod was heating Zorzi busied himself with uncustomary keenness in fetching down and laying out handily for Grandpa the cutters, pontils, wooden moulds and other tools needed for the evening's glassmaking. He so wanted to blurt out the news that Piero had gone off to meet a pirate, together with a foreign sailor - a pirate who for some mysterious reason knew Grandpa's name. However, he was well aware that signor Molin would be very annoyed indeed if he revealed anything that might upset Grandpa. Molin was quick to anger, just like his bruiser sons Bruno and young Aldo. It would only make Grandpa mist over in tears if he probed too directly for more information about his father, so he determined to use Don Tranquillo's 'sideways technique' of questioning: "Did Pa buy the hat for me at the Sensa?

"He bought it for himself, that is, two for the price of one at Rialto. Iridescence - that's the word that comes to mind when I think of your father. It was probably those peacock feathers that made him part with his money. I told him he was a proper feather head and if he ever wanted to be a man of trade he had better know that nothing in life comes two for the price of one. Ever smart with a reply Vincenzo said: 'Well Pa, if one hat blows away I'll at least have the other to fall back on.' Iridescence, that's what I am thinking of now."

"Iridescence? What's that Grandpa?

"It's that rainbow glow you find on oyster and abalone shells. Iride *(Iris)* well she was said to be a messenger for the old Roman gods. Iridescence was something your father sought after all his life. I've been thinking about it a lot over these past days. Trevisan is the one I want to see but I daren't ask for an audience with him just yet. Your father's obsession could be our way out of trouble with the Podestà."

"Just a tick, Grandpa. I'll be back." Zorzi seized the red hot spike with a leather pad and raced out to Molin.

"What's this?" Molin quipped, "Grandpa put you in sackcloth and ashes? What in blazes have you been up to now?"

Zorzi would have liked to stay and watch the hole boring but he raced back to the glasswork shed, Grandpa now being in one of his rare talkative moods. "I remember now Grandpa, you told me all about the rainbow thing ages ago. It's that old beaker in the box under the dresser, the one with with the letters around it."

"You remembered? Now that makes a change. I am going to give the beaker to Trevisan. Trevisan's butler owes me a favour and I know for a fact old Trevisan collects rare and antique things. He is sure want to know who gave him the beaker and all about its story. You're an orphan and he's Patron of San Zianni Guild. You are entitled to his protection. I'll beg on my knees, if necessary. Well, I'll be on my knees anyway – you have to be when you talk to a Senator. Let's hope he'll help me up again!"

"Oh! No Grandpa! But you can't give our beaker away, Grandpa! Anyway, I'm not scared. Aldo's dad and big Bruno could easily give Zustinian a good thumping in an alley somewhere. Aldo says they will 'do' them bulli of his as well, if come near us again."

"What a splendid idea! You'll end up with us all hanged!"

"Anyway, us boys reckon Zustinian is a lily-liver. No one has seen him since the rumpus. Anyway… besides… didn't you say the beaker was Pa's favourite?"

"It was Zorzi. He bought it from a blackamoor, a peddler from some muslim land."

"I know what we'll do. I'll help you make a copy, Grandpa. You can do it Grandpa. You could give the copy to Trevisan. It looks like our girasole glass anyway… You know… well, like those fake pearls you used to make."

Grandpa chuckled, "Don't you think your father would have made a copy if he knew how? It's a complete mystery that beaker, it's full of iridescence. Vincenzo called it his Roman joke."

"What's the joke then, Grandpa?"

"The joke is that you can't drink out of it and I don't suppose the poor heathen who owned it could do either, because it came from his tomb!

That's what the peddler told your father, and Don Toma`, who knows about ancient things, said it was the first bit of truth that he had ever heard of from a moor. Now go and wash that filth off of yourself and see if signor Molin wants another iron…Properly now. Don't dirty the well! Use the waterbutt… cloggs!"

This last was a reminder Zorzi not to walk barefoot through the glass strewn workroom. Grumbling quietly to himself - his probing questions, as usual, had got nowhere very far with Grandpa - Zorzi clambered on to a high stool, pinched his nose tightly and jumped foot first into to the barrel of rainwater. Completely submersed, he rubbed and shook his matted brown hair vigorously to the count of ninety-five, while the displaced flies and mosquito larvae breathed their last on the hot courtyard cobbles. "Not bad," he thought to himself, though his underwater fishing trip with the monster fish must have lasted much longer than it takes to count one hundred. His toilette thus speedily accomplished, he rubbed himself dry with his dusty sack, wrapped the sack about his waist and fixed it again with a frayed length of netting. Molin was not ready yet for another hot iron, so Zorzi slipped silently into the showroom and drew out from its hiding place under the dresser the straw lined box in which the Roman beaker nestled in all its beauty. As he lifted it gently and cast his expert eye over it, he could see now why not even his father would have had the skills to make such a wonder. It was blown or shaped in a mould with separated double layers of glowing iridescent glass. The outer skin had been pierced, carved and possibly drilled through with the finest imaginable looped and inter-twined trellis and around the lip, making it impossible to drink, was a Roman inscription. Each separate and beautifully formed letter was raised on its own stalk of glass. And what made it so shuddermaking now to Zorzi - who was learning how similar Latin is to Italian as he served at Tranquillo's Mass - was that he could now make out what the inscription said:- E D E B I B E S T A L A U D E C R A S M O R S
(*Eat drink and be merry for tomorrow we die!*)

Hastily returning the beaker to its straw coffin, Zorzi scurried out into the sunlit corridor. Was it that frightening inscription, or was it an aftershock from his canal plunge that now made him tremble uncontrollably from head to foot?

89

"Vinegar!" Came the shout from Grandpa, "Use the pickle barrel!"

Vinegar almost ran in Grandpa's veins, it was his solution to every known human ailment, from piles to nits, from cut feet to headache. A long gargle and nose sniff with vinegar ensured survival to eternity after any immersion in that lethal Styx - the Glassmakers' Canal. The canal doubled up as sewer and rubbish tip and was dredged regularly, that is to say every ten years. Zorzi knew better than to dispute with Grandpa. Obediently, he went back into the storeroom, picked up the nearest cup, a work of skill and delicate beauty, but to Zorzi just one of Grandpa's many efforts left unsold from the market. Finding the pickled cabbage barrel he skimmed off some of the surface scum and swilled the green tinged vinegar into his mouth.

Had Satan himself appeared and shoved Molin's burning iron spike through Zorzi's gums and up behind his eye, it would have resulted in no less pain. Zorzi let out a high-pitched wail, dropped the glass on the flagstones, spat-out the burning vinegar and coughed and cried in agony.

 Grandpa and signor Molin came instantly. For a moment they were fearful that he had swallowed one of the glass-making chemicals. Realizing that it was only severe toothache, Grandpa gave him a hug and tousled his damp hair. Such a rare sign of affection made Zorzi half forget his suffering. Signor Molin went off to fetch in the sugar cone and dropped it in a corner of the storeroom with as heavy a thump as the sailor had made.

"What on earth is that?" asked Miotti.

"You'll see," said Molin as he scraped-off a handful of sugar and told Zorzi to lick it slowly. It did the trick and in very few moments the acid burning was neutralized; even the toothache seemed no longer to throb. Knowing from long experience as a family man that distraction can soothe away pain, Molin suggested to Zorzi that he might help him burn the holes for the door hinges. Grandpa went to get the red-hot poker. A pleasant half an hour was then passed with signor Molin pressing down hard with the burning spike then drilling with Piero's auger. Zorzi, filling his mouth from the well bucket, spewed it out over the hard oak whenever flames licked-up from the holes being bored. Between each splutter he nibbled happily at his lump of sugar.

With still no sign of Piero's return, they were beginning to worry. Signor Molin still made no mention whatsoever to Grandpa of the arrival of the English ship 'The Raven.' The young sailor had seemed a pleasant generous sort, for a foreigner. Someone who had saved Zorzi from drowning was hardly likely to do harm to tough old Piero, who anyway wasn't worth robbing.

The pleasant smell of burning oak slowly gave way to a strange musty goat like pong. It came creeping along the corridor and out onto the portico where they were occupied with riveting on the hinges. Grandpa, who had no sense of smell whatsoever, was seated at his workchair with its long extended armrests on which was balanced a wooden tray powdered with burnt plaster: (*molten glass does not adhere to burnt plaster*.) He was lining-up in sequence his long thin sticks of clear and coloured and milk white opaque 'lattimo' glass. The old glassmaker was obviously intent on making just one more masterpiece of spiralling 'latticino' before his beloved furnaces cooled perhaps for ever.

Molin went to investigate the pong. "Fire!" he yelled from the glassworks shed, "Fire!"

Dropping their tools they all ran in, arriving just in time to see the last merry flames leaping up from the seat of Zorzi's breeches, now spread out on the cobblestones. Grandpa had already filled a wooden bucket with glassmaker's sand and doused the blaze.

"Trouble always comes in threes," announced Molin, who had hastily brought in the bucket of well water and after Grandpa's yell of caution was now a wiser man. Cold water would have caused a scalding explosion and most probably would have cracked the furnace walls.

"Let's hope that the nuns of Maria degli Angeli can help us with a new pair," Grandpa grumbled with a sigh of resignation. Then he remembered how unwelcome his presence might be at their convent after the riot he had caused at San Donato.

CHAPTER ELEVEN

By sunset Zorzi was already cocooned in his sleeping blanket listening to the pleasant boom of the Angelus bells echoing across the great Lagoon. Tonight he would sleep with a cool head close to the stone arrow slit that pierced the outer wall of his bedroom. The downward slant gave a clear view of anyone approaching the front door. It was just two hand spans above floor level, sometimes causing a dreadful up-draught and was a built-in feature from more troubled times, when an unwelcome visitor might have been skewered with a swift bolt from a crossbow. Zorzi now used the arrow slit on occasions for dribbling water down onto the heads of passing friends. He removed a small panel of wood blocking the slit, shooed away a pigeon that had chosen to roost there for the night and noticed that Piero's boat was still tied up but had not been covered over with its rainproof sailcloth. Before closing his eyes he said a prayer to St. Peter Martyr, 'him with the axe in his head,' to protect his old friend from pirates and robbers, especially pirates with long daggers, like the ones in the painting by Bellini.

Lost in a delightful dream of wine and fish and freshly baked bread, being served to him by a blue faced and mightily nosed nobleman, he shifted his aching shoulder blades to a more comfortable position on the floorboards. The delicious odours now became so much more intense. Startled by an unusual scraping sound, he woke with a snort. Voices were coming from below. Flickering lights shone between gaps in the thick uneven floor planks. Smells of fresh bread, tobacco and Parmesan cheese drifted up to him together with the more acrid smoke of rushlights. Nolonger a dream though: it was Grandpa, who was sobbing - saying strange things. Zorzi put his ear to the floorboards, fearful of news that Piero had either drowned or had been carried off by the black barge sugar pirates.

"So, in short, your prospects here are nolonger that bright. I'll do what I can to speak with your Podestà." It was the voice of a stranger speaking with a distinctly upper class Venetian command of words. "You are welcome as ever to join us, Daniele, I shan't press you though. Now poor Da Costa is nomore, we are in need of your talents – your experience."

"Gianni Costa dead?" It was Grandpa's voice, cracked with sorrow. "Uncle Antonio taught him….but you must know that. Was he? That is, did they?"

"No, it was his lungs," the stranger replied, "Inhaled litharge I guess, a warning to us all. There was an attempt, a few moths after he joined Uncle George. He fought them off, but got a flesh wound that never healed properly. Soon after that came the London fire. We then dismantled what was left of our works and shipped it all up the Thames to a quiet rural place near Henley. Those murky riverside alleys leading down from Uncle's sheds went up in smoke too, together with the rest of old Savoy slumland, so we no longer had that threat around us. Believe me, there was never a shortage of potash after that fire! But Costa was from Altare, I gather?"

"Well, from somewhere in Monferrato…. Gonzaga territory," Grandpa added. "The Ten don't go in for that sort of revenge anymore. There are so many unemployed, the Marigola *(the glassblowers' guild,)* would be only too glad if half of us us were to hop off abroad with our skills."

With a grim laugh the stranger commented: "Well, I guess a Gonzaga knife in the ribs could be taken as a back-handed compliment to Da Costa's talents. Gonzaga Dukes were always noted for their artistic appreciation!"

Knives in the ribs? Zorzi was fascinated. He rolled over silently, still wrapped in his blanket to deaden any creaking noise. In the middle of the bedroom was a much wider gap in the boards. He could now see straight down to the store room trestle table on which Grandpa displayed his glassware to customers, some prized pieces were on the table all beautifully glistening in the light of expensive looking marine lanterns. He had never seen the candle stumps in the coloured glass wall brackets lit before: they too added their rainbow light to the altogether unusual scene below. Pewter platters, used only at Easter and St. Mark's Day, had been taken down from the dresser and temptingly arranged on them were: a quarter round of Parmesan cheese; two loaves, partly cut; five or six juicy fat oranges and a tapped wooden keg of the kind used for strong liquors.

Below also to his great relief, was Piero, his head glowing pink through the comb-over of his few silvery locks. Piero, helpful as ever and never wasting a moment, was sewing a cloth patch over the burned out seat of

Zorzi's pantaloons. He set down the sail needle, extended his glass and a burly shouldered and sea tanned old man, equally sparse of head hair, refilled the glass with a gush of golden liquid from the keg. It was that grizzly bearded pirate… the one who had given him the sugar cone at the black barge! Excited beyond dreams that Piero was safe and sound, Zorzi was all for running down to greet him. Peering low and further to the right for a better view of the stranger with the fine accent, Zorzi froze with fear - a tall man, a nobleman, wearing splendid clothes and a powdered periwig! A gilded leather baldric and long business like rapier and pistol were dumped on the table top amidst the food and delicate glassware. Costly weapons, silken garments with flowery and minute embroidery, distinctly like those worn by Zustinian and that other swaggering noble who had nearly kidnapped him in San Donato! A shiver of anxiety overtook him: Zorzi kept very still and listened on.

"He certainly had it with him, Vozzignoria. "(Your Lordship.) It was Piero's gruff voice with a slightly tipsy edge to it. "He came late one evening begging me to hide it. Daniele's place here had been burgled, chambers, this store room, the workshop, all ransacked. Nothing taken though: they were after the book."

Piero paused while his wine glass was refilled - one of Grandpa's best pieces - all spirals of contrasting colours and made strictly for sale. He guzzled down the fiery draught, coughed hard and continued: "Young Vincenzo was exhausted, dripping wet, convinced of being followed. Hiding from them amongst the reeds, he recognized one of Bembo's bulli - a murderous a lanky fellow called Adolfo."

"PodestàBembo?" The 'Lordship'queried, "Surely not! I doubt they were doing his bidding. Surely a Podestà would never employ assassins?"

Assassins? They were talking about his father! Shocked and trembling uncontrollably despite the stuffy heat, Zorzi drew his blanket about his shoulders and sat rigid in the darkness, desperate to learn more.

"I urged him to stay the night," Piero continued, "Even loaded my crossbow, but Vincenzo was never much of a hand with weapons. Besides, crossbow or not, I guess we both knew he would have little chance if a bullo like Adolfo caught him. 'He pleaded with me to hide the book somewhere dry. Somewhere dry, I ask you! Like the fool I am, I told him to stow it anywhere else because it would never be secure with me. You see, Vozzignoria Rafenscro, my bilancia – my fishing hut - is not much of a place. I don't have a door, let alone a locker to stow a precious book in. My bilancia, well… it's no more than pine piles, rushes and wattle. I burn samphire weed, you see. Our glass making folk prefer it to the wood potash recipe. Anyway, young Vincenzo made off at dusk in the direction of Our Lady of the Angels: a concealed path few know about goes through the high reeds; no swamps to tumble in and Vincenzo knew every turn, even so, a risky route for others to follow after dark. His plan was to stay overnight in the Convent refuge. You see, Vozzignoria Rafenscro, he was doing some repairs to their stained glass… doing a fine job as well cleaning an old picture for them."

Grandpa interrupted: "Our troubles arose from a silly squabble about that Bellini Madonna. While he was restoring it my poor son had the misfortune to have a few cross words with Zustinian."

"A quarrel with the great Giustiniani, now that sounds to me extremely perilous. Cross words over a Bellini? You intrigue me, Daniele!"

"Well you see Captain, my son could never let another have the last word. So many times I warned him to bridle his tongue when speaking with men of great rank."

"Which of the Giustiniani would that have been?"

"Bastian, the Doge's nephew."

"The Doge's nephew….unfortunate indeed! Not a man to pick a bone with one imagines?"

"Zustinian arrived unannounced at the Angels' Church one day with two or three young dandies in tow. However, they were not there to watch the picture cleaning in progress, as Vincenzo soon found out. He bowed and continued in silence with the slow job of cleaning, waiting respectfully for Zustinian's comment and when it came it was: 'At last I can see my castle through the trees, you are doing a splendid job.' Now instead of having the sense to take the compliment in silence, Vincenzo questioned

Zustinian in a doubting tone: 'So Gradara is your property now?'
Instantly annoyed, Zustinian snapped back: 'Gradara, why did you say
Gradara? Bellini would never paint that evil place next to the Madonna's
throne. Gradara, nonsense man, you've cleaned the western battlements
of my Soave!'

"Alas, Vincenzo insisted that he had seen a very similar Madonna panel
in Pesaro Cathedral with an identical castle painted in the background. He
had been assured by a priest there that it was in fact Gradara. Gradara,
Captain, is a great fortress just up the road from Pesaro. But you may
know of it Captain Ravenscroft? What with your wonderful Italian, I
don't doubt you will have read your Dante. Dante, you will remember,
wrote of Paolo and Francesca, the young lovers murdered in that same
castle…. their souls condemned for ever to wander in the Inferno seeking
one another."

"Of course, of course, Daniele, but I can't yet fathom what annoyed
Giustinian: a yarn about couple of young adulterers, why should that raise
his hackles?"

"Well Captain, Vincenzo learned afterwards from Sister Tecla that
Zustinian had really gone to the Angels' Church with quite another
purpose in mind. He intended to brow beat her into selling him the
Bellini. It's the Convent's prized possession of course: something that had
been hanging in their church for best part of two hundred years.
Zustinian's reasoning was that it had been donated to them by mistake.
He spoke of some ancient document by way of proof that the Executors of
one of his long dead relatives had blundered. They should have given the
Convent another far smaller and unfinished Bellini. Since he now owned
both Soave Castle and the Barbarigo Palace in whose chapel it had once
hung, he felt that it was only right that he should make a fair offer to the
nuns and get it back.

"Does Giustinian have such funds? A Bellini must be worth tens of
thousands. The Giustinian, I'm told, are rolling in wealth, even so…."

"It gets worse, Captain Ravenscroft….It gets worse! Vincenzo ended up
insulting one of his ancestors and scuppering any chance of Zustinian
ever buying the painting. My son knew history too well for his own good:

he knew his Doges, Captain. Alas, he was unaware of Zustinian's connection with the Doge in the painting. He casually informed Zustinian and his friends that Bellini could not have been all that fussy about what he put in his pictures, because the kneeling Doge was in fact Agostino Barbarigo, the biggest thief, extortioner and swindler of a Doge that ever sat on a Venetian throne!"

"Grief! Giustinian must have been pretty riled!"

"Riled he was and all the more because Sister Tecla was present and heard every word, not to metion the sniggering young noblemen with him! Zustinian began to rave at my poor Vincenzo accusing him of keeping our book of recipes, knowing it was stolen form the Library of San Pietro. He then threatened that if our the book was not returned within a month, either to San Pietro or to him, my Vincenzo would soon learn the hard lesson of a Zustinian's displeasure. Sister Tecla intervened and begged them not to raise their voices in the house of God. She then ordered Vincenzo to apologize and leave the church at once, but that was only to protect him from a beating, or worse. Afterwards, she told him how delighted she was about his unwise comment, they had given her a perfect excuse for turning down Zustinian's offer."

Grandpa had never ever mentioned this incident to him and Zorzi now felt offended that he had been told so little about his father's death. Lowering his head to the boards he listened on. Grandpa's voice once again: "We kept our books under the dresser here, under a loose floorboard, wrapped in oilskin, of course. They broke open my cash box, but left the four grossi I had. Lucky too, they didn't get hold of my Darduin book, that's our most precious family heirloom. I'd lent to my cousin, he wanted one of its recipes." Grandpa paused at intervals to cough. "That day was the last I spent with my son, God keep him." The old glassblower then broke down, buried his head in his arms and shook with grief: "I accuse Zustinian, Captain Ravenscroft. Who else, other than the Podestà, has bulli at his beck and call?"

Zorzi was relieved to see the tall stranger's consoling hand reach forward and clasp that of Grandpa: this nobleman was no threat then. "We'll do what we can for you my good friend. Uncle George was very fond of you, that I do know. He often spoke of you as the finest glassmaker he had ever done business with. I shall not dishonour my uncle's memory by leaving you in such... such difficulty."

"It's not unearned money we ask for, Captain Ravenscroft - just the chance of fair trade with you, as we did with your uncle. Take what you want of my glass. I am tired of it."
"The gruff pirate's voice then rumbled and barked for several moments. Grandpa and Piero sensed the anger and menace in his words and were now anxious to know quite what he had said.

"I guess John is right," Captain Ravenscroft observed," If you can endure listening to my poor Venetian, I'll tell you my story. It will explain why John here may be on the right tack. Your Giustinian may innocent after all. A far more mighty noble might well be responsible for his disappearance.

A spasm of cramp gripped Zorzi's calves for a painful minute or two: but he managed to rubbed and stretch it away without making so much as a whimper. Curiosity had overcome all his woes: his aching teeth; the pressure of the floor boards on his hip and arm sores and discomfort of lying so still. Strangely, that dismal news about his father had not greatly affected him, but there was something else that Zorzi had quickly noted, something that had so far escaped both simple hearted Piero and heart-broken Grandpa - a marked change in the stranger's pattern of speech. The Captain had started off, perhaps deliberately, talking in an error strewn mixture of Italian and Venetian. Now relaxed and rum mellow and feeling secure in their friendly company, there was little in his speech that would have betrayed him as anything other than a Venetian nobleman. Not only did he use difficult words, he seemed familiar with the slang and differing pronunciations that there were between mainland dwellers and true islanders. Something about this English Captain did not quite add up! Zorzi was mystified. He listened, fascinated by the stranger's beautiful command of the Venetian tongue.

"The French Duke of Orleans, bother of King Louis knows, far more than he should about your missing book – that is, at least his agent does, for the Duke himself has the brains one would expect of an in-bred Bourbon. This agent knows that you own the Darduin book of your wife's family recipes. The Duke's glassworkers have copies of the Barovier's recipes, as

98

well as those of Antonio Neri, but then most people in the business have Neri's book. Now it's a story involving John here but it's best that I tell it in full. It comes to me all so clearly from childhood because it happened on my birthday. Uncle George went to Court at Greenwich in London and took me with him as a treat. I was dazzled by it all…the silks, the jewels, the scarlet guardsmen, the trumpets and, I guess, the strumpets as well. One of His Majesty's beautiful lady friends indulged me with a heavy golden platter of candy fruit….I stuffed myself full and was sick that night, by way of celebrating my tenth birthday. Much long after, I learned that we had in fact been to a meeting of the King's famous Society of Philosophers. Uncle needed to assert our right to the lead glass patent, which, as you know, we got from your great uncle Antonio's book. Uncle George thought it a good move to present our wise and merry monarch with a cup and cover that Gianni da Costa had made. He took along some fake jewellery and some fine lead crystal lenses that Gianni had made as well. King Charles was astonished, as was the King's natural philospher, a fellow named Robert Hooke. Both King and courtier knew instantly - forgive the pun - what a breakthrough in glassmaking my uncle's gifts represented and what it would mean to everyone involved in star-gazing and studying the world of tiny creatures. The French Ambassador was present, and shortly afterwards, Uncle was surprised by an invitation to St. Cloud: that is to the Duke of Orleans's enormous new country palace, just outside Paris. Can you imagine his excitement? Before he went Uncle George was warned by this Hooke fellow that Orleans was an unreliable devil. Orleans it seems is a fop of a man, quite unlike his warlike half-brother. Orleans is of course the rightful King of France, no doubt about that, but thank God he isn't. Everyone at court, except perhaps stupid Orleans, knows that King Louis is Cardinal Mazarin's offspring."

The sea Captain paused to wet his lips with a gulp of the golden liquid while there were unsurprised comments by both John and Grandpa on this little known piece of French scandal.

Zorzi, doing his best to follow the tale, came close to over tipping the water jug as he stretched his legs to shuffle off another oncoming cramp. The stranger looked upwards from where the scraping and muffled squeal had come, but hearing nothing more continued: "Need I add, Uncle George fell for the trap and was lucky to have John here with him. He never got to see the halls of mirrors in Saint Cloud and waited in Paris for over a week for an audience of the Duke that never came. Eventually he was called to the Palais Royal in the old part of Paris. There our Ambassador introduced him to a very handsome young nobleman who said he was acting on behalf of Duke Orleans. This youngster neither acknowledged Uncle's bow nor treated him with the respect due to an older gentleman. In short he treated Uncle like a common tradesman, asking him to leave his best pieces of glass for further inspection and for possible purchase. Uncle was furious and sorely tempted to challenge him, but John here urged him to restraint. John had noticed duelling scars and that the nobleman's left ear had been part severed. John wisely judged from the young man's build and fitness that he would most likely make butcher's meat of Uncle George. This young villain then made an astonishing offer of ten gold Louis d'or for each page of your Uncle Antonio's precious book of recipes. He even knew the number of pages and that the recipes were all written in the Greek dialect of Constantinople, though some, like the lead crystal recipe, were already translated. Seven hundred and sixty pure gold Louis d'or in all, plus expenses for the trip, was what he offered, if Uncle George could buy, or steal, the book for him. There was even the offer of a French honour of some kind, but that depended on how much of a fortune his friend Duke Orleans could make with the book's recipes. Given that Orleans had the half treasury of France in his purse and was unlikely to be in need of profits from glassware, Uncle guessed that the young noble was out to line his own pockets. But this is the interesting point: the nobleman, a fellow whom we found out later was called Guise de Lorraine, hinted to Uncle that the book held the secret of porcelain and that only he knew how to decipher it. He claimed too that the Grand Duke of Tuscany, had got his porcelain recipe from a similar book, also originating in Byzantium. The whereabout of that too is a mystery, as indeed is the murder of Grand Duke Francesco and his wife. Of course Uncle George refused absolutely to betray a friend in that way. The unpleasant young man then offered to escort uncle around Duke Orleans's own mirror works and laboratories in the basement of Palais Royal. Nodoubt you can both guess what happened next. In no time he and John here were left locked in a room with a heavy door and high windows."

Hearing the words Guise and Lorraine, Zorzi was tempted to cry out aloud. Evidently Grandpa had not remembered those welcoming titles

Don Tozi had given to the French nobleman from his pulpit in San Dona`. He gave another cramp loosening shudder, wrapped his greasy blanket more tightly about his legs and earwigged with growing excitement.

"When night came, Uncle George stacked up some chairs and tables. Climbing on to John's shoulders, he used his glasscutter to remove a pane of glass without the slightest noise and escaped, thanks to John here punching flat the night guard and stealing a horse. Uncle George complained to King Charles, but he did nothing: not surprising, considering it was a crime committed by a high ranking noble of France. Evidently our King was well aquainted with this Lorraine fellow and knew him to be a bit of a rascal. He laughed off the whole matter and, though Uncle felt humilianted, the King advised him to drop his claim. After all the Court of France had given years of refuge to King Charles after his father was chopped in London. This agent of Orleans still owes our Company a mighty sum for the glass he stole: not to mention Uncle's expenses. Where is the book now though, Daniele? I would have heard if it had ended up in Paris. If Bastian has it, he must be holding on to it for some reason. He was always a clever pest though, even as a child he cheated …. that is."

Astonished by the revelation that Ravenscroft not only knew Bastian and may have once played with him, Grandpa exclaimed: "Why, Captain Ravenscroft, did Zustinian live in London then?"

Evading the awkward question, and seeing that Grandpa was now alerted to the fact that he was not all that he seemed to be, Ravenscroft gave no proper answer, other than: "Say nothing of my thoughts, Daniele, keep them to yourself and you as well, Piero. It's best for us all if others call Bastiano to account. One thing more, it would go badly for all of us if your Podestà to get to hear of our meeting this evening. I've reported my landing, so he knows I'm here with cargo and to purchase glass. You know you are forbidden to trade."

By way of distracting Piero and Daniele from this revealing indiscretion, Ravenscroft invited the company to stand while he proposed a toast: "To your talented son's memory. May his good soul rest in peace eternal!"

All seated again, Ravenscroft continued, "Uncle George lived always in

101

hopes that he could persuade you to join him in London."

"Too late for me even to think about it, but Vincenzo should have gone when he had the chance. He'd be alive and prospering now… loyalty to his fellow guildsmen; that's what it was. Now look how they scorn and treat us!"

"Well, you have our gratitude for all your hospitality to Uncle George when he was here. God rest him too, he had a more lingering death than that of Gianni Da Costa. The litharge and arsenate did for them both. Never go near the stuff, Daniele, without a wet mask."

This news brought further cause for alarm to our little earwigger. Litharge, arsenic… Zorzi often dusted them about rather carelessly when helping with the girasole beads and jewellery mix. Grandpa never bothered with a wet mask: from now on Zorzi determined to take more care of his own lungs and to badger Grandpa into wearing one.

"When we dropped anchor yesterday it was ten years almost to the day since Uncle George passed on. To return on his anniversary is a strange coincidence. I ought to leave something here by way of a memorial for the many happy years he spent with you."

"We shall have a Mass sung in his honour." Grandpa proposed, "Tranquillo got to know him well in those years when your civil war was raging.They passed hours together in conversation: though what they spoke of we never knew. Just as soon as it's safe to get out and about, I'll arrange it. Our Dominicans here rarely make a fuss over a dead man's religion. When some foreigner dies on the Island, he's nearly always given a good send-off with a puff of incense for good measure. I guess even Puritans, like yourself Captain Ravenscroft, are consoled by a good send-off: nothing finer than a sung Requiem to cheer you up when grieving!"

"That's a capital idea, Daniele. What better way to remember Uncle George, and on the Island he so loved. I expect many of the older traders will remember him from far back… in more prosperous times. Your priest should invite them all to a memorial breakfast. I shall leave an offering for his expenses, but he must understand that in present circumstances, as matters are in England, I couldn't be seen at a Requiem Mass. Not all of my crew can be trusted to be discreet. The thought of dangling on Tyburn gallows, along the Oxford Street, minus my guts, does not appeal. However, I could slip into San Pietro around about the time of the consecration and pretend to be admiring the pictures. There's a fine Bellini in San Pietro as well, I am told. I must see them both before I leave."

"It's not in the church: it hangs behind Don Tranquillo's desk. No problem in getting to see it though, my Zorzi has the job of cleaning the place. Strange that you should mention it, it happens to be Zorzi's favourite picture….a bit grim for my taste though."

"I had Vincenzo's figurehead re-mounted on our prow. His model, I'm told, was a raven in the San Pietro Bellini, so I really must take a look."

"A raven in Tranquillo's Bellini? Can't recollect anything of that sort, I must ask Zorzi."

Cheered somewhat, with this plan to honour an old friend, now long gone to his rest, grandfather took a generous swig of the powerful Jamaican rum then 'coughed-his-lungs-up.' Hearty laughter followed, putting everyone in a better mood. Grandpa was given a couple of friendly slaps on the back from the big sinewy hands of the pirate, who had now moved out of view from where Zorzi was spying down and trying his hardest to follow the conversation. He would have so much to relate to Aldo and his trusted pals along the towpath - in confidence, of course! Something else now was puzzling the little lad though about this strange gentleman. Something unconvincing had been said which seemed at odds with the nobleman's other comments.

"You must come aboard Daniele, and you too Piero, as soon it can be done discreetly. Bring Vincenzo's little lad. It may be some while before we get the The Raven into the Arsenal so you will excuse the shambles she is in: she needs careening and a re-rig after our crossing from Jamaica and we had to plug a few unexpected holes soon after we left Siracuse. Our Venetian colours saved us though."

"You were showing our colours?" questioned Piero, with a slight hint of disapproval.

"Wouldn't be here otherwise. Beating towards Tangiers we were sighted by a French Second Rater of 84 and its frigate of 32. With that sort of armament we had no choice but to haul-to for inspection. The cut of our stern and its gingerbread betrayed us as English, but our bosun is a perfect Titian when it comes to re-decorating. Way out from the Straits he altered our name to Corvo Nero. Young James here was kitted out as a Venetian nobleman and sent in the cutter to parley in his French and Italian together with a gift of cones and rum. A 'scerzo' like that can't be pulled on the Moors though: to them the lion flag is ever a provocation."
"Cussed blackamoors!" muttered the pirate who, together with the young sailor, was listening with evident understanding of much of Ravenscroft's colloquial Venetian.

"We anchored off Siracusa to take on fruit and cabbage and to water at Arethusa's fountain. They say the Siracusa Spring brings good luck with it, but it didn't do us any good! *(Nelson used the same lucky spring a century later, before the Battle of the Nile.)* Berber galleys tried to board us a league or two out of harbour. But thinking about it, I suppose we did have a bit of good luck: the Knights heard our gunfire and saw our distress signal flying, Venetian style, at top and mizzen. Had they guessed we were under false colours they too would have sunk us with even greater joy than the Frenchmen, I don't doubt. How they charge though for their service. They carried off a good thirty of our cones! The rum didn't appeal to them…being religious, I suppose." The stranger paused to tamp down and relight his tobacco pipe and to savour another glass of that rough Jamaican liqueur so scorned by the legendary Knights of St. John of Malta.

"But you have really got to admire those fighting Friars. The moment their titchy galley flashed red and white on the horizon, the half dozen Xebecs pestering us took to their barbarous heels. But not before our John here had given the Moors a damned good pounding with our 'Mayfield iron.' *(cannons.)* Corsairs….When shall we rid our seas of them? Which reminds me, we didn't bring in the morello cherries for your grandson. He had a bit of a 'run-in' as well this afternoon. Caught a siluro I gather, that's what I call pluck!

"In our canal….a siluro?" queried Piero. "Thought they were sweet water…"

"So it seems," confirmed Ravenscroft. "James noticed its big whiskers on the surface as it swirled and headed straight back towards the little fellow. The lad was so covered in slime it was hard to make him out amidst the pylons."

"Madonna! It would have killed him!" exclaimed old Daniele.

"Indeed, that's just what it would have happened. Siluros have a taste for human flesh, and especially for youngsters who fall in rivers. Some Spaniard with a bright idea brought them back from the Amazon – now they are gobbling up freshwater creatures everywhere, birds and all."

"Eternally grateful to you James: lucky for us all you were passing. To your long life and happiness, Maestro James!"

Young James smiled at the compliment, raised his glass to acknowledge Grandpa's salutation, then in English murmured to the pirate: " Siluro? Fairly sure it was a wels. Saw one in the Avon about the same size…swallowed two swans… one gulp for each."

"It's the Latin for a wels" Ravenscroft explained, "I'm told, there are ten footers in Spain… immense size and weight… devour the very men who fish for them, no Christian should eat one. Leave 'em to the Moors, I say. Which reminds me young man, fetch the morellos, I left them under the stern thwart."

The young sailor moved into the lantern light briefly, and passed close to the pirate. Zorzi wondered why he had not realized before that they were father and son. Innocently unconcerned, as the young so often are about the mortal perils into which they sometimes plunge, it was the prospect of cherries that excited Zorzi now. How though could he find a good reason to go downstairs? Grandpa had seen him take up his water jug and chamber pot, so neither could be used as an excuse. Grandpa would be furious to know that he had been listening - 'earwigging' as he called it. He decided to keep silent in the dark and to learn more.

Talk of battles with Corsair pirates, of Maltese Knights, of how his father may have really died - not drowned, but killed by Zustinian's bulli - just as Grandpa almost was. Talk of stolen books: of kings; of secrets; of dukes; what more would he find out if only he could keep awake and 'earwig' on the conversation just a bit longer?

"Give us a chanty John!" the gentleman ordered: the rum was beginning to work its mellowing spell on the company. "Show these stout glassblowers that we've got puff as well. Give us the 'Snake on the Western Wave.' If there is any truth in John's chanty, our serpent has an appetite for whales rather than wels!"

As the pirate launched into his song, with an expert twiddle on his recorder, Zorzi decided to make another slow silent roll in his blanket towards the top of the stair landing. This manoeuvre he had almost completed when he tumbled straight on to his own booby-trap letting out a yelp of pain.

The pirate's chanty came to an abrupt halt. Grandfather came to the steps and called up, "Are you awake Zorzi? If you are up there ear-wigging, you had better get to sleep at once!"

Zorzi held his breath for a while and then moved slowly to remove the sharp lump of broken pottery pressing through the blanket into the sore on his elbow. The booby-trap was laid carefully each evening as his defence against a possible midnight attack from Gustav and Adolfo. Zorzi had noted, with great satisfaction, how the thin greyish looking jagged shards of pottery had sent the tall, long-necked, 'bullo' limping off.

"My grandson," apologised old Miotti, "Bad toothache... had it for days. Guess he's dreaming of swilled vinegar."

"Well Daniele, I know an excellent fellow, a tooth-puller in the Ghetto. You must get the boy seen-to: teeth can be a plague if left untreated."

"If you are thinking of Rabbi Sterchel, I haven't even got the price of a pair of breeches for the lad let alone dentistry. I am afraid I already owe the Rabbi a deal of money: he used to be a collector of Vincenzo's work…always gave us a fair price. My wife's book is in pawn with him now as well, part surety and part for safe keeping. If Sterchel will let you, you have my permission to copy anything you want from it. In any case, I know all the recipes by heart. My Zorzi, I hope, will redeem the pledge one day."

"I'll be honoured to sort out your loan with the Rabbi, as it happens he is a close partner of ours. Young Zorzi needs to get ship shape as well: kitted out for muster. I owe you a lot more than the price of a few pulled teeth and the Rabbi sells more microscopes for me than I can sell in London. James, fetch me pen and paper from the longboat!"

The young sailor set down a wicker pannier full of gleaming black morello cherries and asked: "Do you want the cash box too, Captain?"

"Sensible lad…. reliable…. trained up well!" He nodded his appreciation to pirate John, the young purser's father.

With another twiddle from his hornpipe, the pirate now continued the entertainment. It was a racy and rude mariners' dirge, telling of shipwrecks; monster squids; mermaids; hurricanes and unfaithful ladies; all of which, fortunately, none but the English company present quite comprehended.

Ravenscroft poured himself another tot from the keg of rum and held his glass to a brass lantern in order to better admire Grandpa's skill. The egg shell thin fluted goblet was decorated with an incredibly fine double spiralling latticework of milk white and jet black glass. As he did so he caught sight of two gleaming little eyes in the darkness at the top of the ladder. Instinctively his hand went across the table to the hilt of his rapier.

"Prepare to repel boarders." The order was whispered in English. John caught the wink and followed the upwards motion of his master's eyes. Leaping from his stool, the pirate came close to overturning his Captain's fifty ducats and more of purchased glass now jangling on the trestle. Instantly steadying the table top, the pirate drew out his great pistol with slow and deliberate menace, then with a roar of feigned anger bounded up the ladder. Alarmed by the sudden commotion, two mariners who were on sentry seated in the Raven's cutter hurled themselves along the corridor cocking and preparing their heavy flintlocks as they ran. Terrified by the swiftness of the attack, for pirate John had scaled the long ladder with no more than two bounds, Zorzi tried to retreat back to the gloom of his bedroom. Instead he tumbled head over heels in his blanket and on to the shards. "My grandson," Miotti apologised.

"Delighted!" Ravenscroft chuckled. "Fetch him down John!"

The young sailor followed his father up the ladder with a lantern. Amidst much laughter, Zorzi made an undignified descent, trussed up in his blanket and slung over the pirate's left shoulder. Dumping Zorzi without ceremony on a cleared patch of trestle top, John ordered, "Open wide!"

Getting the drift of the English command, old Piero assisted by opening Zorzi's mouth gently with his forefingers, whilst the pirate made a thorough inspection with his mirror-backed lantern. "Prettiest dose of scurvy I've seen in a twelve-month, Captain Andrew," he muttered. "What the lad needs is a trip to Siracusa, without delay!" Ravenscroft proposed.

"No, no, not Siracusa! Corsairs will kill me!" pleaded Zorzi, having no notion of how far off the famous Sicilian port was.

"So you have been 'earwigging.' For how long have you been listening?" Grandpa asked. However he didn't seem too displeased. Perhaps it was the rum - he was now on to his fifth glassfull. Popping his arms out of the blanket the lad showed the sores on his elbows and knees to the company.

"Scurvy all right," commented James who had just returned with cash box and writing materials. "Had it twice myself in the South Atlantic."

Zorzi understood little or nothing of what the young sailor said, but felt re-assured by his jolly smile, his nods and his gestures and the pitted scars disfiguring his own neck and forehead.

"Well my young dragon catcher," Ravenscroft commented, "We mariners have a saying about our vitals: 'Bread for your belly, fish for your thoughts and fruit for your fittings.' Your fittings seem to be coming adrift from their moorings. You may lose all those young teeth very soon unless you get some fresh lemons on board. Start now with an orange: it's the next best thing for the scurvy."

Zorzi's eyes widened as he clasped the huge, lusciously sweet Sicilian orange. He had never seen an orange that big, not even in Rialto market: what's more he had never tasted more than an occasional orange segment offered to him by a stallholder in a particularly generous mood.

"Tomorrow, young man, you will go to the Piazza, to the Sensa Fairground, but first you must run me an errand to the Ghetto.....Take a message for me. I will explain all to Piero here. You must follow his instructions carefully. He will ferry you over to Venice first thing tomorrow morning. Now tuck in and when your belly is full, get to your bed."
The exciting prospect of the Sensa Fairground was overshadowed a little by the thought of visiting the Ghetto. "But Capitano," Zorzi begged anxiously, "Jews live there. Can't Piero come too, the Jews will kidnap me?"

"Utter nonsense! The Jews are no better, nor worse than Christian folk. The Ghetto is no great distance from where Piero will set you down. You see, he will be busy with some errands for me as well, tomorrow. You do know your way to the Piazza, don't you?" *(Piazza San Marco - St. Mark's Square.)*

Zorzi acknowledged that he did but, having never been to the Ghetto, he needed more encouragement from Ravenscroft: "Remember young man that Jesus was a Jew. My Jew is a Rabbi, a trustworthy man, once a good friend of your father. He will look after you well, you can be quite sure. He will patch up your teeth and your clothes as well no doubt - better even than Piero can." He nodded in the direction of Piero who was, between swigs of rum, still sewing that patch of sail canvas over the scorched hole in the backside of the precious goatskin breeches.

Zorzi needed no further Captain's Orders. He tucked in to bread and oranges, took a sip of the rum and spat it out in pain and disgust. Encouraged by all, he cautiously drew out Captain Ravenscroft's magnificent rapier. Ravenscroft showed him how to stand on guard for a duel - hilt held at eye level, point dipping down to the opponent's waist. Zorzi could barely hold the weight of the left hand close-combat dagger: a weapon straight out of his nightmares of St. Peter's martyrdom. Raising the tremendous weight of the rapier and holding it out at arms length was altogether too much. Amidst laughter and more rum, John the pirate spluttered: "Toothpick for a gentleman! Useless on board! This is what you call a sailor's weapon!"

Fumbling under the table for a moment, he threw an orange into the air, sliced it clean in two with his cleaver-like marine's cutlass and caught both halves before they hit the floor.

Zorzi clapped and laughed and forgot all his woes. He had never been in such good company. Grandpa told him to bow, to kiss the hand of the generous Capitano Ravenscroft and to get quickly up the ladder to his bedroom. Zorzi bowed with good grace, clinging firmly to his blanket. Almost as an after-thought, while saying goodnight, he added: "Capitano, I have seen the man you were talking about."

"And which man was that, my young shipmate?"

"The French noble - You said he had his ear sliced off, like St. Peter Martyr....No, I think it was Piero's Saint who had his ear... anyway, I saw it under his wig, his ear. It must be him.... a bit chopped off and a shiny pigeon brooch.The priests too were saying bad things about him and all... I heard them. When I accidentally tripped he helped me up. You see, we have to wear clogs in the choir and I'm not used to.... He's a proper prince, you know, Don Tranquillo told me, and he stank.... perfume and garlic. Teeth rotten too... a bit like mine."

For some moments both John and Ravenscroft took silent stock of this news. Then Ravenscroft murmured: "Arethusa has brought us good luck after all. Seems like she's brought us alongside our French Alfio. What a coincidence! I might have guessed Lorraine would be here for the Sensa. "Where did you say you saw him, young shipmate? Was he wearing a blue sash?"

"Yes, and a pink brooch and the cross of Malta. He must be one of those Knights....a very nice sword as well, like yours.... at San Dona`... last Saturday. Loads of soldiers there, and a band and the Podestà. Noble Zustinian was with them as well....you know, the one who you think has killed my pa."

"I said nothing of the kind young man. No one knows yet how your dear father met his end." Ravenscroft spoke in a tone of mild disapproval. "You know, you should not have been listening to the talk of grown-ups, but never mind. You have done me a favour this time, though earwiggers often get their facts in a twist.... isn't that so Daniele?"

"Whatever you have earwigged, Zorzi, you will say nothing about! Nothing ever! Is that clear? Don't let me hear that you have told your friends about this evening. These good gentlemen are here to help us. I don't want you to get us all into trouble again. Is that clear?"

Zorzi nodded, tears of shame in his eyes. Grandpa was obviously very annoyed.

"The poxy-faced Frenchie......fancy that! You must 'call him out,' Captain. But then he's really my quarrel, not yours, let me carve him for you. I'll pardon what he did to me in Paris when he ends up looking like!" The pirate crushed to pulp the two orange halves in his sinewy fist. What little of his face could be discerned from out of his magnificent whiskers, bushy eyebrows and chest length beard was now livid with rage.

"Friends!" Grandpa pleaded, guessing at their intention to get even with the French nobleman. "No duelling for my sake - not at Sensa Time."

"Our only bad luck is that we have so little time left to hook our Frenchie. We need to keep close hauled as well this trip. Maybe it's best after all not to bait him in Venetian waters. But we'll decide how to griddle him once we've caught him. Let's start with young James sounding out for us where he is lodging. The servants at Ca` Lolin- top end of the Grand Canal - may know something. Once we know where he is berthed we might send him an invitation, a welcome on aboard The Raven. We can't do that though until she is clear of the Arsenal. With luck, some day soon we may be asking him to admire the comforts of our bilge deck. Believe me John, compound interest and an apology won't be all I'll ask for! The problem is how to hook him alone. Grandees, big siluros like Lorraine, have friends and flunkeys in tow."

111

"Couldn't we tempt him somewhere quiet on the Lido, Captain? Dad and the crew can deal with any retainers. You could dangle the prospect of the Miotti book. If he's already got it, he won't rise to the bait. If he hasn't, then he might not want his friends to know what he's up to."

"Good thinking, James. We'll discuss this later. Our friends here are looking neglected."

Before climbing back to his bedchamber, Zorzi asked: "Capitano, where did you learn our Venetian? I want to learn Latin and English an' all that, so I can be a spy. Was it very hard to learn our Venetian?"

Ravenscroft stared at the little lad, somewhat taken aback by his question. A wry smile then overtook his rum ruddy cheeks. "Well, my young spymaster, when I was not much more than your age, my dear mother and me had the good fortune to live, shall we say, close by to the Venetian Ambassador in London. I wonder are you clever enough to guess name of that Ambassador? You have already mentioned the name to me a moment ago."

"Not Zustinian!" Zorzi gulped in real consternation.

"Right first time my lad, but not your Zustinian; a relative of his though, a good man named Ascanio. However it was not he who taught me English….that is, that is, I mean Venetian. It was my dear mo....who was herself… well never mind who it was."

Ravenscroft halted, cheeks flushing just that slightly more rummy red - angry with himself for having allowed the drink and the innocent questioning to 'get under his guard.' For whoever signor Ravenscroft really was, be it English gentleman, or sea captain, he was not in Venice simply to sell sugar, nor to enjoy the fun and spectacle of the 'Sensa,' nor even to buy and to export glassware. He was in Venice because he had been requested to come, to give an account of himself and of his reasons for leaving London without permission, and leaving his post in such a hurry. That request had come from a source that no one who valued his life dared disobey.

Zorzi slept fitfully for an hour or so and then awoke, turning over in his mind all that he had gleaned from his ear wigging. That was it! How could a Puritan English captain known so much about the Mass... known that a dead person's name was whispered by the priest straight after the consecration of the bread and wine?" Very few people, not Aldo, not Piero, not even Grandpa had known that when he, Zorzi, had told them. It was a piece of odd and interesting information that Don Tranquillo had not so long ago passed on to him over breakfast. While pondering over this curious contradiction he heard scrapes and jolts coming from the longboat and low voiced salutations from the departing guests. He climbed onto a wooden box beneath his window and looked out onto the moonlit canal. The long white boat glided mid stream beneath the bridge. He was about to step down, when a movement from the opposite bank caught his eye. It was the sliding movement of a closing felze shutter on an expensive looking gondola: the plywood panel seemed to have been burnished with gleaming silver leaf. Seconds afterwards, the lanternless gondola slid smoothly from its moorings and followed the English longboat at a distance and without a sound. Just before it passed under the bridge, a brief shaft of moonlight through the clouds lit-up the gondolier's shoulder length locks of blond hair.

(The felze was a small wooden hut-like compartment in the middle of a gondola. Normally, four or five persons could sit inside, protected from rain by thin plywood shutters, or on sunny days curtained from curious eyes. Though very few have survived and they rarely appear in paintings of the Venetian Lagoon it is certain that Venetian blinds were first made for felze windows in the early years of the 18th century. Felze are hardly ever seen on modern gondolas.)

CHAPTER TWELVE

The dreaded Ten, whose 'requests' were ignored at one's peril, were in fact sixteen elected Senators, plus the least important member - the Doge himself. Their grand hall for full Council meetings has still, to this day, that chilling, 'Consiglio X' inscribed above its door frame. Behind the panelling of that hall is concealed a far more awesome lair, though sumptuously appointed, it is none the less designed to strike terror in any who might have the misfortune to be called to account there. It is a chamber set deep in the centre of the Doge's Palace; a candlelit cavern of a room with a low and oppressive wooden ceiling heavily carved and gilded. This committee room had one more appropriate decoration: a crazy and most entertainingly gruesome triptych by Hieronymus Bosch of 'Hell fire and damnation.' Each month The Ten chose just two of their group to attend in that chamber to the daily matters of State Security. The six Doge's Counsellors chose just one of their members to perform the same duty. So, after much contrived confusion, we end with just three, not ten, noblemen appointed to attend the meeting of the Most Excellent Council of Ten on Friday, 19th May, 1694. Why was it then that a fourth nobleman was present?

'The Ten,' that is the three, entered by way of a swing door set at an angle in a corner of the candle lit chamber. Behind the swing door a hidden staircase and concealed corridors give access to many rooms on the upper and lower floors of that immense labyrinth - the Doge's Palace. That revolving door also led to the gilded and gloomy office of Grand Chancellor Domenico Ballarin. His realm also included the Compass Room and the Inquisitors' Room, where both noblemen and Senators could be grilled, and on rare occasions sometimes suspended painfully from the ceiling by a pulley and rope, drawing their wrists upwards behind their backs.

The three Inquisitors appeared dramatically, like actors on a stage. They were dressed priest like, in cassocks of plain full length red silk, each with a wide sash or 'scarf of office' draped from the left shoulder. After bobbing slight bows to one another, they went over to a table on which was spread out an architect's designs for a grandiose, fifty roomed, country villa. They smiled, behind their frightening white death's-head masks, known as 'bautte,' and made nodding approvals of the beauty of the drawings of the plans and elevations. The villa was very similar in design to an ancient drawing by Andrea of the Gondola, a humble stone cutter's son who grew up to be 'Palladio' - the most renowned of all architects and builders.

Moving silently in their silk slippers, the three Senators mounted the steps to their thrones, tucked their hands up the wide sleeves of their red brocade robes and looked down through the candlelit gloom to where the fourth nobleman was seated. He had travelled hastily a very long way to attend the meeting; in fact seventy miles, from the foothills of the snow capped Dolomite Alps. When The Ten's messenger came, he was in his lovely rose garden playing with his two golden haired toddlers. They were splashing each other with the waters of a sparkling marble fountain and throwing breadcrumbs to the ornamental carp. His beautiful young wife had waved to attract his attention from the balustraded terrace overlooking the newly laid out rose garden.

In a voice resembling the bleat of a peevish old nanny goat, Senator Querini, the most senior Inquisitor, demanded: "Now remind me young Calergi, who presented you with the lead statues – such splendid examples of garden sculpture?"

"The Roman Emperor, your Excellency."

"Indeed, Leopold himself. I wonder what he had in mind when choosing you for such a demonstration of his imperial generosity? Could he have his sights once again on our town of Bolzano? A town that you were duty bound to defend! At the very least you must have known Leopold would want something in exchange. Well, the Austrian Kaiser would be better advised to save his lead for the 'Sons of Allah' when next they come pounding at the gates of Vienna. But if he doesn't know how to deliver his lead to the Turk, then we do. Your statues will go to the Arsenal to be melted for grapeshot!"

From another chalk white death-mask came a more honey toned voice: "And do remind us young nobleman, how you managed to pay for this sumptuous pile of stone?" He waved a languid hand in the direction of the table and the plans.

"From taxes," came the mumbled reply.

"Remind us whose taxes they were."

The nobleman, naked but for a strip of urine-soiled cloth about his nethers, shifted on his stool and winced with great pain at the rope tying his arms at the elbow behind his back: "Yours, your Illustrious Excellencies," was his agonized reply.

"Not ours, the Serenissima's taxes – raised for the Doge's war effort!" came the booming voice of the third Inquisitor, who was none other than Senator Daniele Contarini. *(As a member of The Ten, Contarini was well qualified in dealing swift justice, having slaughtered, amongst others, his runaway mistress and the renowned composer Alessandro Stradella who ran off with her after a music lesson.)*

"Not Marco and Todaro, I beg Your Excellencies! Don't add shame to my suffering... dishonour my family! For the sake of my children and my wife, let it be the Orphans' Canal I beg you! That is my only plea, Your Excellencies!"

The three Inquisitors whispered together for some moments. The Court of Forty Judges meeting in a nearby room had already given the man the death sentence; yet he had fought bravely at the siege of Navarino alongside Doge Morosini. There were sabre scars about his neck and shoulders and a livid white hole just above his knee where a crossbow bolt had entered. The fine new villa could be sold for a far greater sum than the amount of tax he had defrauded from the Serenissima. There would be a slight problem in hanging him between the two huge columns which stood outside the Doge's Palace. The city was swarming with tourists, all of whom knew that it was ten years bad luck to stray between the two columns. Public executions were carried out between Marco's column, topped with the Lion of St. Mark and Todaro's, with St. Theodor spiking his crocodile-like dragon. Compared with other European cities public death spectacles were rare in Venice. The Republic felt that they were degrading to public morals and relied on that deliberately encouraged fear of The Ten and the certainty of capture as their deterrent. Decorating the columns with a dangling corpse, especially at the Feast of the Ascension, might bring bad luck on the Doge's war campaign – not to mention the discouragement to tourism. Their other choice might be a discreet night-time strangling and weighted ankles at the notorious and deep Orphans' Canal near to the Lido.

A knock on the revolving door interrupted their deliberations. The Grand Chancellor entered. He was a neat and elderly little man, his back curved by decades of desk work. Beneath his towering owl's ear wig schemed the cleverest high-domed brain in the whole Republic. He bowed low three times and held out a sealed letter. As soon as he was given permission to speak, he announced: "From the Bocca della Verita` your Excellencies."

The Bocca della Verita` was post box for the convenience of those who sought to betray or restore reputations, or simply grumble. Several of these gaping lions' mouths of stone or marble were to be found set into the walls of the Palace environs.

"Do we know who brought it?" asked Senator Querini.

"A rather thin lady of rank, wearing a mask and a black brocade cloak." The Chancellor was not supposed to have his staff spy on the brave individuals who entered the heart of the Doge's palace to place a denouncement in the 'Mouth of Truth.' The right of free access and complaint was open to all, whether they were the Cardinal Patriarch of Venice or a humble dredger of stinking canals. Free speech for gossiping gondoliers and frequent elections, limited for the most part to the ruling class, had kept the Serenissima going for over one thousand years.

"The denouncement may be of some importance, or else she is just a crackpot out to create trouble. The lady walked with the aid of a gold topped ebony stick and had a limp. She was helped up the Giants' Stairway by her servant, an extremely large and well-upholstered woman." The Chancellor rewarded spies who reported in such detail.

"Open and read it, Ballarin," ordered Contarini. "One moment...." He looked down contemptuously at the prisoner, who had now fallen to his knees, his forehead resting on the floor: "Since you are so fond of lead from the Austrian Emperor, doubtless you will enjoy your stay here as the Doge's guest. You will be confined to the Leads for five years!"

117

The noble prisoner raised his tear-streaked face and blurted out his thanks, calling down a blessing from St. Mark on their Illustrious Excellencies. He knew that he might survive five lonely years, chained beneath the lead roof of the Doge's Palace, suffering agonies in freezing winter and, in summer, blood boiling heat. Yet he would hear the seagulls shrieking their angry quarrels above the rooftops and would hear the faint roar of carnival crowds. He would be spared the final humiliation of the executioner's rope – dangling naked by one leg high between Marco and Todaro.

A guard was summoned to escort the nobleman over the Prison Bridge, *(much later in history called The Bridge of Sighs)* for a brief visit to the nightmare-ish New Prisons. There his crime and punishment would be recorded, his manacles clamped on by the blacksmith and servant to Messer Grande *(Mister Big.)* The Chief Jailer would then assign him to his cell under the rooftop 'Leads' of the Palace itself. On his way back over the bridge he knew he would be allowed to pause for a while and take a last look at the outside world – the beautiful Island of San Zorzi Maggiore *(St. George the Great)* with its church by Palladio floating like a stately red and white ship in the middle of the Lagoon. Ambition to own a Palladian villa, the ultimate status symbol, had brought about the nobleman's downfall....it would be a fitting last sight!

The far too lenient sentence given by Contarini peeved exceedingly old Senator Querini. As senior Inquisitor he had precedence in commuting any death sentence, as well as the right to select from the ghastly written menu of painful forms of dispatch: now he had been upstaged. Old Querini also suspected that Contarini may have taken a bribe from the prisoner's family. His problem though, was not to seem too vindictive in this particular sentence and so dash his own high hopes of ever being elected doge. *(Given that his elder brother, Francesco Querini Stampalia, had been fed to a pet lion kept by the Calergi family, many would have forgiven old Querini for not missing this opportunity for a truly sweet revenge. Three of the Calergi Grimani, a family notorious for violence, brigandage and extortion: Vittore (a priest of sorts) and his brothers Pietro and Giovanni, lured Francesco Querini to his death in the side garden of their palace on the night of 15th January 1658: they were banished, their palace demolished and a column of infamy erected on the site of the crime. After much bribary they later returned and rebuilt. Their splendid Grand Canal palace, re-designed by Mauro Codussi, with that fateful side garden cum lion's den, is now the Venetian gambling casino. NON NOBIS DOMINE is inscribed in the stone just above the water line, which could be translated as that age old criminal plea:- 'It wasn't us, God!')*

"When your sentence is completed," Querini pronounced, "You will be exiled for life. You may go to Austria, where it seems you have treacherous friends ready to inform on you. You have abused your sacred office! You will never again see your wife, nor ever meet up with a member of your disgraced family!"

Senator Pisani ought to have kept his silence. He knew that old Querini was, in the circumstances, being a model of Christian forgiveness. However, Pisani's prime function as one of The Ten appeared to be to annoy old Querini as often as he could and to thwart his ducal ambitions. He now insisted that the sentence be further reduced. Given that Venice was forever short of experienced galley commanders, he added a more hopeful prospect: "Banishment for life will be commuted, if, after your sentence, you volunteer again for the galleys. You will lead the attack and capture in person an Ottoman warship. Only thus will your sentence be expunged from our records!"

The prisoner staggered to his feet, bowed deep and low and cheerfully followed his jailer, praising God and thanking the merciful Senators. The sentence offered hope. It offered too a chance of restoring honour to his humiliated Calergi clan, either through death in battle or through a triumphant return to the Arsenal with the green crescent flag of the Turk tacked to his bowsprit.

Having used the interruption to read through the whole letter, Grand Chancellor Ballarin smelt trouble – indeed, unlidding a barrel of rotting crabs would have been perfume in comparison. The letter was fully signed and correctly witnessed by four signatories, as was the law. Unsigned letters were burned without ever being believed. Fictitiously named writers were only pursued and punished if their accusations proved to be false. The Murano Podestàknew the rules – that is why he gambled on this method of revealing his grave concerns. What's more, The Ten were bound never to discuss elsewhere matters revealed to them in confidence and were as constrained to further silence as were priests in the confessional box. Trying to keep calm and dignified, the Chancellor read on: "To the Most Illustrious, Most Noble Senators and Most Excellent Heads of the Council of Ten." The abbreviations in the letter – Il'mi D.D.Sen'ri et Ecc.mi Capi del Consiglio X – instantly betrayed that it came from someone familiar with government business and the shortened forms of correct address.

He continued reading: "I, Silvestra Valier, Citizen of the Serenissima, denounce to the Most Excellent Council X that I was present on the island of Murano on Saturday 12th May in the year of Our Lord 1694. In the congregation at San Donato I witnessed the outrage upon the person of the Podestà and offence to the persons of the N.H. Sebastian dei Giustiniani *(Zustinian)* and his guest. It is known to me that Il'mo N.H. Podestà Capello Benzon, has punished, as he thought fit, the perpetrator of this sacrilege in a holy place, a glassblower named Miotto Daniele. Your Most Illustrious Excellencies may wish to inquire as to the true reasons for this man's offensive conduct. Though this Miotto Daniele is in advanced age, neighbours confirm that he is neither mad, nor senile. Miotto accuses the N.H. Giustinian of having kidnapped and then murdered his son in order to gain possession of a certain book, said to contain important secrets of the art of glassmaking. He further accuses the N.H. Giustinian of acts of great infamy with male children of the island of Murano and elsewhere; of kidnapping them and transporting them either to Nancy in Lorraine or to Cairo in Egypt, there to be doctored and made into alto singers. Many citizens of Murano are of the same opinion as this glassmaker, hence the riot outside the Church of San Donato – which riot was put down without bloodshed by Podestà Capello Benzon. Further to my denouncement, leading members of the community of Murano are greatly concerned by the presence of a foreign nobleman; namely the Chevalier Prince Guise de Lorraine. Prince Lorraine is notorious in France for his evil habits and his particular friendship with the Duke of Orleans. It is known to all that the French king banished Lorraine for eight years, but has since restored him to favour with the award of the Order of the Holy Spirit. Your Most Illustrious Excellencies may already know that on the last visit of Prince Lorraine to our Islands, many glassworkers were bribed to follow him back to Paris. In consequence both King Louis and his brother the Duke built great palaces of mirrored glass and much damage has since been done to the trade of the Muranesi and of the Serenissima. There are other foreigners from England and the Netherlands on the Island at present, all seeking the aforementioned book.

Podestà Capello Benzon may know, but perhaps out of shame for the N.H. Giustiniano's activities and through loyalty to his Serene Highness the Doge, may not wish to report these matters to your Most Illustrious Excellencies. This, my denouncement, I make and swear before Saint Mark. God preserve the Doge and the Governors of the Serenissima."

"Porca miseria!" exclaimed Senator Contarini.

"Out of shame be damned! This is Capello's doing!" roared Querini. "What Citizen would know of such matters? Why didn't the man have courage enough to write the letter himself? Murano is your territory Ballarin; you must have your nose to the stinks there. Bring us Capello's last report! And one more thing, I can vouch for the fact that there is no such person as Silvestra Valier! This is is a vexatious claim and must be dismissed and…and thoroughly investigated! I mean, the lady must be hunted down and arrested! Is that clear Ballarin?"

Sensing a further opportunity to make mischief with Querini as its target, Pisani, the third Senator, ordered: "Bring us a lens and a reflector lantern so that we may examine carefully the watermark on the paper and compare the handwriting. And find us an example of Silvestro Valier's handwriting. Look at his tax return, you should find it there."

"Silvestro's tax return?" joked Contarini, who held no torch for the Querini clan either. "Why, if we taxed him on his winnings at cards we could fund another Crusade!"

"I can well understand the Podestà Capello's reasoning," mused Pisani, "and for that matter Senator Querini's anxiety. Given that Silvestro is his son-in-law, I move that Senator Querini takes no further part in these proceedings."

"Come now Senators, please!" Chancellor Ballarin interjected, exercising his right to give uninvited advice. "Let us approach this rationally. You may not all know, since they still put up such a prosperous appearance, that the Capello lost most of their treasures and good fortune in '26 when their home burned down on Canal Grande. Bad luck that! Not nearly enough fire fighters! We must look into all such failings and bring our present Superintendent of the Waters to account as well. Ever since the fire the Capello have been quietly selling, or pawning, their Titians: I hasten to say not to foreigners, so they are not guilty of any crime against us – that is to the Serenissima. Bishop Zustinian is one of the Capello tenants and is, I gather, thinking of buying their Murano palace. What could the Podestà do in the circumstances but get someone else to write his letter?"

"His duty!" snapped the now thoroughly irritated Querini.

"More to the point; what shall we do with young Bastian?" asked Senator Contarini.

"Hang him, instead of that thieving young Podestà Calergi, between Marco and Todaro," suggested Querini.

"We can't do that, it would dishonour the Doge. The Doge is a sick man. He would die of humiliation at his nephew's conduct," objected Senator Pisani – who also quietly acted as Doge Morosini's eyes and ears in Council.

"Would that be such a bad thing? Morosini is getting too big for his Corno! Remember Marin Faliero!" thundered Querini.
(Doge Marin Faliero plotted to make himself King, long centuries before. Denounced to The Ten, the Doge's head and Corno crown promptly rolled down the steps of the Giant's Stairway - the site of his coronation.... At least that was the account passed down for dramatic effect. He was in fact decapitated in the palace inner courtyard.)

Calming down under the soothing words and quiet efficiency of Chancellor Ballarin, the three Inquisitors examined carefully the official report of Podestà Capello. The document made known his concerns about certain foreigners and reported his action in setting up the 'breaking-wheel and flail' as a warning to rioters. He had also mentioned the missing book of glassmaking recipes, informing them that it had once been in the great library of Saint Peter Martyr but was given legally to the Miotti in exchange for transporting some church bells from London. 'The Book of Seventy Six Pages,' he reported, had come to the Dominican friars from Constantinople, in 1453, soon after that capital of the Roman Empire fell to the hordes of Sultan Mehmet.

The Inquisitors approved of Don Francesco's report. Their Murano Podestà had so far been a paragon of honesty and good government, nevertheless, they were all quite convinced that he had 'set-up' the denouncement from the falsely named old lady: who else but Podestà Capello would have knowledge of the comings and goings of foreign noblemen? Extraordinary too, they were all in agreement that there was no lady bearing the name Silvestra Valier, for between them they knew everyone of consequence.There was little doubt though in the minds of all three of The Ten as to the truth of this particular denouncement.
The Noble Silvestro Valier loathed like the pox young Bastian Zustinian and his decadent clique of friends. He would have had every reason to make such a denouncement, but he was known to be an idle nincompoop himself, not given to committing his thoughts to paper. Moreover, even though Querini was his overbearing father-in-law, he still could have passed on his concerns in private to The Ten. He would hardly be likely to use his own name in such a declaration of hatred: married as he was to that difficult lady Bettina Querini, he preferred cards and other women to meddling in politics. The Senators removed their uncomfortable masks and took up lenses to compare the handwriting of Silvestro Valier and that of his secretary and accountant. They examined the watermarks on the two different kinds of paper used. They looked at Capello's script and the wording used in both report and denouncement: there were no similarities. They would order the arrest and questioning of N.H. Francesco Capello Benzon, the Podestà of Murano. Most probably he would be the next tied-up prisoner on his knees at the foot of their thrones! Spies would be set to watch all foreign visitors to Murano, both by day and night.

After some further disagreement, the three Senators decided to make a proposal to a full meeting of the Council of Ten. They would not invite the Doge to the meeting: he needed to keep a steady eye on the preparations for battle. The liberation of Constantinople and all Greece from the Sultan of Turkey and Caliph of Islam would not be an easy task. The Pope and the Austrian Emperor would help with money and some troops, but not enough. The French were opposed to the war, they had much to gain from trading with the Turk : trade in luxury goods; in fine waistcoats and fancy Paris clocks. Should the Habsburg Emperor send too many of his troops to fight off the ever-encroaching Ottoman, then the French would stab all Christendom in the back by invading Austrian lands

– they always did! Venice, as ever, would pick up the greater part of the 'bill' in blood and money for defending Europe. That factor of French perfidy would help sway a full meeting of The Ten to their devious design for the 'future welfare' of the Noble Bastian Zustinian.

Bastian had committed a serious offence. Senator Trevisan's report on the riot had already been considered at length. On the pretext of making a recruiting drive, Bastian Zustinian had used his ducal connections to borrow a company of lancers and a state band to swagger about the islands of Murano, Burano and San Michele. Though French noblemen on their home territory might be permitted armed retainers and bands, in Venice such displays of power had been prohibited for many orderly centuries. Bastian had caused a riot and not one single recruit had signed up to join Morosini's war. Lost uniforms and equipment amounted to 20 sequins and loss of dignity to the Serenissima was incalculable. Once Bastian's uncle, Doge Morosini, sailed off with the Venetian fleet, The Ten would propose that his nephew be appointed Ambassador to the Court of King Louis of France. The young noble spoke excellent French; he had no lack of dandified friends at the Court of King Louis, such as the Duke of Orleans and the Batard of Lorraine. The late Doge Marcantonio Zustinian had been Ambassador in his youth to the long-lived King Louis XIV. It would be a popular appointment with the French.

They would also propose that on his way to Paris, the Noble Bastian should meet with an unfortunate carriage accident on the wild mountain pass of Sempione *(Simplon)* and where Mount Lion, that symbol of Venetian justice, is known to let tumble down many a large and convenient boulder.There would of course be no survivors, not even the poor blighter chosen to light the fuse.

CHAPTER THIRTEEN

Zorzi was concerned that the fishing boat was overloaded. Their instructions had been to unload the glassware onto the Raven and then to collect and take a cargo of sugar cones to various clients along the Grand Canal. They left Murano by a longer route than usual via the Canal of St. John. Had they rowed the length of the Glassmakers Canal, prying eyes would have seen their cargo of open boxes which were stacked high with half the contents of Grandpa's dressers. Tongues would have wagged and questions asked at Palazzo Capello. They just caught sight of the Capello Palace as they rowed, as swiftly as they could, past the entrance to San Donato Canal. It shone pink with dawn lit marble; its tall trumpet shaped chimneys brayed to heaven the wealth and power within. When they emerged into the great blue briny Lagoon, at a point called Canal Ondello, they began to ship the odd wavelet over the bow of the boat. Peter seemed unconcerned at how low in the water they were. He ordered Zorzi to stow his oar, take the tiller and hold the boat steady into the wind, while he scrambled about stepping the mast into place and raising a small rusty red coloured triangle of a sail. Zorzi was tired; was queasy with fear of capsizing and was suffering the windy bloating effects of too much overnight bread and oranges. Piero was quite unconcerned as he ordered Zorzi to bring the boat about and to catch the early morning breeze from the far distant Alps. He knew the limits of what his 'bragozzo,' his trusty fishing boat, could do: even though it had more patched holes than a widow's quilt. Soon they were creaming effortlessly through the water in the direction of the Canal of the Ships, an expanse of deep water marked by tall triangular bundles of pine logs chained together. Most of these 'bricola' were topped with candle lanterns or else with rusting iron baskets in which charcoal fires were lit as a guide to ships in the night.

"Look for the bricola with the most cormorants diving from it," he called to Zorzi. "Watch the pennant!" The blue and white pennant flag at the top of the mast was sewn with Piero's emblem - the Crossed Keys of St. Peter. True to his fisherman namesake, old Piero paid out a long fishing line, baited with little scraps of fish from his last catch. Zorzi kept one eye on the little flag, both hands gripped firmly on the tiller. Once the pennant fluttered in another direction, he knew it was time to tack and duck for the sail boom would whiz low over his head with all the deadliness of

Gustav's club. Steadily they tacked towards a forest of tall galleon masts on the horizon.

"Cormorants!" shouted Zorzi.

Piero clambered and crawled between the packing cases towards the stern of the boat and took over from Zorzi. "When we get close give them a shout. Bang an oar on the gunwale to frighten them off!"

Piero steered straight for the busiest bricola. Zorzi had hardly needed to shout or to bang the oar. The cormorants that were diving headlong like happy urchins in a canal game onto a spiralling shoal of golden mullet, took off and winged clumsily back to their perches on the bricola lanterns. They knew when to give way to a superior force. While the birds hung their ragged black wings out to dry, Piero circled amidst the mullet until his fishing line was at breaking point. Never satisfied, even with such a bumper catch, Piero knocked a shower of mussels from the base of the bricola with a deft oar swipe. The mussels landed on board, tinkling amidst the glassware, but doing no damage. While Zorzi netted them into a heap big enough for a week of breakfasts, Piero gutted and stowed the mullet in a basket and covered them with seaweed against the hot sun.

Soon they were in amongst the tall masts. They looked for the Raven but she was not anchored there. Piero stood up and bellowed to all passing: "Corvo Nero! Rafen, Rafen!"

Finally, a young midshipman, giving a lick of white paint to the figurehead of his frigate, pointed forward with his brush and shouted "Corvo Nero!"

The great hulk of the Raven was way ahead, being towed by her longboat in the direction of the Arsenal. Old Piero set sail close to the wind as he dared and within ten minutes drew level with the black and silver painted West Indiaman. The magnificent galleon had been well mauled by Corsair pirates, just as Captain Ravenscroft had described the evening before. In his excitement Zorzi forgot about his queasy stomach. Here was the stuff of boyhood dreams! A large scorched hole just above the waterline and close to the ships rudder had been hastily plugged with tar, rags and wedges of wood. The splintered frames of the captain's cabin

126

windows were part draped and roped over with sailcloth. Other holes peppered the flanks of the great vessel- all similarly plugged. The mizzenmast was less than half its normal height. Fresh wood showed where the mizzen had been shot away and was now neatly sawn at an angle for appearance sake. But where were the galleon's defences wondered Zorzi? Piero pointed them out. There were twelve gun ports on either side, beautifully concealed amidst the swirling silver 'gingerbread' decoration of the hull. The deck guns and carronades had been unslung from their swivelling mounts, there being little risk of pirates in the Lagoon and once inside the formidably defended Arsenal docks not even the theft of a belaying pin would go unpunished.

"Not a good idea to conceal your gun ports: just inviting trouble," commented Piero. "Old Don Zorzi Rafenscro', Capitano Rafenscro's dead uncle, would never have done that.... though he wasn't much of a fighter, as I remember. He left all that cut and thrust stuff to Zianni, *(John)* who is as reliable an old devil of an English pirate as ever I met. Rafenscro's nephew seems civilized enough, but I reckon he must be a real nobleman, nothing like his uncle. There's more to him than meets the eye... a bit of a crafty trader, gentleman pirate, I suspect.... amazing good Venetian accent though!"

A stocky unshaven mariner came to the Raven's gunwale as they sailed close. He watched them for a few moments then levelled a musket at them.

Old Piero raised both hands and yelled "Rafenscro, Capitano Rafenscro!" then pointed to the cargo of glassware. The marine dropped out of sight then re-appeared with a friendly smile on his bristling unshaven chops. He pointed ahead to the longboat and called back "Corvo Nero! Arsenale! Arsenale!" then chuckled with delight at using the only three words of Italian that he knew.

As they sailed in closer, levelling with the bow of the ship, the Raven figurehead itself appeared. Jutting out below the bowsprit was a great carved wooden bird. Its eyes, as wide as dinner plates, were made of ruby red glass. Beak and talons were of dazzling gold and yellow glass. "There you are Zorzi!" shouted Piero above the splash of bow waves, "That's the work of your father! Glad to see that something remains from the old

Rafen; she was more of a frigate though, few could match her for speed. Madonna preserve us! Look Zorzi! There are more crossbow bolts in her than in Saint Sebastian's backside! But Hell! They're not Corsair bolts, they're the quarrels of the Turkish Fleet! Corsairs usually rake the decks when they want to take a cargo. They do it to keep the crew below decks before boarding - but the Ottoman fleet! Why didn't they sink her? For some reason they must have wanted to capture her intact?"

Zorzi was immensely proud of his dead father's talents: not only was he a master glassblower, but a wood sculptor as well! He stood and admired the great carved bird as it floated by. Why then, he wondered, was his father cursed by all the Muranesi as a stinking traitor? It seemed so unfair. He looked in sadness at the dozens of crossbow arrows spiking out from the breast of his father's great black bird and indeed all around the forecastle flanks of the vessel. Their points, now streaking rust brown, had not deep penetrated the tough Cuban mahogany. The shafts and feathers of the quarrel bolts were dyed bright green.

"We must tell Capitano Rafenscro when we see him. He must report to someone in authority pretty soon. The Rafen has had a run-in with the Ottoman! The Turks must be waiting off Siracusa to ambush the Doge!" It then occurred to Piero that once the Raven entered the Arsenal, a full report of the incident would be on the Doge's desk within hours.

Twenty or more shaven and neatly dressed mariners strained at the oars of the longboat. English pride demanded a good seaman-like appearance. Those Venetians should not get the impression that the Turk had defeated them. As they towed the Raven into the repair dock they wanted no one to think that an English crew had 'done a runner.' Little did they know that on sight of those green shafted crossbow bolts, the Arsenal workers would cheer them as heroes and fire a gun salute in their honour.

"I guess the Superintendent of the Waters has given Capitano Rafenscro orders to move sharpish into the dockyard," Piero observed, "he won't want a battered hulk spoiling the appearance of the Lagoon.... Not on Sensa Day."

At the tiller of the longboat was a familiar figure - James the young sailor. When they hailed him he stood and shrugged his shoulders, holding out his hands to show that he had no choice but to proceed to the Arsenal. Then cupping them to his mouth he bellowed back, "Ca` Dario! Go to Ca` Dario!"

Piero waved farewell, showing that he understood the message and tacked away altering sail in the direction of the Fondamenta Nuove, which, despite its new sounding name, was the ancient landward facing quayside of Venice City. Somewhat annoyed at this unexpected turn of events, Piero told Zorzi that he would have to drop him off by the Church of the Misericordia, so called because the priests there took pity on the city beggars. Zorzi was still very frightened of going alone to the Ghetto. He had heard mendacious tales of Jews roasting alive good Christian babies. "Can't I come with you to Ca` Dario?" he pleaded.

"No you can't!" came the sharp reply. "Go and get your teeth seen to as Rafenscro ordered. It's going to take me all day to work this boat down Rio Mendicanti into Canal Grande and then to unload."
Rio dei Mendicanti translates as Beggar's Canal: Canal Grande, in contrast, is the most magnificent of all waterways, lined from end to end with palaces of marble and brick. Ca` Dario, with its distinctive sag to the right and its swirls of marble and porphyry, is on the south side of the Canal, near to the Salute Church. By the 17th Century, Dario's splendid palace had been converted into a hotel well known to English tourists.

"I've sewn a letter inside your hat lining. When you get to the Ghetto, ask someone to point out the Synagogue of the German Rite. Knock on the big door there and when someone comes, only mention Rafenscro's name in a whisper. Make sure nobody else sees the letter in your hat. You must give it in person to Rabbi Sterchel. If signor Sterchel is not there, come away. Don't leave the letter with anyone else. Is that clear?"

Zorzi was surprised that an important message was hidden in his hat. He had not noticed the difference and now, on inspection, he saw the neat stitches of repair and the bulge in its lining. "But what if I lose my way?" he pleaded, knowing that the alleys and canals of Venice were more bewildering than any labyrinth.

"Ask anyone. They will point the way to the Ghetto. Follow the trail of goose feathers along the Misericordia Canal. It's no more than five minutes from where I will set you down."

Resigned to his fate, Zorzi asked, "Can I go to the Sensa Fair afterwards?"
He had been to the fair the previous year with some of his older pals and
like most visitors had a 'sensational' time.
"Of course you can. But be waiting for me at the Misericordia Church,
well before the evening Angelus bell. Is that understood?"

"Yes, yes! I promise," came the excited reply. "But I haven't any money
to spend. Last year Grandpa gave me six bagattini," he added
despondently.

"You are sitting on a silver grosso, a present from the Capitano. I've sewn
it in your pants. If I were you, I'd keep it for an emergency, but there you
are…"

Greatly cheered by the spending prospects of a whole silver grosso, Zorzi
asked if he counds take over and steer the last quarter league.

"There are bulli guards on all three bridges leading to the Ghetto. If you
had any money in your satchel, they would have it off you before they let
you pass. Capitano Rafenscro has arranged for you to have plenty more to
spend at the fair; it says so in the letter. The Jewish Rabbi will give you a
ducat or two when he gets the letter. Are you pleased now?"

Zorzi was mightily pleased. He moved forward from his crouched
position beneath the boom of the sail in order to take over the tiller from
Piero. As he clambered over the last thwart seat, he gave a last glance at
the Raven, now no more than a silhouette on the horizon. He noticed also
a black gondola with a felze, very much like the one he had seen from his
bedroom window. It had, he remembered, glided under the moonlit bridge
soon after Ravenscroft left in his longboat. Of course there were tens of
thousands of gondolas in Venice, but this one appeared to be following at
a distance in their wake. Foolishly, he did not think to tell old Piero. He
was so taken up with the prospect of the Sensa Fairground.

"Remember to buy your old Grandpa a present. Buy him some salted
anchovies - you know how he loves them - the ones they prepare in the
Ghetto are the tastiest. Follow the goose feather trail and ask for the

German Synagogue - Signor Sterchel the Rabbi, remember!"

"I'll get something for you too Piero," Zorzi promised.

"Me, what do I want? I have more than enough. Oh! Maybe a jar of olives, you'll get good olives in the Ghetto. Some bread and a slice or two of ham for our supper wouldn't go amiss either. But you won't find ham in the Ghetto. Look for a salami stall on the way back from the Sensa. Mind you don't get cheated!" The poverty stricken old seaweed burner looked up at the deep blue sky, at the sparking waters of Lagoon and at his decrepit fishing boat. What more could a man want from life?

CHAPTER FOURTEEN

Hunting for goose feathers soon caused Zorzi to lose his bearings.
Because there was such a press of gondolas and other small craft jostling
and bumping one another in desperation, it was impossible to land
anywhere near the beggars' church. Piero managed to tie-up much further
along, well past the landing stage of the magnificent Jesuit Church.
Before handing him his satchel and heading off to battle his way through
the mass of water traffic blocking almost every canal, Piero reminded him
to be at the Misericordia before the Angelus bells. Zorzi gave his promise
and soon found himself tagging along behind a crowd of country folk
who were wearing the most colourful 'glad rags' that they could tack or
pin together in honour of the Sensa. All were eager to make their way to
the Sensa Fairground by the shortest route possible - all were hopelessly
lost. At each turn, some blind alley, some secluded courtyard, dead end
wall, or sudden brink of a bridgeless canal barred the way ahead. Zorzi
was getting into a high state of anxious bewilderment when the honking
noise of geese came from a narrow alleyway leading along to a broad
canal towpath. The promising sound sent him running to where a stout
breasted goose girl of about fourteen years was flailing about her with a
long thin cane, trying her hardest to gather together her flock. Some
horsemen had just cantered straight through her well ordered line of geese
destined for the market and had sent them into a goosey panic: a panic
only matched by that of Zorzi as one waddled up angrily far too close for
comfort. He had a healthy fear of honking geese. One had given him a
severe peck when he was scrumping with his friends in an orchard behind
San Donato and its partner had chased him at high speed across the field.
Nevertheless, he took courage and using his satchel as a shield, shooed
several back from the alleyway and into the care of the goose girl. He
asked her if she knew the way to the Ghetto.

"I should think so," she answered, "I go there twice a day. I am taking
this gaggle there - follow behind and catch any strays!"

He walked at a safe distance behind the waddling white regiment as it
marched on to its heroic death in the cause of humanity and subsequent
plucking. They traversed several small bridges, passed tiny shops selling
salami, goose liver pate and great sides of smoked ham from Parma.
There were coppersmiths and watchmakers, barber shops, picture frame

gilders, mask makers and everywhere little shops stacked with vivid eye-catching glassware from his home island of Murano: all were decked with flowers and blue and white bunting; all with 'bargain prices' to fleece the provincial crowds flocking to the incomparable Sensa Trade Fair. Eventually, they found themselves waddling in line along a canal bank that was clearly signposted 'Fondamenta della Sensa.' "I don't want the Sensa Fair yet!" he shouted ahead to the goose girl. "I want the Ghetto where the Jews live!"

"Silly boy, this is the way to the Ghetto! The Fair is miles away!" she called back. Not entirely convinced, he thought it best to march on in step with the geese for a while longer.

True enough, as Piero had warned him, there were guards standing on the far side of a bridge marked 'Ponte Ghetto Nuovo.' They were checking people who came and went through the lofty metal gates. The goose girl turned on to the bridge ushering forward her flock. Dressed as bulli, with half armour, partizans and side weapons, the guards were expecting her and were ready with their laughing ribald comments. She seemed to be on best terms with them and answered in kind: doubting their manhood and adding a few other insults about their poxy baboon backsided ancestry. One guard retaliated by playfully slapping her on the buttocks with the side of his broad bladed partizan.

Though splitting his sides with laughter at the girl's colourful range of Venetian obscenities, Zorzi judged it best to keep his head down and to do his best to keep a straight face. He followed on over the bridge, passing the guards with a polite nod. Suddenly, he found himself being swung round by the strap of his satchel and hauled-up close in front of the tobacco breath of one of the bulli. "What have we got hidden in here, my fine beggar boy?" the thug demanded.

He tipped the contents of Zorzi's satchel onto the ground. Out came a hunk of squashed bread, a large segment of sugar cone, two oranges, a few cherries and a slice of Parmesan cheese.

"Oranges eh.! Where did you steal these?"

"I didn't steal them," Zorzi answered angrily. "They were given to me by

Mister..." and he almost bit his tongue.

Noticing his swollen left cheek, the other bullo came over and sneered, "A Mister eh? So you have got foreign money to change-up with the Jews. Open your mouth! Don't ever try to hoodwink us, you skinny little brat!"

One bullo held him tight while the other forced open his mouth, hoping to find a silver coin or two. Instead there was a festering abscess. Zorzi let out a shrill cry of pain.

"Leave the kid alone you dirty arsed brutes!" shouted the goose girl and gave the shorter pimply faced bullo a stinging whack across the back of his neck with her goose cane. In the fracas that ensued, a plump gander thrust out his neck, flapped its wings furiously and led the last heroic charge of his goosey platoon - capturing and carrying off Zorzi's hunk of squashed bread. Less courageous birds, who failed to snatch their share of the bread, consoled themselves with the cherries.

A small crowd of onlookers gathered; mostly young Jewish mothers with their babies. The bulli, embarrassed, and also satisfied that he had nothing else worth taking, let him down. Both bulli then played at throwing the oranges to one another. Immediately he was released, Zorzi gave a flying kick at the shin of one of the bulli. It hurt his bare toe and didn't affect in the least the heavily booted thug. But the taller bullo, receiving another hard whack from the goose girl, missed his catch and one of the oranges plopped into the canal. The crowd laughed and applauded. Zorzi ducked under the arm of the pimply faced bullo and scrambled on all fours for his satchel and hat. While he managed to grab his hat and the precious sugar lump, he could do nothing to rescue the satchel. The jeering younger bullo took a swipe at Zorzi with it: missed, and then hurled the satchel into the canal. The goose girl then let loose an even more entertaining stream of obscenities at the vicious guards, which included painful references to their grandmothers' connections with pox ridden camels, to Barbary apes and to their descent from generations of cross eyed diseased bachelors. The listening crowd of Jewish mums chortled with delight at the goose girl's picturesque put-down of the two hateful bridge guards. Seizing hold of Zorzi's arm and scooping up the Parmesan, she dragged him to safety into the busy square called Campo Ghetto Nuovo.

134

She offered him back the Parmesan, but guessing that she was just as famished as he normally was, Zorzi begged her to keep it. "Where is the Scola Grande Tedesca?" he asked.

"I don't know," she replied, "there are so many Synagogues about here. Which is the German one, I couldn't say. You had better ask a Jewish lady. I only herd the geese to and fro for the poultry butchers. Come over here to the well while I wash the dirt off my cheese."

She splashed some water into his cupped hands. His morning nibblings at the salty cheese had given him a great thirst. Anxiously he took stock of his surroundings. Curiosity soon overcame his fear of being baked in a Jewish oven. The square was large and irregular shaped, fringed with very tall plain brick apartment blocks, some were eight and nine storeys high. Several spindly trees sprouted up from the cobblestones. There were tethered cows and mountains of wicker cages packed with cooped-up chickens and geese. Despite the snowstorm of goose feather and obvious gutting going on in some of the butchers' shops, the square had no heaps of refuse. The three well-heads were all very clean and decorated with flags of St. Mark and garlands of spring flowers. The Jews too were celebrating The Sensa, though otherwise forbidden to be present and to take part in the spectacular events to come.

Some boys and girls of about his own age came to stare at him in a slightly hostile fashion. They were all remarkably clean and beautifully dressed: most had shoes. Both girls and boys wore small red skull caps and had identical hair styles - long shiny black corkscrew curls. He was glad that the goose girl was close by him.

"What are you doing here, beggar boy?" one of the girls demanded.

"I've come to see a Rabbi," he answered, feeing humiliated by her comment.

"Which Rabbi? Rabbis don't see Christian beggars. Go and beg outside your own place. Go to the Misericordia: we don't want your kind here, so push off!"

"You had best leave now," suggested the goose girl. "I don't want any more trouble. There are another two bridges off the island. Let me hand over these geese to the butcher and I'll show you the way."

Zorzi sat disconsolate on the well head steps. The children crowded close around him. "Go on, which Rabbi! You don't even know what a Rabbi is," they insisted.

"I do," Zorzi protested. However he was still half convinced that a Rabbi might prove to resemble a wolf-like ferocious dog with rabies. At first encounter, the Rabbi might eat him raw on site rather than roast him like a baby. Perhaps, however, he might need to use a furnace to cook a 'grown-up' boy like him?

"I've come with a message for Rabbi Sterchel. He is expecting me."

The children, who were planning to give him a good thumping before frog-marching him back over the bridge, were mystified as to why the august Rabbi Sterchel would want to meet a Christian beggar boy. Thinking it wise to treat this half naked little mendicant with more respect, given that Rabbi Sterchel might be involved, one of the older girls spoke: "Come along. We will take you to him, but if you are trying to kid us, we'll give you a hiding!"

Hedged in by the small knot of youngsters against any chance of escape, Zorzi was taken to a building with numerous wide arched windows high above ground level. The girl raised a heavy iron knocker and rapped hard on the great studded oak doors. The metal shutter of a spy hole slid back and an angry female voice was heard: "How dare you knock. Boker is still going on!" (*Shaharith is the Hebrew Morning Service: Boker is its Germanic name*)

"Go away at once!"

"We have got a Christian beggar boy here. Says he has got to see Rabbi Sterchel."

"Show him the way to the Misericordia," came the reply, "Now be quiet and go away and play somewhere else!"

136

Knowing that it would be his last chance, Zorzi blurted out, "I've got an important message from Mr. Ravenscroft! I must see Rabbi Sterchel!"

After what seemed an eternity of silence and seething anger around him, there came the sound of heavy bolts being slid back. A little side door creaked open and he was beckoned in. The children, scared now of getting into trouble for being so hostile, ran off.

The Rabbi's housekeeper, an elderly severe looking gaunt thin but upright lady, gave him a stare of disapproval fit to stop a basilisk in its tracks and ordered him to convey the message and be off at once. When he explained that the message from Mr. Ravenscroft was in the lining of his filthy hat, her curiosity got the better of her. She prodded him towards a large X framed armchair. Spreading a duster cloth over its velvet cushion, she told him to sit and not to move a muscle. From his high perch Zorzi sat swinging his legs and taking in the strange room and its contents. The housekeeper donned a pair of cotton gloves and gingerly unpicked the sailcloth lining with her scissors. The expensive notepaper and the 'ravens head' seal impressed in black wax, had the desired effect. She asked Zorzi if he would like a glass of sherbet and a Baicoli ship's biscuit whilst he waited for Boker to end.

Telling him politely not to touch anything, she went off along a corridor. From above came the sound of chanted prayers in a strange language. Zorzi listened with interest. There was something earnest and beautiful in the sounds. He began to relax and to explore with his eyes the room, which was some kind of an office, not greatly different in size and plain decor from that of Don Tranquillo. There were no paintings, nor other decoration on the walls; instead there was a plain wooden bracket supporting the most magnificent model galley that he had ever seen. It had miniature brass cannon and slender carved oars all painted blue and white. An 'out of scale' pennant with a six pointed blue star draped down over its miniature rigging and fine triangular silk sail. He was entranced. Beneath the model was a sideboard with a large glass bowl piled with oranges. It was the bowl that held his attention most. He knew something of the skills of glassmaking, yet had never seen a bigger, nor more colourful, nor more finely made object: except of course for one far smaller, but almost identical, on Grandpa's dresser. In the dim light of the

Rabbi's downstairs office the bowl glowed with an inner light: a glittering light that almost could have been stolen straight from a dramatic sunrise. Bright yellows merged with pink; deep purpley reds and browns as well were smouldering within the glass. But more entrancing than anything else, encased within its iridescent thin walls was what seemed like a storm of millions of tiny golden reflecting snowflakes. The bowl was a collector's gem of chalcedony glass and was worked with gold chloride, copper oxide, uranium dioxide and other rare metals. Only an assured and outstandingly able glassblower would have succeeded in creating such a large and elegant shape: only a wealthy patron could have afforded to purchase such a rare and costly object, namely - a perfect aventurine bowl!

There was a tinkling sound of tiny silver bells. Zorzi got up and peeped along the corridor. There for a fleeting moment he caught sight of the Rabbi as he came along the corridor draped in a white prayer shawl with a patterned blue fringe. He was wearing a strange tall gold and white hat. With him were the housekeeper and another capped and shawled gentleman who seemed to be carrying two large rolls of cloth. All three entered a room off the corridor and were there for the time it took Zorzi to nibble his biscuit and finish off the glass of sherbet.

"Well, well, so it has come to this, has it?" The Rabbi half spoke to himself in a disheartened tone as he inspected Zorzi's skinny ribs, patched breeches and swollen face. Mr. Ravenscroft's two paged letter was opened in his hands. "No need to bow to me my child. Sit back up there while I do a little code breaking."

The Rabbi went over to his desk, opened a drawer and drew out a lemon, a sharp knife and a pair of tortoise shell framed spectacles. Zorzi's mouth sagged open in amazement as he watched the lemon being sliced into slivers and spread all over the second blank page of Mr. Ravenscroft's message. After a few moments the Rabbi shook and scraped the lemon into his waste basket. Then with a silver pencil and frequent reference to a slender leather backed book the Rabbi made notes for five or ten minutes. Zorzi's attention wandered around the room again. His dirty upturned hat was still on Rabbi Sterchel's expensive looking desk: the unstitched hat lining having preceded the lemon slices into the waste bin. He tried to peep at the blank page and thought it odd that the Rabbi should be giving it such close and long attention. The Rabbi looked up at him for a moment and gave him a broad reassuring smile. He then dipped his hand into Zorzi's hat and drew out a large silk handkerchief, blew his nose loudly on it and, popping it back again, got on with his notes. A few moments later, without even looking up, his left hand strayed slowly towards the hat. This time he extracted a large onion and placed it on the desk beside him. A gilded brass and enamel table clock was the next astonishing object to appear. This was followed in slow succession by three oranges, a fluttering pigeon, which shot away along the corridor and an egg. The Rabbi feigned a look of mild surprise at the egg and waved it in the direction to which the pigeon had fled, as though to ask the bird to come back and collect it. While Zorzi filled the room with laughter and clapped his hands in joy, the Rabbi pulled his masterstroke. The great chalcedony aventurine bowl filled with oranges seemed to emerge from the battered hat. On top of the pile of oranges was the large lump of sugar, which instantly Zorzi remembered that he had left on the well steps when he was frog marched off by the children.

"I take it that this is a morsel of your sugar cone?" Sterchel observed with his omniscient humour.

"How on earth did you know that? That's got to be real magic! Wait till I tell my friends! I bet they will think I am spinning them a yarn: can all Rabbis do magic?"

"The odd walking stick into a snake, but only when the occasion requires it," the Rabbi answered enigmatically, adding: "Do you know any codes?"

"What are they?" asked the mystified boy, "Are they magic too?"

"In a way," came the answer. "With codes you can send messages that nobody can read except the person for whom they are intended. Mr. Ravenscroft has told me in code about his adventures and where he is going next. We have lots of things in common, Mr. Ravenscroft and me, such as sugar cargoes." With another look of mild surprise, he made one more lump of sugar appear by scratching the top of his shiny bald head. "Have you seen The Raven? Is it badly damaged?"

"Piero, my friend, knows all about ships. He reckons she is no more than scratched. Says the Ottoman fleet has attacked her, 'cause of the crossbow arrows we saw.... all green they were. We left her early this morning being towed into the Arsenal."

"You really are a most useful messenger. I can see why Mr. Ravenscroft trusted you with his news. Now we must reward you for your trouble: how about the bowl of oranges?"

"Well, it's so beautiful and I might break it. I guess it's a bit heavy too, though very finely made indeed, thanks... as I was hoping to go to the fair, you see. We have got rather a lot of glass at home....I was hoping maybe... to buy something at the fair for Grandpa. He loves salted anchovies. If I had a bagattino or two, instead," he pleaded.

"Only joking; I would not part with my bowl for all the oranges in Sicily. Nor do I want it to go back to its home just yet. You see the bowl was a present to me from Mr. Ravenscroft's uncle. It started off in your house though. I bet you can't guess who made it?"

"I can. My father must have made it, couldn't have been my Grandpa, that's for certain sure!"

"Clever lad!" The Rabbi was impressed by Zorzi's alertness and added: "You never knew your grandmother, did you Zorzi?"

"Grandpa sometimes talks of her. Her name was Angela, that I know, and she was very kind to my friends the Molins when they were a lot poorer than we are now. But I don't know what she looked like though."

"A fine lady was Angela Darduin, even I admired her from afar. And I'll tell you something more, she was a shrewd business woman too. She had no dowry when she married your Grandpa: instead she got a written promise from the Darduin family that their book of secret recipes would be passed on to her first-born son - that was your father, who sadly is no longer with us."

"Was that the missing book that everyone is talking about? I thought that belonged to the Miotti family. Young Daniele, my big cousin, keeps hounding me about it. He say's it belongs to him by rights."

"I think not my young friend. That missing book is almost certainly yet another collection of rare glass recipes. Old Mr. Ravenscroft was convinced that it was copied down by Greek monks from an ancient Roman source. You see, I now have your Granny Angela's recipe book safe and sound with me. Did your Grandpa never tell you?"

Dumbfounded by this news, Zorzi shook his head. There were so many things that Grandpa had failed to tell him straight...."But you are not a....."
"Not a glassblower, indeed. But there are many things left in my safekeeping. Grandpa left it with me as security, just in case there were problems with your house. The Darduin book is yours though and for free - that I promise. When you are old enough to make use of it, you must come and claim it from me, or if my brains have completely unravelled by then, my lawyer will be told to let you collect it. You will need the skills of your father Vincenzo though to make much use of it. When he died, so tragically, the Darduin method of making beautiful aventurine bowls was lost, so you see Zorzi...it is all up to you now to learn the art of glassblowing. Of course, you could one day print and publish the recipes for everyone else to use, if you so wished. That way you might well make a cool fortune....without all the effort and sweat at the furnace."

"But I want to be a spy when I grow up. I am no good at puffing glass, even Grandpa says so. Why can't Grandpa make nice bowls of this aven...adventure stuff?"

"Ah! my young friend, we all suspect that Grandma Angela passed on a few unwritten secrets to your father... which she never confided in Daniele... that is your Grandpa."

"Perhaps so, Grandpa is not always good at keeping secrets. Old Piero gets to know everything, specially when I do something daft. I shall have to be extra careful when I become a spy."

"A spy indeed! Who put that notion into your head? Not signor Ravenscroft I hope? Spying can be a dangerous business. He should know." Rabbi Sterchel was warming to this scruffy little scrap of a child. It was heartrending to see to what a lowly state the son of Guildmaster Vincenzo had descended. He came close to examine the boy. From his long and heavily nit infested hair to his cracked and blackened toenails, the boy was indeed a picture parody of a little vagabond.

"Open wide," he commanded.

While he gently probed and inspected Zorzi's foul smelling gums, the boy marvelled at the Rabbi's own appearance. His was quite the largest tonsured head that he had ever come close to. It was quite different from the long faced Nordic shaped head of Don Tranquillo, or of those of the other shaven friars and elderly balding men that he knew. Different too was what lay beneath, namely the grey matter of a philosopher: a shrewd man of business and a distinguished surgeon; a brain that had once challenged and set the professors of Padua University upon their mettle whenever student Sterchel attended their lectures. Little tufts of silver hair sprouted out sideways above the Rabbi's large pendulous ears and a very wide ever-smiling mouth seemed almost to join one ear to the other. The eyes twinkled with kindness and merriment behind thick tortoise shell framed spectacles. That impressive Old Testament head was set close to rounded shoulders and barrel chest of a stocky middle aged man, who obviously still had much left of his health and strength. "This is going to be unbearably painful to the child," the Rabbi quietly concluded. Instinctively he calculated the exact dose he needed, given the size and age of this little underfed scrap of a child. Calculated risk it was indeed for, God forbid, if news were to get out that a Christian boy had died whilst in his care, the whole ghetto might go up in flames.

"I see you like my model galley. Come and have a close look."

Zorzi jumped down from his chair, eager to examine close-up the exquisitely made model.

"It's called 'The King David.' You will have heard of David: the Jewish boy who killed the giant and wrote the Psalms."

"Oh yes, of course; Don Tranquillo told me all about Goliath. But the Psalms: they were by a Venetian man surely- someone called Monteverdi. I know that because I can sing a whole lot of Monteverdi's Psalms, you see I....."

"Well, well, you can sing some of our Psalms. I am glad to hear that! You must come back sometime and give lessons to my Cantor. He is for ever squawking wildly out of tune. He has a voice like a donkey in distress."

Rabbi Sterchel well understood children. He knew that Zorzi was the sort of bright lad one doesn't want to discourage by correcting his facts like a pedant. Zorzi would learn in time who wrote the Psalms, so he said nothing - other than, "Monteverdi, indeed! Oh yes! A fine music maker! Heard one of his operas once, ages ago in Mantova, I thought that his music had long gone out of fashion in your churches."

Rising abruptly from his desk, Rabbi Sterchel went across to the model. Zorzi noticed that there were bits of thin black string trailing from his wide sleeves and guessed that they had something to do with the magic. However, quite un-noticed, the Rabbi had managed to spirit the bowl of oranges back onto the sideboard. "I'll get the galley down for you to look at, but please don't touch the rigging. It's rather delicate. We presented the real 'King David' to Doge Morosini when he came back from his war in Greece. It was a gift from the Jewish community of Venice."

"What? You mean...a real full sized galley with cannons and things? Gracious me, that must have cost a fortune!"

"It did. But we are indebted to your Doge for his protection, even though some of his bridge guards are no more than cowardly ruffians whom he wouldn't care to have in his army. Doge Morosini, dressed in his full regalia and 'Corno' crown, came to the gates of the Ghetto to show us his appreciation. He swore before all present that, after what had happened in Athens, he would demolish the mosque on our Temple Mount. Should he succeed in his efforts to recapture Jerusalem from the Sultan, then, he assured us, he would let us all return to our Holy City. But I fear that was an idle promise, though made in good heart. The Doge is an old and very ill man. Perhaps, if he were thirty years younger, he might have kept his vow... but there we are! Would you like another drink of sherbet, Zorzi?"

"That's most kind. I wouldn't mind some more: it's so tasty, even though it stings my gums a bit." Zorzi thought that this was the appropriate moment to give another low bow to the Rabbi, who beamed back at him for his politeness. The Rabbi went to the sideboard and casually spooned more of the powdered lemon and sugar and stirred it with water in a fine glass.

"May I ask what happened? I mean, what happened to the Doge in Athens? Someone told me once.... I think it was old Piero... some old building or other fell down on top of him and killed the Doge's cat. I must have been too young at the time to be much interested."

"Drink up. All in one go if you like, there is plenty more. I'll tell you exactly what happened, but sit down comfortably. You wouldn't want to spill sherbet on my beautiful galley."

Zorzi sat back in the armchair and the Rabbi propped cushions around him in a most considerate way and left the largest for him to rest his feet on.

"It was a lieutenant of artillery who did it: he disobeyed the Doge's orders not to bombard the hill of Athens. Seeing some movement of Ottoman cavalry on top of the great hill, the lieutenant let fly at them. With one terrible deafening bang the most famous building in all the world was wrecked. It's said that there were three hundred Christian women inside together with countless children. You see, Ottoman had defiled the place by turning it into a gunpowder store and the women were imprisoned there to serve as a living shield. So the long suffering Greeks not only had to put up with Ottoman terror; they now had to endure seeing their Parthenon, the symbol of their ancient pride, blown sky high by those who came to help them. Such is life! We Jews know about such things! Our Temple in Jerusalem was destroyed too. Morosini was heartbroken of course and was seen with tears moistening his merciless eyes. Some say that the tears came because he knew that his name in history would be tarnished for ever: others think that he wept because his cat was swept overboard on that very same day, together with her litter of kittens. Just one kitten somehow survived, clinging to a sail cloth and the Doge then...."

Zorzi's head nodded onto his chest. The Rabbi caught him gently in his arms as he yawned and toppled slowly forward.

CHAPTER FIFTEEN

Zorzi awoke with a start. He was propped around with cushions so soft that for a moment he thought he was out in the Lagoon treading water. Slowly his eyes focused on a hand that was waving under his nose a tiny bottle of something sharp and vile smelling. A booming pendulum clock nearby struck the hour and other tinkling sounds chimed in soon after. He tried his best, but could no longer count what hour it was. Gradually, it dawned on him where he was. Helplessly relaxed and numb in the limbs, he could neither speak nor sit up properly. His eyes now better focused, he looked down along his body. They couldn't possibly be his own legs stretched out in front of him along the leather couch! Two silky white stockings appeared to be sticking out in front of him from beneath a fluffy cotton towel spread over his chest.

"Feeling better now? Just clear your mouth....Spit it all out. We don't want you choking."

The calming motherly voice was that of the Rabbi's housekeeper. She held a spittoon bowl under his chin. To his horror, he spat out a great lump of greeny brown gunge. He tried to jump up off the couch, but only succeeded in sitting upright. The towel tucked around his chin fell to his lap: no tanned and skinny ribbed chest; no grubby goatskin breeches; all was pure white and azure blue further down; with buttons, lots of shiny mother-of-pearl buttons!

"Don't worry. It's only crushed mallow plant. Rabbi Sterchel has packed your gums with it. It works wonders. You'll need to keep rinsing your mouth with it for a day or so. I've packed a nice big bottle in your satchel."

Zorzi had a vague memory of his satchel sailing through the air and splashing into the canal. He sat for ten minutes or so quite befuddled. The housekeeper tucked a fresh white towel around his chin and patted him gently on the cheek. He felt no pain at all: no more throbbing - just a slight tingling numbness. She left him for a while, carrying away with her a tray of shiny steel instruments and a little glass spirit burner, which was still alight. When she returned she helped him up and asked if he wanted to go to the lavatory. He almost slid from her arms as he tried to stand for

145

the first time - on silk stockinged feet! She supported him along the corridor where they met the Cantor.

"So this is our young Christian Cantor?" he quipped, "I had better watch out for my job! Monteverdi eh! Psalms eh! That's a good 'un!" Though, now the lad is togged up in his 'smutters,' I reckon it will be the Chapel Master at St. Mark's who gets the elbow!"

The Cantor was carrying a heap of fine clothing and leatherwork towards the room they had just left. Unlike the spider and stag beetle infested shack at the end of Zorzi's back yard, the Rabbi's toilette was a thing of beauty and a joy to visit. It took the form of a spacious cedar wood hut projecting over the canal to the side of his home. The Rabbi's private premises occupied the entire ground floor of a large synagogue and a meeting hall. The toilette windows were of patterned stained glass: the two holed lavatory seat made of 'pavonazzo' purple streaked marble and a hand basin of the same costly marble was set into an alcove tiled with mosaic. The clearest of silvered mirrors that Zorzi had ever set eyes upon was fixed above the hand-basin. He was astonished, not so much by all the Rabbi's lavatorial splendours, but by the sight of his own image. His hair was cut short, and he was dressed just like a pageboy he once saw and greatly envied as he was being rowed past up the Glassmakers' Canal. Those shoulder length greasy dark locks had not only gone, but what was left of them was now a fine and fluffy soft brown. He sniffed: he was perfumed allover, even his grimy nails were cleaned! Mightily pleased with his new self, he couldn't wait to meet up with his friends. On second thoughts though, he suspected that they migh well chuck him into the nearest dirty puddle.

When the Rabbi came to say farewell and to check that the effects of the opiate had worn off, he was thanked profusely by the little princeling. He asked if he might keep Zorzi's hat as a souvenir ... as he said, "for future use, since it appeared to have magic properties."

But Zorzi had already noticed with dismay the embers of his precious hat smouldering in the housekeeper's grate, it was the only souvenir he had of his father and had been rescued with great effort after many an escapade. Even so, he thought it polite not to contradict the Rabbi. Finding that both Zorzi and his headgear were crawling alive with bugs and lice, the housekeeper had decided on incineration for the hat and a good spring cleaning with alcohol and lavender water for Zorzi, before dressing him in his new 'smutters.' The fastidious lady had thought twice before throwing Zorzi's breeches on to the kitchen range: the smell of burning goat skin might offend the Rabbi. The housekeeper had made a fair swap - a perfect fitting blue felt hat with yellow ribboned trim and an eagle feather. Long doeskin riding boots and a many buttoned coat of bright blue cloth completed Zorzi's attire. Fearing that Grandpa or Piero might tell him off if he returned without them, and recollecting that grossi sewn inside the patch, he begged the housekeeper that he might keep his old breeches. She relented and dusting them over with some white chemical, she rolled them into a tight bundle and secured them with the string belt. Stuffing them at the bottom of a splendid new leather satchel, she made them into a pad for a bottle of mallow water.

"What was it you were going to get at the Sensa Fair, Zorzi?" the Rabbi asked.

"Well, Grandpa loves Parmesan and anchovies, but I..."

"....Haven't got a bean to spend!" The Rabbi solemnly completed his sentence then handed him a soft leather purse well filled with heavy coins.

Zorzi knew that it would be too impolite there and then to peep at its jingling contents, so he gratefully exclaimed: "Gosh! There must be loads enough to buy everything. I'll get Parma ham now for Old Piero and some cakes as well for Grandpa. Can I get a present as well for you, signor Sterchel, and one for your wife? She has been so good to me. Is there any thing really special you both like?"

Both Rabbi and housekeeper chuckled with mirth: "Certainly not Parma ham! Come again to visit us. Bring something then: one of your Grandpa's lattimo cups would be most acceptable. Behave like someone important and tell nobody about your errand to us. Treat the bridge guards with noble contempt and they won't question you… not in your smart smutters. Now run along - enjoy yourself! Make sure your anchovies are well wrapped and that they don't spoil your satchel. If you feel unwell in any way just come straight back here. Remember to thank signor Ravenscroft for your finery when you see him and give him our compliments. Oh! And watch out for swindlers and cutpurses!"

With the Rabbi's good advice firmly in mind Zorzi swung his leather satchel across his shoulders and bowed low. Slithering and hobbling in his brand new doeskin riding boots, he made his way towards the door.

A trivial action: a slight movement forwards or backwards when crossing a road or the silliest of oversights can transform lives for better, for ill, and sometimes for all eternity. Zorzi's boots were a near perfect fit and about the correct thigh length for riding. It was the fashion when walking to tie them down just below the knee leaving the thigh section to flop over. The housekeeper had done just that, but had tightened the thongs just a little too much for real comfort. When Zorzi loosened one boot thong more than the other he could never, in his wildest dreams, have imagined what a momentous transformation of his life would happen as a consequence.

"Scuff the soles a bit on some gravel. You'll soon get used to them!" the Rabbi called as he waved him goodbye. Then beckoning to the loitering children, he instructed them to accompany Zorzi part of the way towards the Sensa Fair.

"Gracious. I just can't believe it. Are you really a someone – not a beggar after all? Why you look like...like the Doge's messenger!" It was Rachel the leader of the little group who had first mobbed him.

She and the other children knew that Rabbi Sterchel was a great magician; the best in all Venice. During long and tedious sermons in the Synagogue he would sometimes perform an unexpected and often spectacular trick, which would set them and the whole congregation rocking with laughter; but he had excelled himself this time by transforming a ragamuffin into prince in what, to the children, seemed less than no time. The children now chattered to him as though he were an old friend. They admired his clothes and accompanied him to the South Bridge. The two bulli on guard there gave him a smart salute and asked Rachel who he was.

"Doge's Messenger," she answered.

"Oh!" they exclaimed, "No one told us." They thought duty bound to follow on, at least to the next turning beyond the bridge. It was as well that they did. Seated on the paving, outside a tobacco shop, a ragged quartet of thug-faced juveniles was dicing for money. Seeing Jewish children out of bounds, they scrambled up with every intention of beating and chasing them off. The bridge bulli then came into sight, promptly fingering the pommels of their swords with implied menace.

"No you don't!" snarled one of the bulli, "Don't you dare - he's a Doge's Messenger!"

The four young scoundrels were not that dim witted. One of their partners in crime was now serving eighteen months in the galleys, just for wolf-whistling at a passing noblewoman and her maid. They gazed hatefully at Zorzi, sat down and got on with their game.

CHAPTER SIXTEEN

Reason, with its empirical one-eyed needle, had yet to pierce the beautiful fabric of innocent faith and pig ignorance that blanketed late 17th Century Venetian thought. Tailors and their discerning customers knew that red kept winter chill at bay and blue was generally worn for summer cool. Zorzi's outfit seemed at first to be no exception to that rule. After a long brisk walk it was his misfortune to begin to swelter under his blue coat of finest winter wool. He could bear it no more and sat down on the steps of a wide bridge, took off his feathered hat and looked along the towpath of quite the longest canal he had so far come across. He had walked for more than an hour and had only covered less than half a mile as the crow would fly. But there at last was somewhere he recognized - the islands of San Cristoforo and San Michele. Faint and exhausted he tugged off his coat, boots and silk stockings and examined the blisters on his heels. He had given up all hope of getting to the Sensa Fair. Everyone he asked sent him off in a different direction. If only he could walk to the end of the towpath he might be able to pay someone to take him back home. He had some vague notion that he might be able to chalk a message for old Piero at the Harbour of the Misericordia, so that Piero would know why he had not turned up at the Angelus hour. But how would he get to the harbour to do so? If only he had something to eat and drink: if only he had his dirty old calico satchel, instead of the lead weight of Florentine leather that had been dragging on his shoulders for the last hour. He examined the damage to his new hat. It was splattered with black stains. It could have been worse, perhaps even a chamber pot emptied on his head; instead it was no more than flowerpot mud from a pelargonium being watered on someone's balcony. He took a swig from the bottle of mallow water. The Rabbi had advised him rinse his mouth whenever he felt thirsty and under no circumstances to drink well water. The greeny brown mallow tasted warm and foul. He spat it out. On the other side of the bridge there was a huge and beautiful marble building decorated with porphyry and panels of carved scenes of some sort. Attached to its side was an absolutely enormous wooden spiral stairway and at an angle to it a great brick church. He sat down, exhausted at the stone well head. Desperately thirsty, he would wait to beg some passer by to draw-up a cool drink: the Rabbi's advice would just have to be ignored.

As he went to stand up again, the paving of the square seemed to shake and sway. The tall buildings began to spin wildly around his head. He fell heavily on the well steps, smashing the bottle as he toppled. A young Dominican novice was hanging nightshirts on a washing line some way across the square. Hearing the crash, he came running. When he saw the broken bottle, the green liquid and Zorzi out cold, he sensibly guessed that Zorzi had taken poison. He yelled out for assistance. Two elderly Dominican friars passing over the bridge hastened forward to help. Concluding that here was a nobleman's son in the throes of death and on their doorstep, one of them hurried off to fetch Raimondo. Prior Raimondo was Governor of the Scuola Grande di San Marco, the main hospital of the city, and also guardian of San Zanipolo (John & Paul) the gigantic basilica where the bones of numerous Doges and heroes now reposed in marbled splendour.

The Noble Prior sniffed and examined the broken bottle. He felt Zorzi's neck and found a healthy pulse. He opened Zorzi's green dribbling mouth and diagnosed: "Mallow water! The boy has been to the dentist. Someone has done a fine job stitching his gums. Get him into the shade and cool him with wet towels. He will need a drink. Fetch milk cooled with ice. Someone has given him an opiate - not a wise thing to administer to one so small."

While he waited for his commands to be obeyed he examined, with mounting curiosity, the crest cast into the silver gilt buttons on Zorzi's coat and vaguely remembering that he had seen similar outfits worn by the Morosini grandchildren, he announced: "The child is in the livery of the Countess Morosina. We had best get him back to the Palace as soon as he recovers. Look in his satchel."

Discovering a purse with five gold sequins and a great heap of other silver coinage, Brother Denis handed it to the Prior, further convincing him that this boy could only be some member of the ducal family. He concluded that the boy must have got separated from his negligent servants and, confused by the opiate, must have wandered off. Riled by the foolishness of certain members of the ruling class and their recklessness with money, he observed: "Such indulgence, and to a child…. open invitation to a kidnapper. Outrageous that any youngster should be indulged with such wealth, when we scrimp and save and beg for a few grossi to feed our patients!"

151

The Prior was about to return to more important duties when he noticed that a great quantity of nightshirts and infirmary sheets had been strung up beyond reach on three long lines radiating from a rusty old torch bracket on the corner of San Zanipolo Church. Each line was attached at the other end to the hoof of a monumental bronze horse. The horse and the ferocious armoured warrior in its saddle was the work of 'True Eyes' Verroccio with the assistance of his young pupil from Vinci.

Denis bowed his head expecting a reproof for his efforts, but the Noble Prior Raimondo had only thoughts of praise for the initiative shown by the fourteen year old novice."I used the church lamp ladder," the novice explained. "Took it without permission…. apologies Noble Father."

"No apology required, Brother Denis, you have made good use of your brains today. I was wondering where else we could hang the washing. The empty square is a perfect choice. However, Brother Denis, I have a slight concern about your choice of the horse for your clothes prop. I doubt very much if the old general will be granted a spot of leave from his prominent place in hell for the purpose of dicing you up with his sword. Alas, however, he has a living descendent, of similar temperament, of whom you may already have heard?"

Denis, still humbly bent over to receive the Prior's ironic comments, shook his head.

"You are new to us Brother Denis, but doubtless in time you will get to hear of the Cavaliere. The Cavaliere Ettore Martinengo, Brother Denis, is more than likely to ride by here once the Sensa is over!"

"Will he be displeased with me?"

"Displeased with you? Oh no, I shouldn't think so! All that he is likely to do, on noticing this amusing insult to his ancestor, is to perform an instant anatomy lesson upon the body of your humble Father Prior. In short, Brother Denis, he may well decide to fillet my entrails better than any fishmonger!"

The Prior chuckled at his own grim joke and added: "Your penance, for showing such perilous initiative will be for you to accompany this sickly youngster as far as the Doge's Palace, and there to reunite him with his noble family. You may take the short route via the Convent of San Zaccaria. Sister Giuseppina will let you through to the South Gate, since you will be delivering another box of tinctures and ointments to the lady nuns."

Denis gave an involuntary groan and was instantly rebuked by the peppery Prior. "Brother Denis, you will accept my instructions unquestioningly and in silence. Is that understood?"

Denis bowed low and once again murmured an apology.

"And, Brother Denis, you will be extra polite in the presence of the Noble Sisters. You may not call them 'suora,' as I understood you did last time. Should one speak to you, you reply by saying, 'I am Your Ladyship's humble servant.' Is that clear? You may wait at the Doge's Palace, in hope of seeing the Doge himself when he goes in procession to attend Vespers, but be back in the chapel for our own Vespers by five o'clock. No loitering at the Sensa Fair mind you. It is a dreadful den of iniquity ... I tell you.... a den of iniquity! And take care to carry the child's satchel yourself, Brother Denis. Strap it across your shoulders. Keep close to the child in the crowds."

Since leaving home, a remote farmstead in the willow marshes of Friuli, young Brother Denis had seen much less of the world than his pious dreams had promised. Here he was, dwelling in the very heart of the fabled Serenissima, yet his life was no more than an endless tedious round of dawn and midnight prayer, of dirty bedpans to empty and piles of old men's nightshirts to wash and iron. He was just longing to get a peep at some den of iniquity, or better still a glimpse inside that majestic Doge's Palace. Maybe some day in the distant future he might get a gondola trip to Rialto Market and see the wondrous bridge there spanning the Grand Canal. Were they such sinful thoughts for a country lad to entertain?

The little boy must be one of the Doge's own family: what pageboy would have such a splendidly embossed leather bag and such fine boots and clothing? What if he were to meet the Doge himself while escorting the little gentleman? Denis felt certain that he too would faint on the spot in the awesome and unlikely event that the Doge might speak to him. At the very least he would have an attack of the stammering jitters! He guessed that Prior Raimondo would be invited to join the Doge at Vespers that afternoon. If it should come to the Doge's notice that he, Brother Denis, had come to the aid of one of the Ducal Family, it might even mean he could step up a rung or two - at the very least he might be promoted out of the hospital sluice room. He lifted the feather-light little body on to his shoulders and took Zorzi into the shade of the horseman's pedestal. In no time Zorzi was sitting up and slurping down a bowl of white breadcrumbs soaked in milk. Recovering quickly from his faint, he was more than eager to go along with Brother Denis: for the way to the Ducal Palace was, he knew, lined with merchants' stalls and the numerous dazzling attractions of the Sensa Fair!

Denis returned the empty bowl to the pharmacy and shortly after returned staggering under the weight of a large highly polished wooden box. Lowering it to the ground momentarily, he hung Zorzi's satchel about his neck then in one swift move shouldered the heavy box by its brass handles. Assuming that Zorzi would know exactly where to go once they reached the Doge's Palace, he mentioned nothing to him of the Prior's instructions; all he said was: "Off we go, Vossignoria!"

"To the Sensa?" Zorzi queried.

"We'll go that way, but first I must deliver these jalaps to the infernal nuns. None of them are really ill, but they will be tomorrow."

"Tomorrow? How is that?" Zorzi queried.

"Why, tomorrow is not just the Sensa, it is the feast of their founding abbess. You should know that, being one of the family. Wasn't she another Morosini? Oh! A thousand years ago....you ought to know."

Zorzi shook his head, mystified.

Denis gave him a puzzled look, then added: "If I know those pesky stuck-up nuns they will all be bloated by over eating well before mid day, and those who ain't will have a fit of the swooning vapours while they are praying: pretending to one another that they are in some state of holy

154

ecstasy. But never mind, our pharmacist has concocted a pretty explosive mix: prune juice, syrup of figs and a dash of gunpowder. That should keep them all on the hop to the 'cesso' for a day or so!"

Zorzi chuckled. He was beginning to like this lumbering, rather plain faced youth with his wisps of blond fluff on his upper lip and under his chin. And for his part, Denis was beginning to suspect that Zorzi was no Vossignoria, not at all the aristocrat that the Noble Prior had assumed him to be. Chatting happily to one another, they barged their way through the throng. While sitting down on bridge steps from time to time for Denis to get his breath, they soon discovered that they both were sons of Friuli countrymen, and with that they struck up an instant brotherly bond. When Zorzi asked if the horseback statue outside the hospital was of Can Grande della Scala, since it had no dragon, and could not be St. Zorzi, Denis informed him that it was in fact a memorial to some old soldier called Bartolomeo *(Bartholomew)* and that a dangerous man called the Cavaliere sometimes rode by to check up that nobody had damaged it, because he could claim descent from the wicked old general so well portrayed in the statue. Even the Prior was scared of this Cavaliere nobleman who was, the Prior informed him, a Knight of Malta. Unfortunately, he could not reveal the common name given by locals to the horseback statue because it was too rude a word for the lips of a novice, who was trying earnestly to become a holy friar.

"Bartolomeo is my uncle's name too. He's Grandpa's older brother and owns a big glass works. We call him uncle Meo. He doesn't have anything to do with us, after a row he had with Grandpa," explained Zorzi. "You see, we are all of the family Meo of Brayda, a great merchant from Burgundy who went to live in Friuli....who lived ages and ages ago.... about thirteen hundred and something, so Grandpa' claims."

"Oh! I get it," Denis observed, "Meo is the Friuli nickname for Bartolomeo. Bartolomeo is a bit too much of a mouthful for us country clod hoppers. So you are Meotti, sons of Meo. Guess what my Christian name is?"

"Isn't it Denis?"

"No. It's Dionisio - but please don't tell anyone - I'm a bit embarrassed."

"Why?"

"Because it's an old fashioned name…. god of wine, or something like that, and the trouble is even a sip of wine gives me a thumping headache."
"Oh Lord, that's unfortunate! You won't make a priest then…bread and wine and all that?

"Do you know I'd never thought of that. I guess headaches will have to be my cross to bear. We must all have our cross, so Raimondo keeps reminding us; mine is bedpans."

Zorzi was greatly impressed with Denis's explanation of his family name. This novice lad was clever, as well as jolly company. Denis now fully realized that Zorzi was neither a member of the Ducal Family nor even of noble birth, but he seemed nevertheless to be the child of a wealthy glass factory owner. Sometimes factory owners were nobility as well. Trade, he knew, was never scorned by Venetian aristocrats, who prided themselves above all on the success of their business empires.

They were soon speaking together about Zorzi's friend, Don Tranquillo. Denis told him that Tranquillo was something of a legend at San Zanipolo, a rebel angel in fact, who had never 'hit-it-off' with the bossy Prior Raimondo - that was why he had been banished to the Island of Murano. Zorzi learned to his great excitement that Don Tranquillo had killed a man in a duel. Provoked beyond endurance by a rival galley commander from the notoriously violent Calergi family, he had no choice but to defend his honour. In the fight Don Tranquillo received a near fatal wound, puncturing his lung. The Dominicans had saved his life and any assassin employed by the Calergi would think twice about the rope's end, plus eternal damnation, before attempting to slaughter a new recruit to the Dominican order. That affair of youthful honour had spoiled any hope that Don Tranquillo, wise and clever man though he now was, might ever stand for election as Prior.

Immensely entertained by Zorzi's story about the bulli and the 'blowing of the furnaces,' Denis promised on his honour as a novice to tell no one of this latest exploit of the notorious duelling friar. Laughing all the way under his heavy burden, and winding his way through alleys and over bridges Denis took no more than fifteen minutes to get to San Zaccaria. The front of the huge church and the layout of the Convent building beside it looked similar to that of San Zanipolo, except that the whole of the square in front of it was shut off by a high spiked railing.

"Very posh nuns," explained Denis. "Can't shout or spit near the railings, let alone relieve yourself against a wall.... pain of death if anyone does....squeerk!" With his free hand in a chopping motion, Denis tapped lightly on the back of Zorzi's neck. Putting down his box with a thump, Denis went to the railings and shouted "Hey! Suor' Zuseppina. Come and open up!" adding under his breath, "You idle old harridan!"

After much further shouting, at last a wicket gate opened in the great door of the Convent and out hobbled a minuscule nun with a parched white face, her head and shoulders faintly resembling an egg and cup wrapped in a napkin. She peered at the malign world through pebble thick spectacles. Under her large flapping starched wimple her tight-lipped face bore an unmistakable expression of contempt and loathing for the male species in any shape, age or form.

Though she was no taller than himself, Zorzi felt intimidated by her sour looks as she approached with the keys.... he was ever wary of nuns. "Denis, you forgot to call her Your Ladyship," he whispered.

"Don't have to. She's only a 'conversa,' not a proper lady nun of the choir stall, just a sort of holy servant really: just like me I guess. You had better take your hat off though to the lady in the pharmacy. She's a right dragon, daughter of a dead Doge, or something. They all seem to be duchesses and countesses and the like in this Convent. None of them could find a husband, I suppose. All too ugly, or family too hard up for a decent dowry, I guess. Don't suppose any one of them ever wanted to be nunnified for the rest of her life."

Eager for mischief at the expense with the pesky nuns, Denis decided to bow low to Zorzi as Suor Zuseppina approached. Next he waved him with a flourish through the gateway in the railings, adding in a very loud voice: "This way Vossignoria!" *(Your Lordship.)*

Equally eager to pocket a donation from the nobility, Sister Zuseppina curtsied low, managing at the same time to cast a malign eye in the direction of Denis. Zorzi responded with a deep bow and, wondering what Denis was up to, managed to give the little nun a bright smile that seemed for a moment at least to soften her natural loathing of mankind in any shape size or rank. When Denis suggested that Zorzi should follow him into the Convent to meet the ladyship in charge of the pharmacy, he chickened out in a complete panic, his whispered excuse being that the Rabbi's lemonade was still making him feel fuzzy headed and in need of fresh air. Whilst waiting on the cobble stones of the convent courtyard, Zorzi noticed in front of the closed church doors what seemed to be a kind of open-air altar. Silver candlesticks and freshly cut flowers surrounded what appeared to be an upturned pudding basin with a very tatty scrap of dirty linen draped over it. Curious, he sidled towards it and realised that it was nothing more than old nightcap with frayed chin strings and a gnome like peak at the rear. Having locked the gate, the wizened old nun caught sight of his move, and judging that the time was right for the young Vossignoria to tip her a sequin or two, she gathered her skirts and sprinted after him, clucking, "So good of you to come....So good of Vossignoria to come. The Lady Olivia came to see it last year: such grace, such kindly condescension she shows to her inferiors. May I ask how she is? I expect by now she will be betrothed. We quite understand of course that the Doge himself is too busy to visit us, but it is most thoughtful of the Serene Countess to send you along."

Completely befuddled by her comments and not knowing anyone called Olivia, let alone a Serene Countess, Zorzi questioned: "Is it someone's night cap?"

Equally puzzled by the lad's total ignorance, given that the Countess Morosina had obviously sent him along to represent the First Family, the aged nun kept her good temper, answering: "Oh no...No, Vossignoria, that's our 'Zoia,' the cap your ancestor made for the very first Doge." Having noticed Zorzi's two dozen or so silver gilt buttons, the nun had made the reasonable assumption that Denis had brought a Morosini lad along to show him the ancestral relic.

Though still light headed, Zorzi knew that 'Zoia' was a word used to denote a jewel of great price, but no gem stone whatsoever was to be seen on the threadbare moth eaten cap, nor could he recollect Grandpa telling him about a family connection with a cap sewing ancestor. He redeemed himself in the nun's low esteem by commenting: "Ah! Anno Domini 697, his name was, er… Anafesto. Don Tranquillo told me all about him."

"My goodness, how clever, how knowledgeable you are!" the nun exclaimed in feigned delight. She had yet to encounter a young male aristocrat who was other than totally dim-witted. Not wanting to contradict Zorzi outright and risk losing her tip, she tempered her reply: "Strictly speaking your tutor was correct. However, I expect he will inform you some time that we don't count those early Doges. They were nothing better than Podestàs. The Byzantine Emperor sent them to tax and rule us: they weren't true Venetians. This wonderful old Zoia was given to Doge Tradonico - it's a cap of liberty. Doge Tradonico was the first to gain our freedom. No doubt your tutor will also tell of your great ancestress - our holy Abbess - who sewed this 'Zoia' and presented it to him with a diadem of jewels beyond price."

"Zorzi mused for a moment, noticed now that the upturned pudding basin was made of silver and studded with tiny glittering diamond looking stones. He now vaguely remembered that something bad had happened to a Doge called Tradonico: "This Tradonico, wasn't he?"

"He was…. right here where, each Sensa, we place the altar….Murdered, daggered to death on this very spot, it all happened nine hundred years ago...nine hundred years to this very day!" Angling for a generous tip for this piece of only slightly inaccurate dating, she added: "He died in the arms of our great founder, your ancestor our holy Abbess Agostina." The question Zorzi then posed served only to confirm every one of her prejudices about the utter decadence of noble youth. On the way over from Murano with Ravenscroft's glass, Zorzi had asked old Piero to go into all the gory details of the murder of the young lovers, Paolo and Francesca in Gradara Castle.

"Was it her husband who knifed him?" he asked.

The nun's mouth sagged dumbstruck for a moment, then gritting her teeth she controlled her angry response: "What a dreadful suggestion, young man! Are you insinuating something? Our holy Abbess was a saintly unmarried lady…. beyond reproach!"

159

Zorzi's innocent question had indeed touched a raw nerve. Sister Zuseppina was well aware of another and little known legend that romantically connected Tradonico with their holy founder. Flustered by her obvious fury, Zorzi apologised to her and sought to cover his gaff: "So where is the Zoia, I can't see it?"

"The gem stone? Oh! I quite understand the slight confusion; the Zoia is not one stone, it's a diadem of great gems. Whenever His Serene Highness comes visiting we fix it to the cap. Now if you would like to see the circlet itself and the jewels of Queen Catherine, I could ask our Reverend Mother Abbess; she is away at the Sensa celebrations but I am certain she will oblige. We prefer not to make a great show of our little treasures, of course. Poverty and charity are the bywords of our way of life, as doubtless Vossignoria will know. We live frugal and simple lives here, so any donation from our noble visitors is ever welcome. It would go, of course, straight into bread for the underprivileged."

"Not quite able to square the logic of great poverty combined with possession of crown jewels, Zorzi spent a moment pondering the matter, then: "I was wondering....I was thinking. Perhaps your Abbess could find someone rich. I know a rich man called Capitano Ravenscroft. Perhaps he could buy a few things, maybe to help you all out? Now I think about it…. my Grandpa! He knows the exact stall where you can get a good price for gold and gems and things, it's just over Rialto Bridge."

The prospect of flogging off the crown jewels of the Queen of Cyprus, like so many turnips in Rialto market, first stung then horrified the little nun. There was ever much talk amongst the nobility, of the obscene wealth of the Convent of Saint Zaccaria. Once again Zorzi's innocent comment was taken by her to be a subtle jibe at her Order's morality and its stinking riches. Such crafty, oblique, and well calculated insolence was typical of a young male of the nobility. The nun's flushed and angry face drew close to his. All thought of getting a tip from this impertinent young rascal had now vanished from her mind. While Zorzi struggled to think up something to say that would not end in another gaffe, she, on much closer inspection of his bloated and battered looking cheek and rough tanned skin, began to have suspicions as to his Morosini pedigree.

To his great relief, the irreverent Denis sidled up at that very moment. "Still admiring that grubby nightcap, Suor Zuseppina? Open the gate for us will you?"

Denis took a firm grip on her arm and that of Zorzi and hastened them both towards another gate at the south end of the railings. Shocked at this treatment, the peppery nun could find no voice to reply. Denis was in a jovial mood, obviously relieved to have survived his mission to the pharmacy with his brain box un-decapitated. The nun let them out without so much as a parting word. The hubbub of an immense throng was further amplified by a long alleyway leading to yet another iron grilled gate bolted from the inside but without a lock. Denis unfastened this and they passed beneath a stone archway out onto a wide stone paved embankment now packed shoulder to shoulder with revellers, hucksters, beggers, villains, country bumpkins and of course sumptuously clad nobility. This Riva degli Schiavoni was not the slave market, as the name might suggest, but the place where merchant ships from Slavia and Dalmatia once used to anchor and now it was the temporary site of the Sensa Fair, for the two great piazzas of Venice were required for coming ceremony.

The Sensa was in full swing. Hundreds of stalls and attractions lined the long embankment running from the Doge's Palace as far as the distant Arsenal Gates. Full swing was the operative word. A galleon from Hindustan had brought a whole cargo of swings. They were the 'sensation' of that year's fair. They were the first swings ever to come to Europe in any quantity. All were for sale, with disorderly queues of young ladies and their swains eager to try them out before purchase. There were so many swings that they were being sold from at least ten pitches along the embankment. All were elaborately if rather crudely carved in painted hardwood. Their seats took the form of swans, dragons, elephants, peacocks and such like. Several crafty fair ground 'barkers' had already seen their potential for making money. A salesman, dressed as a Hindu Raja, explained to a wealthy looking young couple with children, that swings were superior things in his land; strictly not for child's play, nor for entertainment. Sultanas of the highest rank used them too keep cool in the harem gardens - he made an instant sale!

Zorzi was making careful mental notes: he would ask signor Molin to make one for him. With sequins to spare thanks to the Rabbi, he had more than enough for the timber and rope: more than enough to buy a dozen swings! Denis however seemed eager to distance them both from the cargo of the East Indiaman wherever they came across it. In the wards of the hospital that same morning he had been obliged to deal with several members of its crew who were violently ill with a new form of gut bug that was mystifying Prior Raimondo. Could it be a new form of plague from the East that the Prior had read about in a recent report from The Forty for Trade. The Prior had warned his staff and Denis in particular to use running water from the tank rather than canal water when cleaning up the filth and ordure after attending to patients. In order to distract Zorzi from his new found enthusiasm for swings, Denis suggested that they treat themselves to crushed ice and fruit flavoured granitas followed down by two or three colourful dollops of ice cream: just the thing for a blazing hot afternoon. The ice cream and crushed ice granita selling barges were the only vessels permitted to tie up along the embankment during the Sensa. In the hold of each barge, covered in insulating straw, were huge blocks of ice brought from the glaciers of the Dolomites. Blue and yellow striped awnings shaded the barge decks and on the embankment there were more shaded benches on which one could sit in calm and repose while sipping the mouth watering, fruit juice soaked, granitas: though poor Denis had little or no time to rest his aching shoulders. Again and again Zorzi leapt up the barge gangway to make yet another choice from the luscious display of multi-flavoured granitas. Denis insisted that both he and Zorzi be given clean straws and glass bowls rather than those of cracked crockery. The vendor tended to offer unrinsed bowls to his customers, and as Denis had observed, many had been slurped over repeatedly by grime encrusted snotty nosed little urchins.

Denis held firmly to the satchel, now weighted down with a large wedge of parmesan cheese and a smelly but leak-proof packet of salt dried anchovies. Denis and 'Vossignoria' had more than their fill of fresh bread, cheese and anchovies as well: luxuries that do not mix too well in empty stomachs, particularly when combined with icy and acidic granita. Despite the inevitable burping and queasiness, both lads continued in their exertions adding to the process of fermentation by tumbling several times down the giant slide. This contraption of sailcloth, yard arm spars and pine scaffolding, was lashed together with old rigging, the start being approached by a rope ladder rising up to some thirty feet. Climbing the swaying ropework was no challenge for the boys, but many a brave girl had petticoat problems and few managed to get to the top unaided. The scaffolding and worn old sails were arranged in such a way that when sliding at high speed one was thrown through the air from sail to sail in helter skelter descent. Slithering and tumbling down for the final time, Zorzi almost collided with a very tall and straight backed noblewoman.

 The crowd of laughing parents and happy children that had been waiting at bottom of the slide seemed to have shrunk back to a respectful distance from her. The upper half of the lady's face was concealed behind a white lace 'bautta' giving the disturbing appearance of someone wearing a death mask. From somewhere behind her head of steely grey hair two stiff wires stretched upwards on either side supporting what seemed to be a small and dazzlingly white sail of intricate lacework that added more height to her already stately appearance. A sobbing and complaining little six year old, who desperately wanted to go on the slide, was being scolded by the grand lady and was now being restrained by her nursemaid. Hovering behind this plump and smartly dressed nursemaid was an incredibly tall and muscular man; handsome, but frighteningly grim faced; a man of middle years. He was so enormously tall that he stood head and shoulders above almost everyone else in the crowd. Puzzled, Zorzi stared at the man for some moments. It was so unusual for an aristocrat to be beardless -clean shaven- unhatted and moreover without a wig: he knew that it was illegal even to carry a dagger or a bludgeon at the Sensa, yet this man seemed to be armed to the teeth. Like the elderly noblewoman he was escorting, everything about the giant bravo spoke of steely grey as well, from his cloak and garments to his receeding wiry hair, from those glinting grey eyes to his array of weapons.Twin pistols of superb quality with little silver lions' heads on the end of their butts stuck out from his wide cummerbund and from his embroidered baldric hung an outsized rapier with silver guard and spiralling quillons of shiny steel. Zorzi was so fascinated that his mouth dropped slightly open as he stared in admiration at the splendid gentleman, taking in his every feature. The bravo was wearing an eight pointed cross of Malta, identical with one that Zorzi had seen hanging at the neck of the nasty foreign nobleman in San Donato Church. There was something else terribly familiar as well about that beardless face, that stiff, somewhat menacing, upright bearing, he had seen it somewhere recently, yet it was certainly not in the church. Mr. Ravenscroft had demonstrated to him how those quillons of the bravo's sword could be used to break an opponent's rapier point. He pulled a funny smiling face in order to cheer up the unhappy little girl. She giggled back. He could hardly help noticing that she too, though hardly more than a baby, was dressed with great magnificence in a white brocade gown. About her waist and dangling almost to the ground was a chain of heavy gold, every inch of which was set with great square cut sapphires and rubies. The child held a pretty little spaniel puppy whose ginger coat and tail almost matched the colour of her tightly curled hair. She let Zorzi stroke and admire the little creature. Zorzi loved little dogs and cats and they always responded well to him. None so far had ever scratched or bit him. The little girl asked him if he would help her climb up on the slide.

The grand lady spoke again sharply to the child and then ordered Zorzi to stand where he was. At that moment Denis came up with Zorzi's coat, hat and satchel. Zorzi held the hat to his chest lowering his head ready to bow himself away.

"Just a moment, child!" snapped the noblewoman, "Why are you here… here against my expressed instructions?"

Nonplussed by the question, Zorzi replied, "To see the Sensa with my friend here, Vossignora." He gave a polite bow and flourished his hat.

"Insolent young puppy! How dare you address me in that tone! It is 'Nobil'Zia,' if you are one of my nephew's children, which I suspect you are not. What is your name boy?" Before Zorzi could summon up an answer, she turned to rail at the armed bravo standing at her side: "I don't recognize this face, Ettore… one of our Friuli parasites, I don't doubt!"

Though masked in shadow, Zorzi glimpsed angry and imperious eyes staring down at him: "Did your tutor teach you nothing? Your conduct is unworthy of your rank. Your mother shall account for your disobedience and for your manners! Truly, you deserve a good whipping, young man! Now get to San Marco at once! His Highness progresses at four, you should already be in your place. For Heaven's sake, look at the state of your clothing! Smarten yourself up at once!"

Lost for words, Zorzi bowed low once again. He wanted to get away from this dragon as fast as possible. The lady had been observing with particular disapproving attention his swollen and discoloured cheek.

"And I would remind you child that when you are guest in my house you do not get into fights! You were in that rumpus in the attic last night, were you not?

"Not me Noble Lady....that is Highness....Zia. I think you have mistaken me for...."

"Don't lie to me young scallywag. Just look at that bruised cheek. Look at the state of you!" she exploded. And this lackey of yours, why is he dressed like that? Like...like, a novice monk? The Prior shall have a piece of my mind. How dare he appoint a gormless peasant as your tutor? You boy!" she turned wrathfully to Denis. "Get him brushed and take him at once to the Piazza. At once, do you hear me, or I will have you flogged, novice or no novice!"

The growing crowd kept silent; looking on from a respectful distance, whilst being immensely entertained by every moment of this public scene of noble domestic strife. There was not one amongst them who did not know who the grand lady was, and all looked with awe upon a person equally familiar to them - her fearsome armed companion.

Murmuring another apology, Zorzi bowed low and backed hastily away. The crowd parted respectfully for them both without so much as a word of ribald comment and then swiftly closed behind them, keen to continue watching the tantrums of the little girl. Denis and Zorzi scurried away to safety - quite by chance in the direction of the Piazza.

"Who was that fiery dragon?" Zorzi asked. "What does she mean, telling me go to St. Mark's? I haven't been fighting in her house, honestly Denis. I have only been to Rabbi Sterchel."

"She has mistaken you for someone in her family. Prior Raimondo thought you were someone important - even I did - it's the clothes, I guess. According to Raimondo you are dressed like a Morosini boy: that's the Doge's family crest on your buttons. So where on earth did you get that outfit?"

"The Rabbi's wife let me have them, she called them my 'mutters' or something."

"Well, a Rabbi would never deal in stolen clothes that's for sure, I wonder though how his wife got hold of them? I'll fold your coat for you – best hide the buttons in case they get us into more trouble. I've an idea though Zorzi, let's get to the Piazza like that old woman told you. When the stewards spot you with your coat back on, we'll sail past the barriers. I could pretend to be your tutor… looking after 'Vossignoria' making sure he gets into no more fights!"

"That tall man, Denis, the one with the sword and pistols… I've just remembered who he looks like. He looks like the statue… exactly like the statue!"

"What statue?" Denis queried.

"The one outside your church… with the washing lines….the scary horseback one…. the one like San Zorzi, only with no dragon."

"You mean Colleoni? Oh! My sweet Jesus… I've said his name! You've made me say his rude name! That's a sin! I'll have to confess…!"

Zorzi laughed heartily at the extremely rude name and at Denis's red faced embarrassment. After some thought about the obscene name Zorzi chuckled: "I guess that's why he has lions' heads on his pistol butts."

Denis too now tried to suppress a giggle. But the prospect of going to the Piazza to see the jugglers and the Doge seemed now less appealing to Zorzi. That menacing Maltese Knight and his elderly noblewoman companion were, in his judgment, best kept at a healthy distance. Staying on at the Sensa was now his only wish: hurling skittle balls at turnips and cabbages - the best specimens were securely nailed down to the target boards- riding bright painted rocking horses; laughing at prizewinners in the ugly face pulling competitions; such fun he had not known in ages. Denis suggested that they smarten up anyway. Three bagattini got them a bone comb and a wooden clothes brush. While they enjoyed another sit-down and granita on an ice-cream barge, Denis restored the plumed hat to its former glory. Denis, worried now that he was disobeying his strict orders from the Prior, was all for making straight away at least to the

Piazzetta: the Palace gateway was in the smaller square. He had heard that there would be a spectacular display of clowns and gymnasts in the Piazzetta - possibly a distant glimpse of the Doge as well. He tried again to convince Zorzi, "If we slip a few coins to the stewards they will surely let us pass," he pleaded. He had never seen the Doge. This might be his only chance.

But Zorzi was off and away in the direction of a tent enticingly marked: 'Come see the mermaid freshly caught.' They joined disorderly queue of sniggering juveniles eager to hand over their entrance fees. When it got to Denis and Zorzi's turn to enter the tent, the 'barker' put his hand up to stop them: "Not for you my lord Archbishop, nor you my young Senator... don't want me booth shut down!"

However, the gleam of silver in Zorzi's palm soon overcame his high moral scruples. In his opinion the sons of nobles were all born depraved, so what did it matter; but he'd never had a novice friar as a customer. What was the world coming to? He demanded twice the entrance fee, snatched an extra 'soldo' coin from Zorzi and with a worldly sigh shoved them both into the darkened tent.

In the pitch darkness an eerie wailing sound, accompanied by the drone of a hurdy-gurdy, grew louder and louder; then came the whistling and howling of an oncoming gale; the crash of tinny sounding thunder and flashes of blue light built-up the excitement. Slowly the shutters of a dozen lanterns were drawn back to light the stage set. It was a remarkably well painted shipwreck scene; a view from the inside outwards of a coastal cavern. The waves in front of the picture were unconvincing though - they were no more than strips of blue cloth being undulated by unseen hands. But when the mermaid mysteriously appeared from amidst them, seated on her papier-mâché rock, there were gasps of excitement. These soon gave way to nervous juvenile chuckles. She was what most red blooded men would call a 'gorgeous stunner.' The more discerning punter might have described her as pouting and vulgarly pretty. A mass of real blond hair covered her form down to the waist. The abandoned wife and former model of a distinguished Venetian artist and now suffering from varicose veins, she was far from being freshly caught. Her lower half was clad in sharkskin, shaped into the form of twin siren tails with the aid of wire netting and more papier-mâché.

Wailing her gibberish siren song she began to waggle and flip her tails in a most convincing way. A seashell encrusted hand mirror flashed back the lantern light as she waved it gracefully towards the shipwreck scene. Slowly and provocatively she then began to draw her ivory comb down through her long blond locks. Strand by strand her hair was combed away to reveal, shall we say, the extent of her beauty and two small scallop shells at strategic points. There was a loud groan of disappointment from the audience. This was the new puritan age of the Counter-Reformation in Italy, when underpants and veils were being painted over Michelangelo's manlike women in the Sistine Chapel. Zorzi, in all innocence, was wide eyed with wonder; completely entranced. He had seen carved, he had seen painted mermaids, he had seen book illustrations and heard endless tales from Piero and Don Tranquillo, but nothing could compare with this spell-binding real live siren before him. His beautiful reverie was all too short lived. Whispering loudly, Denis grabbed his arm: "Quick, come away Zorzi. O heavens! What have I done?"

Before he could utter a word of protest Denis had almost whisked him off his feet. Denis blundered towards the exit through the pack of drooling young males, pushing Zorzi ahead of him. The leering lads cursed and tried to aim punches at them in the dark. Within seconds they were out once again into the blinding sunlight. The 'barker' gave a great guffaw of laughter on seeing Denis's embarrassment. Cruelly he pointed him out to the waiting throng. Denis had gone lobster pink.

"A thousand years in purgatory for you my young friar. Wait till the Prior gets to hear of it!" he jeered. It was the best advert for his mermaid show that the 'barker' had had in ages. The young men milling outside the booth were his captive audience. Being a natural comedian, with a repertoire of wicked irony, he knew well how to embarrass and humiliate the poor young novice. As the laughter grew louder and louder the queue of customers grew in proportion; the young tormentors would not let Denis pass and pulled him around by his waist cord, while the barker kept up his invective about the lewd goings-on of Nancy boy friars. Infuriated by this abuse of his friend, Zorzi let fly with boots and fists at the overweight 'barker,' toppling him over from his wooden box and into the tent ropes, almost bringing down the tent. The crowd's raucous laughter was now at the showman's expense. Denis managed to drag Zorzi away before the showman could get to his feet and mangle the little lad. Pulling the hood of his habit over his head he dived into the crowd. They were soon lost amidst the throng of shoppers. Denis felt his heart pounding with fear. His pure young thoughts were now sullied. A puritanical post-Reformation kind of guilt had long supplanted the easy going, easy forgiving, morality of the old Catholic world and Denis now had his full share of complexes about the sinful body. What if the Prior got to hear that he had been seen at a strip-show in the company of a ten year old? If he were to have any hope of salvation, he would have to confess all before his brethren, right down to the scallop shells. He would have to admit to that stern faced Prior of San Zanipolo that he had entered unto 'a den of iniquity.'

They moved swiftly past the silks, the Turkey carpets, the gaudy glassware, the heaps of brightly coloured spices and beans, the map sellers and the juggling clowns on stilts, until they came to a stall selling amber beads. Signora Molin had always hoped to own an amber necklace, she had said so many times, and Zorzi was greatly fond of her. Whenever Zorzi was famished to desperation, she let him join in with her own hungry brood at the family table. When he fell over and cut his knees, or was depressed, she was there to bind him up and to comfort him with a motherly cuddle. He would buy her the best necklace he could afford. He chose a nice big lumpy one with tiny insects trapped within the ancient resin, which was, to his surprise, only a gold ducat. The salesman offered to wrap and box it for him. The salesman was no Rabbi Sterchel though: Zorzi's alert eyes noticed something golden brown slide down into the box from his sleeve.

"Maybe I prefer this one," he said casually, picking up another double-rowed necklace of smaller beads. "Let me compare the two before you wrap that one up for me."

The salesman was completely flustered. He ducked down behind the counter and fumbled for the real necklace amidst a pile of cheap glass imitations. Finding it a last, he handed it back to Zorzi, who gave the salesman a challenging, suspicious look - the look of one who is aware that he is being conned.

"You know," he observed in a loud voice to Denis, "I can make brown glass beads to look just like these amber ones. Grandpa showed me how." Adding cheekily, "It's hard to tell the difference just by weighing them in your hands. There is a test you can do though: amber will always float in sea water. There is another test too. Amber is magic. If you rub it on your sleeve, it can pick-up little bits of paper." Turning to the flustered vendor he asked, "Could you let me have a piece of wrapping paper, so that I can show the trick to my friend?"

The salesman snatched back the double rowed necklace, which was now so obviously false and threw it back into its box, but Zorzi held on firmly to the genuine article and said casually, "I think, after all, I prefer the chunky one with the flies in it. Don't bother about boxing it!" he added cheekily while dropping it into his satchel.

Mightily pleased with his bargain, Zorzi moved away swiftly. The fake amber seller was beside himself with suppressed rage. The little tyke of a nobleman's son had just beaten him at his own game of deception. He had walked-off with his finest amber necklace, worth a least five gold ducats. The salesman could do absolutely nothing. Several other potential dupes of customers were waiting. They had witnessed the sale to this sharp thinking little nobleman. Most of them drifted away, that much more cautious about their Sensa purchases, thanks to Zorzi.

The boys now found themselves mingling with a better dressed shopping crowd. The nearer the stalls and booths were to the Doge's Palace, the more luxurious were the goods for sale: furs from Russia; silver damascened swords from the Lebanon and exquisitely engraved pocket pistols from Pistoia; perfume from Grasse and Egypt; myrrh and incense from the Yemen; caged monkeys; parrots and weird miniature dragons with long tongues; *(chameleons from the Sahara,)* and amidst the mounds of bright saffron and other rare spices there were small dusty heaps of lapis blue stones worth more than their weight in gold to up market Madonna painters. Then, wonder of wonders, quite the biggest booth of all - it took the form of a turreted wooden castle. Two scantily clad carved wooden caryatids held up a notice above the entrance portal. The sign read: 'The Wonders of Mother Nature - The NH. Grimani collection of exotic curiosities - Admission free.'

Zorzi made a dive for the fake drawbridge. Horrified, Denis reined him back, insisting that he was too young to see such lewd profanities. Zorzi had taken rather a liking to the pretty singing mermaid and was getting somewhat annoyed with Denis constantly censoring what he could and could not see.

"Please Zorzi, you will only get me into more trouble; please don't go in," Denis pleaded, "It's not for the likes of you and me."

Zorzi gave in reluctantly then broke into a sudden and excited run towards what was without doubt the worst eyesore of a stall in the whole fair. Denis rushed after him, fearing more embarrassment. The stall was built with ripped, tattered sailcloth. It was little more than an awning to give a bit of shade to the stallholder and was propped-up with broken spars and a splintered oar or two from a longboat. But it was what was on the three barrels that greatly excited Zorzi… the stencilled mark of the Raven! He had seen identical barrels outside Zanetti's sugar shop.

Badly displayed on one barrel were a selection of telescopes and microscopes, all of polished brass and sleeved with green sharkskin. On another barrel was a glittering pile of glass rainbow prisms. The pirate seated on the third barrel was doing a fine trade at three bagattini per prism. Zorzi had already noticed at least a dozen well dressed youngsters staring at the wonderful world through their triangular prisms as they passed by in the fair. He wanted one for himself and now he knew where they came from. He ran up to the astonished pirate and threw his arms about his waist. But Zorzi in his excitement had only focused on the massive white beard, the broad leather baldric and sea boots. This was not John. He stepped back and apologised. The pirated did not understand him at all and was further flummoxed when Zorzi began to mention the names of his shipmates.

"John, John! Where is John? Where is James? Where is Capitano Ravenscroft?"

In one corner of the big sailcloth awning, a little tent-like cubicle had been constructed so that clients could test out the microscopes in semi-darkness. The cubicle curtain drew back: the Most Reverend and Noble Father Prior Raimondo emerged, microscope and spirit lamp in hand. He

171

scowled at Denis who seemed to shrink deep into his hood with utter terror as he bowed, then genuflected, then knelt on two knees, before the grand surgeon of San Zanipolo Hospital.

"You may stand Brother Denis. It is fortunate for you that I am not the Cardinal Patriarch. You need kneel only to him, to God and to the Doge. Stay a moment! You have some explaining to do."

This scene of humiliation and flummery got up the hairy nose of the pirate and when the Prior offered him only one and a half ducats for a superb quality fold-up microscope, he was incensed. Jumping down from his barrel he stuck up two fingers in the face of the Prior and demanded "Dos, deux, due! I'll have two gold sequins, no less. Look!" he added, pointing to some engraving on the barrel of the microscope, "Hooke, Hooke, Robert Hooke! The best!" He made a clawing sign as though hooking the air.

The Prior was taken aback by this show of aggression. He knew well enough what the offensive 'archer's gesture' was supposed to mean. The name of the English philosopher, physician and architect was also more than familiar to him: though friars even of his high rank were not supposed to have prized possessions, his most prized possession nevertheless was a 1665 first edition of Hooke's 'Micrografia.' He wanted that little microscope at all cost, but was not prepared to be insulted by a heathen pirate, nor, in his pride, did he wish to be seen 'climbing down' from his first offer. "Ah! Hook-Key, Hoookey, signor Uncino, he mused, implying that the name seemed to make a slight difference to his first offer. Zorzi wondered for a brief moment how a hook-handed English pirate could have made such a precision instrument, then saw his chance to fish Brother Denis out of the boiling pot. He asked Denis to pass him the heavy satchel. Grubbing down amongst the anchovies, cheese and amber, he found his coins. He was down to his last three ducats and a handful of silver lire and bagattini.

Fishing out two ducats, Zorzi gave them, with a smile and a grimace of resignation, to the pirate. Realizing that Zorzi was paying up in order to save his young friar friend from humiliation and punishment, the pirate presented both of them with free rainbow prisms. As the Prior turned to thank Zorzi for his splendidly generous present, he too received a presentation from the pirate - another traditional two fingered salute!

Both astonished and delighted at the turn of events, the Prior beamed a thin lipped smile at Denis, who dared not raise his eyes. The Prior told Zorzi that the patients and staff at San Zanipolo would pray for the speedy recovery from his gum problem and for the general health and wellbeing of his noble family. Getting Zorzi re-united with his kith and kin at the Doge's Palace was now uppermost in the Prior's thoughts. But there was one more item on the Ravenscroft stall that intrigued his medically trained mind. It was a modest sized box with a spirit burner set on a brass stand beneath it. There were several convex lenses set in the thick lid and movable mirrors designed to reflected sunlight and lamplight.Nailed crudely to the barrel supporting this novel item was a badly written sign. It read: 'Grosso Flea-o, biggisto do Mundo.' An excited little throng of youngsters were jostling to take a peep through the lenses into the box: a peep at the greatest 'flea-o' in the whole of the itchy flea ridden world!

Ushering away the children, the pirate invited the Prior to look down the tube of the strange contraption. When the pirate adjusted the mirror and screw of the tube, the Prior was astonished to see the brightly lit flea-o in enormous magnification, possibly thirty times life size: the very same type of flea that had been illustrated in all its barbed, hairy plated and hook legged glory in his copy of the 'Micrografia.' Greatly impressed, he was now determined that he must have one of these superb instruments for the hospital. Only the Council of the Guild of St. Mark could approve such a purchase and he would have to enter once again into negotiations with the English supplier about the price. It was evident that this particular instrument was not for sale, but the numbskull of an English corsair could not be made to understand that he wanted to order one. Zorzi then intervened between the agitated hand waving Prior and the gruff unhelpful pirate.

"Capitano Ravenscroft, the owner of this stall, is a friend of my grandfather. He is a rich English lord and he has his own big ship in the Arsenal. He makes glass lenses on his island called London. I can arrange for you to meet him. Grandpa says he is a generous man, just like his uncle was, so I expect he won't charge you anything for the flea lens, 'specially as it's for the hospital."

Zorzi's words were heaven's sweet music to the Prior. What a charming generous child... and so usefully connected with a foreign man of great natural philosophy and wisdom. Prior Raimondo looked forward to an encounter with this Ravensco, even though he might prove to be a stubborn heretic of a puritan. How fortunate that Brother Denis had struck up a friendship with the noble little lad. It would be wise, from now on, to favour Brother Denis. Cultivating the friendship between him and this well heeled and well intentioned Morosini child could only be in the hospital's best interests. Of course, now he would have to go out of his way to escort the child back to the Doge's Palace in person. He flicked open the domed cover of his silver 'onion watch.' It was half past three. The Doge, he guessed, would be rising from his afternoon nap and very soon processing in ceremony to St. Mark's. The Palace Watergate was less than five minutes away, even so, the Prior's gondolier would have to lean hard to his oar. There might be other latecomers causing boat jams in the Rio Canonica. Certainly the boy would have to be in his allotted place before the Doge appeared.

The dead flea was at last in focus. Zorzi stared in creepy delight at its grisly hairy legs, its grey transparent body and vicious spiked sting; no wonder it brought up such red itchy bumps, much worse than mosquito bites. He was so absorbed that he hardly noticed that the Prior had turned his attention to the young novice. Denis's hang dog expression and the granita juice stains about his mouth told the Prior all he needed to know. The novice, he noted, was now resigned to some severe penance for flagrantly disobeying orders. But what worse punishment could he hand down to the novice than that of scouring hospital chamber pots from dawn to dusk and washing soiled nightgowns?

"Brother Denis! I have something to say to you. Straighten your back! You need not return for Vespers. I shall take the boy to his relatives. With my authority and blessing, you may stay here and enjoy the Sensa Fair! I would particularly recommend a visit to 'The Wonders of Mother Nature,' of the Noble Grimani, a most informative exhibition for a young man wishing to become a surgeon. There is a calf with two heads, Siamese twins and a giant octopus. You might also like to inspect closely the so-called mermaid."

Denis blushed red. Had the Prior noticed them entering that den of iniquity? Was he being just as sarcastic as that evil showman? Evidently not: the Prior fumbled in his purse and handed him a silver 'soldo,' worth twelve bagattini: quite enough to enjoy every attraction in the fair and still have something left over for an ice cream.

"Brother Denis you may purchase another prism from this crude mariner in order to present it to the other novices who are less fortunate than you in not being permitted to view such marvels. The rainbow, you will know, is a sign of God's redemption given to Noah. As for the Noble Grimani's mermaid, examine it closely: I feel confident that it is not a thing of nature, but a fraud. It appears to be half monkey, half cod fish, and has certainly been opened in the middle for stuffing. You will find it pickled in a large jar of alcohol at the end of Grimani's wonderful collection. Whatever it may be, note the fine and concealed stitching at the join. If you are to study to be a surgeon, that is the skill I shall be expecting of you. Say farewell to your noble friend. Ask him to visit us soon at San Zanipolo."

Zorzi had no desire to go to the Doge's Palace. He wanted to stay with Denis at the fair. But Denis embraced him and obedient to the Prior's commanding gesture wandered off to taste of the iniquities on his own. Noticing this unhappy parting, the pirate clapped a heavy hand on Zorzi's shoulder and pointed towards the nearby Doge's Palace: "Mr. Ravenscroft, John, James, San Marco...San Marco. See Dowj... see Dowjee!"

The pirate put a telescope to his eye and directed it at the Palace. Though horribly mispronouncing the beautiful Doh-jay sound Zorzi got the message. He would find his good friends from The Raven at San Marco.

He stepped into the Prior's gondola and before they had time even to strike up a conversation they passed swiftly under the bridge called Ponte di Paglia. Its wide stone arch was almost groaning under the weight of packed humanity all trying to get somewhere near the Piazzetta to see the parade. The Palace Watergate, in Rio Canonica, is a splendidly arched affair with a wide flight of steps. As a guardsman caught the mooring rope, Zorzi looked up. Almost directly above his head was something he recognized: spanning high above the shadowy chasm between the Palace and the New Prison was that notorious bridge. Nobody in those times referred to it as the Bridge of Sighs, but old Piero often spoke of it in similar terms. Zorzi's heart now began to pound with anxiety. Piero, confident that he would never have the misfortune to cross it - for ignorance of the future is everyone's bliss - had described to Zorzi more than once that condemned prisoners sighed and groaned as they were dragged by their necks onto the bridge. Halfway across, they would be strangled by The Ten - all ten of them tugging on the noose! According to Piero, all ten of them had to pull hard together, because they were such long bearded, such skinny, such bent and wizened old men that not one of them had the strength to do the job on his own! Zorzi was therefore most worried and hesitant about stepping out under the awesome arch. Before he could utter a protest, a guard whisked him out of the Prior's gondola and carried him up the broad and slippery steps.

Only personages of great importance arrived via the Palace Watergate. Its guarding 'Cerberus' was Messer Grande, the out-sized, shaven-headed, bull-necked chief jailer. He came bustling up in his ceremonial uniform, jangling a decorative bunch of keys that might at the very best serve to open a small cash box. Seeing his Excellency the august Prior Raimondo accompanying a young noble, he ordered the guard to snap to attention and to present arms. This they did with a great clutter of halberds, partizans and squeaking armour.

"I take it that you will not be attending the Doge's banquet, your Excellency; tonight being your busy night?" the jailer observed.

"Firstly I was not invited. Secondly you are quite correct in your assumption, Messer Grande. I have two clean wards all ready for the casualties and there are sufficient pine boxes stacked in the mortuary."

"How many do you reckon on this year, Reverend Prior?"

"Last year there were four, but this year, with the extra fun, we are prepared for six at least and fifty or more minor casualties. What with the bull baiting; the falling acrobats; the Cuccagna tower; not to mention the fireworks and the odd exploding cannon, we shall have work enough repairing skin and bone to last us till next year's Sensa. I have begged the Senate many times not to have a Cuccagna. Why on earth can't they distribute food to the poor in a more civilized way?"

"Because the nobility like to see the fun and mayhem, Your Excellency. The Sensa wouldn't be the same without a good Cuccagna," the jailer chuckled.

"Well Messer Grande, unlike the Lord Patriarch, I have my ward rounds to attend to. I must be off. See that this child is taken to his relatives. You will doubtless find them somewhere on the Countess's grandstand. And, Messer Grande, I should like a messenger to be sent to find a certain English lord. His name is Ravenscro. He will no doubt be with the ambassadors from heretic lands. You will find them in attendance on the Doge at the foot of the Giant's Staircase. They too, like me, do not get an invitation to the Doge's Vespers. The child here will recognize the noble foreigner. This Ravenscro must be told to contact me. Is that clear?"

"Quite clear Your Excellency." The jailer wrote on his note pad ' find N.H. Refosco' and handed it to an alert looking flunkey, who hurried-off with his instructions.

"Will Your Excellency be attending the 'Wedding' tomorrow afternoon?" the jailer called out to the parting gondola. He got no answer. The Prior and his gondolier sped off up Rio Canonica, towards the hospital and to his interminable ward rounds.

Messer Grande looked down at Zorzi who had taken off his hat and slung his heavy satchel over his shoulder.

"Well Vozzignoria, what have you been up to, to arrive so late? Been at the Sensa have you? Now that's naughty!"

"Yes Sir. So sorry Sir," Zorzi mumbled, "but I've been to a dentist as well."

"Plucky lad," said the jailer, "been tryin to work-up courage to go meself. Got a terrible rotten molar.... just can't bear going near tooth pullers."

Considering that from time to time this Messer Grande applied his expertise in the Palace torture chamber, this was something of an oxymoron of a remark, but then there was much of the lumbering ox and of the moron about the Chief Jailer's ungainly presence.

"May I ask your name, Vossignoria?"

"Zorzi Sir. Zorzi Mi.........de Brayda of Friuli," The name, not strictly false, seemed to issue from his lips, almost as a defence mechanism. He knew he was now in deep troubled waters and there was no Piero to fish him out, nor even a Ravenscroft in sight. There was just the forlorn hope that round the corner he would find Captain Ravenscroft, or John, perhaps even old Piero. They might be sitting in a room somewhere nearby chatting with the Doge about the Turkish fleet. His presence in the palace and his posh new clothes could then be explained to all.

Messer Grande had no grounds for suspicion whatsoever about Zorzi. The lad had arrived in the care of the Reverend Prior. The Prior of San Zanipolo was the unofficial Minister of Health for Venice. He was often consulted at Senate meetings. The child must be the offspring of someone of great rank for the Prior to concern himself with such a little scrap of a lad.

"I'll take you up to where the Serene Countess is myself. That is, I can't take you all the way. I have my duties." The word Countess sent another flutter of fear through Zorzi's ribs. He had no notion of what a Countess was: somehow, the name did not seem to relate to his pirate friends from the Raven. In fact, the jailer knew that he would be pushing his luck even to enter the palace courtyard. In his realm of prison gloom, rusty chains and hot pincers he was the master. However, part and parcel of the jailer's job was being the scapegoat for any injustices. He was hated, feared and shunned, especially when he strayed beyond the prison confines. In public he rarely ever appeared, even his wife and family were snubbed by all when they ventured out. Appearing now, amidst the Senators and the Doge's guests and on such a grand and joyful occasion, well it would make him resemble the spectre at the feast!

The Countess's grandstand was on the side terrace up and above the porch of the Basilica of St. Mark. From there the Countess and her brood, some of her female friends and their young families would have a panoramic view of the great square and the entertainments in the smaller square, known as the Piazzetta.

Taking Zorzi's trembling hand in his big beefy paw, he led him along a corridor towards the Palace courtyard. Zorzi could hear the occasional dry rattle of military side drums and the harsh shouts of drill officers. Turning a corner, they were confronted with what seemed to Zorzi to be an entire army on parade. Rank after rank they stood at ease, tall plumes and halberds, muskets and gleaming breastplates, trumpets and battle flags. Officers in magnificent gold etched armour, with great swathes of coloured silks wrapped round and round their waists strode and fussed up and down, hoping no doubt to draw attention to their important selves. With their brightly feathered parade helmets, the officers resembled fighting cockerels, strutting, spurred and eager for the cockpit. Along the open cloisters of the upper floor the entire Senate and Grand Council was chatting and weaving about as though at a party. They were paying no attention whatsoever to the yelled commands and clashing of armour below them. Their deadly weapons were soft whispered words of advice or opinion: their armour, those long forged and impenetrable tribal and family alliances.

Apart from the marines, who were guarding the fleet off the Lido, each regiment of the Serenissima's armies had picked a dozen of its fittest fighters to be present at the Sensa parade. Even so, it was a fearsome ordeal for the tough young men to stand for so long in the torrid courtyard. A Water Orderly was moving up and down the ranks. As each soldier gulped down a mouthful from the Orderly's ladle, the spilt water splashed and sizzled on his baking hot armour.

"What are you doing here my good man?" It was the rasping and high pitched voice of a bewhiskered general officer.

"Beg pardon General," the jailer pleaded. "It is this boy; he needs to get up quickly to the Loggia of the Horses. But first I have been asked by Prior Raimondo to get the child to identify a foreign nobleman."

"Well you can't possibly do that now. The Doge will be here any moment. The child should have gone another way, so be off with you!"

The jailer raised his hat to the general and took Zorzi's hand once again. "Sorry your young Lordship. Let's hope that the Countess won't be too

179

hard on you."

The word 'Countess,' set the general's collection of neck-ribboned medals jangling an alarm on his breastplate. A sudden onset of gunfire would have perturbed him less.

"Orderly!" he bellowed, his voice hoarse with anxiety. "Escort this boy to St. Mark's.... to the Countess. You know where she is. Quick, quick! Doge is coming! At the gallop, man! At the gallop!"

The orderly officer hastily clicked his heels, saluted the general with his sabre and swinging Zorzi clean off his feet, tucked him under his right arm as though he were carrying the company pay chest. Zorzi hung there astonished and limp as the officer trotted at a fair speed around the outer edge of the parade ground, passing close by those 'heretic ambassadors' who were waiting at the foot of the Giant's Stairway. The officer with his unresisting bundle then sprinted along the dark corridor leading to the Porta della Carta, *(The grandiose gothic Palace Gateway where legal petitions were handed in.)*

They had almost reached this magnificent gateway when there was a fanfare of trumpets from the courtyard, followed by the rhythmic thud of war drums. The officer broke into another run. They emerged into the bright sunlight of the Piazzetta, where there was an immense throng of wildly excited citizens ready to greet their demi-god; their leader of the pack, their Morosini.

On hearing the war drums, the waiting crowd began their chant: a sound soon amplified by every loyal voice within the city as far as Rialto itself. It echoed and roared, louder and louder, like an oncoming tempest: "Do - ze... Do - ze... Do - ze! .... Mor - o - si - no.... Mor - o - si -no! Evviva Doze Morosino!"

Entering the gorgeously colourful mosaic portico of St.Mark's Basilica, the orderly dodged swiftly to the right thus avoiding the assembling ranks of cardinals, patriarchs, archdukes and bishops. At the foot of the right hand stairway to the Loggia of the Horses he dropped Zorzi saying: "Go up! Go up and hurry! Doge is on his way! Go! Go!" With that he rushed off.

Zorzi took a few anxious steps upward. Each step took some effort: seemingly they were designed for giants. The stairway stretched straight and long up into the gloom. He waited a few moments for the orderly to go away, hoping to make a quick run through the portico and make his escape through the vast throng of spectators that he had noticed were seated on benches around the Piazza. When he crept back down again the portico was packed. Crammed shoulder to shoulder were clergymen dressed in magnificently embroidered copes and mitres. Numerous young acolytes were there as well, all dressed in cassocks of red silk with stiff lace collars. A prelate stared at him disapprovingly as he emerged from the arched doorway and flicked a white glove in his direction in a way that could only mean "Get back up!"

Nearing the top of the stairway Zorzi heard the reassuring sounds of children's laughter combined with loud chattering, squeals and much scurrying about. He stepped out into the huge arched choir loft above the West Porch of the Basilica and found himself not only in a heaven of glittering mosaics but in the midst of twenty or so children and a bevy of musicians who fidgeted with their music scores and tuned with weird noises their very large and wonderfully decorated instruments. After much argument about seating status, the music makers arranged themselves into two separate groups with their stools, sheet music and metal stands and set-to with thrumming and pinging their warm up notes interspersing them with the odd amusing and fruitily rude noise from brass and woodwind. Most of the children were now peering down at the clergy and officials far below by leaning perilously over a balustrade of curiously fretted and pierced stone panels that fenced off a great square gap in the middle of the floor. That gap in the floor was designed to illuminate the rather gloomy loggia far below and those very low balustrade panels were certainly not designed to be leaned upon by a press of excited children. Zorzi took one look down and pulled back, feeling momentarily dizzy. None of the children seemed to notice his presence. With the exception of a very young male child who was still in his blue frock and frilly petticoats, all the boys were dressed in silk and braided suits. The fine quality napped wool that Zorzi was wearing was of an identical shade of blue, with identical buttons and yellow braid trimmings. In the subdued light from the great half moon of an attic window it could hardly be distinguished from silk.

The stairway from which he had just emerged now began to disgorge solemn faced choirboys and adult choristers. Two by two they puffed their way up in their hundreds then divided making their ways towards several other arched and enormous choir lofts high up on either side of the church nave.

As the last of the choristers cleared the stairway, Zorzi made to go down again. A tall ginger haired girl then gripped his arm and snarled: "Not that way, dolt! Get through the window and behave yourself! Uncle Ettore is up here, remember!"

She held firmly onto his sleeve and Zorzi had no choice but to follow the other children through a glass door hinged to the lower left side of the huge semi-circular window. Once out onto the terrace *(known as the Loggia dei Cavalli)* the Roman bronze horses were there right in front of him, prancing in all their golden glory, each hoof balanced on a short marble column. The floor of the open and spacious terrace, set above the church entrance, slopes downwards towards a low parapet of turned marble balusters, the gap between each baluster set alarmingly too wide apart. However, the wildly excited young aristocrats were preserved from tumbling instantly into the grand Piazza, some fifty feet below, by fishing net draped along the whole length of the balcony and its side terraces. Clinging tightly to the netting and suffering once again from a moment of vertigo, Zorzi peered down, now quite overawed by the spectacle. To his left a sidelong prospect of the Doge's Palace with its spectacular white gothic porch and opposite that a perfect view of the Bell Tower, quite the loftiest in the world. Running south from the tower to the waterfront were the endless arches and columns of the Library of St. Marks, a vast classical building with a top parade of elegant statues. At least ten thousand people were seated on stepped benches around the Piazzetta. This Piazzetta was the smaller of the two squares and was enclosed by the Ducal Palace, the waterfront known as the Molo, and the grand library. The high terraced benches gave the merry crowd an unobstructed view of the entertainment: jugglers, stilt walkers, clowns and acrobats. Harlequin and Brighella were there below in the Piazzetta, hammering at one another with their slapsticks and quarrelling over the beautiful Colombine who occasionally did a revealing cartwheel or intervened to slap the cheek of one or the other of her clowning rivals. The Grand Piazza straight in front of the Basilica is still one of the largest and most ancient town squares in the western world and by far the most famous. At first glance the decoratively paved space seemed almost empty, but as Zorzi adjusted his eyes to the glare and the contrasting deep shadows he could make out at least another twenty thousand handsomely dressed spectators seated, either in the shade of the shopping arcades, or crowding the open windows high up on either side of the square.

From down below he had frequently admired the the four golden horses decorating the terrace: now on close examination they looked even more wonderfully lifelike and lively. Piero had assured him that they once drew Caesar's chariot and had been turned to gold by a magician king called Croe...something or other. This wizard sovereign turned absolutely anything he touched into precious metal. Caesar, being a Venetian general, consequently much more nimble on his feet than other commanders, dodged out of the way when he met the magician: his chariot and horses were touched instead. Having slain King Croe... something, by way of revenge for transmuting his favourite animals to gold, Caesar made good use of them as decorations for his favourite church. The chariot, being too large to fit up there above St. Mark's, Caesar had it melted down to pay his army. It was evident now that Piero was misinformed: the horses were not made of solid gold. Some mean vandal had scratched through the surface just to check. Drill holes, where the harness was once attached, also made it plain that they were not even cast in bronze – they were nothing more than old green copper! They were very finely made nevertheless and he stood for a while mouth open in admiration, remembering that at home he had a miniature horse of similar style modelled by his father and cleverly blown in golden tinted glass.

"Anything to scoff down there? What a sweat! Why did they make those stairs so high? I'm starved, absolutely starving!" The child's luminous chestnut eyes looked with friendliness and real pity on Zorzi's bruised and swollen cheek. "Vidal is here!" he whispered in a cautious tone, "Cosying up to scary Aunt Morosina. He's grabbed the almonds... won't share them out. Leastways, if they drool over him, he lets the girls take a handful. Heard the latest? We've got to call him Witale or else Landgrub or something – Auntie's orders. Landgrub! No wonder!" The child chuckled at his own joke.

183

For one who claimed to be starving, the boy now standing next to Zorzi looked exceedingly well nourished. From his plump calves to his cherubic double-chinned face, the child looked a picture of health. He was about Zorzi's own height, but from his high pitched voice and odd way of blurting out his comments, Zorzi guessed that he could be no more than about eight years old."

"Nothing to eat down there, the way I came up…. only bishops and altar boys and things." Zorzi answered.

"What have you got in your satchel?" the youngster inquired, "Got biscuits? Couldn't bring any nosebag, it being church, and what with big Ettore and scary Auntie up here. Custard castles this evening though! Saw them baking. Mean cooks wouldn't let us have a nibble. Let me see! What have you got?"

Hearing talk of food, four or five other youngsters crowded round. Their lightweight silk brocades were now evidently in strange contrast with Zorzi's woollen cloth. However, being boys, they took no note whatsoever of how he was dressed. Their only interest was in his splendid embossed leather bag and its contents. Having the sense to realize that Parmesan and anchovies would not really appeal to the palate of greedy young aristocrats, Zorzi said; "I've been to the Sensa to buy a few things.... for friends."

A loud and instantaneous gasp of half disbelief came from the little crowd: "You've been to the Sensa?"

"Quiet… shut your loud mouths!" an older boy hissed. "He's already in enough trouble with his bashed cheek, God help him if Aunt Morosina finds out he's bunked off to the Sensa as well!"

Zorzi noticed that several of the youngsters had freshly bruised faces. The boy who had hushed the others had a real shiner of a swollen eye, several bruises on his forehead and a small dried-up cut on his lip. Zorzi was about to inquire about the fight, when the boy asked him if he had spent all his money at the fair.

"Well, I've got a few coins left over. You see I had to buy an expensive kind of telescope thing for the Prior... of San Zanipolo and a necklace for the lady who looks after me."

Mentioning the necklace was almost his undoing. Olivia, the ginger haired girl who had first detained him, reappeared with three or four magnificently silk gowned companions in tow, wanting to see it. Zorzi grubbed around in the satchel: it let out an almighty powerful stink of fish and mouldy cheese. He distracted the boys with the rainbow prism, but the girls drew away in disgust at the pong. They then began to notice certain oddities about his clothing. For a start, the newcomer was still wearing the family winter court dress. They were curious to know which cousin he was, or to which old Senator he was related. Zorzi explained that he had been fishing... at sea that morning and this was his fishing bag. He let them handle the fine amber necklace. Their curiosity was soon allayed. They were distracted enough with the curious necklace and its little trapped insects not to insist with their line of questioning.

Zorzi quickly realized that despite their exceptional height and well-fleshed limbs, they were all much younger and more naive than the half-starved and streetwise friends he usually played with. Each girl in turn tried on the amber necklace. The mosquito-like insects made it a rare curiosity and it looked a princely enough gift to them though, in comparison with the great gem stones that they were accustomed to wearing, it was no more than a cheap trinket. Envious, and eager to have one like it, they plied him with questions once again. The boy with the cut lip came to his rescue, whispering that it had come from the Sensa fair. He demanded their promise not to tell anyone about Zorzi's escapade to the fair: a worthless promise since the girls had little else in life to do but to pass on gossip. Some of the children had heard of that important nobleman Prior Raimondo. They thought it most gallant that Zorzi had bought the wonderful magnifying present for the hospital. Not having the vaguest clue as to what the instrument was, they supposed the Noble Prior would apply it to all his poor beggars and peasants who were suffering, with instant healing effect. They were impressed with his daring in going to the Sensa. By way of punishment for fighting in her attic dormitory, the Countess had expressly forbidden all involved from going to the fair. Since her grandson Vitale (Vidal to his young Venetian cousins) had no bruises at all and was clearly not involved in any way with the fracas, he alone was permitted to go, accompanied by an armed manservant - just in case the innocent lamb got picked upon by common ruffians amidst the crowd!

Zorzi's swollen cheek was more useful than a noble pedigree: in the circumstances it was a badge of honour. He too had evidently stood up to Vitale's bullying and had suffered a pummelling for his bravery. Zorzi, they concluded, was both good fun and very clever, particularly when he explained about the horrible great flea, the English pirate who was his friend and the mermaid. All they now wanted to know was how much money he had left.

When he produced his last gold sequin and three silver grossi, there were gasps of astonishment. They were impressed; not to say overjoyed by his show of wealth. Though the parents of these children owned palaces on the Grand Canal, villas, castles, towns and villages, not to mention great swathes of Italian countryside, not one of the children had ever been given much in the form of pocket money. They needed to pay Jasone, *(Jason)* the farrier's son, to beat up their German cousin, the Landgrave Vitale von Wittelsbach. Their devious initiative showed great promise for the future; a first step perhaps on the long progress towards adulthood and eventually, for the most shrewd and ruthless, to membership of the Most Excellent Council of Ten. Zorzi considered their proposal for a moment; then it occurred to him that if Vitale was some relative of the scary Countess, then stable boy Jasone would be sticking his neck out not just for a gold sequin but straight into a hangman's noose. Grandpa had only touched the Podestàs arm, and Don Capello wasn't even a proper nobleman. What would happen to the stable boy's family as well if he were caught? All these doubts tumbled over in his mind and finally he asked quietly. "Where is Vidal?"

"Are you blind or something? He's on the step next to Aunt Morosina."

"Oh! Daft of me! I hadn't noticed…. I was still admiring those horses."

"He's spotted you." whispered the boy with the lip, "Look at him scowling at you. He'll be over to give you a good kicking the moment Aunt Morosina turns her back. You'll see!"

Zorzi turned round and tried not to make eye contact with the great dolt of a bullyboy, as Vitale looked menacingly in his direction. The Countess leaned forward at that moment and gave her charming grandson yet another glass bowl of sugared almonds to tuck into. She caught sight of Zorzi and gave him a nod and a tight-lipped smile. He froze at her recognition. Having had no time to inquire who the dishevelled little boy was, she was satisfied for the moment that he had at least obeyed her commands and got to the stand on time. He looked a forlorn little scrap and so terribly, terribly brown tanned, almost like a peasant's son. Doubtless he was one of the Friuli lot: distant cousins who lived in a rundown Palladian villa out in the sticks. After the State Banquet and when she was less committed with the entertainments for her foreign guests, she would take the sad little creature under her wing. At least she would see him better dressed and less of an embarrassment to the family. He needed learn how to behave like a gentleman and how not to get involved in silly boyish scraps.

Zorzi pretended not to have seen the Countess. He kept up the chatter with the little group whilst surveying the whole scene further along the sloping terrace. Though she was no longer masked, there was no mistaking the Countess Morosina. The little girl with the jewelled chain and the white dress was asleep in the arms of a servant standing nearby. Her ginger puppy dog too was sound asleep in the shadows. Vitale was sitting on a cushion at the feet of his grandmother who, like the other twenty or so ladies surrounding her, was being shaded by servants bearing big bright parasols. Vitale was far too big and aggressive looking for Zorzi to square up to: even Aldo might find him an impossible match in a fight; though nobody under fully grown man-size had ever managed to beat up Aldo.

Zorzi was now more concerned than ever about poor Jasone, the farrier's son. Thinking about his likely fate, he hit upon a plan: "Listen boys," he said. "I'll give my sequin, you promise to dress Jasone like yoursel....like one of us. He'll need a leather mask so Vidal can't pull it off of him in the fight. Lady...that is Aunt Morosina, dotes on him so Jasone might get a proper whipping to death - worse, his family killed too!"

The idea of a leather mask and dressing-up the stable boy appealed to the excited young conspirators. Though some protested that Aunt Morosina wasn't all that cruel, others were less sure about the matter. One of them said: "You'll be with us this time, won't you? Someone must rile him and get chased up the attic, otherwise Jasone won't have a chance. Didn't see you last night….your idea, your turn!"

"Unfortunately, I can't. I've promised Grandpa I'll be home this evening."

The inevitable questions came: "Who's your Grandpa? Where does he live?"

"Er… Murano."

"Murano!" echoed ginger haired Olivia, "Such a pit! But then Bastiano lives there. Are you related? You," she added, sniffing around Zorzi's neck, "You smell! Smell of...of lavender water! Boys should smell of sweat!" This comment caused so much laughter that Zorzi was saved from a reply.

Giving a fake shiver one of the older girls commented:"I've heard there's a castle where they say Cousin Bastian does secret bad things, like.... like magic… trying to turn gold into lead, or something. He keeps common boys there too. What sort of wicked things they do, my maids won't say. They know something, so it must be true: I slapped them all hard….not one of them would tell."

"Your maids should bite their loose tongues!" snapped Olivia. "Don't go about repeating such things," she twisted and caressed with her fingers a gorgeous tripe chained necklace of diamond and black pearl. "I'm very, very fond of Bastiano: he's so handsome and so clever and gives such thoughtful gifts."

"That's because you look like a boy, Olivia… Specially when you go riding in those tight breeches!" This spiteful comment came from a rather plain and spotty, but well developed girl.

Olivia exploded: "It's all lies made up by jealous people… jealous girls like you, pimple face! Why, poor cousin Bastian could be arrested because of your loud mouths. The Ten could even have him burned. You

188

know what happens to people wrongly accused."

The boys weren't terribly interested in this spiteful exchange and went to the balustrade to look down on the jugglers. But Zorzi wanted to know more: the name Bastian rang alarm bells. "I didn't know cousin Bastian had a castle." he observed casually, "Where is it?"

"Why Soave of course," came Olivia's tart reply. "You should know that, you peasant-looking dunderhead!"

"Oh yes," he remarked in a deliberately vague voice, "It's where our wine comes from."

"Soave is mine….Yes, I think it's mine. It doesn't belong to Cousin Bastian, I'm pretty sure it's mine," mused the little fat boy.

"Oh! Do shut up Fatty Gritti!" snapped Olivia. "You Gritti people think you own everything!"

Zorzi gave the little lad a look of amused astonishment mixed with new respect: could this tubby and pleasant natured youngster really be the owner of such a great and famous fortress?

> Having unwittingly gate-crashed a Morosini and Gritti family gathering, Zorzi was now agitated by the knowledge that he was in the midst of Zustinian's folk as well. He just had to find some way of escaping. The hungry little castle owner had mentioned that there was another way down from the terrace. Several other youngsters were now running about rather than keeping to their seats. Zorzi moved away from the older group hoping to avoid further questioning. Whilst affecting to admire once again the magnificent copper horses from every angle, he sought desperately to find another bolt hole amidst the carved stonework and enormous arched windows further along from the wooden grandstand where the ladies were seated. Other than through the glass door there was no way out and Uncle Ettore, that gigantic 'Cavaliere di Malta', armed with rapier and lion's head pistols was standing guardian there.

CHAPTER SEVENTEEN

The muffled noise from the Sensa, not far from his windows, the stifling heat in the darkened room and the usual gripe in the guts caused the Doge to sleep fitfully. When his valet shook his shoulder he sat up dripping in perspiration and feeling quite unwell. After a rubbing down with eau de Cologne and dry towelling he put on a thin cotton shirt. The valet wrapped a silk scarf lightly about his neck and shoulders to pad them against the chafing of his parade armour. The breastplate and neck gorget were magnificently etched with warlike trophies damascened in pure gold: being almost bullet proof, both were extremely heavy. The armour was quite unsuitable, his valet protested, for a long walk in the Piazza. That parade would be followed by an hour or so in a packed and badly ventilated church. But the aged Doge knew better than his valet what his loyal people expected: it was Sensa time and most amongst his adoring citizenry would be howling for 'the dogs of war' to be let loose. He would rise up to the nation's warlike expectations just this once more. The valet covered his thinning grey locks with a lightweight and close fitting cotton cap and tied the strings under his chin. Slinging his ermine cloak over one shoulder the Doge walked on his own through the vast rooms and corridors of the palace until he came to that gloomy portal marked CONSIGLIO X. He knocked, entered and interrupted without ceremony a private conference. The wily Chancellor Ballarin, present with his papers and law books, was the only person to bow low to him.

The 'Tre Capi,' the three duty Senators, had already received a report from Morosini's valet, who doubled up as their spy on the Doge's more personal activities: the Doge had ordered his best parade armour to be unpacked and polished and they were not at all happy with that news; yet they gave no visible signs of displeasure when he had walked in unannounced.

"Doge Francesco, do you not think you will be somewhat overdressed for such a merry occasion? It's terribly hot out there." The honeyed tones of Senator Pisani, a lifelong ally, came at him through the gloom.

"I know what you have in mind my friends," the Doge replied irritably. "We must clip old Morosini's laurels! We must trim his sea boots down a few sizes, otherwise he'll be trampling on the Senate like Caesar back from Gaul! Well, I would remind you that it was you who burdened me with the Captain General's baton! The citizens demand that I wave both 'Corno' and helmet at them today. Which one of you is willing to step on to my galley, eh? Which one will scale a Turkish bastion in my place? Well don't scratch your wigs and find dead fleas! I have no ambitions of the Falier kind and anyway, I'll be out from under your noses very soon, by bullet, or by damned old age!"

"Don't take offence, Serenissimo," the Senator continued, "We know the common folk revere you and we all expect you to play to the gallery. It's just quite what some of the nobility may think of your parade that concerns us. A few of them see you as something of a threat to their privileges and to the ancient freedoms. As you know, we prefer to counsel rather than to direct: our advice is to proceed with extra caution today and to show just a hint of humility when you strut your armoury in the Piazza."

"When you walk out into the Piazza, Serene Highness, you will better understand our concerns." It was the quaky voice of Senator Querini, his sharky old enemy who was ever circling for a bite.

"Well the plebs won't be happy with me if I leave them poaching in the sun for much longer, so open up the trinket box and let me fish out my finery. I'm already late for Vespers."

The Hall of the Ten also served as the ducal treasure house. Doge Morosini selected the biggest and most gem encrusted 'Corno' crown and plonked it on his head. He did not choose anything of great value by way of a ducal ring. Almost certainly the ring would end up in six feet of mud at the bottom of the Lagoon the following day, so he took the one that fitted easiest his big bony wedding ring finger. The original 'Fisherman's Ring' was there of course, amongst the priceless trinkets now displayed like a saint's relics in gold and crystal boxes. That first ring, so worn and thin, was ages old, ancient in the extreme. Its rough cushion cut emerald was quite tiny - a very dull object indeed. And yet a mixture of legend and tradition held that it was the ring handed to a humble fisherman by St. Mark himself who, plucking it from his net, gave the startled fisherman the task of presenting it to Paoluccio Anafesto Tradonico - the very first Doge. Naturally, St. Mark sent an apostolic message with his gift:

namely that the Doges of Venice would reign till Doomsday providing that they threw back into the deep an emerald ring each year on the day of Christ's Ascension. The Ten would have been happier if the one hundred and eighth Doge had plastered himself with every neck chain and gem stone, star and garter that they possessed. Morosini was expected to be the visible proof of the vast wealth of the Serenissima. An ermine caped walking jeweller's shop, would delight the crowd and allay the concern of the nobility. An armour-plated Doge conveyed a different message: one of possible military despotism, with just a hint of kingship in the offing!

The Chief of The Ten then placed a slender chain of gold around Morosini's neck. Attached to the chain was a crudely cast medal of the Madonna, with the date 13th April, 1203. Legend had it that blind Doge Dandolo had worn that neck chain when he sacked Constantinople - in revenge for having his eyes burned out with a sun ray lens by the Byzantine Emperor. Despite his infirmity, Doge Dandolo had managed quite a bit of sacking and pillaging at the sprightly age of eighty-four, before dropping with exhaustion into his Byzantine tomb in the Holy Wisdom Basilica. At only seventy-four, Doge Morosini still had time enough to winkle out the Ottoman from their ill-gotten capitol. Christian Byzantium and its once extensive empire was now crushed and under the dominion of the Sultan. Constantine's city was now Istanbul.

The Doge took his time before emerging into the Piazzetta. He reviewed troops and exchanged pleasantries with the 'heathen' ambassadors in the enclosed palace courtyard. The shouts of 'Do-ze! Do-ze!' had died down. Only the sound of military bands kept up the suspense of the waiting throngs. On descending the Giant's Staircase the Doge greeted with genuine warmth his arch enemy, the Ambassador of the Sublime Porte. From a distance this huge dusky man faintly resembled a giant skittle in a bowling alley, his bulbous body was topped with an enormous tulip shaped white turban: a reminder to all that his considerable brains were bound close to Allah, for the words Allah, turban and tulip looked much the same when written in Arabic. Once chief of the Turkish Sultan's harem, he had been upgraded in rank because of his sound knowledge of French, the language of diplomacy. The Ambassador was being withdrawn, for the umpteenth time by the Grand Vezir of the Ottoman Empire, in protest at Morosini's planned counter attack against the Ottoman occupation of the Greek Orthodox Morea. It was no secret that

Morosini was about to sail straight for the jugular vein with an attack on the fortress Island of Chios close to the Turkish mainland.

"Sad to see you sailing off again," quipped the Doge, "Your presence brings peace and your absence war. That fine turban will be sorely missed, as will your good company. Come back soon and remember... bring your sons and family. They will always be very welcome!"

The Ambassador, a jolly eunuch, laughed heartily: the other diplomats joining in on the rather cruel joke. Not to be outdone, the eunuch struck back with, "Farewell Doge Francesco. There will be a warm welcome for you as well, should you wish to visit Islambol, or wherever else you plan to come ashore. Remember to stop off at Siracuse and buy some oranges!"

The Doge laughed. He always had time for a good straightforward enemy; it was the scheming back-stabbers of statesmen that he hated. He and the enormously fat eunuch embraced one another fondly. Both men knew that the cover of the Turkish fleet had been blown by a passing Englishman and that the rival fleets would be redeployed to ambush one another in bloody conflict elsewhere in the Adriatic Sea.

Turning to Conyers, the Dutch Consul, the Doge inquired with his usual dry humour: "Speaking of fruit, how is your prince? Beg pardon, I should call him King William now. Is his new conquest bearing fruit yet? Oranges tend not to prosper in a cold climate."

Deep down in the Doge's heart was resentment that neither the English, nor the Dutch had ever given a hand in defending Europe from Ottoman aggression, but above all it was for the perfidious King Louis XIV of France that his smouldering rage was reserved. Louis was tearing Europe into beggars' shreds with his quest for 'gloire.' While he pursued his costly, devastating and unprovoked wars with his Christian neighbours, his own peasantry and urban slum dwellers were known to be dying from famine in their hundreds of thousands. Louis was the only European ruler to be directly allied to the Ottoman. After much pleading from the Pope, Louis had sent a squadron of hopeless aristocratic fun fighters to aid in the defence of Candia (*Crete)* who, after losing just one galleon to the Turk, had cut and run, leaving Morosini the hopeless task of defending the island on his own. But at least King Louis helped bankroll Malta, which he did out of self interest as his insurance against Barbary pirates, and the majority of quarrelsome Maltese Knights were from the French nobility. Despite having powerful fleets, the three Protestant powers, Dutch, Swede and English, preferred not to get involved in defending the heartland of Europe and were growing fat on far Eastern trade, whilst the Serenissima was leaking the blood of its sons and the gold of its sequins into the Mediterranean Sea.

"What new conquest would that be your Serene Highness?" the Dutchman asked.

"Why England of course!" came the reply.

The Consul was not amused, but everyone else laughed.

"And, my friend, my thanks to your English captain for the information about the little green arrows. Let us hope that King William produces a Orange very soon.... maybe a little Dutch boy? Though now I come to think of it, he already has a little Dutch boy...Bentinck isn't it?

(This cutting reference to William Bentinck, First Earl of Portland, the boyfriend of his sovereign, offended the masculine pride of the Consul. Since the Dutch invasion of 1688, Morosini's Ambassador to England had been withdrawn and the Venetian State Records show that a spy took his place. There was always a purpose in a Morosini's jibe. Europe had heard a rumour that King William of Orange would make Bentinck his heir, in which case another great conflict in the North would ensue leaving once again the Western World in peril of invasion from Ottoman armies.)

Consul Conyers bowed and turned away angrily. Thinking at first to make a sniping joke about Morosini's many mistresses and his failure as well to produce an heir, he then decided that as a witty riposte it would fall dead flat on the ears of any listener; for although in his tempestuous years the Doge had left more sirens frolicking in his wake than King Neptune himself, it was known that he was now anchored with the Court matriarchs in the calm lagoon of old age. What's more, being elected rulers, Doges were not allowed to have heirs in any case. Amidst the mocking laughter the Consul vowed never again to pass on information to the Serenissima. He was however mystified by the reference to the English captain and the green arrows. Evidently there was some information from England that had not so far been communicated to him.

In fact, Mr.Andrew Ravenscroft had taken measures to insure that the Dutch Consul knew nothing of his unauthorized visit to Venice, not to mention his stopover in the papal port of Ancona. He was already under suspicion of being a secret supporter of the deposed Stuart monarch, James II: a hanging and quartering offence in Orange England. What's more, he had no intention of paying duty, on anything of value that he might bring back from Venice, to a government that he felt had, for bigoted religious reasons, betrayed British interests to those rivals for sea power, the Dutch.

Morosini hitched up his ermine cloak and to the sound of another great drum roll and a blast of silver trumpets strode towards the Porta della Carta and out into the blazing sunlit Piazzetta.

CHAPTER EIGHTEEN

Up on the roof terrace of St. Mark's Basilica the children had stopped running about and were now crowded at the Southern balustrade overlooking the smaller square, the Piazzetta. Something truly spectacular was awaited. The Lenten Carnival of that year had been cancelled. The Doge had been too unwell to make the journey from his country villa and a fierce prolonged winter had continued through February into March keeping the Alpine passes blocked and the wealthy northern fun lovers holed up in their castles and manor houses. Money set aside for Carnival had not been wasted in Bastian's capable hands. The familiar events of Carnival would be added to his own well planned programme, to make what he strongly suspected would be a last farewell and tribute to his aged uncle. Zorzi jostled with the other children to get a better view down onto the square. All childish chatter now gave way to shivers of fear and excitement. The waiting throng below drew breath. Even the seagulls seemed to call with muted shrieks from far above. Little ones hid their eyes or poked their heads against the netting between the columns of the balustrade. Older ones craned heads over the parapet, daring to see the worst that could happen. The Calatafimi, the guild of Arsenal ships riggers and fitters, had saved its last death-defying stunt for the exact moment when the Doge would appear. The renowned feat of gymnastics was called 'The Labours of Hercules.' Twenty five gymnasts were gradually assembling a human pyramid, balancing upon one another's shoulders. Seven were balancing on longboat oars, held in the up stretched arms of the nine below. One acrobat had already fallen with a deadly thud. A replacement was instantly found, while the motionless wreck of a man was carried off in silence. The top man in the pyramid was now in position. Four blazing torches were gingerly handed up the side of the pyramid and were now in his hands.

The trumpets and sackbuts brayed, the side drums rattled and the Doge stepped forth from under his vast gothic archway to honour the event with his presence. No shouts of "Do-ze, Do-ze!".... Utter silence. The juggler threw his firebrands in the air faster and faster, making a circle of flame high above his head, then he caught all four torches in one go and jumped. He managed a treble somersault before swooping safely into the arms of his workmates. That great collective intake of breath was now released as a storm of applause. The young athlete ran forward and flung

196

himself down on both knees before the Doge, his arms gracefully outspread as he bowed his head to touch the paving.

Doge Morosini turned to his treasurer, who handed him a heavy purse made of silver chain and tied with the red and gold ribbon of the Serenissima.

"A boon! A boon!" screamed the crowd. "A boon! A boon!" Zorzi and his little companions joined in the shout.

"Your boon is granted. And what the devil is it?" Morosini bellowed back for the crowd at large to hear. For one so ancient, his voice rang crystal clear and majestically firm.

"My boon, O Serene Highness, is for my mother-in-law. She has long been in jail for debt. I beg that you to keep her there!"

It was a stale old joke but the crowd loved it. The fun of the Sensa had got off to a perfect start. Morosini embraced the athlete, stopped to clap the other members of the human pyramid and walked on. He took care to keep a few paces ahead of his dusky skinned ceremonial umbrella bearer, so that all could see him.

Between the Bell Tower with its magnificent marble loggia and the South West corner of St. Mark's Basilica a triumphal arch had been erected overnight. It was a grand construction of scaffolding, wood panelling and canvas; a full-scale copy of a typical imperial arch of the kind built for returning Caesars along the Sacred Way in Rome. The Noble Zustinian had lavished much time and thought and close supervision over its decoration and had ordered Bastian Ricci, a renowned Venetian artist, to knock up some designs for the arch. However Ricci, though still husband of the varicose veined mermaid so deeply admired by Zorzi, had run off with a rival artist's wife and model; as a consequence of that and of other misdemeanours of the poisoning kind, a death sentence now hung over him. Zustinian even offered to smooth over such trivial obstacles to Ricci's career as part of the contract, but Ricci, now safely living it up in the palace of Duke Farnese in Rome was much occupied converting saucy nymphs into swooning saints for the new Pope. Not wanting to give up the fee for Zustinian's project, nor willing to risk his neck by journeying back to his home town, Ricci sent his 17 year old apprentice, Brusaferro, post haste with a book full of sketches of the Arch of Titus in the Roman Forum. With lightening brush strokes combined with the incredibly refined draughtsmanship required of a Ricci assistant, aided as well by numerous Arsenal joiners carpenters and sail riggers, the young Gerolomo Brusaferro enlarged Ricci's drawings into an heroic arch set in relief with trophies and trumpeting angels and processions of 'Jerusalem swag' carrying centurions and of course a great tablet above the arch with a cod Latin inscription in honour of the Doge. Working in the Arsenal sheds and in a matter of days young Brusaferro, with the illusionistic 'trompe l'oeil' skills learned from his master, had transformed into convincing ancient stone what was no more than splintery pinewood and discarded sail canvas. But it was what was written on the tablet that caused the Doge almost to have an apoplectic fit. Bastian in his usual zeal to ingratiate himself with his uncle had committed an unpardonable offence to the 'SENATUS POPULUSQUE VENETIS.' Steaming with heat and rage, they would now have to walk beneath an arch praising Doge Morosini as their divine emperor, their Caesar, their supreme pontiff, their all conquering great ruler. Not content with all that, the spoof dedication lauded the Morosini family, implying that it would be the perpetual inheritor of the Doge's throne.

Bastian Zustinian was no slouch at school. His command of Latin abbreviations on the fake tablet meant nothing to the crowd of common citizens, who would hardly have recognized their own name had it been up there. However, many senators and quite a few of the nobility had already deciphered his clever abbreviations and were hopping mad. Several of them had already demanded a full meeting of the Senate, to discuss the matter of Morosini's ambition to become their absolute ruler, their Caesar, their Imperator! The PONT MAX bit was quite ridiculous of course: the Pope was the Pontifex Maximus. Leopold, the Habsburg, claimed the title of IMP CAES: not that Venetians would ever accept the Austrian Emperor's claim to that title, for by doing so it would make him their overlord. The nobility were prickly people, ever watchful for attempts to convert into a kingdom their thousand-year-old Republic, that had thrived for far longer than that of ancient Rome. One by one in recent times they had seen generals of Cromwell's kind, Electors of the Palatine and Stateholders, like William of Orange, seek to convert their tawdry titles into kingships. During its long history the Serenissima had seen off more than one attempt by a military despot to seize power.

As was the custom, the Master of the Revels came forward from under the triumphal arch to greet his uncle. He had the self-satisfied grin of the cat that had got the kipper. He knelt to kiss the Doge's ring and as he rose he outfaced the look of fury on the Doge's countenance. He was quite expecting the explosion of rage from his uncle and had his calm reply ready.

The Doge whisked a glove as a sign for his umbrella bearer to draw back; which was also a hint to the Senators following behind to hold off. "What have you done? You imbecile!" the Doge hissed, loud enough to be heard by the Senators. "Do you want my head topped in the palace courtyard? Get that inscription covered-up at once! Tomorrow you will go to the Senate and apologize on your knees to them!"

"Oh, yes uncle. I shall go and I shall give my regrets," Bastian announced in a voice for all to hear. "Embrace me uncle and forgive me."

Bastian was a hand's span taller than his seventy four year old uncle but in appearance resembled him greatly. Curiously, for Venetians of ancient pedigree, both men were golden blonds with bristling eyebrows, fierce deep blue eagle eyes, hinting at Norman descent. Both sported waxed and upturned ginger tinted moustaches and had slight Viking turn-ups to the points of their noses. Identical clipped V-shaped tufts of ginger gold beard sprouted from the end of their chins. Throwing his arms about the Doge, Bastian whispered into his ear, "Why won't you ever grant me an audience in private? Why must I ever confide in you with eavesdroppers at hand? I'll tell you Uncle, The Ten won't remove your head: however, you may well end up like Bragadin. Some of them plot to betray you to the Turk. As for me, I am to be Ambassador in Paris and devoured by Mount Lion on the way. The Ten do enjoy their little moments of melodrama."

"Devoured by a lion? What fantasy of yours is this, Nephew?"

"Buried in a rock avalanche at a place called Gondo on the Passo Sempione. Here are the instructions to their agent in Haute Savoy."

(*Marcantonio Bragadin surrendered honourably at Famagusta to an*

overwhelming Turkish force, after a long and heroic siege. He was
tortured horribly for days then publicly flayed alive. His urn, skin and
monument are in San Zanipolo Church.)

"Then God be with you, Nephew. Once I sail, there will little I can do to prevent it."

Under the pretence of re-arranging the silk scarf about the Doge's neck, Bastian stuffed a tightly folded note, down the top of the gorget of the Doge's armour. "Read that before this evening's banquet," he whispered, "The code is St. Mark's Gospel, Chapter Ten, Verse Ten… letters backwards from the end. I need hardly tell you that they chose the Verses as an insult to us both. Read the note, then you will understand why I put up that inscription. When you return victorious the nation must be ready to acclaim you as king: that is your only hope of survival. I need to smoke out our friends: our enemies we know well enough. Remember the old adage, dear Uncle: 'We need a revolution to keep things as they are.' Now laugh out loud, as though I were whispering a dirty joke to you."

Doge Morosini pushed his nephew away and gave him a slight whack on the cheek with his glove. He was disturbed by Bastiano's news, it sounded highly probable: experience however had taught him that his nephew was far from reliable. "Hold your tongue now, you saucy fellow! That is far too crude even for the Sensa!"

He chuckled merrily and convincingly and beckoned with his glove for the Senators to come within earshot. "Trying to send me up in smoke, my naughty nephew. He's going to blast down the damned archway tonight, by way of a fireworks display! No respect these young 'uns! Take no offence my Lords Senators. Let's have no Caesar, no Brutus and no Cassius at the Sensa. Let's tramp on and enjoy some good old Venetian mockery!"

Master of the Revels, Bastian, was not to be outdone when it came to good old disrespectful pranks. Just as the Doge and Senate were about to process through the arch, Bastian gave a hand signal to someone waiting on top of the arch. From right above their heads came a tremendous rumble and crash. Doge, Senators and terrified ambassadors ducked and ran in all directions, covering their heads. The offending Roman inscription dropped forward like a drawbridge and a great shower of sugared almonds and other coloured sweets pelted harmlessly their shoulder-length wigs and heavy red silk robes. The watching crowd rocked with laughter. Expecting that several similar humorous pranks would interrupt the solemn procession, both Doge and entourage and took it all in good part. The Doge picked up a handful of almonds and aimed them one by one at a hopping and dodging Bastian; thus adding to the fun. Little boys and girls ran from their parents' sides and scrambled like puppy dogs about the feet of the high and mighty rulers of the Serenissima.

Crouching low and quite unnoticed beneath a black cotton veil, Bastian's choir had assembled on top of the arch. The fake cornice surrounding the uppermost part of the arch now flapped noisily outwards to reveal them standing in their bright red choirboys' cassocks. Luanardo was in a cold sweat. He was terrified of ladders and heights. During the climb his thumping heart had almost seized up on him. But it was not just copious flatulence that drove him onwards and upwards. Debt and poverty were even more powerful propellants. He was in arrears with the rent of his tiny room above the sack factory. Both he and his bedridden old mother might soon be out on the pavement. It was not, alas, the Psalms of Monteverdi that he was there to conduct, but a humiliating series of vulgar Venetian serenades; a job that every other choirmaster had disdained to accept. He raised his heavy baton. The comically dressed 'Turkish Band' with an assortment of outlandish and battered instruments struck-up a tune. It was a raucous 'barcarolo' - a gondolier's song, well known to the amused audience. The verses were quite unprintable. Suffice to say that the gondolier's name was Francesco, poking fun at the Doge's first name, and that each verse of the gondolier's lantern-lit exploits, whilst he went out serenading with his mandolin, ended with a rousing chorus from the crowd.... in praise of aged cuckolded husbands!

The Senators revelled in it: their suspicions were mopped away with their sweaty handkerchiefs. They marched happily under the offending arch, admired Brusaferro's painted reliefs of ancient Roman despots and followed their leader around the great square. Behind them came a colourful procession of trumpeters and banner wavers, military bands and trophy bearers. The great officers of state were there with their clerks and equerries. There were Procurators and Generals, Admirals and Podestàs

201

and, stalking amidst the long pageant of exquisitely dressed nobles, were Ten watchful men, whose identity was known only to Senate Committee Members and to the Doge.

CHAPTER NINETEEN

Luanardo's appearance, not thirty feet away and at eye level, was quite disconcerting to our young hero. He froze, and then stepped back from the balustrade, fearful of being recognized. In doing so he collided with Vitale, spilling half the contents of his bowl of sugared almonds. The fiery young bullock of a boy was just about to offer an almond to him. Countess Morosina, with a lifetime's experience of handling aggressive young males, her big brother the Doge being her first conquest, had decided that the friendly young waif in winter clothes (and on such a hot day,) would make an ideal companion for her grandson. She had persuaded Vitale to make overtures of peace to him and instructed him also to invite this strange and unfamiliar looking nephew to come over and speak to her.

Vitale had been commanded forth from his Bavarian mountain fiefdom by 'Nonna *(Grandma)* Morosina,' firstly to meet and be cheered up by his young Italian relations and then to forget his sorrows in the festivities of the Sensa. In March the Countess had received the news of the tragic death of Vitale's father, the Landgrave Wittelsbach. She had loathed the Landgrave from the moment he proposed to her daughter, but the match was politically necessary. It was given out that death came in 'on-foot combat' with a giant boar cornered in a rocky gully. Spies of The Ten reported otherwise to her. It came as no surprise that the dissolute and dimwitted Landgrave had fallen from his horse in a drunken stupor, having imbibed too much schnapps.

Zorzi removed his hat and bowed very low, declaring his profound apology for bumping into Vitale. Raising his head, he noted Vitale's clenched white knuckled fist. Expecting a blow, he ducked low again and set about collecting the almonds, still loudly regretting his clumsiness. With his skinny lightweight frame, Zorzi had found himself in many such tense situations in the back alleys of Murano. He knew that if conciliation did not work the best plan was always that suggested by St. Paul, namely that: 'It is better to give than to receive.' He would throw his puny might behind one swift punch to the solar plexus and then to hoof it away at all speed. Unfortunately that very spot on Vitale's anatomy was covered by a large gold and white enamelled jewel hanging from a bright red and white striped ribbon about his neck.

Right hook ready and left hand full of almonds, he stood-up and gave Vitale his best friendly smile. The smile was returned in part by a not unfriendly grimace. None of the young Landgrave's haughty Venetian cousins had ever greeted him in this way. They called him Vidal, and poked fun whenever they heard him introduce himself as 'Witale fon Vittelsbach.' If any one of them had expressed regret at the death of his father, then he had not understood. He was a bit of a dunce at anything other than hawking, riding and disemboweling deer; but one thing he did understand was their disdain at his oafish manners and their refusal to show any respect and precedence to him, the Landgrave; the heir of his father's mountain fastness.

In the attic gloom of Palazzo Morosini he had been ambushed by several of his cousins and after he had flattened them, he had lashed out at all and sundry young males who were witness to the assault: it was his way of teaching them who was top bullo. Now he felt slightly ashamed of having done such horrible damage to this little scrap of a relation. He touched Zorzi's cheek. Then using one of the few Italian words that he knew and one he had least used since his arrival, he said "Scusa." *(sorry)*

"Nothing to worry about," replied Zorzi with another smile, "it doesn't hurt."

That was the sort of courageous reply that the young Landgrave admired. At last he had found a cousin after his own heart.

The finely modelled pendant covering Vitale's weak spot appealed to Zorzi's discerning eye. "Beautiful, beautiful," he observed and asked permission to touch it.

"Tod....Morto!" *(dead)* Vitale answered and heaving a great sigh, his eyes brimmed with tears. The white enamelled badge seemed to portray in exceedingly fine detail a drooping dead mutton. It had a sparkling ruby eye and reminded Zorzi of his own under arm position when carried off by the orderly officer. He was perplexed to know why a gold and enamel miniature of a dead sheep should make Vitale so unhappy. He touched Vitale's arm in a friendly consoling gesture and realizing instantly that the boy spoke little or no Venetian said, in his best Italian: "Yes, dead... very

204

dead.... so very sorry!"

With this genuine sounding expression of consolation, Zorzi had made a friend. The pendant was of course the most exalted Order of the Golden Fleece; the supreme honour granted by the Spanish/Habsburg Empire. It was Vitale's one cherished souvenir of the father who had brutalized him from an early age; a father whose only merit was that he encouraged Vitale to go hunting whenever his Morosini mother wanted him to apply himself in the schoolroom. Of course the subtle humour of sending a Jason to batter the bearer of the Golden Fleece was not lost on the older boys and girls. Olivia, known to be a sneak, had been kept out of the plot and as for this rough looking newcomer, Zorzi, well the story of the Argonauts had clearly not been part of his classical education.

Vitale of the Golden Fleece wiped his eyes with his long laced cuffs and with a slight bow offered Zorzi the glass bowl. He indicated that he would like him to throw any dirty almonds over the balustrade, which Zorzi did with great pleasure. The hard cased almonds, for the most part, bounced off the wigs and mitres of the waiting dignitaries below and where cheeks and ears were stung they were taken uncomplaining as part of the Sensa fun. With his nodding and tearfully smiling permission, Zorzi offered the bowl around. Only the girls swallowed the sugary bait. In no time the Landgrave and Zorzi were surrounded by a cheerful and chattering gaggle of female relatives, all making eyes at the thuggishly handsome, sad looking and now quite unthreatening Vidal.

Utterly bored with the goings-on in the Piazza, something she had seen more times than she cared to remember, the Countess was most pleased to oversee the happy scene. She had been watching the strange little boy's movements with close interest. Evidently he was a child of some artistic discernment, for he had spent considerable time admiring her horses. Her horses, because she considered the four mighty horses of Constantine's hippodrome personal property of the Morosini clan. One of the horse hooves now served as a powder pot on her dressing table. It had broken off when her light fingered ancestor, Domenico, had looted the horses at the Sacking of Constantinople on his way, in AD 1204, to the Fouth Crusade. For the moment she decided not to intervene and spoil the moment of blossoming friendship by sending one of her maids of honour with a direct summons.

Vitale took Zorzi's arm and tugged him back to the balustrade. The male cousins moved away looking daggers of displeasure at them both. By switching allegiances so promptly this new boy could no longer be trusted. Zorzi could see his friend Matteo quite clearly and there was Toma` as well. In the far row of the choir he could just make out an all too familiar close-shaven head. It would only be a few moments before Aldo turned and spotted him. Pulling his hat low down over his brow he ignored them, stepped back a little and directed Vitale's attention to the Cuccagna and the other curiosities at the far end of the square. Matteo however had already noted the remarkable resemblance the stuck-up pageboy on the ducal grandstand had to his scruffy Murano friend. He beckoned to Aldo who quickly swapped places whilst Luanardo was shuffling the music sheets for the next song. Through the general commotion and bursts of clapping and cheering Zorzi heard Aldo shout, "Hey Zorzi! That's got to be Zorzi!" He waved his song sheet wildly.

Matteo, Toma` and others were now pointing him out. Vitale assuming that he alone was the object of their admiration gave them a slight bow and waved his hat back. After an encouraging nudge from Vitale, Zorzi removed his hat to salute them; taking care to conceal his face as best he could with the broad brim. The choirboy friends were mystified. "What a resemblance, even down to the swollen cheek!" yet the boy on the balcony had a page boy haircut quite unlike the ragged rat-tailed affair Zorzi Miotti normally sported. And how could Miotti be up there in such splendid raiment? Utterly perplexed now, they began to chatter amongst themselves.

Luanardo raised his heavy silver topped staff and bawled at them to pay attention. At long last his moment of triumph had come. His plump chest swelled with pride, though it was not the glorious choir of St. Mark's that would respond to his direction, it was to be altogether something far, far grander. He raised his right hand in a majestic gesture to the crowd and with the end of his staff gave three tremendous thumps on the boards. To his beat... violas, sackbuts, kettledrums, serpents and shawms, deep-noted horn rackets, trumpets, flutes and cymbals struck-up the anthem. Bonding as one with their Doge and Senate, with the Countess and her court and with the San Donato Choir, near half the city populaton stood erect and sang: 'Tremate nemici di Venezia!' *('Foes of Venice, tremble!' a tune that was to resound a century later on the bow of G.B. Viotti at Marie Antoinette's court and thence, ironically, within a few short years to re-emerge, preserving some part of its original verses, as Rouget de Lisle's 'Marseillaise.')*

Though already drenched with perspiration under his ermine cloak, the Doge received a generous sprinkle with holy water, by way of a blessing from the parish priest of San Geminiano. The head of the procession had now reached the far end of the rectangular Piazza and at the foot of the steps of the grandiose baroque church, the Doge stopped for a short while and mopped his brow. "I guess I needed that!" he commented amidst laughter.

Looking up to admire the Cuccagna tower, a thirty foot high wooden cone-shaped precursor of the Christmas tree, the Doges eyes narrowed once more in anger. A swarming black halo - a Pharaoh's plague of buzzing bluebottles - had descended on the dozen jelly coated pigs' carcasses hanging headless at the top of the heap of food. Immediately beneath the smoked carcasses, twelve enormous and elaborately twirled bread loaves added their weight to the pile. "Damnation, nephew!" he exploded, "Is that Aquileia's tribute I see, the left overs from Lent?"

"No, No!" I can assure you Dear Uncle," Bastian replied, raising his voice in an unctuous tone for all to overhear, "I can assure you that Bishop Aquileia's tribute was sent straight to the orphanages, just as soon as the Senate cancelled Carnival... out of respect, of course for your absence and your slight state of ill health at the time."

"Glad to hear it. But they still look fit only to catapult over the walls of some Muslim fort. I don't want any of my young blades dead with the guts-ache, now do I?"

"No indeed Uncle, though I must say that it might be more effective if some of our young riff-raff were catapulted over a Turkish wall or two, instead. However, I can assure you that the bacon up there is freshly cured and from my own farm....and the bread came yesterday from my bakeries."

"Glad to know it Nephew, generous of you, but I've never seen flies like that on the Cuccagna and I've seen a few in my time."

"It's only the sugar glaze Uncle. My cooks were a bit too generous with the sugar in the gelatine: my own fault of course.....Couldn't resist a new cargo just in from Jamaica. I had the ornament made for you as well. Though Capello insisted on paying for it."

Topping the enormous pile of foodstuffs, mostly donated by tradesmen rather than nobility, was a model of the state barge. Confected in spun golden yellow and pale blue sugar around a hull of white icing, the miniature Bucintoro glittered like some sunlit weathercock atop a princely steeple.

"Capello indeed...which Capello would that be? I must thank him."

"A client of mine, uncle - the PodestàCapello," Bastian replied with his customary scant regard for the truth.

"The Murano Podestà? Your client? I find that hard to swallow Nephew. Not even you could buy him! What's the betting you owe him rent! Why do you keep lodgings out there anyway?"

Nephew Bastian gave no answer. He had what he called his 'little sins' to indulge, way out of sight of his nosey peers living along the Grand Canal.

"If only I were fifty years younger," the Doge sighed, "I would risk a broken head, battling with the mob, to rescue my little sugar ship."

"I'll order you another one Uncle and send it on with one of the supply vessels. You have been too long at sea Uncle to notice how rebellious the common people have now become. Nowadays, if a noble gets caught assaulting the Cuccagna, he is likely to end up rent to bits along with the bulls. Though I am not sure what their precedent would be for a reigning Doge....skinning alive perhaps?"

Morosini laughed. His nephew was ever a wit and good company. "Best save my old energies for the Ottoman, I guess."

At the foot of the church steps, six savage looking black bulls were tethered by their nose rings - well apart from one another. The bulls had already left their own comments on the proceedings splattered all over the paving, so the Doge ordered his pages to raise high his ermine cloak. Though it was far from the end of its tether and could easily have gored him, he walked straight up to one of the snorting beasts and gave it an affectionate scratch under one of its ears. "There there, old soldier, I'll see that you get a drink. Orderly Officer!" he commanded, "See that these beasts are watered at once. They will suffer enough later. No need to add to their agony!"

Turning to Senator Loredan, just a few paces behind him, he queried why the Senate still approved of the barbaric practice of bull baiting.

"They are a gift from Milan, from the Spanish Viceroy. We can hardly offend him. Besides, our soft easy going youth needs a challenge. It will toughen them up for your next gory campaign, Doge Francesco. The Sensa Fair would not be the same without a bull run!"

"Maybe, maybe," the Doge replied, "but I would rather good blood were spilt in defending Christendom than in such a senseless sport. Venetian sinew is in short enough supply. You have sailed the Mediterranean, Loredan: we are outnumbered a thousand to one by the Muslims and we would do well always to remember it."

"I do remember it Serenissimo. I wake each day with my son's portrait before me. He was with you at Navarrino."

The Doge too had both wounds and bitter memories from the slaughter on that day and walked across to the Cuccagna, trying to put them out of mind with the pleasant sight before him. "Well, he is with the Good Lord now, Loredan, enjoying the bliss of heaven, no doubt. I sometimes think, Loredan, that we should take a leaf from the crafty Ottoman and promise our idle and reluctant youth six dozen houris apiece as their heavenly reward. That might help with recruiting!"

Loredan observed with a laugh, "Young Venetians are not so easily hoodwinked. Our young men would rather have a cabbage off the Cuccagna today than the promise of a harem in the hereafter. Besides, when I was Ambassador to the Sultan, a wise old Sufi assured me that educated Muslims don't really believe in the six dozen heavenly virgins. It suits their foaming-mouthed imam preachers of world conquest to keep that myth alive. What they were really promised by their Syriac speaking Prophet was not a heavenly bordello but a disappointing bowl of seventy two dried white grapes when they arrived through the pearly gates."

"Really? Raisins? Are you sure of that Loredan? In which case, we'll order the marines to shout back "raisins!" when they come at us like hell's demons shouting their blasphemies. God is great indeed, but it's my belief the Ottoman have mistaken Him for the fiery old fellow down below!"

"Raisins...that's a capital idea, Doge Francesco. However, we'd best inquire what the Turkic word for raisins is - the Ottoman are not likely to pause for a translation. According to my Sufic poet, the old Syriac word for raisin was 'huri,' hence the amusing confusion."

"Well I guess every religion has its element of the absurd, even our own, I suppose. Think what will happen to these poor bulls this evening, Loredan; yet they will be given a good blessing before being dispatched in the cruellest manner one can think of for a dumb beast."

Old Doge Francesco was as passionate in his care of animals, as was his namesake saint from Assisi. He kept his own herd of dairy cattle and was no happier than out and about in the countryside with his dogs and horses.

As for the poor bulls, towards evening, they too would be doused like the Doge with holy water before being released. The bull mastiffs would need no such blessing. They would spring, like the Doge's enemies, straight from hell at sundown. Urged on by daring young hotheads, the dogs would harry the poor beasts about the crowded Piazza and savage them until they collapsed and died a cruel and lingering death.

But first young bodies would be broken in the assault on the Cuccagna. That traditional spectacle would commence once the last bell of the Evening Angelus died away.

The Doge had almost completed his circuit before the last of the dignitaries had managed to tramp into the Square. He had processed under floral arches, had rose petals showered on him in abundance and paused frequently beneath his silk and gold thread umbrella to greet both friends and strangers along the route. The spectators crowding the windows of the State Offices enclosing three sides of the vast square had got their money's worth of splendour. Amongst them, having paid a sequin for each window seat, were Mr. Ravenscroft and his ship's officers. Their pleasure in the proceedings was greatly enhanced by a large zinc pail filled with rum and ice and the presence of a quartet of pretty young houris, though given their geographical location, they might better be classed as sea sirens. The harmony of their siren song may not have been of the best, but their real talents were of the kind that soon have a sailor parted with his purse and abandoned high and dry upon the rocks.

From the lofty gallery of the Doge's Campanile a rope cable a good four hundred feet long was being dragged out at an angle and tethered to an iron ring set in a great stone block near to the Basilica entrance. The cable had been greased and the team from the Arsenal were sweating and struggling to make it taut. The crowd had been primed in their chants by cheer leaders planted amongst them.... all carefully chosen for their loyalty by Bastian. As the Doge approached the vast mosaic encrusted portal of the Basilica, the two rival chants started up. "Peace, Peace - War, War!"

Quite puzzled by this turn of events, the Doge was invited by Bastian to go over to the stone block and to stop his ears with his fingers. The Doge looked up to where the rope seemed to disappear like a gossamer thread into the gallery of the tower. An earth-rending explosion echoed about the square and shook the ancient tower to its shallow foundations. Red and gold rockets shot upwards and outwards in all directions from the belfry gallery. Some, in their glittering arcs, spanned the wide Basin of St. Mark, landing on the Island of St. George. When the smoke cleared, the crowd gasped to see a golden angel balancing on the parapet of the belfry, some three hundred dizzy feet above the Piazza. The angel launched into the void, wings and arms spread wide. In her right hand she held a dove, blown and shaped from lattimo glass and set with coloured gemstones. In her left, a sword with a flame shaped red glass blade: a worthy imitation of the one that chased Adam and Eve out of Paradise. She slid headfirst down the rope at a terrifying speed. Hidden between her wings was a little trolley device of greased pulley wheels; even so she wobbled perilously as she whizzed over the lumpy splices in the great cable.

About her left ankle was a gilded leather thong that was looped around the cable. A scrap of whale brush was sewn on the inside of the loop and this brake she used to good effect to slow her descent, enabling her to land most gracefully almost at the feet of the Doge. She was a tall slender and angelic featured girl of about eighteen. Her head hair and limbs were gilded in pure gold leaf and seemed to merge with the stiffened cloth of gold from which her gown and wings were made. She was the incarnation of the great gilded bronze angel that still tops the pinnacle of the Doge's Campanile.

When the storm of applause died down, she extended her arms towards her sovereign lord and in so doing gave the Serenissimo his symbolic choice of war or peace. For the first few moments some female voices were heard to cry "Pace! Pace," but their faint chorus quickly gave way to a bloodlusting blizzard of roars from the baying throng. The paper masks of peace, merriment and good will to all mankind were instantly blown back to their heavenly abode. Ancient wrongs rose up in hoarse voiced rage; dead brothers in arms cried out from their watery graves for vengeance upon the hated Ottoman:"Guerra, Guerra….Guerrrra!" roared the mob.

The Doge, with feigned reluctance, accepted the flaming blood red sword. At this the crowd went into a frenzy of martial cries that slowly dissolved into rhythmic chants of "Mo-ro-si-no! Mo- ro- si- no! Guerra! Guerra! Guerra!"

In a scene of theatrical humility, the Doge removed his 'Corno' and placed it on the ground. He went down on both knees and pressed his forehead for some moments against the lowest step leading up to the Basilica. The whole occasion was of course a political charade. Venice had some months before entered into a grand alliance with Austria and Poland for a three pronged attack to drive the Ottoman once and for all out of Christian Europe. As he mumbled his prayers in St. Mark's two concerns nagged at his distracted mind: the declining strength and numbers of his land troops and the strong possibility that the French would resume their customary treacherous alliance with the Turk. That same morning he had received reports that a French count and his mercenaries had been appointed by the Grand Vizier to train the Sultan's Janissaries in the arts of modern artillery.

CHAPTER TWENTY

Makò was having his afternoon 'catnap' on a divan beneath a window in the ducal private apartments. He was oblivious to the magical beam of dappled sunlight streaming through the stained glass and making a kaleidoscope of coloured patterns about him. When the rockets went off he opened one eye, gave a deep rumbling snarl of annoyance and arched his back. A strong smell of saltpetre was in the air, the unmistakable call to duty: time now to scamper-up the main mast and out onto the topmost yard arm; there to spit defiance at the hordes of oncoming Ottoman. Or was it? Both ferocious eyes surveyed the empty room. His master had not disturbed his slumber; had dressed and left without him, which thoughtless act offended his feline feelings. It was nothing short of an outrage: in the hour of conflict they were duty bound to be close by one another. No matter; by following to their source the smells and sounds of gunfire, who else would he find but Doge Morosini? So it was that Makò sniffed the air, twitched his long upturned whiskers and in short shrift, bounded down the Giant's Stairway. Sidling close to the wall beneath the great Porta della Carta he trotted out into the packed Piazzetta where, tail held proud and erect, he 'hove to' with perfect timing at the side of his adoring patron. The Cardinal Patriarch of Venice had just descended the Basilica Steps, and with a grand gesture invited the Doge to rise up from his penitent pose and accept the 'Vexilla' the sacred standard of St. Mark.

Morosini clasped the staff of the sacred pennant in both hands and used it to lever himself up from his knees. A searing stab of pain went through his lower abdomen, but his wince of agony was cleverly transformed into a confident smile. Any sign of weakness at such a moment would not be befitting of a Captain General of the Serenissima. Makò was there to console him; he sensed his master's suffering and nuzzled up against his boots. The little 'Lion of St. Mark' had arrived just on cue and the old Doge bent down to scratch behind its ears. The touching scene of affection between wildcat and warrior doge moved the crowd to murmurings of pleasure and wonder. They felt it was a sign, a portent of heaven's approval, for both in size and outline Makò resembled the lion embroidered in yellow thread upon that faded red flag of forked linen. With that extra tuft of fur on the tip of his tail and a middle-aged tomcat mane, all Makò lacked was a pair of wings and a gospel book on which to rest his paw; an open book with PAX TIBI MARCE EVAGELISTA

MEUS incised upon its stony pages. (*Peace to you Mark my Evangelist.*)

Who could object when Makò took precedence by stalking up the aisle of the Basilica, his customary sword's length ahead of his master. Being top cat of the Serenissima had its privileges, the bows and flourishing of long laced sleeves were of course for him and when he curled up beneath the Doge's throne it was his way of indicating that it was high time for Vespers to get under way.

With Vitale's friendly, if heavyweight, right arm clasped about his shoulders, Zorzi was amongst the first to pass through that glass door leading from the terrace into the relative darkness of the choir loft. On close inspection the glass mosaic tessera of the church vault resembled gemstones set in burnished gold. Every arch, nook and surface was emblazoned with glittering mosaic bible scenes. In guessing that Aladdin's cave might look something like the inside of the Basilica, Zorzi was close to the truth. Many of the splendours of the interior had in fact been stolen long centuries before from far off Constantinople by that vengeful old blind Doge Dandolo.

Once his eyes had adjusted to the subdued light, Zorzi was able to make out the elegantly attired adult male choirs and the orchestras of musicians ranged on either side of the vaulted clerestory. Of the several vast and mosaic-ed arches high above the nave, only one was reserved for ladies and children of the court, even so they had by far the best view straight down the nave and over the top of the rood screen with the throne and Pala d'Oro in clear sight. The Countess and her entourage were now being ushered to their allotted seats just behind Zorzi and the children. Makò s reunion with the Doge had been out of sight from the outdoor terrace; consequently the cat's triumphal entry, to a fanfare of silver trumpets and his high tailed stalk up the aisle, left the boys and girls smothering their loud giggles. There were shushing hisses from the noblewomen and loud whispered demands that they should not lean too far over the low marble parapet. The Countess sent Ettore Martinengo, her 'Cavaliere Servante' to keep an eye on them. His overpowering presence and the occasional fearsome scowl was enough to ensure model behaviour from even the youngest. Both boys and girls were made to stand stiffly to attention for almost ten minutes whilst the Doge made his way to his throne.

A majestic figure in his golden armour and diamond encrusted Corno, the Doge paused for a moment beneath the crucifix of the rood screen holding out at arm's length the age-old spear and tattered standard of St. Mark that had once been planted on the walls of Constantinople and at Lepanto had fluttered proudly on the Doge's mainmast. He appeared almost as a symbolic Longinus: a sentinel at the gates of Christendom barring the way to all its enemies. The precious marble and bronze rood screen separated the clergy in the apse from the diplomatic congregation in the nave. It was a real obstruction to seeing the Doge, once he was enthroned; what's more, it made it difficult for those in the nave of the church to catch a glimpse of the fabulous Pala d'Oro. Fashioned from several tons of gold and enamel and set with some of the finest and most ancient jewels in the Western World, the Pala d'Oro, the golden altar panel, was the envy of every Ambassador present. It was also high on the Ottoman Sultan's shopping list, once his long planned visit to the Serenissima was accomplished.

"DIXIT DOMINUS, DOMINO MEO, SEDE A DEXTRIS MEIS..." (*The Lord said unto my lord, sit at my right hand till I make thine enemies my footstool.*) An incredibly high pitched and immensely powerful castrato voice rang out. It came bouncing back again and again from the many vaulted arches of the great church. Zorzi felt a tingling sensation in his hair. It was an unearthly bird-like, angel-like sound, sending shivers up his spine. The voice excited him, yet he felt cheated and angry on hearing his Psalm on another's lips. "When they already had a grown-up who could sing so well," he reasoned, "why did Zustinian cause all the trouble by selecting him as well? It was all a nasty trick. Grandpa must have known. That's why Grandpa was so angry: all those hours of practice, just to be tricked by Zustinian into singing rude songs on top of his rotten, fake wooden arch!"

The Psalm was sung as an invitation to the Doge to ascend to his throne. He bowed to the congregation, handed his tattered standard to the Cardinal Patriarch then disappeared behind the rood screen. Choir echoed choir, orchestra played back to orchestra, counter-tenor vied with tenor and soon the great Basilica was vibrating to the very depths of its mud filled crypt. Old Monteverdi knew to perfection how to use the acoustics of the ancient building. His setting of the Vespers transformed the Basilica into a wonderful echoing sound-box; into one great musical instrument fashioned from marble, brick and glass.

Zorzi found himself in such an exultant state that he lost all awareness of those around him. He was now as one voice with the nearby choir. Except for one brief moment when he lingered too long on an ending note, he kept in perfect tune and time. From time to time the choirmaster would sense a childlike voice and turn to gaze in astonishment across to the distant glittering vault. Vitale and the other young aristocrats shrank back; yet the talented young interloper intrigued them and quite enchanted not only by his fantastic voice, but that he seemed at such ease with all the long Latin verses. They had all struggled unwillingly with Latin tutors. The ladies of the court ceased puffing and fanning themselves in the stuffy heat. They craned forward, eager to catch a better glimpse of the strange little Morosini songbird and whispered to one another: " Such an extraordinarily tuneful voice, but oh so undignified!"

"Performing in public and in such an attention seeking way, is not the sort of thing one should encourage in a young male child of the family! But who the devil's child is he?"

"One of the hard-up Friuli branch, I expect. You can tell from the dusky tan; half peasants I'm told. It's rumoured that they actually farm the land themselves. Quite, quite disgraceful!"

The ladies may have been perplexed, but in the mind of the Countess everything now fell perfectly into place. This was yet another of Bastian's tasteless pranks. She had sent back that very suit of court dress, which was in excess of requirements, because one of her grandchildren had not turned up for the Christmas festivities. The little Jewish tailor, who burned the midnight oil exclusively for her, had the effrontery to request payment for it. Naturally she had refused. Who else, other than Bastian, knew of the tailor's upper floor workshop in the Ghetto? Who else but Bastian had a weakness for the company of little choirboys? Only he could have smuggled the child through the heavy security and up into the ducal grandstand. She would find some way to get back at her nephew for this jape. The child she felt pity for, knowing what his fate might be if left with Bastian - either catamite, or castrato, or both. She greatly disapproved of her nephew's failings, for they were unmanly for a nobleman of such exalted ancestry. However, a noble was free to take his

216

pleasure where he wished so long as it was with the lower orders of society.

Once Vespers were ended she would have the child spirited away. He seemed a harmless enough little creature. Evidently he was educated and seemed better conversant with Latin than any of her brood. Despite the coarse peasant tan and skinny build; the child still had quite a handsome little face. Once taught some manners, he might fit in well as a household servant. When Bastian made his next courtesy call on her at Palazzo Santo Stefano she would produce the little boy at a concert then sit back and enjoy Bastian's squirming embarrassment.

The wonderfully long held notes of the 'Gloria' resounded and echoed away into silence, thus ending the Vespers. Zorzi snapped out of his musical trance and realized from the whisperings of those around him that he had been identified as a gatecrasher. He decided to make a quick dash past the elderly, but very athletic looking, Uncle Ettore and to get down the stairs before anyone could lay hands on him. Should his pursuers get too close when chasing him down the steep stairway, he would swing his satchel and try to trip their ankles. However, there was one more piece of theatre still to be performed in the church that would be his salvation.

Makò much preferred the crackle of gunfire. He had no ear for human caterwauling; no appreciation of the finer points of baroque music, nor of tenor answering counter-tenor, nor of trumpets, flutes, harpsichords and other such un-cattish noise making machines. They sent him straight off to deep sleep; from which a friendly boot in the ribs had now aroused him. He stretched, licked his long white whiskers and crawled out from under the throne of the Serenissimo. Was it time perhaps to lead his master into some new salty and smoke-filled adventure?

The Head of The Ten came forward and solemnly lifted a heavy gold field marshal's baton, cased with red turtle shell, from the altar table. With numerous other Senators in close attendance, he knelt on one knee before the Doge and symbolically offered him the command of the Venetian armies. The Doge stood and made a humble gesture in pretence of being unworthy of the honour now being accorded to him. The Senator insisted and offered the baton once again at arm's length. Fifteen white masked Senators then rose to their feet from amidst the throng extending

217

their hands dramatically with upturned palms for all to see that it was the will of The Ten, something that not even a Doge would be wise to refuse. As he placed an accepting hand on the baton, The Ten, the Senators and Court Officials, the choirs, the congregation and all within earshot of the basilica broke spontaneously into song. It was that shiver-making, somewhat terrifying war anthem of the Christian world, once heard on the lips of both advancing Roman Legionaries and of Crusader Knights - " VEXILLA REGIS PRODEUNT" *(Vexilla, a powerful Latin word, means both legionary standard, cohort and attacking army. The word vexing derives from it. Approx. trans. - 'The banner of (Christ) the King goes forward.)*

His hoarse old voice joining lustily in the battle hymn, the Doge processed towards the great west door with all the dazzling pomp of long forgotten Byzantium: cardinals and croziers, thurifers and generals, acolytes and ambassadors came tailing on behind.

The Doge's Cat scampered to his official position, taking precedence and pride of place ahead of all the mere mortals in the procession. Makò was half way up the aisle when, with an eardrum splitting roar, a siege gun went off. An elderly moggie, who had not seen action since the siege of Malvasia Castle in 1689, could be forgiven for his earlier mistake when Bastian's puny bell tower rockets were fired. Catty instinct and much past experience convinced Makò that at long last a full scale assault was in progress somewhere up ahead. It was his duty as official ship's ratter to beat to his battle station with all speed. He bounded down the aisle and was half way up the curtains of the great west door when the second gun went off. A third thunderous roar sent him clawing his way amidst the flower swags and trophies, some forty feet above the heads of the processing noblemen; hissing and spitting at all below with full feline ferocity.

The Doge could not contain his laughter, nor could the Senators, and high above their heads in the gallery, the Morosini children laughed even louder. The Cardinal Patriarch and his bevy of bishops and clerics tut-tutted their annoyance. The performance of Vespers was quite the finest they had attended for many years. This sacrilegious finale, provided by the Doge's vicious moggie, had quite ruined the solemnity of the occasion.

When he emerged into the Piazza, gold baton in hand and invested with the authority of both Church and Senate, it was customary for the Doge to be saluted with salvos from seven modest sized guns. These were usually ship's iron cannon, resting on simple wooden blocks and pointing out seawards from the Molo, the embankment just in front of Marco and Todaro's columns. Bastian, ever eager to impress the crowds, had arranged for three huge bronze cannon to take their place. These were of little value militarily and would probably have exploded if filled with shot, but they were magnificently cast and decorated with tigers and dragons, elephant gods and six-armed Shivas. They had been captured by a Venetian galley whilst on their way from India - a present from the Mughal Emperor to the Turkish Sultan. When they blasted off, they deafened bystanders in the Piazzetta, shook tiles from the palace roof and set mothers consoling infants who were wailing with fright and ear ache. Bastian's other tasteful contribution to the proceedings was in the process of being torn to bits by Makò in his attempt to reach a vantage point from which to observe the bombardment and siege which, in feline fantasy, was now in full swing. Makò had clawed his way to the extreme end of the great garland festoon of flowers, flags and battle trophies dangling above the west door. The festoon was strung to a thick rope attached at either end to the balcony where the children were standing. Leaning over perilously would be a better description of what they were doing, for the marble balustrade was little higher than a child's waist. Makò had reached the point of no return. His bravado and angry hissings had suddenly evaporated and as he thrashed about amongst the flowers, he let out helpless meowing pleas to be rescued.

To their great annoyance, the children were ordered back from the exciting scene and sent grumbling to their seats. How were they to know that the copper pins and plaster holding the marble balcony panels together had long rotted away? Zorzi however ignored the orders of the Cavaliere and embarked on a dubious rescue plan. He opened up his satchel. An overpowering pong of warm Parmesan cheese, blended with rotting anchovy, wafted downwards towards Makò and upwards to the nostrils of the haughty noblewomen. It made the Cavaliere reel back in disgust, but it was irresistible to a greedy cat and tempted Makò to clamber further upwards to the very end of the festoon rope. There he dangled, desperately trying to get a grip on the swaying rope with his hind legs. Zorzi leaned over as far as he dared, dangling a tempting anchovy, but Makò was just too far below out of reach. Fortunately for Zorzi, a swift firm hand grasped him by the belt of his breeches, yanking him fully off his feet.

"Get back boy. The balcony isn't safe. It could easily collapse!"
When Zorzi turned to see who had grabbed him, he was astonished to come face to face with the first negro he had ever set eyes upon. He was Abele, the Doge's umbrella carrier and general factotum. Abele was a friendly familiar figure to the little Morosinis, but to Zorzi it was as though a genie had leapt up behind him straight from the pages of Sinbad. Noticing Zorzi's open mouthed astonishment, Abele remarked, " Don't look so surprised young master, I'm a genuine black man all over; not one of your wooden blackamoors lighting up the landing stage. You've done your best. Now let's see what I can do to entice the little hellcat further up. He's not too keen on boys: nor on me for that matter. He claws like a goshawk and bites like a cobra, so best keep well back when I catch him.

Abele unwound the cummerbund from around his waist and taking a couple of Zorzi's anchovies, he knotted them into the end of the long length of blue and yellow silk. Taking great care he leaned over the crumbling balustrade panel and dangled his knotted cummerbund in front of Makò , who instantly took the bait. Taking great care, Abele raised the cummerbund with the cat attached until it was level with the handrail of the balustrade. But Makò s ingratitude to his rescuer knew no limits. When Abele tried to grab him, he arched his back, hissed ferociously then spat at him waving angrily the tip end of his tail. He then threatened to leap back into the void. Zorzi broke off a piece of Parmesan and offered it on the palm of his hand. Makò first sniffed Zorzi for friendly pheromones then inhaled deeply the delicious cheese smell. Still balanced precariously on the handrail he set to and polished off the Parmesan. As he licked the last crumb from Zorzi's hand another bigger chunk was produced for him to tuck into: a smelly anchovy followed it down nicely. His repast complete, he licked his paws, rearranged his fine white whiskers and condescended to let Zorzi tickle his ears.

Abele was impressed. The prospect of being bitten and ripped by those talons as he carried the cat down the long stairway was not one to relish. He suggested to Zorzi that he might oblige. Zorzi talked quietly to the cat and stroked it, as he would have done had he met it by chance in an alleyway. He had long desired to have a cat. Grandpa would have liked one too, both to keep the rats out of the privy and from gnawing at the packaging paper in his workshop: but cats were expensive creatures and hard to obtain. Where moreover, would they find food enough for a cat? Whatever Grandpa fished from the Lagoon was essential to his and Zorzi's survival.

"What's he called?" Zorzi asked.

"Makò ," Abele replied.

Thinking that Abele had mispronounced the name, Zorzi commented, "Marco. That's a good name for a big fierce cat: just like Saint Mark's big golden lion, except that he is grey and black, but he has a lovely white face and chest. It's almost like a lion's mane."

"Not sure I'd use the word lovely," commented Abele. "I think he is jealous of my big black face. Whatever; you had better be careful handling him, he is, I promise you, quite vicious. By the way his name is Makò , not Marco. My Doge may be a bit of an old blasphemer, but even he would not call his cat after our Patron Saint. Makò is near enough, I suppose; it's the name given to that sort of linen cloth they use for making sails. They found him hiding under a fallen sail soon after his mother and the other kittens were swept overboard."

"Come along Makò !" Zorzi ordered and wrapped his arms about the unresisting cat.

Makò went limp and compliant. He licked Zorzi's salty ear and quite liked the faint odours of fish, ship's tar and lavender perfume still lingering on Zorzi's body from his morning adventures. For his part Zorzi quickly realized that the cat would provide him with a perfect excuse to get away from what was now an embarrassing and rather threatening situation. Vitale was now studying him with puzzled and far from friendly eyes.

"Would you be kind enough to carry my satchel?" he asked the negro.

Abele obliged, and Zorzi followed him out of the Basilica loft and down the steeply pitched stairway. Being a pampered and well-fed fighting tomcat, Makò was quite a heavyweight to carry and Zorzi had to take each uneven step sideways in order to avoid tumbling headlong. Zorzi soothed and talked to the cat all the while and was so occupied in making friends with it that he failed to notice that he was being followed. When they reached the narthex, the church porch, it was still filled with the smoke and acrid smell of the Mughal cannons. The congregation was now spilling out in noisy disorder after the formal procession. A good hearty cough and a pinch of snuff soon cleared the lungs of most of them and they stood around chatting in the narthex whilst outside in the Piazza yet another parade awaited the Doge's inspection. It was drawn up in a long rectangle beneath the tall flagstaffs of the beautiful loggia at the base of the bell tower. The parade was composed of one hundred and sixty-seven tall and vigorous looking young seventeen to eighteen year olds. These were the select, the privileged few, who would man the oars of the Bucintoro; for on the following day, the feast of the Sensa, the Doge would ride out in his glorious golden barge to 'marry the sea.'

A shrill barked out command: "Stand at ease!" cut through the deafening din of the crowd.

With a great clanking of armour and thudding of halberds on the pavement, the noble young bucks obeyed with smartness and swagger. They now stood legs apart, halberds extended, each sweating with fear that the Doge might stop to criticize some defect in his 'turnout,' but at the same time hoping that Morosini would not pass by without stopping to say a word, or at the very least give a nod of recognition. An encouraging comment from the Doge might lead to the command of a war galley. For the less courageous, a ducal smile of approval might brighten the prospect of an appointment as Podestà of some godforsaken town in Dalmatia. It was important to their noble families that the youngsters cut a fine figure on the parade ground. For that purpose they were tricked out with the finest leather, silk and lace that ducats could buy. Only their axe-head and spike tipped halberds were from the Palace Armoury. None of the famous set of halberds was identical: each had been fretted and gold damascened with exquisite scenes of murder and mayhem; each a minor masterpiece of deadly art and a coveted part of the treasury of the Serenissima. Their own three-quarter suits of mostly Toledo etched and gilded plate armour were family heirlooms. Far too splendid and fancy for use in battle, they

222

were designed strictly for such parades and of course to catch the admiring eyes of noble young ladies.

Through the sulphurous fumes and stench of human sweat, Makò picked up the distinctive scent of his master. He leapt from Zorzi's arms, ran headlong through the crowd and shot between the 'at ease' legs of one of the youthful oarsmen. He responded to a thorough ducal scolding by giving the ermine trimmings of the Doge's cloak the same treatment that he might mete-out to a cornered rat. Honour satisfied, his head and tail returned to the correct upright position for a general review of the guard of honour. This he performed with great solemnity, pausing here and there to sniff around a boot or two and to biff his disapproval with open paw at the odd excessive display of blue and yellow silk ribbon about the calves of the young lordlings.

Zorzi wanted to go after him, but he was held back once again by Abele and told not to disturb the parade.

"You have done well enough by carrying him down for me, young Sir. Another child might have got his eyes scratched. I shall inform the Serenissimo that it was you who rescued Makò. Now please get back up to your family. You don't want to get lost in the crowd.... may I ask your name?"

"Zorzi, Zorzi Miotti," came the surprising answer.

"Not Morosini, not Gritti? How very odd! I have never met anyone from the Miotti family. Are you in the Golden Book? The Serenissimo presumes that I should know all about everyone he has to greet." *(The Golden book with the names of the thousand or so Venetian noble families was closed in the year 1298. From then on, with few exceptions, only those families had the right to vote in the Assembly and to elect the Doge and State Officials. Napoleon had the Golden Books destroyed, with much else of Venetian history, when he conquered the Veneto in 1797. By then the family trees of the nobility had filled four enormous library cupboards.)*

Abele's gentle restraining hand was suddenly struck away and replaced with one clad in embroidered leather. The Noble Cavalier Ettore

Martinengo di Bergamo, bodyguard to the Countess, almost crushed Zorzi's left shoulder with his fearsome grip. Zorzi twisted round and infuriated, glared up to confront his tormentor.

"Let go of me, damn you, you are hurting!" he squealed.

"The little gentleman has been of great help to me. My Doge will be displeased to hear of it... so kindly don't hurt the child," Abele pleaded. Abele would have liked to intervene as Zorzi squirmed and struggled, but he was enough of a survivor not to challenge further the immensely powerful nobleman. Though stockily built with the muscles of an ex-galley slave, Abele was a good head and shoulders shorter than the Countess's 'bravo.' Any Venetian with an ounce of common sense would have known that Martinengo was a law unto himself - quite untouchable. Those of his own rank knew that it was never wise to cross him, for he had the authority of the Countess backing his every whim. It was whispered too that The Ten gave him commissions to fillet with his rapier the odd misbehaving foreigner who proved too difficult for them to get rid of by diplomatic means. He was the only man permitted by The Ten to walk fully armed in public, as it was not unknown for the Turks to kidnap and hold to ransom high ranking noblewomen: though the Countess Morosina Morosini would certainly have made a sharp boned and somewhat withered prize amidst the plump young pulchritude of the Sultan's harem.

"You have some explaining to do young man. The Countess wishes to speak with you at once. Carrying the cat was a clever wheeze. Now forget any plan you may have for slinking away."

"All right, I promise I won't run off. Just let me put my satchel on my shoulder."

Abele helped him on with the heavy satchel whilst the Cavaliere transferred his grip to the back of Zorzi's fine lace cravat. What neither had calculated on was that Denis was not only a Dominican novice but also a hopeless novice in tying cravats. Zorzi jerked forward and bounded away leaving the confounded Martinengo with a yard or so of boyless Burano lace in his leather gauntlet. With the lightening reflex of a consummate swordsman he leapt after him.

224

Zorzi, however, had noticed Makò s preferred method of escape and dived even faster between the armoured legs of one of the Bucintoro's oarsmen. The unfortunate young nobleman, caught in a moment of complete relaxation, was struck hard by Zorzi's satchel in that little weak spot just behind the knee. He crumpled backwards onto the Cavaliere and both sprawled in a heap on the parade ground. His halberd stood on its end, unsupported for a second or so, then did a fine pirouette in the air and slammed down on them both with a mighty whack.

Doge Morosini was about to present an Osella, a specially minted gold coin, to one of the young men who had just distinguished himself in an attack on a village of Dalmatian pirates. He turned and caught sight of a little boy dressed in his own family livery, sprinting away from the two felled warriors, and then disappearing on the other side of the parade ground between the lines of startled young halberdiers.

"Well, well, well!" he commented wryly. "At long last someone has managed to floor Martinengo and that, if I am not mistaken, is the plump young Querini knocked out cold. The little fellow who has just run away seems therefore to be 'one-up' on King David. He felled only one giant, if I remember correctly! Perhaps the little lad thought it was time a young Morosini challenged a Querini for his place on the Bucintoro? Now get up the two of you! Anyone would think you were in love!"

The Doge's sarcasm had the whole clanking armour clad parade convulsed with obsequious laughter. Not having the foggiest idea of what had gone wrong, the crowd in the square joined in the merriment, out of dutiful respect for the Doge.

Old Senator Querini was deeply offended by the Doge's quips at the expense of his humiliated and flattened grandson and began fanning his hot puffy face to conceal his fury. One day, he vowed, he would get even with the Morosini clan.

Meanwhile young Querini was slowly coming to his senses, assisted by the apologetic Cavaliere, who was equally furious with himself at having been outwitted by a mere child. The spinning halberd had landed point first on the flimsy and decorative Querini family parade helmet and had come close to braining their luckless grandson. 'Hard man' Martinengo was on his feet in a trice. Bowing low several times to the Doge, he edged swiftly around the outside of the parade. But he had lost both time and the initiative. Whilst barging his way through the crowd, his great stature and fearsome appearance gave him the advantage, but Zorzi knew well how to beat a hasty retreat. So, despite a careful search of the Piazza and its side alleys and shops, the invincible 'Prince of all Bravi' found himself baffled and beaten by a little runaway boy. Exasperated, he gave up on the search and went to confess his failure to the Countess.

Zorzi meanwhile was stuffing his face with strawberry flan at the back of a baker's shop in a little alleyway near the church of San Zulian. (*St. Julian*) He was seated on a low milking stool well hidden behind the counter and having regained his breath, after a long dash through the warren of alleyways north of the Piazza; he took his time whilst enjoying the juicy cake. The baker's young wife sat amidst the flyblown flans, stale cakes and loaves, admiring Zorzi's beautifully tailored suit. She recognized the gold buttons with the unique Morosini crest and envied the fine lace sprouting from his boots and cuffs. No other Doge before Morosini had been allowed to display a personal coat of arms during his reign, so even a humble baker's wife would have instantly recognized the 'Sabre impaling a Turk's Head' that the Doge had chosen as his tasteful device.

Zorzi was quite the most exotic customer ever to have patronized her shop. When he dashed in, obviously trying to hide from someone, she mistook him for a bag thief, but when he bowed to her and opened his satchel so confidently to display his wealth, she curtsied to him as gracefully as a young plebeian could manage and did him the honour of charging three times the price that one of her commoner customers would have paid. Offering the milking stool as a perch, she inquired if he was in any difficulty. Her shop was on the boundary of the two terrible street gangs that had plagued the alleyways of Venice from time immemorial. She paid 'protection money' to the Castellani whereas the black shuttered shops on the other side of the street were on Nicolotti territory. Naturally, she assumed that the Nicolotti had tried to rob Zorzi and it should therefore have been her right and duty to 'whistle up' protection for this lost little nobleman with all possible speed, but she did not do so. With her big colourful paper fan she continued with her unending task of driving the swarms of flies away back into their breeding ground, which was the cow byre at the rear end of the shop.

"You can't make cream cakes without cow dung," she explained awkwardly and, playing for time until her errand boy brother returned, she offered to show him the cow. "We had two cows, but one died recently," she added. "My good husband sold the carcass to a glue maker and bought me this lovely dress."

She straightened proudly her crumpled, tight fitting and somewhat discoloured red cloth garment. The bodice was so low cut that whoever stitched it together must have had in mind the baker's urgent need to sell loaves to any passing male trade.
Zorzi patted the pathetic under-sized cow. It shuffled so mournfully in its own filth and in semi-darkness at the back of the shop, hardly ever having the energy to moo. He asked how they fed it, since he had only seen cows grazing happily in the wet grasslands beyond the orchards in Murano.

"Hay, stale bread and plenty of water," came the answer. "Would you like a nice glass of warm milk? She asked. "It will only cost a bagatt…that is four bagattini, I mean.""

Having seen the dire and dirty state of the poor creature, even Zorzi's leather-lined guts baulked at the offer. "I should like to buy a loaf, if you please," he asked. "I need to get to the Sacca della Misericordia before the Angelus bell. My friend is going to meet me there and I expect he will be hungry. Do you by any chance know the way?"

"Just wait a while. Unless you know the back alleys really well, it will take you till long after the Angelus to find your way. By that time it will be dark. My young brother will have finished his bread round any time now. I'll ask him. He might ferry you there in his sandolo. We don't often see young gentlemen like you in these parts and there are some nasty folk, robbers and the like coming from the mainland, especially at Sensa time."

It had crossed her mind that with the help of her villainous young brother and some of his pals in the Castellani gang, she might solve all her problems by robbing and disposing of Zorzi in some quiet backwater. Both she and her brother had been 'sold' to redeem an old family debt with the baker. For the last three of her eighteen years, the cruelty and caprices of her near senile husband; the endless monotony of flicking flies and trying to 'palm off' yesterday's stale bread to customers had almost completely addled her wits. She had longed for some handsomely dressed young nobleman to saunter by, take a shine to her red dress and carry her off to a better life. At long last one had fluttered in, as lost and defenceless as a mayfly in a cobweb. The noble child was far too young to notice her charms, but his clothes, second-hand, might fetch ten sequins in the Ghetto. That heavy satchel could well be stuffed with gold coin. With no thought in her mind of that rope dangling between Marco and Todaro, she felt confident that once poor Zorzi was disposed of, she could slip away in the baker's sandolo and make a new life with the wild Uskok folk in some village along the coast of Dalmatia. That foul tempered old husband, who snored all night and woke her at four in the morning to light the baking ovens, might even get the blame for her disappearance. Every neighbour knew of the beatings she got from him.

Zorzi heard the bump of the baker boy's boat and jumped down from the milking stool to greet him with a bow as he entered. The heavily built juvenile was red faced and flustered, obviously in a foul mood, having his basket still laden with unsold bread, amidst which for some reason was buried his red Castellani cap. He suddenly cheered up when he took stock of Zorzi and his handsome outfit. Zorzi instantly offered to pay him well to be rowed to the Misericordia. To his sister's great dismay he agreed to take Zorzi there without further delay. Knowing her brother to be by nature an idle, charmless and disobliging youth, she was quite taken aback by this sudden keenness. Before she could even attempt to whisper her devilish plan to him, he had taken Zorzi by the arm and whisked him into the sandolo. Offering to help with the rowing, Zorzi dumped his bag and the loaf beneath the bow thwart of the flat-bottomed sandolo.

"No need," came the reply. "I know the quickest way there and I'm in a bit of a hurry myself. We'll go by the back canals. That way we'll keep well out of the crowds."

The baker's boy set off at a furious pace rowing up the Rio San Zulian towards the nearest bridge. There he dipped both oars deep and brought the boat to a sudden stop in the shadows of the arch. Peering cautiously out at the other side of the bridge, he announced, "Nicolotti swine! Have to go careful!"

But all too soon it became apparent that he was lying low from his own gang in order to save his skin. As they approached the next bridge, a band of vicious looking youth suddenly appeared with cudgels and sticks, red hats and sashes of various dirty hues and shapes, and steel capped clogs. They were dressed in their finest rags and were evidently on their way to do battle with their rivals in the Piazza. The baker's boy ducked low and tried to hide his face, but he was spotted.

"Eh-oh! It's Lardon! Where are you sneaking off to Lardon? That's the wrong way! Turn about and follow us!" they yelled out.

"Can't just yet....got this boy to ferry... someone important! Meet you at the Cuccagna... later on!" the baker's boy yelled back.
"Stinking coward....pulled the same disappearing trick last year!" one of the youths jeered back. "Scared the Nicolotti will beat you to peach pulp. We'll do the same if you don't turn up! Spread you like the fat lard you are on one of your mouldy loaves! Remember, be with us at the Cuccagna!"

Lardon turned in desperation to Zorzi, "Tell them it's true. Say something or else they are going to beat me up; please!" he pleaded. Ever willing to oblige, Zorzi stood up in the bow of the sandolo, straightened his coat unhurriedly and struck what he thought was an aristocratic pose. Pointing a firm finger at the gaggle of ruffians on the bridge he announced, "I am Giorgio de Brayda, guest of Countess Morosina. If any of you lay so much as a finger on my servant here, err...signor Lardon, I shall have you all whipped! Is that clear?"

'Signor Lardon' was an unfortunate choice of words. The crowd fell about with laughter; mocking Zorzi by repeating his idle threat and pretending to whip one another. One of them bowed low to signor Lardon then hurled a heavy cobble stone that skimmed off the gunwale sending splinters flying just inches from where Zorzi stood firm. The lads were out looking for mischief and now they had found a perfect sitting target. More stones began to fly though they were not aimed deliberately at Zorzi. He however neither flinched, like the baker's boy did, nor ducked at the hail of stones. This show of bravado impressed the tougher

229

members of the mob.

Deciding that whipping was perhaps too mild a punishment to have in mind, now that stones were being hurled, Zorzi shouted above the din and insults: "What's more, my Uncle Ettore, the Cavaliere, will be sent to get each and every one of you! I hope you all know who he is? He will skewer you on the end of his rapier; I promise you! So I hope none of you is in a hurry to die... is that understood?"

Despite his diminutive stature, it was a fine performance. The mob admired his pluck. But what struck home harder than any cobblestone was that threat of the Cavaliere. Zorzi had not the faintest idea who the Cavaliere really was. In the crowd, however, quite a few did know and promptly urged the stone throwers to 'pack it in' and move on. Good fortune ever walked in Zorzi's shadow. By pure chance he had threatened them with the wrath of their local landlord. Many of them came from nearby Calle *(alley)* Martinengo and the prospect of punishment and eviction was not an inviting one. Growling like licked curs, the band of hooligans moved off from the bridge and slunk along the towpath towards better fun: that of pitching-in to their black-hatted Nicolotti adversaries in the Piazza. Zorzi's threat of unleashing Cavaliere Martinengo brought Lardon to his senses as well. He too had harboured thoughts similar to those of his sister, on first sight of Zorzi. Numbskull though he was; he too was now impressed and intimidated by the little nobleman's fearsome connections. Grateful in his own churlish way for the protection Zorzi had afforded him, he now began to add a grovelling 'Vostra Signoria,' *(Your Lordship)* after almost every other word he spoke: this he grunted out as 'Vozzignoria.'

They rowed on under several other handsome stone bridges and were soon in amongst a warren of narrow canals, too small and too tortuous even for a gondola to pass. Other than the occasional wooden bridge spanning high above their heads, connecting together ancient tumbledown dwellings, there was no access by footpath and no prospect of further trouble. Lardon pointed out the palaces of numerous noble families, while Zorzi nodded knowingly, pretending to be familiar with their names. What came as something of a surprise to Zorzi was that, unlike Murano where there were rich and poor districts, here gigantic and noble palaces and crumbling old neglected tenements stood side by side with hardly a gap. Like old comrades of unequal rank returning after a night of drunken revelry, they seemed to prop one another up, stagger backwards, or lurch over on their rotting piles towards the canal at their feet. Should one have fallen, a whole district might well have crumbled with it into muddy rubble. Zorzi noticed too that many of the finest palace facades with their pink marble columns, polished landing steps and white pointed gothic arches and windows could never be seen properly by anyone, because they were so tucked away in such narrow, stinking and rubbish filled backwaters. He guessed rightly that they had all once stood in their own grounds, which over the centuries had been sold off to make money for the noble family.

When eventually they emerged into the crowded 'Canal of the Jesuits,' which directly connected the Northern banks of the Lagoon to the Grand Canal, Lardon's surly and aggressive self-confidence flooded back in full measure. He kicked away, bumped, swore at, or whacked with his oar any boat obstructing his way forward. And so it was that they made rapid progress through the chaotic floating market of peasants' produce which was moored on either side of the *Rio dei Gesuiti.* Great bundles of firewood, punnets of strawberries, copper pots, tubs of honey, butter, turnips and cheap wine turning to vinegar were displayed on board the long rows of mostly battered and unseaworthy craft. Lardon forged ahead like a battering ram, cursing and blaspheming, while Zorzi turned down with lordly gestures to left and right the endless bargains offered to him for purchase. Turning left into St. Catherine's Canal, *Rio di S. Catarina,* a brief and fairly unobstructed five minute row brought them to the great square shaped harbour known as the Sacca della Misericordia.

Lardon tied up to a mooring post and helped Zorzi to scramble on to the slippery landing stage. There they sat together on a stone mooring bollard while Zorzi released once again a rich and powerful stench from his satchel. After fishing out a generous handful of bagattini, Zorzi expected Lardon to row off in his sandolo, but the baker's boy seemed no longer to be in great hurry. He sat there occasionally spitting into the water, cursing and grumbling about the life of drudgery imposed on him by that awful brother-in-law. He hinted that someone like 'Vozzignoria' might take him on, as he was looking for a new and easy going master who knew how to treat generously a hard working and trusty lad like himself.

Now Zorzi was quick to notice the gleaming piggy eyes focusing on his satchel as he grubbed inside for the money. For the first time it dawned on him that this ugly big character beside him might have plans to rob him and was hanging around for that reason. He needed to think carefully how to get rid of this unpleasant companion without giving him cause for anger. Doling out more money might only provoke him to snatch what little was left. There was no sign yet of Piero and the shameful thought came to mind that when his dirt poor and very ragged old friend turned up and hailed him as Zorzi, the illusion of being a nobleman's son would quickly evaporate. After all, being able to quell mobs with a few words of firm authority, being treated with great respect and called 'Vozzignoria' was quite a pleasant new experience.

After a long and silent think, the solution came to him. Evidently the baker's boy was a coward at heart: the best plan therefore would be to scare the wits out of him and convince him that the battle with the rival Nicolotti gang for the prize of the Cuccagna was much the better prospect.
"I think someone will have reported to Uncle Ettore that you were seen helping me escape. Please don't tell anyone where I have gone. You see, I'm running away. I'm running away from my family to join the crew of The Raven... it's an English warship with hundreds of guns.... having a refit in the Arsenal after battling the Turks. The crew are English pirates, you know, the kind who cut your throat if they don't fancy the look of you. You should be be all right though, I know the captain, a fierce brigand called the Corvo Nero. He's all right to me, but I reckon even Uncle Ettore would be scared of him. I happen to know that he is looking for tough hard working lads like you, who are brave enough to man the top rigging in a storm. What do you think? I promise, it will be an exciting life; much more fun than a boring baker's round?"

Lardon did not have to think long to find his excuses: "Well, Vozzignoria will understand that I can't easily leave my poor sister all on her own alone.... with no one to protect her, Vozzignoria, from her wicked husband Vozzignoria."

He coughed and spat several times, "Besides, Vozzignoria will have noticed my lungs.... no good at all for climbing, Vozzignoria, full of flour dust,Vozzignoria. Would love to come but..."

232

"What a pity. I shall miss you a lot. And sadly you will be missing all the fun when Captain Corvo gets back to Siracuse. He's furious with what happened to his ship. The Turks sprang him while he was laden down with cargo. Once his Arsenal refit is done, he's sailing back to Siracuse with a cargo of cannon balls. He'll go at them all guns blazing, I can tell you! Sure you won't come?"

"Well, Vozzignoria, I'd like to but…"

Zorzi screwed up his eyes against the evening dazzle and peered out across the Lagoon to where a number of distant craft were sailing in their direction. "I do believe that's The Raven's longboat," he announced, "Trouble with these English pirates is that they sometimes kidnap young men like you when they are short of a crew…"

Without so much as a 'Vozzignoria,' Lardon leapt down from the bollard, jumped into his boat and with a furious flurry of oars was gone.

The Angelus was rung with special enthusiasm that evening: almost every belfry in Venice joining in the merry din. As the last chimes died on the evening breeze there came a long, deep and throaty roar from the distant Piazza. Had ten thousand mountain bears emerged simultaneously from their gloomy dens they could hardly have made such a fearful bellow. The competing delinquents of the city charged headlong at one another brandishing their staves. Though the wooden frame of the Cuccagna was jointed by some of the best shipwrights in the Arsenal, it could only withstand the shock of the assault for a few minutes before toppling like a giant glittering fir tree, spilling its bounty all over its pillagers. That splendid sugar spun model of the Bucintoro was nobody's prize. It lay shattered into tiny crystals on the flagstones of the Piazza, trampled down amidst the debris of carrots and cabbages, flour and game birds, halves of smoked ham and broken barrels of wine.

There was little or no movement on the Northern Lagoon that evening. The fishing fleet that Zorzi had noticed earlier drifted gently past, trailing its nets on the way home to Chioggia Port. The sun blazed its way slowly downwards transmuting on its way the muddy waters of the Lagoon into an exquisite honey gold shade, tinting with salmon pink and darker indigo the far off hills. Zorzi watched out with growing anxiety for Piero's little blue cross-keyed pennant, but it did not come. In an all too brief twilight the silhouette of a lone gondola could be seen moving swiftly from briccola to briccola, lighting the oil lamps that marked the safest channels across the Lagoon. Soon too the Murano lighthouse would beckon to him in vain and on the horizon the gigantic watch tower of Malghera would create the deception of a long lingering sunset with its bonfire of a beacon. To travellers arriving by night from over the Alpine passes it would serve as a welcoming guide towards that ferry port. A flicker of wine red light now gleamed malevolent eyes through the wrecked window frames of the Ca` degli Spiriti, a ruined mansion at the far end of the pier on the opposite bank of the harbour. Zorzi knew of the mansion's ghostly infamy from old Piero. Now there was no Piero to chuckle loudly at his fears and the haunted ruin of Ca` degli Spiriti was all too creepily close.

With the advancing shadows Zorzi's cheerful self-confidence began to ebb away. Piero's overloaded boat might easily have been capsized in a bump with some other craft in the crowded canals. He knew that like so many other fisher folk, his old friend had never learned to swim. Then there was that mysterious gondola to worry about, so obviously trailing behind them from Murano. He now realized it was very much like the one he had spied following the Raven's longboat along the moonlit Glassblowers' Canal. In all the excitement of the blustery morning's sailing and with thoughts so occupied with the Sensa Fair, he had forgotten to warn old Piero about it- for that he now felt guilty. Anxiety about his own safety now gripped him. Jumping down from the stone bollard he tried to make his way in almost impenetrable gloom along the quayside. Where would he find shelter for the night? The shops were barred and shuttered. Here and there a rush light, or firelight from a cooking stove glowed from an upper window. He made several feeble attempts to bang on doors where he saw better lit windows above them, but no one came down to answered his knocking. In truth, his attempts to get help were no more than half hearted, for shiver making tales of dreadful deeds now came to mind: tales of things done to young children in the velvet darkness of the Venetian night. Piero was the main culprit in passing on these age old city legends. Zorzi was fearful lest the next door he knocked on might swing open and reveal the dreaded Biazio Luganegher, the sausage butcher, who had a soft spot for little boys and girls - inside his crusty meat pies!

The roars and shouts from the distant Piazza grew clearer as night drew on. Every so often his surroundings would be lit up with the white flash of a maroon rocket, or a distant firework would scatter its colours like burning jewels over the rooftops. With the aid of their all too brief light, he stumbled his way over the quayside cobbles towards a flickering blue lantern. There he found a little terracotta shrine to St. Catherine of Alexandria. Her pottery hands were missing and her Catherine wheel cracked and minus a few spikes and spokes, but her blue glass votive lantern lit up the corner of a long alleyway. Just below the statue was a street sign with an arrow pointing down the pitch-dark alley. He could just make out the words 'Scola Grande di Santa Caterina.' Zorzi knew enough about Venetian traditions to be aware that *Scola* did not necessarily mean a school; rather it was most likely to be a room attached to a church where food and shelter were offered to the poor, thanks to the generosity of some guild of rich merchants. As he edged his way down the dark alley, holding close to the wall, he could hear the distinct thump of his own little heart. It was hammering away like hoof beats on a sandbank and his spine tingled up and down with dread. He felt his way blindly past recessed doorways, mysterious gaps, slimy drainpipes and broken railings. At the far end of the alley he stumbled thankfully against the steps of a hump-backed bridge. There was no moon, but faint starlight now reflected in the putrid smelling canal water slowly swirling beneath the bridge. He sat on the steps and, disgusting though they were, he had no choice but to rest on them until dawn came. The stench of urine was all around him. Why, he wondered, did filthy and inconsiderate folk always choose bridge walls to pee against when any decent Christian ought to know that the canal was there for that purpose.

The eerie glow of an extra large green maroon showed enough of his surroundings to make him feel certain that he was now in a rundown and dangerous neighbourhood: a neighbourhood that, from its overpowering pong, had been somehow cut off from the flushing tides of the Lagoon. There was no welcoming devotee of St. Catherine with soup bowl and shelter for the night. The Scola building was boarded up and from its appearance long abandoned, yet he dared not walk much further for the maroon had lit up an absolute maze of slime and rubbish banked canals branching off from the alleyway. One slip would have pitched him headlong into their filth. Feeling his way onto the mossy steps of the bridge he crouched down resting his head on the smooth comforting leather of his satchel. Unable to sleep, he closed his eyes against the living nightmare in which he now found himself. A dog began to bark close by: a deep grunting gruff bark, obviously from the lungs of a very large animal. Exhausted and overtired though he was, he just could not risk nodding off. One of old Piero's lurid and teeth chattering tales now come to mind..... La Saponara! That terrifying hag, wandered the alleyways at night accompanied by a ferocious mastiff that seized lost little children in its yellow fangs and carried them off to the cauldrons of her soap works. There she rendered them down in boiling soda to make soap for her customers, who were mostly dirt caked witches, like herself. True, La Saponara preferred lost little girls, who, being that much sweeter and altogether cleaner, made a better quality product.

Disturbed by a loud scraping noise of a heavy gate being opened, Zorzi lifted his head above the low parapet of the bridge. A hand lantern shed a bright beam across the canal towpath and there to his horror, as though arriving on cue, was La Saponara herself holding her great hound on a rusty chain. Bent backed, like the old hag so well described by Piero, she loomed large black and bony in the lantern light. There was no face to be seen beneath her hood. Just two horrid, shining, yellow disks of reflected light gleamed from out of the darkness of her cowled head.

"Whoever you are there on the bridge, show yourself, or be off at once! Show yourself, I say, or else I'll set the dog on you!"

 Zorzi stood up half petrified. He wanted to run, but all energy seemed to have drained away from his legs.

"Gracious mercy…it's a child! What are you doing out here all alone in the dark? Go home at once! It's not safe for a child to be on the streets at night." Her voice seemed less threatening and crone-like, now that she had formed a hazy outline of his size and shape in the gloom.

 Not wanting to admit to her that he was lost, Zorzi blurted out the first anxious thoughts that came to mind: "You don't make soap do you? You are not a witch, are you?"

"Heavens no!" came the laughing reply. "My husband is the paper maker. If you are looking for Zanni the soap chandler I'm afraid you are out of luck. He is away selling his soap at the fair for the next few days. Now if you want a witch, you had better wait till the next full moon. I'll try and oblige you then!"

Ever curious about the technicalities of things, Zorzi wondered for a moment quite how many sheets of paper could be made with a skinny boy of his age and stature. Clearly witchcraft would have to be involved in any such process. After a thoughtful pause he asked, "So what do you use to make the paper?"

"Not soap, that's for sure. Our paper is for the law courts, best cotton or linen, none of your old sailcloth or wood pulp."

She chuckled at his curious questioning and beginning to read his thoughts, like the wise old lady that she was, she lowered the lantern enabling Zorzi to get a good sight of the massive beast at her side. To his great relief the poor creature appeared to be far more ancient than his mistress. It was overweight and staggering uncomfortably on rheumaticky paws. Its days of ferocious bounding energy had long ebbed away, leaving only that deep unhealthy chesty growl and that slow grumbling old bark.
"You are lost, aren't you? Separated from your parents I guess. Well you had better come inside. I can't offer you a bed, but you can sleep on the rags in the yard, it's a warm night."

She understood his natural caution about being invited in to a stranger's house, so when he politely declined her offer, she did not insist. All the same she was concerned. From what she could make of him in the gloom he was no thief, nor ill-bred ragamuffin.

"Look," she said, "I'll tie up old Leo, not that he would do you any harm. All I can say is, don't sleep on that bridge, or on the towpath. If the rats don't get you, you'll be poisoned by bad air. Donkey's years since our canals were last dredged.... Plague of rats around here!

"Not scared of rats...killed lots of them!" Zorzi answered with returning confidence.

"Very well young man…. Can I ask a favour then? Tip my bucket of slops for me. My sight is not so sharp as it used to be. These specs are near useless at night-time…make me lose balance. I'll give you a drink of orange, freshly squeezed. And I can lend you a stout club for the rats - only lend it, mind!"

Having had nothing to drink since he was on the granita ice barge with Denis, the temptation was great. Courage slowly flowed upwards from his boots as he advanced cautiously towards the old witch and her hell hound. On sniffing him the decrepit old dog promptly flopped down with a thump and a grunt on the towpath and lolled its head to one side. In her astonishment at Zorzi's tiny form dressed in such rich apparel, her own wide-cowled cloak hood fell back to reveal a pleasant looking chubby faced grandma with thick-lensed spectacles. "Madonna!" she exclaimed, "You are a nobleman's son - where are your servants? What are you doing here on your own?"

Tugging off his hat, Zorzi bowed low and received in exchange quite a graceful curtsey from the old lady.

Having disposed of the kitchen waste to the squealing delight of the water rats, Zorzi gulped down with gratitude the orange juice and settled down for the night on a great pile of rags that half filled the courtyard. He slept soundly for a couple of hours or so until awakened by muffled squeaking noises and movement both around and burrowing beneath him. Fortunately the vermin seemed to have no great relish for human flesh so thoroughly scoured clean, and doused moreover in lavender water. However they were now nibbling at his boots and dragging hard at his satchel with their needle sharp ratty teeth.

He sat up, flailed his arms and legs and satchel about hoping to drive them off, but it was all a wasted effort, for within two minutes or so the beady-eyed black pelted and scaly tailed little horrors were back in even greater numbers. A pale half moon was up now: sufficient light to enable him to clamber as high up as he could on the pile of rags and to rummage in his satchel for the anchovies and the parmesan cheese. Reluctantly he unwrapped Grandpa's pungent presents and threw them as far away from him as he could across the paved courtyard. The bread loaf too, had to go.

He threw it over the wall, together with the smelly wrapping paper and a piece of rag on which he had wiped his fingers. Hanging the satchel as high up as he could on something jagged projecting from the top of the wall he settled down to rest once again. In his over weary thoughts he regretted that he had not taken up the kind old lady's offer of a ratting cudgel.

A beautiful dawn with just a few wisps of tiny pink clouds found Zorzi with a bellyache and in urgent need of the privy. He clambered down from the rag heap and finding all doors in the yard locked, had no choice but to bang loudly on the old lady's front door with the side of his fist. She was either slightly deaf, or a sound sleeper, for even heavy kicks on the woodwork did not arouse her. Leo however was aroused. He let out a menacing growl and staggered onto his lion sized paws. He too 'had the rats' after a very disturbed night of firework bangs, shouting humans and nipping rodents and could be forgiven in his old age for not remembering that Zorzi was an invited guest on his territory. Teeth bared, he made a run at Zorzi who scrambled back to the top of the pile of linen with the agility of a squirrel. Leo tried to follow but with his great bulk he dislodged a pile of rags that slid down on top of him, not improving his truculent mood.

It was time for Zorzi to make yet another undignified exit. The top of the wall was spiked with broken glass set in cement. Looking over he could see that there was a drop not much more than twice his own height. Folding his coat he laid it carefully over the glass shards then threw his hat and satchel over the top before scrambling over to join them with an easy leap down. He jumped up several times attempting to retrieve his splendid coat, but it was completely snagged on the glass. He decided to abandon it since there was a more urgent matter to attend to in privacy, under the smelly arch of the hump-backed bridge.

Not wanting to disturb the old lady any further, he made his way up the alley and back to the stone bollard, where he waited patiently after the ringing of the morning Angelus for an hour or more. Small craft of every kind were arriving, landing their passengers or speeding straight southward along the warren of canals. Without that blue and gold coat he was now a boy of little consequence and his pleas for help were either ignored or turned down flat. Offers of extra money were refused: not even for a Doge's ransom would anyone ferry him northwards to Murano. Every oarsman was intent on getting his boatload of ragged peasants and gaily dressed country folk with all possible speed down the clogged canals, out into the sail packed Grand Canal: then onwards to the east and the glorious harbour of St. Mark. Eventually a very overcrowded barge tied up to disembark some of its passengers. One of the bargemen took Zorzi's money, assuring him that they would drop him off at the stone Molo in front of the Doge's Palace, where he would easily be able to hire a gondola to take him home to Murano.

Almost up to his ankles in tarry black bilge water, Zorzi was for the first time glad of his chafing and inconveniently long riding boots. The sides of the canal barge were far too high for him to see over and he had to content himself with listening in to the chatter of those around him. Most of the passengers were plump countrywomen who, with their baskets and bundles of food left Zorzi with barely enough room to steady himself as the barge lurched and bumped. Most were journeying in the forlorn hope of catching a last glimpse of their sons or grandsons who were about to sail off under the Doge's banner. Despite their anxieties they feigned a happy bantering mood, pretending to flirt with the grizzly faced, sinewey, nut-brown bargemen while they plied their long oars.

As ever, food was the main topic of conversation. Like mothers everywhere in such a situation, the women passengers were trying to convince themselves, and one another, that their boys were much more likely to suffer starvation than to fall in some bloody and heroic assault. Hearing their comments, one of the bargemen consoled them with news of an amusing turn of events in the Piazza on the previous riotous evening: - On the ringing of the Angelus bell, a large mob of raggedly dressed young men, who had previously seemed to be in fervent prayer inside the Church of San Gerolomo, rose from their knees, pulled masks over their faces and charged out into the Piazza. They surrounded and beat hell's bells out of both the Castellani and the Nicolotti gangs and carried off the greater part of the spilt goodies piled up around the wrecked Cuccagna. Not content with that, they seized and carried off four of the six bulls. It was only after they had battered their way, in a very organized fashion, out through the Piazzetta and made off in the direction of the Arsenal that the crowd realized, from army boots and glimpses of uniform under their rags, that they were soldiers barracked for the night in

240

readiness for the Doge's parade.

Zorzi joined in the laughter and clapping which followed the bargeman's tale, but was a little less enthusiastic when the bargeman continued: - "Young Zustinian, God bless him, saved the evening though. Instead of the soldiers getting flogged, he persuaded the Doge's guests to load up their plates and napkins and march out into the Piazza. Turkey, ham, peacock, custard pie, iced castle; you name it! Every damned delicacy cooked up for their noble bellies, was given to the mob. None of the fighting and pandemonium that goes on with the Cuccagna: not a mortal soul got killed; not an old lady knocked over! Zustinian knows how to tame the Senate too. Who's ever seen a Senator serving up grub to old grannies and cripples? All lined up in orderly queues. Even the poxy beggars got their mouthful of Doge's dinner!"

"Bastian will be Doge, please God Almighty!" one plump countrywoman called out, to further loud murmurs of agreement, "They say his fireworks were something special. I hope my eldest got a view last night. My eldest is a marine, you know, not one of your ordinary thieving dimwit footslogger!"

"Young Zustinian? Never a chance!" a grey bearded farmer commented, "Senators don't like him, nor do a few merchants that I know. Rumours about his, his 'goings-on'… I shan't repeat them in front of ladies." Better dressed and evidently better informed than others on board, the farmer was immediately plied with questions by the women present, but although he refused to say more, he put his hand on his hip and waggled his backside. This charade and his comment were laughingly dismissed by most on board as wicked scandal.

"He's a great laugh - always up to some prank." added one of the bargemen. "They say the fusty old devils even made him burn down his arch, all out of spite. A pretty sight though, when it went off…. packed with fireworks!"

Zorzi gave a slight shiver at the thought that Aldo, his other pals and even poor fat Luanardo had been singing away like larks on top of what must have amounted to a gunpowder magazine.

The rice barge made achingly slow progress down the busy Rio di Noale: it was too broad in the beam even for that wide canal and of course was dangerously overloaded. Zorzi, exhausted from lack of sleep and from being jostled and jolted against the rough wooden ribs of the barge, finally began to wilt on his feet and feel faint. Noticing that he looked unwell, a young servant girl moved up and let him sit next to her on an upturned wicker basket. "Come to see the parade?" she asked. "My man is in the guard of honour. He's marching from the Palace to the Arsenal soon after midday. Let's hope and pray we get there in time. Sorry I got on this damned slow boat... should have hired a gondola....though they charge you a month's wage on Ascension Day. The old Doge s walking all the way to the Arsenal, most likely it's so he can admire the floats. They say he can't see a thing from the Bucintoro."

"Why's that?" Zorzi asked perking up. He had taken the advice of the kind young lady and held his head low on his knees for a while to recover from his faint.

"Well, I expect there will be a bit of a crowd around his throne. Before he chucks the ring into the Lagoon, there's lots of ceremony. Don't suppose he has much time to inspect all the boats and floats tailing on behind."

"Do you think they will fish up the ring this year?" Zorzi asked her.

"Shouldn't think so. It was only found once during the reigns of the last seven Doges and one of them, I forget which, died shortly afterwards, so it might be a bad omen for old Morosini if the ring is trawled up after this year's Wedding. The mud off the Lido shore is fathoms deep."
"Anyone for Rialto Market? Just coming up!" the youngest and thinnest of the bargemen called out.

"Listen 'celery legs,' no one here wants Rialto. We are all for landing on the Molo, if we ever get there at this rate. Put some backbone into your rowing! If I don't get to see my grandson on parade, your skinny hide will feel the back of my knuckles!" A great hulk of a gruff farmer waved his ham fists at the poor sweating young rower, who was too terrified to reply.

"Calm down Moonface!" a fat countrywoman intervened. "Can't you see the lad's doing his best.... and show some respect! We are passing by Giorgione. You are from Castelfranco like the rest of us aren't you?"

Zorzi was tickled with amusement at the farmer's nickname, which was most appropriate. His round, heavy jowled, peasant's face was so pitted with the scars of smallpox that it looked almost as though he had been caught in the crossfire on a duck shoot. But he was puzzled when the farmer jumped to his feet, removed his straw hat and bowed low with a smug and satisfied grin in the direction of a huge painted stone palace that seemed to go sailing by them. The other men on board promptly followed his example. Seconds later the barge swept under the vast arch of the Rialto Bridge.

"Does Giorgione live there?" Zorzi asked quietly, assuming from their signs of respect that it was the palace of their local overlord.

"No silly," the servant girl replied. Have you never heard of Giorgione, the famous artist? He came from Castelfranco and we are proud of him. Giorgione painted all over that Ca`. *(Fondaco dei Tedeschi.)* Pity you did not see it properly. Stand on my basket or you'll miss lots of other famous sights. Our parish church has his painting of San Giorgio: really lifelike it is, armour looks really real too. You'll have to come and see it. We are only a smallish town, but all our sons are fighters… always make it to the crack regiments."

"Giorgio, that's my name." Zorzi observed.

"Hey! We have a Giorgino on board. That's good luck for our boys!" a servant girl shouted above the chatter and the splash of the oars.
A great cheer went up at this news. Zorzi, the only child on board, was mystified as well as embarrassed by their sudden enthusiasm. He got patted and kissed for good luck by all the old ladies and shoved forward to the best seat at the prow of the barge. There he sat in solitary splendour, acting as their figurehead and good luck talisman, while the four bargemen battled their way up the Grand Canal. Peasant superstition it may have seemed to the bargemen, but it was the passengers' way of dealing with their mounting fear and anxiety. They were all getting more and more desperate to catch a glimpse of their soldier sons, grandsons, or departing lovers. Who could tell if it would be for the very last time?

Though their loyalty to the ferocious old warrior Doge was absolute, they all knew he always took the fight straight to the strongholds of the Ottoman.

Zorzi was peeling a boiled egg offered him by one of the old ladies when the crooked Ca` Dario loomed up on his right. There was no mistaking its squiffy frontage with the vast swirls of deep red porphyry and coloured marble decoration. It leaned then, as it still does, at an alarming angle sideways and tilting slightly backwards from waters of the Grand Canal, its foundation piles having long given way. The longboat of The Raven was moored at its landing stage together with several magnificent gondolas decorated with swags of flowers and bunting. There was no sign of Piero's boat though. Zorzi would have liked to have been landed there and then; to have met up again with John and the Raven's crew, but they were now moving fast in mid canal together with hundreds of other craft, all heading at speed in the same direction. Here and there they passed brightly decked floats in the last stages of preparation for the grand procession of the Bucintoro. One particularly lovely float all covered in flashing bright silver foil was at least the height of a two storeyed building. Two carved wooden sea horses were pulling the seashell carriage of a giant triton that was blowing a conch shell trumpet into the air. Something however had gone wrong with the leather bellows that worked the trumpet sound. Workmen were frantically hammering in tacks and testing it for sound. Despite their efforts, it only let out the most comical squeaks, honks and lavatory noises, adding greatly to the merriment of everyone passing.

Several grand and beautifully flower decked floats supported banners and paintings, or sculptures, of Jesus rising upwards into Heaven; for it was after all the Feast of the Ascension, in Venetian 'La Festa della Sensa,' that was being celebrated. Passengers and boatmen doffed their hats in reverence as they passed each one of these religious masterpieces. Many however were quick to notice and some were scandalised to see that Jesus' white flowing garments were hemmed with yellow and blue... the exact shades of the Doge's coat of arms!

When at long last they drew level with that huge and magnificent domed pile of beauty that is the church of Our Lady of Good Health (*La Salute,*) panic began to set in, especially amongst the young ladies on board. Even

Zorzi's stomach began to churn with anxiety as he willed the leaky old barge onwards amidst the cram of forwards moving craft. Like an oncoming storm the roll of war drums came rumbling up the Grand Canal - The Doge and his army were on the move!

"Get down! Get down!" old Moonface yelled at the exhausted young bargeman. He ripped the oar from his hands and set to in his place, rowing so fast and so furiously that the barge began to drift off course. The other bargemen plied their oars as energetically as they could to keep up with him and to correct the drift.

The gangplank was run out and used as a battering ram on other boats trying to land in the same spot along the Molo: the Sensa Fair embankment and landing stage in front of the Doge's Palace. Finally, with a loud crunch and a groan from its old timbers, the barge was run aground on the steps. Most of the male passengers leapt overboard and hared off in the direction of the thundering drums. There was a great noisy throng moving slowly eastwards through the Sensa Fair, which was closed and shuttered ready to be transferred to a more permanent pitch in the Piazza on the following day. The ladies hitched up their skirts and scampered down the gangplank with their bundles and baskets and slippery clogs, screaming at one another to get out of the way or to hurry up.

The bargemen too, having stowed their oars and hastily thrown the gangplank back onto the barge, made off into the milling crowd with all the urgency that stiff and aching limbs could summon. Zorzi found himself alone once more, pacing up and down the Molo hoping to find somewhere a boatman willing to ferry him back to Murano.

In despair at failing to find anyone even willing to listen to him before they sped off, he turned towards the Piazzetta. Sawdust was being sprinkled and then swept up into heaps, thus cleaning from the flagstones a slippery mess of squashed fruit, litter, charred wood and mixed animal and human bloodstains left over after the orgy of fun and violence that had erupted there on the night before. A team of workmen was smashing and replacing in fresh sand the paving where Zustinian's triumphal arch had burned down. Zorzi, in an unthinking instant and in a daze of heat and anxiety, walked across to have a look.... straight between the gigantic granite columns of Marco and Todaro!

"Madonna Santa!" screamed a passing middle-aged fishwife and crossing herself quickly three times she gave Zorzi such a look of pity and disapproval that for a moment he was quite perplexed to know what he had done wrong. However, on turning round he instantly realized that he was now a condemned soul, quite damned to eternal torment and darkest perdition!

Tears started to his eyes. He ran forward to where a water seller was squeezing out a mournful tune on a goatskin bagpipe to an audience of no one. Slung crosswise on the old man's shoulder was his other shaggy goatskin, this one sealed with a cork bung and bulging with water. Had he robbed a scarecrow of its raiment he could hardly have been more raggedly attired and from the man's fumbling movements and rolling eyes Zorzi concluded that he was blind.

"Oh please tell me what must I do? Must I go to church and pray or something? I have just accidentally gone between the columns, between Marco and Todaro!"

"Don't fret yourself little one, lots of people do it by accident. I daresay some of them goes to hell and others goes to the gallows unshriven, but no more than goes to heaven for doing a good deed. Any road, it's all superstition. You make your own luck in life, little'un."

"What good deed must I do?" Zorzi pleaded.

"Why, you smell sweet, boy… sweet as a minted sequin! Buy a glass of water from a poor old blind man and then help me on my way to the Schiavoni embankment. It's a right swealter of a day so once I'm close to the crowds, I'll get some trade. Just to be sure about the columns, spin three times round to the left, on your right heel; cross yourself seven times and then spit over your left shoulder into Old Nick's wicked squinty eye and you won't ever, ever dangle on a gallows.

To the amusement of the paving breakers, Zorzi performed his spell-breaking ritual at lightening speed and then fished into his bag for a coin. It was one of his two remaining silver lire. That last golden ducat was still warm and shining amidst the greasy folds of his satchel and he wanted to save it for Piero. He was tempted to pay the poverty-stricken water seller with both coins, but it came to mind that should he not meet up with Piero he would need at least half a lire for a ferry back to Murano. The drinking glass was cracked and dirty and the water was warm, hot even, tasting quite, quite rancid, awful in fact... not surprisingly, it had the flavour and aroma of dead goat!

Taking the blind man by the arm, he escorted him along the Molo, past the glittering pink Doge's Palace, over The Bridge of Straw with its gloomy view of the New Prison and along the Schiavoni Embankment. In the brief moments that it took to escort him towards the crowds Zorzi poured out his life story to the ragged fellow and giving him a short account of his recent adventures as well. After the fright of the night before, he felt a compulsion to talk to someone and the water seller 'led him on' with many a friendly question. The stalls and booths of the Sensa Fair had for the most part been dismantled and stacked, to make way for the Doge's procession and for regiment after regiment of proud and plumed young men marching six abreast ahead of him.

Once they caught up with the crowd, the water seller thanked Zorzi and assured him that far from being cursed by Marco and Todaro, he would soon have great good luck for helping a blind old man on his lonely way. It was then, to his joy, that Zorzi recognized the little alleyway with the beautifully carved white stone arch above its entrance. It was the way to San Zanipolo... to the hospital of St. John and St. Paul. He had come to the fair that way with Denis. Denis would help him!

CHAPTER TWENTY-ONE

Other than a stubbly bearded old beggar hunched up against a wall and slumbering in the heat, there was not a soul to be seen along the alley. Finding the gate bolted when he pushed against it, Zorzi felt through the bars and located the latch and bolt. As he shoved with every ounce of effort to close the heavy gate behind him, the man, whom he had taken at first glance to be a beggar, leapt up and ran at him waving an old fashioned ship's blunderbuss. Pinned against the gate, with no chance of wriggling out of the man's excessively rough grasp, Zorzi guessed that he was about to be robbed. The man's breath stank of alcohol and tobacco and from his slightly slurred speech Zorzi judged that the mugger had drunk more than a 'skinful' of strong liquor.

"You little runt, I'll teach you not to open a gate when it's shut on Captain's orders!" the man roared at him. But before he could put down his blunderbuss and carry out his threat, another ruffian, much younger and more heavily built, ran up and pulled the drunkard off.

"Can't you see he's a gentleman's son, you sozzled old fool! It will be you who gets the lash if you hurt him. You'll be beating up a nun next! Ask people what they want, before roughing them up! What sort of a galley scum are you?"

Then clumsily straightening Zorzi's pulled-out shirt, the young man apologised and asked what business Zorzi had in coming that way.

"I was hoping Sister Zuseppina might let me through. You see, I am lost and I am on the way to the Prior of San Zanipolo. He will help me get home."

"Madonna mia santissima! The Prior of Zanipolo! You soused and pickled old fool! See what you have done!" With that, the young man aimed a hefty kick at the leg and then the backside of the drunkard bellowing: "Get back with the others!" An extra mighty swipe on the cheek sent the sozzled sailor staggering away in a bigger fuddle than he was in because of the booze.

Zorzi could hardly conceal a responding smile as the young man grinned pleasantly at him and offered another apology, "You see Vossignoria," he explained, "we're guarding prisoners, Vossignoria, Uzkoks! Don't want the lynch mob out there to find 'em.... Happened a few years back. Galley landed Uzkoks during Carnival week. Nasty it was.... drunken louts lynched the whole lot... flew at them tooth and nail....limbed them apart one by one. Uzkoks again today, mostly women and kids, but that won't worry the Castellani louts and the other trouble makers. God help us all should they get their hands on this lot!"

Now Zorzi had heard a number of blood-curdling tales about Uzkoks from Piero. He knew that Uzkoks were the worst of all sea gypsies, pirates who lived in caves and in concealed villages along the Dalmatian Coast. "Are you taking them to the prisons then?" Zorzi asked and then added excitedly, "Can I see them?"

"We've been stuck here with them since dawn. Prisons closed....no luck at Arsenal cages either....both Governors off to the Sensa. Captain needs galley to entertain new relatives. Just married. Wants to cut a dash. Holding a banquet on board. Listen, Vossignoria, you can inspect the pirate filth if you like, but do us all a favour, some pesky shrimp of a nun won't let us get at the wells. Prisoners are in a bad state, what with this heat. Captain Venier won't be at all amused if we lose any more of them. Hopes to get a decent price for every one of the little vermin. To my mind, though, we ought to have drowned the bloody lot of 'em!"

"Venier? The Lepanto Doge? He's buried in a church near our house."

"Well our Venier is still kicking, but he ain't no Doge. Done his share of Turk sinking though. Not that much comes our way from his booty. So far as I know, he's only ever been crowned with a flying pulley block, but we live in hopes. Maybe we can then swop our slops for Senators' robes."

"The little nun must be Suor Zuseppina. I'll ask her to draw water for you!" Further to impress his saviour as they walked up the alley towards San Zaccaria Zorzi added: "I know Messer Grande as well, the Prison Governor.... met him only yesterday. Perhaps I could....Madonna Santa!"

No previous experience, however unpleasant, could have prepared Zorzi for the scene that met his eyes as he walked into the Convent courtyard.

There were no buccaneers with broken teeth, scars and beefy biceps; no sea gypsies with tattoos and dangling gold ear-rings; just a cowering, skeletally thin and sun blistered heap of women and children. Now Zorzi was no stranger to wasted muscles and bulging joints and there had been days when he too had come close to the reins of that bony horseman of the Apocalypse. But these poor wretches had reached that half human stage of utter and final dejection and were all squatting in their own filth, trussed up in groups to one another by looped ropes about the neck: tetherd like cattle to the high spiked railings of the Convent forecourt. There were half a dozen or so teenage boys, pinioned tightly at the elbows back to back, as for the rest, they were boys and girls of his own age and some much younger. Close up against the retaining wall of the Convent railing were two small bundles of sail cloth, with rigid little blue toed feet sticking out from them. A mother, with her parched mouth wide open to the flies and baking heat, still clung in desperation to a tiny motionless infant.

Rising from his stomach like a sudden attack of the bile came a surge of intense pity; it swirled hot through his cheeks and ears and tingled over the top of his skull. "They're not Uzkoks!" he roared angrily, "just starvelings! For God's sake untie them! Can't you see they are all half dead?"

"Calm it, Vossignoria, or you will have to leave - water, or no water! They are all Uzkoks.... and, I tell you, if I were to loose just one of them boys, you would soon find out what kind they are.They are vermin; sea rats, born to plunder honest working sailors like us. I don't doubt, Vossignoria has mariners in the family. I'd worry about them if I were you."

"There's, well, just my Grandpa and…. and old Piero."

"A grandpa eh? Captain Venier had a grandpa too. Uzkoks slaughtered him in cold blood, and after he surrendered! Not one of them deserves to grow up. I tell you straight...the girls are as bad a lot as the boys… should have been strangled at birth…. all of 'em! Get water drawn up for us, if you are feeling that sorry for the little blighters."

Now disturbed by the news of a murdered grandpa, Zorzi recovered somewhat from his instant rage, lowered his voice and, "But where are the pirates? These people can hardly be pirates...they are all starved and skinny."

"The pirates are dead: hanged, shot, cut down in the fight, every last one of them. Dimwits that they were… tried to 'spring us' while we sheltered in their cove. Must have known we were a patrol galley. Captain gave orders to fire and raze their village. We chased the survivors up a river near Omis. One less nest of vipers for honest merchants to worry about. Now are you going to soft- talk that grumpy little nun, or not?"

Crestfallen, and with the added sobering knowledge that four of the young mariner's friends had been killed in the assault on the Uskok village, Zorzi took off his hat, put his head through the bars of the Convent railing and called "Sister Zuseppina! Your Ladyship! It's me - the friend of Denis!"

Further shouts and pleadings finally brought the irascible, unpitying and black clad Benedictine conversa to the gate.

"I am Giorgio Miotti di Brayda, friend of the Prior of San Zanipolo. I passed by yesterday with Denis. Do you remember me? You told me all about the Doge's hat. It was most interesting, what with your old Abbess and all that.... Could you please let these people use one of your wells?"

Zuseppina looked him up and down. Though now in a far less decorous state, she recognized him from his puffy cheek and remembered his insolence.

"I am sorry Vostra Signoria, it is quite forbidden for me to let men into the Churchyard. As for those ruffian marines, I have told them they are trespassing, disgracing our sacred precinct with their naked gypsies. It is your duty to order them to be off. Oh! If only our Mother Abbess were here!"

Zorzi thought for a moment. He was not that easily put off and since yesterday had found himself rather relishing his new found 'nobility.' Naked; that was his clue.... those catechism morals he had learned by heart, with much help from Grandpa, came in convenient packages of seven. There were seven deadly sins crying to Heaven for justice; seven

251

sorrows, seven sacraments, seven corporate acts of mercy, etc., and he knew instantly which to apply to this situation. Plonking his tricorn at a jaunty angle, he joined his hands reverently, rolled his eyes heavenward in imitation of some saint in a baroque painting and announced to the stony faced nun: "Jesus said, 'The Seven Acts of Mercy'are: feed the hungry; give drink to the thirsty; clothe the naked; visit the sick; visit the imprisoned; comfort the dying and bury the dead!"

"All right, all right.... no need to preach to me young Sir! I suppose if you must give them water, you must. The winch is far too heavy for you to wind though. I will get Suor Brigida to help - that's her job. Just stay out there till I get her."

"And, Suor Zuseppina, Your Ladyship! I have money to buy them bread, or whatever you can spare. They are all starving hungry." He waved his last ducat through the railings.

The flash of a golden ducat and his flattering reference to her Ladyship, had more effect on her mean and uncaring spirit than had he recited by heart the whole of Jesus's 'Sermon on the Mount.'

Her grey face creased into an icy smirk. She curtsied low to Zorzi. Praising him aloud as a true Christian gentleman and complimenting him on his noble good nature, she hurried off to fetch Suor Brigida.

"You had better get someone to help, while I draw water," advised Sister Brigida, "Our trays are quality, don't you know… rather heavy…all silver. Quite a bit left from Sensa Breakfast… feast day, don't you know. Ask that insolent bosun fellow to untie one of the little varmints. Uzkoks, or no Uzkoks, I hate to see people suffering while we have so much going scrap to the pig farm. Make it a girl; a girl is less likely to make a run for freedom. Besides, boys over ten are forbidden to step beyond the railings. You're not yet ten, are you?" she added with a knowing wink. "Those marines…. a bunch of brigands, little different from Uzkoks!"

With that, the plump and very masculine looking Sister Brigida unpinned her sleeves to free up her bulging biceps and began to crank, clank and ratchet the massive well handle with the greatest of ease.

Impressed with Zorzi's diplomacy, the young mariner, who may well have been the galley bosun, tipped his tarry hat and gave a slight bow in amused deference. The other two guards did likewise: a hard clog kick in the ankle by way of a reminder persuaded the drunkard to follow their polite example. Yanking at the neck rope of a slender girl, the mariner pulled four others up with her to their feet: "This one will do. She looks a bit cleaner than the others."

The girl was little more than a bag of bones, blotched red with sunburns on her pallid and sore infested skin. Tearful and trembling at the prospect of what next might happen to her, she held her hands between her legs trying to cover her modesty while the callous mariner unknotted her neck rope and threw about the others attached her as though they were no more than strung up ducks on a poulterer's stall.

Zorzi gave her a reassuring smile and pointing through the railings to the two great marble well heads in the courtyard, he acted a charade of drinking and eating, waving his arms about and rubbing his belly to confirm that both she and everyone else would be given food and drink. Taking her by the hand he shook the metal bars of the courtyard gate. He was about to call again for Zuseppina when the gate swung open silently, almost on its own. Had they wished to, the marines could have entered and taken un-noticed whatever they wanted - Doge's hat, silver candlesticks included!

"Saints in heaven preserve us!" exclaimed Suor' Brigida, half spilling the contents of her copper well bucket, "The girl can't enter the Convent like that! Get a cloth, or something, to cover her…to cover her…parts!"

What few rags of clothes and ornaments the Uskok villagers were wearing at the time of capture had been sold promptly on entering port by the gallant Captain Venier - woollen rags made the best hat felt and when bleached and pulped, linen or cotton made quality writing paper. Their filthy matted hair had been shorn off too and bagged up for a wigmaker. To Zorzi, there was neither embarrassment nor shame, in the girl's unclad state. He and his friends spent half their leisure hours splashing in and out of the Lagoon in the birthday suits that nature had provided for young swimmers.

"None of them seem to have anything to wear, Your Ladyship. Surely you have got a gown or something that she might borrow?"

"I am not a Ladyship - just Brigida, a conversa. And you are asking too much of us young gentleman, we are not a Scuola, not charity! You must know that only ladies of rank dwell here. We have no rags and remnants, nothing that could possibly be given to a....a ...an Uskok! There's been disturbance enough from these drunken galley hands! Never you doubt it, Vossignoria, our Abbess will be making a complaint.... an official complaint to the Procurator. Get one of that foul mouthed scum to lend the girl his cummerbund, otherwise she can't come into our kitchen. It's not decent!" With that, she set to, cranking the well handle for a second bucket of water.

Doubting that any of the marines would be so obliging, Zorzi suddenly realized that he had Jesus's 'Third Act of Mercy' tucked away in his satchel. Undoing the flap he pulled out, with a sigh of regret, his precious and patched goatskin breeches. They fitted the girl well enough, for she was about his own height, and while tightening the drawstring at the waist, he realized that she had not the slightest idea of how to tie knots, which struck him as something strangely lacking in the offspring of an Uskok pirate: after all the Uskok, often called Cravats *(now Croats)* were distinguished by their piratical habit of wearing knotted neckties. The girl gave him a wan little smile of thanks and kept a tight clasp on his hand while Suor' Brigida escorted them in silence to the convent refectory. With high and gilded coffered and beamed ceilings, splendid tapestries, portraits in carved frames of haggard old nuns; crystal, coral and gem studded reliquaries; woodcarvings of tormented saints and martyrs; every nook and carpeted corridor that they passed through seemed to be both adorned and cluttered with holy oddments. On the refectory dressers and cabinets, numerous gold and silver chargers and plates, ewers and intricately decorated flagons were displayed. Passing into the kitchen Zorzi gasped at the absolute cornucopia of fruit, of sugared cakes and of game birds hanging in rows; not to mention the dozens of high-hooked joints of ham and the chandelier like clusters of salami smoking by the dozen near to the kitchen range.

While they were about to carry out the third tray of scraps (the guards having gobbled the choicest morsels from the other trays,) two elderly and grand looking dames came down from the upper cloister rooms to observe what was going on - evidently Suor Zuseppina had thought it wise to alert them. Both ladies were 'dressed to the nines' in the latest fashion. The only concessions they had made to their holy status were their amethyst and diamond pectoral crosses and their rosary beads of rock crystal and pink coral; the Pater Nosters *(Lord's Prayers)* in each decade picked out with large ruby stones!

"What dear little children - such an example of Christian virtue!" One observed loudly to the other, who seemed somewhat deaf. "Oh what fun! We really must show our benevolence in this way more often. That noble little child has put us almost to shame with his truly saintly concern. What a reminder to us of that charming parable of Dives and Lazarus! We really must think of sharing our scraps after next feast day. Are we not exhorted to love our enemies and to do good to those who would harm us, even to Uskoks? I shall propose something along those lines to Mother Abbess at this evening's chapter meeting."

"Mother Abbess? Did you say Mother Abbess?" questioned the deaf one, "Isn't she at the Doge's banquet tonight?"

"Children, children!" squealed the nun who first spoke, clapping her hands in delight, "Do take out all that you want to the poor prisoners. Fill some more trays!"

Zorzi, who was feeling quite peckish himself, decided that it would not be the act of a lordling to stuff down a lamb chop or a meat pie in the presence of such august nuns, particularly while they were eyeing him with such admiration. The little girl seemed very weak and could hardly walk properly, let alone hold her end of the heavyweight silver salvers as they toddled back and forth to the courtyard. He knew that it would only be a matter of moments before the stiff backed haughty faced and more alert looking of the two elderly nuns would begin to probe him about his 'noble' family. She might even ask him how old he was - in which case he might well qualify for a chop that was not of the lamb's rib kind! She had already observed loudly to the other nun, that he had the most handsome profile and the natural gracious manners of a trueborn patrician. As they entered the kitchen on their fourth 'bread run' the nun took Zorzi firmly by the arm.

"Satisfy our curiosity. The little boy helping you...is not a Cravat is he? Sister Amelia and I are convinced that he is either Armenian, or Circassian. It's that pallid skin, the fine features, the greyish blue eyes; you can tell of course.... altogether a better breed of person than those Hunnish tanned Cravats. Where did you find him?"

Now Zorzi had had little time to take stock of his young companion, other than noticing that she had an endearing smile and that she had neither drunk down nor eaten anything. "Tied up with the others in the courtyard, Your Ladyship," Zorzi replied with a hasty bow. He was about to reaffirm that the 'he' was in fact a little 'she,' when the deaf old Amelia, proposed that both he and the poor little sun burnt Circassian should take some refreshment with them: stay for the afternoon and be presented to the Mother Abbess, just as soon as she returned from the Wedding of the Sea.

But in an instant, what was brewing up to be a deeply embarrassing situation for Zorzi was turned completely on its head. A handsomely dressed, masked and beribboned young nobleman, came clattering down the stairway leading from the upper cloisters. He was about to fling his baldric and court sword over his shoulder when he caught sight of Zorzi with the nuns. He made to go back up again and as he did, Suor Zuseppina's voice could be heard on the landing whispering loudly, "Don't go down! Don't go down - for heaven's sake! No! Not that way!"

Dismayed that Zorzi had both seen the man and had reacted to his presence with a very distinct look of puzzlement, the severe looking nun hastened to explain: "Ah, yes... just visiting his sister. She's not terribly well: quite, quite indisposed, in fact." With that she took Zorzi's arm once more and hastened him, with his little Circassian boy out into the Courtyard.

In his innocence, Zorzi believed the old nun and did not quite understand the mirth of the three marines, when ten minutes or so later, they spotted the dashing young cavalier slinking towards the northern gate. With an unseasonable long black cape clutched about him and his large tricorn pulled low onto a 'bauta' mask, he looked the very image of a furtive miscreant.

They watched him shake the locked gate in frustration and knew he had no alternative but to come their way. The young mariner, who may well have been the galley bosun, observed casually: "Time to make a quick ducat or two, shipmates. Our bold buccaneer of the convent sheets seems to have strayed way off course... run himself aground in the heavenly harem! Taken his chance, I bet, while the old Abbess has nipped-off to the Wedding."

The three marines stood together in front of the south gate, their hats held respectfully against their chests. Big built and intimidating though they certainly were, they were not precisely obstructing the way of the young nobleman. However, they left him barely enough room to squeeze past.

"Who is your Galley Commander?" demanded the flustered young man.

"Venier, Your Excellency, Captain Venier."

"Ah! Not a friend of mine... though an acquaintance. You would be well advised to be discreet, master bosun... discreet! Do I make myself plain?"

"Discreet...of course, Vozzignoria! No mention to Noble Captain Venier, Vozzignoria. We men quite understood, Vozzignoria!" The young bosun's reply hit just the right, slightly mocking, tone - not wanting to be accused of outright insolence to a nobleman. "Naturally, Your Excellency will be wanting to make a contribution to the welfare of the poor prisoners?"

"Why, of course... of course!" Only too eager to bribe his way out of the situation, the young dandy rummaged in the pockets of his pink silk coat and drew out a silver chain-purse.

The bold young bosun looked down with slight disapproval at the shining new ducat resting in the palm of his hand and observed, "Naturally my shipmates here are just as concerned for the health of the poor Uzkoks, Your Excellency," adding: "They are such gossiping tosspots, my shipmates, specially when they have had a few drinks. But I can bridle their tongues,Vozzignoria. Specially talkative is my good shipmate here, who is resting after a long spell on duty, Your Excellency."

"Damn you man! I can see clearly enough that he is blind drunk and incapable! What would Venier do if he found that out, eh? I could inform him that you were all drunk on duty and causing a nuisance to the good nuns and that in passing by, I had no choice but to intervene. Here's four ducats. That's all I have on me. Now let me pass!"

 Suor' Brigida, who as a 'conversa' nun was allowed out of the convent precinct, was part occupied with giving water to one of the skeletal mothers, though still keeping a weather eye on the goings-on at the gate. Seeing that the marines had exacted a bribe before letting the young cavalier pass, she made frantic eyes to attract his attention - pointing unobtrusively in the direction of Zorzi, who was feeding scraps of chicken to a tightly bound adolescent boy.

From her worried eye contact and gestures, the nobleman quickly arrived at the conclusion that it was the young lad who was a far greater source of danger to him than the easily bribed marines. Though Zorzi was now slightly dishevelled looking, it was quite obvious that he was the son of some important patrician and might well talk when he returned to his home.

Entering a Convent without the written permission of The Magistrates to the Convents was, as Denis had correctly informed Zorzi, a capital offence. The young nobleman would have known well enough what the penalty was, yet for some reason he was still desperate enough to have taken the risk. If caught just visiting a dying relative without permission, it would be a minimum of twelve years at the oars of a galley; an ordeal few survived. God forbid, that the lady concerned was not his sister.... for then, inevitably, it would be the scaffold and the 'boia's' axe! As with the Vestal Virgins of ancient Rome, the honour of the noble nuns of San Zaccaria should never be compromised: that was the decree of the Senate. There had been very few scandals since they introduced their draconian Convent Laws, some sixty years previously. The Doge was the only male permitted to enter unscathed and that was because every Doge was a bigamist, not to say sometimes a trigamist. In addition to his own wife, if any, the Doge was by tradition symbolically, and certainly only spiritually, married to the Abbess of San Zaccaria. As to his third bride, he was shortly to renew his marriage vow to the deep blue sea.

Striding over to Zorzi, the young gallant observed casually, "Not going to see the Wedding young man? I should be please to take you. My gondolino is close by on the Riva."

"Well thank you for the offer, but I need to get back to Grandpa. He must be worried about me. I've been trying to get home since yesterday. I was hoping the Prior might help me - that's why I came through this way."

"Which Prior would that be, young sir?" the cavalier asked, seeming quite unconcerned.

"Prior of San Zanipolo. I was with him yesterday, and Denis, at the Sensa. Bought a magnifier from my English friends... kind of healing thing for his Hospital."

The young dandy gave a quiet gulp and several further involuntary intakes of breath. In an anxious voice he continued: "You know the.... the Prior.... Raimondo himself was with you at the fair?" He began to stutter uncontrollably. "Look, look, young man, it won't take more than half an hour to see the ceremony. You and I can make, make, friends on the way. I pr, pr, promise I'll row you straight to your palazzo, just as soon as it's all over. You would be missing quite a spectacular show you know. Have you ever seen the Bucintoro close up? Once it's all over, we could whisk you back home, well, well, before dark.... well before Vespers!"

The thought of going off with a complete stranger did not appeal, particularly with one who was cloaked and masked with a frightening looking white bauta. But running counter to his natural concern was the thought that he had spent his last ducat. Even when he had more than enough money to get home, nobody seemed willing to row him back. Murano was quite in the opposite direction to where all the fun was: fun which he knew would continue all night with more feasting and fireworks and perhaps even long into the days after.

Eager to get the troublesome boy off site, Sister Zuseppina then intervened: "Now signorino, you must leave at once with the Noble Rezz....that is, err.... that is, the gentleman here. He is to be trusted, you have my word for it. On official business with us.....an urgent message for our Mother Abbess, from the Magistrates...a secret matter... most unwise to mention yours or his visit to anyone."

Then as if to convince him more, the nun added, "God bless her, our Mother Abbess was so relieved to get the news he brought. I have just come from her office. She thanks you as well for your generosity. Now do be off! We can attend to the prisoners ourselves. No harm will come to them.... no harm at all."

This blatant lie about the whereabouts of the Abbess only served to increase Zorzi's alarm about going with the stranger, but he went all the same.

CHAPTER TWENTY-TWO

Thus it was that Zorzi stepped down onto the leather uphostered stern thwart, like a lost soul boarding Charon's ferryboat, quite unaware of the murderous thoughts brooding behind the nobleman's 'monkey-skull' mask. To be precise, the gondola was a gondolino, built for racing, varnished a honey colour and half the size of its familiar big black brother. Elegant and lightweight, it had no felze and in the hands of the young nobleman it manoeuvred with ease, cutting through the water as fast as a pike in a pond. Within five minutes it carried them into the midst of the great galleons, the frigates and other men-o-war and the swarms of smaller craft all jostling and trying to approach the processional route of the Bucintoro. Sea birds screamed in the azure blue, excited by the clamour and the foam making movements of ten thousand, or more, boats and floats beneath them. From their barnacled briccole, the gannets and cormorants plunged headlong and excited onto the shoals of sprats spiralling and weaving beneath the emerald green calms and the occasional swift currents of navy blue wavelets. The fresh air and salt sea spray soon had Zorzi in a happier mood. He leaned back against the comfortable padded seat and breathed hard and deep, clearing his nostrils of lingering fetid smells: disgusting smells exuded from the bodies of the poor prisoners. Hardest to suffer, as he shared out the water and scraps, had been the rancid stench of breath from shrivelled-up stomachs: stomachs that had held neither food, nor water, for days on end. He tried to put the poor Uzkoks out of mind - in particular that feeble young girl to whom he had not even had the chance of bidding goodbye. Gradually he relaxed and began to concentrate on the astonishing sights all around him, then, to his bitter dismay, he realized that he had left his satchel on the refectory table. The boots were fine in themselves, but that embossed leather satchel would be fair proof to his pals of his incredible adventure. Signora Molin's amber necklace then came to mind and he felt heartbroken. The rainbow prism was gone too. He then cheered himself a little with the thought that retrieving his satchel would be an excuse to meet up with Denis once more. Surely those snooty nuns would not steal, or give away his property? They would realize whose satchel it was and then Denis would be sure to retrieve everything.

Frustrated by the vast jam of craft rowing its way towards the Arsenal Gates, where the Bucintoro was moored, the young nobleman turned about and made for the wide stretch of water between the Island of St. George and the Giudecca Island. Palaces, villas, blossom filled orchards and tall Palladian church spires seemed to skim past to left and right of the gondolino. Once away from the crush, the nobleman pulled off his embroidered long coat and lace trimmed tricorn, dumping them behind him on top of his folded cloak and court sword. He did not unmask however and Zorzi studied what he could of him without seeming ill mannered. The noble could not have been older than twenty years or so. His hair, which was his own though thickly dusted with white lead oxide, was tied in a pigtail with a large black bow. Zorzi wondered to himself, "Was that sweat, or tears, running down the young man's rouged and powdered cheeks?"

They reached mid point between the Island of St. George and the ten mile long strand of mud and sand known as the Lido and were well out of sight of any other vessel. The nobleman still manoeuvred the gondolino with skill and energy, but seemed to be getting more and more tense and agitated. Zorzi had never before seen an aristocrat rowing his own boat and concluded therefore that his mission to the Abbess must indeed have been a matter of very great secrecy and importance.

The nobleman stopped rowing and without any warning call slid the long oars carelessly beneath the thwarts. Had Zorzi not reacted instantly, his shins would have received a nasty knock. Zorzi looked down at the dripping oars in astonishment. As he looked up, there was the nobleman standing over him, scabbard and baldric in one hand, glittering blade in the other.

For an instant the nobleman paused, to direct accurately his aim as well as to summon up fury enough to execute that death thrust taught by his fencing master - namely, to run the boy straight past the collar bone to the left of his windpipe and down into his little heart. Oblivious to the peril, Zorzi smiled back at him - a face lit up with boyish excitement.

"Now that's a fine blade! Gosh! Is it a Pappenheimer? Captain Ravenscroft calls his, my Pappenheimer. His is so heavy though, yours looks a lot lighter. Don't suppose I'll ever wear a sword though. Old Piero, he's a friend, a fisherman, says we can't. But Vossignoria, now if I learn languages and all that, do you think? Do you know if spies, just

262

ordinary citizen ones, can carry swords?"

Taken off guard completely by Zorzi's smile of delight, his calm innocent expression and trusting chatter, the nobleman was overwhelmed with a rush of bitter remorse. Conscience, and the prospect of eternal damnation for such an evil deed, made him shudder. Cold rivulets of perspiration now coursed down his pomaded cheeks staining the edge of his cravat a pinky red. The razor sharp blade flickered in the sunlight as he clenched and unclenched his sweaty grip, then looking up to the blue heavens he uttered a howling, laughing cry of despair. Like a man pole axed by a seizure fit, he then slumped backwards and as the sword dropped it sliced deep into the leather padding just inches from Zorzi's thigh. Instinctively, Zorzi threw himself forward to grab the nobleman's shirt and in the process he almost tumbled overboard himself. To steady the wildly dipping and yawning gondolino, Zorzi rolled to the left as a counterbalance, still keeping a firm grip on the nobleman's sleeve. It was an instinctive move: something he had done more than once when old Piero had stumbled and lost his footing.

Convulsed with sobbing, the man sat for some minutes with his head in his hands. From time to time he would pause and mutter to himself in a sad but still rather maniacal voice: "Why you, Valenzia? Why you? Damn you! Damn you to hell Gradenigo! It's you... it's you, I should kill!"

Zorzi found all this very upsetting. He had never seen a grown man crying so pitifully, nor seen one showing such inexplicable grief and anger. When the man calmed down somewhat, Zorzi put his arm around his shoulder and said, "It must be very hard being a spy. I mean, you must have lots of troubles and worries. I mean, having to kill people and all that. Perhaps, though, I won't become a spy after all."

The nobleman began to chuckle through his tears, "A spy, so that's it, that cursed Conversa! I might have guessed. And you, young fellow, are something special. I am truly blessed to have met up with you. Where did you say you lived? Let me take you home."

"Glassblowers' Canal… our furnace backs on to San Stin."

"Glassblowers' Canal?" the nobleman echoed. "So you are not...that is you are not a..." His voice tailed off, then he burst once more into tearful laughter, "And I so nearly...!"

"You can drop me at the Column Jetty, if you like. Our canal is a bit of a ditch and sometimes boys drop things on rich people as they go under the bridges... dog turds and that sort of thing. And you see, Vossignoria, some bulli have kicked in our front door... just only the other day. Our house isn't really very, very...well... good enough for someone like yourself... being a noble and all that."

The young man laughed and laughed, obviously relieved of an immense burden of anxiety. Now in a mightily cheerful mood and quite enchanted by his alert young passenger, the Noble Rezzonico gave his court sword a hefty kick, drew out again the long oars. With one deft tug he spun the lightweight gondolino eastwards. "Onward!" he yelled above the seagull screams, "Damnation to you Gradenigo and all your clan! Let's seek the glorious Bucintoro! We'll dive for the Doges ring and on we'll row with it to smoky old Murano!"

(And a merry life indeed the young N.H. Abbondio Rezzonico lived thereafter, for though he never again found true love, he did in time rise to the dizzy heights of European power. On learning that little Carlo Rezzonico had just been sired by Abbondio's much older brother, Senator Gradenigo had unwisely concluded that young Abbondio was a poor prospect for his daughter Valenzia and that there was little or no chance now of her offspring ever inheriting Palazzo Fortuna on the Grand Canal together with the Rezzonico jewels and millions. Locking up his daughter in San Zaccaria Convent would in time prove to be a monumental blunder on the part of old Senator Gradenigo.)

CHAPTER TWENTY-THREE

A vigorous ten minutes rowing brought Rezzonico and Zorzi through the lines of great galleons and level with the floats lining the processional route. They hauled-to on the western side close to a raft some twenty feet by twenty feet square from which was coming a most extraordinary wind-like musical sound. Stacked in a crate-like contraption in the middle of the float were a series of what resembled organ pipes - except that they were made of glass cylinders of various heights and thickness. Two musicians were rubbing small pieces of wet leather around the tops of the cylinders and producing powerful and heavenly ringing sounds. Dancing around them in the confined space, were half a dozen scantily clad maidens with feathered wings strapped to their backs. They pirouetted, posed with arms erect, and ducked and weaved under one another's garlands of blue and yellow flowers.

Entertaining though this was, the glass organ soon set up a ringing noise in the young Rezzonico's ears. Zorzi too felt his teeth grind on edge and a severe twinge convulsed his swollen cheek. They decided to relocate and hauled-to alongside a magnificent fountain display, which appeared to be jetting red wine into the Lagoon with all the power of a fire pump. It was a full-scale copy of Bernini's famous Triton Fountain in Rome, except of course that it was made of papier-mâché and gilded to resemble solid burnished gold. By crouching low down on his comfortable padded thwart, Zorzi could just see the feet of the men hidden beneath the beautiful contraption. They were see-sawing up and down on the bars of a ship's bilge pump.

 Spectacular floats of every kind surrounded them. Some took the form of floating gardens, with cardboard Grecian temples at their centres, others were rockeries with palms and live animals: cheetahs, monkeys, tethered parakeets and the like. One construction took the form of a giant golden coach drawn by a team of outsize wooden dolphins. Seated in the coach was King Neptune and a bevy of beautiful damsels dressed as sea nymphs. Most floats though were simply garlanded and flag decked viewing platforms for the ladies of the nobility, with pavilions in the middle and tables set for a picnic. Once the Bucintoro had passed by on its stately progress, the feasting and dancing, the practical jokes and the dousing of one another in water battles would begin in earnest. Hardly any raft was without its band of musicians who, in true Venetian style, sounded off popular tunes in uproarious and discordant rivalry.

The parade barges of the patrician families first came into sight. These fantasies of carving, known as Peotti, were mostly as large as war galleys; magnificent beyond anyone's wildest dreams. Then came those of the visiting Princes of Europe: the Spanish Viceroy, the Papal Legate, the Esterhazy of Austro-Hungary, the Braganza of Portugal, and so on. Outsize flags fluttered, silver trumpets brayed amidst silk lined baldacchinos and carved wooden statuary; every visible angle of each vessel dazzled in gilded excellence. The convoy seemed endless, but young Rezzonico had little difficulty in identifying almost every vessel, pointing them out with as much wild excitement as that of his little passenger.

A flotilla of some thirty, or more, military long boats, known as desdotona, then hauled into view. Each had a large flag of St. Mark fluttering at the stern and a carved and gilded winged lion as a figurehead. They were packed with standing men, dressed like peacocks in parade armour, with medals, plumes and sashes. As though on some watery parade ground, the boats' brightly painted oars dipped and pulled in unison: all moved to a steady rhythmic drum beat; that spine-tingling battlefield beat devised to send hot blood racing in the veins of young warriors; a beat that heralded the arrival of the Bucintoro.

"There it is!" screamed Zorzi in delight, leaping up and almost tumbling out of the gondolino.

CHAPTER TWENTY-FOUR

A most un-serene Doge sat upright in his bed of state, spluttering ship's biscuit crumbs and fig seeds all over the brocade counterpane. Morosini was in a foul cantankerous mood. "Blast you man!" he snapped, "Go sell your purge pills in the piazza. It's cutting for the stone that I need, not purges! And you know damned well that at my age I am not likely to survive your quack pals' shaky scalpels! Haven't you got the sense to know that I am on show all day today? I can't keep running to and fro' to the privy stool."

Maintaining a low bow, the humiliated physician backed towards the bedroom door. It was an unfortunate blunder on his part, to suggest a purge to ease the Doge's pain on the very day of the Sensa. To the Doge's annoyance, the barber surgeon was late as well. He had not yet arrived with bowl and razor to wash and dry the Doge's hair and trim and re-wax the fiery ducal whiskers. However, what had incensed the Doge, more than anything was a pious and hypocritical letter which his Grand Chancellor had just read out - it came from the Cardinal Patriarch.

"Dearly beloved Son, and most Serene Sovereign," it read, "We send you our blessing and urge you in the name of the heavenly Prince of Peace, not to go to the ceremony today in warlike garb. Not warlike, on the holy day in which we remember Our Saviour's glorious Ascension into the Heavenly Kingdom. Go forth in peace to the world, loving and forgiving your enemies. I pray you to wear, in all humility, naught but your ducal robes, your crown jewels and sceptre.
P.S. If you can delay sailing on the eventide, I beg you to do so, for I have sent two cartloads of best sheeps' cheese from one of my farms in Treviso, to provision the fleet. Alas! They are still awaiting arrival of the cheeses at the Arsenal."

"Two faced hypocrite," Morosini snarled at Grand Chancellor Ballarin, "Can you guess who encouraged him to write?"

"Senators Correr, Querini and most of The Ten," responded the Chancellor gloomily, knowing that the Doge would be in a foul mood for the rest of the day.

"Lucky it is, Ballarin, that someone else keeps an eye on the waves while the Cardinal is busy rolling his heavenwards. If it were not for me and my lads in our warlike garb, both he and his College of Bishops would be on their knees on a prayer mat, fat buttocks in the air, facing Mecca!"

"Quite so!" murmured the patient Chancellor. "Shall I send for Makò and Abele?" He knew well that both presences would help to calm the Doge's peppery mood. Makò was in the Palace kitchen taking on board ample provisions of milk and fresh river trout, in anticipation of a voyage that had been long delayed. A pleasant prospect was on the wind of decks awash with human blood and of battle with vermin of the long tailed black rat kind. However, he too was not partial to sheeps' cheese.

Despite the egg-poaching heat, the Doge insisted on wearing his furry robes over his half armour. Abele had taped some goat skin bottles filled with ice into the lining of the ducal cloak and brought along an ostrich fan, as well as the customary gold and gem encrusted umbrella. The Arsenalotti, the Arsenal workers, had the age-old privilege of providing close escort to the Doge wherever he went in town. As he marched behind his regiments, they kept the mob at bay with long thick staves. Using their discretion, they let only the prettiest of young ladies through the protective barrier to kneel and kiss the Doge's emerald ring. Good looking young mothers also qualified and many a startled baby went away screaming after the terrifying old Doge planted a whiskery kiss on his forehead. Makò had a snarling feline jealousy of babies, particularly those taken up in the Doge's arms. He worked out his annoyance during these pauses by pouncing and biffing the ermine fur hem of the Doge's Cloak of State. He had learned from the occasional sharp kick and snagged claw not to attack the gold thread embroidery of the cloak itself.

At the Arsenal the regiments wheeled left through the monumental Lion Gates to embark on their galleys. The Arsenalotti followed them in, thus giving an impression to the crowd that important duties attended them in preparing the fleet for departure. In fact, their main task would be to tap open a few barrels in celebration for, thanks to their efforts, seventy new war galleys of the home fleet were now straining at their moorings. Bristling like wolfhounds on the leash, the galleys were armed, crewed, victualled and manned with criminal oarsmen, ready to dart between the towering gates and out to the blue Adriatic: there to engage their loathed and deadly rivals; the ever probing, ever advancing Islamic fleets. Inside the Arsenal walls and well out of sight of any relatives, provost sergeants were posted to relieve the soldiers of every parcel of goodies that had been thrust at them by their proud and tearful relatives along the march. Orders from on high were that all foodstuffs were to be confiscated for common distribution. The crafty old Doge had calculated that his triumphal march along the Riva degli Schiavoni would bring in enough fresh food to provision the whole fleet for several days.

The procession now considerably shortened, the Doge continued on right to the very end of a mile long promenade which ran past a shanty town district, known as San Piero Castello, (*Now the Public Gardens and site of the Biennale Exhibitions.*) Here were the dwellings of the under-class; the non-Citizens who had no say whatsoever in the governance of the Republic. There were many orphanages there as well, run by orders of friars and nuns who ensured a smart turnout of their forlorn little charges. Shabbily dressed market gardeners, urchins and rag-pants pig farmers now had their chance to see close up their adored Sovereign and equally exciting to them, a glimpse of those mysterious and rather frightening white masked rulers. In their tens of thousands they crowded along the unpaved promenade. Those nearest to the processional route knelt on two knees, as though the Almighty himself was passing by to honour them in their misery. The grumbling old Senators and Procurators, all unmasked, with the exception of those serving their term on 'Ten Duty,' hitched up their red brocades from the mud, held on to their pill box hats in the breeze and constantly adjusted their wide red sashes as they struggled to keep up with the athletic Doge. Some were too senile to make the long march unaided. Their mood was not lightened by the Doge's sarcastic comments about their infirmity, as he strode vigorously ahead, promising loudly to the amused crowd that if the old codgers made him miss the tide he would have them all sweating at the oars of his war galley.

Here and there he would pause and break from the procession to take into his arms some undernourished and under cleansed baby. An arthritic old lady, who was trying her hardest to get down on her knees, found herself tugged upwards, bear-hugged and given a smacking kiss on her hairy lips by the Serenissimo himself. The crowd was ecstatic with laughter and cheering. Grudgingly the Senate had to acknowledge that the old devil knew exactly how to please the crowd: that was really the only role they wanted him to play. They now understood why the crafty fellow had them trudging on such a long march. He could so easily have kept to tradition and embarked onto the Bucintoro straight from the Molo in front of his Palace. A disgruntled half starved mob could rise at any time in insurrection. Once the fleets and the armies were out of sight, only happy memories of pageantry and patriotism kept the nobility safe in their silk canopied beds.

Twin wooden bascules formed a steep arched bridge across the wide canal before them. The bridge also served as a gangway onto the high poop deck of the Bucintoro, which, being too wide to pass through the old Arsenal Gate had to be rowed round from the newer deep dockyard via St. Peter's Canal. To show off his vigour to the adoring crowd, the Doge took the steps two at a time, chasing after his hellcat, Makò . Once on board Morosini swiftly raised both arms in triumph to a tremendous roar of applause. "Do-ze!, Do-ze!, Mo-ro-si-no! Mo-ro-si-no!" they chanted in unison. On hearing the distant uproar, the Arsenal fortresses thundered out their own smoky greeting. Small coins to the value of a thousand ducats were then showered by his almoners into the poorest section of the immense throng.

Once the Patriarch, the Procurators of St. Mark, the Papal Nuncio, the Senators, Ambassadors and finally the dozens and dozens of friends and relatives were embarked and seated back to back along the main deck on red plush armchairs, the Bucintoro cast off its mooring ropes. The Doge was now enthroned amidst much incense smoke and even more trumpeting, blessing, bowing and arm waving flummery. Makò struck a dignified upright pose, seated lion-like at his feet. Silver trumpets sounded a parting fanfare. Noble oarsmen, four to an oar, braced themselves like galley slaves at the command, leaned forward and pulled with all youthful might.

Quite matchless in its artifice and decoration; perhaps the most grandiose vessel ever constructed, the Bucintoro in motion was something that inspired both excitement and awe - it was the ship of dreams - the object the world had come to gawp at. Anthony and Cleopatra might have graced the River Nile in some similar pleasure craft: indeed, the Bucintoro had more than an echo of a Roman State Barge about it. Nemesis, the blindfolded goddess of justice and retribution sat with her

271

raised sword and pan scales under a golden umbrella at the prow of the Bucintoro. She served as its gold plated figurehead and she was beautifully carved in wood - in height about three times life size. Huge twin ramming rostra jutted out from the Bucintoro's bow, giving it the appearance of a giant open beaked water bird. Trailing behind the rudder from the stern and skimming over the water, supported by hundreds and hundreds of little green fishing floats (as Zorzi was to observe later,) was the red and yellow silk Lion's Standard of St. Mark. Whether by mere coincidence, or deliberately intended from time immemorial, the trailing flag appeared to resemble a silken bridal train.

And, moving with all the dignity and beauty of a bride along a church aisle, the Bucintoro began its course, leaving behind a wide tumbling v shaped wake of wavelets. Saluted with song; with music; with screams of delight; with broadsides of blanks from moored galleons; with water jets; rockets and salvos from ships' muskets; its noble oarsmen kept up a steady pace to the rhythmic drumbeat from an escort band of marines. There were no masts or sails on the Bucintoro, just the ancient winged lion flag of St. Mark flapping in a pleasant afternoon breeze from one of the tallest flagstaffs ever turned for a vessel. The seventy-four year old Serenissimo was off to marry, once more, his ever fresh and ever ageless watery bride - the deep blue Adriatic Sea.

The sights of the processional route were of only occasional interest to the Doge. He had seen it all so many times before as a young Senator, though this was only his second Sensa as Doge. With his double duty as Captain General he had spent much of his six-year reign at sea. When the oars dipped deep and held firm, swishing the Bucintoro to a foaming halt, he was still busy poring over coastal maps and adding his signature to state papers. They were opposite the tall campanile of St. Nicholas of the Lido that guarded, at least in spiritual matters, the entrance to the Lagoon. A rumbling message from the immense Fort of St. Nicolas reminded all present that should ever that spirit be put to question, Venetian flesh would show no weakness. The siege guns and the mortars of the fort were trained across the harbour mouth, ever prepared to spit out fire in might and fury at any who came uninvited.

The Six Wise Ones, the Doge's counsellors of state, came forward to invite the Doge to perform the ceremony. With them he walked to the prow of the vessel where, in a pleasant drifting cloud of incense, the Cardinal Patriarch and the clergy were assembled. A curious little bucket, filled with holy Jordan water, was brought forward for the Patriarch to bless. Carved with wonderful miniature panels of ivory, illustrating the watery miracles of Jesus, the bucket was one of the cherished treasures of the Republic, having been stolen in a Twelfth Century raid on Constantinople. (*By an equally strange miracle, the bucket still survives; the only relic of the fabled Wedding of the Sea: for the Doges, their rings and their Bucintoros have passed into the watery mists of time. Napoleon used it for his Champagne; thence it went to the Tsar of Russia; then by purchase to England, at a time when England had become ruler of the waves - the maritime heir of the Serenissima. The National Trust now owns the ivory bucket.*)

Now Morosini had always harboured serious doubts about Jordan water from the time he first learned to decipher Arabic. After liberating some Christian merchantmen from Barbary pirates he found on board several barrels of the stuff. The barrels, it was claimed, were filled from the very spot of river where Jesus was baptised by John the Baptist. This was authenticated on a ticket attached by the local imam, who most likely profited greatly by the trade with gullible Christians. "In the name of Allah, the all merciful," the godly imam had written, "May this Jordan water burn on the lips of the infidel. May it burst their guts and shrivel their manhood in its passing."

Morosini had little doubt that these generous sentiments were reinforced with some bodily contribution of the imam's own making, to defile the holy Jordan water. However he had no qualms about tipping the contents of the holy bucket into the equally polluted waters of the Lagoon. A bit of watered down urine did nobody any harm. Walking forward onto what resembled a carved church pulpit projecting from the bow of the Bucintoro, the Doge waited a few moments. Eventually, silence and a breathless stillness of anticipation spread out across the Lagoon. Then in a loud vice he cried out: "DESPOSAMUS TE, MARE, IN SIGNUM VERI PERPETUIQUE DOMINII." (*We pledge ourselves to you, O Sea, in sign of true and perpetual dominion.*)

With a splendid splash and flourish of his arms, he then emptied the bucket overboard.

Still holding that vast assembly in a thrall of total silence, he slowly removed the emerald ring from his wedding finger. Before tossing it into the sea, he looked down in order to better position his throw. There, some twenty feet below him and treading water silently, was a great ring of young apprentices and other seasoned divers. They were holding one another at bay by locking arms and gripping one another firmly by the side of the neck. It was too late now for any latecomer to break into the locked circle of swimmers. The desdotona, the marine manned longboats, had moved into position to protect the swimmers from further intruders and to ensure that the sacred emerald ring sank properly beneath the surface, before any attempt was made to retrieve it. The swimmers could only guess at the fate in store for any cheat who tried to catch the ring in mid air. In over seven hundred years of Sensas nobody had ever dared.

Flinging back over one shoulder the heavily embroidered side panel of his cloak, the Doge was in the very act of pitching the ring when the Bucintoro received a sudden and violent jolt. The ring sailed in an arc through the air and instead of landing plumb in the middle of the eager swimmers it struck the head of one of them and then slid from his shoulder into the green briny. Pandemonium followed as the circle of swimmers imploded into a wild churning of limbs. The Doge's whiskers twitched: a grimace of fury promptly replaced his amused and affable smile: "Have that imbecile arrested!" he ordered.

The imbecile alluded to was young Abbondio Rezzonico. He had tried to slip through the fence of long boats in his narrow gondolino and had been rammed by one of them right up against the ribs of the sacred Bucintoro. To the Doge's grim satisfaction, the gondolino sank in seconds, but as it did, he saw a tiny little child resurface and struggle desperately to remove what appeared to be sea boots. Almost instantly, he saw the hapless child disappear again beneath the surface, overwhelmed by a tidal wave of violently threshing swimmers. Evidently someone amongst the swimmers had retrieved the ring and all were fighting, kicking and wrestling to wrench it from one another's grasp. Turning away from the unseemly spectacle, the Doge commented that the Provost Marshal would do well to throw a net over some of the healthy looking young ruffians involved in the water fight. They looked just the sort of daring brawlers he needed to conscript into the ranks of his marines.

274

To a drum roll, the enormous flag of St. Mark was dipped and raised again as a signal, for those too distant to witness, that the Wedding of the Sea had been consummated. In answer to the signal, a pent-up roar of artillery was released. From far off it sounded like a Lepanto sized sea battle in progress. Broadside after broadside roared out; the recoil rocking violently from side to side every galley, galleon, frigate and staten-yacht in the Lagoon. Sant'Matteo, Sant'Erasmo and a dozen other surrounding island fortresses sent up veritable volcanoes of coloured rockets from their mortars. Church bells clanged in wild ecstasy; sulphur smoke pouring from the muzzles of cannons and carbines rose in thick black and yellow clouds to the heavens. Choristers, flautists and refined quintets of string instrument players floating by on rafts, were quite unable even to hear their own voices. They therefore contented themselves with just strumming and blowing, or adding their voices at full throttle to the deafeningly discordant din.

CHAPTER TWENTY-FIVE

Zorzi had no memory of being pitched into the Lagoon, or of being trapped underwater by a mass of flailing legs. When a boat hook hauled him in, ripping the back of his shirt, he was grey faced and unconscious. He came-to, slumped on his side at the bottom of a desdotona, when a marine sergeant, long experienced in dealing with such situations, thrust two fingers down his throat and then pressing hard up and down on Zorzi's stomach finally managed to revive him. After sicking up quantities of sea water and boiled egg Zorzi was patted and pampered by the boat crew, congratulated by all on his recovery and still clinging fiercely to one of his boots, he was dried and draped, still shocked and shivering, in a spare regimental flag fished out from the signals locker.

It was a residual bubble of air, trapped in the foot of the waterproof boot that had sent his inert little body bobbing back up to the surface. Confused and still not quite able to take in what was happening to him, Zorzi was helped off with his ripped shirt and stockings, which were wrung-out to dry on the gunwale. The protective father figure of a marine sergeant, then bandaged with his snuff stained neckerchief Zorzi's head, thus stemming the flow of blood from where the hard toenail of a swimmer had gouged a nasty gash. Feeling somewhat better, Zorzi made a fumbling attempt to pull on his wet boot. He was still unaware that he had lost the other. Struggling to pull it upwards on a wet leg, Zorzi now fully unlaced the floppy down-turned fold at the top. He had previously loosened that same riding boot in the Rabbi's kitchen. Something shiny and heavy dropped from between the leather fold and bounced onto the boards. Mystified as to what it was and from where it had come, Zorzi reached down, picked it up and examined it.

"Madonna and Marco!" exploded the old sergeant, "The ring...I can't believe it! The little sprat has got the ring! He's holding the blessed Fisherman's Ring!"

A triumphant shout went up from the crew of the desdotona. Cocking their carbines, they let fly a twenty-gun salvo into the air. While the coxswain wrenched up the sternpost flag from its socket and waved it wildly to attract the attention of the captain of the flotilla, the crew set down their weapons and held their oars proudly on high. Small craft swarmed in from every direction, their occupants curious - guessing that the ring had been found. As the captain's longboat pulled alongside, the finding was confirmed. With hand signals, the delighted captain of marines ordered the drumming to cease and the whole flotilla to ship oars. Despite his best efforts, it took some while for the crew of the Bucintoro to realize that they had lost escort and that frantic signals were being made for them to stop.

Once alongside and while waiting for a rope ladder or a net to be run down, the marines of the desdotona took turns to admire and kiss for good luck the handsome square cut emerald. There was much hilarity, clowning about and preposterous offers of parrots, gin and tobacco in exchange for the ring, all of which soon had Zorzi in a merry mood and helped restore his blood circulation. Eventually, both a net and a rope ladder were let down from a projecting pulley beam jutting out near the bow of the Bucintoro. The flotilla captain took charge of the ring and climbed the ladder alongside Zorzi, who was seated cross-legged in the net. The captain made a fine job of ensuring that the net did not snag, nor that Zorzi should receive a bump from the ornate incrustations of gilded bronze and carved and painted wood decorating the Bucintoro's flanks. Zorzi was hardly in a position to appreciate the beauty of the garlanded cherubs, sea monsters and similar fishy fantasies. He was hauled up steadily, swung in and dumped unceremoniously on to the soft red silk carpeting of the deck.

Kissing the ring once again, the flotilla captain threaded it onto Zorzi's thumb, whispering: "Don't drop it little'un. Tell 'em my name. Say Captain Zen helped you. Remember, Zen's the name. Captain Zen of the 6th Marines, don't forget! It's me, Zen, who helped you. Best of luck!"

With that the young captain, eager not to miss any such a chance for promotion, was ushered away like some low ranking minion, back down the rope ladder; for the silk carpeted decks of the Bucintoro were reserved for the boots of mighty generals and for the lacquered slippers of others who mattered even more.

Accompanied by two gorgeously dressed and bewigged flunkeys, Zorzi hobbled along the main deck, past row after row of seated dignitaries, who whilst applauding him politely with white gloved hands, tried their very best not to burst into laughter until after he had passed by. It could not be denied that he was both a comic and a rather sorry sight. The back of his shirt was ripped in two, revealing skinny ribs and shoulder blades covered in scratches and bruises. One buttock showed through a large L-shaped tear in his breeches and watery blood still dripped from the filthy snuff-stained neckerchief tied about his head. But the main cause for mirth was his dignified straight-backed hobbling, for he had not thought to even up his steps by discarding that fateful riding boot.

Makò sprang out from under the Doge's cloak, where he had been snoozing unobserved on the ermine lining. He bounded along the deck, stopped, arched his back as though to pounce, then, tail cocked high, trotted straight up to Zorzi and wound himself around his wet legs, purring loudly. Zorzi bent down to tickle his ear. Heavy though it was, he lifted the cat into his arms and began to stroke it. There were loud murmurs, astonishment mingling with pleasure at the sight: for nobody who valued his face and hands would ever want to get too close to the Doge's notoriously temperamental moggie, let alone to stroke the evil beast. Loud applause and shouts of "bravo!" now accompanied Zorzi's triumphal progress. Quite a number of Senators got up from their plush thrones and tailed along behind him, eager to see what the Doge's reaction might be. Such a compliment from the Senate to a little ragamuffin was something quite out of the ordinary. As with all changes to Venetian ritual, it set a precedent to be followed in ring finding ceremonies for the next hundred years.

Morosini looked up from a chart of the Peloponnesian coast, which he was studying with some interest, took a long look at Zorzi and his escort of Senators, leaned back in his throne and laughed and laughed as he had not done in many a long month. When the Doge laughed it was diplomatic to echo his sentiments. Even the solemn looking Grand Chancellor to The Ten Domenico Ballarin held a lace handkerchief to his mouth and chuckled – in a most dignified manner, of course.

Zorzi stood there mortified. They were laughing at him. His legs began to tremble and Makò was beginning to weigh heavily in his weakened arms.

Licking the blood from about Zorzi's chin, Makò was purring contentedly, secure in a new friendship: not that he had many friends, other than the Palace head cook. In his long career as mascot and close companion to the warrior Doge, he had smelt and tasted human blood in quantity. Zorzi, despite his dowsing, still had a faint aroma of perfume and well-rotted anchovies and Makò never quite forgot the unique pong of a friend. Zorzi was about to drop the cat and run back to the pulley beam when, in a commanding deep gruff voice, Morosini ordered him to come forward.

One of the flunkeys hissed, "Get down on both knees and address the Doge as Serenissimo – that is, only if he speaks to you. Don't dare to look up at him – just hand him the ring at arm's length. It is impolite to get too close to the Doge."

Overawed both by the ruler's presence and by his harsh commanding voice, Zorzi hesitated. With Makò clinging to him so tightly, it might prove difficult to make a dash back to the rope ladder and net.

"Put that cursed animal down and go forward at once!" the other flunkey whispered and gave Zorzi a firm shove from behind.

Quaking with fear and quite unable to disentangle himself from Makò , who now clung to him, his claws slightly embedded in his shirt, Zorzi edged towards the Doge.

"Sit down here boy!" the Doge commanded, pointing to the footstool that he had just neatly kicked forward from under his feet.

Zorzi obeyed, glancing anxiously at the Doge's dazzling jewels and armour; at those Senators around him and down at the cat, who promptly curled up on his lap.

"So you have come to bring me back my cat. Thank you for that courtesy. Have you anything else for me?"

"Makò won't let go of my arm. I can't hold out the ring like the man told me to do," Zorzi pleaded.

"Good God! The little urchin knows your name. Are you that famous, Makò ? Makò let go of him and come here to me at once!"

279

Makò gave a growl of annoyance, reluctant to stir himself from that fond, if somewhat clawing embrace clamping Zorzi's arms. The ducal voice now changing to a more threatening tone, Makò finally obeyed. The angry end of his tail still twitching, he retired to his own private dominion: the dark cool space beneath the Doge's throne.

Abele, who had been hopping from foot to foot since first sighting Zorzi, could contain himself no longer, "Master! Master!" he called out from behind the ranks of officials surrounding the throne. Then thrusting his ceremonial fan into the hands of an astonished Senator, he pushed forward and threw himself on two knees at the Doge's feet. "Master! Please, it's the boy – the singing boy, who was dressed up in your livery! The very one who saved Makò up in the gallery – he ran away, remember? Ran right across the parade ground! It is him, I swear to God!"

There were gasps of outrage at Abele's impertinence. Abele was a 'non-person,' part of the ceremonial furnishings – a slave, a blackamoor. All knew that he had certain privileges, but to speak to the Doge uninvited in the midst of a state ceremony … that could not be tolerated. Taking a slight nod from a certain long bearded Senator as his cue, the Grand Chancellor Ballarin ordered: "Take him away! Take him below!"

Clanking swiftly forward, two of the Noble Guard seized Abele and dragged him to his feet before the Doge had a chance to intervene. Some of The Ten were present of course, but only Chancellor Ballarin, the Doge and two others knew the duty Senator for that month.

"Thank you Ballarin. That will be enough! I shall hear what Abele has to say, if you don't mind."

A steely glance at the two noble halberdiers was enough to send them bowing respectfully backwards.

"So Abele," the Doge resumed calmly, "You tell me that this is my little giant killer. I can see from his face that he recognizes you. From the state of him, he looks as though he has been duelling once again with Ettore, our formidable Cavaliere! What's the betting, gentlemen, this little'un will make fish paste and knuckle-bones of Ettore Martinengo one day? Shall I promote him to be one of my Generals?"

Another burst of hearty laughter; backslapping and smiles of admiration for the bloodstained urchin came from all around. The Doge's quip eased the mood of the assembly: for many were of the impression that the ceremony was descending into a farce – first that confounded cat, now an impertinent blackamoor. Hanging on the walls of their palaces, they all had picturesque scenes painted by Titian, Bordone and others, showing a grovelling little beggar boy, on all fours, handing back The Fisherman's Ring to some resplendent Doge. In real life though, it was a scene that none of them had ever witnessed. Here was their suitably ragged beggar boy, but where was the ceremony?

"Bring sherbet and biscuits," instructed the Doge. "He looks done in, poor child."

Zorzi gave such a bright smile of pleasure at this news that he instantly won over the old warrior's careworn heart.

"I think you have forgotten to give me back something," he chuckled.

"I've got it here Vossignoria Doge. I don't know who gave it to me. You see, I nearly got drowned and Captain Zen just told me to tell you about him and…well it just fell out of my boot."

Without rising from the stool, Zorzi slipped the ring off his thumb and handed it back to the Doge. Master of one quarter, and one half of a quarter of the Seven Seas, was the title attached to the ring. Both Pope and Emperor had conferred that honour on the Doges of Venice after their 12th Century reconciliation. The Sensa ceremony went with the title, though the ring's donors never specified exactly which three eighths of briny they had in mind, leaving it for each Doge in succession to carve out in battle with the Ottoman the extent of his entitlement.

Yet another interminable drum roll and fanfare announced that the ring was back with its owner. Zorzi was invited to shuffle his footstool to the right hand side of the throne in order to make room for the Six Wise Men, who came slowly and sedately in turn to kneel and to do homage on behalf of the Republic. The homage was not to the Doge in person, for collectively as members of The Ten they were more powerful by far; it was to the ring and to what it symbolised – their dominion and the dominance of Venice over the high seas. Whilst extending his hand for their respectful kisses, the Doge gave an ear to more whispered information from Abele.

Chancellor Ballarin's eyes narrowed. Whispered secrets; information not shared promptly with him and with The Ten were not at all to his liking. Evidently there was much more about this boy that he needed to know. He would have the child taken aside and questioned at the first opportunity. Knowing that Abele would be sailing with a later convoy containing some of the Doge's personal effects, which had yet to arrive from the ducal summer villa, he made a mental note to have Abele interrogated as well.

Delicious little fluffy almond cakes and sherbet water, much sweeter and juicer than that of Rabbi Sterchel, were gobbled and guzzled at lightning speed.

The homage completed, the Doge remarked in a feigned severe tone of voice: "So, my little diving dolphin, what shall we do with you? I shall not ask how you got up on the terrace at San Marco. I would advise you however to keep well clear of my dear sister, given the circumstances. She has been known before now to have bold young boys flogged for their pranks. Tell me, are your parents waiting nearby? I should like to meet them and after that, I too should like to hear you sing. Abele tells me you have a splendid voice."

"There is only me and Grandpa, and Grandpa is not really very well – he keeps coughing, you see, when he wakes up. I had to come on my own to the Sensa and to get my teeth seen to by a rabbi. He's a kind of priest you know, a rabbi, a Jewish priest who does such clever magic. Yes, a rabbi and the rabbi and his wife gave me some very nice clothes, but unfortunately I…well I lost them, you see…"

"I do see," interrupted the Doge, surveying with a grin Zorzi's tattered state. "This rabbi would not be, by any chance, signor Sterchel?"

"Signor Sterchel, that's him Vossignoria!" Zorzi leapt up delighted with the news that the Doge himself knew his benefactor, then sitting down with equal suddenness, he apologized, "I mean Your Serenity…"

"Hah!" guffawed the Doge, "As I guessed, old Sterchel at his sorcery again! Our loyal rabbi always saves his best trick for the Sensa? A little David in my own smutters! Oh, my old bones, how we laughed! Hear me though, all of you. I want none of this to get to Martinengo's ears, is that clear? Floored by a rabbi! What a hoot! Leastwise struck down by Sterchel's little giant killer. How will Ettore ever live it down? No parents then? No mother, no father?"

"They died," explained Zorzi in a matter of fact voice.

"Now that is sad. However, since Abele thinks so much of it, I will hear your voice: many a little song bird has made his fortune. Listen to me though. You're a plucky lad, no doubt about that, some day I would have you a galley captain…captain of a war galley, eh! How would you like that? Not much fun being a warbler in a choir loft. Now what will you sing for us?"

Zorzi liked the idea of becoming a war galley captain very much indeed. "I can sing you the 'Dixit Dominus,' the 'Sancta Maria,' and some other songs. Luanardo chose me to sing to the noblemen, but then Grandpa hit…that is…he took me out of church. People were running about and shouting and throwing things. I don't know why though."

"Were they indeed? Was that by any chance at San Donato?"

Zorzi nodded. The Doge gave a knowing smile. Silence was called for.

And so it was that Zorzi, still half-booted, stood and sang that fateful DIXIT DOMINUS. It was a performance that gave such intense pleasure to the Serenissimo and his guests that for a moment they were left silent; overcome by the melancholic beauty of his rendering of King David's Psalm. When the foot stamping and applause had died away, the Doge gave instructions for his quintet of musicians to be hustled up from the stagnant gloom of the bilge deck. They had been squatting there in some discomfort, on hand for after Wedding entertainment. Not expecting to be

283

called upon for some considerable time, they had been 'pushing the boat out' assisted by a ducal sized flagon of vintage merlot. Mumbled excuses to the Grand Chancellor were on the lines that whilst rehearsing they needed refreshment to prevent them from vomiting, given the nauseous smell of bilge water.

With silver flutes, recorder, multi-stringed chitarrone and viola, they gave nevertheless an intoxicating performance of the sonata and ritornello – a glorious repeat tune which introduce the 'Sancta Maria.' Zorzi somehow knew instinctively when his high-noted voice had to chime in with the strange instruments. In smooth harmony with the quintet, he gave his finest performance.

Tears of joy tricked down the great craggy care worn face of the warrior. Of all old Monteverdi's splendid output this just happened to be his favourite tune. He mopped his eyes and then gave Zorzi a fatherly hug. Zorzi tried not to wince. His back was very sore and as he stepped back a look of absolute fright swept over his face. Chancellor Ballarin and members of of The Ten were quick to notice in which direction the terrified boy's eyes were darting.

Hearing a familiar childlike voice, Zustinian's curiosity was aroused. He made his way swifly along the deck and was now standing amidst the group of Senators behind the throne. As a ducal nephew he had that privilege and nobody dared question his presence there amongst the highest officials in the Republic.

Instantly recognizing Zustinian, Zorzi pleaded in a voice broken with anxiety: "Can I go now Serene Doge? Only, Captain Zen promised to take me. I expect he down there waiting for me, only, Grandpa told me I must keep away… that is from…"

"Hey now! What is troubling you? The Bucintoro can't stop in its tracks again. We'll all be landing at the Lido shortly. Zen, or someone, will see you safely back to your Grandpa. Come now, what's your worry? Besides, you haven't yet asked me for your boon."

Zorzi, now too frightened to give thought to any such request, kept silent: head down he clutched his arms to his chest and began to shiver violently.

All became clear to the Doge when Bastian knelt to kiss the emerald ring and observed in a seemingly casual voice: "I thought I recognized this ragamuffin when Zen fished him out from the net. He's the boy I mentioned to you, from Uncle Torcello's choir, a glassblower's son, I gather. Sound lungs... needs tutoring. Torchello won't mind in the least if I have him. I'll see that he's taken home on my barge, this evening."

The Doge leaned back and looked again towards Zorzi. The child was trembling; downcast, frightened, clenching and unclenching his hands and shaking his head from side to side.

"Christ and St. Mark damn you, Bastian!" he hissed. "Is this one of your Ganymedes? Haven't you got more than enough geldings in your stable? You shall not lay a finger on this child. Your penchant for little choir boys will get you in deep water, if you are not careful. Remember my words, nephew! Remember my warning!"

Crestfallen, and blushing under his lead powder make-up, Bastian bowed low and scurried away beneath the scornful gaze of those present. However, quite unrepentant, he was to be observed shortly afterwards exchanging witticisms and chuckling with a group of male friends at the far end of the vessel. Bastian, after all, was a talented, entertaining and most amusing man. The public reproof from his uncle would have little effect on those many young blades who sought and enjoyed his lively company. Together now they were hatching some new devilment: some diverting and outrageous escapade spawned from their idleness and untouchable privilege.

"Deep water...indeed," mused Chancellor Ballarin. An appropriate idea for disposing of Bastiano had just come to mind. He would present his liquid disposal plan to The Ten at their next meeting. The child's accent was that of Murano's artisan class and it was evident that Bastiano had been up to no good with him, for why should the effete nobleman know where the child dwelled? It was of no direct concern to the Chancellor when the sulphurous cinders of Sodom showered down on some humble abode: that was a matter for the Magistrates. However, the reprobate Zustinian had now set a-smouldering the house of an ancient dynasty. The male heir to a family whose unbroken lineage went back to Roman times, had fallen for his charms. Zustinian's dealings with French courtiers gave off a foul aroma as well, for the skilled workforce that had created the Halls of Mirrors at St. Cloud and at at Versailles had been lured away from Murano by Bastiano's closest friend. Chancellor Ballarin's questing eye looked once again for an approving nod from Number One of The Ten, who, quietly camouflaged amongst the throng of other red robed Senators, was fully alert to what was going on.

The Grand Chancellor stepped forward: "With your leave, Serenissimo, I should like to take the young songbird under my wing. Clearly he is in need of all our protection. Shall you grant him a boon or, given his talents, an Osella?" This was a ripe pun, a clever play on words much appreciated by all, and was met with laughter and polite applause. So the dry old Chancellor was a wit after all, quite equal to the fast thinking Doge. An Osella not only meant 'little song bird,' but also a splendid golden coin of rare and exceptional minting. A few dozen had been minted recently to be awarded either for valour in action, or as a token of appreciation to anyone who had done something of outstanding merit for the Republic. On one side of the coin was an image of the Doge kneeling with his flag: on the other the Bucintoro.

"We'll give him both Ballarin. We'll give him both an Osella for his singing and a boon for his hilarious scrap with Martinengo!" To more laughter and applause the Doge added: "And Chancellor, as ever, you have read my thoughts. Inquire for me as to the law – can a citizen's child be made Ward of State?"

"There may be a precedent Highness, but off hand I know of none."

"Miotto. I read something of that name recently in a report from the Soranzo spy – you know, the fellow just back from England. Yes, it was Miotto… Something about glass for Dutch William and a missing Guildmaster. Miotto, yes… The name rings bells in my memory."

"The bells of St. Peter Martyr, if my memory serves me as well as that of Your Highness." commented the Grand Chancellor.

The rancorous exchange with Bastian and the subsequent banter went completely over the head of Zorzi. All he knew was that the Noble

Zustinian had been sent off humiliated and in disgrace and that the Doge and the skinny and bent old man in purple silk with a wig piled-high like owls' ears and a jewelled court sword, would take good care of him.

It was then that the words of Monteverdi's Psalm suddenly made complete sense to him: 'DIXIT DOMINUS...The Lord said unto my lord, sit at my right hand and I shall make your enemies into my footstool.' Though the transformation of Zustinian into a pouffe had been accomplished long before, and Zorzi was not of the age to comprehend the Doge's public insult to his nephew, he was alert enough to understand that those words of King David's Psalm had now been realized. Grandpa's hated enemy had been crushed and humiliated whilst he, Zorzi Miotti, was now comfortably seated at the right hand of one of God's great elect. He would have to tell Don Tranquillo when he got back. He alone would understand the funny co-incidence of it all. And, that charmed money spider, that he had let free to run under his fishing porch, had honoured to the full its part of the bargain, as Zorzi was soon to discover.

Makò popped a sniffing, whisker twitching, suspicious head out from under the throne. He quite liked the smell of almond cake, but on being offered one by Zorzi he took a nibble and was not so sure. A group of grand looking individuals in gold etched breastplates, elaborate sashes and parade helmets now advanced along the deck. In their hands they had rolls of maps. As they walked they staggered, holding on to one another, for the Bucintoro was now turning rapidly; altering course to come alongside the high jetty of San Nicolo` del Lido. Zorzi guessed that they were not admirals – probably generals of some kind.

The Doge looked down and gave his farewell: "Be off now my little songbird, I have grim work to do. Take the blessing of an old Doge with you. You will find our Illustrious Chancellor to be a kindly person; you will be safe in his care, I promise you. He wants to talk with you, so answer his questions truthfully and all will be fine with you and with your Grandpa. My thanks for restoring the ring – that's certain to bring good fortune on the fleet – blow us the strong North-Easter we now so much need! The Chancellor will speak to you on the lower deck. I expect you will find more almond cakes down there, unless my greedy Senators have gobbled them all."

A caress to Makò 's ear was rewarded with a lick: then kneeling down on both knees, like the others he had seen, he planted a puckered lipped peck on the back of the Doge's hand – after all, he had kissed that glittering emerald several times previously. The Doge had interesting liver marks on his hand and yellowing skin, just like Grandpa's, only much more pronounced. To more applause, Zorzi stood, wobbled on his one booted foot, and then gave the Doge a slow and splendidly executed bow, adding a few extra hand flourishes, having observed that the departing generals had waved themselves off in similar style. In the performance his hand came into contact with the rag about his head: to his dismay he had lost the most precious remnant of his once princely outfit – that fine blue felt hat.

Turning to the Chancellor, the Doge recommended that the boy be rested, poulticed and found some clothes before being escorted safely back home. "Best take him to the 'Buon Pesce' – one of my retired marines, I forget his name, is probably still landlord there. Give him my greetings."

The inn, called 'Al Buon Pesce' was of course perfectly well known to Chancellor Ballarin, as was the name of its landlord. It was an excellent clean establishment at the entrance to the Lagoon, not far from the Church of St. Nicolas. It was set up with funds from The Ten: a loan which had since repaid itself again and again with interest. The landlord was, of course, an agent, a spy, who was encouraged to be hospitable to foreign ships' captains, visiting traders and senior crewmen. All that he overheard and anything incriminating found in their bedchambers was duly reported. Venice, after all, was a trading empire: its exports, imports and manufacturing secrets had to be protected and controlled. Chancellor Ballarin's web of information stretched from Goa in India to the fur trappers of Northern Canada and from Peru to Peking.

CHAPTER TWENTY-SIX

Ex-Captain of Marines, Ezio Lacin was feeding sweet corn to his chickens, scattering it from the downstairs veranda of his inn. Since retiring he had extended the brick and timber property to thirty lodging rooms on two floors, plus a large tavern room decorated with a stuffed crocodile, mother of pearl abalone shells, coconuts and numerous other nautical knick-knacks from far distant lands. His roof was still thatched with marsh reeds, like most lodging houses along the Lido shore, but he intended to remedy that deficiency very soon. The vague resemblance of his premises to an English coaching inn made it a favoured berth for sailors arriving from that rainy land of pirates and Puritans.

Hearing the crunch of feet on shingle Lacin looked up and fair nearly swallowed his wad of tobacco when he saw Grand Chancellor Don Domenico Ballarin advancing towards him with an entourage of advocates, clerks, musketeers and page boys swarming about him. A scruffy bloodstained little boy was trotting along close at his side. "Leave that!" he yelled at his potmen. "Inside at once and hide those damned sugar cones you stacked behind the bar. Get rid of the Oporto casks as well. Roll them out the back. Cover the lot with fish crates or something! Hurry men!"

He need not have agitated himself. The Chancellor was well aware of Lacin's petty tax evasion and the odd bit of smuggling going on at the Buon Pesce Tavern: how else would Ezio have paid off the government mortgage so promptly? Ever fishing for much bigger prey, it suited the Chancellor to leave the sign of the blue swordfish swinging on its hooks and to keep its landlord secure from ever dangling in a similar attitude.

"Hats off! Tankards down! Stand and bow!" Lacin commanded his customers in a bellowing parade ground voice. Seeing who it was marching up the path, almost all but his English guests hastened to obey. "What is it about the Chancellor that makes grown men tremble with unease in his presence?" Lacin wondered. From shoe buckle to tricorn Ballarin was no more than five foot five, with the figure of a dancing tutor, yet his diminutive stature seemed to add to, rather than detract from, his awesome presence. Grand Chancellor and Cavaliere Don Domenico Ballarin just exhuded an aura of power and authority: just to be known to

289

him by name was a tremendous honour. The man had the fascination of a rearing king cobra and always bore down out of the blue when one's guns were unprimed. The Chancellor's international fame derived from that unnerving knack he had of popping up whenever something illicit was in hand and invariably catching the offender 'in flagrante.'

Rising from a deep bow of greeting, Lacin snapped swiftly to attention and head held high with chin jutting like a true marine in a neck stock, he announced to the heavens: "My house is at your command Excellency,"

"Lacin, forgive me for imposing on your hospitality. I am expected at San Nicolo` for the blessing and the departure. Kindly arrange a suitable private room. My advocate will explain everything...a quiet bedroom for the child. See to their necessities. I convey to you the salutation of the Serenissimo himself and bid you my good evening." With that, the Chancellor and his entourage tramped off towards San Nicolo` church, leaving Lacin, part disappointed, part sweating a hot rain shower with relief. Noisy gambling with cards was going on between the English and the Portuguese in the tavern bar. There was no trouble whatsoever, both nations seemed to be getting on very well with one another, for they shared a common enemy in the form of the fleet of King Louis. What was more, several hands in both crews had survived the disaster of Lagos Bay in May '93, when the French had attacked and destroyed the entire English merchant fleet bound for Smyrna. However, both crews were armed to the teeth and both were flouting the laws against gambling in taverns and the carrying of weapons.

Giovanni Maria Licini, the Notaio chosen by Chancellor Ballarin to interrogate Zorzi, was not only a Registrar of Births, Marriages etc., but also kept an eye on any legal concerns connected with the industry of Murano. He was the father of twin boys of about Zorzi's age; a lawyer rising fast in the Chancellor's esteem and, in short, one of his reliable spies.

Over a swordfish steak fried with herbs, buttered aubergines, polenta and a generous carafe of watered-down port, he quietly coaxed out the story of Zorzi's life and that of his family. As a parent, he was greatly relieved to discover, by gentle probing questions, that no harm had yet come to Zorzi, but it was clear that the little lad was still in great danger of being shipped off to Prague, or to Nancy, or to distant Alexandria to be doctored and turned into a castrato singer. There was no doubt now in his mind as to the cause of what was now referred to as the 'San Donato Riot.'

Zorzi's innocent comments confirmed his view that the Podestà, Don Francesco Capello, had dealt with the riot and the public offence given to himself and his noble guests in a wise, merciful and clever fashion. The Notaio, through his own spies, was already aware of the charade of blowing Miotti's furnaces and pretence of dealing-out severe punishment to the consumptive old man. By quietly and deviously permitting old Miotti to continue glass making, Don Francesco had run a grave risk to his own future. The draconian laws of 'The Forty for Trade,' were that the house and furnaces of a traitor should be demolished and the rubble carted off, leaving only a warning notice to anyone else who was considering brighter prospects overseas. The Podestà, was not a bribe taker, of that he was confident; therefore he must have been unconvinced that old Miotti's son, Maestro Vincenzo, had really run away to London. Where else could the fellow be? Such a talented glass blower and artist would by now be feted by kings; celebrated in Paris, Vienna, or Jablonec in Bohemia. Why had he abandoned his infant son, never contacted his family, nor ever tried to smuggle back money to his dirt-poor family? So many glass-blowers, when they prospered overseas, had been caught in that way and if important enough had either been disposed of by a knife in the ribs in some dark alley, or brought back in chains and hanged in disgrace.

Why was a plain English merchant captain making discreet inquiries with the Venetian Magistrates about the missing glass blower? Why for that matter was this sugar merchant being feted in the palaces of important Senators and being left unchallenged about his midnight visit to Zorzi's house? It was all very puzzling. Chancellor Ballarin himself had now ordered him to 'lay off' from having Ravenscroft tailed by Vogalonga. Had Vincenzo been found working in London, it would have already have been reported. Perhaps, after all, the child's belief that his father had drowned in a storm had some truth in it: in which case a great injustice had been done to old Miotti and to his orphaned grandson.

He made a written note to get a clerk to search thoroughly through the archive of reports sent in from spies, from the former Podestà Bembo of

Murano and anyone else for that matter who reported in writing, about the time of the glass blower's disappearance.

Having speedily demolished his own portion, Zorzi was now spooning down the last of the lawyer's plate of crème caramel. He was now drooping with fatigue: a boy's belly requires at least a few moments of repose, before the next meal. In a rather confused and random sequence, he had told all he could remember of his adventures over the past few days. The Notaio put up a friendly smiling pretence of being interested in all the trivia. He had quietly teased out from the boy most of the information he was lacking.

Don Tranquillo's name was underlined twice in his case notes of the interrogation. Of secondary importance was tracing that mysterious young nobleman who had crashed into the Bucintoro and was then spotted swimming away with the speed of a porpoise chased by a killer whale, leaving his little passenger to come near to drowning: that was not an honourable thing for a nobleman to do. He judged Zorzi to be truthful in his statement that the nobleman had not revealed his name. The Notaio had warned his own sons never to tell tales, nor to give names that would get people into trouble, so he quite understood Zorzi's poor pretence of knowing little or nothing about his grandfather's nocturnal visitors, other than that they were: 'English pirates who had only called in to buy some of Grandpa's old glass, because Grandpa was no longer allowed to work anymore and needed the money to buy bread and cough mixture for his lungs.'

A sudden and violent shock wave rattled the parlour windows, followed almost instantly by several very loud booms. Instinctively, the lawyer ducked, but Zorzi continued with the serious task of spooning and licking, quite unperturbed. Peering through the leaded windowpanes, the lawyer realized, with a laugh that what sounded like a powder magazine being blown sky-high, was in fact the parting salute to the Doge as he set sail on board his galleon 'The Serenissima.' The salute signified too that he had to speed up the interrogation. Therefore, he did not insist in his questioning when Zorzi blushed bright red at the name Ravenscroft. The names Soranzo and Sackville drew equal blanks, and those of Worley and Ridley were pronounced so badly by the Notaio that they would in any case have been meaningless to Zorzi. Anxious to get away with his hot news, the

292

Notaio put one further question to the now distinctly sleepy child: "What is your boon, so that I can, if possible, arrange for it to be granted?"

Zorzi thought for a while before answering. He knew what a boon was. He remembered the clowning gymnast in the Piazzetta asking loudly for his boon to be granted by the Doge. "Could I ask the Doge for the Uzkoks to be freed. I still feel sad about them, you know. They are little girls and skinny boys and a few ladies with babies. They can't possibly be sea pirates, not one of them was strong enough."

"All of them?" queried the amazed Notaio. As the prize of a galley captain, it would be hard even for the Doge to grant their release. "Galley captains have their property rights you know Zorzi; the law is on their side. After all, if you let Uzkoks go free, they will only turn back to crime: it's in their blood…. always has been. Perhaps I could apply for just one of them. I could ask about that girl, or else you could always save your boon for some other time, when you are more certain of what you want."

"Yes, the girl….the girl with no hair and my goat pants…. the nuns will look after her… they seemed to like her face for some reason."

"I would warn you Zorzi that she with the rest of them may already have been branded and sold; most probably shipped off to some Arab port. Should we be lucky enough to find her, she will become your slave: sadly that is the law. Once she is branded, the nuns won't take her."

"Branded? That's horrible!"

"Sure it must hurt Zorzi, but slaves are a necessary evil: how else would we man our galley fleets? Even the Doge himself has slaves. Dear old black Abele, in his splendid uniform, is just a slave."

"Well, I don't want a slave. Don Tranquillo says that slavers are an abom…abomibulation crying to heaven for God's venangeance upon us all. That's what he says – so I can't have a slave girl. Grandpa too wouldn't want to upset Don Tranquillo."

"Noble sentiments, young Zorzi, there is always a way around a problem, though. You see, I am a lawyer and I shall write you Grandpa's will for him. Slaves can be freed if named in someone's last will."

"Grandpa hasn't got any money to pay you."
"I rather suspect that your Grandpa will soon be in for a surprise. And, if you remain a good boy, I may ask you for a favour in exchange payment some day soon. Tell Grandpa he need not worry about my fee."

"A favour? That's like a boon, isn't it? What kind of favour?"

"Ah! I shan't say yet. But listen, Uzkoks are branded at the Arsenal, we'll begin by making inquiries there. You would have to keep and feed the girl, of course. However, very soon, my young lad, I suspect that you and Grandpa will be wealthy enough to do just that."

Such a great intake, washed down with much port and lemon water, induced a sudden urge to sleep. As it overcame him Zorzi murmured, "Grandpa will feed her." Eyes now half open, his head jerked a while then nodded downwards to his pewter plate, that was now polished and finger-scoured of its last traces of crème caramel.

"Did you ask her name?"

"I forgot to.... she does't talk Venetian." With that Zorzi slumped forward, eyes closed, gorged, sated and utterly exhausted.

With a deft move, the Notaio swept aside the plate and lowered Zorzi's head onto the food splattered tablecloth. Shuffling together his papers, he patted for good luck the head of the sleeping 'ring finder' and, eager to get away, called for the landlord to present his bill. He had news that the Grand Chancellor might well want to hear at once. If he waited on the jetty to catch his eye, as he was embarking, he might even get a lift back to St. Mark's on the Bucintoro itself. He had followed the Bucintoro in the Chancellor's pinnace, crowded together with a dozen other clerks and lawyers. The Bucintoro would be half empty on the return journey and with the vibes of good luck transferred from little Miotti, his own twin sons might soon be able to boast to their friends that their dad knew the ring finder and also got a ride home on the Bucintoro!"

Knowing that it would be a serious blunder to present one, Lacin waived the bill with much bonhomie, hand flourishing and good grace and set to supervising the washing, bandaging and dressing, of his sleeping guest. His wife found a clean calico shirt and a slightly old fashioned suit of fustian cotton twill which she had long saved for sentimental reasons. The suit had last been worn by her son on his first communion day. Alas, her son was no more - shot and thrown overboard during a sea fight with Barbary corsairs. However she had something else, far more precious than a suit, by which to remember him, in the form of a pretty little granddaughter. Seeing the bruised and lacerated state of Zorzi's head and shoulders, how could she begrudge the child? Both she and her husband concluded that they had found a little warrior worthy of wearing the cherished relic of their son's childhood. Zorzi, still blissfully 'out to the world,' was put to bed fully clothed, on a couch in the landlord's own bedchamber. Though it was still late afternoon, he slept the sleep of a hero home from the wars - except that he was not back at home, nor was he destined to make that journey for some while.

CHAPTER TWENTY-SEVEN

Having had first peek, the potmen and parlour maids of 'Al Buon Pesce' Inn promptly spread news that the boy who had found the Doge's ring was lodging with them. Equally delighted to be host of such a remarkable young guest, Captain Lacin spent some time answering questions from the gathering crowd of neighbours and from their curious children. Calculating that he would sell more ale that way, he built-up a sense of expectation that the young celebrity might wake any minute and come out to greet them all. The crowd waited patiently, chatting and drinking heartily until well after dusk. The bonfires were being lit along the foreshore in honour of the last evening of the Sensa. A strolling group of gipsies from Naples port soon had both adults and children dancing the Tarantella, to the sound of a mandolin, hurdy-gurdy and tambourine. At other times Lacin might have sent them on their way, but the evening was hot and thirsts needed slaking, so he encouraged them to stay with free ale as their reward.

Contented, he retired to the veranda to await with a cluster of young children the fireworks from Sant'Erasmo Fort and those from the Island of St George (*Isola San Zorzi.*) The evening's takings so far were more than enough to compensate him for the cost of the meal for two and the use of his parlour.

Lacin noticed that a long boat was being hauled ashore on his section of beach. In the flickering light of the bonfires he recognized some old acquaintances: There was the flowing grey-beard and the stocky muscular form of 'Maestro Zianni,' together with his son Jacopo. Jacopo (*James)* was the young man he contracted with over payment of food and lodgings of the greater part of the Raven's crew. Jacopo seemed to be the only Englishman amongst them who understood some Venetian. Two fresh-faced midshipmen flopped down on the beach near the long boat, spitting on their blistered hands and obviously exhausted with their long row. Bosun Ridley was with them as well: in appearance to the world a caricature of a pirate of the worst water and yet a man wise in natural philosophy and in good nature. Clearly not in need of accommodation, he guessed that they had come either to check up on the good behaviour of the crew lodging with him, or else to see the firework display. However, from their purposeful strides, and the calling out of foreign surnames as they approached, it now seemed likely that they were engaged in some other business requiring assistance from their shipmates.

Lacin, on greeting them, found out from young Jacopo that they had come to collect a sober crew for the longboat and that they had an errand to run for signor Ravenscroft. Jacopo was quite evasive when asked, seemingly casually, about the purpose of their errand, making Lacin suspect that something illegal might be about to take place while the gaze of most Customs Officers would be directed skywards. He invited Jacopo and his father, whom he addressed as 'Maestro Zianni,' to join him in the parlour for a drink; while Ridley, with some shouting and threatening with his bosun's bull's pizzle, was trying to establish which of his crew were not too 'legless' with alcohol to row the longboat on a long and devious route from the Arsenal to the Ghetto.

After one or two more of his seemingly innocent questions were parried, Lacin decided that he would just make a report of the visit. He had no means, nor spy available, to shadow discreetly the English longboat. Leaving his visitors in the parlour with some fresh bread and soft Asiago Venetian cheese, he went out to the bar once again, still hoping to pick up some more clues from Ridley.

 Someone, in a cultured voice, was asking a potman to be directed to the Landlord. A tall young man then presented himself; he was dressed in the red and yellow uniform of a Palace Guard. What puzzled Lacin was that the man's manner of speaking had suddenly changed to one of an affected rough accent. Further doubt was cast in his mind by the youth of the soldier: Palace Guards were all grey bearded veterans, usually over forty years in age. As a Captain of Marines, Lacin could tell a soldier, even if he was out of uniform. This young guard was no soldier. There were tiny traces of wiped-off make-up under his chin and his shoes, though black and plain, were too new and too well made.

"I come with an instruction from His Excellency the Grand Chancellor. You, I take it, are Landlord Lacin? This is for you." With that he handed him a letter.

Lacin recognized instantly the lapis lazuli blue seal of The Ten. Deeply worried, he hastily opened the letter with his pen-knife and with some relief read: "Countermanding any previous instruction, the child Miotto Giorgio is to be consigned to the escort of the bearer of this note for further questioning at the Palace."

The scribbled signature was quite indecipherable but the rest was in a fine clerical hand. What perturbed Lacin was the absence of an embossed oval shaped Lion of St. Mark, which normally headed letters and instructions from the Palace. He had received one or two letters from the Chancellor in the past and none were quite like this one. Before leaving, the Notaio had told him of some unspecified worries about the little lad's safety and had stressed that only Lacin in person and some stout and reliable fellows of his choice should escort the child back to his home in Murano.

"I do not see the letterhead of The Ten. Where is the upper half of this letter?" he asked.

"Perhaps they are economizing on paper," the Palace guard replied in a seemingly unconcerned voice.

That was it: Lacin's suspicions were now thoroughly aroused. Illiterate Palace Guards were more likely to pepper their sentences with foul language than with words like economize. "I shall not release the child until you give me further proof of your identity. I am not satisfied that you are who you claim to be in that uniform."

"Please yourself," came the insolent reply. "No doubt The Ten will send an armed escort when I report back. You will find the New Prisons very pleasantly cool at this time of year."

"Damn your cheek man! You are addressing an Officer of Marines. Stand to attention when speaking to me!" Lacin spluttered, beside himself with anger.

The Palace Guard obeyed in a slovenly, unsoldierly manner and added, "Come with me to the beach if you want to. You will see that all is in order. I am only the messenger. The Grand Chancellor has not only sent his own gondola but a noble officer to escort the child."

Shaken awake from a deep sleep, Zorzi sat up. His head began to throb:

he ached all over and bilious acid came up, burning his throat. Port wine and crème caramel are not the best of companions in a boy's belly. After allowing him a few moments, the smiling landlord and his plump wife, helped him stand and not wishing to frighten him, told him that he was going home soon.

Lacin decided to show off Zorzi by taking him out and along the veranda rather than through the parlour, thus disturbing John *(Maestro Zianni)* James and the other English guests who seemed to be busy with their own affairs. The tavern bar was now dark and almost empty apart from one or two connubial couples, the lanterns having been carried outside to light up the dancing. Catching sight of Lacin, together with a little boy in a smart fustian suit, the gipsy band stopped in mid tune; sailors unhitched their 'grappling irons' from the waists of fair maidens; children and parents set down their pewter pots and glasses and all hastened forward to hail and clap the young finder of the Fisherman's Ring. With two potman advancing ahead to clear the way, Zorzi made his progress down to the shore, waving feebly to greet the crowd and suffering numerous painful pats. He was not feeling at all well.

Like a stable hand restraining a glossy black thoroughbred, Vogalonga was there holding steady in the wavelets a large and newly lacquered gondola. Its felze was ornamented with silk tassels and gilded bronze finials and as it bobbed in the water its side slats flickered, reflecting back the bonfire light, for they too were gilded with burnished silver leaf.

Lacin was relieved and greeted Vogalonga with a hearty handshake. He was fully expecting to find a battered old sailing craft manned by thuggish kidnappers. Zorzi would be a profitable victim, given that the reward for the ring that would certainly be coming the way of the boy's family. Together with Vogalonga, Lacin had pulled off a number of clandestine operations over recent years, mainly connected with tobacco and silk smuggling. Vogalonga, he knew, was a bit of a rogue and was as freelance with his gondola hiring as he was with the ladies. He was not an official spy, but earned the occasional reward as an informer on the misdeeds of others. Lacin knew that he lived on Murano Island and hired himself as gondolier to various noble families there.

"Go with the gentleman here. He will take you back home. Remember to come and see us again." With that, Lacin lifted Zorzi from around the waist, waded out a yard or two into the shallows and set him down on the rear seat of the gondola. He then gave a leg-up to the Palace Guard, who did not trouble to thank him. With a parting shout of 'Oh Eh!' Vogalonga pressed his long oar into the shingle sending the gondola swishing forward, out into the dark waters of the Lagoon. The crowd gave a cheer, the children screamed their last greetings and a contented Lacin trudged back towards the Al Buon Pesce Inn.

Half way along the path from the shore, three or four boys and girls ran up from behind Lacin, calling "Captain, Captain! What's he done? Did he pinch the Doge's ring? Are they going to hang him?"

"Of course not! Now be off home….go back to your parents!"

"They are going to hang him signor Lacin, I saw them!" announced a dripping little boy, "I swimmed out behind the gondola. They are definitely going to top him, I saw them!"

"Saw what?" exclaimed the exasperated Lacin, "Now hurry off to your parents. The fireworks will be starting-up shortly."

"Don't matter much to us," grumbled the little wet swimmer, "Only the fellow with the load of jewels on his coat shoved a big black bag right over the kid's head. The lanky gondolier bashed him twice very hard, 'cos he was screaming out. He tied up the kid's wrists and shoved him into the felze."

For some moments Lacin stood shaking his head, like a half stunned prize fighter; then, yelling wildly his anger and consternation, he ran back down to the shore. Seeing that all was now lost, he stumbled back to the inn, groaning aloud and shouting incoherently. The mystified customers by the veranda hastened to get out of his way, murmuring their suspicions that he had suddenly gone mad, or had drunk too much ale.

Some degree of reasoning now returning to his confused brain, Lacin ran full tilt along the veranda and without knocking, blundered into the parlour, shouting for help. Over a shared tobacco pipe, Nick Ridley was trying to convince John and James that he had caught sight on the beach

300

of the nobleman's son who had bought a microscope from him at the fair and who had asked after Mr. Ravenscroft and himself. There might be the prospect of another big order for microscopes from the lad, or from the weird old Papist priest who was with him.

When Lacin gave James the boy's name, Maestro Zianni *(John Worley the Raven's Master Mariner)* had no need for further halting translations by his son. With the fury of an aged and dusty lion sighting a rival on his patch, John threw back the table, seized two lanterns and charged down to the shore. There was no need either for Ridley to shout commands in John's wake, the entire crew drunken and stumbling though many of them were, answered the unspoken call to arms. They streamed after their hoary bearded leader, priming pistols and unsheathing cutlasses as they ran. The Portuguese, guessing that their old allies were in some sort of a fix, downed fiddles, tobacco pipes and porter pots, drew their own weapons and followed suit.

At the shore there was much screaming and confusion. Seeing what looked like a pirate raid on full swing, shrieking mothers grabbed their children; lanterns were overturned; dancers took to their heels and gipsy musicians merged silently with the shadows. The Portuguese had beached their longboat and tied down its tarpaulin; even so, they were not long in launching and striking out with deep dipped oars, following silently in the moonlit wake of the Raven's longboat. Though they were heretics and quite often ruthless buccaneers, English sailor men had for centuries stood back to back with their Portuguese shipmates. The crew of the Sao Vicente longboat had no notion of where they were heading or when the enemy would be sighted, but they were game for a fight and trusting of their drinking pals of the Raven.

In mid Lagoon, drawing alongside one another, a council of war was held. Lacin transferred to the Sao Vicente longboat. Both crews now knew what their mission was and what to look out for: namely a superior looking gondola with unlit lanterns and silver gilded slats to its felze. Ridley had seen, if only briefly, Vogalonga. He had looked with disdain on his unseamanlike shoulder length bleached blond curls. However, when Vogalonga took off, Ridley could only admire the stylish power of his rowing: something by which, even in darkness, he thought might well help him to recognize the gondolier.

Using agreed signals to be flashed with the shutters of their lanterns, both crews moved away to make a careful sweep of the Lagoon. The Portuguese scared the wits out of a honeymooning couple. The English disturbed a valiant old granny who was out stargazing in mid Lagoon through a hole in the top of her own silver slatted felze. She threatened to brain with her telescope any thieving brigand who dared to board her. A middle aged auntie with a gondola load of nieces and nephews out to see the fireworks, set up an hysterical screaming when the tail end of her gondola was lassoed by a boatload of foreign pirates. The children though were thrilled by their moonlit encounter; a whole longboat full of armed desperados; what fun! When James called out his apology for the disturbance, they waved their excited farewells with scarves, hats and handkerchiefs.

Fear and panic now sent sweat trickling down Lacin's spine: he peered at the myriad of stem and stern bobbing lanterns each twinned with its reflection on the ink black, satin smooth water, and was convinced now that he was a ruined man. The Chancellor would never forgive him for such a foolish breach of trust. It would only be a matter of days before the Customs would come to search his premises and find, or plant, some evidence to have him thrown into jail. He had taken a gamble that Vogalonga would make towards either the Giudecca, or Grand Canals, there to get lost in a vast maze of narrow waterways, but it would seem that the duplicitous curly haired blond had headed off somewhere else: perhaps directly to Murano. All that Lacin could do now would be to make straight for the Doge's Palace and denounce the kidnapping.

They were now fast approaching the great pink palace: its whole southern facade could be seen clearly lit up with thousands of little oil lamps. The fireworks had started up and wherever they shed their brief and splintered light Lacin could survey the hopelessness of his search. Hundreds and hundreds of gondolas and other oared craft were skimming about: sails and floats were obstructing any proper sighting of hundreds more. A group of revellers on the embankment of the Customs House - a huge stone building, resembling the prow of a ship - had lit a bonfire in an iron brazier and started up their own fireworks display. Their fun in such a fateful place only served to plunge his thoughts into further gloom. As the first batch of their crackling sparklers died down, Lacin noted, one, two, three, flashes; a pause, then three more flashes. It was the agreed signal. His heart leapt, "Remate, remate! Seguite Inglesi!" he screamed at the Portuguese crew.

They got the drift of his instruction and bent their backs to the task.

In the brief glow from one of those fireworks, Nick Ridley spotted the now leisurely drifting gondola, Vogalonga's gleaming blond curls and the shutters of the felze reflecting silver pools in the inky waters as he dipped his oar. John gave orders for the Raven's nameplate to be unhooked from the stern of the longboat. Opening the locker box, he drew out a heavy musket, primed and loaded it with a five ounce iron round. Quietly instructing two of the rowers to move forward and make space for him to kneel on the middle thwart, he rested the weighty weapon on the starboard rowlock. A final signal was sent to the Portuguese then lanterns were extinguished.

Vogalonga was making an easy and unhurried progress towards the mouth of the Grand Canal: in silence the English longboat drew alongside. There could be no mistake; it was their quarry. After a few whispered instructions John crouched and let fly with his five ounce ball. With a flash and a thud it drilled a neat hole right through the gondola and out the other side. It was a perfectly aimed shot, striking below the waterline and just avoiding the cabin area of the felze: the gondola span round out of control. Unable to keep his balance, Vogalonga dropped to his knees and clung to the forcola, a carved hardwood post that serves as a multi-purpose rowlock. Recovering his footing, he leaned overboard and just managed to rescue his oar, which fortunately floated close alongside as the gondola continued its spin towards it. It was then that he saw the longboat closing with him and a white bearded brigand of a man standing amid thwarts with a musket levelled right at his chest. His two companions popped their heads out from the felze, wondering what was going on. Seeing that they were now sandwiched between two longboats filled with armed men, they dived back in again and bolted the flimsy shutters.

Vogalonga, however, was made of sterner stuff - he had done battle with river pirates and Lagoon gypsies on more than one occasion. If he could strike down the ringleader of the robbers, he calculated that it would be an easy task to reverse the gondola with a quick backwards oar sweep. In the confusion that would ensue, he could then dart away from the two boats that were trying to jam him. He raised his oar with both arms above his head in token of surrender whilst allowing the stern of his gondola to drift level with the white haired brigand. Noting his sign of surrender, both longboat crews shipped oars, eagerly reaching out to secure his gondola. Then, with the deadliness of a double-handed broadswordsman, Vogalonga swiped out! It was a blow aimed with such speed, such strength and such ferocity that it would have decapitated anyone but John Worley.

John took the full force of the blow on the butt of his musket, which shattered and splintered into two. He staggered for a second, then ducked and hurled the useless barrel at his adversary, who was already halfway through his lightening reverse move. The flailing gun-barrel missed completely, glanced off the top of the felze and splashed into the canal. Vogalonga laughed loudly - but too soon. The Portuguese had rammed their boat hook through the slats of the felze and for good measure had tangled the comb like steel prow of the gondola with their fishing net. Now harpooned like a luckless whale, Vogalonga had no choice but to stand and to fight. And this he did to his credit, parrying any move to board the gondola with his flailing oar. It was one of the young midshipmen, hands blistered from hard rowing, who saw his chance to pay back Vogalonga with his own coin. While Nick Ridley cocked his pistol with every intention of shooting dead the fighting gondolier, the midshipman swung his oar low and caught Vogalonga a fine cracking blow on the ankle, which swept him clean off his feet and overboard into the canal.

Since it was not officially their fight, the Portuguese conceded the honour of boarding to the English. Unsheathing his cutlass, John scrambled on all fours into the slippery bobbing gondola. Steadying himself - the floorboards were already slopping with water sucked in through the bullet holes - he gave a mighty kick at the seemingly fragile doors of the felze. Made of layers of lacquered plywood, they buckled but did not yield easily. He turned sideways to wrench the heavy forcola from its socket. (It was one of those many lucky moves that he was able to boast about until his ninety-seventh birthday as a Pensioner in Greenwich Hospital.) Twin pistols spat flames of orange through the plywood and into the night, their lead passing within a hair's breadth on either side of him –

one bullet ricocheted off the hardwood of the forcola and struck splinters off the longboat. He battered down the doors with the forcola while the occupants, choking in their own gun-smoke, were unable to reload. He was prepared for the sudden rapier lunge as the doors finally gave way - and it came with lightening speed! Giving a textbook parry to sixte, John riposted instantaneously with a ferocious 'graze,' a twisting sideswipe along the length of the rapier blade, which sent it spinning painfully out of the hand of its masked owner. "Yield! Arrendetevi!" he bawled angrily at the shadowy occupants of the felze.

Nick Ridley was now right behind him with lantern and cocked pistol. The Portuguese were merrily engaged in smashing down the doors at the other end of the felze. His old eyes not fully adjusted to the dim smoke filled light, John failed to notice the squirming little bundle trussed up on one of the leather covered cabin benches.

"Blast you man, unmask!" he ordered. The gem smothered nobleman either failed to understand, or was reluctant to obey. Nick beckoned with his pistol for the 'Palace Guard' to lie face-downwards in the now rising swilling and gurgling canal water. "Unmask! Or I'll slice you like the stinking stale loaf that you are!"

Finally getting the message, the nobleman fumbled behind his periwig to untie the mask strings. Ever willing to oblige in such sartorial situations, John knocked the man's hat and wig off and ripped the white linen *'bautta'* mask from his face. As the Portuguese burst in from the other end, Nick raised the lantern in order for them to distinguish friend from foe. As he did so, John exhaled a long low whistle, which came from deep down in his lungs.

"Blind me if it ain't the Frenchie!" he exclaimed, "My Frenchie - diamond dove and all! I've had a lookout eye for you these past twenty year, Mon-sewer Frenchie! Well your looks ain't improved much with the vintage. You are still the pox-raddled molly that you always were Mon-sewer! Pick him clean Nick and tie his dirty bones up! We'll see what Captain Andrew has to say to him!"

In full ceremonial fig, having just attended a Senatorial reception, the Chevalier Lorraine was a better prize than a Spanish galleon homeward bound from the Americas. Gasping for breath, his nose and mouth caked in vomit, Zorzi could only hear muffled bangs and voices through the thick velvet cushion cover tied over his head and shoulders. But they were English voices...John's voice! He began to shout and to kick and to throw himself about on the padded bench.

Taking the Chevalier's rapier, baldric and scabbard as their prize, the Portuguese hauled the 'Palace Guard' to his feet. Ripping open the top buttons, they pulled his coat down over his arms. With a musket barrel prodding his spine they bundled him overboard into the Portuguese longboat and into the presence of an infuriated Captain Lacin.

When James brought out the little boy and sponged the sick from his face with canal water, the rest of the crew had their chance to see the bruised and lacerated state of Zorzi's head and shoulders. They could contain their rage no more. Quite understandably, they assumed that the Mon-sewer and his red and yellow-coated servant had inflicted the cruel injuries. They demanded that John should execute both men on the spot.

Nick Ridley hauled out from the felze that pathetic shaven headed, ugly and poxey faced freak, who once had been judged to be the second handsomest male at King Louis's court. With his stockings dangling around his ankles and dressed only in his drawers, he pleaded in broken English for his life.

"Top him Bosun! Kill him now!" the crew urged Nick.

Still pressing his pistol hard under the chin of the Chevalier, Nick tossed the sash and badge of the Most Exalted Order of the Holy Spirit, together with a bundle of priceless clothes into the longboat. He looked towards John for confirmation before pulling the trigger.

"Hold it! We can't do it here. Not in mid canal!" James shouted.

In answer to Lacin's frantic pleadings, James had gone over to the Portuguese longboat and had learned from Lacin that both men were high-ranking noblemen. Killing them in such a public place would bring swift retribution from The Ten. More to the point, they were all now drifting towards the palaces of the Grand Canal. Their actions were now lit up by candlelight streaming from ballroom chandeliers and the numerous mirrored lanterns attached to mooring posts. A small flotilla of curious onlookers was now bobbing around them, keeping a safe distance however from what looked like another piratical raid on a nobleman's gondola. It would only be a matter of time before someone alerted the Signor della Notte, (*The Lord of the Night*) who would dispatch a boatload or two of musketeers to hunt them down.

Using the tinplate loud hailer from the Portuguese longboat, Lacin stood up to call out to the surrounding boats. His purpose was save his own skin, as much as that of the two crews and, in the process, that of the captive noblemen. "I am Captain Lacin of the Marines!" he called, "Agent of His Excellency the Chancellor of State! I am arresting two men who have kidnapped and brutalized a young child. With the generous help of these Portuguese seamen - he was careful not to mention the word English - I have succeeded in rescuing the child. I am ordering all who can hear me to look out for and detain a gondolier with long blond hair - his name Vogalonga! He is an accomplice, who must be handed over to the authorities. Here is my badge of authority. While one of the crew held a lantern close to him, he displayed his neck chain with badge of office attached. He looked very impressive, every inch the officer and his parade ground voice carried over the waters. A larger gathering of gondolas, some with noblemen aboard, drew closer as he repeated the message.

Halfway through the repeat message, the silver slatted gondola gave off a loud squelching sound, turned turtle and began to sink gracefully into the canal. Scruffy shirted bosun Ridley and Monseigneur Philippe Le Chevalier de Lorraine Harcourt etc., parted company with a splash in opposite directions, without a shot being fired.

After clinging for some perilous seconds to the ripped Portuguese sardine net, Nick was trawled in by his laughing shipmates from the foul smelling waters. Nick could not swim. His choice of language was more elevated by far than that of the most poetic of Billingsgate fishwives. Not only had he lost his own trusty pistol but, more to the blasted point, a pair of blue steel and gorgeously silver damascened weapons belonging to 'Monsewer' - worth a couple of years pay to an admiral, he reckoned. As for that old raddled pervert he was about to top, he declared: "Good riddance! He wasn't worth the price of a decent English bullet!"

After a brief and half-hearted search for the Frenchie, both crews leaned to their oars, extinguished their lanterns and made off into the dark open waters, in the direction of the Lido.

A further council of war was held once they were well out of sight of any curious gondolier. Zorzi terrified of what might happen to him next, clung to Purser James, his rescuer for a second time. He was determined not to leave the English longboat. Understandably Lacin was unwilling to let the boy out of his sight until he had properly fulfilled his obligation to the Chancellor. Finally it was agreed that Lacin would send back his 'Palace Guard' prisoner under bound escort with the Portuguese.

With the aid of a dimmed lantern he began to pencil a message to his wife, telling her to stow the prisoner 'in the usual place.' As he scribbled, a devious little thought occurred to him. Now that he had retrieved the false warrant from his prisoner, who was obviously a rake from some noble family, he had all the evidence he needed, both to clear up any doubts in the Chancellor's mind about the laxity in his care of the little Murano boy and to hang like a dog this captive accomplice of the Frenchman. For strangled, or hanged, the young noble would be once The Ten were shown that false document issued in their name and with their seal attached. There was however another possibility to consider, namely Lacin's long cherished plan to replace the leaking straw roof of his hotel with good solid terracotta pantiles. A stonepaved forecourt also came to mind: a covered pergola where his customers could dance and revel on wet feast days; perhaps even some new chairs and lanterns for the wine tavern? Thinking about it, the list could be endless but whatever the cost of the improvements might amount to, they would still not add up to the value of a young nobleman's neck! Put like that, his prisoner would soon be eager to reveal his true identity. A handsome ransom note could then be delivered to his noble family, advising them that the false warrant was lodged with a lawyer, who had all the facts, just in case they were planning to send 'bravi' instead of ducats by way of payment. Thus Lacin could sleep contentedly under a dry roof with his ribs well insured against stiletto damage.

Andrew Ravenscroft was expecting a barrel full of silver religious items to be shipped to a London Synagogue when the longboat pulled in at the rear of Ca` Dario: instead he got Zorzi and a moral headache. What to do with a great pink diamond weighing at least thirty carats and twenty or more other precious stones of immense value? Collectively they were worth more than the 'Raven' itself, its cargo and the fair acres of his Kent estate in the Golden Vale of Shoreham.

 Well, the moral side of the problem was promptly resolved by John: "Look upon them as settlement of that swine Orleans's debt. Mon-sewer is his creature, remember? And Captain, we don't know what the blackguard has done to our little shipmate.'Strewth, it ain't decent to think on! I should have sliced the molly when I had him at me mercy! It won't be easy to ditch his diamond dove though. Pity to have it carved, but I suppose you'll have to. I'd the fancy of borrowing it from you when we parade along Wapping High from Katharine's. Why, the ladies of the town would be drooling at me seaboots!"

"More likely a gaggle of molly boys would tack close to your stern." chuckled James, "Specially if they got to know it was Mon-sewer Lorraine who gave you his flash pink pigeon!"

Giving a hearty guffaw, John feigned a swipe at his cheeky son. Ravenscroft poured more red wine into John's and Lacin's glasses. They were seated beside a trickling mossy fountain in the pretty little walled garden at the back of the Dario Palace. James hovered, awaiting further instructions and doing a bit of translation here and there for Lacin. Knowing now that Lacin was some sort agent of the Venetian Republic, he took pains to leave out anything in John's conversation that he thought might compromise Ravenscroft.

John sucked hard and thoughtfully on his clay pipe: "You were too young to know anything about it Captain Andrew, but your dear old uncle George had a trick or two to teach us in situations like this. Arsenal Customs are likely to go through our cargo with a flea comb after this bust-up."

Giving a friendly nod and a smile in Lacin's direction, and knowing that James would have more sense than to translate, he continued: "What's the betting this innkeeper fellow here is about to blab to them about our glassware? I have already seen him eyeing-up old Piero's crates. Now your uncle used to employ Nick on these occasions. Nick ain't only a pretty poxy faced sea-dog and a dab hand at selling microscopes you know, he can make bilge ballast better than anyone else I know!"

"Go on you old devil! Tell me straight what you are proposing?"

"Well, anything pricey, like guineas, silver ingots, jewellery and the like, Nick would plaster cast over and set inside ballast sized blocks. With a bit of dung and dirt coating them, no one, except him, could tell them from any other ballast rocks down in the old Raven's bilges."

"A bit suspicious, loading up one's own ballast in the Arsenal," Ravenscroft commented.

Nick was called for and he soon came up with a much better idea. He had seen quite recently a little back alley statue maker making plaster casts of the Virgin Mary, Saint Mark and the like. He could buy from the statue maker a few bags of plaster and a selection of his gelatine moulds and ferry them, together with Mon-sewers jewels, to the Ghetto. Rabbi Sterchel was a broad minded man: he wouldn't mind old Nick busying himself, breaking the Second Commandment, in one of his spare rooms under the Synagogue. It might even amuse the Rabbi to know that the order he had received from Cree Church Lane Synagogue for silver tabernacle doors, chalices and Torah bell finials would be ferried safely back to London inside the belly of a plaster saint. Rabbi Sterchel had means as well to get a false order printed to fool the Arsenal Customs. The order for statues could appear to come from some wholesaler in Siracuse or Ancona - ports that the Raven had called on during its inward voyage. What bold Venetian official would dare to break open a statue of St. Mark, or the Virgin? The resourceful Nick Ridley had even thought out a plan to hoodwink the far more thorough and puritanical Customs officers in London's Katharine's Dock.

Ravenscroft was happy to go along with this plan, though he appeared to Nick Ridley to be remarkably unconcerned, both about the valuable proceeds from the fight on board the gondola and by the news that a representative from the Lord of the Night was coming later that day to question them all.

Zorzi slept blissfully on his eiderdown mattress till late morning, untroubled by the howling shade of the evil Dario's ghost. *(Venetian folk law had it that a curse laid upon the Noble Dario ensured that his palace would remain forever misshapen and that each subsequent owner would came to a nasty end – as indeed they always have!)* Ravenscroft and Lacin were up and about before dawn. It was agreed that all three perpetrators of Zorzi's kidnap would be reported as either escaped, or drowned. Lacin, in his report to the Chancellor, would emphasize the heroism and self-sacrifice of the English Master Mariner and his crew and would honourably mention the Portuguese. Both Ravenscroft and he would report that it was a French speaking nobleman who had kidnapped the child and though they had no time to get him to reveal his name, he had an uncommonly badly pox marked face. They would both report that they had last sight of the Frenchman floundering in the water when his gondola accidentally capsized and sank. He was treading water and shedding his expensive clothes, weapons and ornaments to avoid drowning.

Well contented with his pact with Ravenscroft, Lacin left in a hired gondola. In a canvas sack he had an entire sugar cone; in another sack a silk brocade coat, waistcoat and breeches. In his purse he had a third share of the gold coinage found on the Chevalier, which had amounted in total to sixty Louis d'Or. The Portuguese share was also entrusted to him - twenty heavy gold Louis would easily settle their unpaid lodgings bill, even if they stayed for a month. As he sat back in the gondola seat and breathed in the early morning air, which was still tainted with the whiff of firework powder, he felt at peace with the world. In a few months the ransom would make him a very rich man. Nobody would be surprised when his little granddaughter appeared on her First Communion day in the most exquisite brocade dress in all Venice. She would advance up the aisle of San Nicolo` del Lido, her waistband and dress bows of purest blue French silk, and appear to all the world like a miniature noblewoman; one might almost say a damsel of the most exalted Order of the Holy Spirit!

CHAPTER TWENTY-EIGHT

Two beefy built topsail men, survivors from the Lagos Bay massacre, were detailed to accompany Zorzi. They were both devout Catholics from Old Ireland and as such unlikely to blab. The gondola was one hailed and hired as it drifted past the watergate of Ca` Dario. Before giving him a parting hug, James reminded Zorzi that there were still bad men about and that he should chat to no one about his adventures until he got safely home, for gondoliers were notorious gossips, indeed the main fount of all news spread about the islands of the Lagoon. Neither of the Irish seamen could speak a word of Venetian and though James would have liked to see the lad safely home he could not be spared. Nick Ridley and the Rabbi Sterchel would not be able to communicate without his presence. James checked that the sailors' pistols were securely loaded, their powder dry and that their short 'boarding hangers' were razor sharp. It would not do to alarm the gondolier, so the weapons were concealed in an innocent looking shopping bag. A small sealed package, addressed to signor Daniele, was entrusted to the sailors and the gondolier was paid a fair price in advance for the return trip.

Familiar with every shortcut in the vast vein of canals, the gondolier entered the narrow Rio dell'Albero, (*Tree Canal*) right opposite the Dario Palace and twisted and turned his craft northwards. He sang rude and merry songs all the way through the city centre, keeping Zorzi and the sailors well entertained, pausing only to shout his "Oh-Eees!" as he approached each sharp bend.

Once out on the Lagoon, with Murano's bell towers bobbing on the horizon, the gondolier got more chatty and curious about Zorzi's tough and suspicious looking foreign escort. Understandably he was a bit concerned about the boy's safety, particularly on noticing his blood stained and battered state: "What were you doing, young man, at Ca` Dario?"

 Zorzi was cautious with his reply: "I took some of Grandpa's glass there. A foreign captain here for the Senza bought it all. He ordered the two sailors to see me home."

"That was kind of him, and wise. I guess you've been in some scrape already? Not surprised you've got extra muscle to look after you, but you'd have been safe enough with me. The city is swarming with villains, bandits, foreigners, Uskok pirates! Now the Doge has gone, even we gondoliers need watch who we take on as a fare. Horrible murder last night, right opposite Customs, a lad no more than your age....just up canal from Ca` Dario."

Curious at this news, Zorzi asked what had happened.

"Son of an inn keeper somewhere out on the Lido. Seems the boy had fished up Morosini's Sensa ring. Gang of pirates followed him back home - after the Doge's reward for the ring, no doubt. Innkeeper now distraught, the swine took his only child. He offered to pay them every sequin of the reward, but kidnappers always hold on to their victims till every coin is paid up!"

Sensing that it would be most unwise to correct the gondolier's bad news, Zorzi was nevertheless curious about his talk of a reward for the ring: "How much does the Doge usually give?"

"Oh! Thousands, most likely, thousands of ducats!" came the reply. "Kidnappers won't get them now though. The lad got shot dead while the swine were fighting one another over him. Nobody on the Canal lifted so much as a finger to save him. Of course, as usual, the pirates rowed off unchallenged. So much for our lilly livered nobles! All the true heroes have sailed off with the Doge. Where was the Signor di Notte al Criminal, I wonder? In someone's bed, or else dead drunk at the casino, I reckon."

Zorzi wriggled and twisted on his seat, almost bursting a button in the effort to hold his tongue. Unable to contain himself any longer; he exploded into singgers.

"I don't think it's at all funny, young man. You should learn to show some concern for your fellow Christians! Learn some manners, you little ape!" With that, the gondolier went into an angry sulk, following but not answering to Zorzi's directions.

CHAPTER TWENTY-NINE

The front door was shut and bolted and when Grandpa did not respond to his calls and his hammering, Zorzi went round the back. Both furnaces were stone cold. There was not even a flicker of life in their embers: it was as though two lifelong friends had just breathed their last, deserting him for ever. So many long hours of his young life had been spent working the steel shutters; pumping the double bellows; pulling blobs of blazing glass in and out of their crucibles. His anxiety was now making his heart thump. He crept up the ladder to Grandpa's bedroom, fearful of what he might find. Grandpa was there, stretched out on his crumbling straw filled trough of a bed, deep in an afternoon nap. Zorzi waved his thanks to the sailors down in the courtyard and shouted that all was well. They left, wondering why the lordly Ravenscroft should be so concerned about a kid who came from such a desperate slum. James, not trusting the Irish men entirely, (since both were newcomers to the crew and recruited at the Lido Tavern,) told them nothing about Zorzi's exploits, nor that they were safeguarding the little finder of the Doge's ring.

Zorzi shook Grandpa, then getting no response other then a snort and a throaty groan, he jumped on him - just like he used to do when he was no more than an infant. Taking an ear in each hand, he gently shook the old man's head while planting numerous kisses on his stubbly cheeks. Grandpa sat up and was immediately overcome by a racking, dry sounding, bout of coughing.

"We've got money now Grandpa. We can buy your cough mixture."

"Madonna and Mark! Where in heaven's name have you been? I've been sick with worry…nightmares... saw you both drowning. Piero should never have over-loaded that leaking tub of his, it needed two trips. Send him up, I want a word with him!"

"He's not here, Grandpa...he never came to ferry me back home. I waited and waited so long, but he never came."

"So what's this.... you've got our money….you went to Ca` Dario then?"

"Yes, that is no. I went to Ca` Dario, but I was kidnapped you see. I saw all the glass crates, so Piero must have gone there, but he never came back for me."

"You are talking riddles boy. What have you done to your poor head?"

"It's a long story Grandpa. I got kicked by someone when I was saving the Doge's ring…. and then some nasty men whacked me and put me in a sack."

Grandpa coughed painfully once again. "Oh! Stop taking nonsense Zorzi. Fetch me my spectacles – they're on the mantelshelf."

Grandpa looped the two strings of his thick goggles over his ears and opened the packet. Twenty bright and heavy gold coins cascaded out onto the straw mattress. Grandpa read the note: 'This is Zorzi's share of the booty. Kindest regards, James Worley.'

"What game is Ravenscroft playing? This is not what we agreed. It was to be twenty seven ducats and another five for the cullet when they came to collect it. These are Louis d'Or! I can't change them up!" (*Cullet: lumps of cold glass prepared in a crucible for shaping and blowing.*)

"That's all James gave me, Grandpa - honest! Perhaps he gave the rest to Piero: I expect he did. The Raven lot wouldn't cheat us Grandpa, they are all good people. John saved me from the red and yellow soldier who bashed me and the nobleman with no proper ear. They all had a proper real fight with pistols and swords and things and I wished I could have seen it.... only, I had a bag on my head and..."

Ignoring his grandson's last remarks as total fantasy, old Daniele took off his glasses, rubbed his sunken, red-rimmed eyes and raised himself unsteadily to his feet. He had been in bed alternately sleeping, weeping, coughing and praying for more than fifteen hours. "Well, where the devil is Piero then?" he half muttered to himself.

 "Bring me up an orange Zorzi, please, and some water. I don't suppose you remembered to get my anchovies?"

"I did Grandpa, but I had to give them to the Doge's cat. You see he got stuck up in the flowers in St. Mark's. I was up on the balcony and Makò , that is the Doge's cat… well… he nearly fell a hundred feet onto the bishops and things."

"I see," said Grandpa, impatiently, "That crack on the head has addled your brain-box: check your satchel to see if there's more money? You had better bring it up for me to have a look. Are you sure Ravenscroft didn't give you any other message? What on earth does he mean saying this is your booty? These coins are no use to us! Only the likes of Ravenscroft can change Franch coins for sequins."

When Daniele learned, to his bemusement, that: his parmesan had been fed to the witch's rats; that Zorzi had crashed into the Bucintoro in the company of a nobleman waving a lovely sword; that the Doge had given him almond biscuits in exchange for his ring and that the satchel, complete with a precious necklace for signora Molin, had been left on the dinner table of the nuns of San Zaccaria; his old eyes narrowed. With another impatient sigh he observed, "Don't tell me any more Zorzi, I know the rest - a four eyed dragon swooped over the Lagoon and swiped off your hat with your brains in it!"

CHAPTER THIRTY

Hearing that old Piero was missing and that Grandpa had been crying, signora Molin gave Zorzi a motherly hug and a slice of bread and lamb's fat dripping, then soaking some old linen strips in vinegar she replaced the filthy rags binding the worst of his grazes and daubed salty lamb's fat on his minor woulds. It stung, but Zorzi gritted his teeth and was cheered up when signora Molin told him he had the best haircut in all Murano. He so wanted to tell her about the necklace and to recount all his adventures, but after Grandpa's scornful dismissal of his stories, he decided not to. Anyway, it all now seemed like an unpleasant dream to be put out of mind. Aldo was not about. Zorzi suspected that he was in the house and had been sent away by the signora when she had caught sight of Zorzi coming along the footpath. Don Tranquillo's instruction was still law in the Molin household.

She tied half of yesterday's loaf and a gooey lump of goat's cheese in a napkin and gave Zorzi a small canister of milk. "Make your old Grandpa some hot bread and milk: that will do his chest good." she said, giving him a kindly parting pat on the bottom.

"Can't hot anything: furnaces have gone out. Now we are shut down, perhaps just Aldo could come across?"

"Let the bread soak for a few minutes, you don't need hot food this weather. I'll talk to Don Tranquillo. Maybe he'll let Aldo come and play. No idle talk mind: everyone thinks Grandpa has been given a beating and that's why he is not out and about. Mind you, they may look at you and think you took a good thumping as well!"

Realizing at once that she had said something rather thoughtless and insensitive, she gave him another smile and a hug. "Cheer up my lad. The worst is over now. There is a lot of sympathy for your old Grandpa. They won't do anything else to him now. They know there will be another riot if they do. And Zorzi, I must tell you something really funny, I'm sure it's a presagio."

"What's that, signora?"

"A heaven sent vision, the sight of something yet to happen, or maybe it's because we all have a double walking the Earth. When Aldo and the lads were singing with fat Luanardo in the Piazza, they saw your double: a young princeling, moving about grandly with all the other nobs on the Loggia. And I know when Aldo is telling me fibs! Whoever he was, the young nob had a shiner on his cheek, just like yours, he even waved his hat back at them. And something else: he had a short haircut like the one you've got from the Sensa. It's got to be a good presagio – who knows, one day Zorzi you may well stand proud as a prince!"

CHAPTER THIRTY-ONE

Hot days drifted by uneventfully. There was food enough, thanks to signora Zanetti of the sugar shop giving poor exchange for a Louis d'Or. Grandpa hid the rest of the French coins behind a loose firebrick in the wall behind the furnaces. Towards the cool of the evening, wild games of wrestling, kicking and throwing the ball at a goal, known as 'calcio,' would start up again in the orchards. Neighbours, as ever, complained about the noise and Zorzi's friends ribbed him occasionally about his princely double. Presagio or no, Aldo and Matteo were still convinced that they had seen their friend dressed in silk and blue moving amongst the grand folk up on St. Marks. For his part, Zorzi kept to Don Tranquillo's advice to speak to no one about his adventure: the added danger of burglary was the last thing Grandpa needed. There was talk of a reading school starting up in the cloisters of St. Peter Martyr and of a young schoolmarm being appointed, but nothing so far had happened. There was gossip too, throughout Venice and the mainland of the terrible fate of the poor little 'Ring Finder,' but Zorzi kept his mouth tight shut on such speculation as well.

And so did Captain Lacin, blatantly holding to ransom his noble prisoner while he raked in the sequins. The Al Buon Pesce Inn was now by far the most popular in the entire Lagoon, people came from miles around to show their sympathy and to drink a glass or two, while Lacin and his wife looked soulful and would neither confirm nor deny the rumour. They busied themselves, for the most part out of sight, counting the takings in the till. Only a few locals knew that the Lacin's son had in fact been shot at sea some years ago and these were paid in free ale to button up their lips: that is when they were not engaged in drinking to the landlord's health.

The Ten then chose their moment to strike!

Vogalonga was taken first. Despite cropping and dying his blond locks, letting his stubble grow and swapping his braided velvet monkey jacket for a beggar's coat, he was betrayed by a rival champion rower and brought in chains from the Port of Chioggia. Once he caught a whiff of burning charcoal and was shown the cauldron of boiling oil and the red hot tongs of Messer Grande, he told all, right down to his two attempts at housebreaking on the Miotti premises whilst employed by Zustinian in the search for the missing recipe book.

Monsieur Le Chevalier de Lorraine received the profound regrets of the Lords of the Night. The entire Senate, deploring his cruel treatment by bandits whilst within the protection of the city bounds, also passed a resolution of apology. He was promised swift retribution and indeed several devious looking but quite innocent gypsies were slung into jail in order to convince Lorraine that The Ten were on the track of his assailants. However, it must be remembered that The Ten often enjoyed introducing a touch of black humour to diplomatic hiccups of this kind: the Dutch and the French were, after all, sworn enemies and a little mischief in that part of the world would not come amiss. For this purpose a high-ranking Procurator of St. Mark's was chosen to be sent with a message of sympathy: one who was much admired for his humorous pranks: one who, by no coincidence, was closely related to the chief beneficiary from the plundering of the Chevalier and his garments. Some token of amends had to be made to Lorraine: the Chevalier was a member of the mighty Guise family that once ruled much of France as well as the vast and independent Dukedom of Lorraine. The Chevalier Batard's suspected father, Duke Charles, had battled alongside the Doge in the Morea Campaign. For many centuries Dukes of Lorraine had been sturdy allies of Venice in fending off the Sultan's armies. Now, with the death of Duke Charles, the dukedom had been gobbled-up by that other menace, Louis XIV, in his ambition to become the second Charlemagne.

With the promise that he would track down the English pirates and their captain and would personally bring them to the Consul for punishment, our prankster Procurator, the Noble Lorenzo Soranzo, persuaded Conyers, the fat Frans Hals of a Dutchman, to come along to give support while he apologized to Monsieur Le Chevalier. The mischief making Procurator also suggested that it might be an occasion on which the Dutchman could boast of the fact that Holland was now a world power and that the English were no more than a subject race. During his apology the Dutchman might also find words to offend Lorraine once more and to hint a threat to King Louis to stay on land and look after his cockerels rather than cluttering up the Dutch shipping lanes.

At Palazzo Lolin, where the Chevalier was honoured guest of the

Zustinian clan, all went swimmingly well, not to say explosively offensive and just exactly as the young Procurator Soranzo had intended. The Chevalier performed his elaborate and carefully rehearsed insult: the Procurator expected nothing less. Still dressed in his nightgown beneath an embroidered Turkish bathrobe, the Chevalier received them in his bedroom: his filled pisspot placed deliberately to obstruct their entrance. As he harangued them both, demanding and presenting a bill for an outrageous sum in Dutch guilders by way of compensation, the Chevalier's young valets minced about him, pomading his grey stubble hair, lacquering his nails, plucking his nostril hairs and adding more perfume and hot water to the footbath in which he was soaking his feet. Lorraine completed his tirade against clog hopping, herring sucking, thieving Dutch and English pirates, by suggesting that the Consul was as welcome in his bedroom as a fishwife's fart.

At that, his face brick red with pent up rage, Conyers tried to aim a kick at the footbath but was restrained by the Procurator. The Dutchman then gave vent in his own language to some gloriously sounding foul oaths, the like of which would certainly have put an extra smirk on the face of a Frans Hals Cavalier. He swore too that it would not just be Lorraine's poncey gondola that would be holed below the waterline in future, but the entire French fleet. Adding that the Chevalier was defiling with his pox raddled feet an otherwise perfectly good Dutch Delft footbath, the Consul flounced out, deliberately dropping the debit bill into the pisspot before overturning it with a deft kick. As he scuttled down the marble stairway the Dutchman fumed within himself. All the insults that he would have liked to deliver about the pederast Lorraine's lifestyle and habit of kidnapping innocent little boys were denied to him. Alas! His own master, William of Orange, was more notorious than Lorraine on that score.

Procurator Lorenzo Soranzo was equally famed for his complete po faced countenance whilst carrying out the most outrageous of pranks. On this occasion even he had to rein himself in from collapsing with mirth. In solemn tones he conveyed the deep regrets of the Senate and as a token of their esteem he presented the Chevalier with a rare and exquisitely bound book of drawings by Gaspare Vanvitelli, showing the great sights and monuments of Venice.

As the two noblemen bid their farewells with much bowing and flourishing of handkerchiefs, the Procurator casually mentioned that the book had been obtained from a delightful little shop in the Square of St. Stephen's *(San Stin now Campo Morosini.)* He mentioned too that the proprietor of the shop, a particularly handsome young man ("Alas! One of easy virtue and inclined to mankind,") had an extensive stock of rare books. Amongst them was a saucy folio of original drawings by Marcantonio Raimondi, a notorious friend of the great Renaissance artist Titian. The young shopkeeper would only show the book to personal visitors and was expecting to sell it soon to some nobleman of wealth and discernment. The Procurator thought the book was very reasonably priced at only thirty-one ducats. Unfortunately, he himself could not afford to offend his wife by purchasing it.

Lorraine eagerly took the bait, his better judgment as ever eclipsed by his libertine lust for low life.

Palazzo Lolin was just a few leisurely paces from Campo San Stin; nevertheless the Chevalier took an escort of four discreetly armed and muscular bravi and wore a plain linen bauta mask so that none should recognize him. The delightful young shop owner proved to be very much a gentleman both in education and manners. He explained that he now kept the naughty volume at home, since there had been a recent complaint from a prudish old nobleman. He suggested that they might adjourn to a nearby chocolate shop while his shop assistant went to fetch it. The offer seemed somewhat unusual. A member of the exalted Guise family, though illegitimate, would not normally accept such an offer from a tradesman. However, the foolish Chevalier saw it as an opportunity to get better acquainted with the handsome young man.

The two men sat sipping their steaming hot drinks and exchanging pleasantries at an outside table. Directly opposite them, was the palace of Countess Morosina. An exceptionally tall and upright middle-aged gentleman strode out from its gateway with a modest sized leather bound book tucked under his left arm. The man seemed an affable enough sort, perhaps out for a morning stroll. As he walked he doffed his hat several times to passing ladies of the humbler class, oyster sellers, laundry maids, nosegay sellers and the like. There was nothing unusual in that, except that none of them did more than curtsey in reply before scurrying away. None attempted to 'button-hole' him for a sale. A more observant passer-by might have noticed however that every itinerant vendor, huckster and mountebank in the square was packing his bags in great haste, almost as though preparing to flee from an expected police raid. Local residents as well were now quickening their steps out of the square towards the nearest alleyway. On sighting the strolling gentleman, Lorraine's bravi as well quietly backed away from the chocolate shop then took speedily to their heels.

Now, as though by casual chance, the gentleman drew near to the Frenchman's table: Lorraine put down his chocolate cup, noticed the leather bound book and gave a slight smile of pleasureable anticipation to the newcomer. In that instant the gentleman swept off his hat to salute a dairymaid hurrying past with her milk churns. Yelping with pain and beside himself with rage, the Chevalier leapt up. The clumsy great oaf of a book shop messenger had knocked flying the chocolate cup with the brim of his hat: its scalding contents splattered and drenched Lorraine; the cup itself neatly swept straight into his silken pantalooned lap.

"Damn you for a clumsy turd of a servant!" bawled the Chevalier, mopping as best he could his breeches with a lace handkerchief, "Have you Venetians no self control? I will have you replace my soiled garments with good coin, Sir, or be damned, I will have you hanged!"

The tall stranger said nothing. Jerking his head to one side, he motioned to the young bookseller to vacate his stool. The young man needed no prompting: he fled back to his musty smelling bookshop and closed the door behind him. There he would await his assistant's return from taking that urgent message to the Countess Morosina's palace, for there was no such book of scandalous drawings to be found in her prim premises, nor anywhere else in his shop for that matter. The bookseller sat down at his desk and whittled a new nib on his quill pen in preparation for writing a full report, as instructed by Chancellor Ballarin. All so far was going exactly to the Grand Chancellor's plan. The bookseller felt fairly confident that he would hear no violent clang and clash of rapier steel echoing around the square.

Cocking booted leg over the stool, the stranger sat down and close faced the Chevalier. Infuriated by this silent provocation, Lorraine turned to order his servants to give a good whacking with their staves to the

323

clumsy, ill-mannered oaf seated so boldly in front of him. But from behind came only a metallic rattle from the shutters of the chocolate shop, as they were slammed and locked shut. It was as though Nemesis, the goddess of justice and retribution, had risen from her golden seat on board the Bucintoro and cast her deathly blindfold over the empty square.

The stranger dropped a leaden hand on the Chevalier's left shoulder. Unable to resist the downward pressure, Lorraine sat back with a squelch into the remains of his spilled chocolate. Wondering nervously and momentarily quite where… at some candlelit diversion or maybe during one of his artistic forays… he had encountered before that awesome grim set face. To his shaking consternation, he then remembered: "Mere de Dieu! C'est le visage de Colleoni!"

The living heir of the bronze horseman of San Zanipolo now held Lorraine clamped like a stumbling poacher in a well set trap. In a paralysis of dread Lorraine now realized quite how gullible he had been. The stranger's ferocious, almost sepulchral, countenance drew closer and in a voice measured, deep and rasping, announced: "My brother, I am the Martinengo di Bergamo."

Lorraine was by no means a coward, nor lacking in skill and experience. He had duelled and killed on several occasions, yet still an icy sweat, a spasm of deep terror overtook him. The expression "my brother" had alerted him to the miniature eight-pointed enamel cross dangling beneath Martinengo's expanse of lace collar. Brotherhood had never deterred a Knight of Malta from scrapping to the death in Valetta's appointed 'Alley of the Sword': elsewhere, brother knights were supposed to forgive one another for any slight to prickly honour: this the Chevalier Lorraine now attempted to do, but the implacable Martinengo would have none of it.

"This evening before sundown on the Lido shore, the choice is of course yours, my brother. Do you still count yourself Noblesse de L'epee, or perhaps your preference would be more inclined to a pouffe of gunsmoke? The choice, I repeat, is yours. Make for the sign of the swordfish, an inn called 'Al Buon Pesce.' The landlord will direct your party to the Ground of Honour." Marinengo rose to his feet, patted the Chevalier on the arm in a feigned brotherly gesture, picked up his his leather bound prayerbook, and strolled slowly away to attend the morning Mass in San Vidal.

Mindful that he would shortly be dispatching his twenty-third inconvenient foreigner, Martinengo had cause to unburden his conscience. Either skewered, or lead ball perforated, their departed souls would travel so much more gracefully down to Hades with the aid of a candle lit prayer. He made the sign of the cross and knelt before Carpaccio's beautifully painted offering to that other horse backed warrior of the Serenissima - Saint Vidal. Whilst on his knees praying and meditating, the 'Coup de Jarnac' came to mind as a suitable method of dispatch. That ghastly 'main gauche' dagger swipe to the kidneys had after all been invented in France, and as a duelling move had the Bourbon seal of royal approval. Following up with a low lunge to a suitable part of Lorraine's anatomy would also seem appropriate for the occasion, given the disgusting information about the French nobleman's habits that had recently been passed on to him together with his detailed instructions from The Ten. In short, he was ordered to decorate the duelling ground with Lorraine's guts.

Sundown saw Lorraine hot hoofing it over the border to the Papal States, leaving his carriages and baggage train of cooks, catamites, flunkeys, astrologers and a magpie collection of straw wrapped curios to be picked over slowly by the Venetian and the Vatican Customs. In a note to Dear Bastiano, Lorraine explained that now that the Sensa was over he had been overcome by a sudden religious urge to visit the shrine of the Holy House at Loreto. In thanking the Giustinani for the gracious loan of their Lolin Palace he offered his sincere apologies for the urgency of his departure. Having ascertained that the Most Noble Brother Martinengo was a close relation of theirs, he should not like to have on his conscience the likely fatal injury to a member of the family; given that the elderly gentleman was perhaps no longer so agile with the sword. As the whole silly episode was nothing more than a matter of a spilled bowl of chocolate, he was quite prepared to forgive and forget.

Not in the least surprised by news of this hasty departure, the Procurator Soranzo - ever a thoughtful and considerate man - had already arranged for the precious volume of Vanvitelli's views of Venice, which the Republic had presented to Lorraine, to be filched back by the Customs. Soranzo had no desire to offend the Chevalier's sensitivities with such a vivid reminder of his Venetian holiday. Moreover the joker of a Procurator had since learned that the great Venetian view painter Gaspare Vanvitelli was in fact a certain Kaspar van Wittel - a Dutch artist and as such an affront to a French pouffe.

Helas! Le Chevalier Prince Philippe de Guise Lorraine Harcourt etc., etc., took care never to 'set foot' on Venetian waters ever again.

CHAPTER THIRTY-TWO

The English longboat slid almost unobserved along Rio Marin in the quiet of the early afternoon and hauled up at the steps of Palazzo Soranzo, a seemingly modern looking dwelling with that kind of simple elegant facade which proclaimed to men of good taste that it was a desirable property - an un-altered survival from the times of the great Palladio. Dismissing his crew, Captain Andrew Ravenscroft bounded up the steps. Servants greeted him as though he owned the place and soon after he reappeared at a side balcony window on an upper floor overlooking the renowned and gorgeous botanical park of Senator Gradenigo. More to the point, that side window gave him a perfect vantage point from which he could oversee the grandiose landing stage and triumphal arch leading to Senator Gradenigo's crumbling Gothic pile. He watched as the Portuguese Ambassador disembarked from a modest gondola. In spite of his great age and matching bulk, the Ambassador seemed quite steady; one could say even nimble on his pins. He climbed unaided the wet steps and bowed, as far as his rotund paunch would allow, to exchange greetings with the Senator and with the Procurator of Saint Mark's. Some time elapsed before the Dutch Consul made his appearance in a gaudy state barge accompanied by an escort of trumpeters, drummers and flag flutterers, who made such a devil of a racket that they brought the whole slumbering neighbourhood to its feet and to its doorways and balconies, for Conyers, the Dutch Consul, was by nature an insecure attention seeker.

Once both visitors had disappeared from sight into the Senator's cavernous hallway, Ravenscroft slipped out through a side door leading directly into the botanical garden and made his way through the clipped parterres and herbal hedges, entering Gradenigo's home via a stairway reserved for servants. He had taken the trouble to dress as a bluff English sea-dog: no wig; no make-up; no rapier; just a heavy three quarter length coat of saffron coloured leather, a calico shirt, sea boots and fustian breeches.

The Portuguese Ambassador, in contrast, was the essence of elegance: a walking advertisement for his nation's favourite tipple. His plum coloured silk outfit and grand expanse of waistcoat were embroidered all over in a vine pattern. Unlike the others who were called to the meeting, who kept their distance, the Ambassador came forward at once to greet Ravenscroft and to introduce himself. In broken English, he thanked Ravenscroft's crew for their bravery and their cooperation with his own countrymen in rescuing the kidnapped child.

When the Procurator of Saint Mark's came to deliver his formal 'dressing-down' to Ravenscroft, he kept up the degree of solemn and offended dignity that he considered appropriate to the occasion. Ravenscroft pretended not to understand a word of what was being said to him, leaving the difficult task of translation both to the Portuguese Ambassador and to the Dutchman. While the Procurator droned on with his long legalistic and flowery worded condemnation of Ravenscroft, the Dutchman's creased and distinctly ugly face grew more and more to resemble that of an elderly pug dog that had just bitten on the proverbial wasp. There was no mistaking his state of mind - his gloomy seething anger with Ravenscroft and his crew was well expressed in his puritanical sober black and grey outfit - only a diamond snuff box and gold knobbed ebony walking cane hinting at his wealth and status. That same bleak mood, fortunately, overclouded the Dutch Consul's powers of observation, for even the most casual of onlookers would have noticed the distinct physical resemblance between the plain English Captain and the majestically red robed and bewigged Procurator.

The involvement of the Portuguese crew in the affray and the strong support they were given by their affable old Ambassador had apparently greatly helped to justify the actions of the English pirates. The noble gossips of Venice, and most diplomats, murmured their approval in strictly off the record terms. France and Holland however were, to everyone's amusement, sworn enemies briefly united in their sense of outrage. The Portuguese Ambassador had been working desperately behind the scenes, hoping to save the Raven from being impounded in the Arsenal and its entire crew from being thrown into jail. Little did he know, poorly informed that he was on such matters, that The Ten was noting his efforts with polite good humour.

The Portuguese Ambassador had taken an instant loathing to the Consul. Moreover, the Dutchman's huffy arrogant manner when greeted at the palace landing stage had not endeared him to that equally haughty patrician, Senator Gradenigo. The vintage of the Gradenigo bloodline was to be savoured in the Senator's hallway and took the form of a vine leafed family tree carved in finest statuary Carrara marble and covering one entire wall of that cavernous space. It was sited so as to overawe any visitor of inferior rank, though, to those with a more discering palate, hints of rhubarb and the odd whiff of raspberry were to be savoured here and there in the make-up of that vintage. Gilt lettering traced his tendrils back to the Roman Consul Sulla via the amorous efforts of three Doges: not to mention those of Cleopatra; Lucrezia d' Este *(Borgia)* and of course Noah. The Gradenigo family vine however, was destined never to sprout the ultimate of all family connections – that of adding the triple crown of the Papacy to its armorials. Now had stubborn old Gradenigo listened to the pleadings of his daughter Valenzia and not locked her up in San Zaccaria Convent, she would certainly have gained the title, power and wealth of a Papal Princess. That, spurned suitor to his daughter, that young upstart of inferior family, Abbondio Rezzonico, became the favourite uncle of clever little Carlo Rezzonico, born in Ca`Fontana in 1693 and later known as Pope Clement XIII.

Talk of the mighty Consul Sulla failed to impress the Dutchman, whose upbringing had been strictly prophets and profits, biblical and businesslike. Genealogies were for a decaying breed of useless parasite patricians, like Gradenigo, and those ancient Roman generals most likely were all papists anyway and of couse he failed to make that obvious family connection he had with the Senator in the person of Mr. Noah. In contrast to the Portuguese Ambassador, the Dutchman showed no concern at all for the likely fate of Ravenscroft and his crew. In an age when religion coloured opposing viewpoints in any dispute, Ravenscroft was strongly suspected by the Dutchman of being a renegade papist Jacobite. The Portuguese Ambassador secretly hoped that the Englishman's religion and politics might be so: the Procurator and Senator Gradenigo had no need for doubts on that matter.

Procurator Soranzo intoned solemnly, *(between pauses for translation,)* that the Republic could not permit foreign nationals to take the law into their own hands, even though it might be in an honourable cause. The right course would have been to call for assistance from the Lord of the Night for that District in rescuing the abducted child, though he conceded that there might well have been a fatal delay by so doing. *(There were six Signori di Notte al Criminal, one for each metropolitan district and, need one add, a thirty year legal dispute as to who was responsible for that section of the Grand Canal.)* The Serenissima would not however follow up the accusation of Lorraine that he had been victim of a gang of English pirates, who had robbed him of his jewels, sword and purse, because there was no shred of evidence to back his claim. (Those witnesses who had come forward were warned that The Ten might submit them to questioning, whereupon to nobody's surprise, they all promptly thought twice about making a statement!) But there were certain conditions required before a metaphorical Venetian blind was closed to the protest from King Louis. First: that Ravenscroft and his crew should depart back to England on the next favourable wind, sailing part way as escort to some provision barges, which would be supplying Morosini's fleet at the Southern end of the Adriatic Sea. Second: that Ravenscroft should act as courier to deliver a sealed and packaged message from the Doge to King William of Orange. Third: that the collection of rare pieces of the art of glassmaking, which he had purchased illegally from Daniele Miotti, be presented to the Sovereign of England as a gift from the Serene Republic of Venice. Fourth: that Ravenscroft should apologize to the Dutch Consul, who represented King William in the absence of any diplomatic agreement with the Serenissima; for by sailing to Venice and trading without his Sovereign's permit he had broken the laws of both nations.

The Dutchman seemed well satisfied with these terms of settlement. A high ranking member of the court of King Louis - his nation's arch enemy - had been robbed, humiliated and personally insulted by an English ruffian. Several of his own informants had overheard English being spoken, so there was little doubt who had perpetrated the crime - Ravenscroft with his crew were the only Englishmen in the city. He would have liked his Dutch lion's share of the booty - of course he would. At heart he was a free-booter too, but at least now he would get the entire credit for the princely gift of Miotti's priceless glassware to King William of Orange. Should the gift lead to a new trading agreement between the two nations, then he might well ask to be elevated from Consul to the rank of Ambassador, with all the extra trading perks that would bring to him. Pleased as he was, he could not resist the chance to lambaste Ravenscroft for his insolence in not reporting to him on first arrival in Venice. He knew that many a sea captain of Ravenscroft's kind were resentful and rebellious after the easy conquest of their country and of Ireland. Ravenscroft had shown his true colours by sailing to Venice without licence. In a heavy Dutch accent he spluttered at Ravenscroft, accusing him of being a renegade; a likely papist; a common brigand and thief of Lorraine's sword and baubles. Had the Senate condemned both Ravenscroft and his crew to hang in the Piazzetta between Marco and Todaro, then he would have come along cheerfully to swing on their legs! Ravenscroft took these insults with feigned humility. He grovelled suitably and presented the Consul with a gem encrusted snuff box in three coloured gold which, strangely yet conveniently, was already engraved with a flowery and profuse apology written in Dutch. Quite taken aback by this most favourable turn of events, the Dutchman's sour mood improved and Ravenscroft fobbed him off further with a tale of seeking refuge in Venice, after having been chased half way through the Mediterranean by a Turkish flotilla. All present then sealed the agreement with a glass or three of the Ambassador's excellent port wine, into which they dipped their traditional rock hard and weevil proof 'Baicoli' ships' biscuits - to make them, like the agreement, just that bit more palatable to chew on. The prospect of losing his beautiful Miotti glass to the Dutch usurper, King William, might have appeared to be a 'hard swallow' for Ravenscroft, but he in fact had first suggested it, having taken time to select the finest pieces for himself. The Ten would be paying for the glassware and their purchases were, as always, for some long term purpose. The princely gift was all part of the charade of diplomacy and in that charade Ravenscroft had his own part to play.

CHAPTER THIRTY-THREE

"Now tell me young Andrea, are we wise to forge ahead with this treaty? I shall never, even if I live to the age of Methuselah, understand the English. You spend best part of the century fighting the Dutch over a few stinking boxes of herring: you let them burn to cinders your capital city and then your entire fleet; next we hear that you have invited a Dutch army to invade and there's an usurper on the Stuart throne!"

Captain Andrew Ravenscroft, (now transformed from bluff English 'sea dog' by wig, lavish lace and silk brocades,) was walking arm in arm with Uncle Gradenigo amidst the aromatic shrubs, enjoying the leafy cool. An evening glow lit up the Senator's botanical garden, transforming to shadows and honey colour his mostly noseless, limbless and otherwise pricelessly battered collection of ancient Greco Roman statuary. The elderly Senator's other arm was being supported by no less exalted a person than Procurator of Saint Marks, the N.H. Lorenzo Soranzo, Deputy Secretary to the 'Quarantia' of forty Senators who oversaw State Security and by far the best hunting spider in Gradenigo's web of nephews. Both Gradenigo and Soranzo were eager to talk politics. Both had speeches to make the next day to the Forty for Trade and needed filling in with Ravenscroft's news and opinions.

"Well, Uncle," Captain Ravenscroft replied, in the leisurely buzzing drawl of a Venetian aristocrat, "I submitted my report on the treaty in person this morning. To my astonishment, The Ten gave it their instant blessing. To be honest, I was expecting a good caning from them for that sugar detour to Jamaica, but then I think they understood that I was left with no choice. It certainly threw the Orange hounds off my scent trail....not to mention the fifteen Catholic families that I ferried to safety in Jamaica. Sadly I had to report that Dutch troopers and their crazed supporters, mostly ignorant Devon bumpkins rather than Londoners, are still pillaging and tearing down any house in London where there is suspicion of a hidden crucifix. You might almost get the impression that Christ himself was a Jacobite: there is not a crossroads in the kingdom without its tarry Catholic carcass. But, to answer your question, we don't seem to have any choice but to do a deal with Dutch William."

Cousin Lorenzo Soranzo then added his observation: "The law of unforeseen consequences will apply to this treaty, as with everything else in life, of that we can all be sure, but we need to keep every puffy French general tied-up in the Dutch borderlands while the Doge sails off to sort out the Sultan. Otherwise, should Morosini ever return, he might well find King Louis's brother lounging with his latest boyfriend on board the Bucintoro...not to mention those fair French courtesans who might take a fancy to your back garden here!"

"Why bless my soul! That last prospect sounds quite appealing. Your old uncle is, let me assure you, still far from shrivelled worm meat! French courtesans eh! I like that! As for your 'law of consequences' Nephew, I am worried about what will happen to you if Morosini sails back triumphant and finds you have backed a papist gutting puritan against the might of two Catholic Kings? Why he might have you and half the Senate topped for treason!"

"Come now, Uncle!" Ravenscroft protested, "Have you taken a close look at the Doge recently? I had that privilege last week. I must tell you I was shocked....shocked and disheartened. He should be in bed, not embarking on what will turn out to be a winter war. The Ten know that the old warrior has little sand left in his hourglass, otherwise they would never have considered this treaty. Brave old Morosini- he has the burden of St. Christopher on him - yet he wades on towards yet another tempest. My bet is that The Ten have already ordered his monument from the stonemasons."

"You may well be right, young Andrea, the Doge is in a bad way, but what now if the London folk rise up and throw out the Dutchman? How would we look then in the eyes of the world? Rumour has it that William was too terrified of the London mob even to turn up at the opening of Paul's new cathedral. Where will your treaty be then....Eh? The London merchants must feel utterly betrayed by that turncoat Churchill: letting the Dutch march through his homeland, without so much as a fight! Is there no one of old Monck's stature to rein in the Orangeman? What of Robert Holmes? He may be a bit of a pirate on the side, but I admire him as a burning patriot, if ever there was one. Can't we bung him a bribe? From what I remember, your entire fleet would turn on his word."

"Sir Robert is dead, Uncle....died last November twelve-month."

"Holmes, dead? Bad news…Sad news indeed, nephew. Went down all guns blazing, I hope?"

"That would have been a mercy, Uncle, but sadly no."

"Not the axe?"

"No, not the axe, though William had it ready sharpened. I didn't want to mention it….but, alas, it was the gout."

"Ouch! Let's keep off that painful topic, Nephew."

"Can we continue then with my own aching bones of contention," Soranzo added with a chuckle, "In my view, Uncle, this treaty is not drawn up well enough - leaves us wide open to that ancient mariner's law of 'arsey-turvey' as Holmes would have called it."

"I don't follow, young Lorenzo. Explain."

"Well Uncle, if you remember, when Holmes lit that firestorm at Vlie then sailed on to make ashes of their fleet, he never calculated that just three weeks later Dutch agents would do the same to London."

"Well, I guess they did everyone a favour by torching the place," Gradenigo observed, "As I remember London, in my days with the merchant fleet, it was an unworthy heap of firewood anyway… stank to high heaven!"

"My concern," Soranzo continued, "is that that blasted spawn of Mazarin *(King Louis,)* may well take an inconvenient page out of history, like the English have done, and with it set light to our Venice. Your treaty, Cousin Andrea, will have its unforeseen consequences - you mark my words!"

"England is a lost cause anyway," Ravenscroft retorted, "We may as well make the best of a bad thing and try to manoeuvre Dutch William to our own purpose. What's more, that unbelievable fire in London just goes to prove by how much the brains of the common folk there have been addled over the last century. Sad to say that when it comes to brains England now seems to breed from the wrong end of its anatomy. Churchill and his fellow landowners calculate on that: they would cheerfully invite the Grand Mughal or even a Barbary ape as king, so long as they they rule England. The mob would be told that the ape was a good puritan ape and that crowning it would guarantee their privileges....but whose privileges? Religion there serves only one purpose - to conserve ill-gotten acres at the expense of commoners."

"Come now Nephew," grumbled Gradenigo, "That's the talk of a leveller!"

"Well, Uncle, it may seem so to one who still has his hospitals, his orphanages and his welcoming abbeys. Come to England uncle, there you'll find honest work seeking folk dying in wayside ditches. Those welcoming shelters are long since turned to silent ruins - turned to quarries; adapted to princely piles high-walled to keep out the dispossessed. The barons give the rabble their patriotic hangings and quarterings of popish suspects - anything to keep the mind of the mob away from the fact that they now hold all that was once farmed for common charity."

"What of your merchant class Andrea?" queried Gradenigo. "Wasn't our old friend Ravenscroft a bit of a Jacobite? His kind would never have supported this conquest, any more than Holmes and Albermarle would have done. Sir Robert, God rest him now, for he knew King James's mind better than the king himself did, once told me that James was at heart a leveller. That could be the real reason why Churchill and the Orange clique threw him out?"

"Little doubt about that Uncle. Had James's lasted, old England would have been a better place for all. You probably know he gave up his Greenwich Palace to his mariners. Alas! Scuttling back to France seems to have affected his health as well as his judgement: I gather he now has terrible nose bleeds. Prospects no brighter than those of our poor Doge, I suspect."

"Too much of their poxy wine." observed Gradenigo. "And talking of Barbary apes, rather than the puritan kind, I'll make you laugh! Moulay

Ishmail has made King James an offer of a corsair fleet and janissaries enough to re-conquer England. And while the puritans debate whether to put a bedknob or a papist cross on the dome of their new St. Paul's, Ishmail will be only too glad to trump it with a crescent moon. But then the imam and the puritan have only a turban to distinguish them."

"Damn it, Uncle! That's from our Morocco agent's 'Relazione' *(top secret Ambassador's report.)* Who the devil leaked that to you?"

"Let me remind you Lorenzo, Ballarin only leaks what he wants to be leaked. England is Andrea's patch, remember, not yours! That is for the present, dear Lorenzo, but you are all due for a game of musical chairs as you may well find out!"

"Ballarin let me read a copy only yesterday," added Ravenscroft. An Islamic England! God help us, it won't only be me and my crew sunk if that should happen! But I'm still not too worried about that bit of arsey-turvey. Mulay Ishmail's overtures have helped us all make up our minds. That beheading barbarian was part of my reasoning for a treaty with the Dutch."

"I guess Louis won't be foolhardy enough to permit a fleet of corsairs to sail up the Channel?" Gradenigo mused.

"Well Uncle," Ravenscroft mused, "Should Ishmail sail in to circumcise England, doubtless King Louis will escort James and the whole Saint Germain's Court back home. Louis keeps them busy at St. Germain making addled plans to restore the Stuart crown, but I'm pretty certain that once Louis has dealt Dutch William a death blow, he will gobble up England for himself. Poor Stuart, when he swapped his sea boots for a crown he turned into a complete loser! Look at that last fiasco in Ireland: it was only thanks to Worley that I didn't leave my own bones amidst the stones of the Boyne Church!"

"Enough of politics!" interrupted Gradenigo, "Let's have some sweet gossip; some mischief while we still have Andrea's company. That pompous Conyers has riled you both too much. How I kept a straight face... how Andrea kept from strangling the blighter in my salon this afternoon, I just don't know!"

"Wringing his fat neck would hardly put me in William's good books, now would it?" Ravenscroft chuckled. I should like to survive long enough to draw my pension….perhaps even build a lead glass works on Murano. Lead crystal is the future Uncle."

"Good grief! Don't tell me I'll have a glassblower as well as sugar shipper for a nephew? Any luck with the Miotti book, Nephew?"

"Not even a sniff. Bastian has it beyond doubt and for certain he has done away with one of our best glassblowers in Vincenzo Miotto. My puzzle is, why he or the French haven't yet used any of the recipes."

"Well, I don't think we are going to leave him much more time for recipe study. Bastian was ever destined for crows' carrion; just a question now of when The Ten find it convenient. So, Nephews, the field is clear for you both. You'll make your fortune when you locate it."

"An old Byzantine tome won't add much more weight to Andrea's purse. Surprised you haven't notice that dear Uncle? Let's sit and enjoy the sunset. I shouldn't hang on to his arm too long, he might well transmogrify into one of your garden ornaments! He's got the Midas touch, has Andrea! He's swanning back to London with un-taxed profits from the Sensa, not to mention his other little trinkets!"

"Would you deny me my fun Lorenzo? I'll swop my Raven for your lawyers' perks any day. Under a lion's mane may seem a good place to hide from your tax ferrets, but remember, I'm risking it with a Dutch lion and The Ten, as usual, aren't paying all my expenses."

"A well earned reward for your work in London" Gradenigo grunted as he sat down with a sigh of pain and scratched for a while at his swollen ankles. "Now, Andrea, that name of yours is surely in need of a change. Conyers's malign toad's eye, is on you now: your run-in with Lorraine will be reported back to London, that's for sure. What's more, I heard some raucous adjutant bellowing 'Refoscro' around the parade ground the other day, just before the Doge's Vespers. He had the Miotti child with him and I guessed he was looking for you."

"Well Uncle, I am open to suggestions? Gradenigo, I guess is not available?"

"There won't be any harm now using your grandfather's illustrious name, will there? We all understood your previous reluctance. You need to have some status when you return to London with the draft treaty."

"I still value my life too highly to risk that name, Uncle. And, if we must move back from sweet Henley and make London once again our headquarters, then I'll have to look carefully to my own. "

"I don't get you nephew. Your own quarters? We intend to provide you with a decent well placed property. We have in mind somewhere on the river bank near Somerset House."

"I wasn't thinking about SoHo, I just had a vision of my head on London Bridge and my tarry quarters flung into the stinkingTyburn stream."

"Come now nephew. There is such a thing as diplomacy. We are not talking of Istanbul."

"In due time, The Ten will doubtless inform us quite who you are, dear Cousin," the Procurator commented with his customary wry humour. "And, apropos of your rebel talk about ill-gotten acres, I take it that you will persuade cousin Charles to give back that great rambling pile I'm told he owns - takes up half of County Dorset, I am told - plenty of room to house the poor amidst cousin Charles's stolen monastic stones!"

Touché Cousin...touché! You have me below the belt there!" laughed Ravenscroft, "It's in Kent, dear Cousin… in Kent, not Dorset. Not stolen stones, if my history serves me well, Knole was only bought by the family at the turn of the century and I seem to remember the place was originally filched by Catholic King Henry from his Archbishop who, incidentally, got roasted as a Protestant. However, you may well find out exactly where it is before many moons pass over the Lagoon."

"What are you hinting at Andrea? I have no plans to join you in your puritan purgatory."

337

Ravenscroft held his silence on that prospect and gave away nothing more than a knowing grin.

Offering snuff to both nephews by way of a diversion, for he too knew about The Ten's plans for the Procurator, Gradenigo remarked: "Amuse us Lorenzo! The Courts are still, I hope, a hive of scalding scandal, profiteering from public office, loopholes in widows' last wills, et cetera."

"They are indeed, Uncle...nothing has changed since your days. But I was thinking of tweaking Andrea's tail, by way of evening entertainment." Turning to Cousin Ravenscroft, the Procurator quipped: "Tell us Andrea, what are you going to say when the English Customs discover your painted statues? Your papist idols will, if I am not mistaken, get them foaming at the mouth in righteous puritan rage? They might after all offer you that long drag to Tyburn to exchange your entrails for them!"

"Damn you too, Lorenzo, for the cunning rascal you always are! How in hell's name did you find that out?"

"We have our eyes, dear cousin, our eyes...ever watchful.... even in the Ghetto! Don't concern yourself however, we all have strict instructions not to meddle with your cargo… that is not to break open anything! The Ten, I gather, have given their blessing to the internal adornments of your sacred images. Such a prompt patch-up too of that ugly pirate's tub of yours: I gather they want the Raven to fly away before it settles too comfortably on its Arsenal perch? Lucky you - as ever their untouchable Andrea - their so convincing Englishman. Indeed, what an apt surname you have chosen!"

Thus provoked, Ravenscroft pretended to squat down next to his cousin, neatly hooked his boot behind the Procurator's heel and gave him a hefty elbow in the ribs, sending him toppling backwards from the stone bench. Bouncing back instantly from the rosemary bush, Soranzo sent Ravenscroft's shoulder length wig flying up to lodge high in a walnut tree. The two then tussled and chased one another around the shrubbery like a pair of eight year olds, laughing and remembering with nostalgia their carefree boyhood together, running wild in that very same garden. Reassuming their airs of dignity, all three men continued their evening stroll.

"You've not answered Lorenzo's question Andrea," Gradenigo insisted. "Tell us, what if Ishmail gets to London before you? Muslims are even more eager to smash up arty statues than foaming puritans!"

"I shall save them both the trouble Uncle. I shall do the job myself - that is - I shall knock the heads and arms off and dump the statues amidst the ballast in the bilges well before we dock at St. Katharine's Wharf. That way I shall be taken for a fervid puritan who has done his righteous and rabid duty by vandalizing a Catholic chapel or two while sailing home."

And so it was that The Ten, acting on their spy Andrea Ravenscroft's report, decided to resume diplomatic relations with Dutch William, whom they hoped would continue to be a painful and distracting thorn in the side of the French. They deducted just a few hundred ducats from Ravenscroft's salary to compensate the Serenissima for his refusal to hand over to them quite the biggest pink diamond in Europe. As an honorary Galley Commander of the Serenissima, Ravenscroft knew his rights to keep and to sell his booty. There were, as ever, conditions of free trade attached to the treaty with England and the obligation that William should write first to them in person and in Latin, politely begging the Serenissima to send an Ambassador - which condition Dutch William hastened to fulfill, being insecure on his throne and eager to have foreign recognition as King of England. Ravenscroft was given the task of acting as 'innocent postman' and courier in this diplomatic exchange. Returning via the Papal Port of Ancona, Ravenscroft picked up more thousands of ducats to convey to Willam of Orange for, astonishing as it may seem, the Pope had long been bankrolling William's campaigns against that greater threat to Italy and to the backdoor to Christendom in the form of King Louis XIV. Ravenscroft had no problem in completing these tricky tasks, for his second cousin was both King William's Chamberlain and his Regent in England. The Illustrious Procurator Lorenzo Soranzo was chosen as the new Ambassador to Britain early in 1695, and landing at the Tower of London Wharf, he was greeted with pomp, with canons, with choirs, with earls and ministers and marching bands and a quick knowing wink through the gun smoke from the mysterious Mr. Andrew Ravenscroft.

CHAPTER THIRTY-FOUR

While turning a page to the next song, the young lady caught one of her bracelets on the edge of the music stand. Thick and heavy, it slid down over her wrist. She widened her fingers just in time to save it falling to the ground. Beautifully crafted from filigree gold, the bracelet was set with a fortune in rubies inter-twined with large cushion-cut diamonds; an ornament worthy of Bianca Capello herself - from whom in fact it had passed down through generations by way of inheritance to Don Francesco Capello Benzon, Podestà of Murano. Now, in gentle harmony with the strings of the harpsichord, the singer's body began to sway. She sang with great passion, yet with careful control: her voice having a surprisingly powerful vocal range for one so slender. At the Incurabili *(The orphanage for the incurable.)* the 'Maestro di Musica' had seen her potential as an opera singer, yet for some reason known only to them, the nuns would have none of her appearing in public. The refrain at the end of each verse of the aria required a 'tremolo' voice. Her vocal chords vibrated with such skill and delight: the notes pitched slowly higher, then falling with a sudden cadenza as though in bitter despondency at unrequited love: *"Amarilli, my beauty. Take Cupid's dart and open up my heart and there you will find writ through your name, Amarilli... Amarilli is my love."*

It was one of Don Francesco's favourite madrigals. He knew every note, often playing the catchy tune with one hand on the harpsichord while sipping his morning tonic. Now that he had once more the companionship at breakfast of a dulcet and sylph-like 'Amaryllis,' he was trying to keep to his doctor's advice by reducing his slight paunch and his sugar intake. His footman stirred just one skimpy spoonful into the Podestàs bitter bowl of green China tea. Amarilli....his late wife had named their daughter after that radiant flower. His wife's baroque pearls now adorned the little laundry girl. The jewelled renaissance pendant and heavy bangles were displayed once more to perfection on Bianca's flawless adolescent skin. He had mourned for what seemed an eternity the loss of his wife and of his seven year old daughter, cut down by pneumonic plague within days of one another, along with so many other friends and servants in the greater Capello household. Spring-like renewal was now before him - making music with him. Giulio Caccini, musician to the Medici princes of Florence, had written the love song way back in 1602, possibly in praise of the murdered Duchess Bianca Capello - a lady of tragic and matchless beauty. However, the sentiments expressed in the madrigal were still for the Podestàs departed loved ones on that May morning. So far as he could interpret what was written within his own heart, his were fatherly protective sentiments towards the laundry girl from the Incurabili. Her intelligent companionship had brought relief from loneliness and the unending cares of his office. Youthful beauty had ever been the mainspring of Venetian art and Don Francesco was noted as a discerning collector and a patron of any who possessed true artistic talent.

Unknown to him were the desires and ambitions of the ex laundry maid with whom he was making music. She, in her youthful innocence, had already misinterpreted his feelings. When quite sure he would not notice, she darted looks that glowed with more earthly sentiments: with an affection that had no regard for age or status. And what of that impassable gulf between them? He was an aristocrat twenty-five years her senior: she no more than a fifteen year old promoted scullion - a child of unknown parentage.

As the last plangent notes of Caccini's aria died away, the footman scooped a bow to the Mona Bianca Silvestra Capello, (her Valier surname quietly left behind with the laundry.) The servant begged her kind permission to take the music sheets from her. With another respectful nod he hastened to bring more tea in a little silver mounted handleless porcelain bowl.

She and the Podestà now sat close together in enormous new armchairs that had just been unpacked. Sipping the bitter amber-green coloured liquid, she was doing her utmost to pretend that she liked it. Between sips their chatter was almost that of a newly married couple. He had suggested that they meet in the Stateroom, which was really the territory of the absent Bishop: the harpsichord there was however the Podestàs property. A warm morning breeze wafted in from the tall windows opening on to the balcony. That balcony was a confounded irritation to the Podestà. He had used up almost half of his inheritance to rebuild in white stone the front facade of the ancient palace, but the architect Gaspari had duped him. The balcony was far too narrow to sit out on and watch the passing shipping. Since his appointment in 1691, Bishop Zustinian had rented the Staterooms from Don Francesco - there being no bigger rooms on Murano

341

Island. Torcello, the bishop's official marshland cathedral seat, had decayed into ruins and malarial swamp. In long ages past Torcello Island had been the cradle of the Venetian Empire. The Podestà was glad of the six hundred ducats rent his palace rooms brought in, but the bishop was a brutal demanding man. He insisted that the carved ceiling of the stateroom, with its ancient Medici pawnbroker's balls and Capello arms be taken down and replaced with those of Torcello and Giustinian, all to be done at the Podestàs expense! Don Francesco didn't mind taking delivery of basic furnishings and even approving of their quality, in the Bishop's absence, but forking out for new ceilings and staggeringly costly armchairs was not something he was eager to do.

Don Francesco disliked intensely the throne like chairs from the moment he first saw them. They reminded him too much of the pompous shape of the over-upholstered bishop. *(It is recorded that 'easy-going' Pope Innocent Pignatelli had baulked at appointing Zustinian to the Torcello Diocese: "Why am I obliged to choose such a sybaritic numbskull for my bishop?" The answer came: "Because The Ten desires you to, your Holiness!")*

The Podestà wanted Bianca's opinion. The chairs had just been delivered by canal barge from Parodi's sculpture studio in Padua. From the invoice it was made clear that Parodi had not carved one bit of them himself. True they were good value, at twenty ducats each, but they were the work of an unknown carver; someone called Brustolon. Whoever he was, he seemed to have got carried away with his swirling elaborate carving of sea nymphs, tritons, dolphins and blackamoors, all tangled up with realistic looking wooden seaweed and shells. In all of it, the artist had overlooked one important thing - comfort. Bianca could not agree. She thought the chairs were absolutely superb. The bargeman waiting below was promptly informed that the Lord Bishop of Torcello would purchase them. Payment would come in due course.... at the convenience of the bishop's purse.

It was a rare moment of peace and relaxation before they applied themselves once more to written orders, to answering letters and to those many pleas for justice or for help in adversity.

Three boats emerged from the dazzling sunlight of the Lagoon and made their way at a steady pace up Murano's 'Grand Canal' in the direction of Palazzo Capello. The middle boat was a large plain gondola with the blinds of the felze drawn down. Fore and aft of the gondola were long, white painted 'desdotona', each sturdy vessel with ten tall and armour-plated musketeers standing alert amidst the rowers. They wore the red and yellow uniform of Palace Guardsmen.

Those who caught sight of them were shocked to silence. Could it be because of the riot? Whatever it was, their sudden appearance could only be bad news for some poor devil!

Gustav had had a wonderful and copious breakfast. The love of his life, Big Marta, had fried him an omelette with half a dozen eggs. He had tasted and spat out a curious swig of the green tea prepared for Don Francesco. To take away the awful taste, he had eaten a whole shoulder of Parma ham. It smelled slightly high, but a good piece of overripe ham was what he enjoyed most. Marta had judged it unsuitable for the Podestàs table, but he Gustav had guts of leather. Since Big Marta had saved him from a second ducking on the day of the riot, they had grown quite close, making big moon eyes at one another - well, small pink bloodshot squinters in the case of Gustav! On hearing of Gustav's plight in defending Zustinian and the French prince while they made their escaped from the furious mob, Marta had led a charge of housemaids and footmen.... headlong, straight at the toughest of the Arsenal workers! Her sudden appearance: her sheer mighty bulky presence; added together with that fearful meat cleaver with which she sliced the air; well it was more than enough to send them all scurrying like mice to the safety of their wine taverns.

Gustav sprawled in the warm sun on the steps of the watergate. He had lit his clay pipe and promptly gone off to sleep, having been condemned to door porter duty for the past several nights. He was having a lovely dream of Marta and married bliss, when he felt a sharp poke in the ribs. Enraged, he started up and tried to focus his beady short-sighted eyes on the offender. It was that blasted little pipsqueak of a jeweller - once again in his puffy high wig - come to demand payment yet again from Bastian. There he was in his black silk suit and his cravat and gold-topped cane. How dare he? How dare he try to enter by the watergate - that was for noblemen only! Bastian Zustinian had given both Adolfo and Gustav

343

strict orders for the jeweller to be 'seen off the premises' next time he came complaining. And there he was again, the smart little man dressed in black silk. What effrontery!

With the roar of a rabid bear, Gustav seized hold of the poor fellow by his lace cravat and his crotch and ran him backwards down the steps. At the water's edge, he raised the pathetic struggling fellow high above his head and hurled him way out into the canal. Gustav stood there for a moment in red-faced rage, shaking his ham-sized fists at the drowning jeweller.

His helmet shot away clean from his head. There was the bright flash and splutter of musket fire - terrible penetrating blows struck his breastplate. Though ripped to shreds by the first volley, Gustav found strength from somewhere to stagger back up the landing steps: after the second volley there was little left of him to go further. Veteran and villain that he once was, an abandoned child of 'The Thirty Years' War,' the German landsknecht's son was now nothing more than a blood stained heap. It was a fitting way for the old devil to exit from his violent, sulphurous smelling world of round shot and gun smoke. What more could one of Morosini's valiant old warriors have wished for by way of an end?

His Illustrious Excellency the Cavaliere Don Domenico Ballarin, Grand Chancellor of State to the Council of Ten, was fished out instantly from the canal. A dozen willing hands helped him stagger ashore. He stood there for a while, confused, shivering and dripping, whilst rivulets of blood from what was once poor Gustav swilled away down the canal steps, and mingled for all eternity with the glorious waters of the Lagoon.

The deafening first volley brought down chunks of rotting wood from the Medici gilded ceiling. Chandeliers swayed and jangled and showered down their candles. Bianca and the Podestà rushed from their thrones to the stone balcony above the watergate. As they leaned over, the second blast sent them reeling back. A flying piece of bullet wadding struck the Podestàs cheek and left a stinging black smear just below his eye. They both choked and coughed, dropped to their knees and held on to one another. Clouds of stinking yellow black musket smoke swept into the room on the morning breeze. As it cleared Don Francesco dared to peep again at the scene below. Though missing his periwig and all dignity and seen from above in a filthy bedraggled state, there was no mistaking the dapper form, the high forehead and the balding dome of Don Domenico.

"Oh God and saints preserve us....It's Chancellor Ballarin! I am done for!" he whispered to the crouching girl.

His Excellency the Grand Chancellor had done him the honour of coming in person to make arrangements for a presentation ceremony. A golden 'Osella' coin impressed with the image of the Bucintoro was to be awarded to one of the Podestàs islanders, a certain Giorgio Miotto, a child, together with a reward of ducats. Such an enormous sum would have to be handed over to the Podestà to administer. The Grand Chancellor's decision to make a personal visit was a singular mark of gentlemanly respect for someone he knew as a neighbour. The Chancellor was himself born on Murano, elder son of the distinguised Ballarin family of glassblowers. His father, a tragic martyr at the hands of the Turk, had also been Grand Chancellor and the family chapel was in St. Peter Martyr where there were marble monuments to heroic deeds. In the absence of the Doge himself, the PodestàFrancesco Capello would be given the honour of handing over the 'Osella' coin to its young recipient.

In the circumstances following the riot, the Chancellor intended to advise against using the public square outside San Donato. He had in mind a select gathering of aristocrats and glass traders in the ballroom of Palazzo Capello or else, if the Podestà thought it secure against the mob, the cloister yard of St. Peter Martyr would be chosen - half the population of the island could be accommodated there. Once the place and date for the ceremony were agreed, the Grand Chancellor would then place the Podestà under arrest and cart him off discreetly in his gondola for a short sojourn under the rooftop 'Leads' of the Ducal Palace.

Having considered that mysterious letter from Bianca Valier, The Ten had pointed the white glove straight at Don Francesco. The arrest would be a formality, for vigorously defended by the Chancellor himself and with proof already found, that the Podestà had acted in the best interests of the Serenissima, the Podestà might have expected at the most a week's confinement chained up in a comfortable cell. The poor man would endure some sleepless nights under the Leads, amidst the bats and the beetles, and be submitted to hostile questioning by those three masked and ever mysterious Inquisitors of State, but then he would be released and reinstated with honours and apologies heaped upon him. A long and detailed report from Captain Lacin of the Buon Pesce Tavern had clinched a matter that had been pending action for all too long. The 'proof already found' took the form of a sunken gondola, dredged-up at the entrance to the Grand Canal: its ownership had been traced to the Noble Bastian. After being shown the iron instruments in the room of punishment, Vogalonga had talked volumes and had been dispatched promptly to deploy for five years his rowing talents in a war galley.

But now...!

The Podestà stepped back into the room. Clasping his arms about Bianca's shoulders he gently kissed on her forehead. "God bless and keep you in His care my child. Should I be put to shame in the Piazzetta, do not come and witness it, I beg you, just remember me always and pray for my soul. Take the keys: go quickly to my cabinet. All that is there is yours - then get out of here! Use the lavatory stairs!" The Podestà then strode towards the great staircase.

Bianca let out a shriek of anguish and defiance. "No! Never! If you will walk to your death Don Francesco, then I go with you!" She hopped and stumbled across the room, threw herself at him and gripped his wrist with both hands so that he had to drag her behind him for several paces. But it was a far more terrible scream from below that saved the Podestà from the hangman's padded noose.

Big Marta was rolling pastry for a fish and parsley pie when the shots rang out. A scullery maid ran into the kitchen, open-mouthed, quite speechless. The fearless cook dropped her rolling pin and moved like lightening out into the great reception hallway. It was now filling with marines and musketeers who were buffeting, disarming and shoving against the walls the footmen and bravi. Someone yelled above the shouting and confusion, "It's Gustav!"

Marta caught sight of the faceless heap of ripped flesh, of metal and of bloodstained garments. That terrible cry of a soul in deep torment burst from her lungs. The power of a dozen demons then possessed her. She set about flooring, hurling in the air and kicking with all her might the Chancellor's guard. Had she armed herself with her rolling pin, had she

346

succeeded in snatching a musket from one of her victims, then with certainty she would have swung by her treble-chinned neck between Marco and Todaro. But her hands were so slippery with pastry dough that she could grip nothing. Judging instantly and correctly, that the most feather-plumed and beribboned of the musketeers had given the order to fire, she struck him with her fist with such speed and violence that she broke his jaw: she knocked him out stone cold! Before she was brought down with a crack to the head from a pistol butt, she had mauled and maimed, dazed and downed at least half a dozen well-built marines.

All twenty stone of ferocious female valour was now unconscious, face downwards on the hall floor. Still caked with white flour, her arms reached out towards her crumpled hero. Tied tightly over her face and knotted behind her neck, her egg stained pinafore served both as blindfold and gag. When they pounded her with their musket butts, when they twisted and bound her without pity, she felt nothing. She had fallen like an Amazon warrior avenging her Gustav and all her Amazon spirit went away with him. Sadly, as she fell, she broke her hip. But Marta was made of sterner stuff than most viragos. She would survive to mourn long years into a docile and fairly comfortable old age. It would be Adolfo's task in years to come, to rise grumpily to the sound of the Marangona bell and trundle her off to Mass at San Donato... in a wheelbarrow.

The Podestà looked down from the halfway landing at the scene of confusion below him. Bianca still clung to him. He did not want to be arrested and dragged away in the midst of such chaos and in such a humiliating way. Nobody, he well knew, could ever evade the Council of Ten's vengeful claws. He needed time therefore, to think and to surrender with dignity. So it was that Bianca managed to drag and coax him back up the second flight and into his private rooms.

The lavatory was a modest sized wood panelled alcove, leading off a corner of the sitting room overlooking the orchards. Inside to the left was a marble washbasin fixed to the wall: to the right was a barrel-sized chamber pot comically decorated with colourful baby cherubs relieving themselves. It had the usual dirty ditty of the Deruta potteries in fine lettering around the rim: *'Popes and princes may have power, and pomp and pedigree. But when they sit upon this throne they're just like you and me.'*

She drew the curtain and then dragged to one side the heavy chamber pot. Pressing hard and sliding to the right a strip of walnut beading she opened the lock. The door gave way to a tiny landing and spiralling steps covered in dust and cobwebs. It was a perfectly carpentered concealed access for servants, who could come and go emptying and replacing the chamber pots whenever there was a ball, or grand reception. But there had been no such event in many years, not since the Lord Don Vincenzo Medici, a Florentine mercenary hired to be a Venetian General, had rented the palace as his headquarters.

The trusty housekeeper was the only servant who knew of the concealed stairwell; she kept secret as well the location of a comfortable little hiding space between the rafters and a chimneystack. It was a centuries old, purpose built, sanctuary for troubled times. Once Bianca was installed as Podestàs secretary and mistress of the palace, the housekeeper had revealed to her every nook in the ancient building. The housekeeper had somehow gained the impression, from the Podestàs evasive hints, that Bianca might be one of his nieces who was in hiding from a jealous and unpleasant aged husband, to whom she had been married off for money. But then she had certainly come from the 'Incurabili.' Damaged daughters of the aristocracy were sometimes dumped there and obliged to become nuns, when a suitably wealthy but modest born Citizen partner could not be found. Escaping was not uncommon, even for vowed choir nuns. Both stories about Bianca's background were current gossip on the island and aroused much female sympathy.

"Please, I beg you Don Francesco," Bianca whispered," Go up and wait for me. I'll find a way to smuggle some old clothes to you."

The Podestà urged her to leave at once and to make for the Dominicans.

"Let Tranquillo know all that has happened. He will decide what's best to do." Before he had time to say "Take off your jewels!" she was gone. The brass locks clicked back and he was on his own.

She slid the pot close against the panelling and hurried back to the stateroom. There was just time to dash one of the tea cups into a waste bin and swing one of the Brustolon thrones around and away from the other before musketeers blundered in. They pointed their weapons at her: she stopped them in their tracks with a haughty gaze and sat down resting her arms regally on the gilded woodwork. She was so obviously an important noblewoman: they dared not even approach her without first informing the Grand Chancellor.

Domenico Ballarin entered unannounced, his diminutive frame enveloped in a musketeer's coat. In place of his magnificent piled 'owl's ear' wig, he wore a short cheap horsehair wig with black bow, borrowed from the knocked-out captain of the guard. It restored to him some semblance of dignity. Bianca stood and curtsied to him. It was a dreadful mistake on her part and could have led to her instant arrest - the wily Chancellor was intrigued.

"What the devil! Who can this delightful little lady be?" he murmured to himself and shivered once again in his sodden undergarments. The smelly canal water was still squelching in his boots. Something vaguely familiar about her face he noted instantly. Then there was that haughty bearing and that inviting aura of mystery - and how he liked solving mysteries! Yet, she could not be a Venetian noblewoman: had she been so, she would have remained seated, extended a languid left hand and waited for him to bow low and feign to kiss it. This he would do by touching his lips with the tips of his fingers and flourishing his hand towards her in a graceful gallant gesture. He did none of these things. He walked to within four paces from where she stood: far too close for politeness. No angry reaction came, as it should have done from a great lady who would have demanded that he stand off until invited to come closer.

"Who are you madam, may I ask?"

Bianca tried hard to keep calm and not to blush with embarrassment when she gave a false answer. She knew that she would need to lie like a gipsy fortune teller if she were to get away without being arrested. Gipsies.... that would be her story to explain Don Francesco's absence: "The Podestà is not here, Your Excellency. He went out some while ago towards St. Mary of the Angels. Sea gipsies have anchored off there and people are concerned about them. They are raiding the orchards for fruit and roses. I expect they will want to sell them at Rialto Market." The last bit of her lie had some truth. A report about gipsies had come that very morning.

"Yet Madam, he went without his guard. Is that not strange? I asked Madam who you are. You have given me no answer."

"I am... that is, The Podestà likes to resolve problems on his own in a peaceful fashion your Excellency." Bianca at once realized the stupidity of her answer. She had hoped in her innocence to pass herself off as a visitor.
"For one so young, you seem to know much about the Podestà's affairs. You also appear to have been perched on some kind of ducal throne. Are you perhaps the Doge's daughter?"

His questioning was now in a mocking ironic tone that frightened her. In her growing panic she tried to hide the ruby bangle behind her back. It was a foolish move for the Chancellor had the gimlet eye of an aerial predator; no effort to conceal, nor finicky detail escaped his notice. A Ming dynasty tea bowl in the waste bin? Tut-tutting his disapproval at such opulent wastefulness, he fished it out and held it up to the light pretending to admire the translucence and the fine chiselling on the silver parcel-gilt mounting, whilst in fact simply checking to see if its tea dregs were still warm. By good chance it was the one Francesco had drunk from before that Caccini madrigal began. The porcelain had gone stone cold and the green grey tea leaves had congealed in the draught from the open window.

"You have costly tastes Madam!" he snapped, "Now who the Devil are you? Tell me where the Podestà is hiding, or I will lose patience with you!"

"It fell. It fell.... by accident in the bin....when the guns went off."

The foxy Chancellor smiled faintly at her flustered and pathetic efforts to conceal the Podestà's whereabouts. He was not really annoyed, rather he was curious to find out why such a pretty young girl should be attempting to deceive him. She was cornered for the kill like a young hen and he had vulpine cunning in full measure. Opportunities for interrogation were ever a delightful challenge. Getting at the truth in a calm and civilized way bolstered his sense of superior intellect - so much more satisfying than having her carted off to the New Prisons and subjected to the water torture.

"One of the Podestàs bulli is now dead. Are you not concerned?"

"O heavens! Dead! Was it Adolfo... that is, who is it?" she blurted out.

 It was evident now that she was a member of the Capello household, but he knew that the Podestà's only child, young Amarilli, had died in infancy. She might be a visiting relative: though much more likely, with those jewels and the scattered music sheets, she was his singer and courtesan. "The old goat," he thought to himself. His high regard for the Podestà took a dive for the worst for Ballarin had daughters of his own, one of about this child's age.

Knowing that she would betray them both if she gave her true name - she had after all signed and delivered in person that denunciation to The Ten - she tried desperately to think of a suitable substitute. The invoice and bill headed: 'Filippo Parodi at The Hermitage, Padua,' was still open on the serving table.

"I am Filippa Parodi of Padua. I have come with these chairs and to collect payment - that is, if the chairs are acceptable to the Podestà."

"Well indeed....Parodi! I should think they might well be acceptable even to the Doge, that is of course if they are not considered good enough for the Podestà!"

Ballarin was nevertheless taken aback by this unexpected answer, but he persisted in his mockery. The deceitful little minx stood there in front of him, radiant in her satin gown. Brustolon's carved and gilded ducal crown seem to hover in the air behind her head. Indeed, she could almost have been a Doge's daughter - that was a thought he would never entirely dismiss from his mind.

"Parodi must be prospering, to dress his daughter so finely to run errands for him. There are laws Madam - you know them surely - a commoner may not dress in jewels and noble regalia."

"I am not his daughter your Excellency. I am a distant relative. These

351

jewels belong to a Paduan Jew who begged me to display them to the Noble Zustinian. Look, here is the invoice for the chairs."

That made more sense to the Grand Chancellor. Though Zustinian admired boys rather than youthful courtesans, he knew that the depraved young nobleman was an obsessive collector of jewellery. "Don Giacomo. How is he now?"

Not knowing who on earth Don Giacomo was, she replied, "Oh! Fine, very well….very well. Thank you for asking."
It was the Chancellor's job and enjoyable hobby to know by name everyone of any note and what their state of health was. He knew, of course, that Filippo Parodi's real name was Giacomo. Not many years back Parodi had spent months in the Doge's Palace, creating a magnificent life-like bust and monument to honour Doge Morosini's conquests. He knew too that Parodi was gravely ill and was farming-out his furniture work to talented young sculptors like Brustolon. He had quickly concluded too that this girl had something to do with that denouncement to The Ten that was signed Silvestra Valier. There was something of a Valier about her stature and mannerisms, but much more alarming to him was her face: even without his spectacles, now lost in the canal, he could see it was exactly the face of a very grand dame of the Ducal Family! He had to proceed cautiously for he dared not cross swords, even metaphorically, with the terrible Martinengo. He could have asked her why she had no Genoese accent, since the Parodi family came from that rival City State, but he would be satisfied with a specimen of her handwriting.

He sent for pen and paper and ordered her to write her full name and address. As expected, her reply came that she was illiterate. Illiterate: despite the fact that she had been singing madrigals to the Podestà from a music sheet! He had had enough of the silly one-sided duel. It was all too simple for his talents as an inquisitor and he had more important matters to attend to.

Long hours of scheming by candlelight on behalf of The Ten had made him somewhat short sighted. He now drew much closer to inspect his victim. Had Bianca given him the slightest sign that she had a clubbed foot, he would have guessed instantly her parentage and identity and judged her above and beyond even his powerful clutches. Like that experience Don Francesco had on first meeting Bianca, Chancellor Ballarin had an uncomfortable sensation that he was in the presence of someone very familiar, someone of importance, someone who might be useful to know; someone he could not quite put a name to. Like the Podestà, he was a political survivor. This seemingly innocent little liar had rung loud alarm bells in his scheming skull. By dragging her off to give account for herself before the almighty Ten he might be making the biggest mistake of his life!

"I am not satisfied with your answers Madam. You will be confined here until I have time for further questioning." He had to get on with the search of the premises and the collection of evidence.

Three marines entered. They checked all exits, searched every room including the lavatory closet. Bianca wanted to sob in despair, but she held back her tears and thought hard what to do next. An hour passed, then two, with noises of running and rummaging from the Podestàs rooms across the first floor landing. The Bishop of Torcello and his nephew, the Noble Bastian, had suites of rooms leading off from the stateroom; their bedrooms were on the upper floor. The Chancellor had to supervise any search with respect for their privacy: not that the Bishop had made much use of these rented rooms - they were to him no more than a prestige address. And as for Bastian, the real occupant, - this was a golden opportunity to rummage through his many possessions for evidence. Bastian's days on earth were already counted, right down to his last hour on that mountain pass, but every bit of incriminating paper; every perverted print would help justify his sad departure.... and at such a promising moment in the young nobleman's diplomatic career.

"I must go to the lavatory," she announced. The guards were quite amused to see such an exquisitely dressed young noblewoman hobbling with a stick. They followed her across the landing and into Don Fancesco's paper strewn apartments. Two assistants to the Chancellor were still ferreting in drawers and cupboards. With their usual policeman efficiency they had already parcelled-up the Podestà's rude Riccio inkstand and labelled it: 'Evidence NH Zustinian.' Don Francesco's prized possession, the dreamy little painting by Bellini of a Madonna and Child, both sleeping and seated in a meadow with the sunlit towers of Soave in the background, had a diagonal strip of official tape sealed across it: 'NN.HH.Dom Vesc.Torcello - STET' was written in bold letters on the tape. In other words, the painting was presumed to belong to the Most Noble Lord Bishop of Torcello, namely Bishop Zustinian, and was not to be collected.

 Bianca noticed, with a fleeting glance of amusement, that a piece of card by way of a fig leaf was hung with a string about the nethers of the Podestàs Farnese Hercules. On this too was written 'Evidence NH Zustinian.' The bronze statue weighed well over a ton. Quite how the Chancellor would cart away such weighty evidence, Bianca had no time to consider. Luckily for her escape plan, the wily Chancellor was occupied upstairs in Bastian Zustinian's bedroom. There he had already seized a whole pile of Parisian prints. His puritanical post-Reformation mind was now outraged beyond measure. He had stumbled on a den of vice, a den of turpitude worthy of an Inquisition bonfire - moreover in the holy Bishop's Palace! He now had more than enough to make ashes in Campo San Polo of the Noble Bastian Zustinian and all his disgusting vanities. (*St. Paul's Field - the second largest open space in Venice - once used for burnings at the stake - an extremely rare occurrence in easy-going 17th Century Venice)*

A marine drew back the curtain of the privy, checked the panelling once again for any possible escape route and then stood guard outside. Guessing that a used chamber pot would be less likely to be moved by the smartly dressed and superior looking guardsmen, Bianca relieved herself. She heard the guard moved away towards the Podestàs office, boasting to one of his companions of how he had downed that old harridan of a cook with just one clout from his pistol butt.

By jerking up and down the pump lever above the washbasin she let a gush of water splash out from the little brass dolphin tap. Leaving the tap running to cover any scraping sound, she slid the heavy pot clear of the inward opening door. Unwinding her long silk-ribboned waistband, she looped it round the pot. That concealed door panel clicked open once again. On the cramped stair landing, she carefully tugged at the ribbon, manoeuvring the pot back into position as near as she could manage. Though now quivering with fear she took time and care whilst withdrawing the ribboned waistband through the closing gap. Once closed, she jammed the door for good by stamping on and breaking one of her enamelled bracelets and twisting the jagged metal into the sliding door-lock mechanism.

Don Francesco had been careless in leaving footprints in the dust of the spiral stair. Her judgement confused for a moment, Bianca climbed up some way, thinking to join him in the hide behind the chimney stack. She had been ringleader in several pranks whilst at the orphanage, mostly night time adventures, escaping from the ever watchful nuns. On one occasion she had stolen keys and got out just to gaze in awe at the wonders of the candlelit shops around the Rialto Bridge. Now was the time to cover both his and her tracks and to get away undetected. She pulled off her wig and stuffed every bit of jewellery inside it. Next came her silk slippers and stockings; but the struggle to remove her dress proved hopeless. Fashion dictated that one had to be either laced or sewn into a gown by a servant dresser and all the fastenings were behind Bianca's back. Undaunted, she tore off the stomacher, the pearl and embroidered chest flattener and gathered up her skirts into a bundle with the wig. Her layers of cotton shift undergowns might just pass at a glance as a maid's dress.

At the bottom of the stairs she put her ear to the door panel: neither sound nor movement came from the other side. The brass lock had greened over and needed a desperate tug to slide it back. Bianca's sudden apparition caused the little laundry girl to let out a squeal of terror. Bianca managed to hush and calm her and by the time a guard came to investigate the noise, both girls were bent down gathering arms full of bloodstained shirts, sheets and rags from where they were piled on the linen room floor. Marta's mayhem had left many a bloody head and nose and several days' work for the washer girl. The guard laughed and joked, assuming that their squeamishness in handling the blood drenched linen had cause the commotion. He insisted on escorting them out to the washhouse, but grew suspicious as Bianca walked ahead of him. He was no fool. The taller laundry girl was wearing make-up and her tucked up skirt was made of costly brocade. Bianca's disappearance had as yet gone un-reported: otherwise he would have detained her there and then. But there was also a gruesome distraction in the courtyard, which took his mind completely off the matter.

Gustav's corpse was dumped close to the stone well that he had so recently been obliged to scrub clean. Its timeworn carving of the Lippomani crest was now splashed with his lifeblood. A meandering red streak across the flagstones traced where he had been dragged. Bianca shuddered and felt close to fainting: bile and bittersweet tea rose up in her throat. The marine made a hasty 'sign of the cross' on himself, whilst the twelve year old clung tightly to Bianca's arm and sobbed - overwhelmed with pity for the kindly giant she had known for no more than a few weeks, while working as Bianca's replacement in the laundry.

Bullet torn boots and a bloody shot riddled and caved-in head stuck out from under a rag of sail cloth thrown for decency's sake over the mostly missing torso. To one who knew of Gustav's misdeeds, it would not have taken a long stretch of the imagination to compare his state to that of a temple familiar to us all, for that too has only its two wrecked ends surviving. Death's angel would certainly have known what an exceptional weight of crimes he ferried to Hades Gate - where the blind scales of Nemesis would have wobbled under that burden for some time. In one pan, rising in glory, that Sergeant Gustav who launched an heroic charge in Candia to rescue his encircled comrades and in recompense stopped a Turkish bullet with his forehead, rendering him short sighted, short tempered and somewhat imbecile. Dropping down fast in the other pan, however, would be that Lieutenant Gustav of Count Koenigsmark's army, standing gallantly by his mortar cannon on Mouseion Hill with linstock in hand and squinting at his target through the setting sunlight while a squadron of Turkish cavalry was close assembling on the Acropolis of Athens.

Dipping the pen of eternity, the Recording Angel might have written as follows: Monday 26th September, 1687, at seven in the evening; Athena looked down, with Pericles at her side and saw in dismay that smouldering linstock ....for it was Gustav who blasted apart the Parthenon of Athens!

Lena, an aged washerwoman, who had worked for the Podestà and his late wife for more than twenty years, was gutting fish and pigeons for the servants' meal. Now that Marta was no more and the housekeeper was under arrest, she alone would have somehow to make do. She caught sight of the two girls and the marine approaching her washhouse. The look of haunted dread and desperation on Bianca's face was enough to complete a story she had just heard from a house maid - Bianca's elderly husband had turned-up to claim her back! He was a nobleman with a troop of bravi and would slaughter without warning anyone who got in his way. Poor Marta and Gustav had already paid the terrible price for doing so. Lena herself had just caught a glimpse of the outraged, peppery, skinny old man in black as he stood dripping in the great hallway. She thought it best to keep out of the way during the commotion and retreated to her washhouse. But she was a woman of spirit, a born actress, deserving of a career as Harlequin's comic Colombine at the Comedy Theatre. Her impressions of the mincing Noble Zustinian and lower creatures like Adolfo, had kept the staff in constant fits of laughter. Bianca had been extremely kind both to her and her family since becoming Mistress of the Palace. Puffing herself into an artificial rage she sallied forth from the washhouse. To Bianca's utter amazement Lena ran at her brandishing the gutting knife in her face, then began to scream and curse at her: "You little painted Jezebel! You wanton wicked girl! How could you do this to me? I have been up all night - worried sick about you. Where have you been? I can well guess where. Your poor dear mother will be turning in her grave! Just look at you! Dressed and made up like a tart! How dare you do this to your poor old grandmother?"

Bianca and the little laundry girl froze with astonishment, but before they could utter a word that might have betrayed them, Lena turned in red-faced anger and began to abuse the marine.

"So this is your fancy man is it? I thought he was a gondolier, not a soldier!" She swiped the knife within an inch of his nose. "If you have laid so much as a finger on my granddaughter, I'll gut you, I will! By St. Mark, I will damned well gut you!"

The poor dumbfounded marine stepped back out of range of the knife, protesting loudly his innocence.

To Lena's intense relief Bianca grasped quickly what the whole charade was about and pretended to sob. "No grandma, it's not him. I don't know him at all."

"Then who is it? Tell me who is it? I'll geld him, I will. And he bought you that dress did he? Well you can take it off at once and give it back.

No granddaughter of mine will flounce around like a courtesan! Who is he then? Tell me girl, or I'll skin you alive!"

Bianca mumbled and tried desperately to think-up a name, but Rita the little washer girl piped up with a perfect tell-tale voice: "It's Vogalonga, signora Lena, I saw him kiss her!"

The marine had heard of Vogalonga, and guessed he was as fast with the girls as he was with his gondola. It was time for him to back away out of the argument.

"Look lady, this has got nothing to do with me. I only..." But before he could complete the sentence Lena told him to 'clear off' and in the same tone of matronly authority ordered Bianca to get inside and to remove that offending dress. He retreated in a complete fluster back to his guard duties: he too had a wayward daughter and was not too offended by the old lady's abuse.

Within moments the loyal washerwoman had stripped Bianca using her knife to slice through the ribbons and fastenings. She ripped holes in two turnip sacks and clad her in them, using a piece of washing line to hold-up the skirt. Guessing that Lena and most of the palace staff would now be dismissed and left unpaid, Bianca begged Lena to take whatever she thought fit of the jewellery to cover their lost wages, but Lena refused the offer outright. Dumping a pile of wet washing over the wig, the bracelets and a fortune in the form of a diamond necklace, and then stuffing Bianca's gorgeous dress behind some dirty rags under the granite washing slab, Lena observed with a laugh: "The likes of me would only dangle like the day's washing if I got caught trying to sell any of this. Rinse off your make-up girl and take some washing out to the orchard to dry. Best leave it to me to bring out your bracelets and baubles. You had best find somewhere else other than here in the wash house to hide them. There's a very keen guard on the orchard gate: I have already spoken to him. He's bound to search you, as you are such a pretty lass - just put up with it though and don't complain too much. Confuse him with a bit of coming and going: tell him you need more pegs. Start hanging the washing at the back of the orchard. I'll distract him while you duck behind the wall. Make towards the marshes as fast as you can. After dark I'll meet you in the old shack where the fruit baskets are kept."

"Where do I find the shack?" Bianca asked.

"Rita will show you....No, I'll show you myself. It's overgrown with hawthorn, not so easy to spot. Whatever happens, I'll do my best to leave something there for you to eat, a blanket as well for you to sleep on."

Bianca decided to confide in no one about her intention to seek refuge with Don Tranquillo in the vast and rambling complex of St. Peter Martyr Convent.

CHAPTER THIRTY-FIVE

In Palazzo Capello, Bianca's absence was reported at last to the Grand Chancellor. He was incandescent with fake rage at his incompetent guards. He would have them dismissed. He would have them shot. He would have them hung between Marco and Todaro! But it was no more than huff and bluff. His immediate concern was no longer the mysterious young lady. Searching the house any further for her, or for the decent hard working Podestà was no longer a priority on his precious time. He had concluded that Don Francesco had done his duty, obliquely through that mysterious Valier lady's denouncement, to expose Bastian's foul living, his treachery and his contacts with French noblemen intent on damaging the Serenissima's trade.

He had read Don Francesco's morning correspondence, inspected his well kept accounts and studied various pending memoranda proving the Podestà was worthy of his high office. There was, he found, a written appeal from the orchard farmers of St. Mary of the Angels to come at once to deal with the gipsies. The Podestà was either brave, or very foolish, to go on such a mission without his guard of bravi. Upstairs, however, there were two colossal unpaid bills from a Paduan jeweller, stuffed in a bedside commode drawer. Both were addressed to NH Sebastiano dei Giustiniani. Perhaps, after all, the young lady was telling something of the truth?

What incensed him most was a letter from the 'Palais de St. Cloud,' signed by the Duke of Orleans, no less, thanking Bastian for some service or other. The Chancellor's French was not good, he was of necessity a scholar of Turkic, but the letter smelled of Grasse perfume: it stank of treachery. Zustinian was nailed as well for yet another state crime: keeping bulli. Armed retainers were prohibited, even to the highest nobility. Only a Podestà had the authority to keep men-at-arms, and that for public order reasons. The violent wretch, who had pitched him into the canal, had shouted something about a jeweller. Evidently he was a private bullo placed there on guard, not by the Podestà but by Zustinian to fend off his debtors.

The girls wrung out two large panniers of washing and went to the orchard gates. Bianca muddied her feet and legs and scrubbed her forearms raw with a pumice stone. The guard hesitated at first. He was ordered to look out for a lady and a man in any guise, but here were two little scrubbers. They kept within his sight as they strung out the washing between the apple trees. Then they moved further off at a leisurely pace taking time to collect washing that had already dried. Taking a bold risk, Bianca returned to the gates as Lena had suggested and told the guard she needed to get some more pegs. He let her through to the washhouse and then back out once again.

Lena came with Bianca's treasures knotted into an old headscarf. All three sauntered with their laundry panniers towards the edge of the orchard and began to pick morello cherries from trees sticking out from an overgrown hawthorn hedge.

"Hey Lena, what's going on?" It was an all too familiar nasal voice whispering from inside the shack.

Lena went in and as her eyes adjusted to the gloom she caught sight of Adolfo's bird-brained head and lanky black locks sticking out from under a pile of wicker baskets.

"What are you doing there?" she asked sarcastically, knowing full well Adolfo's heroic temperament.

"Err... I'm setting rat traps," he replied unconvincingly.

"Using yourself as bait, I suppose?" Lena quite enjoyed taunting the cowardly beanpole.

"What's all the shooting and shouting about, Lena? I was out here picking cherries for Marta."

Marta had in fact sent him off cherry picking: his great height being the only virtue of any use to the household. At the first sounds of conflict he had 'hared it' to the end of the orchard and burrowed under the pile of baskets.

"Marta's dead and so is poor Gustav," Lena announced with half a sob.

"Dead! Who killed them?" Adolfo gasped, though he was not entirely shattered by the tragic news. He had no real feelings of comradeship and was shrewd enough to reckon that Gustav's demise would mean his own promotion.

"A great nobleman has turned up out of the blue with dozens of armed retainers. He wanted to take back Bianca: she must be his wife or maybe his runaway daughter! Gustav and Marta tried to interfere, poor souls, but...."

Lena's revelation came as a considerable surprise to Bianca, she almost half believed her, then concluded that Lena was still letting her splendid imagination fly in order to protect her.

"Has he gone now? Inquired Adolfo, "Has he carted her off? I always knew she was trouble, that stuck-up hobbling young bitch."

Lena signalled with a hand behind her back for the two girls to get away at once before Adolfo saw them.

"The mistress is safe, no thanks to cowardly mongrels like you. I have hidden her," announced Lena.

"Where have you put her, you crafty old devil?" There could well be a reward. We could share it!"

"You know what the reward is? A bullet in the brain, you oaf!" came the angry reply. "Now get out of there you lily-livered coney and get to San Dona`. Poor Marta and Gustav will need a priest. They died unshriven I am certain sure... only the Last Rites will save them... so use your damned long shanks and fetch Monsignor Tosi straight away. If Don Tosi is not about, fetch some other priest!"

Adolfo staggered up on his stilt-like legs and, fortunately for the Podestà, directed them straight to the nearest tavern, where the hot gossip might be exchanged for a free flagon or two.

CHAPTER THIRTY-SIX

Don Tranquillo was steadied by oarsman Molin but declined the aid of other sturdy male parishioners who hastened forward as he stepped swiftly out of the 'sandolo' and mounted the watergate steps. Though a dark pool of blood and other smears and splatters had already been sluiced down, he paused at the top to sprinkle the fateful site with holy water from a miniature bottle - silver screw topped and beautifully decorated in Miotti blue and white latticino. A great crowd of idle gawpers and gossipers was still standing around the entrance and joined with him in the 'De profundis' a well known prayer, crossing themselves repeatedly against the evil and bowing low to receive his blessing as he strode through the marine guarded gateway. Grumbling Don Toma` had already been assisted up the steps of a nearby side canal entrance to the Podestàs palace. Telling him that he would explain everything later, Tranquillo had asked Toma` as a favour, to walk round and enter by the less well guarded orchard gate, drawing as little attention upon himself as was possible in the circumstances.

Signor Molin unloaded two dusty and discoloured white bundles: "Shrouds!" he announced gloomily.

"Shrouds!" the onlookers echoed his word and crossed themselves once more as he carried in the bundles of linen.

Chancellor Ballarin had departed over an hour previously together with a dozen or so of his battered and bedraggled escort. It was a situation of acute embarrassment for him to have to return to the Doge's Palace in such disarray; nevertheless, he carried with him a substantial pile of evidence to gloat over. It had proved a most profitable escapade for him after all, though he was feeling distinctly sick and groggy from his canal dip and took with him no prisoners to interrogate. His next move would be to send warrants to convene a meeting of the four Murano Deputies. Once the Podestà was found and arrested they would assume the authority, that is the 'Podestia,' until Capello was reinstated or a new appointment made. Meanwhile a senior clerk and a marine officer were instructed to reside at the palace and attend to administration and security.

Despite their presence, and with those God given rights of authority bestowed for life upon galley commanders and on priests, Don Tranquillo took instant charge of the situation. Now quite out of her wits at being placed under house arrest, the Housekeeper and the frightened and bruised staff each knelt in the hallway and kissed the hand of their new and undisputed master. The Don then moved swiftly into action. Willing hands lifted Marta on to her kitchen table. As she was untied from her apron she breathed a faint groan. Don Tranquillo splinted and bandaged together her legs, washed with vinegar her minor wounds and, having nothing more suitable immediately to hand, used the stiff covers of his prayer book to secure her head and neck against any jolting movement. Strapped with several towels to some sturdy broom handles she was made ready for her journey to hospital.

He angrily ordered some marines idling in the courtyard to lift Gustav's remains away from the well head, which they did reluctantly, aided by signor Molin. It was a messy, unpleasant task. Don Tranquillo quietly asked the housekeeper which was the linen room door. Gustav's body was manhandled with some effort through the door and placed on the floor. Signor Molin brought in the shrouds.

"Leave us now," Tranquillo ordered, "Pray for his soul. Attend to your guard duties. See that nobody unauthorized enters or leaves."

Some ten minutes later, signor Molin emerged and inquired loudly as to the whereabouts of Don Toma`. The old librarian was outside, hood raised against a chill draught and pacing up and down the courtyard praying quietly in his quaky old voice from a large, elaborately gilt tooled and leather bound, 'Office for the Dead.' Signor Molin accompanied him back into the linen room. Some ten minutes later, in the midst of much deliberately created confusion and bustle, Don Toma` and Molin came out once more from the linen room and while crossing the courtyard were evidently deep in discussion about the dimensions of the pine coffin. Snapping shut his splendid prayerbook, the monk murmured in a shaky voice, "Very well, I shall go and arrange that…..Anything else needed?" With a nod and a sign of blessing to the guards, he made off through the Orchard Gate slowly at first, then once out of sight, he broke into at a surprisingly brisk jog, for one apparently so ancient and arthritic, across the fields and towards the footpath leading to the ferry.

Bandaged, splinted and semi-conscious, Marta was carried out. A dozen willing hands cushioned her bruised and bulky limbs as she was lowered into the Palace Guardsmens' launch and without questioning Tranquillo's commands , they ferried her to Venice and to the expert care of Prior Raimondo.

Some moments after their departure, Don Toma` emerged from the palace doorway onto the towpath; for a person rarely seen up close, even in St. Peter Martyr Church, Don Toma` was greeted with much respect by the on-lookers. His arthritic and stiff bones playing him up as ever, he was helped down the slippery watergate steps and into Molin's sandolo. Ashen faced, slow moving and grumpy though he was, he was held in great awe as the holy brain-box of the Island. Indeed, for one who had spent a lifetime caring more for books than for parishioners, he seemed remarkably unconcerned that he had somehow managed to mislay his precious and costly leather bound 'Office for the Dead!' Throwing back their black cowl hoods for all to see them, both priests gave their blessings to the onlookers before Molin rowed them off to San Zanipolo Infirmary and to a none too friendly encounter with His Excellency Prior Raimondo.

CHAPTER THIRTY-SEVEN

On 29th June, the Feast of old Piero's namesake, a memorial was held. It could not be a proper Requiem, for neither he nor his boat had been dredged up and in any case corpses were not admitted on feast days. It was an evening affair and being a public holiday was very well attended. Grandpa put on his black cloak and was received at the church door as chief mourner. At the conclusion of the Mass and ignoring all festive, not to say clerical, tradition Don Tranquillo permitted Zorzi to sing Thomas of Celano's 'Dies Irae' *(The Day of Wrath.)* With much garbled Latin, Zorzi stumbled solo through the numerous verses with just the odd prompt here and there from Fra Zeri. At the end, when Zorzi's plangent 'Dona eis Requiem' tailed away there was a great rustling of handkerchiefs, a snuffling of noses and much eye mopping.

Drowned fishermen were bid farewell when a model boat was floated out into the Lagoon at sunset bearing a lighted candle. Aldo Molin, with the aid of his carpenter father, took time and care with its making; fitting it with an ochre painted triangular sail and a paper pennant on which Zorzi took care to draw in blue chalk the crossed keys of St. Peter. Witnessed by a silent crowd, the matchwood model was blessed and launched from the landing stage by the Roman Column. It twinkled away for some fifteen minutes into the evening gloom.

A week or so after Piero's 'Requiem,' a schoolroom opened in the former pharmacy and then promptly closed. Quickly tiring of the children's unruly behaviour, Don Toma` abandoned his lessons and retreated to the dusty peace of his library. Tranquillo had calculated that his old rival would demand of his little charges at the very least a post graduate level of Latin. Toma`s dismal start gave him the freedom to appoint a pretty young school-marm who, although she had a bit of a hobble, was an instant success. She in turn appointed monitors to wash the writing slates, monitors to paint lampblack on the upturned table top that served as her blackboard, and monitors to shape the rough lumps of chalk with which the children wrote their alphabet and numerals. Zorzi's duty was to fill and empty the barrel in which the children washed their hands before touching any of the illuminated books from the convent library, not to mention the less pleasant task of emptying the slop barrel, which for convenience was placed behind a screen in the cloisters. Don Tranquillo always managed to sneak out three or four precious volumes each school day from under the suspicious nose of Don Toma`.

Aldo was adept in keeping the more disruptive boys in order and the wise young school-marm soon appointed him her 'disciplinarian.' Lucia, despite her size, excelled at blackboard cleaning, sprinting off with messages and exclaiming loud and flattering compliments about the beauty of the visiting ladies. Inevitably, the ladies came: Don Tranquillo actively encouraged them, their donations of silver grossi were needed to buy bread and second-hand clothing for the ragamuffins who attended. Unannounced, these grande dames would breeze in to interrupt Bianca's lessons with wafts of perfume and stunning displays of satin and needlepoint lace and, frequently idiotic, questions to the children. Questions of the historical, biblical or mental arithmetic kind were often posed for the purpose of demonstrating to accompanying gallants the superior intellect of the questioner. Taking Don Tranquillo's advice, Bianca dressed in cheap fustian covering her hair and her face as much as possible with an old fashioned nun like wimple. A pair of thick spectacles promptly donned whenever the door flew open and her servile bowing completed her disguise. Valier good looks and Morosini genes would, otherwise, have been noted instantly by these visitors and with equal rapidity tongues would have been set a wagging in every island salon.

Don Tranquillo's other useful piece of advice to Bianca was to teach the children to distinguish between their left hand and their right. Once this great skill was mastered by all, the children were instructed to put up their right hand if they thought they knew the answer to a visitor's question and to put up their left hand if they had no idea at all of the correct answer. An impression of class enthusiasm, good instruction by the school mistress and value for money was thus created and helped in loosening the purse strings of the visiting ladies. With the loud flattery of ragged hungry eyed Lucia still ringing in her ears, even the most ugly, hatchet faced, grand dame departed feeling that she had performed her charitable duty to the deserving off-spring of the under class.

Games took place noisily, at regular intervals, in the great cloister courtyard that extends behind the Church of St. Peter Martyr. Bianca made up a few safety rules for boisterous team games, but her limp and her special footwear made it impossible for her to do other than ring her hand bell angrily and to plead with Aldo to intervene whenever her rules were fouled.

Bianca was in the middle of explaining, with blackboard and chalk, some clever adding patterns with the nine times tables when she was interrupted by a loud rumpus of noise coming from the cloister. Lucia was back in an instant after being sent to investigate: "Miss, Miss," she urged, tugging at the young lady's gown sleeve, "There are soldiers and crowds of people. They are all marching into the cloister, shall I run and tell Don Tranquillo, Miss?"

The schoolmistress went pale with fear. To the consternation of her pupils she began to tremble and perspire as though she were about to faint. Recovering her composure she instructed Lucia and two others to search with all possible speed for Don Tranquillo and to tell him that she would wait for him in his office. "Children," she announced, "I have to leave at once. Go home to your parents now. I will let you know when lessons will start again."

Without waiting for anyone to clear up, or to pose awkward questions, she picked up her canvas school bag and hastened out through a side door in the direction of the friars' living quarters.

It was an extraordinary and quite unexpected happening - there was a band that instead of sounding out a doleful gallows beat, was making loud and merry dance music to the tunes of Tielman Susato. Some forty grey-bearded veterans, dressed in Palace Guard uniforms were advancing in step with the music, along the towpath of the Glassblowers' Canal. With them came noblemen in their civic robes and a number of noble ladies in court gowns of the kind they would only wear on meeting a Senator, or indeed the Doge himself. The Gastaldo, the Captain of the Palace Guard, whose many duties included presiding at public executions of felons of the highest nobility, headed the procession. From time to time he either twirled in great circles or threw into the air and caught with great dexterity his gold topped baton of command. He paused in his stately prancing only to call aloud, inviting all to come out from workshops, taverns and houses to join in the procession. Bringing up the rear of the throng, to everyone's surprise, was old Senator Trevisan. Evidently, from his presence, something quite momentous was about to happen. Would it be an execution? Some idle tongues were wagging with the rumour that the Podestà Capello had been captured after running away following the terrible insult to the Grand Chancellor and the well deserved shooting dead of that thug Gustav on the palazzo landing steps.

When he got the news from a breathless Lucia, Don Tranquillo seemed not in the least surprised. The schoolmistress hobbled into his office soon afterwards. He quickly calmed her fears and asked Lucia to wait outside. Closing the door he lowered his voice: "Don't fret. It's not Chancellor Ballarin on his way to arrest us - just old Trevisan making a bit of a show for the crowds. He's here for rather a special occasion. All the same, just tell the Podestà to make himself scarce for what I hope will be no more than an hour or so. Both of you had better make your way to the library loft. The Podestà knows the way well enough: he has mattresses, candles, water jars, weapons and the Lord knows what else stashed away up there; the roof is too low to stand, but the floor boards are all sound. No fond embraces mind: take something to read! Remember it wasn't the apple on the tree that caused all the trouble in Eden, it was the 'pair' on the ground!"

Lucia, who was waving down to her friends from one of the corridor windows, was instructed to find Zorzi: "Take him to the schoolroom. Bolt the door. Stay with him and to keep him out of mischief until I send for him. Here is a comb. Make sure he looks tidy and has cleaned his hands and face."

On the bell tower side of the cloister a wide outdoor stone staircase gives access to the upper rooms of the monastery. On these steps and on the top landing the party of noblemen, ladies and clerics assembled. Monsignor Tosi from San Donato Church had joined them and was making loud Latin prayers from his breviary, for no particularly good reason, to which prayers the noble ladies and others present were obliged to mumble with uncertainty the appropriate Latin responses. Down below in the vast cobbled cloister the band played and the palace guard stood at ease until the whole cloister and its approaches right to the canal edge had filled with pushing, shoving and curious humanity.

Making their way with some effort through the crowd, escorted by two guards, came Grandpa and signor Molin. Grandpa was dressed in a faded and moth-eaten long garment. It was his livery coat, bearing the badge of the 'Arte' the Honourable Guild of Glassmakers. It had last seen daylight on the shoulders of his son Vincenzo. A number of furnace owners and workers in the crowd reacted with anger and annoyance that old Miotti had dared to appear in public wearing the 'Arte' livery. Others felt sorry for the poor old devil who was wheezing and walking with difficulty, propped up by signor Molin. Most of the women present were convinced that old Miotti was about to be given a public thrashing, if not summary execution: why else would the Gastaldo be present? It would not be the first time that a band played before an execution; it was common enough practice in most states throughout Europe. Yet, how could such an horrendous thing take place on sacred ground?

Monsignor Tosi called for silence - something only he could command of the crowd.

Senator Trevisan stepped forward clutching nervously at a handful of memory aids for his proclamation: "Citizens and common folk of Murano," he announced. To his surprise his voice carried rather well in the echoing cloister, "In the name of our Serene Prince Doge Francesco, I am here to present an Osella to a child of our Island home."

It was quite the last thing they expected: yet another rumour having gone round to the effect that old Trevisan was to be announced as the next Podestà of Murano.

Trevisan continued: "A boy who by courage and singular good fortune retrieved the sacred ring of the Sensa. May his achievement be an example to all young males here present." The Senator paused while prolonged cheering and clapping rang round the cloister. But who was the child?

"Let it be known," he resumed, "that the Senators of The Most Excellent Council have extended their protection to this young citizen of your homeland and will show their displeasure to any who might seek to do him harm."

Awe-struck with the news that one of their fellow islanders should be in need of such powerful protection, many in the crowd began to exchange

370

murmurs of curiosity. Their buzz of whispers was amplified by the stones of the enclosed courtyard and when silence finally returned Trevisan delivered his true surprise:

"Let it be known to all that Giorgio, heir to Vincenzo the former esteemed Master of the Glassmakers' Guild has, by the generosity of his Most Serene Highness, been awarded an Osella. This token of peace and of the Doge's fatherly love is given both to the boy and to all who dwell in Murano and today I have the honour to present it. Doge Morosini has been much taken by the example of fortitude in adversity that the boy has shown and wishes to compensate for the injustices done to his family. This same Osella token serves to mark his pleasure with the boy for returning the sacred ring of the Sensa."

At this news a great cheer went up; but it was short-lived, as some in the crowd began to circulate the name Miotti; while blissfully unaware of the changing mood of the fickle throng Trevisan continued: "The Senate has examined the charge against Miotto Vincenzo and finds him innocent of treason. Furthermore, it has concluded that grave injustice has been done in that he was abducted and done to death at the instigation of foreign powers. Let it now be known throughout the Veneto that license to manufacture and to trade in glass has been restored to Miotto Daniele. I, Trevisan am appointed Podestà, but as tradition demands, depute my authority to the Four Deputies until such time as Podestà Capello is found. I ask your prayers for his safe return. God preserve the Serenissimo and his people."

Quite dumbstruck, the crowd in its gawping stillness seemed reluctant to accept the news: it then resumed its murmurings and subdued protestations. For five years and more the mob had been 'worked upon' by Bastian's agents with stories of Miotti treachery. The band struck up a solemn and subdued tune, allowing those present to adjust their thoughts and to chatter more loudly. Murder? Kidnap by foreign powers? It was all too astonishing. Then a gasp of sympathy went up as the crowd saw Grandpa buckle forward and collapse unconscious on the steps. No one had prepared him for the unexpected news of his son's murder. He was now prostrate and cold, overcome with grief. Molin, his own eyes half blinded with tears, carried his old friend into Don Tranquillo's office. Molin had always hoped that one day Vincenzo might return and suspected that Bastian held him captive somewhere. Molin and the crowd knew well enough that the Ten would not issue news of that kind without some firm evidence: evidence which of course would never go beyond the walls of the Secret Council Chamber.

While Zorzi was accompanied from the schoolroom, Trevisan called for his snuff box, flipped open the double layered lid, and took a generous pinch. The gorgeously gem studded and enamelled gold box was passed around by his page for the noblemen and the clergy to partake. By way of thanks, it was good manners for the snuffer to make loud and complimentary comments on the beauty of the snuff box. While this ritual was still in progress, Trevisan had a moment to savour the mood of the crowd: he went once again to the balustrade of the stairway. To his astonishment, an instant roar from the crowd greeted him, mingled with shouts of "Trevisan! Trevisan! Trevisan!" The crowd had 'chewed over' his news and were now on his side and were now 'as one' with the victimized Miotti family.

Someone in the crowd shouted: "Trevisan Doze!" and the mob took up the chant. Now that was dangerous stuff to encourage, particularly when witnessed by the other noblemen present, and he begged the crowd to desist. Yet Trevisan would have been deceiving himself if a desire for the ducal crown had not come mind with that shout. His gravelly old voice had carried well across to the crowd. His delivery, aided by the cloister acoustics, was he thought, quite dignified, not to say magisterial: he was a Senator, a bachelor with no legitimate heirs; a bachelor not by inclination but because his elder brother, being the Patriarch of the Trevisan family, was the only male allowed to marry; he was now a member of The Ten and might expect in turn to do his monthly duty as one of The Three; he was in reasonable health, was over sixty years in age and had fought with courage and serious wounds at the siege of Candia. In short, instead of looking to a pleasant retirement keeping bees and breeding hunting dogs at his villa in Friuli, he might, when the time was ripe, throw his hat into the ring and with luck, pull out in exchange the Ducal Corno! There was a well kept little secret that made him entertain such daring thoughts: Morosini might seem quite the most vigorous, virile and athletic Doge that the Republic had elected in the past century, but even he had his 'Achilles Heel' - that vulnerable spot was in Morosini's case his bladder, with its inoperable bladder stone! Why not smile indeed, and pretend to

372

be embarrassed on hearing those repeated shouts?
"Doze....DozeTrevisan!"

Zorzi came up the steps with little Lucia holding his hand. Don Toma` the librarian, who had been sent to escort him, grumbled aloud that his hip and his arthritis was killing him and that furthermore he was not a footman to be commanded by Monsignor Tosi and this bunch of idle noblemen. Zorzi was curious. Nobody had told him what was going on. Don Tranquillo brought his high backed chair from the office and closed the door so that Zorzi could not see what had happened to Grandpa. Propping the chair against the parapet he invited Zorzi to clamber up on to it.

Looking down at the great throng Zorzi was quite bewildered. Loud expressions of sympathy for the young child of a murdered father now gave way to polite clapping. Wasn't this the very same boy who had caused the San Donato riot? So there was truth after all, in what those thick-skulled Arsenal workers had long believed.

Zorzi thought to wave back, but the chair was rather loose at the joints and wobbly and he felt a bit dizzy standing at that height with only the low parapet in front of him to stop him plummeting down, so he clung firmly to the chair back.

Trevisan came forward holding high the glittering snuff box. He flipped its spring lock once again and from between the double-layered lid took out the Osella coin. It was a subconscious gesture, quite unintended on the part of poor Trevisan, but it certainly dashed any hope he might have of ever becoming the next Doge. Holding the Osella coin between index finger and thumb, he displayed it to the crowd from right to left. It was exactly the gesture that a priest makes when he consecrates the communion host and shows it to the faithful. Being the same size as a communion wafer, the golden Osella had an identical effect! Stumbling and tumbling over one another in the cramped space, first the old ladies in black, then the children wiggling noisily for space, then the men and finally the band and Palace Guard fell to their knees. Zorzi knelt down on the chair and made a hasty 'sign of the cross' half expecting Trevisan to pop the coin into his wide-open mouth. The nobles could contain themselves no longer - they fell about with laughter. They rocked on their feet, holding their side with tears of laughter streaming down their cheeks: they patted one another's arms in merriment. Don Tranquillo could see at once the funny side of the situation: his own damaged old lungs were now aching with mirth.

"Get up! Get up! Confound you!" Monsignor Tosi bellowed at the confused crowd, "Get up you blithering fools! It is only a coin for heaven's sake! It's not the Blessed Sacrament!"

Trevisan was now mortified: his blush almost matched the hue of his satin Senator's robe; he knew well enough the pettiness of his peers. From then onwards, whenever he passed amidst a gathering of the nobility, he would be their laughing stock. Hastily he shoved the Osella coin in Zorzi's hands. Any words of praise and congratulation he intended to say now failed him. He turned to hasten down the steps, then, almost as an afterthought, added: "Oh! And the Senate has granted your boon. You may have a prisoner released...just anyone you wish to name... that is within reason of state security. Oh! Never mind, you won't understand that yet. Don Tranquillo has the papers. Don't spend all your bounty on sweets and sherbet, save some for your education. I must go now, I have other duties."

On Don Tranquillo's instruction, Zorzi went down on one knee and kissed the Senator's hand in gratitude. He could not bow, for as yet he had not the wherewithal for a hat to flourish at Trevisan. In exchange he received a pat on the head and an invitation to visit Trevisan in his Murano Palace - adding that Zorzi might like to tell of his kidnap and adventures, by way of entertainment at some reception for guests.

As the noblemen and clergy descended the stairway, the band struck up a parting march. Lifting Zorzi onto the chair once more, Tranquillo called to the crowd, who were about to depart, somewhat deflated by the turn of events, but nevertheless eager to pass on the extraordinary news. "Hey! Don't go away! Give a cheer to our finder of the Fisherman's Ring - our little orphan! He too is the victim of those wicked foreign men. Give him a cheer, won't you?"

Half an hour later, having entertained the ever-growing crowd with folk songs and having taken the lead in a noisy singsong of popular ballads,

Zorzi stepped down to one last storm of applause. The honour of the Miotti was restored and his arm ached from waving the Osella coin.

That night and into the early hours of the morning there was rejoicing. Murano Arsenalotti could now boast and claim the Sensa honours like champions of some rough inter-island calcio ball encounter. Ring shaped bouquets of summer flowers dangled from almost every shop front and tavern doorway. Even curmudgeonly old Meo, Grandpa's cousin, on receiving the news, sent a friendly message and got his team of glass-blowers at the 'Del Jesu' works to make a giant Doge's ring in yellow and green glass. This he displayed in his showroom window and smirked with pride when clients congratulated him on his young nephew's bravery and good fortune. Trevisan, his hopes of the ducal throne still not quite dashed, hung a green and rose-red circular garland from his palace balcony. Taverns and wine cups everywhere were filled to capacity: common-folk put on their finery and danced in pairs the 'saltarello' up and down towpaths of the Glassmaker's Canal. They linked arms in a seemingly endless chain for the noisy 'carmagnola' dance. There were a few fireworks on the bridge of Saint Peter Martyr and torch lit droves of well-wishers descended on the Miotti home. Only Palazzo Capello remained in deathly silence, its great doors and shutters slowly accumulating dust from nearby furnace chimneys. Bastian Zustinian and the Podestà Don Francesco Capello had both vanished.

Molin, his wife and eldest son, stood guard at the Miotti open door, receiving gifts of every kind from home made salami sausages to half a dozen slightly shop-soiled angels, left over from signora Zanetti's Christmas stock. Being a good business woman, she guessed that Zorzi, once in receipt of his new-found wealth, would soon be making tracks towards her sugary paradise of a shop. Upstairs, Grandpa snored soundly on his straw bed, having consumed an entire bowl of bread and milk slops liberally laced with the last of the Ravenscroft rum. He had not bothered to remove his moth-eaten master glassblower's robe, which would serve as his dressing gown, now that he had both the right to wear and the means to pay for having a new one tailor made.

CHAPTER THIRTY-EIGHT

Now Don Tranquillo knew full well that bright children living wretched lives sometimes escape into a world of fantasy and that little boys in particular were no respecters of the fine boundaries that lay between truth, downright lies and make-believe. He blamed himself for over stoking Zorzi's imagination with too many tales from Voragine's 'Book of Golden Legends' and from the adventures of San Bao. (*Sinbad as he is now known- the Chinese Admiral who mapped the world 1421- 1423*) He felt a certain amount of guilt in having first encouraged the lad to join San Donato's choir. For all these reasons he had listened to Zorzi's fantasies of recent days with a certain amount of amusement, but with little or no conviction that he was telling the truth. After all, what little Venetian boy did not dream of diving for the Fisherman's Ring?

A week or so before the Osella Ceremony took place Don Tranquillo had received a summons from the Procurator's Office in the Doge's Palace. He feared at once that someone in the parish had betrayed him: that someone knew that he was hiding the Podestà in the warren of corridors, lofts and rooms that made up the Convent of St. Peter Martyr. When he met the Notary Licini, Registrar for Murano, he was greatly relieved, not to say honoured, that his opinion of the events surrounding the riot was thought to be more trustworthy than that of any other. Archpriest Tosi, he learned, had already been grilled by the lawyer about another child who had been abducted from his choir. The Archpriest had clearly done a thorough investigation at the time, and reported the child's disappearance both to the Bishop and to the Podestà. All that Tosi could remember was that the boy's disappearance happened six or seven years ago - just a few days after another singing competition at which Bastian had been present. When asked if he could recollect a French noble being with Bastian in San Donato Church, his memory was quite clear. Similar reports of child abductions from other choirs about the islands were found in the archives of the Procurator of St. Mark's.

In the Procurator's Office, with the aid of Notary Licini, Don Tranquillo drew up the arrangements for the presentation of the Osella coin. He learned that old Senator Trevisan, who lived opposite Palazzo Capello, had been chosen by the Chancellor for the honour of making the presentation. How the Republic's generous gift to Zorzi was to be both paid and spent was also agreed. Zorzi would collect fifty ducats each year, on or about the Feast of the Ascension, with a first down payment of one hundred and fifty ducats. The total amount of six-hundred ducats would mark the six years of the Doge's reign and would include a reward for rescuing the Doge's cat and the value of the Fisherman's Ring. The generosity of the Republic was, as ever, tempered by the greater need to pay for the war effort. In fact, since The Ten controlled every sequin spent, Zorzi's reward, was most unlikely to be paid in full, and if remembered after a year or so, would be deducted from the Doge's wage packet. Deliberately, though seeming an oversight by his copy clerk, the Notaio had not included a name, nor a description of the citizen who, by Doge's boon, would be released from jail, commenting that Don Tranquillo might one day find it useful, given the number of lawbreakers he had living in his parish. Without stating who the generous donor was, the Notary then handed Tranquillo twenty-seven gold ducats and two English silver coins, instructing him to use the money to provide for the immediate needs of the Miotti family and to distribute the greater part of what was left over amongst the poor in his parish. He allowed Tranquillo to assume that the generous donor of the ducats and the two curious English coins was Senator Trevisan.

Licini also informed Tranquillo of the Doge's expressed wish for the child to be made 'A Ward of State,' so that he would be protected against his nephew's vile intentions, and of the Doge's desire that Zorzi should receive a military and naval education and would not at any stage be barred by inferior birth from training to be a galley commander. The Senate had not granted the Doge's wish in full, for it had dealt in its own ruthless way with that threat and concern about Zorzi's safety. Don Tranquillo would have to dismiss any thoughts of turning the boy into a friar, for in exchange for their six hundred ducats the Senate would insist on getting a young warrior to sail one day to defence of its watery empire.

CHAPTER THIRTY-NINE

Messer Grande's unventilated office beside the Watergate had become unbearable. The rank stench from the prisons was always at it worst towards midday. He sat tooth picking the debris of a walnut cake from his rotting molars. Cake confiscation and the subsequent eating thereof, was all part of his official duties...alas! His majestically proportioned girth left no doubts that he was in any way negligent. Since his appointment, very little by way of escape tools had entered the prisons via the baked cake method. The fine silver toothpick that he had recently nearly swallowed was further testament to his thoroughness! He sat outside his office in the corridor running from the watergate steps to the palace courtyard. Even on the hottest of days there was a cooling draught there, funnelled in from the gloomy shade of Rio Canonica by the rising scorching heat of the courtyard.

Was his memory playing him tricks, or was it just a touch of deja` vu? A Dominican friar in his black and white robe and a little boy were being off-loaded from a gondola. As they drew nearer and his old eyes focused better, he realized from the friar's threadbare tunic and rough replacement patches at the knees that it was not Prior Raimondo: though in stature, walk and proud bearing the friar much resembled the august Prior of San Zanipolo. The child was wearing good quality fustian though. The guard had saluted the friar out of respect and checked his papers. Normally Messer Grande would have let them pass without even bothering to rise from his creaking x-framed armchair, but he had nothing much else to do, having completed his prison round and for his lunch consumed all that was worth confiscating. Touching his forelock to the friar, he requested to see his papers again. Noting the official blue seal of The Ten he put on his horn rimmed spectacles and invited the visitors to enter his steamy office. He flicked some lavender water from a brass dispenser and apologised for the smell, which was in great part of his own making. "I see! A Doge's Pardon. We don't get many of those these days. But what is this, no name?"

"I regret we don't know the name of the prisoner. It is a child, an Uskok girl who is to be released," Don Tranquillo explained.

"Good God! That is beg pardon Your Reverence, an Uskok? We don't take such kind in here. Why I'd rather have an hyena on a watch chain than an Uskok in me prisons!"

"Where might we find the child? She was with a group of women and children under guard, just over a month ago on the Day of the Sensa. They were landed at San Zaccaria from a galley."

"Sold, most likely. Have you tried the Arsenal?"

"We haven't, but these prisoners must have been some captain's prize. As an old galley captain myself, I know someone has to list them for the State, get the sale money and pay the bounty. Isn't that part of your duties?"

"Well, err...yes and no, Reverend Father. The Clerk to the New Prisons does that. You had better inquire with him. You know the way across."

"Yes, but our gondolier was ordered away from the steps."

"Well, I'll see you out through the Gate of the Papers, (*Porta della Carta*) then you can walk round via the Molo and the Bridge of Straws (*Ponte di Paglia*) no more than five, or six minutes."

As Don Tranquillo gave a slight bow and Zorzi followed suit, Zorzi observed: "I hope your teeth are not troubling you any more, Sir?"

"By Saint Mark!" exclaimed the jailer, levering himself to his feet and bowing low. "I thought it was you. I didn't recognize Vossignoria in your hunting clothes! My deepest compliments to His Excellency, Prior Raimondo, and of course to Her Highness the Countess. My teeth are fine thank you," he added, wincing slightly. "I shall be honoured to escort you myself to the Clerk."

Intending to glean some reward in exchange from stirring his bulky stump up the steep flights of the Doge's Golden Stair and over the Prison Bridge he added, "No doubt it is all too familiar to you Vossignoria, but your reverend tutor might like a look at some of the State Apartments on the way."

"While Messer Grande fussed and fluttered around Zorzi, Don Tranquillo filched back the warrant from the jailer's desk, hastily concealing it in the folds of his habit. Carelessly, Messer Grande had already endorsed it with his stamp, but had omitted to complete any description of a child to be released, furthermore he should have filed away the Doge's warrant amongst his important documents and given his visitors, in exchange, a prisoner release docket. As they walked out, the friar gave Zorzi a sidelong knowing grin and silently murmured a prayer, begging pardon of Saint Dominic for his venial sin. Uppermost in his thoughts was the idea that the warrant might one day come in useful to spring from prison his good friend the Podestà. The Ten were certain to track down the Podestà and Don Francesco Capello might well expect a life sentence in jail as a sad consequence of poor Gustav's short sightedness. Tranquillo was also quite certain that Zorzi's little Uskok would long have been sold and if she wasn't then he planned to bribe the jailer to release her, as a person of no consequence, and to persuade Zorzi to hang on to the Doge's boon for the time being.

"Pretend that you have seen it all before," he whispered to Zorzi. "Leave all the gasping in amazement and the silly awestruck comments to me."

The unbelievable splendour of the State Apartments left Zorzi speechless anyway. He was impressed by the craftsmanship and beauty of all that he set eyes upon. Tranquillo had inspected the opulence of the Palace interior on several past occasions and had contrasted the Halls of State with the hovels of his parishioners. However, he well understood that all was designed to impress the ambassadors of foreign powers rather than for the pleasure of the Doge and his officials. He took care not to tax too much the knowledge of their thick looking guide. Their tour included the immense and noisy Hall of the Great Council, where there were agitated groups of cloaked and wigged noblemen, either craning their necks to read the most recent news pinned on the notice boards, or waving their arms in animated arguments about what should be done about the latest crisis. The Hall of Scrutiny, where votes were counted at elections and the Halls of the Senators were busy hives of lawyers and Senators, scurrying here and there, clutching bits of important looking paper. The cavernous and equally splendid halls of the College, of the Three Heads and of The Ten were of course not places into which idle gawpers were permitted to stray. Scenes of saints, senators, Doges and sea battles seemed to adorn every wall and ceiling that was not already smothered in marble and woodcarving. Zorzi played his disinterested role with great patience, longed to ask and to know who the artists were and quite how they set about creating art on such a gigantic scale. The carved wooden ceilings, with their brooding swirls of baroque gold seemed almost poised to descend and crush the mere mortals treading beneath them. Finally, via a series of stairways and narrower passageways, they approached the Prison Bridge. To Zorzi's relief there was no sign of the ten skinny old men performing their rope trick on some hapless victim. He was saddened by the thought that he would no longer be able to tell old Piero that there seemed to be no truth in his tale. It was obvious that the rather dull and narrow inside of the bridge would leave little room for such gruesome goings-on. Alas, old Piero had now gone the watery way of so many hard-working fisher folk. Zorzi had sung at his memorial Requiem on the previous Friday.

From the bridge they descended into the semi- darkness to the dank rotting human smells: to the stark stone and iron warren that is the New Prison. Entering a wide corridor with a whitewashed stone vault, they turned right past four dreadful prison cells crowded with clanking-ironed and awful stinking humanity. The Room of the New Admissions was lined with the records of several hundred years of malefactors. The shelves sagged under the weight of their neatly written sins. Though there was a high window giving on to the prison courtyard, each clerk's desk was candle lit. Don Tranquillo quietly palmed a coin into Zorzi's hand, whispering "Wouldn't do to make him suspicious. Make sure nobody sees you giving it to him."

Checking to see what was in his half closed hand, Zorzi saw one of Grandpa's Louis d'or. They were introduced to the Clerk to the Records as Sua signoria, the Noble de Brayda and his tutor Fra Tranquillo Selvo. In the distant tone of one parading his great authority, Messer Grande ordered the Chief Clerk to release whoever it was that the young nobleman specified. He then hovered expectantly for his tip. All credit to him, he had given an exciting and informative tour. There was nothing now for him to explain, nothing to contemplate but great stone blocks, rusty iron grilles and the festering smelly misery of his own infernal realm.

Tranquillo gave Zorzi a nudge. Confident and relaxed now in his false status, Zorzi took the jailer's arm and walked with him to the office exit, thanking him most politely for showing the apartments to his tutor. Out of sight of the clerks he slipped the heavy gold Louis d'or into Messer Grande's already well-greased palm. Concluding that only a child of the ducal family could have dispensed such a tip, Messer Grande had no reason to concern himself further with the name of the prisoner, nor why the Chancellor had issued the release warrant. He presumed that the Prison Clerk would get one of his assistants write all that down. By happy coincidence the Clerk, an almost illiterate man, was also Messer Grande's son-in-law.

After many a fumbling effort to locate the right place in the current ledger of recorded crimes, the Clerk passed the heavy book across his desk to Don Tranquillo. Flicking quickly to the pages dated from a week onwards before the Sensa time, the friar scanned his eye swiftly up and down looking for any entry for a female prisoner. Standing close by to inspect the book as well, Zorzi felt the Don's sudden grip on his forearm. "What is it? What's wrong Don Tranquillo? Has she been sold?" he asked in alarm.

"Afraid so Vossignoria: wasted journey!" Don Tranquillo replied, as casually as he could manage to do in the circumstances, "Nevertheless, if you are in agreement, Vossignoria, we could use the pardon to release some other poor prisoner from his misery....perhaps and elderly and infirm person?"

Not waiting for a reply and now addressing the slow-witted Clerk, he observed: "We shall choose some aged person at random, if you don't mind. Ah! This one will do." He read out the entry, omitting the prisoner's name: " Prisoner No. 319 -Male, aged 73. Money found - 27 ducats and two foreign coins of silver; means of livelihood confiscated, namely sandolo boat to be burned for kindling at Arsenal. Sentence -ten lashes - commuted to three lashes on appeal for old age and infirmity by the Procurator for Trade - three years incarceration for complicity in illegal trading with foreigners. Consigned - Cell Lione della Mal Paga. *(Lion of Bad Debt - curiously Colleoni's castle bears the same name.)* May I borrow your pen?"

Taking out a small knife from the money pouch concealed within folds of his friar's habit, he gave the Clerk's quill nib a quick trim - obviously it had not been used for ages. Then unfolding the warrant he wrote: 'Tacca, Pietro.' Turning to Zorzi, he commented, with no hint of excitement in his voice," You see Vossignoria, how important it is for all to learn to read and write well. Only thus through learning will we all grow in wisdom and efficiency."

"Quite right! Quite right! Your Reverence," the Prison Clerk added in an unctuous voice, "Vossignoria, I am sure, will learn to be a great scholar, with such a good tutor."

Infinitely more retarded in his studies than Zorzi, the Clerk was quite oblivious to the fact that Don Tanquillo's sarcasm was intended for him and that the friar had utterly hoodwinked him as well.

The Clerk's 'Vossignorias' brought just a hint of boyish regret that nobody would ever be likely to address him again in that way. However, when Tranquillo whispered, "Piero," he was hardly able to contain his joy and relief, for he could see that with a quick scan of a book, a quick scribble with a pen and an even quicker thinking brain, Don Tranquillo was about to release from a gloomy dungeon their dear old friend Piero the seaweed burner, for so long thought by all to have been drowned.

Had they both gone down with the jailer to release Piero, there would have been an immediate noisy and emotional reunion, which would have betrayed their subterfuge and certainly cast doubts upon Zorzi's nobility. Don Tranquillo was about to send Zorzi off to hire a gondola when the most awful fetid pong that he had ever inhaled came wafting into the office. The stink heralded the entry of Celestine, the 'Lady of the Night Soil.' By far the most useful and effective person in the whole prison; she it was who, with the aid of her two stout limbed sons, kept the cells in some reasonable state of cleanliness. By emptying the sewage tubs daily into large portable metal vats and having the lot rowed away in her nephew's barge, she earned her daily grosso, as well as the extra silver grosso or two from selling the urine to the Arsenal gunpowder factory. In more peaceful times Celestina had been obliged by the prison rules to collect the liquid emanations of the noble prisoners for further refinement into quality saltpetre for pistol shot. Now that war was afoot she no longer bothered and pooled it, so to speak, with the common pee of the criminal classes. When dried in the sun, the urine provided the essential potash and nitrate ingredients for cannon powder. The more solid waste was transported to the fields about the islands where, once dissolved into uncomposted slurry, it completed the cycle of human misery by contaminating the lettuce, cabbage and root crops.

Rejoicing in her beautiful name, the 'Donna del Cesso' was also blessed at birth with that most useful of all 17th Century gifts, the gift of having no sense of smell whatsoever. Celestina, more than anyone, knew what made the prison hum. Not a rat keeled over, not an ounce of quicklime was spread without her knowledge. She it was who diagnosed cases of jail fever and carefully noted the comings and goings of prisoners, both of the head first and feet first kind: the number of sewage barrels required and the quantity of quicklime in each cell were adjusted by her accordingly.

Sniffing noisily and reaching for his rosemary and sage nosegay the Prison Clerk yelled: "Celestina! Shut down that hellish stinking lid! Tell me, are there any young girls downstairs in the female prison?"

"Just a minute. I can't put the lid on the vat till I've emptied this lot. Your turn-keys have some filthy habits…. worse than the jailbirds. Tell them to aim more careful in future! It ain't my job to clean up their mess you know!"

She had just finished the unpleasant task of emptying the sewage tubs in the adjoining rest room. The Room of the Navara was little more than a large unventilated prison cell with partitions and wooden benches around the walls where the night guards diced, played cards or stretched themselves out for long spells of illicit sleep that it would be unwise for any prisoner to disturb by crying out for help.

"There are two little sluts," she continued, "Caught thieving coins from the charity box in San Marco....the usual honey on a stick trick. Oh! And a wretch of a child sent back from the Arsenal. Mistook her for a boy, it seems.... nearly went for a galley slave till they stripped her for the branding. What's she done? Don't understand why we are keeping her with the women.... by rights ought to go to an orphanage."

"Is she wearing my....that is, leather breeches?" interrupted Zorzi in an excited voice.

"Why yes, Your Excellency, dirty patched leather ones. Now how would Your Excellency know a thing like that?"

Don Tranquillo gave Zorzi's arm another warning squeeze and addressed himself to the Chief Clerk: "Sua signoria de Brayda, did come to the aid of a female child who was captured, together with Uzkoks, by one of our brave galley captains. He asked the Sisters of San Zaccaria to find her some clothing for decency's sake. They were, I understand, male breeches provided by the noble nuns: a curious fact, which stuck in my mind, given the fate awaiting any male who strays within their perimeters. If this child is the one my noble pupil is looking for, she will of course not be a Venetian: the Doge's boon states that the prisoner to be pardoned shall be of Venetian birth."

Tranquillo offered up silent penance for his venial lie. Secure in the knowledge that the Clerk could not read, he continued: "How unfortunate that we cannot alter the document, now that this elderly prisoner's name is written on it. Should you find the girl, my kind hearted pupil will willingly purchase her from you: that is of course, from her owner, the galley captain."

The distinctly unpleasant features of the Chief Clerk twisted into a half-smile of understanding. Like the thieving little sluts of San Marco, he too had sticky fingers. In a quiet aside, Don Tranquillo added: "I should think it almost certain that the galley captain has sailed off with the Doge's convoy. I doubt if he is concerned anymore about the small bounty. A young female can't be worth more than a half sequin at the most. My pupil saw the girl suffering from exhaustion amongst some prisoners, when visiting the precinct together with Prior Raimondo. Doubtless he will recompense for your trouble in arranging the release. Such concern shows a noble spirit, don't you agree? In time no doubt he will learn to be of harder heart with pirates. However, I understand that the nuns thought the girl to be Circassian rather than Slav. She may well have been an Uskok captive."

More than delighted with the prospect - he would demand at least a full gold sequin for his trouble - the Clerk asked Celestina to accompany

Zorzi to the female prison, whilst he, complaining of a recently broken finger, asked Don Tranqillo to complete the written formalities of the release warrant.

Zorzi might well have come barefoot to the prison, had signora Molin not insisted that he wore his newly washed stockings of fine cotton crochet and the well-waxed leather shoes inherited from Lacin's son. The mixture of quicklime and urine in which he was now treading would have stung the most calloused of feet. Barefoot, he could never have claimed title to the many respectful 'Vossignorias' now being addressed to him by all and sundry of the prison staff. Groans, maniacal laughter, screams of agony and despair and echoing whispers now came at him from every direction, as he passed in lantern lit gloom a labyrinth of stinking cells and descended with Celestine to the ground floor. Zorzi was astounded by the thickness of the cell walls: the mighty weight of their rust covered iron doors; the fat bolts thick as anchor shanks; the enormous size of the hinges; and the vile and greasy stone funnel holes down which food and water was passed into each pitch dark receptacle of inhumanity. Here and there outstretched arms and emaciated hands writhed in the gloomy space between the double barred cell windows. Voices beseeched him for mercy - filled his impressionable heart with pity - yet even so, he found those very pleas extremely scaring. The empty alleyways of Santa Catarina at night time held only imagined horrors... here all around him was a wide awake nightmare.

Apart from a few pale tufts sprouting at the back of her neck and above her ears, the girl was now quite bald, but there was no mistaking his patched goatskin and that wan famished look; that same smile of gratitude that he had last seen in the refectory of San Zaccaria. Celestina took her out into the prison yard, slapped a handful of soft soap on her head and while scrubbing and dowsing her down with several buckets of well water observed entirely for her own amusement: "Why you're the lucky one aren't you? No branding on the bum; no slavery in some dirty heathen's seraglio; a handsome young nobleman come specially to carry you off. You'll soon have a fine satin dress, little missie. They won't let you in his palace wearing this filthy pelt, I'll bet. You don't understand a damned word of what I am saying, do you?"

As she helped the girl to pull back the breeches over her soaking limbs she added, "Where those shrivelley nuns got this disgusting bit of old goat from, I don't know! Why it ain't Christian, not with all their wealth!" Giving the girl a friendly pat on the bottom she dismissed her with a final piece of completely uncomprehended advice: "You ain't branded, so Venice is your oyster! Use your fine skin and your fair locks as well when they grows back. You won't never make a noblewoman, so try for a courtesan, there ain't that much difference!"

Leaving a trail of wet behind her, the girl stumbled into the guardroom. Half blinded by the combination of dazzling sunlight and caustic soap and totally confused as to what fate might still await her, Elenca sobbed quietly as the order of release was formally read out and a slice of dry bread and two worn and wafer thin silver soldi from the prisoner's charity box were pressed into her hands as formal tokens of her freedom: there she was signed out by Celestina together with seventeen vat loads of stinking ordure. Though traces of stinging soft soap may have added to her streaming eyes, there was no mistaking deep felt gratitude when she was re-united with her somewhat embarrassed young gallant. The girl took hold of Zorzi's hands, held them a long time to her cheeks and unable to express her relief in any other way, cried her heart out.

On the Bridge of Straws they sat down together in the shade of the ballustrade and waited for Don Tranquillo to emerge. Elenca seemed an odd name: to a Venetian it sounded more like a list of things. Zorzi was still trying, with much pointing and expansive gesturing to establish whether it was the girl's Christian name, or her country of origin, when he caught sight of old Piero staggering feebly out through the prison gate, propped on the Don's sturdy right arm. Letting out a whoop of delight he let go of the girl's hand and ran towards them, only to be checked by a severe frown from Tranquillo and a hand raised in warning to restrain Zorzi's excitement. "Over the bridge and go quietly. Walk casually 'til we join the Piazza crowds. Someone is bound to be watching. That imbecile clerk is suspicious, though I have paid him to mind to his own affairs."

Tranquillo was aware that jail birds on release were often shadowed for the purpose of locating and identifying their associates in crime and, just as he surmised, the little group was followed by one who was the eyes and the ears of the Republic along that bustling section of the Molo. He dogged them at a discreet distance as far as the base of St. Mark's

Campanile, where a dozen or more refreshment kiosks, mostly cobbled together from yellowing canvas and rough hewn pinewood, sprouted like mushrooms beneath the shadow of a mighty elm. Before following Tranquillo and Piero into a tent chosen for its relative cleanliness and display of fierce and colourful liqueurs, Zorzi turned to admire two stilt walkers dressed as Harlequin and Brighella: there to his great surprise and delight was the ragged bagpiper! Weighed down by his sagging skin of tepid goat tainted water, the blind beggar seemed nevertheless to be merrily occupied in playing a jig to accompany the jerky steps of Harlequin's comic stilt dance. Once again Zorzi felt the compulsion to talk to the blind man who, as ever, was trailing rags and tatters from his person like so many leaves in autumn: indeed the poor man might have been better attired by standing in a blizzard in a rag merchant's yard. The beggar's cruel affliction, his heart rending appearance of poverty, his rolling eyes and his cheery smile all seemed to invite people to open their hearts with pity and to confide in him things that they were unlikely to tell to others of his lowly kind. Zorzi ran across to remind him of who he was and to tell him that his 'blind man's promise' of good fortune had indeed at last come true. When he confided that his little companion was suffering from soft soap in the eyes and needed a beaker of water to rinse them, the begger willingly allowed himself to be guided towards the kiosk.

Her stinging eyes almost miraculously soothed by a couple of beakers of goat water, Elenca now smiled happily and with *'grazie'* repeatedly mispronounced alerted the waterseller to her foreign origins. Though faintly surprised he did not attempt to question her accent and willingly joined them for *un'ombra* of fierce Grappa liqueur in the five o'clock shade - the 'ombra' of the Doge's immense Bell Tower. Tranquillo, suspecting at once from the blind man's line of questioning to Piero that he might be an informer to the prison authorities, kept up the pretence that Piero was a complete stranger to them all: a lucky old prisoner released on Doge's writ by the generous hearted and noble little 'Ring-finder.' As for the little scrap of a girl, the water seller seemed nolonger even aware of her presence. However, the ever famished Zorzi drew further attention to the two released jailbirds by suggesting that they go to some nearby 'bacaro' tent and tuck into a solid meal together. Tranquillo, anxious to get away from the prison environs with all possible haste dismissed this proposal with: "And who is going to pay for it all? You don't have any tin on you and I've just got enough for the ferryman."

"Eager as always to jest with the wily Don, Zorzi countered: "Elenca will. Would you lend me your pen knife Don Tranquillo, just for a moment?" Giving a knowing wink to old Piero, he pointed to the patch on the girl's breeches. The old fisherman's ribs shook with laughter for the first time in many months: "Oh Lord! No Zorzi! Only you could come up with such a daft idea. Unpicking a young lady's pants in public? I don't know what the penalty is for baring a bum at the Doge's Palace, a good flogging from Messr Grande would be only part of it, I reckon."

The mystified Don Tranquillo was soon informed about the silver grosso still stitched firmly into the seat of the goatskin pantaloons. And, to the Don's great consternation, while the tale of the burned pants was being told, Capitano Ravenscroft's name was mentioned several times. In an attempt to distract the now curious beggar he offered him his own drink and to further curb Piero's tongue he urged him to drink *un'ombra* or three more of the fiery Grappa while the children were sent off with a couple of 'baghetini' to the adjoining refreshment tent, where they tucked into fresh bread and large 'granitas' of cherry ice. When the water seller finally wandered off, Piero began to suffer from the effects of fiercely strong spirit on an empty stomach and became rather maudlin and emotional: "How will Daniele forgive me?" he sobbed, "Neighbours will think of me as no more than an old swindler to be hunted down!"

The confiscation of his rotting sieve of a fishing boat and his precious nets was a small matter of concern in comparison with the terrible loss of Daniele's fortune in gold ducats that had been entrusted to him by the English. Though pasty faced, hollow eyed and tottering from weeks of confinement in semi-darkness, Piero had in fact put on some weight. Thanks to sharing the Mala Paga cell with a crazy nobleman, he had eaten in a style never before experienced. Concern about Grandpa's misplaced trust in him had affected his health far more than the confinement, the stagnant air and the infected sores from the humiliating whipping that he had endured in silence. He had convinced himself thoroughly that everyone in Murano would damn him as a common thief who had run off with Grandpa's earnings.

When the children returned, both Tranquillo and Zorzi assured him of the outburst of loving memories expressed at the Requiem service. Once again he began to chuckle through his tears. He then entertained them with his account of his time with the kleptomaniac nobleman, who had even tried in dead of night to slip the key to Piero's boat locker from around his neck. The senile nobleman had spent many months plundering the palaces of his friends and neighbours, collecting the most extraordinary items of trinkets, clocks and dressing table items. He was only caught when he tipped the whole lot into the Grand Canal from an upper window of his palace, announcing loudly that he was giving it all back to Saint Mark and Saint Theodore to pay for their daughters' dowries.

To their great pleasure little Elenca laughed with them. Though she understood nothing of what was being said, she was more relaxed now and old Piero's voice was familiar to her. She had heard it many times before, though muffled, through the ventilation shaft of the Womens' Prison. The 'Lione della Mala Paga' was the prison reserved for harmless old men, who posed no threat of insult to the women in the neighbouring cells.

In a suite of palatial rooms overlooking the fashionable shoreline of Giudecca, the 'blind' water seller sat down at his walnut and ivory inlaid writing desk and debated with himself as to whether to mention the Circassian girl at all in his report. Information that he had received was still at a delicate stage of interpretation. Further unobtrusive checks would have to be made before reporting fully to Chancellor Ballarin. There was too the damned inconvenience of that interfering Sub Prior from Murano. Evidently there was more than one venal clerk in the Chancellor's department. Someone must have tipped off Tranquillo as well about the girl's identity: why else would the friar have sprung her from jail in such a clever and casual manner. Tranquillo would have to be stopped before he could lay first claim to the inevitable reward for information about her that would soon be on offer from the The Ten.

A clerk, trusted with opening the post in the department monitoring daily events in Istanbul, had given our 'blind' water seller a most useful tip off. There had been an appeal to Venice from the Florentine spy Anton Maria Del Chiaro, now working for Venice as well in the Wallachia region, to seek out a girl kidnapped in a raid on a Turkish harem. Far from being a waif of no consequence, the Circassian girl might well be the very one sought after. A young female, named in Turcic as Ilinka, had certainly gone missing while under the Sultan's protection and Islamic honour had been held to ridicule. The child's disappearance was causing diplomatic tremors of earthquake proportions along the northern borders of the Ottoman Empire. Sipping an 'aperitivo' in the form of a sparkling glass of Bardolino before his man servant brought in the first course of his supper, the 'blind' water seller set down in swift and elegant calligraphy and in remarkable detail a report on the developing Murano intrigue. As the wise Chancellor Ballarin had anticipated, the Sub Prior Tranquillo had used the Doge's Pardon to gain the release from prison of his aged parishioner. This Pietro Tacca, an illiterate ferryman, whilst employed by His Excellency the English Sea Captain, had been seized and confined by Customs Officers. In short, a complete cock-up had taken place, caused entirely by Vogalonga's gannet like greed: for when it came to bounty hunting and betraying the misdemeanours of his fellow men Vogalonga had the persistence of a fly on a fish stall. Old Tacca would have been released in any case, once Captain Ravenscroft got to know of his capture and the English Captain's payment in ducats for the glassware would now have to be restored by the Treasury- even though Miotti had no license to trade. Such payment would need to be made in a manner that would not arouse any suspicions about Ravenscroft's senior and undercover role in the Department of Information. As a middle raking spy, the blind water had of course been told all that was necessary for him to know about the 'English Captain.' His carefully composed report was designed to add fuel to the Chancellor's existing suspicions about Don Tranquillo. The friar was up to something: most likely he was also hiding the Podestà Don Francesco Capello in that labyrinth of halls and corridors at St. Peter Martyr. Tranquillo was clearly a devious and subtle mover. Short of desecrating the Convent premises and provoking Prior Raimondo's powerful lobby of Senators, Chancellor Ballarin was advised by the 'blind' water seller to find some way of dealing Tranquillo an incapacitating blow from which he would not easily recover.

A few days later, while passing through the Map Room in the Doge's Palace, Licini, the promising young Notary and Registrar in whose care Zorzi had been entrusted, encountered Chancellor Ballarin studying an ancient plan of Soave Castle. Don Domenico confided in him that he had

391

had no intention of causing internal strife and military weakness by laying siege to its massive hill top walls; moreover, he just could not spare troops for such a difficult assault. There was always the risk of an overland attack on Venice while Doge Morosini was away at sea. *(Ottoman hordes had swept through the Balkans in a lightning strike just ten years previously and were at the gates of Vienna before any Western nation could organise a counter attack.)* The Noble Bastian may have considered himself to be impregnable, holed up as he was with his alchemists and with other seekers of illicit pleasures. Bastian was hopeful as ever that he would discover the 'philosopher's stone,' the formula that would transform lead or iron pyrites into a shower of desperately needed gold ducats. The Grand Chancellor had a three pronged plan and was poised to turf out Bastian from his hide-away with little need for violence or bloodshed. Little Fatty Gritti's lawyers had issued a writ for repossession; for to nobody's great surprise, that plump, flatulent and eternally hungry Croesus of an eight-year-old was the rightful owner of the castle and lands of Soave. Secondly, the Chancellor had discovered in that ancient plan that there was a secret gallery, an escape route cut many hundreds of yards up through the rock leading from the cellar of an old dwelling in Soave village: a house known as the Palace of the Counts of Saint Boniface. This tunnel-cum-stairway terminated at a trapdoor beneath the castle's guardroom. A swift night attack by a dozen marines might overwhelm the garrison; otherwise the marines might plant a gunpowder charge beneath the trapdoor that would have the same result. Finally, he had already planted a 'time bomb' - a cuckoo within the castle's nest - a young rake-hell who was short on brains but long in purse and likely to appeal physically as well to the cash-strapped Bastian. His cuckoo was none other than that 'convent gatecrasher', the Noble Abbondio Rezzonico, over whom Chancellor Ballarin had his usual life or death stranglehold.

Before dismissing the lawyer Licini, Chancellor Ballarin instructed him to report regularly on the comings and goings of the Sub Prior Tranquillo and all others resident in the Convent of St. Peter Martyr. He suspected that the Tranquillo knew more than he cared to admit about the disappearance of Podestà Capello and that the Sub Prior also knew the reason why the Miotti child had been the subject of two kidnapping attempts.

CHAPTER FORTY

Piero's homecoming across the Lagoon was a triumph. The astonishing sight of their old pal waving to them and hailing them from a smart gondola like some tipsy Lazarus, soon had fishermen hauling in their nets. Eager to find out where their Requiem'd pal had been buried for the past months, they reset their sails and tagged on behind. Neighbours shouted their greetings, or in amazement, waved from their windows or from their rickety balconies. As the small procession rowed its way along the Glassmakers' Canal, rumour spread with the speed of old maids' gossip that Piero had been locked up on the orders of the Noble Zustinian. There was news too that Vogalonga had been sentenced to the galleys, having been somehow involved in both Piero's capture and Zorzi's abduction. Piero was feted and invited to celebrate with many *un'ombra,* by tradesmen and glassmakers living along the canal: for at some stage in the past he had obliged almost all of them either with transport, with fish, or by giving a hand with some heavy communal task. In his absence, his own tumbledown fishing hut had been plundered for wood by sea gipsies and many, including Molin, were now eager to help him rebuild. Piero spent the first weeks of freedom as guest in Grandpa's newly replastered downstairs parlour.

Elenca's entry into the Miotti household was in contrast less than cordial. First came the severe shock to Grandpa's ever glassy edged nerves: she was not a hated Uskok, she was something far, far worse - an Ottoman Turk! While serving with the fleet, Grandpa had lost the top halves of two fingers on his left hand - severed by an Ottoman axe! During the long return gondola ride to Murano Elenca's origins had become fairly obvious, fortunately at that stage only to Tranquillo. She had mumbled incomprehensibly between sobs and smiles, but the mumbling was in Turkic, of that the former galley commander had no doubt. When Tranquillo left her with the Molin girls to be soaped and scrubbed once again of the prison stench and dressed modestly in a cream linen smock, he gave instructions that they should treat her in a kindly manner, but as the new servant for Grandpa. He told the Molins that she was a Circassian slave girl from somewhere near the Black Sea. Breaking the bad news to his old friend was not easy, but he reminded him of his Christian duty to love his enemies and to protect the innocent. This sermon came with the practical advice not to bring her anywhere near a church until she had learned how to bless herself by making the correct Sign of the Cross: she seemed to know the Orthodox method of doing this. Harbouring a Turkish child, even though she might yet prove to be Greek Orthodox, was still probably the quickest way to get lynched by the mindless mob.

Attempting to deceive signora Zanetti only made matters worse. In the sugar bowl of that lady's many virtues crawled a buzzing wasp, a wasp with a tongue that could spread gossip faster than that of an out of work gondolier. Anything that Elenca communicated to Eldeniz, her Turkic speaking porter, went straight to the signora and thence via her customers to Don Tranquillo. Even though the Don had bribed Eldeniz to inform everyone that the child was a Circassian Christian who only spoke in Greek to him, the calamitous news eventually seeped out. Elenca had been captured from the coastal harem of a certain Koprulu Hussein, a member of a family from which Grand Vezirs of the Ottoman Empire were often chosen. Elenca was possibly one of Hussein's countless offspring: pale skinned Circassian concubines were very much to the Turkish taste. Before matters could get out of hand and the Miotti family became once again the target of insults and threats from their neighbours, Grandpa, with Don Tranquillo's advice, moved quickly to dowse down the rumours. He confronted signora Zanetti - prosperously plump and matronly in her pearls and Sunday brocades. The sudden encounter took place on the steps of St. Stephen's while a small crowd of her friends and family were well within hearing distance should Grandpa have chosen to raise his voice. Holding Elenca's emaciated little hand firmly in his, and in blunt words, he told the grand signora that if the name Koprulu was ever mentioned again then it would be on her conscience if the innocent child was sent back to the dreadful prison cell from which she had just been released. In that eventuality, her conscience too would be troubled with rumours about her curious unmarried relationship with the Turk called Eldeniz. Eledeniz, in turn, would have no need to whisk Zorzi away from her shop front, for Zorzi would take his prospective small fortune in gold coins to a rival sugar shop in Rialto Market.

The signora and her obliging porter took stock of the threat to both good name and trade. In any case, the shrivelled and ill looking child servant in her grubby kitchen smock hardly looked the part of a Koprulu, who were the bogeymen of Eastern Europe, having plundered much of its wealth. From then on there was no further gossip about Koprulus, nor of offspring from the harems of the 'Satanic Empire.' Murano accepted the strange girl as no more than a Circassian slave employed in Grandpa's now prospering household. It would be many months before news of her presence in Murano came to the office of the new Podestà whereupon the full attention of the almighty Ten swiftly descended upon the poor scrap of a girl.

Elenca *(Helen)* seemed to be neither a name on the Roman Christian calendar, nor a Moslem name, therefore to re-assure the local community, Tranquillo made a bit of a public spectacle of her baptism. On that Saturday afternoon bags of 'confetti' of sugared almonds, a gift from signora Zanetti (who was wise enough to offer to be godmother,) were distributed to the many children and parents present. The handsome silver cross and chain that Don Tranquillo blessed and gave to Elenca had been purchased earlier at the church door by Grandpa from a dubious looking pedlar, with much haggling over the price: luckily nobody in the congregation could lay claim to its loss.

Don Tranquillo, with an escort of cudgel carrying parishioners, presented Zorzi's first banker's draft for one hundred and eighty ducats at the Rialto Exchange. From then on the Doge's gift was conveyed via the Notary Licini, who was appointed to be Zorzi's adviser and accountant.

Understandably, after his smart sartorial adventures with the young Morosini 'nobs' at San Marco, Zorzi wanted expensive summer and winter clothes for himself and for all his pals. Grandpa, however, restricted his generous spending sprees to the Molin family. Several bales of top quality Bradford wool cloth, yards of printed Egyptian cotton and sewing materials were purchased at Rialto Market. The Molin girls set to with needle and thread and much observation of the ladies of fashion entering and leaving Zanetti's. When Zorzi offered to replace his patched and threadbare cassock, Don Tranquillo refused. Zorzi then suggested that maybe Don Toma` the librarian, Brother Gerolamo, (known as Fra Zeri the cook,) and 'that other friar' would like to have new clothes, Don Tranquillo then realized that his schemes of confusion and deceit about the presence of the Podestà were about to unwind. An unnamed friar on the premises would always invite curiosity. Children could not be expected to keep silent about the extra hooded presence that they glimpsed from time to time about the Convent corridors.

As for Zorzi's offer of smart new raiment, Don Tranquillo explained that the threadbare habits that the Dominicans wore were a sign of their obedience to Jesus's commandments. "How could he," he asked, "go visiting his shivering and sick parishioners in winter, while he was garbed in warm new English wool?" As for the other friar, he explained that he was just a visitor, a scholar from Padua University, who was researching medical cures in the great library. Signorina Bianca was just acting as this scolar's copywriter. Zorzi then stumped him with two innocent questions: "Is signorina Bianca a noblewoman...only, she wears such costly dresses?" And, "Can ladies get married to friars?"

Piero and signor Molin were soon fully occupied directing and giving a hand to a team of laid off Arsenal carpenters and stone masons. There would be little demand for their skills until Morosini returned victorious with a fleet of Turkish galleys in tow, or equally likely he had need to replace some of his own losses. After weeks of hammering, chipping, sawing, re-beaming and tiling of the roof and replacement of window frames and shutters, Zorzi's house began to resemble once more the prosperous merchant's dwelling that it had been in centuries past. Grandpa now slept on a quilted woollen mattress, in a wood panelled room smelling of lavender and fresh varnish. His bed was built into a corner next to a new fire hearth. The bed was boxed in with long hinged wooden shutters on the two exposed sides rising to a decoratively carved wooden canopy – all carefully devised to keep out the winter draughts and the biting bugs of summer. The windows of the upper rooms were leaded with small lozenge shaped pieces of coloured glass that cast their magical Harlequin rays down onto bright new woven rush matting. Zorzi dismantled his booby traps of broken pottery; for there were now oak doors fitted with latches and locks at the top of each of the two open staircases now rising from the courtyard. These steps and their handrails were now re-built with delicately carved Istrian stone. Apart from a lick of lime wash to the walls and replacemant of the rotting mattress on the family marriage bed, Grandpa insisted that no alterations whatsoever be made to Vincenzo's room. Still hanging on a row of wall pegs and now riddled with moth holes were Vincenzo's Guild Master's gown, his working clothes and his glassmaker's leather apron. Numerous other silent reminders of happier times long gone littered the room as well. Zorzi had no choice but to share with Elenca. He did not argue the matter

- understanding that the middle room would always remain a shrine to his father's and to his mother's memory. The respective territories of Elenca and Zorzi were divided up by a row of beautifully carved and painted 'cassoni' linen chests. Piero bought them as an out of fashion job lot from a dealer in the Ghetto. The chests of Spanish walnut proved to be a most practical purchase - receiving many a heavy knock, during wild indoor games with friends. Zorzi was happy to lay claim to just one chest. In it he stored his shirts, stockings, fishing tackle and most important of all, under a planked false bottom, his own 'Cabinet of Curiosities of Mother Nature' namely: an assortment of sea shells and dried crabs; one beautifully painted but slightly chipped pot from the pharmacy; a stuffed squirrel that he had found on the side of a rubbish heap and one must not forget that collection of glass bottle badges.

New suits of clothing were either left 'hung up' on the floor, or dumped in with Elenca's dresses, clogs and shawls in the three other cassoni. Common ground was the fireplace area, where they sat and toasted bread on cold evenings and struggled with their jointly challenged minds to read and spell the lists of words that signorina Bianca set as homework.

In all this new comfort, there were inevitably disadvantages to be found. Zorzi sometimes reverted to sleeping on his old goatskin, finding his sturdy rope framed bed, his duck down mattress and blankets too soft and far too hot for a good night's sleep. Elenca sometimes woke him from her cotton curtained couch with nightmare screams and sobs: her past was still a mystery. With fixed multi-coloured glass windows it was nolonger possible to shout across the canal to Aldo Molin. Similarly, he could no longer scramble high up onto wooden packing cases in order to catch a glimpse to the north-west of those pink snow capped peaks of the Dolomites. Dragons lurked in their caves there, in wait for hapless travellers along the wilderness tracks to Austria. Now that he and Grandpa had the means, he longed to journey to those distant Alps and to play, perhaps with friends like Aldo, amidst the shining pink snow. As for any dragons that they might encounter: if a generous gob of spit failed to send them howling back to their caves then there were Grandpa and Piero's newly purchased hunting guns. The open draughty eaves ventilator from which he used to view the mountains was now closed off with a 'Saint Dona` and Dragon' set against a deep blue starry sky and disappointingly white mountain tops: all painted expertly on soda glass by signor Barovier, the father of Matteo, one of his friends. Even the little arrow-slit beside his bed, giving that overhead view of the new front doors, was now glazed with a panel of thick clear glass. He could no longer play the trick of sprinkling water down onto the heads of visiting pals and pretending it was something worse.

As for the beautifully carved and painted cassoni - they too proved to have their down side as Zorzi soon discovered. Thinking to give his rather timid friend Matteo a good fright, Zorzi invited him round at a time when he knew Elenca would be off to Zanetti's sugar emporium for a long chat with Eldeniz. All was ready - ghostly sheet and lid of cassone chest opened ready to jump into, once he spied Matteo entering through the front door. The wails and groans of a soul in torment somewhere in the empty bedroom and the loud knocking and scratching noises had the desired effect on Matteo - he fled in terror! The self-locking external latch on the cassone lid had a similar effect on Zorzi. Scrambling around in pitch darkness and sweltering heat amidst the heap of junk, clothes and linen, he made numerous attempts to heave upwards the heavy lid. Now in a blind panic, he realized that he had the added inconvenience of a full bladder. After two hours of shouting, knocking and misery he suddenly realized that Don Tranquillo's 'alborello' pharmacy pot had more than purely decorative use. Grandpa, occupied as ever with clanking furnace doors and roaring fire bellows, was too far off to hear any cry for help and what's more that oak bedroom door was a most effective soundproof. It was Elenca who at last came to his rescue. His pride dented, Zorzi kept the misadventure to himself and hinted to Matteo that perhaps there was a ghost somewhere haunting the Miotti bedrooms. Elenca was highly amused and fortunately quite lacking in words to say anything to the contrary.

CHAPTER FORTY-ONE

The owner of 'The Dragon Inn,' a boarding house and cooked meat tavern just over the bridge from San Donato, fell ill with a 'mighty griping of the guts.' A few herbal remedies from Fra Zeri would have had him on his feet within a day or so, but he had the misfortune to have enough ducats to consult a renowned and expensive quack physician. Despite prayers to the dragon slaying saint and copious candle lit devotions, he was finished off in a delirium of pain and infection by repeated bleeding with dirty scalpels: not to mention the enemas, cuppings and emetics. At the age of twenty-eight he left a widow, two infants and more to the point, an almost brand new fishing smack.

When Don Tranquillo got to hear of the tragedy, he came to confer with Grandpa and Piero. It was agreed that, after a respectful day or two for mourning, they would approach the widow and make a generous offer. Meanwhile Piero would make a seemingly casual inspection of the fishing smack at its mooring.

The deal was done in due course and to the great joy of Zorzi and his pals the fishing smack came with its own little 'topo' sailing dinghy on board... all for forty five gold ducats! To celebrate the purchase, another four ducats were to be lavished on an evening banquet that was to be held after a decent interval at the widow's tavern – both for her consolation and as Grandpa's thanksgiving to friends and neighbours who had helped him in his own adversity. Fifteen-year-old Daniele Miotti (Junior) was the only family member invited to represent the Miotti del Jesu. Zorzi got on quite well with Young Daniele, Grandpa's namesake, remembering that he had come to his rescue one afternoon and had pushed one of the louder offensive name-calling taunters straight into the Glassmakers' Canal. Grandpa made a great show of affection to the lad whenever they chanced to meet: remarking how much he resembled his great grandfather Antonio their common ancestor and once owner of that contested book of recipes. Getting even with the del Jesu clan was, however, never far from Grandpa's thoughts. Old Meo Miotti del Jesu had been abusive to him and had refused to attend the traditional Requiem held some months after Vincenzo's disappearance: convinced, as Meo was, that Vincenzo had traitorously taken that priceless family volume to London. In the past five years there had been no help, nor contact, between the elderly cousins.

399

Now Grandpa had a half-formed plan to buy out the Miotti del Jesu and to take over their furnaces and work force.

Piero was now co-owner of the sturdy vessel, which was re-named 'St. Peter in Chains,' partly because it did not lack for chains, in the form of a derrick-hoist on its mizzen mast and other chain tackle for net hauling. The choice of names was appropriate as well as a reminder of Piero's ghastly sojourn in the New Prisons. Don Tranquillo blessed the vessel with holy water and for further good fortune tipped a generous splash of Soave over its bow from a handsome straw coated demijohn which afterwards, to Zorzi's disappointment, was carried back to the Convent kitchen in Fra Zeri's brawny arms.

Since the arrival of that unnamed scholar from Padova University, the housekeeper of Palazzo Capello had moved her devotions from the Church of San Donato to Saint Peter Martyr. The vile tasting and Spartan burnt offerings of Zeri suddenly improved beyond belief. There was now a ready supply of exceptionally princely fodder in the Convent refectory: vintage reds from Savoy and fromTuscany being poured at most meals. The ascetic librarian, Don Toma`, was ever in good humour now, for some reason unrelated to food, for although he ate as heartily as the others he did not put on an ounce of fat. At supper one evening he quipped about Tranquillo's improved girth, suggesting that he might be in competition with the plump Prior of Verona, once a celebrated preacher of fasting and abstinence and now, to everyone's amusement, finding it difficult to fit into his own pulpit.

"Medical condition....opposite to yours....nothing to do with grub!" was all that Tranquillo could find to snipe back at his old sparring partner. But something more devine than pasta and fine wine was livening up the dreary existence of grumpy Toma`. He was now holding long conversations with his intellectual equal - that reclusive scholar from Padova. There were whispers though about the stranger, mainly emanating from the praying widows in black Burano lace. Despite their great age and their poor sight, they were quick to notice, on just one occasion, a cowled figure kneeling in the shadows of the high altar.

Zorzi's collection of slightly whiffy junk now included part of a dragon's backbone *(a sperm whale's vertebra,)* and a huge ivory coloured egg guaranteed to have been laid by Sinbad's great auk; both of which he picked up at a very reasonable price in Rialto Market from a dealer who promised him that even a Renaissance prince could not have boasted of better specimens. In Zorzi's estimation, the Grimani collection of the 'Wonders of Mother Nature' that he had so envied at the Sensa Fair might soon find a close rival: all that he now lacked was a stuffed mermaid, or two. The great auk's egg, or more precisely its setting in an unpleasant looking nest of black wire fused on to a heavy base, provided an extra motive for a celebration. Grandpa was annoyed about the egg: he had seen several others of that kind on the stalls of shifty Berber traders, but when he examined the nest he seized Zorzi in his arms and gave him a great hug and a kiss on the forehead. It was not often that Grandpa gave way to such dispays of affection. Old Daniele reckoned that a bit of criticism, frequent disappointments and the occasional hard knocks of everyday survival were better character builders than sloppy shows of affection. When he had untangled and polished the seventy ounces of pure silver wire and sawn the base into malleable strips, he set about making three tiaras: one to sell to recover his costs; one for Marcella out of thanks to her and signor Molin's family and the last and most stunningly beautiful was for Elenca. From a distance she resembled a May Queen crowned with a chaplet of wild flowers. Close up her diadem seemed to flashed a fortune – a trembling emerald leafed fantasy mounted with pearls, with ruby and with sapphire. By mounting numerous stones on coils of thinned wire, Grandpa created this dazzling effect of movement. The gemstones were of course made of silver foil backed glass and the pearls too were 'girasole,' but at a glance they would have fooled all but a jeweller. A bolt of blue Como silk that had survived a dip in the Grand Canal and had ended on a remnants stall in Rialto Market was, with much cutting out of damage, transformed into an evening gown for Elenca. Delighted by Marcella's skill with the needle Grandpa announced: "We must hold a banquet and show off both of you to the neighbours."

The 'Taverna Dragone'was situated immediately over the bridge and on the opposite bank to San Donato: the three friars arrived there after Vespers carrying between them that great demijohn, still almost full but minus its protecting jacket of woven straw. Though also invited, the mysterious scholar friar from Padova failed to turn up. The celebration banquet in fact was held as Grandpa's thanksgiving to the Clergy and to his many neighbours, as well as to mark the purchase of the fishing boats. It had been delayed for six weeks out of respect for the widow and her two infants, in whom it must be said few signs of sadness were to be noticed. The late boat and tavern owner had been a bit of a slave driver to his family and employees. Don Tranquillo had some slight hope that Zeri might pick up a few culinary tips from the widow's cook, for the Padovan scholar friar and the Podestàs housekeeper would not be staying for much longer at St. Peter Martyr. Nobody wanted a return to Zeri's sacrificial burnt polenta offerings, over which Don Tranquillo often felt he should be saying the Office for the Dead instead of the prayer before meals. Don Tranquillo had long since explained to Zorzi that his puns at the expense of poor old fuzzy bearded Zeri had a lot to do with his unfortunate name. Zeri was a nickname for Zerolamo. *(Gerolamo = Jerome.)* A fanatical puritan friar called Gerolamo Savonarola once rose to be ruler of Florence. He held his 'bonfires of the vanities,' burning everything of beauty and luxury in that famous city, until came the day when the Florentines tired of him and roasted him by way of a change.

During the banquet, held under the vine clad pergola at the back of the Taverna, Don Tranquillo made a proposal for the spending of Zorzi's money that did not 'go down' so readily as the delicious spread. He explained that Luanardo the Choirmaster had an ancient bedridden mother to care for. Both had been evicted for non-payment of rent. The mother was sleeping on straw in the stable of San Donato rectory, having been carried there on the shoulders of her son, amidst the mockery and insults of the lower dregs of glass blowers' apprentices. Meanwhile, Luanardo was spending uncomfortable nights sleeping on the bench of his church organ. Monsignor Tosi was unhappy with the arrangement, but can find no one who would accept Luanardo as a lodger, given that he owed on his last rent. Luanardo's fee for his heroic performance on top of the Roman Arch had of course not been paid. The Noble Bastian Zustinian was nowhere to be found and there were numerous other creditors searching for him. Luanardo's dingy one room flat above the sack factory was now up for a ten-year lease at only eight ducats. But why, Zorzi wondered, should he oblige the tetchy Luanardo?

"Well Zorzi," the friar explained,"Luanardo might be the butt of local fun and name-calling but he is, I know, a hard-working fellow, who not only takes every care of his elderly mother, but is unpaid for his job as choirmaster; contrary to what everyone thinks. Maybe he is hot tempered at times, but he only wants the best from his choirboys."

"Well he was not too friendly with me and everyone calls him fartso and eunuch....What's a eunuch Don Tranquillo?"

"A eunuch? That you will understand better when you grow up! A lung disease, which he survived when he was no more than little older than you, is thought to have left him fat and hairless. Being called a eunuch is God's cross for him to bear and no fault of his own. God sends trials sometimes to test worthy people and even those who mock Luanardo still go along to hear his fine organ playing in San Dona`. People who are taunted about their handicaps sometimes get bad tempered with everyone. Didn't you get annoyed when people used to curse you and call your Grandpa a traitor? Look how happy you and Grandpa and Elenca are now! You should share some of that happiness. You say Luanardo is not friendly, yet after all, he did choose you as his best singer."

"I guess you are right as ever Don Tranquillo. But eight ducats! Why that would buy all of you your new cassocks and hoods and all the sweets in Zanetti's ten times over."

"Maybe, but I have got a suggestion. Let's offer him six ducats for music lessons. He could teach you to play the organ and to read music. Think of the lovely noises you could make on the organ: your pals would be so envious! Now that Zustinian has bolted, Senator Trevisan has gone back to San Dona` and likes a bit of music whenever he attends Mass. I am certain Monsignor Tosi could squeeze another couple of ducats from the Senator to keep the Choirmaster from the debtor's prison. Trevisan, I am told, is never tight with his money; unlike Zustinian, who was generous with other people's cash. I say was, because I don't think we shall be seeing much more of the Noble Zustinian, from the rumours that I hear."

Zorzi stopped feeding breadcrumbs to the sparrows that were hopping on and off the trestle table, much to the annoyance of the waiter. He mused for a moment: "Don Tranquillo, I would much prefer to be a Galley Commander, like the Doge said I should.... better still, the Doge might make me be one of his spies. He is a kind man you know, the Doge, a bit like Grandpa, not really fierce at all once you know him and his nose turns up a bit at the end, just like yours. The other nobles on the Bucintoro all seemed to have big hatchets for noses. I think I shall be a spy and have a long rapier, like signor Ravenscroft's, a big black cloak and a gold bauta specially made for me by Grandpa: he made Elenca that crown, you know, from my bird's nest."

"A gold bauta? Wouldn't that make you rather conspicuous?" Fra Zeri chuckled; then seeing the look of puzzlement added, "Everyone would see you coming a mile off in a golden bauta!"

"Ah! Well! Maybe I would not wear my gold bauta while I was doing my spying, that way nobody would notice me. Spies aren't supposed to be noticed, you know, Fra Zeri."

Zeri conceded that he was defeated by Zorzi's profound logic and continued chewing contentedly on a wine marinated goose leg fried in butter. By his own highly flammable standards he felt that, in the cooking, justice had not been fairly done to the poor bird.

"If we buy Fartso...that is Luanardo's lodging," Zorzi mused," Couldn't he come and play your church organ, instead of giving me lessons? Aldo then wouldn't have to keep fighting the boys at the ferry."

"Well that idea makes sense, but I don't follow what you mean about fighting."

"If you had a choir we wouldn't have to cross the ferry to San Donato and Lucia could join - she can sing pretty well, better than most boys. I don't think they really want me back at San Dona`, Don Tranquillo, even though I am famous. Anyway, Aldo's fed up with bashing the boys who hang around the ferry. They pick on him, now he is on his own."

"Monsignor Tosi is the 'bigwig' who might object, but the Bishop is away, so he can't appeal to him. I shall speak to Don Tosi about the ferry problem. It sounds as good an excuse as any. I shall write to my old friend Prior Raimondo for permission to have a school choir that sings from the nave occasionally: you see we friars are supposed to do our own singing – God help us with Zeri's groans! As for Lucia, she will have to be disguised as a boy to sing in church. I may leave the disguise to you - you seem to have done a convincing job with Elenca. Look at your pretty girl friend now….she looks altogether like a true princess. Who now would ever mistake her for a grubby boy?"

"Elenca is not my girlfriend! She's only a...well...sort of family," protested Zorzi.

"So it's the little Vianella, is it?" teased the old friar.

Zorzi blushed and blustered a denial amidst laughter and much ribbing. The plane trees surrounding the open courtyard and the vine draped pergola rustled above their heads in a pleasant breeze that came in from the orchards with dusk. The sparrows went home to their rooftop nooks well contented. The lanterns were lit on the trestle tables and the singing, eating and merriment went on into a mild mosquito-free night.

Silent as moths in the moonlight they crept towards the pergola out of the orchard's shadows: a desperate and hungry ragtaggle band of twelve or fourteen men and women, attracted to the glowing lanterns and to the sounds of merriment. One of the guests who had gone to relieve himself behind a bush hared back to the patio yelling in terror "Zingari!" Fra Zeri tightened his grip on the long bone handled carving knife. Don Tranquillo started to his feet, fists clenched, and searching in the gloom for a weapon found only the water jug, but he had fought and killed with less. 'Sea gipsies!' the waitresses shrieked. The landlady ushered her staff and all the children she could trace in the confusion into the safety of the tavern; then calmly went about bolting doors and window shutters as though such raids were an everyday occurrence. Grandpa dropped his table napkin into his lobster soup and seized hold of a wooden stool: those guests who were armed looked to their daggers. Noting the swift reaction, the strangers backed off, calling: "Musica! Musica!" in a strange accent and holding forward their fiddles and tambourines. They were outnumbered anyway and when Grandpa, with the formidable escort of Zeri, Don Tranquillo and young Young Daniele, approached them they proved to be more like troubadours of the Roma race than desperados. Their bright woven sashes, beads, sequins and short jackets of torn and faded embroidery looked vaguely Eastern in style; possibly Turkish? Male and female,

Tranquillo frisked them nevertheless, before offering them food in exchange for entertainment. He consigning to the widow's parlour for safe keeping five long knives and two ancient pistols. On close inspection Tranquillo concluded that the pistols could only have been carried for bravado, being rusted up and with their wheel-locks quite jammed. Their copper beating hammers soldering irons and other kettle repairing tools reassured him that they were, sometimes at least, honest working folk. Whatever their original intentions may have been, the Zingari gave great value in exchange for their food and wine and that hat full of baghettini coins collected in advance from the guests. As the evening drew on the fantastic tempo of their fiddles, rhythms and dancing increased and they invited the guests to join them. To everyone's great surprise Elenca proved to be as skilled in her steps, graceful arm gestures and twirlings, as some of the gipsy girls. But there were frowns from many of Grandpa's guests when she seemed to be responding to questions put to her by the 'count' and his 'princess' (as by tradition the gipsy leader and his wife were called.) The long bearded and brilliant old fiddler and his bone thin wife, who played her wooden recorder with equal skill, were evidently impressed with Elenca's dancing as well as by her silk dress and dazzling coronet. It was clear too that Elenca had made suggestions as to one or two dance tunes that they played.

Grandpa was quietly dismayed: the little girl of whom he had grown so very fond was no more than a gipsy after all. Something curious then happened during a pause for all to draw breath from the frantic music. A brief exchange of words between Elenca and the old fiddler, with whom she had been dancing a tarantella, made him gasp aloud. He leapt away from her as though stung by a wasp. Remorse at offence given was now in his every gesture and expression and evident to all despite the dim lanternlight. Now with that same mortified expression and head hung low he stood for a while as though he had made some some completely unpardonable social blunder. Stepping further back from Elenca, he whipped off his hat bowing very low six or seven times in rapid succession. Grandpa's friends laughed and applauded this gallant gesture, taking it to be a compliment to Elenca's dancing talent. But when the old fiddler instructed his ragged companions to gather around Elenca and they too hesitantly began to bob low curtseys and bend their heads almost to the ground in deep bows every one of Grandpa's guests was left perplexed.

Tranquillo had no such uncertainty as to the intentions of the Roma. Elenca's pretty face, dancing skills and headdress had their value and this was their distracting ploy before making off with her. He gave Grandpa a nudge in the arm and the two men strode into their midst. Elenca came back with Tranquillo's firm grip on her arm, red faced and embarrassed and was seated between Grandpa and Fra Zeri. Though they tried to question her with the simplest of slowly spoken phrases she failed to respond, so the whole episode was left unexplained - like many other little mysteries connected with her. The Roma showed signs of being deeply offended at Grandpa's show of mistrust and his rough handling of the girl, but their music contined into the night. After some hours of fast fiddling, rhythmic twirling, clashing of tambourines and truly delightful dance music the Roma had exhausted their repertoire and everyone else to the bargain. They approached Grandpa to collect their gratuity and to reclaim their weapons. With the cautious habits of a good galley commander, Don Tranquillo had trussed the weapons together with the tinkers' tools into a heavy single bundle secured with sacking and knotted rope. However, the Roma did not bow to him, nor did they to Grandpa, after receiving their generous tip. One by one each solemnly genuflected with straight back then bowed head to the ground on both knees by way of a farewell salutation to Elenca. It was evident that they had assumed that she was the hostess. As each gipsy rose to his feet he murmured "Doamna" and backed away respectfully while flourished his hat at her: the females nodded heads low down to their knees, but kept their distance. Elenca remained seated and acknowledged each "Doamna" with a regal wave of her little hand as though it were a salutation to which she was accustomed. Then one by one the Roma disappeared as silently as they had come into the pitch darkness of the surrounding fields.

"Doamna," when had she heard that title last used? A fleeting memory came: it was of a chubby nursemaid calling down from a balcony; a huge balcony that was carved and supported with granite winged corbels in the form of ravens. Tears then came to her eyes together with a sad longing for someone half forgotten, someone who once loved her. Zorzi noticed her weeping and cheered her up by making his own comic genuflexion before her. In the shadows of the lanternlight he used his fingers to pull grotesque faces and when his antics finally made her chuckle through her tears he demanded to know what on earth 'Doamna' meant.

"Oh!" she replied, "In my language it means princess."

"What a hoot! Just goes to show Granpa is right. It's all down to appearances. It's not who you are; it's what you wear. I was a prince too, you know, Elenca…so we are quits."

Elenca, Zorzi Aldo and the younger Molin girls now began to droop with fatigue, having eaten their way enthusiastically through seven or eight courses and danced their feet sore. When the waiters came to clear the trestles and to claim their tip from Grandpa as well, one of them attempted to carry off the heavy demijohn on a wooden tray that was already overloaded with plates and glasses. It fell onto the cobblestones - a great pity, since it was such a shapely and well blown bottle. Zorzi scrambled around in the gloom helping the waiter to clear up the broken pieces. The jagged bottom and foot ring of the flask had somehow survived in one piece and as Zorzi was about to dump it into a canvas sack together with the other large pieces that would be melted down for Grandpa's cullet, he noticed something. Holding it up to the lantern light he could see, worked onto the hollowed inward curving base, the image of a beautifully sculpted glass monkey with a curly tail, that appeared to be climbing in the midst of a distinctly V shaped bush. Zorzi decided he would trim off and grind down the jagged edges as usual, but he would do that the next day in better light. It looked by far the best example that he had found so far: something that might now take pride of place amongst his very private cabinet of curiosities.

Zorzi was sorely tempted to show the glass monkey to Grandpa and then to Don Tranquillo, but the Don was in wise conversation with the widow and her unlamenting young children, possibly attempting to console them, if indeed consolation for the loss of their tyrant father was what they still required. Grandpa was drinking steadily and in a very merry state and what's more was about to win a fair sum of grossi in a game of dominoes. One momentary glimpse in the flickering candle light of that curious glass emblem would have been all that was needed to brim over for ever Grandpa's beaker of happiness, but it was not to be. Zorzi hesitated, decided not to distract him and slipped the bottle base into his satchel having carefully wrapped it in a dirty dish cloth.

CHAPTER FORTY-TWO

The Miotti furnaces were not lit again until the first frosts of late autumn. Grandpa took a long and profitable holiday with Piero. Sometimes both friends, aided by tough young Young Daniele, cousin Meo Miotti's grandson, were away fishing from dawn to dusk. Large catches were winched on board the 'San Pietro ad Vincula' with such regularity that Grandpa was able to supply the Murano market as well as a wholesaler at the Pescheria, the elegant fish market just beyond the Rialto *(stylishly rebuilt in modern times.)* The break from breathing toxic glass making fumes; the salt sea air and the hard physical labour seemed to have reinflated Grandpa's lungs and raised his drooping spirits enormously. Zorzi had never seen him so fit and so enthusiastic. He was even making plans to buy new tools and glass shaping moulds made of iron rather than of hardwood. He also intended to employ through the winter some stout young apprentices in the glassworks to learn all the tricks and to do all the hard and repetitive tasks. Most glassworks were shut down for the winter so there would be no shortage of talent needing extra training. Grandpa was no longer so exhausted and breathless in the afternoons. Instead of sleeping for hours, he would often be content with a short nap. Refreshed, he would then set to with vigour making drawings for an improved furnace, or designing new patterns for glassware.

When evening came he would be seen sitting on a bench surrounded by a group of Zorzi's friends in the cool of the front porch. Neighbours passing along the towpath would pause to greet him with warmth and friendship. The cruel and unwarranted ordeal to which they had once subjected him now weighed heavily on their consciences. Grandpa was ever a fine raconteur and though Zorzi knew most of his lively stories, he still took pleasure in hearing them repeated in the company of his pals. With his battle-scarred face, his missing fingers, his glass of freshly brewed ale and frequent vigorous sucks on his clay pipe, Grandpa would captivate the youngsters with tales of perilous voyages and crossbow battles with the Turk. These light-hearted and much embroidered tales usually involved Grandpa, or Don Tranquillo blundering into some utterly daft situation. Faced with hopeless odds against them, the two adventurers always managed in some hilarious and not too gruesome way to scatter to the four winds the treacherous Ottoman, or else to effect some spectacular escape. Tales of tempests amidst the isles of Greece, of being smashed to matchwood on the rocks of Dalmatia, or spooked by some headless Knight of St. John in a Candia castle, would invariably end comically. After rolling about on the paving in fits of laughter, his enthralled young audience retired to their beds with demands for more stories tomorrow and the certainty of a night of undisturbed dreams.

Elenca was far and away the most attentive of the little audience seated on the warm pavement at his feet. How much she understood was never clear, for she spoke so very little despite much praise and extra lessons from Bianca. Without a word of farewell, come mid September, Bianca disappeared from her lodgings at the home of the former Podestàs housekeeper. The elusive scholar who once dwelt in the San Pietro library preceded her by several days in his departure back to the Paduan University. One of the four Deputy Podestà's appointed by Trevisan had taken a far too keen an interest in signorina Bianca's activities. Much to the annoyance of Don Tranquillo, this gentleman would make surprise visits to the school room in St. Peter Martyr Convent, his excuse being always some quite trivial matter.

Tranquillo had no choice but to close down the school on Bianca's departure. There were other tutors on the island but they were either employed in the households of great families or expected a living wage for their services.

Left to their own devices, Zorzi and company roamed once again as freely as nature ever intended for children of that carefree age. Now unencumbered by formal lessons, they schooled themselves in the topography of the Lagoon: learning to be familiar with the ebb and flow of the tides over dangerous mud flats; the places where there were fast flowing undertow currents; the ever capricious cloud formations over the Lagoon that promised good sailing weather, or presaged an oncoming storm. In a very short space of time Zorzi was the complete master of his little 'topo' that he could tack into the wind, bring about suddenly and haul alongside another sailing vessel in full sail without so much as a bump. At night, the topo was chained by its bow to one of the middle columns of the portico, so that Zorzi could keep a watchful eye by looking down from his arrow slit. The 'San Pietro ad Vincula' *(St. Peter in Chains,)* was far too large to pass under the bridges of the Glassmaker's Canal without unstepping both masts. It would have caused a real obstruction and bad

410

feeling with neighbours if it had been moored there permanently. For a modest fee, Grandpa agreed with the night porters and house 'bravi' of Ca` Da Mula' for the boat to be moored just to the side of the landing stage of that ancient and most elegant gothic palace.

One of Grandpa's strict rules was that Zorzi should not sail past the Island of San Michele and into the busy waters separating that island from the busy Fondamenta Nuove *(The New Landing Stage,)* the place where Zorzi had found himself abandoned at the Sensa before enduring that night of terror. Sailing to far off islands like Burano and long abandoned Torcello was also out of bounds. A myriad of mud flats and scrub covered islets were still within bounds for them to sail around, or to land on and to explore. The 'topo' was little more than a flat bottomed plaything, which enabled it to pass easily, punted or under oar, through the acres of reed beds and up the shallowest of muddy creeks. It could hold no more than four children safely, but despite Grandpa's strictures Zorzi would sometimes pick up an extra friend once out of sight. His permanent crew were Aldo and Lucia, both of whom could manage the little craft with skills almost equal to his own. Young Daniele joined their expeditions less frequently, preferring to fish in deep waters. Elenca, who still could not swim, was happy to stay about the house helping Grandpa with minor chores: grinding the sweet corn grains to polenta flour, or preparing glass cullet for the winter furnaces by baking light coloured flints and quartz stones on the steel tray. As she threw cold water onto the blazing stones, making them pop and explode into fragments small enough for grinding, she would either squeal with mad delight or sometimes dance around the charcoal burner, shielding her eyes and singing in a strange language. She preferred playing solitary games of hopscotch or knucklebones while most of the young girls in the neighbourhood joined in with the boys in playing tag, or whatever vigorous game was currently popular.

Grandpa insisted that Elenca should learn to swim before permitting her to venture out in the cramped and unstable little topo. Any attempt by Lucia or the young Molin girls to teach her left her trembling, some times hysterical with a fear amouting to hydrophobia. Given the humiliating state in which Zorzi had first found her, she was understandably anxious to preserve her modesty, but lacked the words to express her concern. The young Molin girls found amusement in her habit of staying crouched gingerly into the foreshore while they were splashing about carefree.

411

They had no such reservations, nor did any other girl they knew. Marcella finally guessed at the reason for Elenca's timidity - she did not want to display her shrivelled ribs and limbs and in particular her part bald and part tufted scalp, for she was still suffering with shock alopecia.

In the early weeks after her release from the New Prisons there had been much concern about Elenca's severe emaciation as well as her state of mental health. Signora Molin's and Grandpa's loving concern and care seemed destined never to be rewarded. Evidently something dreadful had happened to her, either in the Venetian galley or with the Uzkoks. Marcella, Aldo's eldest sister, finally got at the truth by questioning Eldeniz. The traumatised child had survived an Uskok raid on the coastal citadel where she had been brought up in the Ghazi Koprulu Hussein's harem. In the slaughter she had lost her childhood companions and possibly her mother, though she was not quite sure which of the many ladies in the harem might have been her mother. Whilst being conveyed to the raiding galleys of the merciless Uzkoks, she had come close to being drowned.

Eventually, in the familiar surroundings of the recently built Turkish bathhouse, and with the encouragement of Marcella, she learned to float in the cold plunge pool. From that beginning she quickly progressed to swimming a few floundering yards. A simple but essential skill, once mastered, transformed her from a wizened skeletal figure, with hollow-eyed sunken features to a plumped-out child with a distinctly pretty face. From being almost neurotic and fearful, she now seemed relaxed and happy even in the company of strangers. It became obvious too that the noble nuns of San Zaccaria had not been wide of the mark on Elenca's pale skinned Circassian origins. High cheekbones and a well-rounded flattish face hinted that the hordes of Genghis Khan had some minor part as well in her Byzantine and Slavonic ancestry.

With such blossoming good looks, Lucia became convinced that Elenca had supplanted her in Zorzi's affection, though any preference for girls, as opposed to male pals, was far from Zorzi's thoughts. What mattered to him was that Lucia was an affable adventurer, with whom he hardly ever quarrelled: though fiery and argumentative, Lucia provided the daring and the comedy in their exploits. Despite her diminutive stature, her pluck and speed outpaced that of any boy he knew. For her part, Lucia would not admit to herself that she was deeply envious of her rival, in particular when that gleaming pale straw coloured hair began to grow back. Elenca was dismissed as a tufty head: a 'foreign freak' and far too timid to be worthy of Zorzi's company. Fortunately, Elenca's poor command of Venetian left her blissfully unaware of Lucia's taunting.

Leaving instructions for Zorzi not to fiddle with his papers but to beat the carpet and to dust and polish anything that needed such attention, Don Tranquillo shouldered his wicker basket and went off on his 'cadge;' namely his weekly charity round of the Market stalls at closing time. Some age old unwritten prejudice, forbade girls from entering the sacristy: Zorzi knew that well enough, but through the sacristy was the only internal way to the upper floor office. Don Tranquillo's departure and his own disinclination to do anything in the way of chores tempted Zorzi. He was suitably delighted by Elenca's squeals of fear as, broom and bucket in hand, she hurried past the carved and frighteningly grim looking wooden caryatids that projected from the sacristy's walnut panelling. Entering the office, Zorzi promptly hoisted himself into Don Tranquillo's padded chair, flourished with grand gestures the various quills, fussed with the lid of the porcelain inkpot, studied without attempting to read, various papers and pretending to be engaged in writing crucially important letters which required a great deal of sighing, pauses for deep thought and head scratching. He then set to with the great brass seal of the Convent Prior stamping down on any odd bit of paper that came to hand. While he dangled his legs in this fashion Elenca got on with the cleaning.

His fantasy of bureaucratic self importance was interrupted by a sudden scream of terror. Elenca backed away from the desk towards the door pointing at something dreadful behind Zorzi's head. Leaping down from the chair he turned, prepared to lash out with his clog at some intruding rat or large spider, but there was nothing….nothing more than Don Tranquillo's cracked old Bellini in its woodworm riddled frame. Elenca was pointing to the soldier with the large shield on the left of the scene of St. Peter's martyrdom. She then shut her eyes, shook violently from head to foot, went limp and very very white, then collapsed with a thud to the floor knocking her head on the wooden bucket. Zorzi shook her, begged her to get up or to say something to him. After a moment her eyes opened but stared blankly as though in a trance. In a strange language she then begain to babble, her mouth frothing slightly as she did so, distinctly repeating several times the word 'corvin.'

In a complete panic, Zorzi dithered for a moment trying to prop her up, but with no sign of normal breathing he ran out along the corridor yelling for help. Fra Zeri by chance was in the cloister below looking for red beetle amidst his precious Madonna lilies. He leapt the steps of the great stone external stairway three at a time. Cold water from his watering can and a compress of lavender essence on her forehead was applied to good effect. Soon she was being cradled and soothed in his arms, sobbing and convulsing from time to time. He smeared some lint ointment on the cut above her ear and carried her back home. Zeri's best suggestions to Grandpa as to the cause of the fit were dehydration and the grim Bellini scene. And good sport that he was, in exchange for a promise never to take Elenca into the convent without permission, he agreed not to mention the incident to Tranquillo. Zorzi however, was curious for an explanation, though it would be some months before he got one. She was definitely pointing to the raven painted on the soldier's shield when it all happened. The only understandable words about the episode that now came from Elenca were 'corvin' which he correctly assumed meant raven and 'bad, bad men.' Then there was 'Brancovan' the other strange word that she now sometimes used when referring to herself. 'Brancovan' he surmised was her surname, but he gave the matter insufficient importance to mention to anyone other than Grandpa, who suggested that they never use it since it sounded foreign and possibly Turkish sounding. Zorzi wondered nevertheless whether her fright had something to do with the Raven, but that was impossible: she had never met the English pirates.

The sight of that raven emblem on the warrior's shield had by some trick of the mind pierced through to Elenca's distant memory so long blanked out by cruel experiences. Like a sudden shaft of light through an opened window shutter, memories flooded back to a time of blissful happiness: then to a moment of bitter betrayal. It was that knife cut of a memory in particular that had caused the onset of her fit. There she was, leaning out at the upper casement, just turned seven years old. On her mother's arm was baby sister, Smaragda. Her other sisters were present too…. now they were Safta, Ancuta and Balasa… no not quite, her eldest sister Maria was grown up and married… to whom? They were all waving down to their handsome brothers…down there in the courtyard. They had come to say farewell and horse hooves clop clopped on the cobblestones. Radu and Stefan were mounted, legs stretched wide, on sure footed little mountain ponies but Constadin was prancing and showing off on his dapple grey war horse. The younger boys were cloaked with arctic fox and trimmed about with woven sashes, with bright red leather hunting boots and Hungarian style fur hats sprouting eagles' feathers. Pinned under Constadin's fluttering feathers was a jet brooch shaped like a raven and set with pearls: another brooch in his fur bonnet took the form of a red stone, almost the size of a small cobblestone, and framed too with pearls. Now, she remembered that big brother Constadin sometimes joked about that red brooch: it had once belonged to someone very, very bad indeed – an evil ancestor who did dreadful things to people with wooden stakes.

Soon after her brothers had clattered away under the stone arch, a troop of cavalry men who had escorted the boys swept into the courtyard: the defiant open beaked raven was on their gleaming breastplates and on their saddle cloths and shields… they had come to take her away! A tear dropped onto father's massive black beard as he knelt down to kiss her goodbye and to pat a blessing on her head. But no… it was not father; it was Fra Zeri smiling down at her now: she was very cold and focusing on nothing more unfamiliar than Zeri's unkempt tangle of fuzz.

As the days grew longer Grandpa and Piero took to fishing out into the Adriatic Sea. In their absence, the young crew of the topo began to range further into the Lagoon. Young Matteo Barovier, another glassmaker's son, often joined them. The islands of Carbonera, Tessera and San Secondo were now their playgrounds. Each of these islands contained a star fort battery with gun emplacements facing outward either towards the mainland or to the Adriatic. As a precaution against an invader who might turn and train the captured guns onto the Serenissima itself, the city facing side of each island was deliberately left overgrown with immense thickets of hawthorn, berberis and acacia. Throughout the violent and gloomy 17th Century, famine had cropped the poorest of the former inhabitants of those islands. Malaria, bubonic and typhus fever as well had raged amidst the ranks of both the high-born and the low, carrying off many a wealthy villa owner and all his family with him, leaving their properties to wreckers, salvagers and winter storms.

With a cloth bundle of cooked polenta, an old but effective tinderbox and fishing tackle, the friends would sail out soon after dawn. Landing on one or other of the islands, they would make camp, hiding the 'topo' under the overhanging willows and then run wild about the thickets, playing Moors and Christians, battling on pickaback with willow stick swords. After cooking whatever fish they caught on the way and scoffing down quantities of lumpy reheated polenta, seasoned 'Savonarola fashion' with the flavour of burnt wood, they would throw themselves back into the long grass and listen for a while, trying to identify the calls and twittering of the estuary birds, while digesting their meal. It was common knowledge that swimming on a full stomach was fatal, so they would set about 'finding things' for two hours or so before swinging out on the willow branches and bombing with great splashes into the clearest gravel bottomed water that they could find about the island's shore.

It was while 'finding things' and during a half-hearted pursuit of a sleek green lizard through the undergrowth of hawthorn and acacia, that the friends made their most exciting discovery - a wrecked villa covered with an almost impenetrable blanket of poison ivy! One wing of the modest sized villa, built when the flamboyant Gothic style was fashionable, was a mess of fallen masonry brambles and sprouting young trees. The atrium and remaining traces of a stone stairway could be made out and three floors of rooms on the right were open to the elements but not completely blanketed in creepers. But it was what could be seen of the decoration in the staterooms and roofless bedrooms above them that challenged the young adventurers. Elaborate wall paintings of galloping old knights and damsels, strange looking beasts and swags of flowers, beautifully painted fruit and vegetables, could be seen peeping out from behind a curtain of brambles, ivy and dangling moss. It was quite obvious that treasure was to be found somewhere up there in one or other of the rooms. While discussing just what wonders of ancient weapons and jewels might lay in store for them to plunder, they hacked their way forward, taking turns to use the boat hook and finally making a complete circuit of the building. The ground floor rooms were easy enough to penetrate, but here and there were great holes in the tiled flooring, down which they peered to gloomy darkness of unknown depth. For the most part, whatever plaster wall decoration was once there had peeled off in decay and dampness. Other than a bent pewter spoon, a rotten leather slipper with long pointed toe and the skull of what might have been a dog, there was nothing there precious, or curious enough to satisfy their high hopes. How to get at the more splendid and well-preserved 'piano nobile,' the staterooms above, still remained an infuriating challenge. There were large promising footholds in the rear wall of the hallway where someone had torn out the stone stair treads, but they were cut off by a mass of sharp vegetation sprouting up from where the hall floor had collapsed into the cellars. Aldo climbed a young sapling and scrambled up from there, finally standing triumphantly on top of the rear wall. From there he could only progress so far, before coming to the remaining stone tracery of a fine pointed arch that may once have been a gothic hall window. There was a gap wide enough for a fearless boy to jump but Aldo suspected that any such move would cause all the stonework to give way underfoot. He edged gingerly backwards and jumped back into the sapling scratching his chest and knees. Lucia had her own plan. She would take the same route, but then climb down below the window gap using some of the stair tread holes. Then, since she was so light, she would clamber up to the rooms through the mass of ivy, which she judged, had tendrils and branches as thick as any ship's mooring hawser that she had ever shinned up.

In half the time that it had taken Aldo she was high on the wall, balancing confidently amongst the crumbling bricks and powdery mortar. To their screams of encouragement and advice she made her way, foothold by foothold, like a little spider. There were numerous empty birds' nests as well as spiders in and amongst the ivy tendrils. The prospect of meeting a giant tarantula or a scorpion up there was of more concern to her than her perilous progress; not that tarantulas of any size could have survived that far North in the bitter winters of the Lagoon. Using the carved stone sill as an elbow rest, she traversed the window gap and got to the easy climb through the ivy towards the doorway and the part demolished partition wall of the upper room. She could now see clearly that the room was splendidly frescoed with battling knights. Narrow waisted ladies, with shaven-back foreheads and hair-pieces knotted with jewels, were prancing through little hills and castle filled countryside: other walls further on showed scenes of courtiers sitting around fountains reading, or dallying, or playing on strange musical instruments. On what was left of a deep azure ceiling were more beautiful damsels sitting amidst the stars on zodiac signs.

As she shouted news of her exciting find across to the waiting friends and encouraged them to follow her, a great spider scuttled up her arm and tried to bury itself into her hair just behind her ear. It may not have been a tarantula; more likely it was a hairy, overfed and long-legged wolf spider, but it had the same effect. Lucia let out a horrified cry, tried to brush it away and lost both her hand and foot holds. She slid down for a second, made another successful grab at the ivy and swung her legs frantically to find another foothold. Though her weight was little more than 25 kilos, it was enough to tip the scales in favour of the ivy in its age-old struggle with the wall. Mercifully, the wall did not yield completely. Instead, an extensive section of the fresco rendering flaked off and descended with a thud in a cloud of grey dust. For the most part it was still firmly attached to the fine tendrils of the ivy. Instantly, without even time to cry out, Lucia was buried deep in the basement, beneath a thick blanket of foliage and plaster rendering.

When there was no answer to their desperate calls, the friends began to run about in tearful panic. Summoning up all his courage, Aldo threw himself down into the basement and began to hack wildly with the boat hook, but he was quickly torn by the thorns and bramble and had to give up. As they pulled him to safety and a tearful Elenca began to pluck the hawthorn from his arms and chest an idea came to Zorzi. The little iron grappling hook that they used for anchoring in the shallows could be thrown into the mass of brambles and some of it at least could be dragged away, if only they could find planks or something to stand on. Leaving Elenca to shout and plead with Lucia to respond, they crashed through the undergrowth, back to where the boat fittings were hidden. They always kept the fittings well away from the topo itself, which could not easily be stolen without its single oar, its 'forcola' rowlock and its detachable rudder. Grabbing the grappling hook anchor, some lengths of rope and the oar, they were about to start back when they sighted a fishing boat some way off. Zorzi was all for stepping the mast and sailing out to get help. Aldo however had a better idea. Without even asking permission, he cut the foresail from its pulleys and rigging with his fishing knife and bundled it under his arm.

When they got back Elenca was smiling through her tears: she had heard Lucia moaning feebly and crying-out for their help. Aldo wound the thick sailcloth around his chest and legs, but there was far too much of it. Cut and ripped into three, the triangular foresail provided more than sufficient body armour for Matteo and Zorzi as well. Armed with oar, grappling hook, knives and boat hook, they plunged like furies into the thickets of the basement. Tearing and tugging away at the brambles, and hurling plaster chunks and ivy in all directions, they came at last to where Lucia was almost impaled face downwards on a young hawthorn and smothered from head to toe in a blanket of ivy and plaster fragments. As she fell she had twisted her body in a desperate attempt to jump clear. To their great relief and admiration the timid Elenca joined them, ripping her own way through the bushes. The boys were utterly exhausted and were grateful for her amazing burst of strength in lifting Lucia high and clear without any help whatsoever from them.

The breath had been knocked out of Lucia's lungs, leaving her unable to cry out: blood oozed from deep scratches on her forehead, her nose, her slender torso and even skinnier limbs. On regaining her voice, the only sobbing worries were about the rips, the plaster dirt and the blood stains that had soiled beyond any hope of repair her cotton smock of printed Indian pine cone patterns. Zorzi swore he would buy her a new dress, a new shawl, a proper paper fan and whatever else she wanted when next she came with him to Rialto Market. They helped her to her feet and to their consternation she fainted again. It was obvious that something was wrong with her bulging collarbone: her left shoulder too began to swell up. Using a length of the sailcloth as a stretcher they carried her down to the boat. With no space for Matteo Barovier to get a useful handhold on the sailcloth, he strode ahead giving mighty swipes with the forcola at any obstructing hawthorn on the way.

With great speed and efficiency they reattached the rudder and raised the mainsail into a good off shore breeze. Lucia was lowered carefully between thwarts, cushioned and resting on the three scraps of foresail. Thrusting the oar into the muddy bank Aldo pushed off. Within minutes they were well out on the Lagoon with the tall towers of San Stin, San Dona` and Pietro Martire bobbing up and down in the distance, seeming almost to be urging them to make haste homewards. The wind then dropped and without the extra spread from a foresail they were almost becalmed. It was then that they realized that Matteo had left the forcola behind on the beach. They could hardly heap blame on him, as they sometimes did for such oversights, because Aldo had left the anchor and rope in the bushes and Zorzi had forgotten just where he had put down the boat hook. Undaunted, Zorzi dipped the oar over the stern of the boat; jamming it as best he could against the tiller and rudder. He waggled it about just like he had seen gondoliers do. Alas, his unskilled efforts had little effect: without the forcola the oar kept slipping away along the transom. They seemed to be drifting backwards! Aldo took over with more strenuous strokes and in no time lost the oar. He dived over to retrieve it and as they pulled him onboard, Zorzi spotted a desdotona with full eighteen rowing crew not too far off. They were practising starts for the September festival races around the islands, known to all as the Voga Longa. (*The long 17 mile row - hence Vogalonga's nickname.*)

Taking off his shirt, Zorzi waved it wildly at them. Their coxswain gave a friendly wave back and prepared the crew for another racing start. In desperation Zorzi tied his shirt to the oar and began to dip it and to raise it slowly while instructing Aldo and Toma` to stand and to make big slow 'signs of the cross' on their bodies, alternately pointing down to the gunwales of the topo. Chancing to look in their direction, one of the racing rowers was puzzled by their strange behaviour. The children were either taking a rise at their prospects for winning the long race, or they were in serious trouble. Fortunately he decided that they were after all making signals of a crew in distress. He yelled out, alerting the coxswain to turn about.

Having deposited Lucia with the greatest of care on signora Molin's freshly scrubbed kitchen table, the racing crew's rescue efforts were rewarded with a large jar of elderflower wine. They were clapped by the usual crowd of idle onlookers clustered round the Molin doorway as they made their way back to their boat. They pulled away to cheers, content in the knowledge that news of their rescue efforts would soon be spread about the isles. Come September, their neighbourly deed would certainly ensure them a favourable place at the starting line: despite the fact that they were a mixed team from the mainland communities of Malghera *(now Marghera)* and Mestre and in the eyes of many, not considered worthy to take part in the famous race as proper Venetians.

Signora Molin cut up her second best sheet and set about cleaning and poulticing with lint ointment Lucia's badly scratched little body. The boys, together with Aldo's eldest sister, Marcella, were sent to find signora Vianello, Lucia's mother. Zorzi knew that she lived with some other ladies in rooms above the main tavern of the island, a place of little repute, which nevertheless prided itself in displaying 'The Snake & Cockerel' as its inn sign. (*A cockerel with its beak snapping a snake was the coat of arms of Murano.*) Signora Vianello was not to be found there and after making a long search, inquiring at several other 'dens of drunkenness' they eventually found her seated with some sailors and fishermen at a gaming table outside the 'Star and Crescent' along the towpath of the Murano Grand Canal.

Breathless, after the long run, Marcella told her that Lucia had fallen from a wall and had injured her shoulder.

"So what?" the mother replied casually, "Serves her right, the useless little alley cat: how many times have I told her not to go playing rough games with boys!" She darted a malevolent look at Aldo and Zorzi, who stood there looking guilty, dirty, rough indeed, and rather sheepish.

"But she's hurt badly signora. Please come; my mother is looking after her at our house. It wasn't the boys' fault, really!" pleaded Marcella.

"Well, if your precious mum is looking after her, why do I need to come? I've got better things to do than dancing off to pick up Lucia every time she falls over. Now just clear off will you? I am in the middle of a game here!"

Marcella stood there dumbfounded for a moment at this unexpected and callous response. This was her first encounter with that frequently drunken widow, signora Vianello. Then her hackles rose, "What kind of a mother do you call yourself ? Can't even be bothered to take care of your own daughter!"

La Vianella threw down her hand of cards, seizing an empty wine bottle she made a wild lunge at Marcella screaming: "I'll show you what kind of a mother I am, you smug little minx!" adding to her threat a few choice and unmentionable foul epithets.

One of the sailors managed to wrestle the bottle from her hand, but as she let it go she knocked over the bench against his shins and then leapt at Marcella. Grabbing her hair with both hands, she dragged the startled and unresisting Marcella towards the ground. The sailors, ever keen on enjoying a cat-fight, formed a ring and began to whistle and clap their encouragement. Zorzi was appalled. He hopped from foot to foot, not quite knowing what to do. Finally he shouted, "Go on Aldo! Don't stand there and let her pull your sister about!"

Aldo still hesitated. His gentle mother, knowing what a strong lad he was, had instilled in him the sensible notion that it was forbidden to strike a female of any age. As he dithered, Zorzi dashed through the ring of sailors and leapt onto signora Vianello's back. He crooked his elbow and managed to get a firm lock on her neck, gripping his wrist with the other hand and tugging with all his might against her windpipe. As she tried to throw him off, she fell backwards onto him taking two hands full of hair from poor Marcella's forehead. Zorzi still clung on as she staggered back to her feet. This time though, she faced Aldo's narrowed eyes and big fist poised to break her nose.

He was not quite her height, but she could see, even in her blind rage, that she was no match for him. Aldo had no need to strike her. He told her that if she said one more word to his sister he would 'knock her lights out' there and then. Zorzi let go of his choking grip as she sat down on the edge of the upturned bench and began to slobber in a drunken voice, bemoaning the fact that there wasn't a sailor there who was man enough to stand up for her when she was being attacked. Hearing the rumpus, the landlord came out with a cudgel and told everyone to leave, or he would break a few heads.

The three returned home in silence. Zorzi felt his legs trembling, but he tried to convince himself it was only the fatigue of the long and strenuous effort to save his friend Lucia. When they got home, the lanterns were already lit and Fra Zeri was there putting the finishing touches to Lucia's bandages. Lucia was now lost in a deep drug induced sleep. Zeri was a big built upright broad shouldered man - very jovial, with a fine jungle of beard, quite unstreaked with grey, though he was well into his seventies. After years with the fleet patrolling the Mediterranean, he was turned down as a lay brother by the Knights of Malta, possibly because he was a Venetian. Should it come to a showdown with the Ottoman Sultan, the Doge would always have first claim on poor Zeri - the son of a potter from Bassano. Maybe, as well, a combination of humble birth and even humbler cooking expertise failed to make him appeal to the fierce and fastidious Knights of St. John. *(However, they could not have been all that fussy: the Batard of Lorraine had been accepted into the exclusive brotherhood- thus allowing him to boast the title of Chevalier; amongst knights of all European orders, including those of the Garter and the Golden Fleece, the highest possible rank. The Grand Master of the Order ranked above the Doge of Venice as a sovereign king. Martinengo was also proud of being a Cavaliere. As warrior friars, Knights of St. John of Malta could not marry – which of course posed no problem for Lorraine.)*

Fra Zeri took to the Dominicans instead, where he had spent many years as a medical orderly at San Zanipolo and in the public infirmary run by the Scola Grande di San Marco. *(The Guild of St. Mark dedicated to caring for the city's poor and sick.)* Savonarola would have never employed him as a cook, but Fra Zeri's expertise might well have come in handy after that fanatical art-burning friar had finished his final stretch on the Florentine rack. Fra Zeri, in short, was an expert bonesetter and had already fixed back into its socket Lucia's dislocated shoulder, relieving greatly her pain. While persuading her to suck on the drugged lump of sugar, he had prepared himself to give the necessary violent tug and jerk on her arm and shoulder. Urging her to be very silent and not to cry out, he gave her the charming explanation that only then would she be able to hear the quiet snoring of the little chicks nesting for the night in his great black beard. While she chuckled through her tears, half believing him, he made the sudden and essential move. There was little he could do about the fractured collarbone other than binding her up and making her more comfortable on the table, where she would have to rest immobile for the night. Signora Molin could see from all the cuts and bruises on the boys and from the torn hair of Marcella that something unpleasant had happened to the trio, but she was too tired to ask. A long sleepless night was ahead, watching over Lucia. It was not until the latter part of the next day that Marcella troubled her mother with the full story.

A greatly exaggerated account of the scuffle at the tavern was reported to the prickly tempered 'Abbot' of the church of San Stin; though everybody referred to the miserable fellow as the 'parroco' since he was now no more than a lonely incumbent of a church in terminal slime green and black damp and decay. That slovenly slang abbreviation of the name of his church was something else that raised his instant ire. He was an unyielding man who felt even more offended by the interference in the affair by a Dominican friar right opposite him on the other side of the Canal. After all his church, with its vaunted bones of the Holy Innocents, had once been the most imposing brick pile on the island. The Glassmakers' Canal was, when correctly named, the 'Canale di Santo Stefano' and even its murky waters were legally part and parcel of his parish. He took a very masculine pride in the fact that his bell tower was the tallest and the grandest, despite those few minor cracks that for long time had worried Grandpa. He was always being slighted by the other clergy who, in his estimation, belonged mostly to devious orders of monks and friars. Now was the time to act. He demanded a meeting with the Four Deputies to discuss how best to put down vice and brawling taverns in his parish and to re-establish his authority once and for all. Signora Vianello was condemned to being shaven of her hair, tied to the back of a mule cart and whipped by a bullo through the crowds on market day. The landlord of the 'Star and Crescent,' where fighting involving children had taken place, and where illegal gambling was subsequently reported, lost his licence and was taxed heavily for its restoration . Little Lucia Vianello was given over to the nuns of Saint Mary of the Angels, for her moral well-being and future upbringing.

Don Tranquillo went to plead with the Deputies, taking with him the offer, from signora Molin for the young girl to be employed as a servant in her now prospering household. They refused. However, he did succeed in convincing them that the scene of a woman, however vile, being lashed half naked through the town would be worse for public morality than keeping open a rough haunt of a tavern, mostly used by foreign sailors. The Four Deputies suspended the public whipping, on condition that signora Vianello should enter a convent on the western shore of Giudecca Island. This convent for fallen Magdelens was known as the 'Convertite' *(the ones who repent.)* The Deputies decreed that she should never attempt to see her child again: a harsh decision, but worse sentences were within their powers.

After Lucia's own downfall at the ruined villa, it was felt by many to be an unfair ruling, but others, including Tranquillo, knew it was in the interest of the child's health and her moral welbeing. The friends lost their most adventurous companion, but Lucia did not slip completely from Zorzi's life. Her confinement at Santa Maria degli Angeli Convent was to lead to an important discovery that could have so easily transformed the life and fortunes of Zorzi and Grandpa.

CHAPTER FORTY-THREE

Senator Trevisan was up to something. Very few of his invited guests had any knowledge as to what that something was. On returning from his country villa he gave a series of select, delightful and small-scale entertainments. The modest scale of the staterooms in his Murano residence would permit nothing grander, however, they made up for their lack of size by the rarity and magnificence of their frescoed walls. Veronese himself had painted the cycle of gods and temptresses of Mount Olympus that disported themselves so realistically in candle light that Zorzi was half convinced, on first sighting, that they were living beings; and as for Trevisan's smart little canal side abode, well the Great Palladio himself may well have built it. To the clink of Murano goblets and to the ping of sprung gold and enamelled snuffboxes, political gossip and news of the Doge's war were exchanged at these soirees; all to the background music of Trevisan's own quintet. Zorzi sang frequently, rehearsing his programme first with Luanardo. Having paid the full ten-year lease on Luanardo's room, Zorzi was now doted on, not to say fawned over by the adipose choirmaster. Zorzi was satisfied with the deal too, learning many a trick of voice control and emotional emphasis when singing madrigals, hymns and love songs. Lessons in how to identify the guest with the biggest purse and the most generous nature did not come amiss either. Zorzi soon found that concentrating his most charming smile and addressing his verses in the appropriate direction nearly always reaped a reward of silver 'grossi' at the end of the performance. From Trevisan's man servant he learned the airs and graces; the degrees of bobs and bows appropriate for the occasion; the etiquettes of eating with a fork; of first addressing an aristocrat; the more problematic art of keeping a solemn, reserved and straight backed stance: not to mention keeping out of mischief whilst circulating in grand company. Luanardo was a most competent harpsichord player and smelled far sweeter, now that performance fees allowed him to eat a more varied diet than chickpeas boiled for hours with fish heads. As accompanist to Zorzi, he was now employed quite regularly and quite generously by the Noble Senator, as well as occasionally at the villas and palazzi of Trevisan's guests.

Whenever the Senator invited a new audience, Zorzi was instructed to retell the tale of the Doge's ring and to pass around for admiration his ducal Osella coin. For the feast of San Stin, the day after Christmas, Zorzi had the Osella mounted on a gold chain, which he presented to signora Molin during the traditional exchange of gifts on the steps of San Stin, straight after the crowded and solemn High Mass held there by the unpopular Parroco. Consequently, when he received an invitation from Trevisan to perform with Luanardo's quintet on the Feast of the Epiphany, 1694, Zorzi no longer had the Osella to show off.

"Bring along your bits of fresco. Tell the tale of the hidden villa," Trevisan suggested. "Add a ghost or two. I would prefer a spooky yarn for Twelfth Night, so embroider the tale as much as you like, but kindly leave out the brawl with the loose Vianella woman at the tavern: that would be too indelicate for the ears of lady guests."

Zorzi thought this a capital idea. He would ask Grandpa about a suitable ghost, but the rest he would tell as truthfully as he could remember, whilst attributing the sad downfall of little Lucia to her mother's sudden death. That would be it... He would make signora Vianello into the villa spook, and her sudden appearance would cause Lucia to fall! Maybe the grand ladies present would sympathize and then intervene to release Lucia from what he was sure must be an unhappy and regimented life in the Convent of the Angels.

The aristocracy, especially its grand dames, was entranced by his lively tales and his charmingly naive way of describing his experiences. From him they had learned much about the Countess and her equally haughty German grandson: not to mention the dark doings of her dreadful nephew Bastian. Secretly, most of the ladies envied the Countess for her supposed lover, the ageing but still very handsome and formidable Martinengo. Zorzi's innocent words backed up to perfection what gossip they had already heard. What's more, they had titillating glimpses into the hardships of life amongst the common folk. Bit by bit the grand ladies teased out of Zorzi little snippets, identifying details, pointing to the young nobleman whom he, unintentionally, had to admit that he had met.... in San Zaccaria Convent! They guessed correctly that Rezzonico had drawn his sword with every intention of disposing of the only witness to his infamy who might talk. Knowing that the little innocent telling the tale had come so unwittingly close to death, gave an extra frisson to the tale.... Such deliciously shocking news! News that only confirmed gossip that the rich young Rezzonico was now a grovelling client, dancing at the beck and call of the Grand Chancellor Ballarin!

For the worst of the winter season, Trevisan had retreated to the warmth and comfort of his apartments in the family home on Rio Canonica, just a few yards up from the Ducal Palace. Trevisan had hot news as well from Nauplia Castle in the Bay of Argos where the Doge too was holed up, unable to sail further because of icy rigging, violent snow storms and certain other more severe complications. Twelfth Night would be the occasion for Trevisan to throw his dice in the direction of the ducal 'corno.' He would give a reception for two hundred of the most influential in the public affairs of the city. It would be a time for revelry, lavish food and costume: a masked ball and gambling to follow. The invitation letters would expressly ban all talk of politics, on pain of being bopped on the head with slapstick, or inflated pig's bladder. The Trevisan patriarch, his arthritic elder brother, had sailed south to Palermo, seeking the winter sun. It would therefore be Trevisan's pleasure and duty to welcome guests on the grand staircase. As their humble host, he would be there to greet them in a plain red senatorial robe and sash. The family baubles and glitter would of course be on display on the shoulders of his nieces and the fists of his nephews. It would not do to appear to be a poverty stricken clan in the run-up to a ducal election. The incorruptible Serenissima had, nevertheless, its share of hard up nobles who sometimes needed a bit of financial assistance in casting their votes in the right cause. It would not go amiss either, for a certain little celebrity, to be seen at his side as his pageboy. It would show that he was not aloof from the plebs….had the common folk at heart. In his dreams, only Rio Canonica now separated him from that horn shaped crown and from treading a kingly path in the footsteps of the Magi.

He had completed the 'groundwork' in the manner of all ambitious politicians, dismissing any suggestion that he had his eye on the ducal crown; frequently declaring that he was far too old to interfere in public affairs anymore. It was now known to all who mattered that he had done some modest duty to the Republic in his youth; leading the way in a couple of bloody engagements with the Turk, served here and there as Ambassador, sat in judgment as a Procurator of St. Mark's. His only wish now was for peace and quiet in his dotage. Idle gossip had it that he was now one of The Ten, for he tended to disappear from time to time. As for his position, he was rich enough and unattached. He might make it known as well, that he had made a will and testament leaving part of his worldly wealth to the Republic. He was not after all someone with family ambitions - not head of the Trevisan clan, like his brother. As a younger son he had of course not been allowed to marry, but he was still fit and virile in his old age, though he had no embarrassments 'born on the other side of the blanket' to ruin his image. Most of all he was quite unworthy of even being thought of as a candidate. In short, such serious shortcomings made him the perfect candidate for the job. Trevisan was but a stone's throw from the ducal crown. And now hot secret news had come that the stone was of a quite different kind from that which propelled King David to his throne!

CHAPTER FORTY-FOUR

Dressed in a suit of silk brocaded magnificence, with the 'Trevisan' a golden sea horse badge on a chain about his neck, our shivering little hero stood at the top of the triple flight of steps leading up from the central courtyard of the palace. In his hands a silver salver piled with marzipan sweets beautifully crafted and coloured to resemble miniature fruits, ships, wild animals and the like. A bitter wind was being funnelled into the courtyard from the Canonica Canal, via the ground floor reception room, where charcoal braziers could do little to relieve the icy damp air and where even the Neptune fountain in its grandiose marble niche was dripping icicles. Outside, torch lit gondolas bumped and jostled, eager to disembark as swiftly as possible their exalted passengers. Nevertheless, lady guests were more than eager to be relieved of their sable furs by Trevisan's flunkeys: for what mattered a little suffering? Bedecked with a king's ransom of glittering gem stones, each expanse of goose pimpled bosom was bared for the sole purpose of flaunting wealth before female rivals. The men, for the most part un-impressed by this display of elderly pulchritude, clung to their cloaks and to one another against the icy blast. The palace Major-domo announced, without so much as a snigger, the titles of the guests as they arrived in the courtyard - his loud voice echoing up the stone stairway: "The Marquis of Omnium and his fair companion the Duchess of Utopia! Abbott Adipose of Pietropollo!" (*Chickenstone, rather than Peter* and *Paul, a reference to a comic tale of a greedy friar, by Boccaccio.*) When the Abbott approached, rattling his iron begging pot and crying "Alms for the love of Allah!" Zorzi dropped two sweets into the pot and was startled to see that the Abbott really had a large stone and a smallish boiled chicken nestling at the bottom. The Princess Confetti and her handsome swain Count Caramella of Rottenteeth; Baron Gorgonzaga of Putridville and the Princess Topolina *(little mouse)* followed immediately in the Abbott's very plump wake. Baron Gorgonzaga's chosen title was just a gentle snobbish hint that the 'baron' was both partial to that pungent cheese and connected by ancestry to the equally overpowering Gonzaga family, the Dukes of Mantova.

Zorzi's ribs ached with laughter as each title was announced and each hilariously costumed couple mounted the steps and exchanged courtesies with Trevisan, who with great solemnity addressed them by their spoof titles, his face not so much as twitching a smile, though he was clearly

430

enjoying it as much as everyone. Once Zorzi had offered his tray of sweets and gently bopped with his beribboned pig's bladder any guest who refused, the couples moved onwards into the'sala del portego' the vast corridor, which was dazzlingly lit with an infinity of glass girandoles and candelabra. Thence they proceeded in twos to the 'sala da ballo' where a royal spread of refreshments and a dance band awaited.

Regretting that he had not put on the scratchy woollen under vest that Marcella had knitted for him, Zorzi began to consider the possibility that he might die of the 'coughing lungs' like some people did after going to the public steam baths in mid-winter; something that Grandpa had obliged him to do that morning. He stopped his teeth from chattering by popping a couple of marzipan sweets into his mouth each time he went to the sideboard to replenish the tray. After what seemed a freezing eternity, the last of the guests were helped from their gondolas, disrobed of their furs and directed up the stairs. It was then that, instead of conveying his pile of sable cloaks to the cloakroom on the right of the entrance lobby, a splendidly dressed footman bounded up the stairs towards them. When Trevisan did nothing to rebuke the man or to send him back, Zorzi looked up at him quite puzzled. He saw Trevisan shiver and hastily straightened his senatorial sash with agitated fingers. Giving a loud nervous cough, he ordered Zorzi to stand up very straight. He then asked the Major-domo to call for silence. As the fur-carrying footman passed them at the top of the stairs he gave Trevisan a quick bobbing bow. In doing so, he almost let drop two pistols folded inside the cloaks. Zorzi saw instantly the silver lions' heads decorating those all too familiar ebony butt ends! A powerful shock - a spasm of fear shot through Zorzi's shivering frame. Panic brought an adrenalin rush to aid his flight. He turned, only to find a pressing throng of curious, excited, but silent guests closing in behind him.

"From the moon, come down to us by celestial silver beam..." announced the major-domo, "We are honoured to receive this evening the goddess Diana and her legendary huntsman, the most unfortunate Acteon!"

Zorzi had no choice but to stand where he was and to look down as a tall lady in black silk and bombazine advanced towards him. Her gown was spangled with diamond set starlets, her face, fully masked, resembled that of a silver statue with a great quarter moon balanced above her powdered

431

grey hair. In her hands she held a silver bow and quiver. Her antler-horned companion carried a hunting spear, finely made in papier-mâché, and was dressed and high-booted in animal skins. His helmet, fashioned as well in papier-mâché to resemble a deer's head, only came down to his bushy eyebrows, underneath which glittered out those familiar ferocious grey eyes! Those eyes, gimlet- like yet showing utter surprise, came to rest on Zorzi, who, for a second or two stood mesmerized like a coney in the beam of a huntsman's lantern.

Thrusting the salver of sweets into the hands of an astonished and masked Colombine, Zorzi burrowed into the throng of curtseying ladies and bowing nobles behind him. Uttering a bellow of rage, worthy of a monarch stag in rut, and shaking his spear wildly to clear the way, the gigantic Acteon bounded up the stairs. There was the briefest of nods to poor dismayed Trevisan as he charged by - scattering the crowd in all directions - for he had sighted his long sought prey.

"A hunt! A hunt!" screamed the youngest of the lady guests. Acteon paused momentarily to blow a rude blast on his ox horn to add to the excitement. Zorzi ducked and dived hoping to find the service stairway leading down to the kitchens, where an hour previously he had left Grandpa ensconced in the major-domo's chair, warming himself with a glass of red wine, close to a wood stove. Finding the ballroom less crowded, Zorzi crawled under the cloth of a long refreshment table, but accompanied by more bellows and hunting whoops from the crowd, Acteon was right behind him. With astonishing agility for one so tall and well built, Acteon vaulted over the table top without so much as disturbing a crumb from the cake trays and delicious confections set out thereon. However Acteon had to pause, to retrieve his dropped paper deer's head and set of horns, giving Zorzi just enough time to back out from the way he had entered and leaving Acteon stranded on the other side of the table. The crowd roared their applause and encouragement at Zorzi's deft move.

While Luanardo drooped his head in utter dejection over the keyboard and held his hands to his weeping eyes, the horn players in his band entered into the spirit of the occasion by blowing a French boar-hunting tune. "What was it about this boy?" Luanardo moaned to himself. "Can he go nowhere without causing a riot?"

Luanardo had come close to losing his job after the incident at San Donato. The parish priest had accused him of enrolling the boy in his choir, knowing full well that he was from a troublesome family. Once again Zorzi had created havoc. Would Trevisan employ his band ever again? An endless gloomy prospect of sack selling, of cold rowing for hours across the Lagoon and of the abuse of insolent and mean customers, rose up in poor Luanardo's thoughts. The thoughts of Senator Trevisan were on similar disaster lines. His well-planned party had collapsed into anarchy before even beginning. His prospects now of the 'Corno' crown were about as bright as candle smoke. This was far, far worse than that silly gaffe in front of the crowd at St. Peter Martyr, which had now almost been forgotten. As with most aristocrats he had a lurking suspicion that children of the lower orders, once encouraged, tended to abuse their benefactors by cheating or stealing. He wondered what it was of such high value that Zorzi had stolen to provoke such an instant and ferocious reaction from his two most important guests.

Egged on by the wildly excited younger nobility and to the tut-tuts and outrage of the old dames, Zorzi dodged hither and thither to escape from the outstretched arms of Acteon. Finally, mistaking the entrance to the library for an exit corridor he was cornered. Acteon advanced towards him, like the Minotaur in his maze, with lowered horns, snorting and growling and with arms outstretched. In his terror, Zorzi seized a heavy brass bound book and was about to launch it at his tormentor's head when Trevisan entered with Diana, Goddess of the Hunt on his arm. "Put down the book Zorzi! It is my brother's and beyond price! Put it down!" Trevisan ordered with a half plea in his distraught voice.

"Enough Ettore! Enough! You have terrified the wits out of the poor child!" commanded the Moon Goddess.

Acteon obeyed, paused, and straightened up his gigantic stag horned frame. Yet, knowing the wiles of his young adversary, he could not resist the temptation to spread wide his legs. Zorzi saw his chance and dived. Acteon snapped his legs together with a speed and accuracy that only he knew how to employ. Zorzi was trapped neatly at the waist! It was an appropriate conclusion, one could almost say a poetic end, to a seven month long chase. Seizing Zorzi by the ankles, Acteon swung him into the air, caught him in his arms and gave him a kiss on the forehead of the kind a father reserves for greeting his young offspring after a long absence. Still holding the breathless Zorzi in a fatherly embrace, he announced in a voice like the thunder of doom, "It shall not be said that Ettore Martinengo failed to track down his quarry! He is all yours Countess!" With that, he let Zorzi down and bowed low to the assembled guests.

Utterly mystified, the crowd held silence until Trevisan spoke: "For whatever he has done to you, Countess, I can only beg pardon. Whatever he may have taken from you, I shall willingly replace. Forgive me for his outrage to you and to the Cavaliere in my home."

"Outrage? Theft? What on earth are you nattering about Trevisan?" the Countess exclaimed, giving Trevisan a sharp tap on the arm with her silver bow, "Why, I wanted the child detained so that I might offer my apologies to him and to make amends. Up until now he has always managed to escape me, that is to outwit my fleet-footed Acteon here."

"Your apologies to the child? How so, Countess?"

"Why, Trevisan, I once threatened the boy with a whipping, when he was entirely innocent. It was all a matter of mistaken identity. I took him for one of my own brood, but I should have known better: he is far more of a gentleman than any of them!" Turning to Zorzi she continued, "Young man, I am most sorry for my mistake and for giving you such a fright. How can I ever make amends?"

Realizing for the first time that the chase had all been a bit of rough fun, Zorzi knew it was time now to give a gallant bow, a wide grin and to edge away as soon as politeness allowed from the Countess and her Cavaliere, but she would have none of it: "Stay a moment!" Her firm voice was addressed as much to Trevisan and his guests, "Prior Raimondo speaks to me of your graciousness and your generosity, as does the Noble Abbess of San Zaccaria, for that we give you our thanks. But you are dear to my heart for another reason: my brother commends you to my care in this note I have just received from Nauplia." She waved the Doge's letter.

At the mention of news from the Doge, there was a tumultuous shout and a great stamping of feet in sheer delight on the ancient timber floor: nothing but bad news had been expected from Nauplia in the Bay of Argos. The prolonged applause set jangling and glittering the myriad of chandelier droplets. Showers of bees' wax from them, and from candles branching out from silver girandole mirrors, dropped onto unconcerned silks and satins.

"Great fun! Tremendous fun Trevisan! What a celebration! Never been to a better!" exclaimed the Lord Bishop and Patriarch of Grado, slapping a relieved and gratified Trevisan heartily on the back. "Fancy! The old harridan apologizing to a child, and in public...that must be a first; what? I want the child from you Trevisan. Name your price. I am told he has a rare voice. I'll have him for my choir and give him a rich living as a Monsignore somewhere before he is eighteen, no matter what that old sybarite Torcello thinks of me pinching from his territory- what?"

Turning to the ragged 'Abbott of Pietrapollo" and acknowledging at the same time the cheers and clapping from his delighted guests, Trevisan observed: "Your Grace, I regret to disappoint you, but he's not mine to sell. He is the grandson of a Citizen: what's more, he's likely to become a Ward of State. It seems the Serenissimo himself is his patron and would have him for a galley captain. Now the Countess has the poor scrap commended to her clutches, there's nothing either of us can do to keep him. I doubt very much that I shall have the young skylark much longer to entertain my guests."

It was evident to Trevisan that his guests wanted more rumbustious fun of the same nature. Zorzi, despite his shock, still seemed game. Trevisan gave him an encouraging hug and a pat on the head and slipped him a gold sequin.

'Baron Gorgonzaga' bustled forward in his cardboard cheese outfit. A fun loving character and considered a bit of a buffoon by those who invariably lost to him at cards, 'Gorgonzaga' was ever eager to make light mischief. Behind his blue veined cheese wedge and mousy-eared hat, he was a tall, stately and fit looking man, though from his wrinkles and greying hair well into his early sixties: "Martinengo!" he challenged, "The

dashing young 'gentleman' has now not only supplanted you as the Countess's Cicisbeo: he has drawn your blood Sir! He has clipped your ear, Sir, as you grabbed him. You are bleeding, Sir! And which of us did not see him bring you down with a bump in the Piazza, Sir! And in front of the Serenissimo himself! Ettore, you are losing your touch! You have no choice but to challenge Trevisan's young champion to a duel!"
(A cicisbeo was a male champion of a lady of high rank. It was an ancient custom of Venice - husbands did not in the least object to having these bodyguards cum companions for their wives - so long as they were of noble birth.)

"Readily I shall, Silvestro, you damned old trouble-stirrer!" replied Martinengo in a feigned menacing voice, "If the lad is willing and you will stand as my second in the fight. What's more, if you agree to pick up the laundry bill, I shall slay him here and now on Trevisan's new Persian rug!"

In truth, Zorzi had clipped the Cavaliere's ear with his gem encrusted 'Trevisan' sea horse badge and there was the slightest trickle of blood on Martinengo's leopard's skin costume. It was entirely an accidental wound, as Zorzi protested to the chuckling crowd, who were now determined: "A duel! A duel!" they urged.

"Your second? That I shall not be!" the cheesy-dressed Senator Silvestro Valier replied, "For how else shall I bring you down in a duel, Ettore? The lad shall fight on my shoulders. You shall have the fat friar with his chicken pot as your second; for when you are defeated, he will pray the 'last rites' over your sinful corpse!"

"Pistols or slapsticks?" inquired the Lord Patriarch of Grado, putting down his chicken pot.

"Alas! We have no pistols in the house!" announced Trevisan, "It must therefore be slapsticks."

Zorzi was about to contradict him about the pistols, then thought better of the matter. In his young mind he was still a little unsure as to how far the fun might extend and did not fancy the prospect of being shot at by one of the Cavaliere's dangerous looking lions' head weapons. As 'Baron

436

Gorgonzaga' was divested of his cardboard cheese wedge and came forward to lift him onto his shoulders, Zorzi noted something. It was a small matter....Baron Gorgonzaga had a limp.... and kindly eyes.... just like those of signorina Bianca, the pretty little schoolmistress who had disappeared!

The irony of this comic duel was that only the blissful ignorance of both 'Gorgonzaga' and his opponent 'Acteon' prevented it from taking place for real - and on Martinengo's preferred killing ground! Had either noblemen known of the existence of Bianca then that strip of Lido reserved for such bloody purposes, would have seen the cheesy 'Baron' promptly transformed into a slice of riddled Emmental.

Cheered on by the crowd and accompanied by martial music from the band - even Luanardo was thumping the keys wildly, half blinded with tears of joy and relief - the unequal duel commenced. There was no shortage of slapsticks for at least half a dozen guests had arrived costumed as Harlequin, Colombine, or Brighella.

Martinengo advanced menacingly, waggling his brightly painted stick. The guests let forth many an 'ooh' and 'aah' as he pranced back and forth, side to side, in manoeuvres of such speed and admirable precision that they were almost too hard to follow with the eye. Rocking elegantly on the soles of his feet, from toe to heel, in the classic stance of a fighter, Martinengo launched himself at lightning speed with a bounding rush, known in the duelling trade as a fleche-attack. Zorzi and 'Gorgonzaga' stood their ground fearlessly. Zorzi raised his stick to parry the lunge that never landed: for Martinengo pretended to slip and topple headlong towards them, extending his horns within range of a swift riposte from Zorzi.

The colourful slapsticks were confectioned from two layers of thin plywood bound together loosely with leather thongs, so that they made the devil of a clatter when they struck. Zorzi swiped the horns clean off the head of the Cavaliere, who stood for a second as though pole-axed, then threw himself into a double backward somersault, hardly touching the ground. Finishing his gymnastic display with a perfectly steady handstand, he slowly rolled over from that position onto his back. Crossing his arms, he closed tight his eyes and played dead.

The Lord Bishop of Grado, alias Abbott Adipose, came forward with great solemnity to perform the 'last rites;' which ceremony concluded with the Bishop administering a hefty thump on the Cavaliere's rock hard chest with his boiled chicken. This resurrecting blow proving quite ineffectual, Martinengo not even opening an eye, let alone twitching a muscle, when he was struck; the Bishop then performed an on the spot miracle with the aid of the contents of an ice bucket.

To loud cries of "A miracle! A miracle!" the Cavaliere leapt to his feet and chased the Bishop round the tables, threatening to give him "a right Papal Blessing" with the boiled chicken. The Bishop, a slight and nimble man under his cushion padding, claimed sanctuary by leaping onto a chair, from which he preached a short sermon explaining that under no circumstances could it be said that he had performed a miracle. The reality was that Lucifer had barred the burning gates, on catching sight of Martinengo. Having sent far too many bad customers to him, and not wanting any more trouble in hell, the devil had made it clear to Martinengo that he was not welcome there. As for that other heavenly place... Martinengo's penchant for shooting dead anything with wings on... well what more explanation could he give them for the Cavaliere's sudden return from Hades, other than a desire to continue disturbing the serenity of the Most Serene Republic?

Zorzi laughed and laughed, until he almost choked on his marzipan cake. Never had he been in such entertaining company. Yet he had overheard enough to note that jolly 'Baron Gorgonzaga' and his more acidic faced 'Princess Topolina' bickered all the time under their breath. Curious: he soon overheard that the plump mouse princess in her grey satin, black velvet ears and stunningly fabulous jewels, was really called Bettina. He wondered what she had to complain about with a husband like jolly old Silvestro, alias Baron Gorgonzaga, who must have loved her at least as far as the jeweller's shop. When another noblewoman inquired after the health of Bettina's father, referring to him as Senator Querini, Zorzi felt certain he knew who she was. Remembering little Lucia, shut-up in her gloomy convent and now no longer able to skip and hop to her favourite rhyme, his eyes became rather misty and moist; though he put it down to tiredness:

"Betta Querina, e` ducessa o reina?"

438

Elisabeth Querini, is she our duchess, or our queen?

Zorzi's rendition of Monteverdi's madrigal, 'The Lament of Ariadne' had a similar lachrymose effect on the old ladies clustered around the harpsichord. The band of musicians set down their instruments to join in the applause for his performance. Thereafter and throughout the evening, old ladies came forward to give him motherly squeezes against their sharply bejewelled stomachers and to press a ducat or two into his palm. It was fortunate that his finery, borrowed from the Trevisans' family wardrobe, was provided with new fangled pockets in which to stow away the loot with all speed, thus leaving an ever empty sweaty little palm for the ladies and for Senators in their dotage, to refill.

The library with its painted beams and ceramic tiled corner stoves was the comfortable setting for those who wished to be entertained with stories. The door was closed against the stately noise of the sarabands; minuets and voltas being weaved with intricate dance steps in the ballroom. When it came to Zorzi's turn, he was not on his best form and omitted to mention the 'ghost of Lucia's mother' altogether, but his bits of plaster were a sensation. As they were passed around he was inevitably subjected to a certain amount of half understood ribbing. One old Senator, with tongue in cheek, reminded him that abandoned properties belonged to the State; therefore as a Procurator he should confiscate all the plaster paintings at once, as stolen property. A bright young noblewoman objected, saying that she thought that she knew who owned the villa, for she recognized the backsides of the twin little boys portrayed on one of the plasters. When she murmured behind her hand held mask, Bastian's name and that of another nobleman, there was much sniggering as well as tut-tuts from some of the elderly dames who were within earshot. Fortunate for her that the Countess Morosina was seated in the front row of armchairs, studying Zorzi from behind that silver Diana mask and giving him more jitters than any villa spectre could ever have done.

In his naivety, and with a desire to impress 'Abbott Adipose' with his knowledge of the Scriptures, Zorzi suggested that the baby twins shown embracing one another from a back view might be John the Baptist and Jesus. The painted lady seated on a blue wave in a flimsy dress with the word 'Virgo' written at her feet must surely be a portrait of Mary, because she was surrounded with silver stars. Since she was in her nightgown, she was obviously going to bed. When the chuckling and guffaws subsided, the 'Lord Abbott' asked him what the pictures of the crab and the two fishes pointing in opposite directions were doing up in the sky. Unhesitating, Zorzi suggested that Joseph might have caught them for Mary's breakfast.

"And the Sagittarius, the half horse, half man with the bow," inquired the Abbott, "Where does he come into the pages of the Bible?"

"Oh! He must be one of the four horsemen of the Apocalypse," came the instant reply. "Anyway Aldo found him. That one belongs to him. Aldo got him down with our boat hook while sitting on my shoulders. He's so heavy he nearly broke my neck! And do you know, Lord Abbott, some low-down sea gipsy must have stolen our forcola off the beach, but Aldo's dad is going to carve me a new one!"

The Countess Morosina sat there in silence until Zorzi had concluded his rescue tale and the account of his and Aldo's subsequent trip to the island, on their own. "But there is no ghost in your story, Maestro Zorzi," she commented, "but I can suggest one who should have been there to haunt you. His name is Vettor Carpathius, better known to some here as Victor Carpaccio, our greatest artist!"

There were gasps of half disbelief. Crowding round the large lump of plaster showing the centaur, the guests began to look more carefully. Many of them were experts, not to say traffickers to overseas noblemen in Venice's ancient heritage. They could only agree with the Countess's opinion and this time it was not out of sycophancy, or fear of her wrath.

"I shall order a guard to be placed on the island and for the remains of this cycle of paintings to be covered for the winter. Once they are retrieved and suitably mounted, they will be displayed in the Great Hall," she announced to polite clapping. The Hall of the Great Council in the Doge's Palace was technically out of bounds even to ladies of her exalted rank. It should have been no concern of hers what went on, or was displayed there; but who was brave enough to dispute the matter with the Countess?

Towards the end of Abbott Adipose of Pietrapollo's magic show, the major-domo interrupted to announce that Rio Canonica was now completely iced-up, despite every effort from waiting gondoliers to break up the ice with their oars. Lamplighters and guards would escort anyone home who wished to return by foot, or by Sedan chair. Servants then began discretely to clear away plates and glasses close to the magician, when suddenly he pulled off his second and far more spectacular resurrection trick. Placing once again the boiled fowl and the stone into his empty iron pot, he waved his hand in benediction, then promptly pulled out a real live clucking hen and immediately afterwards - a huge 'Sinbad' egg. Zorzi was entranced. Even the Rabbi had not managed to equal that for magic and he was sitting behind a desk where he could hide things, whereas the Lord Bishop of Grado was surrounded on all sides by guests and by 'seemingly busy,' servants. Of course, Zorzi could hardly help noticing that the abbot's adiposity seemed gradually to thin down as his act progressed. His only disappointment, immediately following the display of holy magic, was to learn from the Lord Bishop that he had been cheated by that damned plausible rogue trader in Rialto Market. His own identical giant egg was not, after all, that of a dragoness or a giant Auk, but had been laid by a very big long-legged African bird called an ostrich.

That night all Venice froze at its moorings, transforming itself into a phantom fairyland. The natural humidity of the Lagoon remained suspended in still air in the form of tiny crystals which glittered in the faint moonlight and cloaked with diamond dust every wall and rooftop, every toppling tower and odourless stony bridge. Zorzi slept, cradled by Grandpa in the Major-domo's armchair with his arms thrust, for reasons of both security and warmth, into the pockets of his borrowed suit, which at evening's end had left him sagging at the knees with the heavy weight of golden ducats. Deprived of their beds by Trevisan's stranded guests, exhausted servants huddled in cloaks and whatever coverings they could find for mutual body warmth on the flagstones of the ground floor kitchens and store rooms. They were joined in their discomfort by numerous household gondoliers who had failed to smash their way out of the icy grip of Rio Canonica, whilst attempting to ferry home their noble masters.

When the Angelus rang through the darkness and was followed an hour or so later with a faint foggy dawn, the grand Feast of the Epiphany brought gold in plenty to the side of the green baize topped gaming table where Senator Silvestro Valier, alias Baron Gorgonzaga, still sat. Surrounded by spluttered candle wax, half empty wine glasses and holding yet another winning hand of cards, he was now almost alone. Only Abbott Adipose, on another gaming table, had a bigger pile of ducats at his side. His winnings, he had vowed, would be donated to the poor as a penance for his tipsy state and other venial sins. In the absence of the Lord Bishop, frankincense, that other gift of the Magi, would be wafted in great clouds that morning over the shivering congregation at High Mass in his cathedral at Grado: whilst in the unheated attics, in the gutters of grubby alleyways and in sheltering doorways there were rigid and grotesquely crouched shapes a plenty; vagabond children; naked babies; elderly beggars - half the myrrh in Arabia would hardly have sufficed to anoint them all. And in a far distant harbour, that kingly gift, that bitter perfume, had been offered to an aged mortal man, a once mighty warrior who, with the coming of the dawn, was nolonger aware that he had been 'with myrrh anointed.'

CHAPTER FORTY-FIVE

Nauplia Harbour (Nafplion Greece) - 6th January, 1694 - The Feast of the Epiphany (N.B. in the 17th Century the New Year always began on 1st March)

Depriving another old warrior of his breakfast, particularly one of such exalted rank, was tantamount to gross insubordination; though breakfast in Bourtzi Castle in recent weeks had consisted of little more than frozen rat, seasoned occasionally with the soft crunchy bones of a boiled pigeon which had previously been well plucked of its flesh by a garrison cook. He would have to make a stand. He would have to lodge an official complaint, to protest that he was being overlooked by his overlord. The call for his presence on ceremonial duties had dwindled from infrequent to none at all. Feeling deeply offended by all this, Makò smartened up his whiskers, gave himself a quick paw licking and made off across the wind-swept battlements to the citadel tower. The slanting drop from the bastion walls to the freezing waters of the harbour was quite a dizzy prospect, even for a sure-footed cat. In compensation for his low crouching, scrambling effort along the icy and exposed parapet there was a reassuring view of almost the entire Venetian battle fleet frozen at anchor in the bay. From the base of the castle's main tower an immense chain of thick steel links ran just above water level to the mainland. Its purpose was to protect the fleet from a surprise attack. Now the chain seemed to take the form of a precious necklace, sparkling and dripping with icicles where it rose and dipped into the water between each supporting trunk of cut timber. The galleys at least had not abandoned him in this godforsaken place. Their yardarms pointed heavenwards at a slant with neatly furled sails, though their jolly flags and bunting were no longer strung out. From the mainmast of the great galleon, 'The Serenissima' the yellow and red lion flag drooped stiff and miserable and at half-mast. Regularly every ten minutes, came the muffled boom of a shore gun. Half way in time between each blank shot the towers of Saint Anthony's and of Holy George Cathedral gave out single doleful bell chimes. At his master's oak and iron studded door Makò was spurned away yet again by the steel boot of an ignorant and uncaring palace guard, in parade uniform, who was clearly badly instructed about Makò s absolute right of entry. The guard was leaning with bowed head on his partizan: its broad spearhead pointed downwards. A partizan was not the sort of weapon one disputed with cats' claws. Exasperated, Makò prowled the icy, barrel vaulted, corridors until he found a narrow gunport opening through the walls with a short drop down to an expanse of wooden scaffolding, now abandoned by its repair masons. For some days now as well, the stonecutters and slaves toiling on high Palamidi Hill, building a new and formidable fortress, had ceased their irritating chip chipping. Both Turkish and Venetian fleets had generously peppered over the years the walls of Bourtzi Island Citadel, determined to possess that clasp which held together a chain of other similar anchorages along the fighting edge of Christendom.

Treading and clawing his way cautiously along the slippery scaffolding, Makò eventually leapt up and through the wide-open window of his master's bedchamber. There was a faint smell of decay. An odour to which Makò was well accustomed, having picked his way, a sword's length ahead of his master, over many a corpse strewn deck. The cat's sudden bounding presence in their midst disconcerted the knot of generals, priests and dignitaries surrounding the simple camp bed. On the arrival of this 'familiar' of the Serenissimo - this miniature sign from heaven of St. Mark's presence - all pretence of putting on a brave front was given up. Battle scarred generals dripped tears onto their steely gorgets; clerics paused in their prayerful mumblings only to mop their misted eyes; hunched in a corner of the room sat Abele, no longer a slave, but a Citizen of the Serenissima under the terms of the Doge's last will and testament. Yet so distraught was he after his final act of service to his master, that of gently tugging off the emerald ring, he could no longer be reasoned with. Hopping onto the bed, Makò went to lick, as was his custom, those sinewy fingers. There was usually just a trace of butter to lick off where Morosini eased on the ring each morning over his swollen finger joints. Some trace of rancid butter was there still and Makò licked, but there was no familiar warmth, no friendly caress, no tickling behind the ears, nor any heartbeat through the covering blanket to purr and to nuzzle against. Escorted by a flotilla of war galleys, the glistening emerald green stone of authority, together with the Corno crown, were already on their way back to Venice, to adorn the hand of a successor.

As concerned as a cat can be on such an occasion, Makò padded off to hunt for a rodent breakfast in the darkened depths of the castle grain store.

CHAPTER FORTY-SIX

The Scaligero Castle, Soave - 16th January, 1694

Rezzonico was utterly exhausted. This was his third journey as intermediary between Bastian and The Ten in as many months. This time he had to slog his way on foot for the last half-mile or so of what was once a reasonable mule track. Now it was bristling with wood and metal spikes and dug at unknown intervals with murderous stake bottomed and well concealed pits. The dry stone walls which had once held back fertile vine clad terraces had been thrown down in disorder across the pathway and without the aid of guides, who more resembled brigands than servants of the Zustinian family, he would have been impaled several times on his way up - the only way up to Castle Scaligero. Or was it? As on previous occasions, he was curious to notice that two of the more senior ranking brigands, who had accompanied him into Soave Village were already in the castle guardroom on his arrival.

Passing through three barbicans with fireproofed steel plated drawbridges and watched through loopholes by musketeers at every step, he came at last to the inner bailey, the third of the courtyards which rise step-like with tall fork tailed battlements up the side of the hilltop fastness. The great courtyard is still to this day overshadowed by its enormous whitewashed watchtower from which traffic on the road to Verona may be surveyed. Bastian awaited him at the foot of the external staircase to his retreat: a Lombard style palace set against the highest battlements on the unassailable side of the mountain. It was clear to Rezzonico from Bastian's haggard looks and far away voice that he had become more paranoid with each passing day since they had last met. Already fully informed of his uncle's death, he expected his own to follow shortly. "What else could he hope for?" wondered Rezzonico, "By not responding to a request from The Ten, Bastian had sealed his doom."

The Noble Bastian could now be counted amongst the walking dead - Rezzonico had no doubts about that. A nervous concern that he himself might be suspected, or even required at some stage, to be the chosen assassin of The Ten had left him in a state of nervous agitation throughout the whole journey. The crimes recorded against Bastian now ran into several pages. At least the evidence that he, Rezzonico, had taken back to the Chancellor after his first visit had resulted in the charges of witchcraft and consorting with the devil being dropped from the list of crimes. The Serenissima had a far more gentlemanly exit in store for Bastian, which fortunately for him did not require a bonfire in Campo San Polo, nor a one legged dangle between Marco and Todaro, nor a prolonged bloody siege of Scaligero Castle. In his satchel Rezzonico brought an invitation. Signed by the Grand Chancellor and witnessed by the Lord Bishop of Aquleia, as given under oath, it was a plea from The Ten for Bastian to return to Venice to oversee and organise the state funeral of Doge Francesco Morosini. On return for this great favour he would be permitted afterwards to take himself into exile together with the proceeds from the sale of his estates and chattels and with all civic debts against his name cancelled.

Bastian's Palladian villa, set picturesquely out of sight of the common gaze amidst the Soave vine slopes, was now boarded up and entrusted to the safe keeping of a much feared local bandit. The best pieces from his collection of sculpture, paintings, coins and hardstone cameos now littered the floors of the castle's modest sized staterooms. Bastian paced up and down amidst the packing cases, reading and rereading the terms of offer. Should anyone be foolhardy enough to do so, volumes could been written about the ever varied, ever devious methods used by The Ten to lure their victims; starting with the entrapment of poor Count General Carmagnola who gave his name to that 'strung out' dance. Yet, so far as Bastian was aware, Rezzonico had nothing whatsoever to gain by betraying him. That wealthy young nobleman, though of inferior pedigree, had proved himself a generous friend who had negotiated the best deal he could and had brought with him a genuine looking copy of the State Funeral Notice, which proclaimed to the public in the small print that the 'N.H. Sebastiano dei Giustiniani, nipote del Doge defunto, *(in other words Bastian nephew of the late Doge,)* would be responsible for the State Funeral arrangements and the distribution of alms to the poor thereafter. Another reliable source, an adolescent toff to whom he was particularly attached, had written with condolences and a passionate plea for his return to Venice, assuring him that he had seen the notices pasted up in the Doge's Palace and on the streets. The dates and times fixed for the Doge's funeral that 'Dearest Renato,' had mentioned in his letter, all seemed to correspond with Rezzonico's copy of the poster. Marcantonio Zustinian, Lord Bishop of Torcello, had sent news as well, that he was returning from Milan to take part in the Doge's Requiem. Marcantonio, he knew, would create outrage in the courts of Europe if anything unpleasant happened after the funeral to his depraved, heathenish, yet - 'Dearly beloved Cousin in God....'

In spite of all these assurances the cautious Bastian dithered for a whole day and a half. It was only when Rezzonico packed his bags with every intention of departing back to Venice that Bastian finally gave orders for his treasures to be smuggled via the secret tunnel into Soave Village, thence over the least frequented mountain passes in Austria. Certain of his alchemists, potters and glass blowers, with their tools and portable equipment, were to be conveyed under armed escort by the Lombardy route to France. Genuine French passport papers, with which he had been well supplied by Lorraine, would be drawn up, stating that the occupants of the carriages were in the service of the Duke of Orleans. By that same route and method Bastian had dispatched many a corrupted glassblower, not to mention numerous innocent little songbirds of Zorzi's age and talents, *(known as 'Nancy boys' because they were mostly dispatched to Nancy, the capital of the Duchy of Lorraine.)* Once his instructions was seen to be under way, he left with Rezzonico to make the cold and uncomfortable four day journey by horseback down slippery country tracks, and by barge when they could, then onwards through the final lock-gates of the Brenta Canal.

There were many opportunities for Bastian to rail at his fate while they were out of earshot of their escort. Shivering over the charcoal braziers in barge cabins; between bites at the meagre fare in country inns; and whilst sipping mulled wine at some ill lit corner table of a canal side tavern; Bastian railed and ranted. He lamented that his best intentions were always misunderstood whenever he tried to help the underclass. The ignorant and superstitious Senators who made up The Ten wished to burn him for a wizard, whilst he was practically the only philosopher doing serious research for the good of the Republic. His researches were near to bearing fruit. He was close to finding that elusive method of transmuting base metal to gold, not to mention discovering secrets of fine glass and fine white porcelain making. Soon they would hail him for the wealth and other benefits his researches would bring to Venice. He felt certain that a cussed and stubborn glassblower in his employ already knew more about such matters than he would concede. He had been obliged to put him painfully to the question more than once, in the interests of Venetian trade, and to threaten that the glassblower's family might come to harm, but he, Zustinian, would have his laugh on his detractors in the Senate. He would now rather go over to the Ottoman and take his experiments with him than let his fellow nobles profit from his discoveries. Amongst his other laments, which in truth Rezzonico had some sympathy for, came the extraordinary claim that a certain family of low born traitors living on the island of Murano had the answers to all his research problems. The solutions to all his furnace and glassmaking headaches had alrady been found and recorded in a book back in the times of his ancestor, Caesar Augustus Justinian, grandest of all Roman Emperors. That book was rightfully his as a direct descendent of the Emperor. A Greek friar had brought it to Venice at the time of the sack of Constantinople in 1455. Now, somehow, it had got into the grubby hands of a glassblowing family, a family of illiterate peasants who not only could not read it, but would have no clue as to where to obtain the rare earths and minerals needed for the recipes detailed in the book.

Though, to his great satisfaction, both Zustinian and Rezzonico had had their careers knocked permanently off course by their contact with Zorzi, Grand Chancellor Ballarin was still convinced that Bastian had either done away with, or imprisoned in Soave Castle the Podestà Francesco Capello. Capello must have known something even more incriminating about Bastian's activities than spying for Orleans, gelding boys of the lower class and collecting pornography. Somehow he still hoped that either with Zorzi and his book as bait for Zustinian, or perhaps through Rezzonico's terror about his Convent crime, he would get at the truth behind Capello's disappearance.

When that smouldering red poker of Messer Grande was held close to his eyes, Rezzonico confessed to a list of heinous crimes against the honour of the Serenissima, for some of which he was totally innocent, as the Grand Chancellor well knew. When the accusations were read out before the Magistrates to the Convents, who were present to witness his ordeal in the torture chamber, Rezzonico immediately realized that it was not the child Zorzi who had betrayed him. Who other than that venal, pebble-eyed midget, Zuseppina, knew the dates on which he had made his illegal visits to the Convent of San Zaccaria and the exact day on which he intended to spring his half-baked plan to elope to Austria with that pretty novice nun - Valenzia Gradenigo. Zuseppina was, he concluded, The Ten's planted spy in San Zaccaria. Her thick glasses, her seeming deafness and myopia were no more than an act to entrap any foolish noblemen who dared violate the holiest of all Venetian convents. Fortunately, the Magistrates and the Abbess herself did not want another great scandal like that which engulfed the Republic in 1614, when a certain Suor Laura Querini was sprung from the convent.

Rezzonico had reported on all that he had observed at Castle Soave. In the outer bailey there were three large beehive shaped glassblowing furnaces with separate fume stacks: two of these were in constant use, making bottles for the local wines. The Grand Chancellor was more interested however to learn that there were two modest sized pottery kilns positioned on steeply rising ground to the east of the castle. These kilns, used for high temperature experiments, were cleverly linked by firebrick tunnels which created a flaming up draught - raising temperatures in the top kiln to white heat. The former Romanesque Chapel had been converted into a laboratory and in the Great Tower of the Keep, there were more alchemy laboratories, well provided with contorted glass alembics and retorts for distilling rare liquids. Two men, he noted, worked long hours there in the cellar dungeon and were always shackled with leg irons. One of them was in his mid thirties, tall and thin with a hangdog expression: the other, a long bearded Greek, was in his late middle age. Both men were very knowledgeable about dye stuffs, metals and mineral compounds. Despite their leg irons, they seemed to be the managers of some twenty staff working the kilns and furnaces: yet they were guarded like criminals at every turn. An armed escort of bulli always accompanied them whenever they waddled out from their dungeon to resolve some problem with the stacking of the kilns, or some technical hitch in the glassmaking process.

 Of all the things that Rezzonico reported, the ill-treatment of these two workers was the only illegal act that he felt could be held against Bastian. No 'Witches' Sabbaths' were going on; no devil-raising orgies; no poisons were being brewed; other than those required for glassmaking, for dyes and for glazing pottery. The catamite-looking youths who lounged idly in fine clothes around the salons of the castle all seemed to be enjoying life and were there at their own volition. As a red-blooded lover of female beauty, Rezzonico found these ill-mannered juveniles of the lower orders quite repugnant: however, he had to put up with their company only at meal times. Bastian and his work team had certainly made remarkable progress with making fine hard lead glass, though not in commercial quantities - it all tended after a while to craze with tiny cracks when subjected to natural temperature changes. His alchemists had also created something that might well in Rezzonico's opinion make a fortune for the Serenissima: a yellowish and very hard form of pottery, a mixture of fine kaolin type clay from nearby Tretto and a frit of soapstone and mica rock from the Dolomites. Once given a milky white tin glaze, this product was almost indistinguishable from that imported at enormous cost from Far off Cathay. Knowing that both Chancellor Ballarin and the Convent Magistrates had private collections of Chinese porcelain, he suggested, in an ingratiating and repentant tone, that the whole of Bastiano's workforce and equipment might be transferred profitably to Bassano Town where there was even more expertise and a huge trained workforce of potters.

CHAPTER FORTY-SEVEN

Grandpa got window seats for the obsequies in St. Mark's Square: it would be Doge Morosini's second funeral - his first was in Saint Anthony's Basilica at Nauplia. There, it was just his innards and heart that, with much holy smoke and ceremony, were immured within an urn. Whilst embalming the Doge, with great quantities of myrrh to preserve him for his homeward journey, they found the four-ounce gallstone in his bladder that had caused his tragic end. So far as Christendom was concerned Morosini had the soul and the courage of King David of old. The Sultan however, rejoiced and went on his knees to Allah for sending that vengeful stone to bring down, like another Goliath, his infidel foe.

Bastian, as Master of Ceremonies, put on his finest ever show in honour of his late uncle. The entire processional route from the Piazzetta and all around the great square was covered with a blue and white canopy, supported with garlanded and flag decked poles. The bier passed beneath triumphal arches, and past large-scale painted scenes of Morosini's many acts of heroism. St. Mark's Basilica itself was adorned with a huge portrait in oils and Parodi's life-like bronze bust of the Doge was carried with solemn ceremony from the Palace and placed in front of the porch, framed with a green laurel wreath. The seemingly endless procession of silent mourners trudged to the slow and eerie beat of muffled drums, zigzagging its way four abreast up and down the Piazza and taking several hours to pass. Wrapped in his fur cloak, for there was that cold east wind of sorrow blowing, Zorzi marvelled at the twenty enormous siege guns, whose iron wheels and massive beamed trucks creaked and rumbled their final tribute to their once lord and master. But beyond doubt the most moving tribute came from the Arsenalotti - the Arsenal men. Barefoot and stripped to the waist in the bitter wind, they exercised their right to take turns in carrying the Doge from the deck of the Bucintoro to the portal of St. Mark's and then onwards - all the way to his Requiem in San Zanipolo and finally to his burial place beneath the nave of Saint Stephen's - the church next door to the Morosini palace.

Though orders came from The Ten that there should be no mourning weeds, no black arm bands nor drooping flags, no slow ringing of funeral bells, their decree was for the most part defied by the throng of witnesses. The Senators felt that this should be a day of celebration for Morosini's glorious victories and a tribute to his life as servant of the Serenissima. Nor did they deny popular rumours that he had died in battle, sword in hand at the head of his marines.

As was the age-old tradition, the warrior Doge was carried on an open bier four times around the Piazza and came four times to the door of the Basilica. Four times the Patriarch raised his crosier as though to deny him entry: for St. Mark's was the ducal chapel and only living Doges were permitted to celebrate there. Each time they hove to at the Basilica door, the assembled multitude held a deathly silence while the rough and ragged Arsenalotti raised his waxen corpse at arm's length towards heaven, shouting in heart-felt unison their prayer: "San Marco! San Marco! San Marco! San Marco!"

Tears were in every witnessing eye. With hushed sobs too, Zorzi mourned the passing of his own special friend. His twinkling-eyed, cat loving, old benefactor was now stiff and shrunken, in armour and ermine, resembling from the distance little more than a painted statue. He half hoped that San Marco would call down his welcome from the gathering winter clouds, in answer to that shouted invocation - but no sound came.

They had planned to follow the procession to the Requiem but there was now a multitude of tight press of bodies in the Piazza and hardly any movement at all in the narrow alleyways and on the bridges leading to San Zanipolo Church - all far too perilous for the young and for the elderly.

CHAPTER FORTY-EIGHT

From her armchair placed some two or three paces in front of him the Lady Olivia glared at him malevolently. Zorzi had never felt so ill at ease and so humiliated in all his life. Twice he had missed his cue and the group of madrigal singers and musicians were thrown into confusion. Luanardo, looking smart in his second hand wig, was now hissing at him in exasperation. There had been a pleasing and harmonious rehearsal in the Countess's music room up to the time when the younger Morosini, Gritti and Zustinian children entered. Sighting Zorzi amongst the players, they crowded around to greet him. Little Fatty Gritti had grown several inches in all directions since Zorzi had first observed his girth at the top of the stairs to the Loggia of St. Mark's. He was now as tall as Zorzi and welcomed him with a friendly embrace, as did several others who remembered Zorzi from St. Mark's. All had been told of the 'singing boy's' exploits with their great uncle's ducal ring and were warned that he was to be treated not as a servant but as an honoured guest. However, the atmosphere changed when the Lady Olivia, entered and caught sight of Zorzi in his stunningly embroidered Trevisan waistcoat, his blue silk stockings, silver trimmings and shoes of the finest black lacquered leather. Noticing that the contemptible little upstart was now far better turned out than she, or any of the other Morosini children, she stood at the back of the knot of children bristling in a pose of upright rage. She was every inch a scaled down version of her great aunt Morosina. Though still flat chested under her whalebone and satin stomacher, Olivia was already in the marriage market at thirteen and ready to flaunt her importance in front of some of the sillier young noblemen present. Her eyes narrowed and she let fly with juvenile venom: "And who precisely do you think you are?" she demanded... "A singing boy, an impostor, that is all you are! You have not bowed to me! You greeted my cousins as though they were equals. Bow down, singing boy and do not raise your eyes until I tell you to!"

It occurred to Zorzi, for the first time in his young life, that the age-old and commonplace ritual of bowing was in essence no more than what a dog does when putting its tail between its legs. It was craven show of humility in front of a threat from a superior force. He would not be threatened by a girl, no matter how mighty in rank she might be: "I'll bow if you curtsey!" he snapped back.

There were gasps of outrage from those who heard his reply and before servants could be called to throw him out and to give him a cuffing, Luanardo hastened forward to mumble an apology. Bowing low several times to the haughty young harridan, he stage whispered to Zorzi, "Bow down you little idiot. I have got a harpsichord to pay for. You will be the ruin of us all!"

Put like that, Zorzi had no choice but to obey. Already jittery and overawed by the importance of the occasion and by the splendours of the Morosini Palace decor, the other musicians hastily joined him, But Zorzi's bow was more of a crouch, for as ever on perfect cue, Makò made his entry to diffuse a tense situation. With good reason now to stay crouching, Zorzi gave the cat an affectionate tickle behind the ears and was rewarded by having his nose thoroughly licked. A Senator's wife then quietly ordered Olivia to go to her allotted seat and to stop making an undignified exhibition of herself. Olivia deliberately chose a seat right in front of Zorzi with every intention of being off-putting.

Unlike most felines, Makò was partial to the taste of rose water. Marcella had taken great trouble earlier in the afternoon to given Zorzi a perfumed scrub about the ears, face hands and neck. Fatty Gritti, still too young to comprehend all the fuss, walked over to join Zorzi. Cautiously, he too began to caress the Doge's cat - it was something he had longed to do. Like all the other children he had been scared off with tales of Makò s fiery temperament. Alas, an allergy to cat hairs caused the boy to begin to sneeze violently. His crouched pose combined to make him relieve the tension even further with a series of rude and most embarrassing reports, finishing with a belch loud enough to have graced a sultan's breakfast. Accustomed though he was to having his presence announced with salutes of musketry, Makò thought little of Fatty Gritti's efforts. He got up and walked away in mild disgust. The impertinent sparrows on the ballroom balcony now had Makò s full attention.

So it was in the midst of merry laughter that Grand Chancellor Ballarin entered the room with the Countess on his arm. Bringing up the rear of a small escort of gentlemen at arms and secretaries came the Cavaliere Martinengo. He was linked arm in arm to a regal looking lady of great beauty though nearing her middle years, who was unmistakably the daughter of the Countess. And yet there was something even more recognizable in her features: something that should have astonished Zorzi, but he completely failed to notice the lady; smarting still, as he was, with hurt pride and fidgeting with his song sheets. Lastly, Senator Trevisan made his entry with the ex slave Abele at his right hand.

Don Domenico Ballarin, Grand Chancellor of the Serenissima, surveyed the room. He noted with satisfaction that Bastian was present and that the only head not bobbing and bowing to him was that of the errant nobleman. A wiser man would have acknowledged the Chancellor's feigned smiling glance in his direction, with a bit of humility and at least a polite nod, but Bastian was not a wise man. He smirked, and made an overheard remark about Don Domenico's diminutive stature to his young male companion. In so doing he sealed his own fate. The Chancellor was 'on the skids' himself. His future was far from certain and Bastian knew that. Whoever was elected Doge within the next few weeks would bring with him his own entourage of favourites. Should the Querini or Correr families come to power, as many thought, then the Chancellor would be doomed for various interfering annoyances given them during his long years in office. It was not a time for anyone to make enemies by taking drastic action of any kind. Holed up with his disapproving, but ever protecting Aunt Morosina, Bastian thought that he could bide his time until he could buy favour with the next Doge. In that he was wrong too, for the wily Grand Chancellor of State had set up this very occasion - this Osella presentation - with the sole purpose of sending Bastian to his watery doom.

Holding the Osella in both hands to steady a nervous tremble, Abele made a beautifully composed and sincerely expressed speech, thanking Chancellor Ballarin and the Noble Trevisan for presenting it to him. He spoke of his long ambition to return to his beautiful native Nuer people, who lived amidst the reeds where a tributary of the River Nile meandered out of the marshlands. He described how his people took refuge in the marshes from the Arab raiders from the north who came regularly each season to plunder their crops and to enslave them. There was applause and nods of approval as he reminded those present that Venice herself had come into being in such dire circumstances, when their noble ancestors had sheltered in the marshy reeds of the Lagoon from Attila and his Huns. Now that he was a freed man and a full Citizen of the Serenissima and, under the terms of the Doge's will, a prosperous man, it was his duty to return and to defend his people. There was more applause as he spoke with tearful eyes of his Master: of how he had saved the Doge from being brained from behind with an iron mace in the fight on board a Turkish galley: how he had slid his oar out from its rowlock to trip up and hold down the Doge's assailant, thus giving the old warrior a few seconds time to recover and to slaughter all three of his attackers. He spoke of the Doge's gratitude: it was something a lesser man than Morosini would have overlooked in the confusion of battle. But the Doge had freed him from his bondage and had given him the choice of service with him, or money and freedom to return to wherever he wanted. At his own request and in gratitude, he had swapped the rusty galley slave's collar for a circlet of silver gilt provided by the Serenissima. He would wear that circlet with honour when he returned to his people, but for the time being would not flaunt it in the lands of the Sultan, through which he would have to pass, disguised as a rich merchant on his way to capture yet more unfortunate African slaves.

It was a thoughtful and sincerely expressed speech. Almost every word of it had been vetted and well rehearsed. Such minor details were never left to chance when The Ten were poised to pounce. In conclusion, Abele wondered, almost casually, what sort of gift he could give in exchange to the Serenissima for the great honour he had received.

"Unlike our handsome little rascal Zorzi here present," Abele added jokingly, "I am not a man of immense wealth and fine discernment. I have no library of rare books; no finely bound volumes of strange recipes to present, nor the ability to write a letter of thanks with such elegant handwriting."

Zorzi remembered that he had spent the best part of a week copying out that letter of thanks to the Doge, which Don Tranquillo, in his turn, had composed for him. Much to everyone's exasperation, he had wasted at least half a dozen sheets of Don Toma`'s finest rag paper in the process. Beautifully hand illustrated though it was, the book on the preparation and cooking of game had failed to inspire the culinary efforts of Fra Zeri, and Don Toma` was not too concerned at its loss from his precious library. The Doge's cooks would at least make good use of its recipes. However, Toma` had insisted that the ancient volume be bartered for

456

some winter blankets which Grandpa went to purchase at Rialto Marked and which Don Toma` distributed to the needy old folk of the parish.

In a loud enough aside to Zorzi, intended to be overheard by all, Abele added, "Don't worry Zorzi, you will get your precious volume back. Captain Zen will be going to fetch it with the rest of my Master's belongings at Bourtzi Castle that, in all the haste and confusion, I had no time to pack. Meanwhile see that Makò is well looked after."

Turning to the audience he raised his voice once again: "One of my Master's last wishes was that I should hand over Makò to the care of our young ring finder and it is evident that neither the Noble Countess, nor her curtains and chair covers are prepared to withstand another tomcat onslaught. As all of us know, once that tail begins to twitch, Makò transforms himself into a fearsome force - a miniature Lion of St. Mark! Give him another chance, young gentlemen here present: let him sail with you one more time and I promise you he will swipe that vile and insolent Hassan Messomorto's turban right off his head!"

With these 'bon mots' Abele bowed and sat down to a storm of stamping and clapping.

(Hassan was a Barbary corsair *who became Supreme Admiral of Sultan Ahmed's fleets. His Venetian nickname 'Halfdead' came from his miraculous recovery from injuries received in battle with the Doge's fleet.)*

CHAPTER FORTY- NINE

Zorzi's Wels catfish could not have taken the bait with more vigour. Later that evening Bastian drew Abele aside to confirm the nature of the book and its contents. Being semi-literate, Abele had not even bothered to look inside Zorzi's gift, nor for that matter had Doge Morisini. So many parting gifts had been shipped out to Nauplia with the Doge's personal baggage. As instructed, Abele simply reported that the book seemed to be no more than a dull list of recipes: of what he did not know. However, he confirmed with seeming innocence that His Excellency the Chancellor was anxious to have the book back, because it held important secrets useful to the trade of the Serenissima.

Repeated mention of his name by Zorzi now drew Captain Zen into Chancellor Ballarin's web. Zen was instructed to make casual aquaintance with as many as possible of Bastian's closest friends and to spread the happy news that at long last promotion from Captain to Galley Commander had come his way. His first cruise would be for the purpose of retrieving the late Doge's personal effects from Bourtzi Castle. This unexpected news caused Bastian to throw caution to the wind. He promptly sent Zen a most cordial invitation to a musical soiree in Ca` Granda. As an executor of his late uncle's affairs, the contents of the Ducal apartments both in Venice and in the castle at Nauplia were Bastian's to divide up amongst relatives, according to the Doge's testament. That meddlesome nuisance Domenico Ballarin, had no authority to appropriate any of it. The long sought Miotti volume would soon be within Bastian's grasp and with entirely legal right of possession. Should he fail to make neither head nor tail of its contents, he could always dispose of it to Orleans. The duke had scholars at the Sorbonne in Paris and decoders of every known script and language at his private disposal and Orleans would pay handsomely, as ever.

In the guise of an officer of marines, with a manservant in tow, Bastian was piped on board the war galley 'Vendetta.' Some three days out from Venice, Commander Zen signalled orders for his flotilla to shelter in a cove off the Island of Zante and to ride out an oncoming storm. Calm finally came with the dawn. Bastian wiped the condensation from his cabin windows and looked out. The flotilla had dispersed, yet his vessel was still riding gently at anchor stem and stern. There was nothing disconcerting in that: it was quite normal for small galley fleets to drift off on patrol and then to re-assemble for the onward voyage when visibility improved. He climbed back into his bunk, drew the blankets tighter around his fur lined overcoat and went back to sleep.

A slight commotion of running feet and sounds of clashing steel from the main deck woke him. Cocking both pistols he tumbled out of his bunk and went to draw the oilskin curtain that divided his poop deck cabin from the long run of middle deck boards. It was all too late. The convict oarsmen, half asleep, chained and slumped over their oars, hardly made a murmur of concern as the Uzkoks clambered on board. There were no officers on deck, no marines no pleasant young servant companion to fire a shot in his defence. To his credit, Bastian put up a fight worthy of a Venetian. Severely wounded by a successful jab in the abdomen with a boarding pike, he knew that there was no longer any alternative. Uskok women were notorious for their prolonged torments of any who fell wounded into their menfolks' hands. Grabbing tight hold of one of the heavy swivel guns mounted to the rear of his cabin, he hurled himself through the cabin window and into the icy waters. It was not the millstone promised by Jesus of Nazareth that took the Noble Bastian straight down to the abyss - just a plain brass cannon - but it fulfilled the Good Lord's promise.

CHAPTER FIFTY

The 'Broglio' leading up to the election erupted with much noise and minor scuffles each morning in the Piazza. Some two thousand who had the right to vote and to write N.H. (*Nobleman*) before their illustrious surnames milled about, dashed one another's wigs onto the wet paving, poked angry fingers at one another's chests, or danced in fury on one another's tricorn hats. Old enemies embraced with flamboyant gestures in new found loyalty, age old friendships were split asunder with bitter words and thousands of gold sequins slipped from hand to hand in attempts to buy votes in each round of the election. Not surprisingly the word 'embroil' still has its place in most European languages.

When the final round came, Querini and Trevisan, being the most senior Senators, were dispatched to the Basilica of St. Mark's. Their task was to choose a ten-year-old boy to distribute the final voting counters and to witness the addition and the result. It was a custom dating back a thousand years and a peculiarly Venetian way of involving the lower orders of society in the choice of the Doge. Packed to the doors with the well-washed and well turned-out sons of the citizenry, St. Mark's was a buzzing hive of pushing, shoving confusion. After struggling for several minutes to get through the doors, even the palace guard made little headway. It was then that Querini pounced on a pathetic urchin trying to sneak out through the crowd. The child let out a scream when the guards seized him. Bursting into tears, he dropped the little candles that he had filched from the offertory box at the shrine of the Byzantine Madonna of Victories. His sobbing excuse was that he was intending to light them in memory of his poor dead mum, when he was pushed away from the pay-box by the crowd. Pleading again and again not to be hanged, he then wet himself in utter terror. His pleas unlistened to, he was promptly bundled off to the Palace, for he suited to perfection the role required by Senate for such a momentious occasion. In his now thoroughly soiled sailcloth breeches he distributed the final voting tallies and brought about the election of the one hundred and ninth Doge of Venice.

CHAPTER FIFTY-ONE

In his second week of office the Doge limped his way gingerly down the Giants' Stairway on his way to afternoon Vespers. He had not quite perfected the sideways stepping that he needed to avoid taking an undignified tumble. Balancing the gem encrusted Corno over his wig; coping with the heavy cloak of state, which Morosini once twiddled and swished with such ease, and trying to look relaxed with the even heavier state sceptre resting on his arm: all were skills yet to be perfected. To his mild amazement, waiting at the foot of the stairs was the trim, purple silk clothed figure of Don Domenico Ballarin.

"What the devil!" he muttered to himself and averted his eyes hoping to pass by and ignore the ex Chancellor without incident. But then his common sense quickly brought him to the conclusion that Don Domenico Ballarin would not have risked neck and limb by straying into the web of his enemies without good reason. The ex Chancellor was ever a calculating man - one who made no move without covering his back. The 'Quarantia Criminal,' had brought about his suspension from office. The Doge knew that that the forty Procurators had sifted through every document, every accounts ledger, and every written denunciation that had passed through the capable hands of Chancellor Domenico Ballarin: so far they had found nothing to pin on him, not even the murder of Bastian, for the clever little man had it recorded in the minutes of The Ten, that he, the Grand Chancellor, had disapproved of that fateful decision. All feared that, once out of office, the Chancellor might become a magnet for the mettlesome war faction made up of Morosini, Foscari, Gritti and Giustiniani clans. Four of The Ten were for having Don Domenico quietly and quickly done away with. Typically, they were the Senators of the peace and appeasement faction, concerned only about their wealth being frittered away in war taxes. Don Domenico's digestion was notoriously poor and all knew that he dined alone on most evenings at an eating-house off the Piazza. In their plan, the unfortunate cook of that establishment would have to be intimidated into mixing the poisoned potion with something flavoursome. Alas, he would have to perish too, either by a dose of his own cooking or by being accused of Don Domenico's murder and promptly hanged. However, none of the inefficient four had bothered to send agents to check out the restaurant. Since his suspension from office, Don Domenico had taken the precaution of no longer eating in such close proximity to the Palace. Another four of The Ten had the better plan of sending Don Domenico on a peace mission to Istanbul. In his youth Ballarin had been on two previous peace missions, both of which had ended disasterously for his father, the former Grand Chancellor, Giobattista Ballarin. Far away in Istanbul, Allah's Caliph on Earth would show his infinite mercy and peaceful intentions by having ex Chancellor Domenico skinned alive and by demanding a ransom for his carcass. The remaining Senators were all for having Don Domenico reinstated, once it was proved that he had always acted in the best interests of the Serenissima. Only the seventeenth member of the full masked assembly in the Room of the Bussola sat hesitantly on the fence, or to be more precise, sat hesitantly on his throne. Feeling insecure since his unexpected election, uncertain of quite who to trust, the Doge sat shamefaced at his own cowardice. The Grand Chancellor had always played fairly with him, both at cards and during the election process.

When the ex Chancellor stepped out in front of him at the bottom of the stairs without so much as a bow and when, with a slight flick of his lace handkerchief, Don Domenico Ballarin sent the Captain of the Guard and the ducal escort of halberdiers pacing swiftly backwards up the stairs, the Doge was mildly outraged. When his angry eyes met with those of Don Domenico, the Doge had no doubts whatsoever about who held the 'ace hand' in the deck of deadly cards. The new Doge, it should now be remembered, was far and away the sharpest card player in the Serenissima.

"Most Serene Highness, a lady seeks audience of you. With your leave, I should like to introduce her."

"Not now, Ballarin. Not now! It is neither time nor place. You should know the rules: ladies should first seek audience with my wife, the Dogaressa." Out of force of habit, the flustered Doge then found himself addressing Don Domenico with his former title.

But Ballarin insisted: "I rather think, Serenissimo, that this particular lady would be the last person you would wish to have introduced to the Dogaressa."

It was then that the Doge noticed the young noblewoman standing in the midst of a small entourage of expensively dressed servants. She herself was veiled with fine lace entwined with silver thread - the veil of an engaged lady of high rank. If he needed further confirmation of her status, it took the form of an ermine cape and jewels beyond price about her waist, neck and wrists.

"I may be new to office Don Domenico, but I believe it is no part of my duty to approve, or disapprove, of marriages: if that is why the lady is here. I leave such matters to my good wife. Now out of my way - I am late for Vespers!"

"The lady's pedigree is not noted in the Golden Book - yet your Highness must approve her marriage all the same. Nor will she be recorded in the Golden Book, unless it is your desire to have her legitimized by the Vatican."

"You are talking riddles, Ballarin....Legitimised by the Pope? Explain yourself and then be off!"

"With some pleasure, Highness. Your approval of marriage will be necessary for the lady, who also begs your fatherly blessing." Don Domenico, solemn faced as ever, lowered his voice to a half whisper whilst dealing his 'trump card.' Raising his voice just so slightly once again, he added, "The lady desires to marry Don Francesco Capello Benzon, the former Podestà."

"Don Francesco, from Murano? Wasn't he taken by Uzkoks about a twelve month ago? You are mistaken, Ballarin. Have you fallen victim to some confidence trick? You, who are so worldly wise!"

"Let me be brief and introduce the lady concerned without further delay. I notice that your good Lady, the Dogaressa, is approaching along the upper loggia together with some of her court."

The ex Grand Chancellor's timing was perfect as ever. To a fanfare of silver trumpets the Dogaressa Bettina Querini Valier (alias Princess Topolina) was fast approaching her Baron Gorgonzaga (alias His Serene Highness Doge Silvestro Valier.) A nod in the direction of the veiled lady brought her hobbling forward and curtseying low to the Doge. She raised her veil.

"Graziella! How can it be? Bones of Saint Mark! It cannot be!" The Doge came close to collapsing on the steps.

Instinctively touching his arms to steady him, a gesture no other mortal would have dared attempt in public, Bianca whispered: "It's Silvestra, father... please call me that, for now I know I am your child." Lowering her veil on the instructions of Don Domenico and without a moment to lose, Bianca hobbled swiftly away.

"You were speaking to a noblewoman, Silvestro. Why did she not wait to be introduced?"

"Well...that is….well, let me see. The Grand Chancellor will explain," flustered the ashen faced Doge.

"Chancellor? There is nolonger a Chancellor, husband. To whom are you referring?"

Turning imperiously and puzzled towards the slightly bowing Ballarin, the Dogaressa commanded: "And you Don Domenico, I marvel at your temerity in presenting yourself at court uninvited! You have business here no longer."

The reply came swiftly and in a familiar commanding tone: "His Serene Highness is aware that I am here on matters of State - matters of confidentiality. The lady is a foreign visitor with important news from abroad: she is travelling incognito. She came also to pay her respects to his Highness before departing to her Sicilian estates - this very afternoon."

"Sicilian estates," snarled the rightly suspicious Bettina. "The Lady looked remarkably well festooned for one hailing from that arid backwater. Was she by chance a Bourbon, Silvestro, or one of those common courtesans certain people I know are so fond of? Much the same thing in my judgement!" From what I saw of her, she looked like one of the Morosini girls - only better dressed!"

Doge Silvestro Valier's ashen face now flushed with deep purple: "I thought it courteous not to ask of her family, Bettina. No... No... No relation at all to the Morosini! As the Chancellor explained to me, the noble lady wished to remain incognito and her news was a matter of concern only toThe Ten, so I may not discuss it at present."

All that now remained to be said, was said by Doge Silvestro. It was his first firm ducal decision - one of very few he ever made, for Bettina wore the breeches in that partnership: "My gratitude to you Grand Chancellor. I shall come to your office tomorrow at noon to discuss the matter." Turning to his escort he ordered in a newly found confident voice: "Officer of the Guard! Leave us to proceed alone. See that His Excellency the Grand Chancellor is escorted with all ceremony back to his office. Mount a full guard outside the Hall of the Bussola. Be at His Excellency's command and no other. Admit only those Senators with whom he wishes to consult!"

Suddenly, contemplating a swift and violent end to his reign at the hands of Cavaliere Martinengo, the Doge mopped the cold sweat from his brow and said: "Bettina, we must delay no longer, it is bad form to be late for Vespers. We don't want to get into old Morosini's habits!"

CHAPTER FIFTY-TWO

Fra Zeri was in an exceedingly cheery mood. His young replacement had arrived the previous evening and he had just cooked his last and most successful of breakfasts: boiled asparagus topped with fried egg, elegantly served with a slightly singed slab of polenta and a dash of dried origano powder. The bread oven had not played up, as it so often did. Only one of the fried eggs had ended up in the plug hole of the washing up sink, but he had retrieved it, given it a quick rub on his sleeve, added a liberal sprinkle of salt to disguise any foul taste and restored it to Don Toma`'s plate. Fra Zeri was on the move, back to his native town. There he would live out his retirement years, fishing in the mountain streams and singing off-key in the slumbering geriatric back rows of the Bassano Convent choir stalls. Don Toma` was on the move too, back to San Zanipolo Convent. From there he would take up his long desired post as Archivist in the Doge's library. It would be his reward - on condition that he kept his mouth tightly shut and his quill pen un-inked on the matter of recent events in Murano.

Don Tranquillo kept pausing, mopping his sweating forehead and giving vent to rather breathless sighs. Unable to fathom out what was wrong, Zorzi decided that he must have had some personal affection for the aged gentleman in whose memory the Requiem was being held, a glassblower who had died of burns several years previously and had left a few grossi for this annual memorial. The 'Dies Irae' with its resounding verses was sung at the conclusion of every Requiem. Now word perfect, Zorzi had learned from Luanardo how to wring every ounce of emotion from Celano's magnificently disturbing poem: to his satisfaction there were sobs and sighs and the fair certainty of an extra soldo or two from the mourners present. Pitching high notes in the right places, elsewhere lowering his tones to match the words of anguish, he got as far as '*Salva me fons pietatis*' then paused open mouthed in astonishment. Unchecked tears were glistening in the eyes of the steely old warrior. Zorzi had never thought Tranquillo capable of such emotion: smiles of true pleasure certainly or, on provoking occasions, perhaps a thundering glance of anger….but tears!

After breakfast Denis came in to the office to clear the table and to return Zorzi's by now almost forgotten satchel. There was hardly time to express

466

his excitement on meeting once again the novice friar and retrieving that amber necklace with its curious trapped insects when Don Tranquillo announced: "This afternoon Zorzi, you and Piero will be ferrying me to Fusina with some ladies. Be so good as to give a good clean to St. Peter-in-Chains....No fish heads, no worm bait, no nets to trip the Podestàs housekeeper. A servant will be travelling with us, a pleasant old lady called Lena. They'll have a fair bit of luggage for you to stow. No room for Elenca, but send her to me to me, I've something private for her ears. Keep the news to yourself for the moment: best we have no fuss in the parish. At Fusina we can say our goodbyes."

"Goodbyes, Don Tranquillo, Goodbye? I don't understand."

"I'm leaving, Zorzi. I've been sent to Verona."

"But you can't. I mean you are coming back, aren't you?"

"Sadly no. I travel by coach from Fusina: the ladies are in no hurry, they go by barge along the Adige route."

"Coach? That's not a good idea Don Tranquillo. Matteo's dad got shot at in a coach and then he was robbed by brigands."

Don Tranquillo's solemn face now lit up with a grin of knowing amusement. "There will be an escort of soldiers and if they can't cope with a few brigands it will be my Christian duty to give them a helping hand."

"Grief! Soldiers! Have you done something bad? They are not taking you to, that is ...to Verona Castle?"

"No, my little friend.... leastwise, I hope not! They are just a courtesy escort for someone who is now, so it seems, quite an important fellow. But don't worry about me, I am pretty certain there will soon be a very happy occasion when you can come and pay me a visit. Zeri tells me the Verona friars eat breakfast in silence and apparently the chewing there is so tough on the old gnashers that it's hard to hear the Lector's daily dip into the Gospels. I just can't fathom why they want me: I've never met even one of them. Someone wants rid of us all from here, that's for sure.

467

Politics, Zorzi, all politics! It's those unseen hands again. We are but pawns on a chequer board, being slid around by unseen hands!"
Anxious to get home with the terrible news, and feeling too stunned and upset to question Don Tranquillo further, Zorzi scraped the grizzled remains of the polenta into his satchel and without so much as a farewell to Denis, he scampered down the steps from Don Tranquillo's rooms for what might well have been the last time. The lumpy yellow mess, salvaged from force of habit rather than from need, oozed fried olive oil over signora Molin's amber necklace, but that was now the least of Zorzi's concerns.

On passing the high altar, instead of his customary swift and sliding genuflection, he paused to say fervent prayer to San Marco: "to protect his friend from the politics and from the 'unseen hands' and to keep the Don safe from brigands with long knives when travelling through woodland." It was Zorzi's reasonable assumption that 'the politics' and the 'unseen hands' where the equivalent of Uzkoks on the Verona highway: if not, they could quite possibly be a deadly disease rampaging in those parts. It was reasonable also to assume that San Marco's protective net would extend at least as far as Verona, which was, after all, a Venetian city. Grandpa had received the sad news a day or so previously, but had kept it to himself. After Grandpa's long explanation of what was going on, Zorzi concluded that 'the politics' were more or less the same as the practice of bowing - a way of bending another person to one's will.

CHAPTER FIFTY-THREE

From their ancient fortress palace the Capello (Capulet) clan and their guests rode out in their hundreds. They processed through the town with drummers and fifes and banner wavers and garland bearers and numerous ornate carriages protected by halberdiers in parti-coloured uniforms. Swarming through the magnificent pink portal of the Dominican Cathedral of Sant'Anastasia they swiftly covered the entire floor space in the great nave with their embroidered kneeling cushions. Prominent amongst the guests was the N.H. Emo in his scarlet robe. Luanardo Emo was the newly appointed Podestà of Murano and in his own appointed place in the choir stalls was Zorzi.

Zorzi had travelled by barge and carriage to Verona in the company of Emo's servants. Earwigging on their conversations, the only news of real interest that he learned was that the Countess Morosina derived her title from a French husband who, relieved of her overbearing company, was enjoying his declining years wrapped in furs and star gazing: making calculations from a watch tower that he had built on one of his estates. As well as a telescope on his tower top, the Count had a large mortar cannon trained on the moon. The cannon blasted off from time to time in the depths of night, violently awaking and terrifying the peasantry and gentlefolk of half the county. So far, his astronomical efforts had been rewarded with limited success, though he was quite convinced that at least one of the craters was a direct hit of his own making and marksmanship. When not engaged in peppering the moon, the Count was busy writing and re-writing a learned paper on his ballistic blastings for the enlightenment of scholars and lunatics and of course for the French artillery. Zorzi had the sense not to name drop, nor to make much of his newly made noble connections when in the company of Podestà Emo's servants. Had he done so, they might well have shunned him and turned his journey with them into a misery. Emo's clever butler however was most amused when told that the Countess had come to Trevisan's ball dressed as Diana. His comment: that given the old Count's hobby, it would be wise for Zorzi to keep clear of the Morosini palace until the Countess reinforced her roof, left our hero rather puzzled; but he thought it impolite to ask the Podestàs butler for further explanation.

Bianca had sent wedding invitations to many of her former pupils and friends on the island, all but one of which were intercepted by the Chancellor's clerks. It was Ballarin's decision that all memory of Bianca and of her future husband, the former Podestà Capello, should quietly fade from Venetian memory. That decision formed part of a long and complex deal Ballarin made with Bianca's real father - that philandering card-sharp, the newly elected Doge Valier.

In the marriage register Bianca would soon signed herself as Bianca, Baronessa Roccella Valdemone, daughter of Marquis and Prince Domenico Spadafora, Peer of the Realm of Sicily. Doge Silvestro Valier was so evidently Bianca's natural father that it was useless to deny it, yet concealing her parentage from both the Querini and Morosini clans was essential to his own survival. As for her other parent - who so promptly dumped her baby at the Incurabile Orphanage to avoid the wrath of her illustrious family - Chancellor Ballarin had seen Bianca's mother often enough at court, on the arm of Cavaliere Martinengo!

The Dogaressa, Bettina Querina was not the sort of woman to permit a rival on her patch. Once seated firmly on her Parodi throne she had arrived at a feminine solution to the problem of disposing of Chancellor Ballarin into retirement. By appointing him to the honorary post of Inspector General of Overseas Territories, he would nolonger be available in Venice to serve as focus of opposition to her imperious rule. Any thought of progressing Ballarin from kinghthood to nobility as a reward for his near thirty years of service as Grand Chancellor was out of the question. The Ballarin family was not of the Golden Book of ancient nobility, they were descended from a humble glassblower, also called Zorzi, from Dalmatia, who began his brilliant career in the Barovier Factory.

Though Doge Valier would never acknowledge Bianca as his daughter, fatherly pride demanded that she too should have a title - better a foreign title- and would have need of a quiet and distant country estate. No better estate was available on the market than that of the late lamented hero - the N.H. Bastian Zustinian. There would of course be the additional expense of a memorial chapel somewhere in Soave village dedicated to: N.H. Sebastian dei Giustiniani, who fought and died so valiantly, defending his nation against the invading Ottoman.

Having been one of those Senators who voted for Bastian's watery death, Doge Valier coughed and chuckled at the proposed lettering on the memorial slab, but he willingly paid for it! It was a nice touch, reconciling both the Giustiniani and Morosini to the knockdown price offered for Bastian's delightful Palladian Villa and Soave vinyards.

In exchange for a pension and a written guarantee from The Ten that he would be free from all blame, persecution or inquiry, Ballarin set to work covering up the new Doge's youthful misdeeds, making arrangements for Bianca's ennoblement and marriage and procuring the essential baronial patents and religious certificates before she could have a proper church wedding. The Benzon were an ancient and haughty clan and Capello hat feathers too would have been crumpled by a marriage of one of their leading members to a skivvy of unknown parentage. The latter problem could have been overcome by applying to the Vatican: for the only man on earth with the remarkable gift of expunging the stigma of bastardy was the Pope. His Holiness however, would have expected first to study the evidence, at least in the form of a birth certificate with the name of one genuine parent - so that avenue to Bianca's legitimacy was out of the question.

The Chancellor's method of aquiring Bianca's barony can only be described as a lasting tribute to his administration, for having achieved so much in this world, Grand Chancellor and Knight Domenico Ballarin obtained his heavenly reward just four years into his retirement. With his written guarantee from The Ten well publicised about court, Ballarin had nothing more to lose personally. Being a man who had both a passion for tying up loose ends and a delight in poetic justice, he struck out with all his thoroughness and brillance for the very last time as Grand Chancellor of the Serenissima. His last delicious piece of mischief was to restore to Bianca a title that she might well have inherited.

Having been informed that Marquis Spadafora was in need of cash, gunpowder and weapons with which to pursue a slight dispute with one of his good neighbours, the Chancellor sent his agent to Sicily. Prince Spadafora was something of a volatile character. It was known to the Chancellor and just a tiny few at the very highest level of Venetian aristocracy that he was a wife beater. Domenico Spadafora weighed-in at near nineteen stone of feudal ferocity. All his impetuous actions were inclined to send shock waves throughout Sicilian society and that was the last thing Cancellor Ballarin wanted. Therefore he sent his Sicilian agent with most careful and detailed instructions on how to proceed:-

Thus it was that Archpriest Risicato, of the little town of Rocella Valdemone on the slopes of Mount Etna, fell to his knees, reduced to sobs and tears and prayers to the Good Lord, when a heavily armed band of ruffians drew up outside his church of Saint Nicolas. They carried instructions from the Bisop to dismantle the famous Gagini side altar of the Nativity and carry it off for re-erection in Messina Cathedral. The Gagini sculptors were once considered to be the Sicilian equivalent to Michelangelo and Leonardo combined. Their masterpiece of a side altar had long been a place of artistic pilgrimage and offerings at the shrine were the poor priest's only source of income. The colourful thugs, who looked as though they had just stepped out of a painting by Salvator Rosa, had masons' tools and two huge ox wagons with them. But not to despair – Marquis Spadafora came gallopping to the rescue. He happened to be riding in the neigbourhood and was desirous of showing off Gagini's splendid scuptures to his foreign friend, a Venetian. There was also the small matter of a Birth Certificate for his 'daughter' as well as a Confirmation Certificate. No need for the priest to look it all up in his parish register, the Venetian gentleman had all her details right down to his 'daughter's' unfortunate affliction of a limp. The Archpriest dried his tears and wisely took the hint: then he suddenly remembered with startling clarity the newborn baby baroness whom he baptised some months back - that is of course many years ago, a charming little new born baby who walked with a limp – a very distinct limp – quite a miracle indeed! She was such a beautiful child, who could forget her, with true aristocratic Spadafora blond hair and blue eyes: well… no…more correctly both hair and eyes were brown, distinctly brown with ginger hints – that is the hair, not the eyes.

With a dramatic shout of "Fora!" and an even more dramatict brandishing of his sword, the Marquis promptly drove off the ragtaggle band of ruffians. The villagers took up their overlord's battlecry of "Fora! Fora!"*(Out! Out!)* though it must be said that even the lumbering oxen dragging away the great haycarts seemed well resigned to this outcome. Marquis Spadafora left with his Venetian guest and with the applause and blessings of the entire community ringing in his ears and further loyal

472

shouts of "Fora! Fora!" However, before his departure, the thoughtful Marquis reminded the Archpriest that a candle light would most likely tip over in the vestry that evening, causing a small fire that would consume one particular volume of parish records. With great sadness, the Marquis also reminisced for a while on the terrible accident that had occurred some months back to the parish priest of nearby Randazzo. Tragically, whilst cleaning his baptismal font, that kindly, but so unfortunately slack mouthed and gossipy priest fell head-first in and drowned!

Zorzi thought Bianca looked gorgeous in her scarlet and gold gown: besides being the traditional colours of a bride, they were appropriately chosen - the red and yellow of the Valier arms. As she advanced towards him veiled and guided by ex Chancellor Ballarin, Zorzi decided that if only he were eighty or so years older, like the bridegroom seemed to be, he would have willingly married her himself. Luanardo's choir sang an anthem in welcome. Occupied though he was in modulating his voice for the higher notes of his solo piece, Zorzi could not help but notice a familiar gem encrusted hilt of a court sword. He had last seen it, as well as the elderly gentleman wearing it, from close-up, whilst on board the Bucintoro. The two figures, 'godfather' and Doge's daughter seemed to float up the aisle as though engaged in a dance. The dapper elderly and appropriately named balletic knight was guiding Bianca by her finger tips at arm's length, because of the width of her skirts. Zorzi wondered to himself why it was that Bianca had worked so hard as a schoolmarm when she had a godfather who, when first observed on board the Bucintoro, had seemed almost as important as Doge Morosini.

Tranquillo celebrated the nuptial Mass with that very satisfying combination of pomp, drama, magnificence, glittering robes and clouds of incense that only the Latins can summon up at an instant, without need for rehearsal. Fat Luanardo, now Chapel Master to the His Excellency the Illustrious and Most Reverend Lord Tranquillo, Prior of Verona, was resplendent in red slippers comfortably shaped around his bunions, a tall white wig, and silken beribboned cassock hand tailored to his increased girth.

In a long 'thanksgiving' at the end of the Mass, the bridegroom, ex Podestà Francesco Capello Benzon, spoke of his happiness after a time of trials: trials which he was careful not to specify. (Those trials had

included two months in the shivering dungeon of Can Grande's Castle
Prison, by the bridge of Verona, where he was 'banged-up' for insurance
purposes by his future 'godfather-in-law,' immediately after news broke
of Doge Morosini's death. The ever-scheming and now ex Grand
Chancellor had the habit of keeping his 'Insurance Policies' safely under
jailer's lock and key.) Don Francesco rambled on in his oration, thanking
the Noble Prior Tranquillo who had always supported him in his hour of
need and praising the important official who had helped resolve the slight
misunderstanding over the exact ending date of his 16 month term as
Podestà of Murano. (That again was crafty Chancellor Ballarin, who had
released him from the Verona cell after he had 'done a deal' with the new
Doge and Ten to save both their necks.) With all the sermonizing, Zorzi's
attention began to wander, first to the marble floor, then to the carved
choir stalls, then to the frescoes painted high up in the vault of the
Pellegrini Chapel to the left of where he was standing. There were city
walls, a procession, the gruesome scene of a man hanged by his twisted
neck and there was San Zorzi, his own patron saint, in splendid armour
and old knights and damsels and castles and things! Why, it was so
obvious; this was the same artist who had done the wonderful wall
paintings in Lucia's ivy clad ruin of a villa! He remembered too that the
Countess had not yet returned his bits and pieces, nor that bit of a funny
'Horseman of the Apocalypse' belonging to Aldo. Aldo was annoyed
about that. He would have to summon up courage to go and see the
Countess and ask for them back. There was no need to make an excuse
for such a visit for he was obliged from time to time to assure her that
Makò was still alive. Her generous provision for cat food, some ten
ducats per annum also had to be pocketed. Besides, the big Cavaliere,
Uncle Ettore, had promised him a real fencing lesson next time he came
visiting with the cat. He would need to know how to handle weapons, like
the armoured Saint Zorzi up in the fresco, if he were ever to carve a
career as a galley captain.

He came to from his reverie with a sharp nudge from Luanardo,
"Recessional hymn, boy!" Now that he was secure in his grandiose job of
'Maestro di Cappella,' fat Luanardo was becoming once again a bit of a
bossy boots.

The bride and groom arrived at Ca` Capello an hour or so before the
wedding breakfast, accompanied in their carriage by Prior Tranquillo in

his ceremonial vestments. While the seemingly interminable line of guests was greeted Zorzi sang love madrigals, amongst them was Caccini's 'Amarilli' and that re-evoked sad memories of a lost wife and of a beautiful seven years old daughter. To Don Francesco's graceful young bride it brought back grim images of musket smoke, of trails of blood, of screams and shouts and of the perilous events that came directly after, perils that were still not entirely resolved by her wedding. Zorzi's performance continued with 'Idolo del cor mio', yet another beautiful if somewhat forlorn sounding Monteverdi love song. Thereafter he cheered everyone up with his and Luanardo's repertoire of rude and raucus 'barcaroli.' At the end of the recital, just when he had squatted comfortably on the floor to marvel at the clowns, the acrobats, the lady contortionist and the fire jugglers who were assembling for their performance, Zorzi was called away into a side room. There stood Don Licini in his braid trimmed lawyer's togs and and Prior Tranquillo looking absolutely magnificent in his gem encrusted cope of ancient splendour. Zorzi guessed what they were going to say and wanting to get back as quickly as possible to the acrobats, anticipated their warning: "Nobody knows I am here Don Licini, I promise. Grandpa told me not to talk. I've said nothing to everyone, that is, to no one, not even Aldo, not even old Piero. They all think I'm away singing for Senator Zianni."*(Giovanni Trevisan.)*

Taken aback somewhat, for he had prepared a long fatherly warning about possible dangers should certain people in Venice get to know of Bianca's whereabouts, Don Licini decided that flattery rather than counsel was his best recourse: "Zorzi, you had already proved worthy of our confidence. You did not gossip to servants. They didn't even know you were the boy who caught the Doge's ring. Well done! Tight lips are essential to a future galley commander."

"Don Licini, could I ask, only I won't tell anyone. Are the 'unseen hands' more dangerous than The Ten. Have you seen the 'unseen hands' Don Licini?"

Completely flummoxed by the question, Tranquillo intervened: "When we talk of unseen hands Zorzi, what we really mean is some unknown power. You see, the Baronessa Bianca may still have problems, maybe coming from more than one unseen hand."

"So you can't really tell how many there are, 'cos you can't see them?"

"Indeed Zorzi. But I don't suppose they are more than two or three and the less we talk the fewer they will be."

"Good then, Grandpa was wrong. It can't be The Ten then, 'cos they have twenty."

"Twenty?" queried Licini. He paused, scratched his head, then laughed out loud: "Ah! Yes of course, I must tell that one to Baronessa Bianca. I shall compliment her too on educating such a profound mathematician. Perhaps we should be offering you a professor's chair at Padova insead of a leaky galley!"

A handful of grossi was all that was needed now to seal up the lips of the little song bird.

"Off you go Zorzi. I've got to get out of my vestments. I don't want to spoil them with burnt polenta, now do I? Oh! And Zorzi, there is going to be a talking monkey as well as fire eaters after the wedding breakfast. A real talking monkey who tells jokes and asks for fruit: how your pa would have loved to see one! Watch its trainer's lips though. Surprizing what can be done when lips are sealed up tight!"

As Zorzi scampered away, content with his handful of silver, Tranquillo turned to his companion: "You know Licini, I reckon even that monkey keeper could learn a trick or two from Ballarin. He is the absolute master of the art of putting words on the mouths of others."

Thus it was that both Bianca and Don Francesco were able to start life anew in Bastiano's fine Palladian Villa, with its picturesque view of Soave Castle in the hilly distance. All record of the happy couple was erased by the new Podestàfrom the archives of the Island of Murano.

CHAPTER FIFTY-FOUR

Fish and glass now seemed to turn into cash with much less effort than they once did in the Miotti household. Gleaming ducats were being banked at Rialto to ensure that neither Zorzi nor Elenca would be constrained to swelter at the furnace doors in future years. Cousin young Daniele, who had glassmaking in every sinew of his sturdy body virtually took over production, leaving Grandpa leisure to fish and to design a new range of colourful wine cups and cruets which were much sought after by Northern European visitors to Rialto Market. Young Daniele had a prodigious appetite only matched by that of his pal Denis. There were few evenings when Denis did not dine with the family: an arrangement that suited the thin and abstemious Don Anselmo, the new and rather aloof Dominican priest at St. Peter Martyr's, who never joined them. Grandpa would have willingly taken on Denis as an extra pair of lungs in his glassworks, but he knew that any attempt to lure the novice friar away from his devotions would cause great offence to the Dominicans. Knowing that Denis had a way of charming and disarming belligerent nuns, Zorzi asked him during supper one evening if he could weave his spell on Sister Tecla, the dragoness who stood guard at the door of Saint Mary of the Angels where little Lucia was being held. Lucia had only been seen once since she entered the convent. Marcella had been invited to her first communion ceremony and had found her neat and well fed, but looking pale faced, depressed and listless in her movements.

The friends: Elenca, Aldo and Zorzi had made numerous attempts to see her, all of which had ended disastrously. Zorzi's inventive plan to supply Lucia with rosary beads made of coloured sugar was turned down flat by signora Zanetti of the sugar shop, even though it was an order coming from a valued customer. The giant Eldeniz suggested that they try to pass off a 'Doge's pistol' prayer book as a real one and to have it parcelled and delivered from the shop with a message. This seemed a splendid notion and might have succeeded had not Zorzi's note been so badly written that Lucia took it to the dragoness for translation. It read: "Lucia you mast be hattin it with fat ole nones there an all that rune away wen the cruch door is opin an we wil hid you louv Zorzi Elenca Matteo an Aldo."

When the hairy faced and broad beamed old nun stormed into the shop and demanded not only an apology but also a full refund of the value of

477

the sugary confection, signora Zanetti was embarrassed before her customers. Elenca and Zorzi were banned from shopping there. Eventually, Eldeniz made the peace between his employer and the children. Elenca was, understandably, by far his favourite visitor to the shop. The tall 'bashi-bazooker' in his strange outfit and the diminutive Elenca held long soulful conversations together in a mysterious language, further intriguing customers and rather annoying Zorzi. Whenever he questioned Elenca about what was said between them, she would only reply, "Bad things done to us and to our families....only bad things. You would not understand. Such bad things....I cannot speak."

Makò was Denis's suggested solution. Being close to the market midden, next door to a rice and wheat wholesaler and never being short of candles to nibble on, Santa Maria degli Angeli was running a close rival for vermin with the legendary Brunswick town. The bearded nun was quite terrified. Finding one day that she was sharing a confessional box with a rival, a particularly whiskery black rodent, she had leapt out in such tearful hysterics that the priest was half convinced that she had just committed a dreadful sin; a sin so mortal that she could not bring herself to confess.

Makò was the best companion when you went to visit the privy in the black of night and the slaughter of a mere confessional box rat would not weigh too heavily on his catty conscience. So it was that, with Aldo in tow, they moored the 'topo' against the jetty opposite St. Mary of the Angels and approached the unfriendly looking 'Daughter of the Charity of Saint Augustine' who was working at a piece of bobbin lace in the shade of the church porch. On demanding their business there, Aldo explained to her that Makò was greatly attached to little Lucia and that they would happily leave him with Lucia for a day or so, if they were allowed to talk with her for a while. Before any deal could be struck with the suspicious nun, Makò shot out of Elenca's arms and disappeared into the darkened church. They all piled in after him, calling aloud for him to come to heel. When the puffing and remonstrating nun finally drew back the sun blinds from the upper windows, there was Makò silently occupied in mangling the remains of a large black and revolting rodent. From the still twitching corpse blood trickled onto the gleaming white marble of the high altar steps. Horrified, but nevertheless greatly impressed, the nun agreed to fetch Lucia, on condition that the boys should clear up the mess with the sawdust and water that Lucia would be instructed to bring. But before she had time to retreat to the safety of the sacristy, Makò gave a deep throated snarl and scampered off again. Within as many seconds he had flushed out two much more sizeable specimens, one of which turned to attack him with an angry squeak. Makò was not the creature to submit to such impertinence. His talons had been honed amidst the spars and the high pulley blocks. Few tomcats could rival his success rate in speed chases along the ratlines of storm tossed galleys, or whilst neck deep in foul bilge water. It was his opportunity to treat the delighted children to a display of aerial acrobatics. Repeated exclamations of "Merciful God!" and "Saints in Heaven preserve us!" came from Sister Tecla while she tried to avert her eyes - yet still could not resist peeping. Pouncing from on high and with a graceful balletic twist of his body and tail, Makò swiped downwards. Slaughtered instantly, the impudent rat was sent slithering across the nave. The other less heroic specimen only made it halfway up a barleysugar type spiralling altar column. Then Makò disappeared and so did Sister Tecla, though she went through the sacristy door.

From behind a side altar, that was overmantled and adorned with a magnificent painting, the children could hear squeals and scuffling. The alabaster altar table with its elaborate wrought iron front grille and its brightly cleaned painting was detached from the wall by the space of two feet or so; a sensible practice which ensured the survival of so many great works of art, that otherwise might have rotted away in the humid climate of the Lagoon. Poking his head around the back of the altar, Zorzi called again to Makò . There was no response, only the occasional rat squeal. Then a tiny ratling ran out between the children's feet. Zorzi stepped back laughing, almost colliding with Aldo who was gazing upwards with a surprised look. "I guess Makò is too busy to answer," Zorzi commented, "Bet he's found a nest in there."

It was then that Aldo then gave him reason to be puzzled: "Take a look at the picture, Zorzi! Do you see anything odd?"

"Nothing special… it's by Bellini… who did our Peter Martyr….you know, the one with the the meat chopper stuck in his head."

"A Bellini? Here? You are kidding! Only Doges have Bellinis….reckon

479

you're an art expert now!"

"No, but I can read. You can't. It says there under the Madonna - Giovanni Bellini 1482."

Remembering that curious episode when Elenca screamed and fainted in Don Tranquillo's office, Zorzi added: "And I tell you something else; my father cleaned and mended it, that's how I know about it. Fra Zeri told me it was here…. He knows all about paintings and things. My Dad mended this one before he died….so my Dad would have gone straight up in heaven for mending this one as well….that's what Zeri told me…so that's for sure."

"Stumped for a smart reply that would not offend Zorzi's cherished image of his lost father, Aldo could only insist: "Look again Zorzi… recognize something?"

"Can't say I do…there's a Doge kneeling to the Madonna; then a peacock; a balcony; another beardy old bishop holding up his book; a castle on a hill; some angel heads with wings… O hell!" exploded Zorzi, "Just like my Soave bottles! Look at the towers…exactly the same! And look, an angel girl with a fiddle and another one with a mandolin!"

"Exactly, Zorzi…. your bits of bottle!"

"So, someone at the Soave furnace must be trying to copy this picture. You are dead right Aldo. How very odd…. must tell Don Tranquillo. Oh dear! I can't do that anymore! Better not say anything to Grandpa though, Aldo, he will only pinch my bits for cullet."

Elenca pushed past them. She called once more to Makò and then squeezed herself into the confined space beneath the altar table. Grabbing Makò by the scruff of his neck she emerged and said: "Wicked devil cat…. he kill them all, even little mouse ones. He play games. Some little one…. half kill, half live."

Makò, exceedingly annoyed at being interrupted in the middle of a successful hunt, squirmed out of her grasp, made to scratch her and bolted back behind the altar again.

"Big treasure box inside.... I fetch it....We look inside, yes, no?"

"I'll get it." Zorzi insisted, "I'll tease Makò with the rat. He'll come back out like a shot.You'll see!"

Tossing the baby rat for Makò to chase into the middle of the nave, Zorzi dragged out an old copper green metal candle box covered in rat droppings and cobwebs. Not really wanting to touch it further, he gave the hasp a deft kick and then slowly opened the lid with the point of his clog.

"Why bless me with a scrubbing brush!" exploded Aldo, "if it isn't the one in the picture! Look at the leather cover! It's the book that the saint in the mitre is holding."

Undoing the brass and leather thongs holding together the magnificent bookbinding, Zorzi flicked through its pages - whilst groans of disappointment came from all around. No Sinbad, no colourful bestiary monsters, no grizzly slaughterings of saints and martyrs, no galloping knights and castle walls being besieged - there was not a vellum page that looked in the slightest bit interesting - all faded ink and lists of things unreadable - all most uninteresting for a volume that had been coveted and sought-after by the rivalling economic powers of Europe for well over two hundred years.

"No pictures... hymnbook, I reckon," announced Zorzi greatly disappointed. "Nice cover. Reckon these gemstones on the cover are just glass! You are right, Aldo. It does look just like the book in the picture. We had best put it back. Expect it belongs here with the Bellini...some sort of relic, I guess."

"Greek," announced Elenca, looking with some interest over his shoulder, "I can't much read Greek.... many book like it in my zenana. I can't read it. No... not hymns...sums...lot of sums, lot of...of places names. Look here!" she pointed proudly a some of the text that she could read: "Bursa, Constantinople, Trebizond! When they capture us, kill our men, Uzkoks! With book like this, they burn house....make me light up galley-stove with book like this."

481

"Do you think Eldeniz might be able to read it, if we show it to him?" Aldo asked.

"Eldeniz no Greek he read. He Greek, but he only talk Turkic. I talk him Turkic."

"Better put it back," advised Aldo. "The hairy nun will think we want to pinch it."

Though sorely tempted to keep it to show to the nun, Zorzi decided to drop the volume back into its thick copper box and to stamp down the lid before stowing it once again beneath the alabaster altar. He brought out the half dozen or so limp and pink fleshed ratlings and the last of the big black ones and lined them up neatly in order of size on the altar steps: convincing evidence of Makò s taloned talent. The bearded Sister Tecla was mightily relieved; furthermore, she was overwhelmed with the revelation that she had been honoured by a visit from Doge Morosini's very own cat. To her, Makò s presence was little short of a miraculous apparition. With good reason, she was concerned that the far more worthy bones of the great Doge Venier, victor of the battle of Lepanto, whose monument was the church's greatest treasure, were being gnawed at by rats. She had been praying, it must be said with little fervour, for Doge Morosini's soul for many weeks past. Makò s intervention with the rat problem was sufficient proof, if further proof were needed, that her prayers still held serious clout 'up there.'

Yielding place to no mortal on earth, the diabolical old Doge had qualms nevertheless about his exact status in the hereafter. He had therefore ordered in his will that astonishing heaps of ducats be set aside for the repose of his soul: ten thousand Masses, no less, were to be sung so that his spirit might not wander downwards to a hotter place; stained as it was with much blood of his fellow men. Funds for two hundred of those Masses were handed to the chaplain of St. Mary's. The orphans and the Daughters of Saint Augustine had therefore done well out of the Doge's last bequest.

Lucia then entered carrying a box of sawdust and a broom. She looked in fair health and it was evident from her glowing smile that she was happy with her new situation. She spoke of many new friends amongst the orphans. As a consequence of the fall she had now lost mobility in her arm: she could hold things close to her side but nothing more. But there were compensations: she was now in charge of the laundry. Other youngsters did all the hard work and all she had to do was to starch a few ruffs and to keep an account of the linen as it came and went. Reading the adventures of Don Quixote and of the grisly lives of the saints and martyrs of old, was now her preferred pastime. She could now read music as well, something Zorzi had not yet fully mastered. He still found it easier to learn lines by rote and to follow Luanardo from memory, inventing his own vocal ornaments as he went. Lucia was eager to hear about their escapades in the wide world outside her cloisters; however it was evident that she had lost all desire to leave her comfortable life with the nuns and to return to her miserable former existence, sleeping on the floors of taverns and scrounging and sometimes stealing where she could. The rowdy games of football and the hare-brained adventures she would leave to them. Visits from Makò and his escort of polite and well behaved friends were from then on always welcomed by the bearded nun.

CHAPTER FIFTY-FIVE

When a bankers draft for twenty ducats arrived, signed by Podestà Emo, Zorzi thought he would be spared the ordeal of attending any more at Palazzo Morosini to collect his cat fees. On every past occasion the contemptuous Olivia had gone out of her way to make him bow to her, after which she would do her best to make him feel as welcome as a polecat in a perfume parlour. However two days after the arrival of the draft, Don Zianni Maria Licini appeared 'out of the blue' in the downstairs parlour. The newly appointed Notary of the Serenissima had kept a close eye on Zorzi's safety and wellbeing since that Sensa evening in the Lido tavern when he had first questioned the boy. Licini came masked and with only his armed gondolier as escort. A bowl of crème caramel came with him, as a present to Zorzi and it seemed just a social visit, until he mentioned that he would like Zorzi to teach his sons, Primo and Arnoldo, to sail and to swim somewhere safe and he would like them to join in football games, from time to time, without being picked upon by young 'bulli' in the making. Zorzi assured him that with Aldo's rock hard fists to count on, no one would dare offend the twins. Licini seemed content with these arrangements and then added that his twins were being instructed in fencing at the Morosini Palace by no less an expert than a noble lady, who was also a 'close friend' of the Cavaliere Martinengo. Zorzi, therefore, might like to pay his respects to the old Countess, who was far from well. Zorzi was puzzled, for he had always imagined that the Countess and the Cavaliere were a married couple, but he thought it impolite to ask for an explanation from Licini. There, in the armoury at Palazzo Morosini, with Martinengo himself on hand to advise, he could meet with the boys for as may lessons as he wished. Laughingly, Licini added that he had never yet met a gentleman who had not at sometime in his life been 'called out' for a duel. If Zorzi wished one day to be a galley commander he would need to master the art of self defence: Licini hardly needing to remind Zorzi quite who would be the best instructor in that deadly art.

The Countess sat with her head wedged against one of the wings of a high backed embroidered armchair. Zorzi was shocked and saddened. The eagle like glitter had gone from her eyes and she had shrunk almost to the husk of her former regal self: her face and neck now a cobweb of lines and wrinkles. A lady in waiting went forward at frequent intervals to dab the dribble from the side of her mouth and the hand that she extended for his kiss shook so much that Zorzi had for a moment to hold on to the cold fingers to aim his lips accurately at her emerald.

"How are you nephew?" she asked in a feeble voice. "No more fisticuff battles up in the attic I hope? Remember, young Wittelsbach wants you.... only you at his court.... none of the others. They were so spiteful to him, so spiteful... the poor orphan. Promise me you will visit him soon. You made a conquest there you know, with my dear kind grandson. He lacks good friends and friends amongst the family - alas! All so sad...so sad, but don't worry about me. Be off now... have fun with Uncle Ettore. Be a Doge my boy! Be a Doge! Our bloodline must go on. Oh my poor clever Bastian!" Her slurred and far away voice trailed to silence.

Perplexed as to how to reply, Zorzi looked in desperation towards one of the ladies-in-waiting. "Say yes. Say you will go," she mouthed at him. More audibly, she added, nodding vigorously in the direction of the stricken Countess, "Say, I promise to go, Great Aunt."

"I do promise, Great Aunt, I will go soon. And I do hope you will get much better very soon," Zorzi blurted out.

"Kiss your Great Aunt and go now," the same lady-in-waiting advised.

Zorzi rose from his knees and plonked a firm kiss on the icy cheek of the Countess. Her mouth twisted as best it could into a satisfied smile. He was wearing the blue silk and velvet coat bought at great cost for Bianca's wedding.

"Where is my daughter?" the Countess slurred feebly, "Where is Graziella? She must see how well my nephew is dressed. Why can't she dress her own brood in similar fashion?"

"She is in the armoury, Countess, giving a fencing lesson," one of the ladies in waiting answered.

"Tomboy.... always was a tomboy!" the Countess commented and turning to Zorzi in a kindly voice she dismissed him, sadly, for the last time: "Good boy....always so smart and polite. Be off now, I am tired.... Tired." The Countess patted Zorzi's sleeve and his cheek.

Unobserved, and seething with rage in the background, was Olivia. She had witnessed the whole scene, but was held in check by two of the other elderly dames present. Olivia was by no means her Great Aunt's favourite. As Zorzi turned at the saloon doorway to bow and salute the company with a courtly sweep of his velvet hat, Olivia sidled forward. In a clear enough voice for most to hear she hissed: "Be damned to you cat boy! Get off with you! How much more of your imposture do we have to take?"

Zorzi bowed to her as well, just slightly, and hastened down the stairs.

Elenca was waiting in the 'topo' with the Pisanello fresco fragments already loaded. Zorzi had wanted to show off his newly acquired knowledge about them to the Countess, but...no matter now. The arrangement was to meet up with Piero and Grandpa at the Fish Market quay, but not for a couple of hours or so. He was about to push off from the watergate when a middle-aged, very tall, and extremely good-looking lady called out to him from the top of the steps. The lady was dressed from head to toe in black brocade and with silken mourning bows at her elbows. "Ah! The Miotti boy. You are here for a lesson, I understand."

Dumbfounded, Zorzi's mouth sagged. He was about to comment on how astonishingly, how exactly, she resembled his crippled schoolmarm, who was now a Baroness of Sicily and moreover Don Francesco's bride. Remembering his promise, he held his tongue. He had sworn an oath before St. Mark and in Prior Tranquillo's presence that he would never ever again make mention of Bianca. Puzzled when she got no reply - only the sight of a confused boy opening and shutting his mouth - the lady repeated: "You are the Miotti boy, are you not? Hurry in, I've been waiting for you."

Zorzi was expecting meet the frightening Cavaliere on entering the armoury, instead there were two boys of about his own age; they introduced themselves as Primo and Arnoldo. Both were barefoot, shirtless but wearing short leather tabards laced up at the back. Their slender necks and shoulders were protected by rather large decorated steel gorgets of the kind worn by officers. From the elbow length leather glove that each was wearing Zorzi observed that they must both be left handed, which he knew gave them an advantage when fencing a right-hander. He watched, greatly amused, as they ran hell for leather at a padded bench, bounced off it and tumbled backwards or sideways, each time quickly regaining their feet and standing on guard. Each held a very heavy looking iron weight in his gloved hand and once or twice each boy managed to drop his weight with a loud clank onto the sawdusted floorboards. Each time they lost grip, they apologised to the lady with the words, "Scusi Marchesa." Now dressed in leather skirt and half armour the lady insisted: "Again! Faster, faster! Again! It is speed that counts. Remember it is all over in less than thirty seconds: no duel lasts longer than that! Any longer... and you are dead mutton! Throw your weight arm out much quicker as you come on guard! Again!"

This was serious stuff: not the silly larks with pea sticks that he and his friends were used to playing for hours on end in the orchards. Zorzi felt the red blood of excitement surge in his veins.

"Shirt off!" ordered the grand lady, "You'll find a glove and tabard on the end table. No stockings! You must get used to running in bare feet! When you are ready, I will help you lace up."

Zorzi chucked to himself and made a mental note to tell Aldo of the lady's concern about him running in bare feet.

Zorzi joined in with gusto for half an hour or so of faster and faster exercises. While all three were sitting down in a swelter and making friends over glasses of fizzy lemon sherbet, the Cavaliere entered. "Tired gentlemen?" he inquired, then pretending to be surprised by Zorzi's presence, he turned and crept with long slow comical strides towards the door, announcing: "Holy hell and St. Mark! He has tracked me down at last! Now I am done for! I shall have to plead to Marchesa Graziella to defend me... Cavalier Zorzi has come to carve me up for supper!"

The Licini twins fell about with laughter while Zorzi, still a bit afraid of the gigantic Ettore, was uncertain as to whether to join in the merriment.

"Show us the Doge's things again, please Uncle Ettore!" the twins urged. "Zorzi hasn't seen them."

Now the armoury was stacked from wainscot to ceiling with weapons, shields and battle flags of all kinds. Most were arranged in decorative patterns and were for the greater part trophies from encounters with the Turks and Arabs. In pride of place though, in a locked glass topped box, was the Doge's sabre. The blade, to Zorzi's surprise, was etched all over with a calendar. There was the Doge's onion pocket watch, which when picked up began instantly to tick, his telescope, a cameo portrait of him with a lock of his golden ginger hair swirling on the other side, his gloves, several golden and jewelled batons of command and of course his renowned 'Doge's pistol.' It was a small weapon, an insignificant looking thing, nesting in the hollowed-out pages of a very plain prayerbook.

"Did he ever use it?" Zorzi asked.

"Does it still work?" the twins wondered.

"Shouldn't like to try," Martinengo's replied. "I'm told our Doge, God rest him, threatened to use it on cousin Torcello when he rambled a bit long with a soapy sermon."

Well satisfied, the boys sat down to watch with growing fascination and frissons of anxiety as the Cavaliere and Marchesa circled one another with rapier and 'main-gauche' triangular bladed dagger in hand. The Marchesa moved with such smooth grace, as though performing a ballet in her soft doe skin slippers. Heavy jawed Martinengo, even though he had a bright smile about his eyes and lips, could not help but look utterly and horribly menacing. First they explained their moves; then performed them in slow motion; then repeating the move leapt like panthers at one another with lightening flashing blades. Within less than thirty seconds, the Marchesa had well nigh struck with what would have been a fatal lunge to the Cavaliere's abdomen had he not stepped aside in the last instant, embraced her with a quick kiss on the forehead and then sent her spinning backwards. Zorzi now realized that this was the Cavaliere's true lady love. He had always supposed he was somehow attached to the Countess, perhaps even her husband. He realized too, inexpert though he was, that Martinengo was just playing with the lady and was not using his reach and strength to fend her off, as he would have done with a real opponent.

In a brief interlude, while servants came and helped the Cavaliere and his

Marchesa equip themselves with three quarter plate, in order to demonstrate weapons used when boarding or defending a galley, Zorzi whispered to the twins: "Who is she? She can't be his wife 'cos I just saw her dressed in widow's weeds."

"No," Arnoldo whispered, "She's the Marchesa Graziella."

"What's a Marchesa?"

"Next step down from a Duchess."

"Like a Doge's wife, only far lower down," added Primo when Zorzi still looked mystified. "She's a Sicilian princess as well, but, father told us that there are more princesses in Sicily than there are beggars at Rialto. She's the Countess's youngest daughter as well, you know. She and the Cavaliere can't ever marry, 'cos he's a friar."

"A friar!" gulped Zorzi, raising his voice slightly.

"Yes… a friar. He's a Knight of Malta, didn't you know? He's called a Religious, or something. Knights of Malta are proper friars, you know… they can't ever get married."

"Oh!" exclaimed Zorzi; extremely puzzled by this news.

Young Primo then whispered: "Can you keep a secret? If you can't, I won't tell you."

"Course I can. Your dad told me one in Verona and I've never split."

"The Marchesa's husband got blow up, that's why she's wearing black. Blown to smithereens…. just a month back."

"Gosh! How terrible…. But she don't seem too unhappy now."

"Nor should she be," added Primo, "The Marquis was a brute who often beat her up. I overheard papa telling mamma. Uncle Ettore was ordered to call on him but the marquis got wind of it and sailed off to Sicily."

"And now he's all blown up," added Arnoldo, "Serves him right...not a toe nail left of him or of his castle. Went up like a volcano... middle of the night....stones raining down for miles around."

"I'd hate to live near a volcano."

"Wasn't a volcano, but don't you dare tell anyone this, 'cos I overheard papa. The Marchese was about to gunpowder a neighbour.... all over who owned some peasants and a plot of land. Someone must have tipped off the neighbour about where the Marchese stored his powder. No one else got hurt, so the old devil's servants must have been well in on the plot."

"Killing baddies... that's the Cavaliere's job: someone on the Verona barge told me."

"No, it wasn't Uncle Ettore; anyway, he was here in Venice when it all happened. Best not talk about what he does for The Ten, though I'm pretty sure Uncle Ettore would never pull a dirty trick like that! Mind you," Primo added with a merry snigger, "He would have killed him in a duel: he's won every duel he's ever fought and slaughtered regiments of Ottoman...Never once got so much as a scratch!"

Zorzi was about to contradict Primo, but then thought it wiser not to tell the twins about the parade ground episode, nor of his slapstick duel with Ettore while seated on the shoulders of Doge Valier: nor mention that bloody scratch he gave to the Cavaliere's ear. Grandpa had always impressed upon him never to tell tales that might embarrass others. Friendly as they were, and clearly much cleverer and more well spoken than any of his pals, Zorzi's instinct alerted him to the likelihood that the twins could never keep such a piece of gossip to themselves.

The call to arms then came with the Cavaliere's shout of: "On guard gentlemen!" The boys were poised to do battle with blunted court swords, when Zorzi heard Elenca screaming hysterically outside in the long corridor. Dropping his blade into the sawdust barrel he hastened out to her.

"Makò !" she sobbed, "She throw him into canal! I see her! She throw him from window in sack! He go under Zorzi..... I don't know how I get

490

him!"

Tugging at his metal gorget and leather tabard, but failing to undo them, Zorzi, with mounting panic, sprinted down the servants' stairway through the stone corridor below and out to the steps of the landing stage. There was a sack, a flour sack of some kind, floating in the filth towards a tunnel that appeared to pass beneath the apse of a very big church. *(Santo Stefano –San Stin- where Doge Morosini is now buried.)* With the reflection of its low arch and with two oblong windows, placed like eyes in the brickwork above; the tunnel looked frighteningly like a monstrous head gulping in the foul and feculent waters of the narrow canal. Leaving Elenca tearful and trembling on the palace steps, he cast off from the mooring post and rowed with every sinew of his being until he came alongside the sack just as it was about to be sucked into the tunnel. Blocking it with his oar, he could hear Makò s wails of anger as he was struggling inside. Trying desperately to pull the sack on board, the weight of metal about his neck caused him to overbalance and to fall in, half swamping the topo as he did so. It was a fearful effort to resurface, but he kicked with all his might as he had learned to do when practising 'drownings' with his pals off the lighthouse beach. He managed to heave Makò on board, but any attempt to clamber onto the topo himself would have resulted in capsizing the little craft. Clinging on to the stern and half choking with the vile tasting water he managed to push the topo towards the landing stage. Two servants pulled him from the most unsuitably named Rio del Santissimo *(Canal of the Most Holy)* and undid his tabard and heavy gorget, while he sat and coughed and spat stinking mire. The steps were now crowded with helpers and as another two stout and obliging servants upturned the topo to empty it of water, the Pisanello fresco bits dropped out, together with Zorzi's precious leather satchel, into which he had tucked two of them. All promptly sank into the murky black depths. The Cavaliere, the twins and Marchesa Graziella arrived on the scene just in time to hear a shrill laugh and a call from a window above: "Torna nea fogna da dove ti x'e venuo, garzon de gat!" *"Go back into the filthy sewer from where you came, cat boy!"*

Zorzi wanted to weep but rage held back his tears. Instead he stood up, bared to the waist, his pale blue velvet breeches were now an off-black mud colour, his hair streaked with stinking human ordure. He looked up and shouted back: "Bastarda! Fia de na curtezana! Ziuro che te coparo`!"

Sadly for him, Zorzi's foul language was ill chosen. Far from being a courtesan, Olivia's late mother had been very much a saintly noblewoman; in character quite the opposite to her quarrelsome daughter. An educated young gentleman would certainly have offered some more picturesque and cutting insult to the young harridan. All that Zorzi succeeded in doing was to confirm Olivia's opinion of him to some who heard him. Ladies took offence at his unprintable words, but from the long-suffering male staff there were chuckles and quiet murmurs of agreement. Olivia gave a loud and disdainful laugh, then hurled back at Zorzi: "Volgaraccio! Vigliacco! Bifolco!" *"You vulgar, villainous piece of low life!"* With a splintering thud she then slammed closed the external shutters to her bedroom window.

Makò with his fur all slippery and caked with muddy white flour paste, was held in the arms of a tearful Elenca as tightly as she dared. Like all cats when agitated he tended to lash out at the nearest human. Zorzi steadied the boat for Elenca to board then, leaping in after her, he thumped violently the Morosini jetty with his oar and pushed off with a swirl and a splash, vowing never to go near the place again.

The Cavaliere Ettore Martinengo, who had only been present for the last moments of the episode, got a full account of what had happened from his manservant. Calling for his hat, cane and gondolier, he too left without saying a further word. He made for St. Mark's Square: to the Offices of the Magistrates to the Convents, seeking an immediate interview with the Mother Abbess of San Zaccaria. If she would not take Olivia, then he knew of a very pleasantly situated convent on the Isle of Ischia in the Bay of Naples. It had wonderful panoramic views from its terraces and the nuns there were confined perpetually in underground cells carved from the black rock: their penitent devotions lit only by rushlight. Olivia had already been deemed surplus to the breeding requirements of the Morosini clan. The modest dowry still allocated to her could now be put to better use.

CHAPTER FIFTY-SIX

Makò was soon placated with a wash of seawater and a freshly caught mackerel. Once again he had been saved by that tightly woven and almost waterproof linen after which he had been named. Zorzi's ruffled fur soon settled as well. He spent the next two days fishing and playing with his true friends and in the early morning of the third day he awoke with violent abdominal pains. Not wanting to wake Elenca, he lit the bedside lantern and ran through the glassworks shed to the privy. The cramps, the gripes, the vomiting and the diarrhoea got worse. He made it back to the shed before collapsing sideways onto the glass-strewn floor. There, doubled up in agony Makò found him and licked his ear. Makò left, came back again and then returned, meowing loudly, to his couch at the foot of Elenca's bed. His meows unanswered, he then decided to pounce on her angrily with claws extended.

By mid morning Zorzi's condition worsened. The drinks of lemon water, the sponging with diluted vinegar, the wet cloths held to his brow had no effect. He was drifting in and out of consciousness and whilst conscious was wailing in agony. Grandpa sent Young Daniele to fetch Denis and ordered him not to alarm the Molin family on the way, just in case whatever Zorzi had might be contagious.

Denis came, took one look at the rice coloured contents of the bedroom bucket and knew what it was. He had seen its like before, cutting its swathe amongst the patients in the infirmary. It had come at Sensa time with the crew aboard the East Indiaman, together with those cursed swings. Greatly disturbed, he began to shout orders at Grandpa: "Must get to San Zanipolo straight away! Young Daniele,come with me to row! Send Elenca away at once - anywhere - to the Molin family, if they will have her! Bury the bucket slops in the orchard. Don't, whatever you do, throw them in the canal!"

Before leaving, Denis hastily sought out Don Anselmo. Without his written authorization to the pharmacy of San Zanipolo, Denis knew that he would have problems in obtaining the opiate, the wormwood, the other herbs and refined clay compound that were urgently needed. Don Anselmo was horrified. "You know the rules Brother Denis! Go at once to alert the Podestà. The house must be closed off! You should know from your experience that you are wasting your time getting drugs. What's more, you of all people should know that there is no cure for this new flux! Stay and pray with me for the child's soul, if you must do something useful!"

"At least then come with me and give Zorzi the last rites!" pleaded Denis angrily.

"Don't lose your temper with me young boy!" the priest snarled back. He lives in the parish of San Stin and is no concern of ours. Already I am in trouble with the bishop for poaching parishioners from over the canal. Go to Padre Zuffi: the boy is his responsibility. And Brother Denis, kindly be obedient.... that was your vow was it not? Now get to the Podestà to alert him!"

But Denis could no longer care a damn for his vows, nor for the laws of the Podestà. He would save his little friend, if it were the last thing he ever did as a novice friar. Taking turns at the oars, the boys sped in the little topo across the choppy waters of the Lagoon and through the maze of backwater canals to the church and hospital of San Zanipolo.

After an argument that was resolved by Young Daniele offering a half ducat and the threat of violence with his large fists, they got the drugs that were needed. But within the three hours it took to obtain them and to return, all sign of life had convulsed and then quietly ebbed away from our young hero. Denis put his ear to Zorzi's rib cage and listened long and desperately. He held a piece of looking glass over the wide opened mouth in hope of detecting some condensation, but there was none. Finally, he pressed closed the staring little eyes and shouted a tearful prayer to that demanding God who gives so much and then takes all away.

Denis went once again to confront Don Anselmo, but came back alone, streaming angry tears. Grandpa and Elenca were kneeling, holding hands in front of a cheap printed image of San Marco nailed above a small mirror. From time to time Makò would jump up onto the bed to lick the ashened and now yellowing little face.

They waited for what seemed an eternity. Evidently, neither Don Anselmo nor Padre Zuffi could summon enough courage to come and administer the last sacrament. Denis got up from his knees and asked Grandpa if he had a missal prayer book with the 'rite for the dead.' Grandpa unlocked from an oak box the plain brown leather covered book, last used at the time of Grandma Angela's demise. Pressing Zorzi's hands together, Grandpa bound them around with Grandma Angela's glassy jet rosary beads. Denis then sent Elenca to see if she could find some olive oil, or any other flower oil that might be about the kitchen stove. She came back with the bottle of rose water essence that Zorzi had given her as a present on St. Stephen's Day. It was far from the fatty 'oil of extreme unction' that he had seen used by priests in the infirmary, but it would do.

Denis was not even a deacon. He knew he had no licence to anoint the dead, nor had he really much idea how to go about it, other than to chant the sorrowful Latin.

He lit a candle then made little crosses with the rosewater on Zorzi's forehead, lips, ears and chest and on the backs of his hands. He knew that babies when being baptized, were anointed between the shoulder blades, but could not quite remember if this was done to corpses as well. To be safe and certain, he put his arms round the frail body to lift and to lean it forward. There was a gurgle and a splutter of the kind made by a swimmer who emerges from a deep, a profoundly deep dive. Zorzi saw sparking sunlight and flailing arms and legs swirling about him and above his head. He fought and thrashed and writhed his body upwards, upwards towards the shining surface of the living.

CHAPTER FIFTY-SEVEN

It was to be the last of Zorzi's misadventures: the one that would best
equip him for his assured future as Citizen Galley Commander; he was
now quite bug proof! Under a month later, well on the mend, but having
lost almost a third of his body weight in the long mean struggle with that
deadly scourge, (as yet to be named and a century after identified as
Cholera,) Zorzi was lost in his dreams in the deep sleep of recovery. The
time for the Sensa Fair was drawing near once again and Grandpa had
bought tickets for a window in St. Mark's Square to see the Dogaressa
Bettina Valier Querini parade the Piazza in all her coronation finery - the
first Dogaressa to appear at a Sensa ceremony for well over a century.
Zorzi's dream was of luscious crushed ice granita: of brightly painted
swings; of English pirates armed with microscopes and of Denis in
earnest conversation with a beautiful mermaid; when his dream was
shattered. He was startled awake by a resounding crash right next to his
ears.

....

Elenca, had promised Grandpa to keep an eye on Zorzi, for when he
awoke he still often felt nauseated and needed much persuasion to gulp
down his bitter tasting 'physic.' Elenca had also offered to have breakfast
ready when Piero and Grandpa returned with their catch and their lanterns
from an over-night fishing trip to far off Punta Sabbione, where an
underground stream of clear water leaked out amidst the reeds into
marshy vastness of the Lagoon: there great eels abounded.

The bedchamber shutters with their colourful iron frames and expanse of
stained glass had been fastened back so that the first rays of dawn would
rouse her from comfortable slumber. Mosquitoes never troubled her at
night and heavy ornate grilles and fine steel mesh set into carved stone
casements were a deterrent to any larger intruders. For a moment she
stared at the enormous silk corded canopy draped above her head then sat
up to ponder for a while on her strange and now rather lonely situation.
First she inspected her fingernails: they had been manicured and waxed
by the housemaid who had helped her undress on the previous evening.
Changing dresses several times a day with the aid of jewelled pins and
maids had been exciting at first but had quickly turned into a very
tiresome ritual. How she missed those lightweight and often grubby

cotton smocks that she once wore in Grandpa's house.

They could be pulled on and tied in an instant and were no obstruction when running about or squatting down on the warm flagstones to play marbles or knucklebones Now, with four or five layers of silk skirts and petticoats restricting one's legs, even sitting down in a chair could be a hazardous undertaking. But there were other beautiful luxuries a girl from humble surroundings could be to be thankful for. Opposite to her bed hung a dressing mirror in a huge silver frame sculptured with mermaids and tritons, their long fish tails intertwining down either side. The mirror now radiated a magical pinky hue in the dawn light. It came as a gift together with a silver gilt and well filled jewellery box, washbasin, jug and commodious but very heavy silver chamber pot: the pot too had sea nymphs, shells and tritons decorating its twin handles and exterior and could well have doubled up as an ice pail at a royal banquet. The Ghazi's harem had its luxuries as well, but they were mostly of the Grasse perfume and embroidered cushion kind and then the harem, she remembered, was no more than a cramped and overcrowded gilded cage, with no privacy at all. Sometimes both in her dreams and in her waking thoughts, that stifling hot harem became confused with the primitive horrors of the Uskok huts; sometimes too with the foul indignities of the Doge's prison. Podestà the Noble Emo had been most kind and continued still to shower her with his gifts, toys and trinkets as well, some of which, like the mirror and wash stand fittings, she guessed had enormous value. He had been thoughtful too in his largesse, for cresting the silver mirror was the open beaked raven of Wallachia! It was picked out in red and black enamel and in semi- precious stones. In return for his calculated generosity, Podestà Emo had been most gratified and re-assured when Elenca had wept tears on recognizing once again that open beaked emblem.

She waited, warm and comfortable between fine cotton sheets until the Marangona bell began to ring its distant call to the Arsenal workers, then without disturbing the still sleeping da Mula household, she crept out onto the towpath holding in her straw shopping basket a well filled purse and the key to Grandpa's front door. At the bakery, which was just opening, she purchased eight deliciously smelling bread rolls, some eggs and a small slab of fresh butter. Dropping the rest of her change into the grubby hand of a near naked waif at the church door, she recollected that not many months previously she had languished in a similar state. Now she was wearing a full-length Florentine green brocade dress, trimmed and bowed in the smartest of fashion, a thick hedge of starched lace about her neck and a Burano shawl of crocheted silk draped over her head and shoulders to give herself some slight degree of anonymity. A kindly afterthought made her turn back, to insist that the shivering beggar girl should take and keep the shawl, together with an egg and a bread bun. Hurrying over St. Peter Martyr Bridge Elenca encountered two elderly and prosperous looking ladies who evidently were in some haste to get to the morning Mass. Nevertheless, they instantly froze in their tracks and backed against the low parapet in order to let Elenca pass and with heads bowed low curtsied to her. "Principessa," they murmured politely and smiled with admiring and demure glances. When, as she had been instructed to do, Elenca acknowledged their greeting with a just a slight inclination of the head, both ladies beamed in delight, for a nod was more than their lowly status merited. Without warning, a sudden abyss that no bridge could ever cross had opened up, separating Elenca from the common folk of Murano and much worse from her loving friends, like the Molin girls. Each greeting, each departure, each exchange of words now required a rigid etiquette appropriate to her rank: there was a bewildering range of hand, fan and body gestures to master and always, always, that rigid backed deportment. Podestà Emo's housekeeper and the Nobildonna da Mula were her strict tutors. On the first day of appointment as one of Elenca's maidservants, that thoughtful, plump and caring friend, Marcella Molin, had received a severe tongue lashing from the Nobildonna who had overheard Marcella call along the palace corridor: "Elenca, are you there?"

Storming out in her curlers from her boudoir, Donna da Mula had threatened a thrashing and dismissal if she ever again heard Marcella address her young mistress in such a familiar fashion. From then onwards it would be a grave social gaffe for any person of quality on the island to address little Elenca other than as the Doamna Basarab Brancoveanu, or else in plain Italian as - La Sua Eccellenza Principessa. For the more ragged backsides of society, which also included all those of the serving class, it would be a matter of bowing low, keeping a respectful distance and not speaking until spoken to. Failure to do so could merit an instant bludgeoning by the servants of any noble person who witnessed the offence. But the greatest victim of such social injustice was now Elenca herself. Her meteoric rise in rank trailed with it those seemingly endless sparking points of irksome restriction that had never been there when she was settled happily at the rock bottom of society - the strata reserved for slaves of foreign origin. There were to be no more fishing trips; no more wild and noisy explorations; no carefree swimming; no wild games in the orchard with Zorzi's friends; no smashing up of glass cullet for Grandpa's furnace. Instead, there was a seemingly endless throng of stuffy and unknown adult visitors to meet and to greet both at Palazzo da Mula and at the Podestà's villa. But at least when Grandpa's front door closed behind her she could still slouch and scratch and spit out the odd bit of eggshell and raise her voice and whistle a tune. Zorzi had taught her to whistle and to sail the topo into the wind; to create real exploding sparks by spitting into the furnace 'glory hole,' to fish and to fire a catapult. And as for Elenca's sudden uplift to the dizzy heights of ancient European princedom well it was all a bit of a joke between her, Grandpa and Zorzi and a temptation for the occasional disrespectful prank by Zorzi's pals.

Elenca looked along the towpath towards Grandpa's house and then froze in horror...Uzkoks! Bandits! Two big, hairy and very shabby men with fearsome looking clubs were seated with their backs to Grandpa's door. She thought to run back to the da Mula Palace to alert the staff, but the night guard of the palace was now at some distance and had in any case been sprawled out, sound asleep on his porter's armchair, when she left. The worrying thought came that the iron back door to Zorzi's orchard might be unlocked, as it almost invariably was, and that the Uskok bandits might soon enter by that way to murder Zorzi in his bed - just like they had done to that poor eunuch of Ghazi Koprulu's household, splattering in the gloom and candlelight both her child companions and herself with the eunuch's hot blood.

 Soon Elenca would find herself once again snatched from familiar surroundings and from those she had grown to love dearly. The longer she remained in Venice the bigger the embarrassment she became to the Serenissima. The Ten were eager to see the back of her and approved the devious plan that Podestà Emo presented to them. Princess Elenca would be returned to her Bucharest home with all due care and ceremony and by the safest overland route, which was through Austrian territory. On the long slow journey she would be feted and bobbed to at the stifling courts of the Austrian Emperor and those of various Herzogs, Grafs and Grafins in their cliff top castles and lakeside palaces. Other than sad recollections of her handsome brothers and sisters she had no other memory of her homeland, nor of the savage magnificence of Dracula's Buchuresti Palace, nor of the splendid renaissance villas at Potlogi and at Mogosoaia, nor of her father's numberless other fortresses guarding the remote passes to Transylvania.

Gossip, that seeping, oozing, reputation wrecking pastime, on some rare occasions exposes truth. Gossip from Zanetti's had percolated like slow melting sugar, first to the office of Podestà Emo, from thence to Captain Venier, hero of the attack on the Uskok village, and finally to the office of the Grand Chancellor to The Ten. The report pending action on the Chancellor's desk that the blind water seller knew so much about proved to be correct. Ilinka fitted the description therein. Further fierce questioning of poor lumbering and innocent old Eldeniz, signora Zanetti's shop porter, provided the new Chancellor with full confirmation of Elenca's identity. A copy letter, obtained from a corrupt eunuch at the Sultan's court filled in the rest of the mystery about the little Miotti girl. Addressed to the Sultan of Islam, the letter contained threats against Venice and her trade as well as dismay and anger with Sultan Ahamed's Grand Wazir the Ghazi Koprulu. He, Constantin Basarab Brancoveanu the Hospodar of Walachia and Voyovod of Transylvania, had offered honourably his child as a guest to the Sultan - *(In fact a hostage guarantee of peace between them, sealed in 1690.)* The mighty Sultan Ahmed II had failed to protect her from just one galley of Venetian pirates. To compound the insult, he had learned that Venice had since sold her into slavery. *(Elenca was the fourth of his six daughters. Three of his four ill-fated sons were already adult but Matei, who was to die so cruelly and yet so heroically at the age of twelve, had not yet been born.)* The Hospodar demanded revenge: he demanded the customary blood money as well from the Sultan and instant retribution upon Venice and its commerce.

Under an oath of eternal damnation, Sister Zuseppina attested that she had brought her deep concern, comfort, sustenance and shelter to the poor prisoners abandoned by Captain Venier outside her convent; moreover she had extended especially her loving maternal care to that famished little Circassian girl: all this she did out of her Christian sense of duty and at her own time and expense. Severely rebuked by the Senate, the gallant captain Venier was demoted to a slow and leaking transport galley. The

500

Ten then brought swiftly into operation Podestà Emo's plan for Elenca's disposal. His cousin, Admiral Emo had been captured in a sea fight and was now in chains and in Istanbul. Elenca's return would be promised in exchange. Some poor innocent look alike, possibly from the prisons, or from the sea gipsy community, would be dressed up to resemble the Hospodar of Walachia's daughter and dispatched to Turkey with a few trinkets of Paduan silver and Murano glass: for how could a Christian princess be returned to a Muslim harem? Neither ally of Venice nor of Austria, the Hospodar and Voyovod of Transylvania might yet be persuaded into friendship once the 'truth' was known to him about Elenca's capture. The Ten were well aware that whenever it suited him the Prince Constantin could cause useful trouble on the boundaries of the Ottoman Empire, (and, for that matter, to that other old rival of Venice, the Austrian Emperor.) Elenca would eventually make her journey home by a devious Austro-Hungarian route dressed modestly as the daughter of the Donna da Mula, whose carriages in turn were hitched up to the numerous and well armed entourage of Prince Ghika of Wallachia. Before being safely escorted home in this manner - and with Marchella as her handmaid - Elenca was carefully schooled by Podestà Emo. Young Miotti, was instructed to convince Elenca never to speak of her brief spell in the Doge's prison. A few honest lies, told in the best interests of the Serenissima neither saddened the Confessional box of San Pietro Martire, nor troubled the conscience of our astute and patriotic little ring fisher. In return for his cooperation more gold ducats would tumble into the boy's satchel.

Podestà Emo had reported that the Princess Brancoveanu was still utterly confused and traumatised by all that she had endured. Zorzi would convince her that it was the Uzkoks who had captured her and that it was the Uzkoks who had imprisoned her and had sold her little friends of the Ghazi's harem to the Arabs in Cairo. Eventually she would inform her illustrious father, Prince Constantin, that a certain heroic Captain Venier, ever concerned for the welfare of poor captives, and young Zorzi Miotti in particular, had come to her rescue and had subsequently taken great care of her. Elenca would be urged to correspond with Zorzi, though any expression of affection between them would be censored from both ends of the letter trail. Zorzi was the son of a glassblower: she was a Brancoveanu. Whilst the Ottoman Sultan could boast of his descent from those kindly benefactors of mankind, Gengis Khan and Mohammed, she,

Elenca Basarab Brancoveanu, could lay claim to an equally interesting pedigree, for the blood line of Vald II Tepes ran in her veins: in short, Vlad the Impaler *(Dracula)* was her distant grandpa!

Ever eager to exploit an opportunity, The Ten had already made plans for the girl to be 'nurtured' from afar. In time Elenca might well become a client of The Ten - an informer who could be manoeuvred into a key position at the Austrian or some other European court.

A devious plot of The Ten rarely concluded with some happy consequence but it did so on this occasion: Eldeniz found a job with them and so was able to make an honest woman of the Widow Zanetti. He was given the post of chief Turkic translator in the Chancellor's Office and the task of schooling the substitute child in the essentials of the Turkic language. He succeeded, for she was a bright little gipsy girl and to the satisfaction of The Ten, Eldeniz passed on to her every useful scrap of information that he had gleaned from Elenca in their long conversations. The girl was dispatched to Ragusa with an escort of Croat mercenaries and expendable servants where, with sufficient drumming, parading and flag waving to attract the attention of any Turkish spy anchored in that port, she was piped aboard a French man-o-war bound for the Sublime Porte. With luck, the orphaned gipsy girl might pass muster at the Sultan's divan and be destined for the glided cage of some Ghazi's harem. There was of course the possibility that the Sultan and his ministers might not fall for the ruse and might have the child substitute tied up in a sack with a billygoat and then hurled from a tower down to the skeleton strewn sea bed of the Bosphorus - but that time honoured tradition of the Ottoman was never mentioned to the little gipsy 'Doamna.'

Scuttling down the side alley, Elenca went through the orchard with all speed and double bolted behind her the door to the glassworks. Summoning all her courage and removing her leather trimmed clogs, she tiptoed down the corridor to the front door… 'Bandits! Uzkoks! Men talking a Greek sounding language on the other side of the door!' Though she tried to slide shut the heavy door bolts as smoothly as she could, the bandits heard her and began at once banging and calling for her to open up. Still petrified, she ran barefoot up the new stone stairway and entered Zorzi's room. He was sound asleep in his four-poster which had been placed close to the hearth as safety permitted in order keep up the temperature in his emaciated little body. The embers of a great log were still smouldering in the hearth. She drew back the silk-corded bed curtain.

Pushing at his shoulders, tugging back the duck down quilt and slapping at his ears had no effect. He was well and truly in the land of nod. In desperation she stood on a stool and tried to wrench Grandpa's old crossbow from its place of honour above the chimneybreast. It was then that she toppled Zorzi's fine pharmacy 'alborello;' the only souvenir surviving, though slightly cracked, from Gustav and Adolfo's grand smash-up.

Elenca's elbow had completed the bulli's task. The last of the unique 15th Century Venetian porcelain pots was now dust and thin shards! All that remained now was the recipe for making it and that was concealed amidst the faded ink, the vellum and the untranslatable Byzantine Greek of the mysterious 'Book of Seventy Six Pages.' "Wake! Wake, Zorzi! Bad beggar man at door. He wants come in. He robbers. He get big stick. He....they must be bad Uzkok....Won't go away!"

Though Elenca's command of Venetian was growing at a commendable rate, there were times when it proved most difficult to follow, and this was one. Still drowsy, Zorzi dragged back the silk quilt around his shoulders. "Oh! Leave me alone Elenca. It's hardly yet dawn. Go and wake Grandpa, or Piero!"

"Grandpa, Piero, go lantern fishing. Not back Angelus, maybe not back breakfast. I tell bad men, go away. I lock back door. I get Grandpa's crossbow for shoot bad man."

"Elenca, don't touch that for heaven's sake! It's too heavy for you. You'll drop it and end up killing me instead. Beside we have no bolts for it, Grandpa keeps them on the boat. They'll go away. Stop getting all in a panic! No one can break in now. Most likely they are poor beggars. Slip a coin under the door for them, like Grandpa does. Tell them to go over the ferry and get food from Sister Tecla."

Zorzi eased himself up, rubbed his eyes and now fully awake, saw to his great annoyance the remains of his lovely pot. "Oh Elenca... do you have to be so clumsy? I promised that to old....old... Oh! What was his name! I wanted to give it to him... for all that he has done to help me get better."

"Trevisan," suggested Elenca.

"Yes, Trevisan; now who was he? I can't quite remember."
There were disturbing blanks, bubbles of emptiness in Zorzi's memory that his close friends now noticed with consternation. They noted too that his once witty and observant quips, his entertaining chatter and swift reactions seemed to have deserted him as well. Every thought and body movement seemed now to be cumbersome, as though he were labouring under a heavy coat of chainmail. So, with little adult prompting, his young companions in adventure would come together from time to time in St. Peter Martyr church to light a 'one bagettino' candle and to beg with their prayers that brain-battered saint to take pity and to restore Zorzi's health and wits in full and proper measure.

Zorzi swirled and drank down the dregs of a glass of lemon water, a concoction prepared by Denis, made murky and slightly unpleasant tasting by a tinge of morphine and a bottom sludge of fine kaolin clay powder from Vicenza.

"Pa!" came a muffled voice from below. "Pa, wake up you old lazy bones and let me in! It is me!"

Zorzi rolled over, raised himself unsteadily and wrapped his shoulders in an exquisite Kashmiri 'moon shawl;' a gift from Senator Trevisan. His legs felt like two sticks of boiled celery. A few slow paces took him to the spy hole where he collapsed onto his knees. He peered through the glass panel. The strangers, well built tramps, were sitting with their backs to the oak doors. Propped against the doorframe were their long, knobbly, dangerous looking cudgels: beside them blanket rolls and odd bundles tied with bits of old string. One of the strangers had removed his hat and placed it on one of the bundles. Zorzi could see a sunburned balding patch, surrounded with thick matted and unkempt shoulder length brown locks, which straggled over a very dirty and ragged calico shirt. The stranger's hat was trimmed with a familiar clipped plume, plucked from a peacock's tail. "Quite impossible!" Zorzi knew full well that he had lost that peacock plume to the siluro catfish. "Absurd!" He had seen the

504

remains of that floppy greasy old hat smouldering amidst the flames of the Rabbi's kitchen range, yet both hat and plume were clearly visible below him! Zorzi tapped on the glass. The stranger stood up from the box on which he had been sitting. His clothes were in tatters, his beard straggly and unkempt, yet there was something about him, an echo of a memory in Zorzi's confused thoughts. Nut brown hair, peeling sun blistered skin on nose and forehead, eyes just like Grandpa's, twinkling moist and grey.... Grandpa's eyes, no mistake about that. And that green copper box: had he not kicked its lid shut and stowed it under the Bellini altar in St. Mary of the Angels some months ago?

Confounded, he called down: "If you want food, take the ferry to St. Mary of the Angels. Ask for Sister Tecla. Tell the ferryman... tell Sister Tecla that Zorzi Miotti sent you....tell them I will settle up later for the cost."

"Why?" answered the stranger with that disturbingly familiar grin of mild amusement, "That's generous of you Don Zorzi Miotti...mighty generous! But I have already paid off the ferryman and had a fine bellyful of breakfast with our friends at St. Mary's. Tecla told me I might well find the noble Don Zorzi ladling out charity at the gate of Palazzo Miotti. I've met your pretty playmate too, the little washer maid! Now what's her name? Ah yes - Lucia! I seem to remember a cheeky little sparrow would serenade my homecoming with a verse or two of La Bella Lavanderina! *(The pretty washer maid – an age old nursery song.)* No song for me now Zorzi? No serenade for me through the spy hole? I'm told you have a fine voice!"

"Oh no! No! It can't be," Zorzi sobbed, half terrified, half delirious with joy, "You can't be...you are dead!"

"Only dead on my feet....dead on my feet my boy. With Pavlos here, I have walked best part of the way from Soave. We are in need of our beds. Now go and wake your lazy Grandpa. Just whisper in his hairy old ear... just tell him....that your Pa is back home at last."

With that perfect timing which he never failed to manifest throughout his long eventful life, Makò appeared on the towpath and sidled along to the front door. After a most satisfactory night of wooing, howling and scrapping with rival toms, amidst the stars and the chimney pots, he

505

was more than ready for his breakfast. Giving a cursory sniff to the sweaty odours of the two unsavoury strangers, he pounced on the copper box, which still insolently exuded a distinct rat pong, and gave it an indignant clawing.

"So this is the Doge's Cat," observed Maestro Vincenzo, bending down to give Makò a welcoming tickle. "My, how we Miotti have risen in the world: a new front door; a princess for our hall porter and the Doge's ratter to reign over our vermin!"

-*END*-

ZORZI

Giorgio (George) Miotti, imagined as the son of Vincenzo and grandson of Daniele, (See below.) Zorzi's adventures link together characters, both fictional and real, representing every rank and level of 17th Century Venetian society. As Zorzi travels about the islands and gets caught up in stupendous ceremonies as well as diabolical intrigues,he acts as our innocent guide to the politics, society and traditions of 'La Serenissima,'- the world's most beautiful city and its longest enduring republic.

DOMENICO BALLARIN
(1632 -1698.)

Knight and Grand Chancellor of Venice from 1666-1694, son of Giovanni Battista Ballarin also Grand Chancellor. The distinguised Ballarin family, who are still important manufacturers of glassware on the Island, descend from the Dalmatian Zorzi (Giorgio c.1440-1506) from Spalatro (Split.) According to Island legend this other Zorzi, as a foreigner, was resented by his colleagues for being the most able glassblower amongst the staff of Angelo Barovier, the renowned Renaissance glassmaker. Zorzi's rivals dropped a great block of burning glass onto his foot causing him to dance with pain (ballare.) Crippled for life and nicknamed Ballarin (little dancer) he succeeded nevertheless in founding his own glassworks and dynasty. Domenico Ballarin was one of the diplomatic talents of his age. When just fourteen he was appointed as a senior secretary by The Ten. Aged fifteen, he witnessed his own father being dragged through the streets of Istanbul tied by his feet to a donkey, tortured in the Istanbul Arsenal and threatened with being skinned alive. Ottoman rulers were no respectors of ambassadors, nor of the conventions of Western diplomacy. On a second mission to the Sultan and a further brave attempt at peace making between Venice and Turkey, Givanni Battista was once again tormented and died chained up in a Turkish prison. Domenico took over the Grand Chancellorship on the death of his father in 1666. Understandably, from then on he was one of the leading diplomats in advancing Morosini's campaigns, Morosini's election as Doge, and in co-ordinating the forces of Venice, Austria, Poland, the Papal States and Lorraine in their League against the Turk. Domenico Ballarin had three daughters. Elizabetta and Emilia, married into the ancient and ducal families of Michiel and Barbarigo, thus making the Ballarin clan semi-noble and a third daugher, Angela, entered the convent of S. Bernardo di Murano. The Ballarin Chapel with its family monuments is in the Church of St. Peter Martyr and the largest of their palazzi is near to the Roman column.

*The N.H. FRANCESCO CAPELLO BENZON
Don Francesco inherited Palazzo Capello from his aunt, yet another Bianca Capello, who was the widow of the N.H. Piero Benzon. The aunt had previously rented the palace for 200 ducats per annum to the then Bishop of Torcello, Marcantonio Martinengo. By deed of 16th June, 1707, Don Francesco finally managed to sell the palace to Bishop Marco Giustinian, who used it as his residence until his death in 1736. By Island tradtion Palazzo Capello (now Giustinan) was the childhood home of Bianca Capello and was also the palace chosen by Henry III of France to lodge in overnight during his buying tour of Murano's glassworks. Don Giovanni Medici, a Florentine in the employ of the Serenissiama as governor of Friuli Province at one time owned the palace. Now called Palazzo Giustinian it has become the much visited Murano Glass Museum. Some changes have been made from the way the palazzo would have looked in the days of Don Francesco: domestic outhouses and attachments to the Gothic style building to the rear and side of the palace have been removed; the double headed 'Justinian' imperial eagle, (first used by Constantine the Great to show that he ruled both to East and to

West,) now surmounts the entrance and the apotheosis of a Giustinian saint now adorns the Stateroom. Don Francesco is not recorded as a Podestà of Murano and all other trace of his tenure on the island has disappeared. I have inserted him as a fictional Podestà between the tenures of Podestà Bembo and Podestà Emo.

ELENCA BRANCOVEANU
(also written as Ilinca/Ilinka.)

A seemingly unimportant Wallachian *(Romanian)* girl captured by the Uzkoks in a raid on Turkish Vizier Koprulu's seaside harem: saved by Zorzi from the New Prisons and later the cause of consternation in the both the Turkish and Venetian courts. She was the fourth of seven daughters and four sons of Voivode Prince Constantin Basarab Brancoveanu, ruler of Wallachia from 1688 -1714, when he was deposed and taken in chains to Istanbul. There, together with his four sons: Constantin, Stefan, Radu and eleven year old Matei, Prince Brancoveanu was horribly tortured for many days while confined in the Fortress of the Seven Towers (Yedikule). The Grand Vizier Gin Ali Pasha wanted the Wallachian princes to convert to Islam, which they refused to do. August 15th 1714, the Feast of St. Mary, an important date in Orthodox worship, was chosen as a further insult for the day of their execution. They they were all decapitated in that vile way now familiar to us from islamist videos. The Sultan Ahmed III was present at the executions and demanded that all the Ambassadors of the West, including Britain, be present as witness to his ruthless power. Ahmed ordered that the heads to be paraded through the streets and the bodies to be exposed on stakes outside Topkapi Palace and later thrown in to the Bosphorus. During his twenty five year reign in Wallachia, Prince Constantin presided over a re-awakening of Romanian artistic life and identity as a nation and was a true scholar and Renaissance man. He and his four sons were made saints of the Orthodox Church in 1992 in memory of their Christian fortitude. Prince Constantin was betrayed by his own cousin, Stefan Cantacuzin, *(trans. 'the singing cousin')* who revealed secret correspondence between Brancoveanu and the Tzar of Russia. Stefan subsequently took the throne of Wallachia, collaborating with the Sultan and in due course was also decapitated in Istanbul. Constantin's wife Marica and his daughters were made hostage for long years, but there is a legend that one daughter escaped capture by hiding amidst the sweeps of tall iris bordering the lake at Mogosoaia, sometimes holding her breath under water. Princess Marthe Bibescu restored the ancient and beautiful Palace of the Brancoveanu Princes at Mogosoaia, near Bucharest. She replanted with her own hands the great swathes of irises leading down to the lake and it was she who in my childhood told me a number of thrilling tales from Romania, including that of Elenca's capture by pirates and of her subsequent adventures in Venice.

BIANCA CAPELLO 1548-1587

There were conflicting accounts of her ill starred life and tragic death circulating in the European courts in the late 16th Century. Shakespeare's celebrated drama Romeo & Juliet would have had extra significance to a courtly audience, given the recent poisoning of the Grand Duke and his wife. It is one of history's extraordinary coincidences that the fates of Francesco Medici and Bianca Capello should so closely match those of Juliet Capello and Romeus Montecchi, for example: the Capello/Capulet family legends; the historically recorded wooing of Bianca under a (Florentine) balcony; the Medici family opposition to their wedding and the poisonous ending. The original tale of course pre-dates by centuries the murder of Bianca and Grand Duke Francesco Medici. The 'novello' was founded on a feud between Capello and Montecchi in 13th Century Verona and given style and fame in one of the 214 'novelle' by the Lombard Dominican and later French bishop Matteo Bandello 1485-1561, who provided the plots for many of Shakespeare's (Edward de

Vere's?) plays and for the novels of several renowned 19th Century French and Spanish authors. Bandello's tales have been overlooked and under-rated: they are of pivotal importance in the development of European Literature. Arthur Brook's poem of 1562, the *Tragicall Historye of Romeus and Juliet, was* lifted from Bandello and Shakespeare in his turn failed to acknowledge his plagiarism of both Bandello and Brook. The exhumation of Bianca's bones and those of Grand Duke Francesco and subsequent forensics on their visceral remains kept in the Church of Santa Maria a Bonistallo, have proven beyond doubt that both were poisoned with arsenic trioxide. (See: article in British Medical Journal Vol.333 Dec. 2006.) No portrait of Bianca survives showing her with the Medici crown jewels – Cardinal Ferdinando would have seen to that! By all accounts she never flaunted her wealth and rank, although she acted for a considerable time as ruler of Tuscany while her husband spent much of his life in his Pitti Palace laboratory, where together with his assistants the sculptor and architect Bernardo Buontaleni and alchemist Francesco Fontana, he finally cracked the mystery of 'vasi alla porcellana'in 1570. Though hopeless as a ruler, compared with his fratricidal younger brother Cardinal Ferdinando (who certainly poisoned Bianca as well) none should underestimate Grand Duke Francesco Medici's contribution to methodical scientific progress. There is a portrait of Bianca Capello by Angelo Bronzino in the National Gallery, London.

GRADENIGO. The botanical garden of Senator Gradenigo on Rio Marin, so admired by Henry James and other 19th Century writers, is now much reduced in size and what remains is in a rather neglected state. The present Gradenigo Palace replaced the old gothic style building some twenty years after the old Senator's death. Only the grand arch of the original palace watergate remains.(See also Rezzonico.)

Sir ROBERT HOLMES (1622-1692.) The most successful admiral of the Restoration Fleet. Personal friend and ally of James Stuart (James II) and Prince Rupert, he was a firm Jacobite and evidently a Catholic. On 9th August, 1666 he struck at the Dutch merchant fleet destroying 150 vessels with fireships. He had earlier destroyed, creating a vast firestorm known as 'Holmes Bonfire,' the Dutch East India Warehouses and townships on Vlieland Island. The Great Fire of London was the prompt Dutch retaliation, as was the burning of our own fleet in the Medway in the next year. Aware that the Dutch would seek revenge for his actions, Holmes pleaded furiously that our fleet should not be stood down for the winter, but his pleas were ignored. Remembering what had happened to his father when he went to Parliament seeking 'ship money,' Charles took that risk and left his mariners unpaid and cheering on the Dutch when their fleet arrived at Chatham. Charles II never quite forgave Holmes for provoking the Great Fire of London, passing him over for promotion on several occasions. However, he and his brother James had the Dutch involvement hushed up in order to protect Holmes from any blame. Naturally, when Dutch William came to power French papists got the blame for the Great Fire. Holmes was Governor of the Isle of Wight until his death from gout.

*GIOVANNI LICINI - Notaio (Registrar) of the Veneto throughout the period covered by the story.

LORRAINE, CHEVALIER PHILIPPE CAMBOUT HARCOURT
(1643 - 8th December 1702)

Lorraine and his elder brother the Comte de Marsan were members of the Guise family and close relatives of the exiled Duke of Lorraine, whose territories Louis XIV annexed. By all accounts the Chevalier was as handsome as an angel in his youth and a thorough rascal. He was the lifelong companion of the gay Duke Philippe d'Orleans, the 'brother' of Louis XIV. The dull witted and foppish Duke was cunningly manipulated by Lorraine and did little or nothing without his consent. Orleans, nevertheless outlived two wives and had eight legitimate children, from whom every present day European monarch is directly descended. From time to time Le Chevalier de Lorraine was either imprisoned in the Chateau d'If, or banished from court by King Louis. He was also suspected of being involved in several murders of persons of high rank.. However, he always seemed to bounce back from these periods of exile or prison. He obtained his Cordon Bleu from King Louis XIV by acting as go-between in the unpopular marriage of King Louis's last illegitimate daughter with the Duke of Orleans eldest son. This son, Philippe II d'Orleans later became Regent of France and by all hereditary rights should have been crowned king. The Sun King Louis XIV himself was beyond any serious historical doubt the bastard son of Cardinal Mazaran and his lifelong lover Queen Anne *(Habsburg)* of France. Philippe I d'Orleans was almost certainly the rightful kingly heir of his otherwise gay father King Louis XIII. Both Duke Philippe I d'Orleans and the Chevalier Lorraine were decadent, wasteful and rather dreadful characters and noted pederasts. France was perhaps spared even more misery, war and poverty than was ever heaped upon it by Mazarin's son. With the Chevalier's advice Duke Philippe built the (now demolished) palace of Saint Cloud, upon which Versailles was modelled, and filled it with mirrors made for the most part by workers enticed from Murano. The Chevalier had a vast inheritance from his father Henry de Harcourt and hoarded many of the jewels, art collection, plate and furniture of the Guise Lorraine family in his appartments in the Palais Royal in Paris. He was also Abbot of four of the most wealthy abbeys in France, nevertheless he died penniless and of apoplexy after a night of thorough debauchery. He had several illigitimate children but only one, Alexandre, is recorded. A 'niece' inherited what little was left of his estate and then married the Prince of Monaco.

MAKÒ - *Pronounced Mah-Koh with emphasis on a short sharp 'o' sound, as in off.*
After Dick Whittington's companion, the Doge's cat must surely rank as the most famous feline in both legend and history. Makò s remains are no longer on display, because they are considered by some to be too gruesome an exhibit. They now rest in a storage box in the Correr Museum *(Museo Correr)* at the opposite end of St. Mark's Square to the Basilica. Though Makò may now be quietly mouldering and neglected in an edifice named after the arch enemies of his ducal master, nevertheless he is still close enough to the locations where he once prowled in triumph. Makò s mummy came to the Correr Museum in 1895, together with Doge Morosini's pistol concealing prayer book, his calendar sword, his golden baton of command and much of the contents of the armoury of the Palazzo S. Stefano. All were purchased from the executors of the last of the illustrious race, Countess Morosina Morosini-Gattenberg.

514

MARTINENGO - There were several Ettores in the Martinengo dynasty and all descended from Bartolomeo Colleone *(Lion's testicles)* who, before Francesco Sforza, was the greatest of Italy's mercenary generals, known as Condottieri. Colleone's superb statue outside San Zanipolo *(Saints John and Paul)* is attributed to Verroccio assisted by Leonardo da Vinci.

MIOTTI ANTONIO, VINCENZO & DANIELE & ANGELA DARDUIN - In order not to confuse the reader I have tried to avoided using the singular form of the Miotti name - Miotto is the correct form - and both Daniele and Vincenzo (1644-1729) signed themselves as such. The Miotti glassworks in Murano seems to have been sold in its entirety to an Amsterdam company in 1606, though this may have been just a transfer of technology to a branch of the Miotti family already living in Holland, who had their glassworks at Middelburg. The family obviously had Netherlandish origins with de Brayda as an ancestral name. The Miotti regained possession of their Murano premises around about the 1640's when a Daniele married Angela Darduin and thus combined the talents of both families in the form of their son Vincenzo. Angela's ancestor Nicolo` Darduin was one of the first glassmakers to record his recipes for lead crystal glass which were added to and bound in book form by his son Giovanni Darduin (1585-1654) The secrets of making 'aventurine' glass and the so called 'girasole' *(sunburst rather than sunflower)* glass were also contained in this book. Girasole glass was used to make a wonderful opalescent glass which imitated pearl and was used from then on for costume jewellery. Very few pieces of the fabulous 'aventurine' have survived the ravages of time. Vincenzo's quest in the story to imitate Roman glass was of course to no avail. The iridescence in such glass is caused by gradual decay over centuries of burial and the crystallizing of the lime content in the glass combining with minerals in the earth. Examples of 'caged' Roman glass of the kind admired by Zorzi are so rare that today they fetch millions of dollars at auction. One good example is the Trevulzio Cup in the Archeological Museum in Milan. That one reads: BIBEVIVASMULTISANNIS (Drink up and live a long life.) The Darduin recipe book went missing about the 1680's and re-appeared in 1693 (1694 in the old calendar.) It is now in the State Archives of Venice. Other famous Italian recipe books from early Renaissance times onwards also contain recipes for lead glass. Of particular note are: Antonio da Pisa's 14th Century manuscript now in Florence; The Montpellier manuscript of 1536, of Murano origin; An anonymous part book of recipes also from about the year 1536, marked however with the Barovier family emblem of a star. This fascinating document has only recently emerged from private ownership. Recipe thirteen in this document describes how to make lead glass. As for knowledge of lead crystal in England, Antonio Neri's 'Arte Vitraria' of 1612 was translated in 1662 by Christopher Merritt: his commission came from King Charles II. From its inception, the Royal Society was eager to have good lenses made in England, rather than purchased from the Dutch, for their scientific and heavenly research. Antonio Miotto went to London (possibly with the Miotti's book of recipes,) in the early part of the 17th Century. His fame was such that he was recorded as working for Sir Joseph Mansell from 1618 to 1623. The Duke of Buckingham and Mansell had the royal monopoly of glassware and mirror making. It is my presumption in the story that *George Ravenscroft, whose glassworks was on the site of the old Savoy Palace, where the hotel is now located, got his successful recipe for making lead crystal in quantity from Antonio's book. The Duke of Buckingham imported the pure and rare silica from the Wicklow Mountains for the purposes of mirror making for his own and the royal Stuart palaces. No evidence has yet come to light showing contact between Ravenscroft and Antonio Miotti. Antonio was however the leading expert in London up to the time of the Civil War. Ravenscroft's long sojourn in Venice co-incided with Cromwell's reign, and for that some have suggested that the glass merchant was either Catholic, royalist or both.

Vincenzo di Daniele Miotto is recorded as proprietor of the Del Jesu Glassworks in 1701. Maestro Vincenzo Miotti became one of the Four Deputies to the Podestà in that year and with it the right to issue his own silver 'Osella' coinage. The Miotti family continued to use the Jesuit IHS mark of the ancient foundry near to the Bridge of Santa Chiara and frequently used the monkey and apple, (symbolic of the desire to imitate,) as their mark and crest. Vincenzo may have remarried after his reappearance in 1693/4 and either a son or his cousin Daniele (1678-1763) took over the glassworks from him. I have used this Young Daniele as Zorzi's cousin in the story. Family first names continued, for there was still a Vincenzo Miotto as Deputy issuing Murano coinage in 1785. Miotti milk glass, in imitation of Chinese porcelain, may be seen in the Murano

Glass Museum, formerly Palazzo Capello, and now Palazzo Giustinian. Tin oxide was used from ancient Egyptian times to give a milky whiteness to glassware. 'Lattimo' was improved upon by the Miotti family, substituting litharge and arsenates for the tin to give an enhanced brightness. In the Wallace collection in London there is a wonderful example of chalcedony and aventurine glass in the form of a goblet c.1500 in date, which may well have been of Darduin manufacture - given that it has an internal flashing of lattimo milk glass. It would be fanciful to think that the small rather wobbly glass vase in the Palazzo Giustinian collection and decorated with a monkey in a bush was a trial piece by our fictional character - Zorzi Miotti. A superb plate decorated by Vincenzo is in the Victoria and Albert Museum, London. As for the mysterious book of 76 recipes that may have come to Venice after the fall of Constantinople to the Islamic Ottoman Empire, I was told about it in 1952 by a Canadian, Mr. Myot, who claimed descent from the famous Miotti, but where the book of recipes is now, nobody knows. There is still a vast treasure of unexplored texts in the State Archives and in the numberless Palace Libraries of Venice. The original may have been looted or destroyed by Napoleon's troops when they sacked Venice in 1791, or later in 1806, when Napoleon ordered the Marigola Arte the age-old Guild of Glassmakers to disband. Could the mysterious book also have held the ancient secret of porcelain, and the locations of kaolin type clay in Europe? There were deposits of kaolin in nearby Vicenza and also in Bologna. Antonio di San Simeone of Murano was claimed to be the first porcelain maker in 1470 - hence those ancient pharmacy pots at St. Peter Martyr? A document, discovered to be a forgery created in the late 19th Century, also laid claim to Venice as the place where porcelain was first manufactured in Europe. This document may well have been a modern copy of an original. As the home of Marco Polo, who gives a detailed account of its manufacture, one assumes that many attempts were made in Venice over the centuries to imitate Chinese porcelain. The alchemist Grand Duke Francesco Medici had a Byzantine recipe book of the Miotti kind. He produced the first porcelain in the Western world that has survived down the ages: porcelain that was made long before the success of Tschirnhaus and Bottger in 18th Century Saxony.

DOGE FRANCESCO MOROSINI
Reigned 1688-94

The last of the warrior Doges was born on 26th April, 1619 to Pietro and his distant cousin Maria Morosini. One of the outstanding military strategists of his time, he held off an Ottoman Islamic invasion of Western Europe and was often obstructed by other European nations - France in particular. Smaller nations with emerging wealth, like England and Holland were far off geographically from the conflict and were content to sit back and to profit from the economic and military weakening of the ancient European powers: - Spain; Austria; Poland; Venice; the Papal States and Russia - who were for long ages the bulwark against the Western expansion of Islam. Even in death Doge Francesco still bears a great weight upon his shoulders in the form of a vast floor slab tomb in the nave of San Stin. The church is to be found next door to his Palazzo Santo Stefano; both buildings are opposite to the Accademia Bridge. There are more grandiose monuments to him in the Doge's Palace. Sadly, he is now only remembered as the Doge who blew-up the Parthenon, and his many warlike efforts proved futile, for the lands that he liberated were either re-captured or given back to the Ottoman by later treaty.

CAPTAIN ANDREA (Andrew) RAVENSCROFT - A fictional character based on 'the spy who was left behind' by the departing Venetian

Ambassador at the time of William of Orange's invasion of England. Many recusants, both Catholic and Puritan, escaped the harsh religious laws of the time by migrating to the West Indies. Many more, who were caught and sentenced in England and Ireland, became slaves on the sugar plantations before the trade in negro slaves expanded. We must assume that Ravenscroft would have taken Catholics outward bound and sugar on the return trip.

GEORGE RAVENSCROFT was not, as proud English tradition has it, the inventor of lead crystal. Litharge, or lead oxide was used from late Roman times as an ingredient for making fake jewels and for encasing gold and other coloured metals used in mosaics. Ravenscroft was not as such a glassmaker. He was an expert businessman who traded with Murano and lived there for at least fifteen years. Yet much credit must go to him and to his chief glassmaker, Gianni da Costa of Monferrato, for modifying existing recipes by increasing the lead content to 30% and reducing the potassium traditionally used as a catalyst. That same recipe may have been in that lost book passed down to Antonio Miotti, which, I have presumed, dated from Byzantine times. Lead crystal production in great quantity may well have helped to make England prosperous after the Civil Wars and misery of Cromwell's time. When one considers the telescope and microscope lenses of high quality that were produced subsequent to the discovery of 30% lead glass, one realizes what a gigantic leap forward in science resulted from that simple discovery. It is thought that Maestro Antonio Miotti may have died in London about 1680. Its lack of colour and unsuitability for fashioning into elaborate shapes ensured that lead crystal never appealed to Venetians, but it was nevertheless manufactured there from the early 18th Century onwards until the Napoleonic destruction of Murano's trade.

REZZONICO Abbondio – A madcap and wealthy young nobleman whose girlfriend Valenzia Gradenigo has been locked way by her Senator father in the Convent of San Zaccaria. In later life the real Abbondio became a lay Cardinal and Papal Prince at the court of his nephew. His and the Pope's failure to stand up to the bullying of the King of Portugal led to the the violent events in South America when the free and Utopian native communes established around Jesuit Missions were suppressed by slavers. That magnificent film 'The Mission' with Morricone's haunting 'Gabriel's Oboe' music so well evokes those tragic times. Ca` Rezzonico, once home of the Papal family and now one of Venice's grandest museums was restored by the son of of Robert Browning the English poet. Some of Brustolon's ornate chairs may be admired there. The real Valenzia Gradenigo was an idealized example of constancy in love and a subject of both 19th Century history painting and French romantic literature. In a reversal of roles with the Rezzonico of our story, she tried but failed to spring her lover from jail hours before he was sentenced to death by The Ten. She is sometimes depicted swooning in the arms Messer Grande while being condemned to eternal imprisonment by her own father, Senator Piero Gradeningo. Valenzia was besotted with love for Ambassador Antonio Foscarini, who so legend has it, did not return her affection because he was allergic to blond hair. Foscarini was falsely accused of treason by consorting with foreign powers. In 1621 a great scandal was whipped up by the bitterly Calvinistic English Ambassador, Sir Henry Wotton, who wanted the Catholic Alatheia Countess of Arudel, and daughter of Bess of Hardwick, driven out of Venice on the pretext that she was spying and in league with Foscarini. He failed, but poor innocent Foscarini dangled by one leg between Marco and Todaro. At least, when they got to the truth, The Ten had the decency to give Foscarini a monument in San Stae church inscribed with a fulsome apology.

N.H.LORENZO SORANZO (dates unknown) Ambassador to Britain appointed in 1695. Venice broke off diplomatic relations when William of Orange invaded in 1688. A letter from The Ten of that year instructs the Embassy to withdraw from London for its own safety, since all Catholic premises were under fanatical mob attack at that time. The Ambassador was asked to leave behind a spy to deal with the affairs of the Serenissima and to send covert reports - hence the character of Andrea Ravenscroft. I have presumed that a relative of the famous Sackville family of Knole in Kent was that spy, since Charles Earl of Dorset (Regent of England in William's absence) was involved with the re-establishment of the Venetian Embassy and the family had close connections with other Venetian Ambassadors e.g. Nicolo` Molin c. 1622. Lorenzo Soranzo lived in the Palazzo Capello Soranzo that has been recently restored and is next to the Gradenigo Palace on Rio Marin, near to the modern Scalzi Bridge.

SPADAFORA Domenico, Prince of Maletto and Baron Rochella Valdemone. (1640-1703.) Apologies to his shade for portraying him as a wife beater: most probably he was a man of true nobility. He is used as a character because the Spadafora had a Venetian connection and a palace there. Domenico had two sons, Nunzio and Francesco and was in fact married to Giuseppa Branciforte Borgia. With such a 'strong armed,' alliance one might suppose the family could well have teamed up for a bit of arm wrestling with their neighbours.The Spadafora (Spatafora in Sicilian) barons claimed to have been sword bearers to the Emperors of Byzantium, hence their name 'Sword Out,' their battle cry, and and their emblem of an armoured arm brandishing a sword. Baron Giovanni Michele Spadafora commissioned the famous altar of the Nativity from Antonello Gagini in 1526 and it was completed by his son Giacomo in 1540. According to local tradition several attempts were made to carry off the sculptures and relocate them in Catania or Messina because Rocella, though a picturesque little town, was never easily accesible. The altar is still in situ and a good road from Catania now winds its upward to Rocella around the slopes of Etna. As for the widely scattered ruins of the Spadafora Castle, no one is now sure how it was destroyed, but gunpowder was certainly involved. Most of Rocella's history went the same way on 23rd August 1943, when in a moment of madness and anarchy following the German retreat, a bunch of illiterate delinquents thought to destroy tax and criminal records by hauling out the entire historic and Municipal archive and burning it in the Piazza.

STERCHEL – Rabbi, doctor, dentist and magician. Rabbi of the German Rite Synagogue in the Ghetto, a character based on a famous Venetian Rabbi of that name who lived at an earlier date c. 1600.

ANDREA TOSI - Archpriest of San Donato 1667-1700

TREVISAN - Andrea Trevisan was active on the Island about the time of our story and was patron of several charitable foundations for children as well as patron of the Guild of St. John the Baptist. His Murano palace, thought by some to have been designed by Palladio, is now in a ruinous and abandoned state. Worse still, the important cycle of frescoes it contains, which were completed in 1557 by Paolo Veronese before his world renowned works at the Villa Barbaro Maser, are at risk of damp oblivion. (This is by way of a plea to the Venetian Prefettura. Wake up!)

DOGE SILVESTRO VALIER

The so-called 'Decorative Doge' was born on 28th March 1630, eldest son of Doge Bertuccio. He was handsome, astute, wayward and profligate with his wife's fortune and had a clubbed foot. It was known that he had an illegitimate daughter. After many candidates failed at the last voting session and with the aid of many more bought votes he was elected by way of a compromise candidate in February 1694. His wife, whom he was obliged to marry at the age of 19 years; the formidable Elisabetta Querini, insisted that she be crowned Dogaressa; something that had not been permitted in Venice since a Morosina Morosini was crowned in 1597. Bettina was in effect queen of Venice and acted as such, while her card sharp husband was regarded as being no more than the 'cavaliere servente.' Her coronation took place on 4th March 1694. After a row with his wife, Silvestro died suddenly of apoplexy on 7th July, 1700. (Did Bettina finally discover Bianca's parentage? One can only guess!) The grandiose baroque tomb of Bertucccio, Silvestro and Bettina is in San Zanipolo. The larger than life sized marble figures of Bettina, flanked by the two Doges were acclaimed as accurate likenesses. All three grandees peer down from their monument as though about to take a haughty bow at the final curtain of life's cruel comedy. Naturally, being both Valier and Querini, the final curtain is made of six or seven tons of precious yellow Siena marble!

JOHN WORLEY

Born Haverfordwest, Pembrokeshire 1624, died a Greenwich Pensioner in 1721. A trader in coal from South Wales and a mariner for over seventy years, mostly in the service of the British Navy, his portrait by Sir James Thornhill may be seen in the Queen's House. He is depicted as 'Winter' on the ceiling of the Banqueting Hall, Greenwich. A fine drawing of him, also by Thornhill, is kept in the Naval Museum. He is regarded as the archetypal Ancient Mariner and his portrait may well have inspired Coleridge.

CAPTAIN ZEN

Antonio Zen got the promotion he long desired. He was given supreme command of the fleet and drove the Turks from the Island of Chios where they later returned and after a century or more of cruel rule perpetrated one of the most dreadful massaces of Christians in recorded history. Misfortune dogged Zen though and he lost the island partly as a consequence of his fleet being caught in a flat calm followed by a storm that favoured the Ottoman. For his supposed lack of leadership and his bad luck, he was arrested by The Ten - passed over the Bridge of Sighs and died in Messer Grande's prison on 6th July, 1697.

ZUSTINIAN - Sebastiano dei Giustiniani - imagined as a wayward nephew of Marcantonio Giustiniano (Doge from1684-1688.) Though little in detail is known about this family before the early twelfth century, when it was recorded that all but one of the male heirs were wiped out in a disastrous naval expedition, the Giustiniani nevertheless claimed descent from the great Roman emperor Justinian, who ruled from Constantinople. They were listed amongst the founders of the Venetian State in the 7th century, along with the Morosini, Gradenigo and Bembo. In order to continue the family line, in 1172 AD., the Pope obliged a young Giustinian monk to pop out of his monastery at San Niccolo` on the Lido in order to procreate via the Doge's daughter. Promptly after the birth of his heir, he returned to his cold and loveless cell. The Giustiniani family owned no less than six palaces along the Grand Canal. Ca` Granda, mentioned in the chapter about the San Donato riot, was their main residence, it is the triple fronted gothic palace attached to Ca` Foscari University and half way along the Grand Canal. On 26th July, 1944, the central part of Ca` Granda was blown up by partizans. It was being used as a headquarters, prison and torture chamber by the Nazis. As a reprisal, the Germans took thirteen prisoners and machine gunned them to death in the ruins two days later. Ca` Lolin, where Lorraine is said to have been a guest, is also on the Grand Canal near to the Accademia Bridge and is acclaimed as one of the architect Baldassare Longhena's finest constructions.

OTHER CHARACTERS in the story for the most part belong to the realm of the writer's imagination. Historical characters act as they might well have done in the context of real events in the years 1693/4. The ceremonies, vespers, parades, and Sensa Trade Fair did take place on the dates given and, with the exception of the Pisanello ruined villa, all locations still exist.

LOCATIONS REFERENCE & WORKS OF ART
San Pietro Martire and San Donato are both splendid churches to visit and are to this day frequently filled with the singing of enthusiastic youngsters. San Donato no longer has its baptistry. During his disastrous improvements to the church, an ancient wonder of Romano Byzantine architecture, Bishop Marco Giustinian had the marble choir stalls and the two tub like lecterns, (mentioned in the story,) demolished. The ancient wooden statue of "San Dona`" now in the church may have come from

the demolished baptistry. It is more likely that a wall fresco, of the kind described in the story, would have adorned the north wall of the church. San Pietro Martire Convent was plundered and lost its library and half of its monastic buildings in Napoleonic times, but later acquired paintings and art works from Santa Maria degli Angeli and other Murano churches, including the Bellini masterpiece mentioned in the story: 'The Virgin with St. Mark presenting Doge Barbarigo.' The large open cloister square and the steps to the upper floor have survived. There is a small, but fascinating local history museum in the upper rooms where, in the story, Don Tranquillo shared his breakfast with Zorzi. The Ballarin memorial chapel is to the right of the high altar. The ancient Whitechapel bells were damaged in the last war and re-cast. St. Peter Martyr himself rests in his magnificent gothic tomb next to that of the Three Magi in the church of Saint Eustorgio, Milan. Sant'Anastasia, Verona, with his Pisanello Chapel and other gothic splendours is also dedicated to the Dominican martyr who, in real life was something of a provocative character.

The church of Santo Stefano (San Stin) Murano with its gigantic bell tower either fell down earlier, or was pulled down in Napoleonic times. St. Stephen - the Boxing Day Saint - was the patron of glassmakers. He was stoned to death and by tradition flintstones were used in his martyrdom. Ground up quartz flint from the River Tagliamento was one of the main ingredients of Murano glass: hence the choice of name for the Glassmakers' Canal, which up to the 19th Century was called Canal di San Stin. The other San Stin in Venice itself contains the tomb of Doge Morosini.

Several Synagogues in the New Ghetto are open to the public, but there is nolonger one specific to the German rite of Rabbi Sterchel.

Doge Morosini's Palazzo Santo Stefano is private property. He rests nearby in the nave of the Church of San Stin. San Vidal Church with its high altar surmounted by Carpaccio's magnificent painting of the warrior saint is now a concert hall open to the pubic. It was reconstructed in the early 18th Century. All these buildings are close to the wooden Accademia Bridge.

Two versions of the 'The Murder of St. Peter Martyr' by Giovanni Bellini have survived. The larger is in the National Gallery London and the smaller in the Courtauld Gallery in Somerset House, London. The Courtauld version re-appeared in 1910 in the stock of a Viennese dealer. A coat of arms, shown to the left on one of the assassin's shields, displays a raven with a bar beneath and is very much like the Brancovan arms. It is hard to imagine that any donor would want to have his arms thus displayed in such a cruel scene. However, other than the Black Raven of Wallachia, the closest match would be the emblem of the Toso (Tosi) family of Murano. The third Bellini painting, mentioned as being in Don Francesco's study, the 'Sleeping Virgin and Child in a Meadow' may also be found in the National Gallery.

A series of engravings called 'Le feste ducali' (the Ducal festivities) were published almost a century after the events recorded in this story. They were engraved by Giambattista Brustolon after drawings by Canaletto and vividly depict the Sensa ceremonies and Shrove Tuesday carnival. Copies may be seen in the Correr Museum and the British Museum.

Can Grande della Scala's Castle of Soave, where in the story Vincenzo was imprisoned, is now open to visitors in the summer months. The long rocky climb to its impressive battlements and interior staterooms is well worth the effort. I am reliably informed that the secret tunnel up to the guardroom is still there, but has collapsed in several places and is now impassable.

I have drawn mostly on S. Romanin's 'Storia documentata di Venezia' (1912, 2nd Edition, ten vols.) for background information. Morosini's cat gets an honourable mention there, as he does in a more recent and concise account, 'A History of Venice' by John Julius Lord Norwich. (The Folio Society 2007.)

I leave it to the reader, who might now wish to visit Murano, to decide which of the surviving glassmakers' homes along the Rio dei Verieri best resembles that described in the story. Ca` dei Sodeci and Ca` degli Obizzi all have some external features that may readily be identified, but the area once occupied by San Stin and its surrounding dwellings and glassworks has long been transformed. A modern clock tower is nearest to the site I had in mind for the story. Calle Miotti, the alleyway at the South end of the Canal is the site of the defunct Miotti Del Jesu Glassworks and the corner of Calle Zannetti is the location of the imagined sugar shop.

My original motivation for writing this tale was to mark the 4th Centenary of Claudio Monteverdi's Vespers. To the greatest pleasure of all present in the Albert Hall, as well as that of millions tuned in to radio and T.V., the Scola Cantorum of the Vaughan School and the choir of the London Oratory School were chosen to sing at the 4th Centenary Celebration of the Vespers on the penultimate night at the Prom. Monteverdi's sublime and now frequently performed work was almost unknown when, as a Grammar School boy and chorister, I too sang Psalms from the Vespers 1610.

V.W.